This book belongs to.

EDWARD G. DRUM.

TREASURY OF
GREAT
SHORT
STORIES

TREASURY OF
GREAT
SHORT
STORIES

Exeter Books

NEW YORK

This edition first published in USA in 1986 by
Exeter Books
Distributed by Bookthrift
Exeter is a trademark of Bookthrift Marketing, Inc.
Bookthrift is a registered trademark of Bookthrift Marketing
New York, New York

Produced by
Octopus Books Limited
59 Grosvenor Street
London W1

ISBN 0 671 08624 3

Printed and bound in the United Kingdom by
William Clowes Ltd, Beccles.

CONTENTS

No Kaddish for Weinstein

WOODY ALLEN

WEINSTEIN LAY UNDER THE COVERS, staring at the ceiling in a depressed torpor. Outside, sheets of humid air rose from the pavement in stifling waves. The sound of traffic was deafening at this hour, and in addition to all this his bed was on fire. Look at me, he thought. Fifty years old. Half a century. Next year, I will be fifty-one. Then fifty-two. Using this same reasoning, he could figure out his age as much as five years in the future. So little time left, he thought, and so much to accomplish. For one thing, he wanted to learn to drive a car. Adelman, his friend who used to play dreidel with him on Rush Street, had studied driving at the Sorbonne. He could handle a car beautifully and had already driven many places by himself. Weinstein had made a few attempts to steer his father's Chevy but kept winding up on the sidewalk.

He had been a precocious child. An intellectual. At twelve, he had translated the poems of T.S. Eliot into English, after some vandals had broken into the library and translated them into French. And as if his high I.Q. did not isolate him enough, he suffered untold injustices and persecutions because of his religion, mostly from his parents. True, the old man was a member of the synagogue, and his mother, too, but they could never accept the fact that their son was Jewish. 'How did it happen?' his father asked, bewildered. My face looks Semitic, Weinstein thought every morning as he shaved. He had been mistaken several times for Robert Redford, but on each occasion it was by a blind person. Then there was Feinglass, his other boyhood friend: A Phi Beta Kappa. A labor spy, ratting on the workers. Then a convert to Marxism. A Communist agitator. Betrayed by the Party, he went to Hollywood and became the offscreen voice of a famous cartoon mouse. Ironic.

Weinstein had toyed with the Communists, too. To impress a girl at Rutgers, he had moved to Moscow and joined the Red Army.

9

When he called her for a second date, she was pinned to someone else. Still, his rank of sergeant in the Russian infantry would hurt him later when he needed a security clearance in order to get the free appetizer with his dinner at Longchamps. Also, while at school he had organized some laboratory mice and led them in a strike over work conditions. Actually, it was not so much the politics as the poetry of Marxist theory that got him. He was positive that collectiviz-ation could work if everyone would learn the lyrics to 'Rag Mop.' 'The withering away of the state' was a phrase that had stayed with him, ever since his uncle's nose had withered away in Saks Fifth Avenue one day. What, he wondered, can be learned about the true essence of social revolution? Only that it should never be attempted after eating Mexican food.

The Depression shattered Weinstein's Uncle Meyer, who kept his fortune under the mattress. When the market crashed, the government called in all mattresses, and Meyer became a pauper overnight. All that was left for him was to jump out the window, but he lacked the nerve and sat on a window sill of the Flatiron Building from 1930 to 1937.

'These kids with their pot and their sex,' Uncle Meyer was fond of saying. 'Do they know what it is to sit on a window sill for seven years? There you see life! Of course, everybody looks like ants. But each year Tessie – may she rest in peace – made the Seder right out there on the ledge. The family gathered round for Passover. Oy, nephew! What's the world coming to when they have a bomb that can kill more people than one look at Max Rifkin's daughter?'

Weinstein's so-called friends had all knuckled under to the House Un-American Activities Committee. Blotnick was turned in by his own mother. Sharpstein was turned in by his answering service. Weinstein had been called by the committee and admitted he had given money to the Russian War Relief, and then added, 'Oh, yes, I bought Stalin a dining-room set.' He refused to name names but said if the committee insisted he would give the heights of the people he had met at meetings. In the end he panicked, and instead of taking the Fifth Amendment, took the Third, which enabled him to buy beer in Philadelphia on Sunday.

Weinstein finished shaving and got into the shower. He lathered himself, while steaming water splashed down his bulky back. He thought, Here I am at some fixed point in time and space, taking a shower. I, Isaac Weinstein. One of God's creatures. And then, stepping on the soap, he slid across the floor and rammed his head into the towel rack. It had been a bad week. The previous day, he had got a bad haircut and was still not over the anxiety it caused him. At first the barber had snipped judiciously, but soon Weinstein realized he had gone too far. 'Put some back!' he screamed unreasonably.

'I can't,' the barber said. 'It won't stick.'

'Well, then give it to me, Dominic! I want to take it with me!'

'Once it's on the floor of the shop it's mine, Mr Weinstein.'

'Like hell! I want my hair!'

He blustered and raged, and finally felt guilty and left. Goyim, he thought. One way or another, they get you.

Now he emerged from the hotel and walked up Eighth Avenue. Two men were mugging an elderly lady. My God, thought Weinstein, time was when one person could handle that job. Some city. Chaos everyplace. Kant was right: The mind imposes order. It also tells you how much to tip. What a wonderful thing, to be conscious! I wonder what the people in New Jersey do.

He was on his way to see Harriet about the alimony payments. He still loved Harriet, even though while they were married she had systematically attempted to commit adultery with all the *R*'s in the Manhattan telephone directory. He forgave her. But he should have suspected something when his best friend and Harriet took a house in Maine together for three years, without telling him where they were. He didn't *want* to see it – that was it. His sex life with Harriet had stopped early. He slept with her once on the night they first met, once on the evening of the first moon landing, and once to test if his back was all right after a slipped disc. 'It's no damn good with you, Harriet,' he used to complain. 'You're too pure. Every time I have an urge for you I sublimate it by planting a tree in Israel. You remind me of my mother.' (Molly Weinstein, may she rest in peace, who slaved for him and made the best stuffed derma in Chicago – a secret recipe until everyone realized she was putting in hashish.)

For lovemaking, Weinstein needed someone quite opposite. Like LuAnne, who made sex an art. The only trouble was she couldn't count to twenty without taking her shoes off. He once tried giving her a book on existentialism, but she ate it. Sexually, Weinstein had always felt inadequate. For one thing, he felt short. He was five-four in his stocking feet, although in someone else's stocking feet he could be as tall as five-six. Dr Klein, his analyst, got him to see that jumping in front of a moving train was more hostile than self-destructive but in either case would ruin the crease in his pants. Klein was his third analyst. His first was a Jungian, who suggested they try a Ouija board. Before that, he attended 'group,' but when it came time for him to speak he got dizzy and could only recite the names of all the planets. His problem was women, and he knew it. He was impotent with any woman who finished college with higher than a B-minus average. He felt most at home with graduates of typing school, although if the woman did over sixty words a minute he panicked and could not perform.

Weinstein rang the bell to Harriet's apartment, and suddenly she was standing before him. Swelling to maculate giraffe, as usual, thought Weinstein. It was a private joke that neither of them understood.

'Hello, Harriet,' he said.

'Oh, Ike,' she said. 'You needn't be so damn self-righteous.'

She was right. What a tactless thing to have said. He hated himself for it.

'How are the kids, Harriet?'

'We never had any kids, Ike.'

'That's why I thought four hundred dollars a week was a lot for child support.'

She bit her lip, Weinstein bit his lip. Then he bit her lip. 'Harriet,' he said, 'I . . . I'm broke. Egg futures are down.'

'I see. And can't you get help from your *shiksa*?'

'To you, any girl who's not Jewish is a *shiksa*.'

'Can we forget it?' Her voice was choked with recrimination. Weinstein had a sudden urge to kiss her, or if not her, somebody.

'Harriet, where did we go wrong?'

'We never faced reality.'

'It wasn't my fault. You said it was north.'

'Reality *is* north, Ike.'

'No, Harriet. Empty dreams are north. Reality is west. False hopes are east, and I think Louisiana is south.'

She still had the power to arouse him. He reached out for her, but she moved away and his hand came to rest in some sour cream.

'Is that why you slept with your analyst?' he finally blurted out. His face was knotted with rage. He felt like fainting but couldn't remember the proper way to fall.

'That was therapy,' she said coldly. 'According to Freud, sex is the royal road to the unconscious.'

'Freud said *dreams* are the road to the unconscious.'

'Sex, dreams – you're going to nitpick?'

'Goodbye, Harriet.'

It was no use. *Rien à dire, rien à faire*. Weinstein left and walked over to Union Square. Suddenly hot tears burst forth, as if from a broken dam. Hot, salty tears pent up for ages rushed out in an unabashed wave of emotion. The problem was, they were coming out of his ears. Look at this, he thought; I can't even cry properly. He dabbed his ear with Kleenex and went home.

Alopecia

FAY WELDON

IT'S 1972.

'Fiddlesticks,' says Maureen. Everyone else says 'crap' or 'balls', but Maureen's current gear, being Victorian sprigged muslin, demands an appropriate vocabulary. 'Fiddlesticks. If Erica says her bald patches are anything to do with Brian, she's lying. It's alopecia.'

'I wonder which would be worse,' murmurs Ruthie in her soft voice, 'to have a husband who tears your hair out in the night, or to have alopecia.'

Ruthie wears a black fringed satin dress exactly half a century old, through which, alas, Ruthie's ribs show even more prominently than her breasts. Ruthie's little girl Poppy (at three too old for playgroup, too young for school) wears a long white (well, yellowish) cotton shift which contrasts nicely with her mother's dusty black.

'At least the husband might improve, with effort,' says Alison, 'unlike alopecia. You wake up one morning with a single bald patch and a month or so later there you are, completely bald. Nothing anyone can do about it.' Alison, plump mother of three, sensibly wears a flowered Laura Ashley dress which hides her bulges.

'It might be quite interesting,' remarks Maureen. 'The egg-head approach. One would have to forgo the past, of course, and go all space-age, which would hardly be in keeping with the mood of the times.'

'You are the mood of the times, Maureen,' murmurs Ruthie, as expected. Ruthie's simple adulation of Maureen is both gratifying and embarrassing, everyone agrees.

Everyone agrees, on the other hand, that Erica Bisham of the bald patches is a stupid, if ladylike, bitch.

Maureen, Ruthie and Alison are working in Maureen's premises off the Kings Road. Here Maureen, as befits the glamour of her station, the initiator of Mauromania, meets the media, expresses

14

opinions, answers the phone, dictates to secretaries (male), selects and matches fabrics, approves designs and makes, in general, multitudinous decisions – although not, perhaps, as multitudinous as the ones she was accustomed to make in the middle and late sixties, when the world was young and rich and wild. Maureen is forty but you'd never think it. She wears a large hat by day (and, one imagines, night) which shades her anxious face and guards her still pretty complexion. Maureen leads a rich life. Maureen once had her pubic hair dyed green to match her fingernails – or so her husband Kim announced to a waiting (well, such were the days) world: she divorced him not long after, having lost his baby at five months. The head of the foetus, rumour had it, emerged green, and her National Health Service GP refused to treat her any more, and she had to go private after all – she with her Marxist convictions.

That was 1968. If the state's going to tumble, let it tumble. The sooner the better. Drop out, everyone! Mauromania magnifique! And off goes Maureen's husband Kim with Maureen's *au pair* – a broad-hipped, big-bosomed girl, good breeding material, with an ordinary coarse and curly bush, if somewhat reddish.

Still, it had been a good marriage as marriages go. And as marriages go, it went. Or so Maureen remarked to the press, on her way home (six beds, six baths, four recep., American kitchen, patio, South Ken) from the divorce courts. Maureen cried a little in the taxi, when she'd left her public well behind, partly from shock and grief, mostly from confusion that beloved Kim, Kim, who so despised the nuclear family, who had so often said that he and she ought to get divorced in order to have a true and unfettered relationship, that Maureen's Kim should have speeded up Maureen's divorce in order to marry Maureen's *au pair* girl before the baby arrived. Kim and Maureen had been married for fifteen years. Kim had been Kevin from Liverpool before seeing the light or at any rate the guru. Maureen had always been just Maureen from Hoxton, east London: remained so through the birth, rise and triumph of Mauromania. It was her charm. Local girl makes good.

Maureen has experience of life: she knows by now it is wise to watch what people do, not listen to what they say. Well it's something to have learned. Ruthie and Alison, her (nominal) partners from the beginning, each her junior by some ten years, listen to Maureen with respect and diffidence.

And should they not? After the green pubic hair episode, after the *au pair* and divorce incident, Maureen marries a swinging professor of philosophy, a miracle of charm and intelligence who appears on TV, a catch indeed. Maureen's knowledge of life and ideas is considerable: it must be: lying next to a man all night, every night, wouldn't you absorb something from him? Sop up some knowledge, some information, some wisdom?

Someone, somewhere, surely, must know everything? God help us if they don't.

Maureen and the professor have a son. He's dyslexic – the professor tries to teach him English at two, Latin at three, and Greek at four – and now, away at a special boarding-school, is doing well on the sports field and happy. She and the professor are divorced. He lives in the South Ken home, for reasons known only to lawyers. All Maureen wants now (she says, from her penthouse) is another chance: someone familiar, trustworthy, ordinary. A suburban house, a family, privacy, obscurity. To run Mauromania from a distance: delegating: dusting, only pausing to rake in the money.

Mauromania magnifique!

'Mind you,' says Maureen now, matching up purple feathers with emerald satin to great effect, 'if I was Brian I'd certainly beat Erica to death. Fancy having to listen to that whining voice night after night. The only trouble is he's become too much of a gentleman. He'll never have the courage to do it. Turned his back on his origins, and all that. It doesn't do.'

Maureen has known Brian since the old days in Hoxton. They were evacuees together: shared the same bomb shelter on their return from Starvation Hall in Ipswich – a boys' public school considered unsafe for the gentry's children but all right for the East Enders'. (The cooking staff nobly stayed on; but, distressingly, the boys, it seems, had been living on less than rations for generations, hence Starvation Hall.)

'It's all Erica's fantasy,' says Ruthie, knowledgeably, 'A kind of dreadful sexual fantasy. She *wants* him to beat her up so she trots round London saying he does. Poor Brian. It comes from marrying into the English upper classes, old style. She must be nearly fifty. She has this kind of battered-looking face.'

Her voice trails away. There is a slight pause in the conversation.

'Um,' says Alison.

'That's drink,' says Maureen, decisively, 'Poor bloody Brian. What a ballbreaker to have married.' Brian was Maureen's childhood sweetheart. What a romantic, platonic idyll! She nearly married him once, twice, three times. Once in the very early days, before Kim, before anyone, when Brian was selling books from a barrow in Hoxton market. Once again, after Kim and before the professor, by which time Brian was taking expensive photographs of the trendy and successful – only then Erica turned up in Brian's bed, long-legged, disdainful, beautiful, with a model's precise and organised face, and the fluty tones of the girl who's bought her school uniform at Harrods, and that was the end of that. Not that Brian had ever exactly proposed to Maureen; not that they'd ever even been to bed together: they just knew each other and each other's bed partners so well that each knew what the other was thinking, feeling, hoping. Both from Hoxton, east London: Brian, Maureen; and a host of others, too. What was there, you might ask, about that particular acre of the East End which over a period of a few years gave birth to such a crop of remarkable children, such a flare-up of human creativity in terms of writing, painting, designing, entertaining? Changing the world? One might almost think God had chosen it for an experiment in intensive talent-breeding. Mauromania, God-sent.

And then there was another time in the late sixties, when there was a short break between Brian and Erica – Erica had a hysterectomy against Brian's wishes; but during those two weeks of opportunity Maureen, her business flourishing, her designs world-famous, Mauromania a label for even trendy young queens (royal, that is) to boast, rich beyond counting – during those two special weeks of all weeks Maureen fell head over heels classically in love with Pedro: no, not a fisherman, but as good as – Italian, young, open-shirted, sloe-eyed, a designer. And Pedro, it later transpired, was using Maureen as a means to laying all the models, both male and female (Maureen had gone into menswear). Maureen was the last to know, and by the time she did Brian was in Erica's arms (or whatever) again. A sorry episode. Maureen spent six months at a health farm, on a diet of grapes and brown rice. At the end of that time Mauromania Man had collapsed, her business manager had jumped out of a tenth-floor window, and an employee's irate mother was bringing a criminal suit against Maureen personally for running a brothel. It was all quite irrational. If the employee, a runaway girl of, it turned out, only thirteen, but looking twenty, and an excellent seamstress, had contracted gonorrhoea whilst in her employ, was that Maureen's fault? The judge, sensibly, decided it wasn't, and that the entire collapse of

British respectability could not fairly be laid at Maureen's door. Legal costs came to more than £12,000: the country house and stables had to be sold at a knock-down price. That was disaster year.

And who was there during that time to hold Maureen's hand? No one. Everyone, it seemed, had troubles enough of their own. And all the time, Maureen's poor heart bled for Pedro, of the ridiculous name and the sloe eyes, long departed, laughing, streptococci surging in his wake. And of all the old friends and allies only Ruthie and Alison lingered on, two familiar faces in a sea of changing ones, getting younger every day, and hungrier year by year not for fun, fashion, and excitement, but for money, promotion, security, and acknowledgement.

The staff even went on strike once, walking up and down outside the workshop with placards announcing hours and wages, backed by Maoists, women's liberationists and trade unionists, all vying for their trumpery allegiance, puffing up a tiny news story into a colossal media joke, not even bothering to get Maureen's side of the story – absenteeism, drug addiction, shoddy workmanship, falling markets, constricting profits.

But Ruthie gave birth to Poppy, unexpectedly, in the black and gold ladies' rest-room (customers only – just as well it wasn't in the staff toilets where the plaster was flaking and the old wall-cisterns came down on your head if you pulled the chain) and that cheered everyone up. Business perked up, staff calmed down as unemployment rose. Poppy, born of Mauromania, was everyone's favourite, everyone's mascot. Her father, only seventeen, was doing two years inside, framed by the police for dealing in pot. He did not have too bad a time – he got three A-levels and university entrance inside, which he would never have got outside, but it meant poor little Poppy had to do without a father's care and Ruthie had to cope on her own. Ruthie of the ribs.

Alison, meanwhile, somewhat apologetically, had married Hugo, a rather straight and respectable actor who believed in women's rights; they had three children and lived in a cosy house with a garden in Muswell Hill: Alison even belonged to the PTA! Hugo was frequently without work, but Hugo and Alison manage, between them, to keep going and even happy. Hugo thinks Alison should ask for a rise, but Alison doesn't like to. That's the trouble about working for a friend and being only a nominal partner.

'Don't let's talk about Erica Bisham any more,' says Maureen now. 'It's too draggy a subject.' So they don't.

But one midnight a couple of weeks later, when Maureen, Ruthie and Alison are working late to meet an order – as is their frequent custom these days (and one most unnerving to Hugo, Alison's husband) – there comes a tap on the door. It's Erica, of course. Who else would tap, in such an ingratiating fashion? Others cry 'Hi!' or 'Peace!' and enter. Erica, smiling nervously and crookedly; her yellow hair eccentric in the extreme; bushy in places, sparse in others. Couldn't she wear a wig? She is wearing a Marks & Spencer nightie which not even Ruthie would think of wearing, in the house or out of it. It is bloodstained down the back. (Menstruation is not yet so fashionable as to be thus demonstrable, though it can be talked about at length.) A strong smell of what? alcohol, or is it nail-varnish? hangs about her. Drinking again. (Alison's husband, Hugo, in a long period of unemployment, once veered on to the edge of alcoholism but fortunately veered off again, and the smell of nail-varnish, acetone, gave a warning sign of an agitated, overworked liver, unable to cope with acetaldehyde, the highly toxic product of alcohol metabolism.)

'Could I sit down?' says Erica. 'He's locked me out. Am I speaking oddly? I think I've lost a tooth. I'm hurting under my ribs and I feel sick.'

They stare at her – this drunk, dishevelled, trouble-making woman.

'He,' says Maureen finally, 'Who's he?'

'Brian.'

'You're going to get into trouble, Erica,' says Ruthie, though more kindly than Maureen, 'if you go round saying dreadful things about poor Brian.'

'I wouldn't have come here if there was anywhere else,' says Erica.

'You must have friends,' observes Maureen, as if to say, Don't count us amongst them if you have.

'No.' Erica sounds desolate. 'He has his friends at work. I don't seem to have any.'

'I wonder why,' says Maureen under her breath; and then, 'I'll get you a taxi home, Erica. You're in no state to be out.'

'I'm not drunk, if that's what you think.'

'Who ever is,' sighs Ruthie, sewing relentlessly on. Four more blouses by one o'clock. Then, thank God, bed.

Little Poppy has passed out on a pile of orange ostrich feathers. She looks fantastic.

'If Brian does beat you up,' says Alison, who has seen her father beat her mother on many a Saturday night, 'why don't you go to the police?'

'I did once, and they told me to go home and behave myself.'

'Or leave him?' Alison's mother left Alison's father.

'Where would I go? How would I live? The children? I'm not well.' Erica sways. Alison puts a chair beneath her. Erica sits, legs planted wide apart, head down. A few drops of blood fall on the floor. From Erica's mouth, or elsewhere? Maureen doesn't see, doesn't care. Maureen's on the phone, calling radio cabs who do not reply.

'I try not to provoke him, but I never know what's going to set him off,'mumbles Erica. 'Tonight it was Tampax. He said only whores wore Tampax. He tore it out and kicked me. Look.'

Erica pulls up her nightie (Erica's wearing no knickers) and exposes her private parts in a most shameful, shameless fashion. The inner thighs are blue and mottled, but then, dear God, she's nearly fifty.

What does one look like, thigh-wise, nearing fifty? Maureen's the nearest to knowing, and she's not saying. As for Ruthie, she hopes she'll never get there. Fifty!

'The woman's mad,' mutters Maureen. 'Perhaps I'd better call the loony wagon, not a taxi?'

'Thank God Poppy's asleep.' Poor Ruthie seems in a state of shock.

'You can come home with me, Erica,' says Alison. 'God knows what Hugo will say. He hates matrimonial upsets. He says if you get in between, they both start hitting you.'

Erica gurgles, a kind of mirthless laugh. From behind her, mysteriously, a child steps out. She is eight, stocky, plain and pale, dressed in boring Ladybird pyjamas.

'Mummy?'

Erica's head whips up; the blood on Erica's lip is wiped away by the back of Erica's hand. Erica straightens her back. Erica smiles. Erica's voice is completely normal, ladylike.

'Hallo darling. How did you get here?'

'I followed you. Daddy was too angry.'

'He'll be better soon, Libby,' says Erica brightly. 'He always is.'

'We're not going home? Please don't let's go home. I don't want to see Daddy.'

'Bitch,' mutters Maureen, 'she's even turned his own child against him. Poor bloody Brian. There's nothing at all the matter with her. Look at her now.'

For Erica is on her feet, smoothing Libby's hair, murmuring, laughing.

'Poor bloody Erica,' observes Alison. It is the first time she has ever defied Maureen, let alone challenged her wisdom. And rising with as much dignity as her plump frame and flounced cotton will allow, Alison takes Erica and Libby home and installs them for the night in the spare room of the cosy house in Muswell Hill.

Hugo isn't any too pleased. 'Your smart sick friends,' he says. And, 'I'd beat a woman like that to death myself, any day.' And, 'Dragging that poor child into it: it's appalling.' He's nice to Libby, though, and rings up Brian to say she's safe and sound, and looks after her while Alison takes Erica round to the doctor. The doctor sends Erica round to the hospital, and the hospital admit her for tests and treatment.

'Why bother?' enquires Hugo. 'Everyone knows she's mad.'

In the evening, Brian comes all the way to Muswell Hill in his Ferrari to pick up Libby. He's an attractive man: intelligent and perspicacious, fatherly and gentle. Just right, it occurs to Alison, for Maureen.

'I'm so sorry about all this,' he says. 'I love my wife dearly but she has her problems. There's a dark side to her nature – you've no idea. A deep inner violence – which of course manifests itself in this kind of behaviour. She's deeply psychophrenic. I'm so afraid for the child.'

'The hospital did admit her,' murmurs Alison. 'And not to the psychiatric ward, but the surgical.'

'That will be her hysterectomy scar again,' says Brian. 'Any slight tussle – she goes quite wild, and I have to restrain her for her own safety – and it opens up. It's symptomatic of her inner sickness, I'm afraid. She even says herself it opens to let the build-up of wickedness out. What I can't forgive is the way she drags poor little Libby into things. She's turning the child against me. God knows what I'm going to do. Well, at least I can bury myself in work. I hear you're an actor, Hugo.'

Hugo offers Brian a drink, and Brian offers (well, more or less) Hugo a part in a new rock musical going on in the West End. Alison goes to visit Erica in hospital.

'Erica has some liver damage, but it's not irreversible: she'll be feeling nauseous for a couple of months, that's all. She's lost a back tooth and she's had a couple of stitches put in her vagina,' says Alison to Maureen and Ruthie next day. The blouse order never got completed – re-orders now look dubious. But if staff haven't the loyalty to work unpaid overtime any more, what else can be expected? The partners (nominal) can't do everything.

'Who said so?' enquires Maureen, sceptically. 'The hospital or Erica?'

'Well,' Alison is obliged to admit, 'Erica.'

'You are an innocent, Alison.' Maureen sounds quite cross. 'Erica can't open her poor sick mouth without uttering a lie. It's her hysterectomy scar opened up again, that's all. No wonder. She's a nymphomaniac: she doesn't leave Brian alone month in, month out. She has the soul of a whore. Poor man. He's so upset by it all. Who wouldn't be?'

Brian takes Maureen out to lunch. In the evening, Alison goes to visit Erica in hospital, but Erica has gone. Sister says, oh yes, her husband came to fetch her. They hadn't wanted to let her go so soon but Mr Bisham seemed such a sensible, loving man, they thought he could look after his wife perfectly well, and it's always nicer at home, isn't it? Was it *the* Brian Bisham? Yes, she'd thought so. Poor Mrs Bisham – what a dreadful world we live in, when a respectable married woman can't even walk the streets without being brutally attacked, sexually assaulted by strangers.

It's 1973.

Winter. A chill wind blowing, a colder one still to come. A three-day week imposed by an insane government. Strikes, power-cuts, black-outs. Maureen, Ruthie and Alison work by candlelight. All three wear fun-furs – old stock, unsaleable. Poppy is staying with Ruthie's mother, as she usually is these days. Poppy has been developing a squint, and the doctor says she has to wear glasses with one blanked-out lens for at least eighteen months. Ruthie, honestly, can't bear to see her daughter thus. Ruthie's mother, of a prosaic nature, a lady who buys her clothes at C & A Outsize, doesn't seem to mind.

'If oil prices go up,' says Maureen gloomily, 'what's going to happen to the price of synthetics? What's going to happen to Mauromania, come to that?'

'Go up the market,' says Alison, 'the rich are always with us.'

Maureen says nothing. Maureen is bad-tempered, these days. She is having some kind of painful trouble with her teeth, which she seems less well able to cope with than she can the trouble with staff (overpaid), raw materials (unavailable), delivery dates (impossible), distribution (unchancy), costs (soaring), profits (falling), reinvestment (nonexistent). And the snow has ruined the penthouse roof and it has to be replaced, at the cost of many thousands. Men friends, come and go: they seem to get younger and less feeling. Sometimes Maureen feels they treat her as a joke. They ask her about the sixties as if it were a different age: of Mauromania as if it were something as dead as the dodo – but it's still surely a label which counts for something, brings in foreign currency, ought really to bring her some recognition. The Beatles got the MBE; why not Maureen of Mauromania? Throw away clothes for throw away people?

'Ruthie,' says Maureen. 'You're getting careless. You've put the pocket on upside-down, and it's going for copying. That's going to hold up the whole batch. Oh, what the hell. Let it go through.'

'Do you ever hear anything of Erica Bisham?' Ruthie asks Alison, more to annoy Maureen than because she wants to know. 'Is she still wandering round in the middle of the night?'

'Hugo does a lot of work for Brian, these days,' says Alison carefully. 'But he never mentions Erica.'

'Poor Brian. What a fate. A wife with alopecia! I expect she's bald as a coot by now. As good a revenge as any, I dare say.'

'It was nothing to do with alopecia,' says Alison. 'Brian just tore out chunks of her hair, nightly.' Alison's own marriage isn't going so well. Hugo's got the lead in one of Brian's long runs in the West End. Show business consumes his thoughts and ambitions. The ingenue lead is in love with Hugo and says so, on TV quiz games and in the Sunday supplements. She's under age. Alison feels old, bored and boring.

'These days I'd believe anything,' says Ruthie. 'She must provoke him dreadfully.'

'I don't know what you've got against Brian, Alison,' says Maureen. 'Perhaps you just don't like men. In which case you're not much good in a fashion house. Ruthie, that's another pocket upside-down.'

'I feel sick,' says Ruthie. Ruthie's pregnant again. Ruthie's husband was out of prison and with her for exactly two weeks; then he flew off to Istanbul to smuggle marijuana back into the country. He was caught. Now he languishes in a Turkish jail. 'What's to become of us?'

'We must develop a sense of sisterhood,' says Alison, 'that's all.'

It's 1974.

Alison's doorbell rings at three in the morning. It is election night, and Alison is watching the results on television. Hugo (presumably) is watching them somewhere else, with the ingenue lead – now above the age of consent, which spoils the pleasure somewhat. It is Erica and Libby. Erica's nose is broken. Libby, at ten, is now in charge. Both are in their nightclothes. Alison pays off the taxi-driver, who won't take a tip. 'What a world,' he says.

'I couldn't think where else to come,' says Libby, 'Where he wouldn't follow her. I wrote down this address last time I was here. I thought it might come in useful, sometime.'

It is the end of Alison's marriage, and the end of Alison's job. Hugo, whose future career largely depends on Brian's goodwill, says, you have Erica in the house or you have me. Alison says, I'll have Erica. 'Lesbian, dyke,' says Hugo, bitterly. 'Don't think you'll keep the children, you won't.'

Maureen says, 'That was the first and last time Brian ever hit her. He told me so. She lurched towards him on purpose. She *wanted* her nose broken; idiot Alison, don't you understand? Erica nags and provokes. She calls him dreadful, insulting, injuring things in public. She flays him with words. She says he's impotent, an artistic failure. I've heard her. Everyone has. When finally he lashes out, she's delighted. Her last husband beat hell out of her. She's a born victim.'

Alison takes Erica to a free solicitor, who – surprise, surprise – is efficient and who collects evidence and affidavits from doctors and hospitals all over London, has a restraining order issued against Brian, gets Libby and Erica back into the matrimonial home, and starts and completes divorce proceedings and gets handsome alimony. It all takes six weeks, at the end of which time Erica's face has altogether lost its battered look.

Alison turns up at work the morning after the alimony details are known and has the door shut in her face. Mauromania. The lettering is flaking. The door needs repainting.

Hugo sells the house over Alison's head. By this time she and the children are living in a two-room flat.

Bad times.

'You're a very destructive person,' says Maureen to Alison in the letter officially terminating her appointment. 'Brian never did you any harm, and you've ruined his life, you've interfered in a marriage in a really wicked way. You've encouraged Brian's wife to break up his perfectly good marriage, and turned Brian's child against him, and not content with that you've crippled Brian financially. Erica would never have been so vindictive if she hadn't had you egging her on. It was you who made her go to law, and once things get into lawyers' hands they escalate, as who better than I should know? The law has nothing to do with natural justice, idiot Alison. Hugo is very concerned for you and thinks you should have mental treatment. As for me, I am really upset. I expected friendship and loyalty from you, Alison; I trained you and employed you, and saw you through good times and bad. I may say, too, that your notion of Mauromania becoming an exclusive fashion house, which I followed through for a time, was all but disastrous, and symptomatic of your general bad judgement. After all, this is the people's age, the sixties, the seventies, the eighties, right through to the new century. Brian is coming in with me in the new world Mauromania.'

Mauromania, meretricious!

A month or so later, Brian and Maureen are married. It's a terrific wedding, somewhat marred by the death of Ruthie – killed, with her new baby, in the Paris air crash, on her way home from Istanbul, where she'd been trying to get her young husband released from prison. She'd failed. But then, if she'd succeeded, he'd have been killed too, and he was too young to die. Little Poppy was at the memorial service, in a sensible trouser-suit from C & A, brought for her by Gran, without her glasses, both enormous eyes apparently now functioning well. She didn't remember Alison, who was standing next to her, crying softly. Soft beds of orange feathers, far away, another world.

Alison wasn't asked to the wedding, which in any case clashed with the mass funeral of the air-crash victims. Just as well. What would she have worn?

It's 1975.

It's summer, long and hot. Alison walks past Mauromania. Alison has remarried. She is happy. She didn't know that such ordinary everyday kindness could exist and endure. Alison is wearing, like everyone else, jeans and a T-shirt. A new ordinariness, a common sense, a serio-cheerfulness infuses the times. Female breasts swing free, libertarian by day, erotic by night, costing nobody anything, or at most a little modesty. No profit there.

Mauromania is derelict, boarded up. A barrow outside is piled with old stock, sale-priced. Coloured tights, fun-furs, feathers, slinky dresses. Passers-by pick over the stuff, occasionally buy, mostly look, and giggle, and mourn, and remember.

Alison, watching, sees Maureen coming down the steps. Maureen is rather nastily dressed in a bright yellow silk shift. Maureen's hair seems strange, bushy in parts, sparse in others. Maureen has abandoned her hat. Maureen bends over the barrow, and Alison can see the bald patches on her scalp.

'Alopecia,' says Alison, out loud. Maureen looks up. Maureen's face seems somehow worn and battered, and old and haunted beyond its years. Maureen stares at Alison, recognising, and Maureen's face takes on an expression of half-agony, half-entreaty. Maureen wants to speak.

But Alison only smiles brightly and lightly and walks on.

'I'm afraid poor Maureen has alopecia, on top of everything else,' she says to anyone who happens to enquire after that sad, forgotten figure, who once had everything – except, perhaps, a sense of sisterhood.

February 1999: Ylla

RAY BRADBURY

THEY HAD A HOUSE OF CRYSTAL PILLARS on the planet Mars by the edge of an empty sea, and every morning you could see Mrs K eating the golden fruits that grew from the crystal walls, or cleaning the house with handfuls of magnetic dust which, taking all dirt with it, blew away on the hot wind. Afternoons, when the fossil sea was warm and motionless, and the wine trees stood stiff in the yard, and the little distant Martian bone town was all enclosed, and no one drifted out their doors, you could see Mr K himself in his room, reading from a metal book with raised hieroglyphs over which he brushed his hand, as one might play a harp. And from the book, as his fingers stroked, a voice sang, a soft ancient voice, which told tales of when the sea was red steam on the shore and ancient men had carried clouds of metal insects and electric spiders into battle.

Mr and Mrs K had lived by the dead sea for twenty years, and their ancestors had lived in the same house, which turned and followed the sun, flower-like, for ten centuries.

Mr and Mrs K were not old. They had the fair, brownish skin of the true Martian, the yellow coin eyes, the soft musical voices. Once they had liked painting pictures with chemical fire, swimming in the canals in the seasons when the wine trees filled them with green liquors, and talking into the dawn together by the blue phosphorous portraits in the speaking room.

They were not happy now.

This morning Mrs K stood between the pillars, listening to the desert sands heat, melt into yellow wax, and seemingly run on the horizon.

Something was going to happen.

She waited.

She watched the blue sky of Mars as if it might at any moment grip in on itself, contract, and expel a shining miracle down upon the sand.

Nothing happened.

Tired of waiting, she walked through the misting pillars. A gentle rain sprang from the fluted pillar tops, cooling the scorched air, falling gently on her. On hot days it was like walking in a creek. The floors of the house glittered with cool streams. In the distance she heard her husband playing his book steadily, his fingers never tired of the old songs. Quietly she wished he might one day again spend as much time holding and touching her like a little harp as he did his incredible books.

But no. She shook her head, an imperceptible, forgiving shrug. Her eyelids closed softly down upon her golden eyes. Marriage made people old and familiar, while still young.

She lay back in a chair that moved to take her shape even as she moved. She closed her eyes tightly and nervously.

The dream occurred.

Her brown fingers trembled, came up, grasped at the air. A moment later she sat up, startled, gasping.

She glanced about swiftly, as if expecting someone there before her. She seemed disappointed; the space between the pillars was empty.

Her husband appeared in a triangular door. 'Did you call?' he asked irritably.

'No!' she cried.

'I thought I heard you cry out.'

'Did I? I was almost asleep and had a dream!'

'In the daytime? You don't often do that.'

She sat as if struck in the face by the dream. 'How strange, how very strange,' she murmured. 'The dream.'

'Oh?' He evidently wished to return to his book.

'I dreamed about a man.'

'A man?'

'A tall man, six feet one inch tall.'

'How absurd; a giant, a misshapen giant.'

'Somehow' – she tried the words – 'he looked all right. In spite of being tall. And he had – oh, I know you'll think it silly – he had *blue* eyes!'

'Blue eyes! Gods!' cried Mr K. 'What'll you dream next? I suppose he had *black* hair?'

'How did you *guess?*' She was excited.

'I picked the most unlikely color,' he replied coldly.

'Well, black it was!' she cried. 'And he had a very white skin; oh, he was *most* unusual! He was dressed in a strange uniform and he came down out of the sky and spoke pleasantly to me.' She smiled.

'Out of the sky; what nonsense!'

'He came in a metal thing that glittered in the sun,' she remembered. She closed her eyes to shape it again. 'I dreamed there was the sky and something sparkled like a coin thrown into the air, and suddenly it grew large and fell down softly to land, a long silver craft, round and alien. And a door opened in the side of the silver object and this tall man stepped out.'

'If you worked harder you wouldn't have these silly dreams.'

'I rather enjoyed it,' she replied, lying back. 'I never suspected myself of such an imagination. Black hair, blue eyes, and white skin! What a strange man, and yet – quite handsome.'

'Wishful thinking.'

'You're unkind. I didn't think him up on purpose; he just came in my mind while I drowsed. It wasn't like a dream. It was so unexpected and different. He looked at me and he said, "I've come from the third planet in my ship. My name is Nathaniel York –"'

'A stupid name; it's no name at all,' objected the husband.

'Of course it's stupid, because it's a dream,' she explained softly. 'And he said, "This is the first trip across space. There are only two of us in our ship, myself and my friend Bert."'

'*Another* stupid name.'

'And he said, "We're from a city on *Earth*; that's the name of our planet,"' continued Mrs K. 'That's what he said. "Earth" was the name he spoke. And he used another language. Somehow I understood him. With my mind. Telepathy, I suppose.'

Mr K turned away. She stopped him with a word. 'Yll?' she called quietly. 'Do you ever wonder if – well, if there *are* people living on the third planet?'

'The third planet is incapable of supporting life,' stated the husband patiently. 'Our scientists have said there's far too much oxygen in their atmosphere.'

'But wouldn't it be fascinating if there *were* people? And they traveled through space in some sort of ship?'

'Really, Ylla, you know how I hate this emotional wailing. Let's get on with our work.'

It was late in the day when she began singing the song as she moved among the whispering pillars of rain. She sang it over and over again.

'What's that song?' snapped her husband at last, walking in to sit at the fire table.

'I don't know.' She looked up, surprised at herself. She put her hand to her mouth, unbelieving. The sun was setting. The house was closing itself in, like a giant flower, with the passing of light. A wind blew among the pillars; the fire table bubbled its fierce pool of silver lava. The wind stirred her russet hair, crooning softly in her ears. She stood silently looking out into the great sallow distances of sea bottom, as if recalling something, her yellow eyes soft and moist. '"Drink to me only with thine eyes, and I will pledge with mine,"' she sang, softly, quietly, slowly. '"Or leave a kiss within the cup, and I'll not ask for wine."' She hummed now, moving her hands in the wind ever so lightly, her eyes shut. She finished the song.

It was very beautiful.

'Never heard that song before. Did you compose it?' he inquired, his eyes sharp.

'No. Yes. No, I don't know, really!' She hesitated wildly. 'I don't even know what the words are; they're another language!'

'What language?'

She dropped portions of meat numbly into the simmering lava. 'I don't know.' She drew the meat forth a moment later, cooked, served on a plate for him. 'It's just a crazy thing I made up, I guess. I don't know why.'

He said nothing. He watched her drown meats in the hissing fire pool. The sun was gone. Slowly, slowly the night came in to fill the room, swallowing the pillars and both of them, like a dark wine poured to the ceiling. Only the silver lava's glow lit their faces.

She hummed the strange song again.

Instantly he leaped from his chair and stalked angrily from the room.

Later, in isolation, he finished supper.

When he arose he stretched, glanced at her, and suggested, yawning, 'Let's take the flame birds to town tonight to see an entertainment.'

'You don't *mean* it?' she said. 'Are you feeling well?'

'What's so strange about that?'

'But we haven't gone for an entertainment in six months!'

'I think it's a good idea.'

'Suddenly you're so solicitous,' she said.

'Don't talk that way,' he replied peevishly. 'Do you or do you not want to go?'

She looked out at the pale desert. The twin white moons were rising. Cool water ran softly about her toes. She began to tremble just the least bit. She wanted very much to sit quietly here, soundless, not moving, until this thing occurred, this thing expected all day, this thing that could not occur but might. A drift of song brushed through her mind.

'I –'

'Do you good,' he urged. 'Come along now.'

'I'm tired,' she said. 'Some other night.'

'Here's your scarf.' He handed her a phial. 'We haven't gone anywhere in months.'

'Except you, twice a week to Xi City.' She wouldn't look at him.

'Business,' he said.

'Oh?' She whispered to herself.

From the phial a liquid poured, turned to blue mist, settled about her neck, quivering.

The flame birds waited, like a bed of coals, glowing on the cool smooth sands. The white canopy ballooned on the night wind, flapping softly, tied by a thousand green ribbons to the birds.

Ylla laid herself back in the canopy and, at a word from her husband, the birds leaped, burning, toward the dark sky. The ribbons tautened, the canopy lifted. The sand slid whining under; the blue hills drifted by, drifted by, leaving their home behind, the raining pillars, the caged flowers, the singing books, the whispering floor creeks. She did not look at her husband. She heard him crying out to the birds as they rose higher, like ten thousand hot sparkles, so many red-yellow fireworks in the heavens, tugging the canopy like a flower petal, burning through the wind.

She didn't watch the dead, ancient bone-chess cities slide under, or the old canals filled with emptiness and dreams. Past dry rivers and dry lakes they flew, like a shadow of the moon, like a torch burning.

She watched only the sky.

The husband spoke.

She watched the sky.

'Did you hear what I said?'

'What?'

He exhaled. 'You might pay attention.'

'I was thinking.'

'I never thought you were a nature lover, but you're certainly interested in the sky tonight,' he said.

'It's very beautiful.'

'I was figuring,' said the husband slowly. 'I thought I'd call Hulle tonight. I'd like to talk to him about us spending some time, oh, only a week or so, in the Blue Mountains. It's just an idea — '

'The Blue Mountains!' She held to the canopy rim with one hand, turning swiftly toward him.

'Oh, it's just a suggestion.'

'When do you want to go?' she asked, trembling.

'I thought we might leave tomorrow morning. You know, an early start and all that,' he said very casually.

'But we *never* go this early in the year!'

'Just this once, I thought —' He smiled. 'Do us good to get away. Some peace and quiet. You know. You haven't anything *else* planned? We'll go, won't we?'

She took a breath, waited, and then replied, 'No.'

'What?' His cry startled the birds. The canopy jerked.

'No,' she said firmly. 'It's settled. I won't go.'

He looked at her. They did not speak after that. She turned away. The birds flew on, ten thousand firebrands down the wind.

In the dawn the sun, through the crystal pillars, melted the fog that supported Ylla as she slept. All night she had hung above the floor, buoyed by the soft carpeting of mist that poured from the walls when she lay down to rest. All night she had slept on this silent river, like a boat upon a soundless tide. Now the fog burned away, the mist level lowered until she was deposited upon the shore of wakening.

She opened her eyes.

Her husband stood over her. He looked as if he had stood there for hours, watching. She did not know why, but she could not look him in the face.

'You've been dreaming again!' he said. 'You spoke out and kept me awake. I *really* think you should see a doctor.'

'I'll be all right.'

'You talked a lot in your sleep!'

'Did I?' She started up.

Dawn was cold in the room. A gray light filled her as she lay there.

'What was your dream?'

She had to think a moment to remember. 'The ship. It came from the sky again, landed, and the tall man stepped out and talked with me, telling me little jokes, laughing, and it was pleasant.'

Mr K touched a pillar. Founts of warm water leaped up, steaming; the chill vanished from the room. Mr K's face was impassive.

'And then,' she said, 'this man, who said his strange name was Nathaniel York, told me I was beautiful and – and kissed me.'

'Ha!' cried the husband, turning violently away, his jaw working.

'It's only a dream.' She was amused.

'Keep your silly, feminine dreams to yourself!'

'You're acting like a child.' She lapsed back upon the few remaining remnants of chemical mist. After a moment she laughed softly. 'I thought of some *more* of the dream,' she confessed.

'Well, what is it, what *is* it?' he shouted.

'Yll, you're so bad-tempered.'

'Tell me!' he demanded. 'You can't keep secrets from me!' His face was dark and rigid as he stood over her.

'I've never seen you this way,' she replied, half shocked, half entertained. 'All that happened was this Nathaniel York person told me – well, he told me that he'd take me away into his ship, into the sky with him, and take me back to his planet with him. It's really quite ridiculous.'

'Ridiculous, is it!' he almost screamed. 'You should have heard yourself, fawning on him, talking to him, singing with him, oh gods, all night; you should have *heard* yourself!'

'Yll!'

'When's he landing? Where's he coming down with his damned ship?'

'Yll, lower your voice.'

'Voice be damned!' He bent stiffly over her. 'And *in* this dream' – he seized her wrist – 'didn't the ship land over in Green Valley, *didn't* it? Answer me!'

'Why, yes —'

'And it landed this afternoon, didn't it?' he kept at her.

'Yes, yes, I think so, yes, but only in a dream!'

'Well' — he flung her hand away stiffly – 'it's good you're truthful!

I heard every word you said in your sleep. You mentioned the valley and the time.' Breathing hard, he walked between the pillars like a man blinded by a lightning bolt. Slowly his breath returned. She watched him as if he were quite insane. She arose finally and went to him. 'Yll,' she whispered.

'I'm all right.'

'You're sick.'

'No.' He forced a tired smile. 'Just childish. Forgive me, darling.' He gave her a rough pat. 'Too much work lately. I'm sorry, I think I'll lie down awhile – '

'You were so excited.'

'I'm all right now. Fine.' He exhaled. 'Let's forget it. Say, I heard a joke about Uel yesterday, I meant to tell you. What do you say you fix breakfast, I'll tell the joke, and let's not talk about all this.'

'It was only a dream.'

'Of course.' He kissed her cheek mechanically. 'Only a dream.'

At noon the sun was high and hot and the hills shimmered in the light.

'Aren't you going to town?' asked Ylla.

'Town?' He raised his brows faintly.

'This is the day you *always* go.' She adjusted a flower cage on its pedestal. The flowers stirred, opening their hungry yellow mouths.

He closed his book. 'No. It's too hot, and it's late.'

'Oh.' She finished her task and moved toward the door. 'Well, I'll be back soon.'

'Wait a minute! Where are you going?'

She was in the door swiftly. 'Over to Pao's. She invited me!'

'Today?'

'I haven't seen her in a long time. It's only a little way.'

'Over in Green Valley, isn't it?'

'Yes, just a walk, not far, I thought I'd —' She hurried.

'I'm sorry, really sorry,' he said, running to fetch her back, looking very concerned about his forgetfulness. 'It slipped my mind. I invited Dr Nlle out this afternoon.'

'Dr Nlle!' She edged toward the door.

He caught her elbow and drew her steadily in. 'Yes.'

'But Pao —'

'Pao can wait, Ylla. We must entertain Nlle.'

'Just for a few minutes —'

'No, Ylla.'

'No?'

He shook his head. 'No. Besides, it's a terribly long walk to Pao's. All the way over through Green Valley and then past the big canal and down, isn't it? And it'll be very, very hot, and Dr Nlle would be delighted to see you. Well?'

She did not answer. She wanted to break and run. She wanted to cry out. But she only sat in the chair, turning her fingers over slowly, staring at them expressionlessly, trapped.

'Ylla?' he murmured. 'You *will* be here, won't you?'

'Yes,' she said after a long time. 'I'll be here.'

'All afternoon?'

Her voice was dull. 'All afternoon.'

Late in the day Dr Nlle had not put in an appearance. Ylla's husband did not seem overly surprised. When it was quite late he murmured something, went to a closet, and drew forth an evil weapon, a long yellowish tube ending in a bellows and a trigger. He turned, and upon his face was a mask, hammered from silver metal, expressionless, the mask that he always wore when he wished to hide his feelings, the mask which curved and hollowed so exquisitely to his thin cheeks and chin and brow. The mask glinted, and he held the evil weapon in his hands, considering it. It hummed constantly, an insect hum. From it hordes of golden bees could be flung out with a high shriek. Golden, horrid bees that stung, poisoned, and fell lifeless, like seeds on the sand.

'Where are you going?' she asked.

'What?' He listened to the bellows, to the evil hum. 'If Dr Nlle is late, I'll be damned if I'll wait. I'm going out to hunt a bit. I'll be back. You be sure to stay right here now, won't you?' The silver mask glimmered.

'Yes.'

'And tell Dr Nlle I'll return. Just hunting.'

The triangular door closed. His footsteps faded down the hill.

She watched him walking through the sunlight until he was gone. Then she resumed her tasks with the magnetic dusts and the new fruits to be plucked from the crystal walls. She worked with energy and dispatch, but on occasion a numbness took hold of her and she caught herself singing that odd and memorable song and looking out beyond the crystal pillars at the sky.

She held her breath and stood very still, waiting.

It was coming nearer.

At any moment it might happen.

It was like those days when you heard a thunderstorm coming and there was the waiting silence and then the faintest pressure of the atmosphere as the climate blew over the land in shifts and shadows and vapors. And the change pressed at your ears and you were suspended in the waiting time of the coming storm. You began to tremble. The sky was stained and coloured; the clouds were thickened; the mountains took on an iron taint. The caged flowers blew with faint sighs of warning. You felt your hair stir softly. Somewhere in the house the voice-clock sang. 'Time, time, time, time . . .' ever so gently, no more than water tapping on velvet.

And then the storm. The electric illumination, the engulfments of dark wash and sounding black fell down, shutting in, forever.

That's how it was now. A storm gathered, yet the sky was clear. Lightning was expected, yet there was no cloud.

Ylla moved through the breathless summer house. Lightning would strike from the sky any instant; there would be a thunderclap, a boll of smoke, a silence, footsteps on the path, a rap on the crystalline door, and her *running* to answer . . .

Crazy Ylla! she scoffed. Why think these wild things with your idle mind?

And then it happened.

There was a warmth as of a great fire passing in the air. A whirling, rushing sound. A gleam in the sky, of metal.

Ylla cried out.

Running through the pillars, she flung wide a door. She faced the hills. But by this time there was nothing.

She was about to race down the hill when she stopped herself. She was supposed to stay here, go nowhere. The doctor was coming to visit, and her husband would be angry if she ran off.

She waited in the door, breathing rapidly, her hand out.

She strained to see over toward Green Valley, but saw nothing.

Silly woman. She went inside. You and your imagination, she thought. That was nothing but a bird, a leaf, the wind, or a fish in the canal. Sit down. Rest.

She sat down.

A shot sounded.

Very clearly, sharply, the sound of the evil insect weapon.

Her body jerked with it.

It came from a long way off. One shot. The swift humming distant bees. One shot. And then a second shot, precise and cold, and far away.

Her body winced again and for some reason she started up, screaming, and screaming and never wanting to stop screaming. She ran violently through the house and once more threw wide the door.

The echoes were dying away, away.

Gone.

She waited in the yard, her face pale, for five minutes.

Finally, with slow steps, her head down, she wandered about the pillared rooms, laying her hand to things, her lips quivering, until finally she sat alone in the darkening wine room, waiting. She began to wipe an amber glass with the hem of her scarf.

And then, from far off, the sound of footsteps crunching on the thin, small rocks.

She rose up to stand in the center of the quiet room. The glass fell from her fingers, smashing to bits.

The footsteps hesitated outside the door.

Should she speak? Should she cry out, 'Come in, oh, come in'?

She went forward a few paces.

The footsteps walked up the ramp. A hand twisted the door latch. She smiled at the door.

The door opened. She stopped smiling.

It was her husband. His silver mask glowed dully.

He entered the room and looked at her for only a moment. Then he snapped the weapon bellows open, cracked out two dead bees, heard them spat on the floor as they fell, stepped on them, and placed the empty bellows gun in the corner of the room as Ylla bent down and tried, over and over, with no success, to pick up the pieces of the shattered glass. 'What were you doing?' she asked.

'Nothing,' he said with his back turned. He removed the mask.

'But the gun – I heard you fire it. Twice.'

'Just hunting. Once in a while you like to hunt. Did Dr Nlle arrive?'

'No.'

'Wait a minute.' He snapped his fingers disgustedly. 'Why, I remember *now*. He was supposed to visit us *tomorrow* afternoon. How stupid of me.'

They sat down to eat. She looked at her food and did not move her hands. 'What's wrong?' he asked, not looking up from dipping his meat in the bubbling lava.

'I don't know. I'm not hungry,' she said.

'Why not?'

'I don't know. I'm just not.'

The wind was rising across the sky; the sun was going down. The room was small and suddenly cold.

'I've been trying to remember,' she said in the silent room, across from her cold, erect, golden-eyed husband.

'Remember what?' He sipped his wine.

'That song. That fine and beautiful song.' She closed her eyes and hummed, but it was not the song. 'I've forgotten it. And, somehow, I don't want to forget it. It's something I want always to remember.' She moved her hands as if the rhythm might help her to remember all of it. Then she lay back in her chair. 'I can't remember.' She began to cry.

'Why are you crying?' he asked.

'I don't know, I don't know, but I can't help it. I'm sad and I don't know why, I cry and I don't why, but I'm crying.'

Her head was in her hands; her shoulders moved again and again.

'You'll be all right tomorrow,' he said.

She did not look up at him; she looked only at the empty desert and the very bright stars coming out now on the black sky, and far away there was a sound of wind rising and canal waters stirring cold in the long canals. She shut her eyes, trembling.

'Yes,' she said. 'I'll be all right tomorrow.'

According to Celsus

MARY RENAULT

THE WOMAN WENT ALMOST RUNNING along the road from the Necropolis to the city, unaware of her speed, which was that of desperation seeking outlet. A funeral procession, walking ahead, slowed her down; women in white linen beat their bared breasts with rhythmic ululations; the bier with the gilded and painted mummy-case was drawn by softly pacing mules. It would be unseemly to overtake, still more to join them; she had to keep behind their crawl till they turned off towards a tomb. Then she hurried again, as relieved as if she had some appointment to keep, till she reached the suburbs. Here she collected herself; it was the Egyptian quarter, where she might be known, though she was a Greek and lived in the Bruchion.

Before leaving home she had smeared her face with dust and put on over her robe, which was professionally thin, a mantle borrowed from her slave. She had never visited an embalmer's shop before, but everyone said what scum they were, and that no one sent them a handsome woman till the third day in hot weather or the fourth in cool. She had laughed about it with her Greek friends; if one was supposed to keep forever the looks one was embalmed with, she for one would risk a short bout with them, to be pickled fresh. Among Egyptian friends, of course, she took such matters with due solemnity; good manners, or at least appropriate ones, were a mainstay of her calling. As she walked, she recalled these moments with anguish, clutching her mantle which she would have torn had she been alone.

She had almost joined the wailing women, to have her grief out. She had wept, but not rightly bewailed her dead. Her very body craved the release of ritual lamentation; under her veil, her lips moved in ancient words she had heard in childhood at young men's funerals. Woe to me, woe to me, alas! How have you left me? My lamp is broken, my sun is darkened, my rose is dead. My shining jewel, you lie in the dark shades. How did we wrong the fates, that they took you in your youth, while I breathe the air and walk among the living? . . . The words flowed from her, mindless as tears, till she was aware she had grown audible; someone had turned to look. She bit upon her veil. He should be mourned in the proper words of his people, such as the hired women on the road had used; but she did not know them. They had always spoken Greek together. All well-bred Egyptians in Alexandria spoke Greek. But they did not lament their dead in it.

She had entered the Canopic Way, the axis of the city, already filled with its morning crowd, complexioned from jet to ivory. In the flat delta land, no skyline showed beyond the ornate roofscape, except the cone-shaped Hill of Pan, man-made for the mountain god. Not a week since, they had climbed its spiral steps together to look at the lights by night, and the path of the Pharos beacon on the water. Had he known even then what he meant to do?

The morning sun picked out the gilded wings of sphinx and gryphon acroteria, crowning the pediments of the royal palaces; the laurel wreath of solid gold flamed over the tomb of Alexander. There his imperishable body lay; and all around it the imperishable bodies of later kings whose fame had perished sooner. There lay Kleopatra, the last Ptolemy; a fellow-whore, but one who could afford to bury her man like a king; even he had an imperishable body in a painted tomb. There would be no more Macedonians lying here in spices. Alexandria had been Roman for sixty years.

She turned aside into the Greek quarter, and went to her house to make herself presentable. Dropping the borrowed mantle, she saw the fleas she had felt. Dull habit told her the slut should be whipped for letting down the house; but that was in another life. She washed her face, but did not paint it. She had been a customer of the man she was going to see, but he had never been one of hers. She was going to beg, not sell. That must be clear from the beginning.

Her Nubian doorkeeper had been told to deny her to everyone; but coming out she met dawdling before the house a callow youth, eager for fashion, and aware that it cost nothing to be seen in the street exchanging quips with a hetaira at a good address. It seemed that at some time she must have been to bed with him. She had forgotten his name, and almost his face; feigning to have forgotten it entirely, she turned her back and walked away. In protecting her grief, it seemed to her she was protecting the dead as well. When she had left him, she knew she must have behaved like a woman who has only time for rich men, and remembered that he was young.

She returned to the great highway, walking east again. This stretch she knew like her own doorstep. Straight as a ruler where Alexander had paced it out, it led to the Canopic Gate, and on to the canal; which was the work of others, and doubtless not in his style. Kleopatra, they said, had known it very well, and much as it was now; its barges moored to the palms, swaying and plashing when lantern-lit revellers danced to harps and flutes; the bright-awninged booths on shore, selling beads and birds, sweet gums and ivory toys and wine; the little tents for hire, with someone in them to any taste for those who came alone, or empty for those who came together. The Canopic Life, the waterstreet of pleasure, drew tourists from all over the Empire. In one of its tents she had started her career. She had been taken up by a moneyed young Roman, resolute to be Hellenized, and had made enough out of it to rent her house, before he moved on to Ephesos. After that she had kept going, with a good sort of client who could afford to start the evening on the canal, or end the night there; till she had met Inaros, and shut her door to all the rest.

They had lived their own Canopic Life, on the water-palace of their private barge; it had been made new for her, as if she had been some sightseer from Rhodes. Her house had been full of the toys and gems and scent, alabaster vases, flaskets of jewellers' glass, the scarves sewn with gold and pearls, that he had bought her on the canal. He had given her something every day. She was starting to cry again, and wiped her face with her veil. It was time to leave the Canopic Way; she turned north, into the Jewish quarter.

It was quieter here. At the west end, nearest to the palaces and the houses of rich Greeks, the rich Jews lived, behind high walls, with heavy teak gates spiked at the top. One was still blackened from last month's riot, when an Egyptian mob must have tried to burn it down. Only two kinds of Jew lived on the fringes of the quarter: those who could afford protection, and those who could not afford the safer streets inside.

She passed a house whose owner had once called on her. Over the greeting-wine, he had apologized for not taking her to Canopus, lest his family should get to hear he had been seen there. She had shown him the door and directed him to a brothel. She was a hetaira, a companion; she had kept her professional pride. Now she remembered he had not been a bad sort of man, and she might have made as much from him as from the Roman; but once set up, she had never been one to save. The rioters had been at his door too, there were axe-marks on it.

She had been forgetting the riot; the first thing she saw when she got to the poorer streets was a burned-out house. Would the shop be gone? They had broken into it, she knew, the time before, in search of magicians' scrolls, but had found no one at home. He had gone off somewhere as he often did; if he had had books he had returned them, or had them looked after, so they had only stolen his tools. He had come back looking as lean and tanned as if he had crossed a desert; when he came to repair her broken shutter (some drunken reveller had tried to get in that way) she had made him eat a good meal. The money she had lent him for new tools, he had repaid her within a month. That money was spent like all the rest; she wished it had still been owing.

Yes, the shop was standing. They must have stoned the roof; it had been patched with offcuts, and with part of an old sail. (He had friends, she remembered, among the river boatmen; he had told her, while he was fixing up the shutter, that he had worked his passage to Memphis, and even once to Thebes.) He had been back since the riot, then. But it was a day of adverse stars; he would be out.

She heard a laugh; a Jew in a smith's apron came out smiling and walked away. Through the open door she saw him at work inside.

He was putting in a box the nails that the smith had brought him. On the bench was the lid of a bride-chest, which he had been sanding; the cypress-wood showed a gloss through the drifts of dust. Even when he had been gone a month, he was never long without work, having a name for never skimping it; people saved up for him anything that would wait. The sun through the doorway reddened his chestnut hair and beard. Her shadow fell on the new wood; he looked up and said, 'Shalom.'

It recalled to her the taboos of his religion; she had forgotten even that. Drawing back upon the threshold she said, 'I shouldn't come in here. I have touched the dead.'

'Come in, Myrrhina.' He stood up, powdered with wood-dust up his arms and down his short working tunic. He was tall. Still fearing a bad start with him, she said, 'I don't want to make you unclean.'

'You look clean to me. Cleaner than this chair is.' He dusted it down with a polishing rag. She thought, as she had done before, how good his Greek was, despite his strong Jewish accent; more like a scholar's than an artisan's. It must be true about the scrolls. 'Sit down. Try it and tell me how it feels. They're coming for it tomorrow.'

'It's smooth. It's restful to the back.' This in fact was true. She had been very tired. She wondered whether she was ritually polluting some strict Jewish home to which the chair would go; but from all she heard, the very orthodox took their custom elsewhere.

He dusted off his hands on his tunic skirt, took down from the shelf a wine-flask, a water cooler, and a jug, and mixed for both of them; giving her the guest's cup of red-glazed clay, and untying a workman's bronze one from his girdle. The wine was good. Someone would have given him that, like the sailcloth on the roof. It reminded her to express sympathy for the damage. It was not only her training in good manners that made her put off declaring her errand.

'I had warning; and this time I took my tools with me.' He smiled and touched the plane, a gesture of thanks. But still unready, she said, 'You had no roof, in all that rain.'

'Oh, yes, I slept warm and dry. I was fixing new mangers in a stable, and they let me use the loft.'

'A stable! That isn't right, that isn't fit for you.' She could see that his usual sleeping-place was a shelf above the shop; but men's dignity must always be taken care of; it was second nature. 'Why, I'd gladly have lent you the price of an inn room. A stable, what a place, for a man like you.'

'It should have been just like home. I was born in one.' She looked up, shocked. He half laughed, then said, 'I am sorry. That put me in mind of my mother, when I was so-high, and she heard me telling my friends. "So we were late on the road, and why? Because your father took on extra work to have you well provided for, and wouldn't leave the apprentice to make your cradle. God should be so good to you, you should be half the workman your father is. So now you run about telling all the street you were born in the straw, as if we had been beggars. Children today, they have no gratitude."' He was a startlingly good mimic, apparently without thinking about it. 'Poor Mother, she never knew what I might say next.'

Seeing he had ceased to smile, she asked, 'Is your mother dead?'

'No.' He took the empty cup from her. She had only felt her thirst when she began to drink. 'It is you who are mourning.'

The word released her. She lamented as she had only begun to do beside the dead, when the neighbours ran her out of the house, the ruinous Greek whore, and chased her off with stones. She cried out the ancient words, and tore at her hair, till he came forward from the bench on which he had been leaning, and laid his hand on her head.

Her grief, which had been her own, was no longer hers. But she bore it all, like a great black tower built up on her, tier on tier. She wept for the mothers of dead children; for men dying in deserts or drowned at sea; for the great Alexander laid in spices and the soldiers unburied in his wars; for the very robbers whom the Romans crucified: for every agony she had heard of since she was born. She felt the weight would crush her into the earth. He withdrew his hand; she heard him say, 'No. I did not mean . . .' His fingers brushed her forehead. 'Peace, peace.' Her wailing ceased, without any will of hers; the visions left her; the darkness thinned, a remote glimmer, faint and discontinuous, promised some answer beyond comprehension. Coming to herself, she found she had torn her robe, and drew it together, knowing he was a modest man. She remembered she had told him nothing yet.

'Inaros is dead.' But he would never have heard the name. 'I left the others. He was the only one. You will think we were mad. Everyone thinks so. We wanted to be Antony and Kleopatra. Children believe in their games like that. I should have known, he didn't understand money, he'd never had to think of it, he had so much; but it was only what his father gave him. I didn't know how they all hated me. His father died and left him nothing, he said his portion was spent. He never told me. He never told me everything was gone. Everyone tells me now, now it's too late. When he went to the house his brothers shut the door in his face. They said for all they cared, he could go herding swine.'

'Just people need no repentance.' He swept an angry hand across the work-bench; the dust from it made her cough.

'He'd never been taught a trade, he was ashamed to beg. He knew I would never leave him, that I'd starve with him unless he'd let me keep him. He wrote to me, asking me to forgive him for choosing to die instead.'

There was a deep silence. It came back to her that some superstition forbade the Jews to die when they chose, like Greeks and Romans. He turned to the work-bench, and drew with his finger in the sand. At last he looked up.

'And have you forgiven him?'

She was stunned to silence, only now perceiving that she had not. 'Yes,' she said presently, 'Yes, I can forgive him.'

'So will his father. Go in peace.'

But she was ready with her errand now, and no longer ashamed to beg. 'I came to ask – would you make a coffin for him? I must tell you first, I don't know when I can pay.'

'A friend in grief,' he said. 'Don't speak of it, in God's name.' He looked about the shop, at the timber stacked by the walls. 'Was he a tall man? Say, about as tall as I am? No, it's better I come to the house.' He fell silent. She saw him withdraw into himself. Presently he lifted his large shadowed eyes – she understood why people called him a magician – and asked, 'How long has he been dead?'

'You can't see him. He's gone to the Necropolis. He was a hand's breadth shorter than you. About a hand's breadth.'

'To the Necropolis?' He took a step backward. 'For the rites of the Egyptians?'

'That's why I can't pay.' She could scarcely bring herself to speak of the morning's horrors. 'I've never been there before. They didn't tell me, until I'd brought him there, that the coffin was extra.'

She saw him stiffen, and cried out, 'He gave me everything! Look at this dress, you can pull the stuff through a ring.' It was indeed revealing; he looked aside. 'How can I leave him to be sundried and wrapped in a rush mat like a beggar? I've given him my tomb, I paid for one in the plague year. . . . He's an Egyptian. He must be embalmed in the proper way. It's taken all I have, they make you pay them first. . . . Someone said you made a poor man's coffin for nothing.'

'But that was one of our people.' With a sinking heart she saw him now wholly Jewish. 'The only son of a widow, a good son too. For the rites of the idolaters, God forbid I should make coffins.' Having known many men, she saw his harshness came more from shock than anger. 'They will paint a heathen god on it, an Osiris. I am not a maker of idols.'

'You promised!' she cried childishly. But she had had promises from other men. She rocked herself silently in the chair with its smell of new wood and wax. After a while she said, 'O Zeus, if I could have died instead. They could have thrown me on a dunghill, with only a pinch of earth on me. Our gods don't care. But he's an Egyptian. If his body perishes, he can't rise up again.'

He turned away from her; was he telling her to go? Walking to the little window, he drew the back of his hand, still dust-streaked, across his eyes. They focused on something outside; he turned and beckoned her. She came up, caring only that she had not been dismissed yet, willing to be shown whatever passing sight he chose.

He pointed instead into a corner of the window-square, silted up with dust and twigs and dried leaves. Among them a chrysalis, plump glossy-brown, clung to the wooden frame. He stroked it, delicately, with his finger end.

The polished carapace dulled and dried. A flaw appeared in it, then a lengthways crack. It widened, showing the veined, tissue-thin folds inside. Faintly they heaved, as the crack grew bigger; a head emerged, with round eyes of polished bronze. The black threadlike forefeet followed. Labouring, moist and weak, the creature dragged itself free, and crept into a patch of sunlight. It sat there a long time, faintly quivering, before, as if only now aware of them, it began to stir its pleated wings.

Softly, without disturbing it, he picked up the split dry husk and showed it her in his palm. 'I should make you a box for this?'

She glanced at it; then turned again to watch with a fixed painful intentness the slow tentative shrugs and stumbles, the exploring, vague antennae, the falling back. One of the pale-green wings had a fold that would not part; the downy thorax kept lurching sideways, and struggling erect again. 'Sometimes,' he said over her shoulder, 'it takes too long.' Pursing his lips he sent a soft breath towards it. It rocked on its feet, twice; then the wings opened and beat, and it launched itself on the air.

She walked back into the shop. The sun-patch on the cypress wood had moved and deepened. Dust-motes danced in its beam. Her mind dazzled like her eyes; the wood itself seemed a shaft of whirling motes whose motion bonded it like shuttles in a loom; it, and the flask, and the clay cup on the bench, were all inhabited by powers which could be released if some god pronounced the Word. She remembered she had watched all night; but she felt, rather than weariness, like a dancer in step with the dance. It returned to stillness, and she to the wooden room. He was still standing there, waiting, with the chrysalis in his hand.

After taking time to think, for time was not important, she answered, 'He will still be wishing it. Six thousand years, he told me, the Egyptian records go back. It takes a long time, you said. It was better he had his rights from me. . . . But you're a good Jew, I

know. I know you're a holy man. I shouldn't make you unclean. I'll
buy an Egyptian coffin. . . . I can get the money.'

'No!' He tossed the brown shard from him. She had never heard
him raise his voice before. 'Better I should be thrown in the deep sea
with a millstone tied to me. Be comforted. I will make the box.'

He went back to the wall again, and started to turn the timbers.

'Oh, the blessing of all the gods on you!' She ran on, garrulous
with relief, forgetting that for him Zeus and Osiris were alike
idolatrous. He up-ended the longest plank and measured it against
himself. It was tall enough.

'May you never want, may your good mother rejoice in you! Finish
your other orders first. Don't lose paying work. They don't need it
yet. I could have – earned it – but it wouldn't be doing right by
him, he wouldn't wish it, it was why he died. While he's lying
unburied. . . . The proper way takes seventy days.'

'You shall have it in seven. I am leaving; I have sold the shop.'

'Leaving?' Even on such a day, she found it could still upset her,
'Oh, it is wicked the way these mobs behave. What harm do the
Jews do? They work and mind their own business. Why, even the
great Alexander welcomed them here. You know, he gave the Jews
of Alexandria the right to be Macedonians.'

'No doubt he meant it kindly.' (They were all alike, she thought,
convinced they were something particular; it stirred up the mobs
against them.) 'But I am from Judea, in any case.'

'I thought you had always lived here.' She was well trained in
showing interest, and had done it often for far less return.

'Once I believed I had been born in this very shop. It was the first
place I remembered, sitting on this floor and pulling the shavings
straight. I was a baby when we came away; there was a pogrom in
our village. My father left everything, except his tools and his savings,
just enough to buy this place. It was for his sake I took it, when I
came back. Look, those are his notches on the doorpost, where he
measured me on my birthdays. He made this bench; look at the
work.' He pointed fondly to fine chamfering and smooth-ended
dowels. She admired them with animation, as she had admired men's
horses and houseboats and battle-scars. She too had craftsmanship.

'He's buried among our people. He saved for years, to take us back
in time for my barmitzvah.'

'Yes?' she said at last. The pause had been long. She knew nothing
of the rite; no doubt it was one of the Mysteries, about which, as

always, it was unlawful to speak. Those of Isis, she had heard, were very awesome; and there was that cave in Boeotia, after which people said you could never laugh again. At the sound of her voice, his eyes returned to her.

'Yes. I learned my father's business both there and here. But it is time now to be taking it up at home.'

'We shall miss you, dear man. May you live long and die rich.' Privately she resolved to offer a votive for him to Hephaistos. The artificers' god would surely consent to favour an honest craftsman; and he would be none the wiser.

Note

According to Celsus, an eclectic philosopher of the second century A.D., Jesus of Nazareth had lived and worked in Egypt, and there 'learned the arts of thaumaturgy'. According to Matthew, it would be likely that his early years were spent in Alexandria, containing as it did the first large and established Jewish community which refugees from Judea would encounter. The city is described at some length by Strabo the geographer, who lived there from about 25-20 BC.

Flight

JOHN STEINBECK

ABOUT FIFTEEN MILES BELOW MONTEREY, on the wild coast, the Torres family had their farm, a few sloping acres above a cliff that dropped to the brown reefs and to the hissing white waters of the ocean. Behind the farm the stone mountains stood up against the sky. The farm buildings huddled like little clinging aphids on the mountain skirts, crouched low to the ground as though the wind might blow them into the sea. The little shack, the rattling, rotting barn were gray-bitten with sea salt, beaten by the damp wind until they had taken on the color of the granite hills. Two horses, a red cow and a red calf, half a dozen pigs and a flock of lean, multicolored chickens stocked the place. A little corn was raised on the sterile slope, and it grew short and thick under the wind, and all the cobs formed on the landward sides of the stalks.

Mama Torres, a lean, dry woman with ancient eyes, had ruled the farm for ten years, ever since her husband tripped over a stone in the field one day and fell full length on a rattlesnake. When one is bitten on the chest there is not much that can be done.

Mama Torres had three children, two undersized black ones of twelve and fourteen, Emilio and Rosy, whom Mama kept fishing on the rocks below the farm when the sea was kind and when the truant officer was in some distant part of Monterey County. And there was Pepé, the tall smiling son of nineteen, a gentle, affectionate boy, and very lazy. Pepé had a tall head, pointed at the top, and from its peak, coarse black hair grew down like a thatch all around. Over his smiling little eyes Mama cut a straight bang so he could see. Pepé had sharp Indian cheek bones and an eagle nose, but his mouth was as sweet and shapely as a girl's mouth, and his chin was fragile and chiseled. He was loose and gangling, all legs and feet and wrists, and he was very lazy. Mama thought him fine and brave, but she never told him so. She said, 'Some lazy cow must have got into thy father's family, else how could I have a son like thee.' And she said, 'When I carried thee, a sneaking lazy coyote came out of the brush and looked at me one day. That must have made thee so.'

Pepé smiled sheepishly and stabbed at the ground with his knife to keep the blade sharp and free from rust. It was his inheritance, that knife, his father's knife. The long heavy blade folded back into the black handle. There was a button on the handle. When Pepé pressed the button, the blade leaped out ready for use. The knife was with Pepé always, for it had been his father's knife.

One sunny morning when the sea below the cliff was glinting and blue and the white surf creamed on the reef, when even the stone mountains looked kindly, Mama Torres called out the door of the shack, 'Pepé, I have a labor for thee.'

There was no answer. Mama listened. From behind the barn she heard a burst of laughter. She lifted her full long skirt and walked in the direction of the noise.

Pepé was sitting on the ground with his back against a box. His white teeth glistened. On either side of him stood the two black ones, tense and expectant. Fifteen feet away a redwood post was set in the ground. Pepé's right hand lay limply in his lap, and in the palm the big black knife rested. The blade was closed back into the handle. Pepé looked smiling at the sky.

Suddenly Emilio cried, 'Ya!'

Pepé's wrist flicked like the head of a snake. The blade seemed to fly open in mid-air, and with a thump the point dug into the redwood post, and the black handle quivered. The three burst into excited laughter. Rosy ran to the post and pulled out the knife and brought it back to Pepé. He closed the blade and settled the knife carefully in his listless palm again. He grinned self-consciously at the sky.

'Ya!'

The heavy knife lanced out and sunk into the post again. Mama moved forward like a ship and scattered the play.

'All day you do foolish things with the knife, like a toy-baby,' she stormed. 'Get up on thy huge feet that eat up shoes. Get up!' She took him by one loose shoulder and hoisted at him. Pepé grinned sheepishly and came half-heartedly to his feet. 'Look!' Mama cried. 'Big lazy, you must catch the horse and put on him thy father's saddle. You must ride to Monterey. The medicine bottle is empty. There is no salt. Go thou now, Peanut! Catch the horse.'

A revolution took place in the relaxed figure of Pepé. 'To Monterey, me? Alone? *Sí*, Mama.'

She scowled at him. 'Do not think, big sheep, that you will buy candy. No, I will give you only enough for the medicine and the salt.'

Pepé smiled. 'Mama, you will put the hatband on the hat?'

She relented then. 'Yes, Pepé. You may wear the hatband.'

His voice grew insinuating, 'And the green handkerchief, Mama?'

'Yes, if you go quickly and return with no trouble, the silk green handkerchief will go. If you make sure to take off the handkerchief when you eat so no spot may fall on it. . . .'

'*Sí*, Mama. I will be careful. I am a man.'

'Thou? A man? Thou art a peanut.'

He went into the rickety barn and brought out a rope, and he walked agilely enough up the hill to catch the horse.

When he was ready and mounted before the door, mounted on his father's saddle that was so old that the oaken frame showed through torn leather in many places, then Mama brought out the round black hat with the tooled leather band, and she reached up and knotted the green silk handkerchief about his neck. Pepé's blue denim coat was much darker than his jeans, for it had been washed much less often.

Mama handed up the big medicine bottle and the silver coins. 'That for the medicine,' she said, 'and that for the salt. That for a candle to burn for the papa. That for *dulces* for the little ones. Our friend Mrs Rodriguez will give you dinner and maybe a bed for the night. When you go to the church say only ten Paternosters and only twenty-five Ave Marias. Oh! I know, big coyote. You would sit there flapping your mouth over Aves all day while you looked at the candles and the holy pictures. That is not good devotion to stare at the pretty things.'

The black hat, covering the high pointed head and black thatched hair of Pepé, gave him dignity and age. He sat the rangy horse well. Mama thought how handsome he was, dark and lean and tall. 'I would not send thee now alone, thou little one, except for the medicine,' she said softly. 'It is not good to have no medicine, for who knows when the toothache will come, or the sadness of the stomach. These things are.'

'Adios, Mama,' Pepé cried. 'I will come back soon. You may send me often alone. I am a man.'

'Thou art a foolish chicken.'

He straightened his shoulders, flipped the reins against the horse's shoulder and rode away. He turned once and saw that they still watched him, Emilio and Rosy and Mama. Pepé grinned with pride and gladness and lifted the tough buckskin horse to a trot.

When he had dropped out of sight over a little dip in the road, Mama turned to the black ones, but she spoke to herself. 'He is nearly a man now,' she said. 'It will be a nice thing to have a man in the house again.' Her eyes sharpened on the children. 'Go to the rocks now. The tide is going out. There will be abalones to be found.' She put the iron hooks into their hands and saw them down the steep trail to the reefs. She brought the smooth stone *metate* to the doorway and sat grinding her corn to flour and looked occasionally at the road over which Pepé had gone. The noonday came and then the afternoon, when the little ones beat the abalones on a rock to make them tender and Mama patted the tortillas to make them thin. They ate their dinner as the red sun was plunging down toward the ocean. They sat on the doorsteps and watched the big white moon come over the mountain tops.

Mama said, 'He is now at the house of our friend Mrs Rodriguez. She will give him nice things to eat and maybe a present.'

Emilio said, 'Some day I too will ride to Monterey for medicine. Did Pepé come to be a man today?'

Mama said wisely, 'A boy gets to be a man when a man is needed. Remember this thing. I have known boys forty years old because there was no need for a man.'

Soon afterward they retired, Mama in her big oak bed on one side of the room, Emilio and Rosy in their boxes full of straw and sheepskins on the other side of the room.

The moon went over the sky and the surf roared on the rocks. The roosters crowed the first call. The surf subsided to a whispering surge against the reef. The moon dropped toward the sea. The roosters crowed again.

The moon was near down to the water when Pepé rode on a winded horse to his home flat. His dog bounded out and circled the horse yelping with pleasure. Pepé slid off the saddle to the ground. The weathered little shack was silver in the moonlight and the square shadow of it was black to the north and east. Against the east the piling mountains were misty with light; their tops melted into the sky.

Pepé walked wearily up the three steps and into the house. It was dark inside. There was a rustle in the corner.

Mama cried out from her bed. 'Who comes? Pepé, is it thou?'

'*Sí*, Mama.'

'Did you get the medicine?'

'*Sí*, Mama.'

'Well, go to sleep, then. I thought you would be sleeping at the house of Mrs Rodriguez.' Pepé stood silently in the dark room. 'Why do you stand there, Pepé? Did you drink wine?'

'*Sí*, Mama.'

'Well, go to bed then and sleep out the wine.'

His voice was tired and patient, but very firm. 'Light the candle, Mama. I must go away into the mountains.'

'What is this, Pepé? You are crazy.' Mama struck a sulphur match and held the little blue burr until the flame spread up the stick. She set light to the candle on the floor beside her bed. 'Now, Pepé, what is this you say?' She looked anxiously into his face.

He was changed. The fragile quality seemed to have gone from his chin. His mouth was less full than it had been, the lines of the lips were straighter, but in his eyes the greatest change had taken place. There was no laughter in them any more, nor any bashfulness. They were sharp and bright and purposeful.

He told her in a tired monotone, told her everything just as it had happened. A few people came into the kitchen of Mrs Rodriguez. There was wine to drink. Pepé drank wine. The little quarrel – the man started toward Pepé and then the knife – it went almost by itself. It flew, it darted before Pepé knew it. As he talked, Mama's face grew stern, and it seemed to grow more lean. Pepé finished. 'I am a man now, Mama. The man said names to me I could not allow.'

Mama nodded. 'Yes, thou art a man, my poor little Pepé. Thou art a man. I have seen it coming on thee. I have watched you throwing the knife into the post, and I have been afraid.' For a moment her face had softened, but now it grew stern again. 'Come! We must get you ready. Go. Awaken Emilio and Rosy. Go quickly.'

Pepé stepped over to the corner where his brother and sister slept among the sheepskins. He leaned down and shook them gently. 'Come, Rosy! Come, Emilio! The mama says you must arise.'

The little black ones sat up and rubbed their eyes in the candlelight.

Mama was out of bed now, her long black skirt over her nightgown. 'Emilio,' she cried. 'Go up and catch the other horse for Pepé. Quickly, now! Quickly.' Emilio put his legs in his overalls and stumbled sleepily out the door.

'You heard no one behind you on the road?' Mama demanded.

'No, Mama. I listened carefully. No one was on the road.'

Mama darted like a bird about the room. From a nail on the wall she took a canvas water bag and threw it on the floor. She stripped a blanket from her bed and rolled it into a tight tube and tied the ends with a string. From a box beside the stove she lifted a flour sack half full of black stringy jerky. 'Your father's black coat, Pepé. Here, put it on.'

Pepé stood in the middle of the floor watching her activity. She reached behind the door and brought out the rifle, a long 38–56, worn shiny the whole length of the barrel. Pepé took it from her and held it in the crook of his elbow. Mama brought a little leather bag and counted the cartridges into his hand. 'Only ten left,' she warned. 'You must not waste them.'

Emilio put his head in the door. "*Qui 'st 'l caballo*, Mama.'

'Put on the saddle from the other horse. Tie on the blanket. Here, tie the jerky to the saddle horn.'

Still Pepé stood silently watching his mother's frantic activity. His chin looked hard, and his sweet mouth was drawn and thin. His little eyes followed Mama about the room almost suspiciously.

Rosy asked softly, 'Where goes Pepé?'

Mama's eyes were fierce. 'Pepé goes on a journey. Pepé is a man now. He has a man's thing to do.'

Pepé straightened his shoulders. His mouth changed until he looked very much like Mama.

At last the preparation was finished. The loaded horse stood outside the door. The water bag dripped a line of moisture down the bay shoulder.

The moonlight was being thinned by the dawn and the big white moon was near down to the sea. The family stood by the shack. Mama confronted Pepé. 'Look, my son! Do not stop until it is dark again. Do not sleep even though you are tired. Take care of the horse in order that he may not stop of weariness. Remember to be careful with the bullets – there are only ten. Do not fill thy stomach with jerky or it will make thee sick. Eat a little jerky and fill thy stomach with grass. When thou comest to the high mountains, if thou seest any of the dark watching men, go not near to them nor try to speak to them. And forget not thy prayers.' She put her lean hands on Pepé's shoulders, stood on her toes and kissed him formally on both cheeks, and Pepé kissed her on both cheeks. Then he went to Emilio and Rosy and kissed both of their cheeks.

Pepé turned back to Mama. He seemed to look for a little softness, a little weakness in her. His eyes were searching, but Mama's face remained fierce. 'Go now,' she said. 'Do not wait to be caught like a chicken.'

Pepé pulled himself into the saddle. 'I am a man,' he said.

It was the first dawn when he rode up the hill toward the little canyon which let a trail into the mountains. Moonlight and daylight fought with each other, and the two warring qualities made it difficult to see. Before Pepé had gone a hundred yards, the outlines of his figure were misty; and long before he entered the canyon, he had become a gray, indefinite shadow.

Mama stood stiffly in front of her doorstep, and on either side of her stood Emilio and Rosy. They cast furtive glances at Mama now and then.

When the gray shape of Pepé melted into the hillside and disappeared, Mama relaxed. She began the high, whining keen of the death wail. 'Our beautiful – our brave,' she cried. 'Our protector, our son is gone.' Emilio and Rosy moaned beside her. 'Our beautiful – our brave, he is gone.' It was the formal wail. It rose to a high piercing whine and subsided to a moan. Mama raised it three times and then she turned and went into the house and shut the door.

Emilio and Rosy stood wondering in the dawn. They heard Mama whimpering in the house. They went out to sit on the cliff above the ocean. They touched shoulders. 'When did Pepé come to be a man?' Emilio asked.

'Last night,' said Rosy. 'Last night in Monterey.' The ocean clouds turned red with the sun that was behind the mountains.

'We will have no breakfast,' said Emilio. 'Mama will not want to cook.' Rosy did not answer him. 'Where is Pepé gone?' he asked.

Rosy looked around at him. She drew her knowledge from the quiet air. 'He has gone on a journey. He will never come back.'

'Is he dead? Do you think he is dead?'

Rosy looked back at the ocean again. A little steamer, drawing a line of smoke sat on the edge of the horizon. 'He is not dead,' Rosy explained. 'Not yet.'

Pepé rested the big rifle across the saddle in front of him. He let the horse walk up the hill and he didn't look back. The stony slope took on a coat of short brush so that Pepé found the entrance to a trail and entered it.

When he came to the canyon opening, he swung once in his saddle and looked back, but the houses were swallowed in the misty light. Pepé jerked forward again. The high shoulder of the canyon closed in on him. His horse stretched out its neck and sighed and settled to the trail.

It was a well-worn path, dark soft leaf-mould earth strewn with broken pieces of sandstone. The trail rounded the shoulder of the canyon and dropped steeply into the bed of the stream. In the shallows the water ran smoothly, glinting in the first morning sun. Small round stones on the bottom were as brown as rust with sun moss. In the sand along the edges of the stream the tall, rich wild mint grew, while in the water itself the cress, old and tough, had gone to heavy seed.

The path went into the stream and emerged on the other side. The horse sloshed into the water and stopped. Pepé dropped his bridle and let the beast drink of the running water.

Soon the canyon sides became steep and the first giant sentinel redwoods guarded the trail, great round red trunks bearing foliage as green and lacy as ferns. Once Pepé was among the trees, the sun was lost. A perfumed and purple light lay in the pale green of the underbrush. Gooseberry bushes and blackberries and tall ferns lined the stream, and overhead the branches of the redwoods met and cut off the sky.

Pepé drank from the water bag, and he reached into the flour sack and brought out a black string of jerky. His white teeth gnawed at the string until the tough meat parted. He chewed slowly and drank occasionally from the water bag. His little eyes were slumberous and tired, but the muscles of his face were hard set. The earth of the trail was black now. It gave up a hollow sound under the walking hoofbeats.

The stream fell more sharply. Little waterfalls splashed on the stones. Five-fingered ferns hung over the water and dripped spray from their fingertips. Pepé rode half over in his saddle, dangling one leg loosely. He picked a bay leaf from a tree beside the way and put it into his mouth for a moment to flavor the dry jerky. He held the gun loosely across the pommel.

Suddenly he squared in his saddle, swung the horse from the trail and kicked it hurriedly up behind a big redwood tree. He pulled up the reins tight against the bit to keep the horse from whinnying. His face was intent and his nostrils quivered a little.

A hollow pounding came down the trail, and a horseman rode by, a fat man with red cheeks and a white stubble beard. His horse put down its head and blubbered at the trail when it came to the place where Pepé had turned off. 'Hold up!' said the man and he pulled up his horse's head.

When the last sound of the hoofs died away, Pepé came back into the trail again. He did not relax in the saddle any more. He lifted the big rifle and swung the lever to throw a shell into the chamber, and then he let down the hammer to half cock.

The trail grew very steep. Now the redwood trees were smaller and their tops were dead, bitten dead where the wind reached them. The horse plodded on; the sun went slowly overhead and started down toward the afternoon.

Where the stream came out of a side canyon, the trail left it. Pepé dismounted and watered his horse and filled up his water bag. As soon as the trail had parted from the stream, the trees were gone and only the thick brittle sage and manzanita and chaparral edged the trail. And the soft black earth was gone, too, leaving only the light tan broken rock for the trail bed. Lizards scampered away into the brush as the horse rattled over the little stones.

Pepé turned in his saddle and looked back. He was in the open now; he could be seen from a distance. As he ascended the trail the country grew more rough and terrible and dry. The way wound about the bases of great square rocks. Little gray rabbits skittered in the brush. A bird made a monotonous high creaking. Eastward the bare rock mountaintops were pale and powder-dry under the dropping sun. The horse plodded up and up the trail toward a little V in the ridge which was the pass.

Pepé looked suspiciously back every minute or so, and his eyes sought the tops of the ridges ahead. Once, on a white barren spur, he saw a black figure for a moment, but he looked quickly away, for it was one of the dark watchers. No one knew who the watchers were, nor where they lived, but it was better to ignore them and never to show interest in them. They did not bother one who stayed on the trail and minded his own business.

The air was parched and full of light dust blown by the breeze from the eroding mountains. Pepé drank sparingly from his bag and corked it tightly and hung it on the horn again. The trail moved up the dry shale hillside, avoiding rocks, dropping under clefts, climbing in and out of old water scars. When he arrived at the little pass he stopped and looked back for a long time. No dark watchers were to be seen now. The trail behind was empty. Only the high tops of the redwoods indicated where the stream flowed.

Pepé rode on through the pass. His little eyes were nearly closed with weariness, but his face was stern, relentless and manly. The high mountain wind coasted sighing through the pass and whistled on the edges of the big blocks of broken granite. In the air, a red-tailed hawk sailed over close to the ridge and screamed angrily. Pepé went slowly through the broken jagged pass and looked down on the other side.

The trail dropped quickly, staggering among broken rock. At the bottom of the slope there was a dark crease, thick with brush, and on the other side of the crease a little flat, in which a grove of oak trees grew. A scar of green grass cut across the flat. And behind the flat another mountain rose, desolate with dead rocks and starving little black bushes. Pepé drank from the bag again for the air was so dry that it encrusted his nostrils and burned his lips. He put the horse down the trail. The hooves slipped and struggled on the steep way, starting little stones that rolled off into the brush. The sun was gone behind the westward mountain now, but still it glowed brilliantly on the oaks and on the grassy flat. The rocks and the hillsides still sent up waves of the heat they had gathered from the day's sun.

Pepé looked up to the top of the next dry withered ridge. He saw a dark form against the sky, a man's figure standing on top of a rock, and he glanced away quickly not to appear curious. When a moment later he looked up again, the figure was gone.

Downward the trail was quickly covered. Sometimes the horse floundered for footing, sometimes set his feet and slid a little way. They came at last to the bottom where the dark chaparral was higher than Pepé's head. He held up his rifle on one side and his arm on the other to shield his face from the sharp brittle fingers of the brush.

Up and out of the crease he rode, and up a little cliff. The grassy flat was before him, and the round comfortable oaks. For a moment he studied the trail down which he had come, but there was no movement and no sound from it. Finally he rode over the flat, to the green streak, and at the upper end of the damp he found a little spring welling out of the earth and dropping into a dug basin before it seeped out over the flat.

Pepé filled his bag first, and then he let the thirsty horse drink out of the pool. He led the horse to the clump of oaks, and in the middle of the grove, fairly protected from sight on all sides, he took off the saddle and the bridle and laid them on the ground. The horse stretched his jaws sideways and yawned. Pepé knotted the lead rope about the horse's neck and tied him to a sapling among the oaks, where he could graze in a fairly large circle.

When the horse was gnawing hungrily at the dry grass, Pepé went to the saddle and took a black string of jerky from the sack and strolled to an oak tree on the edge of the grove, from under which he could watch the trail. He sat down in the crisp dry oak leaves and automatically felt for his big black knife to cut the jerky, but he had no knife. He leaned back on his elbow and gnawed at the tough strong meat. His face was blank, but it was a man's face.

The bright evening light washed the eastern ridge, but the valley was darkening. Doves flew down from the hills to the spring, and the quail came running out of the brush and joined them, calling clearly to one another.

Out of the corner of his eye Pepé saw a shadow grow out of the bushy crease. He turned his head slowly. A big spotted wildcat was creeping toward the spring, belly to the ground, moving like thought.

Pepé cocked his rifle and edged the muzzle slowly around. Then he looked apprehensively up the trail and dropped the hammer again. From the ground beside him he picked an oak twig and threw it toward the spring. The quail flew up with a roar and the doves whistled away. The big cat stood up: for a long moment he looked at Pepé with cold yellow eyes, and then fearlessly walked back into the gulch.

The dusk gathered quickly in the deep valley. Pepé muttered his prayers, put his head down on his arm and went instantly to sleep.

The moon came up and filled the valley with cold blue light, and the wind swept rustling down from the peaks. The owls worked up and down the slopes looking for rabbits. Down in the brush of the gulch a coyote gabbled. The oak trees whispered softly in the night breeze.

Pepé started up, listening. His horse had whinnied. The moon was just slipping behind the western ridge, leaving the valley in darkness behind it.Pepé sat tensely gripping his rifle. From far up the trail he heard an answering whinny and the crash of shod hooves on the broken rock. He jumped to his feet, ran to his horse and led it under the trees. He threw on the saddle and cinched it tight for the steep trail, caught the unwilling head and forced the bit into the mouth. He felt the saddle to make sure the water bag and the sack of jerky were there. Then he mounted and turned up the hill.

It was velvet dark. The horse found the entrance to the trail where it left the flat, and started up, stumbling and slipping on the rocks. Pepé's hand rose up to his head. His hat was gone. He had left it under the oak tree.

The horse had struggled far up the trail when the first change of dawn came into the air, a steel grayness as light mixed thoroughly with dark. Gradually the sharp snaggled edge of the ridge stood out above them, rotten granite tortured and eaten by the winds of time. Pepé had dropped his reins on the horn, leaving direction to the horse. The brush grabbed at his legs in the dark until one knee of his jeans was ripped.

Gradually the light flowed down over the ridge. The starved brush and rocks stood out in the half light, strange and lonely in high perspective. Then there came warmth into the light. Pepé drew up and looked back, but he could see nothing in the darker valley below. The sky turned blue over the coming sun. In the waste of the mountainside, the poor dry brush grew only three feet high. Here and there, big outcroppings of unrotted granite stood up like mouldering houses. Pepé relaxed a little. He drank from his water bag and bit off a piece of jerky. A single eagle flew over, high in the light.

Without warning Pepé's horse screamed and fell on its side. He was almost down before the rifle crash echoed up from the valley. From a hole behind the struggling shoulder, a stream of bright crimson blood pumped and stopped and pumped and stopped. The hooves threshed on the ground. Pepé lay half stunned beside the horse. He looked slowly down the hill. A piece of sage clipped off beside his head and another crash echoed up from side to side of the canyon. Pepé flung himself frantically behind a bush.

He crawled up the hill on his knees and one hand. His right hand held the rifle up off the ground and pushed it ahead of him. He moved with the instinctive care of an animal. Rapidly he wormed his way toward one of the big outcroppings of granite on the hill above him. Where the brush was high he doubled up and ran, but where the cover was slight he wriggled forward on his stomach, pushing the rifle ahead of him. In the last little distance there was no cover at all. Pepé poised and then he darted across the space and flashed around the corner of the rock.

He leaned panting against the stone. When his breath came easier he moved along behind the big rock until he came to a narrow split that offered a thin section of vision down the hill. Pepé lay on his stomach and pushed the rifle barrel through the slit and waited.

The sun reddened the western ridges now. Already the buzzards were settling down toward the place where the horse lay. A small brown bird scratched in the dead sage leaves directly in front of the rifle muzzle. The coasting eagle flew back toward the rising sun.

Pepé saw a little movement in the brush far below. His grip tightened on the gun. A little brown doe stepped daintily out on the trail and crossed it and disappeared into the brush again. For a long time Pepé waited. Far below he could see the little flat and the oak trees and the slash of green. Suddenly his eyes flashed back at the trail again. A quarter of a mile down there had been a quick movement in the chaparral. The rifle swung over. The front sight nestled in the v of the rear sight. Pepé studied for a moment and then raised the rear sight a notch. The little movement in the brush came again. The sight settled on it. Pepé squeezed the trigger. The explosion crashed down the mountain and up the other side, and came rattling back. The whole side of the slope grew still. No more movement. And then a white streak cut into the granite of the slit and a bullet whined away and a crash sounded up from below. Pepé felt a sharp pain in his right hand. A sliver of granite was sticking out from between his first and second knuckles and the point protruded from his palm. Carefully he pulled out the sliver of stone. The wound bled evenly and gently. No vein nor artery was cut.

Pepé looked into a little dusty cave in the rock and gathered a handful of spider web, and he pressed the mass into the cut, plastering the soft web into the blood. The flow stopped almost at once.

The rifle was on the ground. Pepé picked it up, levered a new shell into the chamber. And then he slid into the brush on his stomach. Far to the right he crawled, and then up the hill, moving slowly and carefully, crawling to cover and resting and then crawling again.

In the mountains the sun is high in its arc before it penetrates the gorges. The hot face looked over the hill and brought instant heat with it. The white light beat on the rocks and reflected from them and rose up quivering from the earth again, and the rocks and bushes seemed to quiver behind the air.

Pepé crawled in the general direction of the ridge peak, zig-zagging for cover. The deep cut between his knuckles began to throb. He crawled close to a rattlesnake before he saw it, and when it raised its dry head and made a soft beginning whirr, he backed up and took another way. The quick gray lizards flashed in front of him, raising a tiny line of dust. He found another mass of spider web and pressed it against his throbbing hand.

Pepé was pushing the rifle with his left hand now. Little drops of sweat ran to the ends of his coarse black hair and rolled down his cheeks. His lips and tongue were growing thick and heavy. His lips writhed to draw saliva into his mouth. His little dark eyes were uneasy and suspicious. Once when a gray lizard paused in front of him on the parched ground and turned its head sideways he crushed it flat with a stone.

When the sun slid past noon he had not gone a mile. He crawled exhaustedly a last hundred yards to a patch of high sharp manzanita, crawled desperately, and when the patch was reached he wriggled in among the tough gnarly trunks and dropped his head on his left arm. There was little shade in the meager brush, but there was cover and safety. Pepé went to sleep as he lay and the sun beat on his back. A few little birds hopped close to him and peered and hopped away. Pepé squirmed in his sleep and he raised and dropped his wounded hand again and again.

The sun went down behind the peaks and the cool evening came, and then the dark. A coyote yelled from the hillside. Pepé started awake and looked about with misty eyes. His hand was swollen and heavy; a little thread of pain ran up the inside of his arm and settled in a pocket in his armpit. He peered about and then stood up, for the mountains were black and the moon had not yet risen. Pepé stood up in the dark. The coat of his father pressed on his arm. His tongue was swollen until it nearly filled his mouth. He wriggled out of the coat and dropped it in the brush, and then he struggled up the hill, falling over rocks and tearing his way through the brush. The rifle knocked against stones as he went. Little dry avalanches of gravel and shattered stone went whispering down the hill behind him.

After a while the old moon came up and showed the jagged ridge top ahead of him. By moonlight Pepé traveled more easily. He bent forward so that his throbbing arm hung away from his body. The journey uphill was made in dashes and rests, a frantic rush up a few yards and then a rest. The wind coasted down the slope rattling the dry stems of the bushes.

The moon was at meridian when Pepé came at last to the sharp backbone of the ridge top. On the last hundred yards of the rise no soil had clung under the wearing winds. The way was on solid rock. He clambered to the top and looked down on the other side. There was a draw like the last below him, misty with moonlight, brushed with dry struggling sage and chaparral. On the other side the hill rose up sharply and at the top the jagged rotten teeth of the mountain showed against the sky. At the bottom of the cut the brush was thick and dark.

Pepé stumbled down the hill. His throat was almost closed with thirst. At first he tried to run, but immediately he fell and rolled. After that he went more carefully. The moon was just disappearing behind the mountains when he came to the bottom. He crawled into the heavy brush feeling with his hands for water. There was no water in the bed of the stream, only damp earth. Pepé laid his gun down and scooped up a handful of mud and put it in his mouth, and then he spluttered and scraped the earth from his tongue with his finger, for the mud drew at his mouth like a poultice. He dug a hole in the stream bed with his fingers, dug a little basin to catch water; but before it was very deep his head fell forward on the damp ground and he slept.

The dawn came and the heat of the day fell on the earth, and still Pepé slept. Late in the afternoon his head jerked up. He looked slowly around. His eyes were slits of wariness. Twenty feet away in the heavy brush a big tawny mountain lion stood looking at him. Its long thick tail waved gracefully, its ears were erect with interest, not laid back dangerously. The lion squatted down on its stomach and watched him.

Pepé looked at the hole he had dug in the earth. A half inch of muddy water had collected in the bottom. He tore the sleeve from his hurt arm, with his teeth ripped out a little square, soaked it in the water and put it in his mouth. Over and over he filled the cloth and sucked it.

Still the lion sat and watched him. The evening came down but there was no movement on the hills. No birds visited the dry bottom of the cut. Pepé looked occasionally at the lion. The eyes of the yellow beast dropped as though he were about to sleep. He yawned and his long thin red tongue curled out. Suddenly his head jerked around and his nostrils quivered. His big tail lashed. He stood up and slunk like a tawny shadow into the thick brush.

A moment later Pepé heard the sound, the faint far crash of horses' hooves on gravel. And he heard something else, a high whining yelp of a dog.

Pepé took his rifle in his left hand and he glided into the brush almost as quietly as the lion had. In the darkening evening he crouched up the hill toward the next ridge. Only when dark came did he stand up. His energy was short. Once it was dark he fell over the rocks and slipped to his knees on the steep slope, but he moved on and on up the hill, climbing and scrabbling over the broken hillside.

When he was far up toward the top, he lay down and slept for a little while. The withered moon, shining on his face, awakened him. He stood up and moved up the hill. Fifty yards away he stopped and turned back, for he had forgotten his rifle. He walked heavily down and poked about in the brush, but he could not find his gun. At last he lay down to rest. The pocket of pain in his armpit had grown more sharp. His arm seemed to swell out and fall with every heartbeat. There was no position lying down where the heavy arm did not press against his armpit.

With the effort of a hurt beast, Pepé got up and moved again toward the top of the ridge. He held his swollen arm away from his body with his left hand. Up the steep hill he dragged himself, a few steps and a rest, and a few more steps. At last he was nearing the top. The moon showed the uneven sharp back of it against the sky.

Pepé's brain spun in a big spiral up and away from him. He slumped to the ground and lay still. The rock ridge top was only a hundred feet above him.

The moon moved over the sky. Pepé half turned on his back. His tongue tried to make words, but only a thick hissing came from between his lips.

When the dawn came, Pepé pulled himself up. His eyes were sane again. He drew his great puffed arm in front of him and looked at the angry wound. The black line ran up from his wrist to his armpit. Automatically he reached in his pocket for the big black knife, but it was not there. His eyes searched the ground. He picked up a sharp blade of stone and scraped at the wound, sawed at the proud flesh and then squeezed the green juice out in big drops. Instantly he threw back his head and whined like a dog. His whole right side shuddered at the pain, but the pain cleared his head.

In the gray light he struggled up the last slope to the ridge and crawled over and lay down behind a line of rocks. Below him lay a deep canyon exactly like the last, waterless and desolate. There was no flat, no oak trees, not even heavy brush in the bottom of it. And on the other side a sharp ridge stood up, thinly brushed with starving sage, littered with broken granite. Strewn over the hill there were giant outcroppings, and on the top the granite teeth stood out against the sky.

The new day was light now. The flame of the sun came over the ridge and fell on Pepé where he lay on the ground. His coarse black hair was littered with twigs and bits of spider web. His eyes had retreated back into his head. Between his lips the tip of his black tongue showed.

He sat up and dragged his great arm into his lap and nursed it, rocking his body and moaning in his throat. He threw back his head and looked up into the pale sky. A big black bird circled nearly out of sight, and far to the left another was sailing near.

He lifted his head to listen, for a familiar sound had come to him from the valley he had climbed out of; it was the crying yelp of hounds, excited and feverish, on a trail.

Pepé bowed his head quickly. He tried to speak rapid words but only a thick hiss came from his lips. He drew a shaky cross on his breast with his left hand. It was a long struggle to get to his feet. He crawled slowly and mechanically to the top of a big rock on the ridge peak. Once there, he arose slowly, swaying to his feet, and stood erect. Far below he could see the dark brush where he had slept. He braced his feet and stood there, black against the morning sky.

There came a ripping sound at his feet. A piece of stone flew up and a bullet droned off into the next gorge. The hollow crash echoed up from below. Pepé looked down for a moment and then pulled himself straight again.

His body jarred back. His left hand fluttered helplessly toward his breast. The second crash sounded from below. Pepé swung forward and toppled from the rock. His body struck and rolled over and over, starting a little avalanche. And when at last he stopped against a bush, the avalanche slid slowly down and covered up his head.

Murder. 1986

P.D. JAMES

THE GIRL LAY NAKED ON THE BED WITH a knife through her heart. That was the one simple and inescapable fact. No, not simple. It was a fact horrible in its complications. Sergeant Dolby, fighting nausea, steadied his shaking thighs against the foot of the bed and forced his mind into coherence – arranging his thoughts in order, like a child piling brick on colored brick and holding its breath against the inevitable tumble into chaos. He mustn't panic. He must take things slowly. There was a proper procedure laid down for this kind of crisis. There was a procedure laid down for everything.

Dead. That, at least, was certain. Despite the heat of the June morning the slim, girlish body was quite cold, the rigor mortis already well advanced in face and arms. What had they taught him in Detective School about the onset of rigor mortis, that inexorable if erratic stiffening of the muscles, the body's last protest against disintegration and decay? He couldn't remember. He had never been any good at the more academic studies. He had been lucky to be accepted for the Criminal Investigation Department; they had made that clear enough to him at the time. They had never ceased to make it clear. A lost car; a small breaking and entering; a purse snatch. Send Dolby. He had never rated anything more interesting or important than the petty crimes of inadequate men. If it was something no one else wanted to be bothered with, send Dolby. If it was something the C.I.D. would rather not be told about, send Dolby.

And that was exactly how this death would rate. He would have to report it, of course. But it wouldn't be popular news at Headquarters. They were overworked already, depleted in strength, inadequately equipped, forced even to employ him six years after his normal retirement age. No, they wouldn't exactly welcome this spot of trouble. And the reason, as if he didn't know it, was fixed there on the wall for him to read. The statutory notice was pasted precisely over the head of her bed.

He wondered why she had chosen that spot. There was no rule about where it had to be displayed. Why, he wondered, had she chosen to sleep under it as people once slept under a Crucifix. An affirmation? But the wording was the same as he would find on the notice in the downstairs hall, in the elevator, on every corridor wall, in every room in the Colony. The Act to which it referred was already two years old:

PRESERVATION OF THE RACE ACT - 1984
Control of Interplanetary Disease
Infection Carriers

All registered carriers of the Disease, whether or not they are yet manifesting symptoms, are required under Section 2 of the above Act to conform to the following regulations. . . .

He didn't need to read further. He knew the regulations by heart – the rules by which the Ipdics lived, if you could call it living. The desperate defense of the few healthy against the menace of the many condemned. The small injustices which might prevent the greatest injustice of all, the extinction of man. The stigmata of the Diseased: the registered number tattooed on the left forearm; the regulation Ipdic suit of yellow cotton in summer, blue serge in winter; the compulsory sterilization, since an Ipdic bred only monsters; the rule prohibiting marriage or any close contact with a Normal; the few manual jobs they were permitted to do; the registered Colonies where they were allowed to live.

He knew what they would say at Headquarters. If Dolby had to discover a murder, it would have to be of an Ipdic. And trust him to be fool enough to report it.

But there was no hurry. He could wait until he was calmer, until he could face with confidence whomever they chose to send. And there were things they would expect him to have noticed. He had better make an examination of the scene before he reported. Then, even if they came at once, he would have something sensible to say.

He forced himself to look again at the body. She was lying on her back, eyes closed as if asleep, light brown hair streaming over the pillow. Her arms were crossed over her chest as if in a last innocent gesture of modesty. Below the left breast the handle of a knife stuck out like an obscene horn.

He bent low to examine it. An ordinary handle, probably an ordinary knife. A short-bladed kitchen knife of the kind used to peel vegetables. Her right palm was curved around it, but not touching it, as if about to pluck it out. On her left forearm the registered Ipdic number glowed almost luminous against the delicate skin.

She was neatly covered by a single sheet pulled smooth and taut so that it looked as if the body had been ritually prepared for examination – an intensification of the horror. He did not believe that this childish hand could have driven in the blade with such precision or that, in her last spasms, she had drawn the sheet so tidily over her nakedness. The linen was only a shade whiter than her skin. There had been two months now of almost continuous sunshine. But this body had been muffled in the high-necked tunic and baggy trousers of an Ipdic suit. Only her face had been open to the sun. It was a delicate nut-brown and there was a faint spatter of freckles across the forehead.

He walked slowly around the room. It was sparsely furnished but pleasant enough. The world had no shortage of living space, even for Ipdics. They could live in comfort, even in some opulence, until the electricity, the television, the domestic computer, the micro-oven broke down. Then these things remained broken. The precious skills of electricians and engineers were not wasted on Ipdics. And it was extraordinary how quickly squalor could replace luxury.

A breakdown of electricity in a building like this could mean no hot food, no light, no heating. He had known Ipdics who had frozen or starved to death in apartments which, back in 1980, only six years ago, must have cost a fortune to rent. Somehow the will to survive died quickly in them. It was easier to wrap themselves in blankets and reach for that small white capsule so thoughtfully provided by the Government, the simple painless way out which the whole healthy community was willing for them to take.

But this girl, this female Ipdic PXN 07926431, wasn't living in squalor. The apartment was clean and almost obsessively neat. The micro-oven was out of order, but there was an old-fashioned electric cooker in the kitchen and when he turned it on the hot plate glowed red. There were even a few personal possessions – a little clutch of seashells carefully arranged on the window ledge, a Staffordshire porcelain figurine of a shepherdess, a child's tea service on a papier-mâché tray.

Her yellow Ipdic suit was neatly folded over the back of a chair. He took it up and saw that she had altered it to fit her. The darts under the breasts had been taken in, the side seams carefully shaped. The hand stitching was neat and regular, an affirmation of individuality, or self-respect. A proud girl. A girl undemoralized by hopelessness. He turned the harsh cotton over and over in his hands and felt the tears stinging the back of his eyes.

He knew that this strange and half remembered sweetness was pity. He let himself feel it, willing himself not to shrink from the pain. Just so, in his boyhood, he had tentatively placed his full weight on an injured leg after football, relishing the pain in the knowledge that he could bear it, that he was still essentially whole.

But he must waste no more time. Turning on his pocket radio he made his report.

'Sergeant Dolby here. I'm speaking from Ipdic Colony 865. Female Ipdic PXN 07926431 found dead. Room 18. Looks like murder.'

It was received as he had expected.

'Oh, God! Are you sure? All right. Hang around. Someone will be over.'

While he waited he gave his attention to the flowers. They had struck his senses as soon as he opened the door of the room, but the first sight of the dead girl had driven them from his mind. Now he let their gentle presence drift back into his consciousness. She had died amid such beauty.

The apartment was a bower of wild flowers, their delicate sweetness permeating the warm air so that every breath was an intimation of childhood summers, an evocation of the old innocent days. Wild flowers were his hobby. The slow brain corrected itself, patiently, mechanically: wild flowers had been his hobby. But that was before the Sickness, when the words flower and beauty seemed to have meaning. He hadn't looked at a flower with any joy since 1980.

1980. The year of the Disease. The year with the hottest summer for 21 years. That summer when the sheer weight of people had pressed against the concrete bastions of the city like an intolerable force, had thronged its burning pavements, had almost brought its transport system to a stop, had sprawled in checkered ranks across its parks until the sweet grass was pressed into pale straw.

1980. The year when there were too many people. Too many happy, busy, healthy human beings. The year when his wife had been alive; when his daughter Tessa had been alive. The year when brave men, traveling far beyond the moon, had brought back to earth the Sickness – the Sickness which had decimated mankind on every continent of the globe. The Sickness which had robbed him, Arthur Dolby, of his wife and daughter.

Tessa. She had been only 14 that spring. It was a wonderful age for a daughter, the sweetest daughter in the world. And Tessa had been intelligent as well as sweet. Both women in his life, his wife and daughter, had been cleverer than Dolby. He had known it, but it hadn't worried him or made him feel inadequate. They had loved him so unreservedly, had relied so much on his manhood, been so satisfied with what little he could provide. They had seen in him qualities he could never discern in himself, virtues which he knew he no longer possessed. His flame of life was meagre; it had needed their warm breaths to keep it burning bright. He wondered what they would think of him now. Arthur Dolby in 1986, looking once more at wild flowers.

He moved among them as if in a dream, like a man recognizing with wonder a treasure given up for lost. There had been no attempt at formal arrangement. She had obviously made use of any suitable container in the apartment and had bunched the plants together naturally and simply, each with its own kind. He could still identify them. There were brown earthenware jars of Herb Robert, the rose-pink flowers set delicately on their reddish stems. There were cracked teacups holding bunches of red clover, meadow buttercups, and long-stemmed daisies; jam jars of white campion and cuckoo flowers; egg cups of birdsfoot trefoil – 'eggs and bacon,' Tessa used to call it – and even smaller jars of rueleaved saxifrage and the soft pink spurs of haresfoot. But, above all, there were the tall vases of cow-parsley, huge bunches of strong hollow-grooved stems supporting their umbels of white flowers, delicate as bridal lace, yet pungent and strong, shedding a white dust on the table, bed, and floor.

And then, in the last jar of all, the only one which held a posy of mixed flowers, he saw the Lady Orchid. It took his breath away. There it stood, alien and exotic, lifting its sumptuous head proudly among the common flowers of the roadside, the white clover, campion, and sweet wild roses. The Lady Orchid. *Orchis Purpurea.*

He stood very still and gazed at it. The decorative spike rose from its shining foliage, elegant and distinctive, seeming to know its rarity. The divisions of the helmet were wine-red, delicately veined and spotted with purple, their somber tint setting off the clear white beauty of the lip. The Lady Orchid. Dolby knew of only one spot, the fringe of a wood in old Kent County in the Southeast Province, where this flower grew wild. The Sickness had changed the whole of human life. But he doubted if it had changed that.

It was then that he heard the roar of the helicopter. He went to the window. The red machine, like a huge angry insect, was just bouncing down onto the roof landing pad. He watched, puzzled. Why should they send a chopper? Then he understood. The tall figure in the all-white uniform with its gleaming braid swung himself down from the cockpit and was lost to view behind the parapet of the roof. But Dolby recognized at once that helmet of black hair, the confident poise of the head. C.J. Kalvert. The Commissioner of the Home Security Force in person.

He told himself that it couldn't be true – that Kalvert wouldn't concern himself with the death of an Ipdic, that he must have some other business in the Colony. But what business? Dolby waited in fear, his hands clenched so that the nails pierced his palms, waited in an agony of hope that it might not be true. But it was true. A minute later he heard the strong footsteps advancing along the corridor. The door opened. The Commissioner had arrived.

He nodded an acknowledgement to Dolby and, without speaking, went over to the bed. For a moment he stood in silence, looking down at the girl. Then he said, 'How did you get in, Sergeant?'

The accent was on the third word.

'The door was unlocked, sir.'

'Naturally, Ipdics are forbidden to lock their doors. I was asking what you were doing here.'

'I was making a search, sir.'

That at least was true. He had been making a private search.

'And you discovered that one more female Ipdic had taken the sensible way out of her troubles. Why didn't you call the Sanitary Squad? It's unwise to leave a body longer than necessary in this weather. Haven't we all had enough of the stench of decay?'

'I think she was murdered, sir.'

'Do you indeed, Sergeant. And why?'

Dolby moistened his dry lips and made his cramped fingers relax. He mustn't let himself be intimidated, mustn't permit himself to get flustered. The important thing was to stick to the facts and present them cogently.

'It's the knife, sir. If she were going to stab herself, I think she would have fallen on the blade, letting her weight drive it in, then the body would have been found face downwards. That way, the blade would have done all the work. I don't think she would have had the strength or the skill to pierce her heart lying in that position. It looks almost surgical. It's too neat. The man who drove that knife in knew what he was doing. And then there's the sheet. She couldn't have placed it over herself so neatly.'

'A valid point, Sergeant. But the fact that someone considerately tidied her up after death doesn't necessarily mean that he killed her. Anything else?'

He was walking restlessly about the room as he talked, touching nothing, his hands clasped behind his back. Dolby wished that he would stand still. He said, 'But why use a knife at all, sir? She must have been issued her euthanasia capsule.'

'Not a very dramatic way to go, Dolby. The commonest door for an Ipdic to let life out. She may have exercised a feminine preference for a more individualistic death. Look around this room, Sergeant. Does she strike you as having been an ordinary girl?'

No, she hadn't struck Dolby as ordinary. But this was ground he dare not tread. He said doggedly, 'And why should she be naked, sir? Why take all her clothes off to kill herself?'

'Why, indeed. That shocks you, does it, Dolby? It implies an unpleasant touch of exhibitionism. It offends your modesty. But perhaps she was an exhibitionist. The flowers would suggest it. She made her room into a bower of fragrance and beauty. Then, naked, as unencumbered as the flowers, she stretched herself out like a sacrifice, and drove a knife through her heart. Can you, Sergeant, with your limited imagination, understand that a woman might wish to die like that?'

Kalvert swung round and strode over to him. The fierce black eyes burned into Dolby's. The Sergeant felt frightened, at a loss. The conversation was bizarre. He felt they were playing some private game, but that only one of them knew the rules.

What did Kalvert want of him? In a normal world, in the world before the Sickness when the old police force was at full strength, the Commissioner wouldn't even have known that Dolby existed. Yet here they both were, engaged, it seemed, in some private animus, sparring over the body of an unimportant dead Ipdic.

It was very hot in the room now and the scent of the flowers had been growing stronger. Dolby could feel the beads of sweat on his brow. Whatever happened he must hold on to the facts. He said, 'The flowers needn't be funeral flowers. Perhaps they were for a celebration.'

'That would suggest the presence of more than one person. Even Ipdics don't celebrate alone. Have you found any evidence that someone was with her when she died?'

He wanted to reply, 'Only the knife in her breast.' But he was silent. Kalvert was pacing the room again. Suddenly he stopped and glanced at his watch. Then, without speaking, he turned on the television. Dolby remembered. Of course. The Leader was due to speak after the midday news. It was already 12:32. He would be almost finished.

The screen flickered and the too familiar face appeared. The Leader looked very tired. Even the makeup artist hadn't been able to disguise the heavy shadows under the eyes or the hollows beneath the cheekbones. With that beard and the melancholy, pain-filled face, he looked like an ascetic prophet. But he always had. His face hadn't changed much since the days of his student protest. People said that, even then, he had only really been interested in personal power. Well, he was still under thirty, but he had it now. All the power he could possibly want. The speech was nearly over.

'And so we must find our own solution. We have a tradition in this country of humanity and justice. But how far can we let tradition hamper us in the great task of preserving our race? We know what is happening in other countries, the organized and ceremonial mass suicides of thousands of Ipdics at a time, the humane Disposal Squads, the compulsory matings between computer-selected Normals. Some compulsory measures against the Ipdics we must now take. As far as possible we have relied on gentle voluntary methods. But can we afford to fall behind while other less scrupulous nations are breeding faster and more selectively, disposing of their Ipdics, re-establishing their technology, looking with covetous eyes at the great denuded spaces of the world. One day they will be repopulated. It is our duty to take part in this great process. The world needs our race. The time has come for every one of us, particularly our Ipdics, to ask ourselves with every breath we draw: have I the right to be alive?'

Kalvert turned off the set.

'I think we can forego the pleasure of seeing once again Mrs Sartori nursing her fifth healthy daughter. Odd to think that the most valuable human being in the world is a healthy fecund female. But you got the message I hope, Sergeant. This Ipdic had the wisdom to take her own way out while she still had a choice. And if somebody helped her, who are we to quibble?'

'It was still murder, sir. I know that killing an Ipdic isn't a capital crime. But the Law hasn't altered yet. It's still a felony to kill any human being.'

'Ah, yes. A felony. And you, of course, are dedicated to the detection and punishment of felonies. The first duty of a policeman is to prevent crime; the second is to detect and punish the criminal. You learned all that when you were in Detective School, didn't you? Learned it all by heart. I remember reading the first report on you, Dolby. It was almost identical with the last. "Lacking in initiative. Deficient in imagination. Tends to make errors of judgment. Should make a reliable subordinate. Lacks self-confidence." But it did admit that, when you manage to get an idea into your head, it sticks there. And you have an idea in your head. Murder. And murder is a felony. Well, what do you propose to do about it?'

'In cases of murder the body is first examined by the forensic pathologist.'

'Not this body, Dolby. Do you know how many pathologists this country now has? We have other uses for them than to cut up dead Ipdics. She was a young female. She was not pregnant. She was stabbed through the heart. What more do we need to know?'

'Whether or not a man was with her before she died.'

'I think you can take it there was. Male Ipdics are not yet being sterilized. So we add another fact. She probably had a lover. What else do you want to know?'

'Whether or not there are prints on the knife, sir, and, if so, whose they are.'

Kalvert laughed aloud. 'We were short of forensic scientists before the Sickness. How many do you suppose we have now? There was another case of capital murder reported this morning. An Ipdic has killed his former wife because she obeyed the Law and kept away from him. We can't afford to lose a single healthy woman, can we,

Dolby? There's the rumor of armed bands of Ipdics roaming the Southeast Province. There's the case of the atomic scientist with the back of his skull smashed in. A scientist, Dolby! Now, do you really want to bother the lab with this petty trouble?'

Dolby said obstinately, 'I know that someone was with her when she picked the flowers. That must have been yesterday – they're still fresh even in this heat, and wild flowers fade quickly. I think he probably came back here with her and was with her when she died.'

'Then find him, Sergeant, if you must. But don't ask for help I can't give.'

He walked over to the door without another glance at the room or at the dead girl, as if neither of them held any further interest for him. Then he turned: 'You aren't on the official list of men encouraged to breed daughters in the interest of the race, are you, Sergeant?'

Dolby wanted to reply that he once had a daughter. She was dead and he wanted no other.

'No, sir. They thought I was too old. And then there was the adverse psychologist's report.'

'A pity. One would have thought that the brave new world could have made room for just one or two people who were unintelligent, lacking in imagination, unambitious, inclined to errors of judgment. People will persist in going their own obstinate way. Goodbye, Dolby. Report to me personally on this case, will you? I shall be interested to hear how you progress. Who knows, you may reveal unsuspected talents.'

He was gone. Dolby waited for a minute as if to cleanse his mind of that disturbing presence. As the confident footsteps died away, even the room seemed to settle itself into peace. Then Dolby began the few tasks which still remained.

There weren't many. First, he took the dead girl's fingerprints. He worked with infinite care, murmuring to her as he gently pressed the pad against each fingertip, like a doctor reassuring a child. It would be pointless, he thought, to compare them with the prints on any of the ordinary objects in the room. That would prove nothing except that another person had been there. The only prints of importance would be those on the knife. But there were no prints on the knife – only an amorphous smudge of whorls and composites as if someone had attempted to fold her hand around the shaft but had lacked the courage to press the fingers firm.

But the best clue was still there – the Lady Orchid, splendid in its purity and beauty, the flower which told him where she had spent the previous day, the flower which might lead him to the man who had been with her. And there was another clue, something he had noticed when he had first examined the body closely. He had said nothing to Kalvert. Perhaps Kalvert hadn't noticed it or hadn't recognized its significance. Perhaps he had been cleverer than Kalvert. He told himself that he wasn't really as stupid as people sometimes thought. It was just that his mind was so easily flustered into incoherence when stronger men bullied or taunted him. Only his wife and daughter had really understood that, had given him the confidence to fight it.

It was time to get started. They might deny him the services of the pathologist and the laboratory, but they still permitted him the use of his car. It would be little more than an hour's drive.

But, before leaving, he bent once more over the body. The Disposal Squad would soon be here for it. He would never see it again. So he studied the clue for the last time – the faint, almost imperceptible circle of paler skin round the third finger of her left hand. The finger that could have worn a ring through the whole of a hot summer day . . .

He drove through the wide streets and sun-filled squares, through the deserted suburbs, until the tentacles of the city fell away and he was in open country. The roads were pitted and unmended, the hedges high and unkempt, the fields a turbulent sea of vegetation threatening to engulf the unpeopled farmlands. But the sun was pleasant on his face. He could almost persuade himself that this was one of the old happy jaunts into the familiar and well-loved countryside of Old Kent.

He had crossed the boundary into the Southeast Province and was already looking for the remembered landmarks of hillside and church spire when it happened. There was an explosion, a crack like a pistol shot, and the windshield shattered in his face. He felt splinters of glass stinging his cheeks. Instinctively he guarded his face with his arms. The car swerved out of control and lurched onto the grass verge. He felt for the ignition key and turned off the engine. Then he tentatively opened his eyes. They were uninjured. And it was then he saw the Ipdics.

They came out of the opposite ditch and moved toward him, with stones still in their hands. There were half a dozen of them. One, the tallest, seemed to be their leader. The others shuffled at his heels, lumpy figures in their illfitting yellow suits, their feet brown and bare, their hair matted like animals', their greedy eyes fixed on the car. They stood still, looking at him. And then the leader drew his right hand from behind his back, and Dolby saw that it held a gun.

His heart missed a beat. So it was true! Somehow the Ipdics were getting hold of weapons. He got out of the car, trying to recall the exact instructions of such an emergency. Never show fear. Keep calm. Exert authority. Remember that they are inferior, unorganized, easily cowed. Never drop your eyes. But his voice, even to him, sounded feeble, pitched unnaturally high.

'The possession of a weapon by an Ipdic is a capital crime. The punishment is death. Give me that gun.'

The voice that replied was quiet, authoritative, the kind of voice one used to call educated.

'No. First you give me the keys to the car. Then I give you something in return. A cartridge in your belly!'

His followers cackled their appreciation. It was one of the most horrible sounds in the world – the laughter of an Ipdic.

The Ipdic pointed the gun at Dolby, moving it slowly from side to side as if selecting his precise target. He was enjoying his power, drunk with elation and triumph. But he waited a second too long. Suddenly his arm jerked upward, the gun leaped from his grasp, and he gave one high desolate scream, falling into the dust of the road. He was in the first spasm of an Ipdic fit. His body writhed and twisted, arched and contracted, until the bones could be heard snapping.

Dolby looked on impassively. There was nothing he could do. He had seen it thousands of times before. It had happened to his wife, to Tessa, to all those who had died of the disease. It happened in the end to every Ipdic. It would have happened to the girl on the bed, at peace now with a knife in her heart.

The attack would leave this Ipdic broken and exhausted. If he survived, he would be a mindless idiot, probably for months. And then the fits would come more frequently. It was this feature of the Disease which made the Ipdics so impossible to train or employ, even for the simplest of jobs.

Dolby walked up to the writhing figure and kicked away the gun, then picked it up. It was a revolver, a Smith and Wesson .38, old but in good condition. He saw that it was loaded. After a second's thought he slipped it into the pocket of his jacket.

The remaining Ipdics had disappeared, scrambling back into the hedges with cries of anguish and fear. The whole incident was over so quickly that it already seemed like a dream. Only the tortured figure in the dust and the cold metal in his pocket were witnesses to its reality. He should report it at once, of course. The suppression of armed Ipdics was the first duty of the Home Security Force.

He backed the car onto the road. Then, on an impulse, he got out again and went over to the Ipdic. He bent to drag the writhing figure off the road and into the shade of the hedge. But it was no good. Revolted, he drew back. He couldn't bear to touch him. Perhaps the Ipdic's friends would creep back later to carry him away and tend to him. Perhaps. But he, Dolby, had his own problem. He had a murder to solve.

Fifteen minutes later he drove slowly through the village. The main street was deserted but he could glimpse, through the open cottage doors, the garish yellow of an Ipdic suit moving in the dim interior and he could see other yellow-clad figures bending at work in the gardens and fields. None of them looked up as he passed. He guessed that this was one of the settlements which had grown up in the country, where groups of Ipdics attempted to support themselves and each other, growing their own food, nursing their sick, burying their dead. Since they made no demands on the Normals they were usually left in peace. But it couldn't last long. There was no real hope for them.

As more and more of them were overtaken by the last inevitable symptoms, the burden on those left grew intolerable. Soon they too would be helpless and mad. Then the Security Force, the Health Authorities, and the Sanitary Squads would move in, and another colony of the dispossessed would be cleaned up. And it was a question of cleaning up. Dolby had taken part in one such operation. He knew what the final horror would be. But now in the heat of the sun-scented afternoon, he might be driving through the village as he had known it in the days before the Sickness, prosperous, peaceful, sleepy, with the men still busy on the farms.

He left the car at the churchyard gate and slipping the strap of his murder bag over his shoulder, walked up the dappled avenue of elms to the south entrance. The heavy oak door with its carved panels, its massive hinges of hammered iron creaked open at his touch. He stepped into the cool dimness and smelled again the familiar scent of flowers, musty hymn books, and wood polish, saw once again the medieval pillars soaring high to the hammer beams of the room, and, straining his eyes through the dimness he glimpsed the carving on the rood screen and the far gleam of the sanctuary lamp.

The church was full of wild flowers. They were the same flowers as those in the dead girl's apartment but here their frail delicacy was almost lost against the massive pillars and the richly carved oak. But the huge vases of cow-parsley set on each side of the chancel steps made a brave show, floating like twin clouds of whiteness in the dim air. It was a church decked for a bride.

He saw a female Ipdic polishing the brass lectern. He made his way up the aisle toward her and she beamed a gentle welcome as if his appearance were the most ordinary event in the world. Her baggy Ipdic suit was stained with polish and she wore a pair of old sandals, the soles peeling away from the uppers. Her graying hair was drawn back into a loose bun from which wisps of hair had escaped to frame the anxious, sun-stained face.

She reminded him of someone. He let his mind probe once again, painfully, into the past. Then he remembered. Of course. Miss Caroline Martin, his Sunday School superintendent. It wasn't she, of course. Miss Martin would have been over 70 at the time of the Sickness. No one as old as that had survived, except those few Tasmanian aborigines who so interested the scientists. Miss Martin, standing beside the old piano as her younger sister thumped out the opening hymn and beating time with her gloved hand as if hearing some private and quite different music. Afterward, the students had gone to their different classes and had sat in a circle around their teachers. Miss Martin had taught the older children, himself among them. Some of the boys had been unruly, but never Arthur Dolby. Even in those days he had been obedient, law-abiding. The good boy. Not particularly bright, but well-behaved. Good, dull, ineffectual. Teacher's pet.

And when she spoke it was with a voice like Miss Martin's.

'Can I help you? If you've come for Evensong services, I'm afraid it isn't until five-thirty today. If you're looking for Father Reeves, he's at the Rectory. But perhaps you're just a visitor. It's a lovely church, isn't it? Have you seen our 16th century reredos?'

'I hoped I would be in time for the wedding.'

She gave a little girlish cry of laughter.

'Dear me, you are late! I'm afraid that was yesterday! But I thought no one was supposed to know about it. Father Reeves said that it was

to be quite secret really. But I'm afraid I was very naughty. I did so
want to see the bride. After all, we haven't had a wedding here
since —'

'Since the Act?'

She corrected him gently, like Miss Martin rebuking the good boy
of the class.

'Since 1980. So yesterday was quite an occasion for us. And I did
want to see what the bride looked like in Emma's veil.'

'In what?'

'A bride has to have a veil, you know.' She spoke with gentle
reproof, taking pity on his masculine ignorance. 'Emma was my
niece. I lost her and her parents in 1981. Emma was the last bride to
be married here. That was on April 28, 1980. I've always kept her
veil and headdress. She was such a lovely bride.'

Dolby asked with sudden harshness the irrelevant but necessary
question.

'What happened to her bridegroom?'

'Oh, John was one of the lucky ones. I believe he has married
again and has three daughters. Just one daughter more and they'll be
allowed to have a son. We don't see him, of course. It wasn't to be
expected. After all, it is the Law.'

How despicable it was, this need to be reassured that there were
other traitors.

'Yes,' he said. 'It is the Law.'

She began polishing the already burnished lectern, chatting to him
as she worked.

'But I've kept Emma's veil and headdress. So I thought I'd just
place them on a chair beside the font so that this new bride would
see them when she came into church. Just in case she wanted to
borrow them, you know. And she did. I was so glad. The bridegroom
placed the veil over her head and fixed the headdress for her himself,
and she walked up the aisle looking so beautiful.'

'Yes,' said Dolby. 'She would have looked very beautiful.'

'I watched them from behind this pillar. Neither of them noticed
me. But it was right for me to be here. There ought to be someone
in the church. It says in the prayer book, "In the sight of God and
of this congregation." She had a small bouquet of wild flowers, just
a simple mixed bunch but very charming. I think they must have
picked it together.'

'She carried a Lady Orchid,' said Dolby. 'A Lady Orchid picked by her bridegroom and surrounded by daisies, clover, white campion, and wild roses.'

'How clever of you to guess! Are you a friend, perhaps?'

'No,' said Dolby. 'Not a friend. Can you describe the bridegroom?'

'I thought that you must know him. Very tall, very dark. He wore a plain white suit. Oh, they were such a handsome couple! I wished Father Reeves could have seen them.'

'I thought he married them.'

'So he did. But Father Reeves, poor man, is blind.'

So that was why he risked it, thought Dolby. But what a risk!

'Which prayer book did he use?'

She gazed at him, the milky eyes perplexed. 'Father Reeves?'

'No, the bridegroom. He did handle a prayer book, I suppose?'

'Oh yes. I put one out for each of them. Father Reeves asked me to get things ready. It was I who decorated the church. Poor dears, it wasn't as if they could have the usual printed service sheets. Emma's were so pretty, her initials intertwined with the bridegroom's. But yesterday they had to use ordinary prayer books. I chose them specially from the pews and put them on the two prayer stools. I found a very pretty white one for the bride and this splendid old book with the brass clasp for the bridegroom. It looked masculine, I thought.'

It lay on the book ledge of the front pew. She made a move to pick it up, but he shot out his hand. Then he dropped his handkerchief over the book and lifted it by the sharp edges of the binding. Brass and leather. Good for a print. And this man's palm would be moist, clammy, perhaps, with perspiration and fear. A hot day; an illegal ceremony; his mind on murder. To love and to cherish until death us do part. Yes, this bridegroom would have been nervous. But Dolby had one more question.

'How did they get here? Do you know?'

'They came by foot. At least, they walked up to the church together. I think they had walked quite a long way. They were quite hot and dusty when they arrived. But I know how they really came.'

She nodded her unkempt head and gave a little conspiratorial nod.

'I've got very good ears, you know. They came by helicopter. I heard it.'

A helicopter. He knew almost without thinking exactly who was permitted the use of a helicopter. Members of the Central Committee of Government; high ranking scientists and technicians; doctors; the

Commissioner of the Home Security Force, and his Deputy. That was all.

He took the prayer book out into the sun and sat on one of the flat-topped gravestones. He set up the prayer book on its end, then unzipped his murder bag. His hands shook so that he could hardly manage the brush and some of the gray powder was spilt and blew away in the breeze. He willed himself to keep calm, to take his time. Carefully, like a child with a new toy, he dusted the book and clasp with powder, gently blowing off the surplus with a small rubber nozzle. It was an old procedure, first practiced when he was a young Detective Constable. But it still worked. It always would. The arches, whorls, and composites came clearly into view.

He was right. It was a beautiful print. The man had made no effort to wipe it clean. Why should he? How could he imagine that this particular book would ever be identified among the many scattered around the church? How could he suspect that he would ever be traced to this despised and unregarded place? Dolby took out his camera and photographed the print. There must be continuity of evidence. He must leave no room for doubt. Then he classified its characteristics, ready for checking.

There was a little delay at the National Identification Computer Center when he phoned, and he had to wait his turn. When it came he gave his name, rank, secret code, and the classification of the print. There was a moment's silence. Then a surprised voice asked, 'Is that you, Dolby? Will you confirm your code.'

He did so. Another silence.

'Okay. But what on earth are you up to? Are you sure of your print classification?'

'Yes. I want the identification for elimination purposes.'

'Then you can eliminate, all right. That's the Commissioner. Kalvert, C.J. Hard luck, Dolby! Better start again.'

He switched off the receiver and sat in silence. He had known it, of course. But for how long? Perhaps from the beginning. Kalvert. Kalvert, who had an excuse for visiting an Ipdic Colony. Kalvert, who had the use of a helicopter. Kalvert, who had known without asking that the television set in her room was in working order. Kalvert, who had been too sure of himself to take the most elementary precautions against discovery, because he knew that it didn't matter, because he knew no one would dare touch him. Kalvert, one of the four most powerful men in the country. And it was he, the despised Sergeant Dolby, who had solved the case.

He heard the angry purr of the approaching helicopter without surprise. He had reported the armed attack of the Ipdics. It was certain that Headquarters would have immediately summoned a Squad from the nearest station to hunt them down. But Kalvert would know about the message. He had no doubt that the Commissioner was keeping a watch on him. He would know which way Dolby was heading, would realize that he was dangerously close to the truth. The armed Squad would be here in time. But Kalvert would arrive first.

He waited for five minutes, still sitting quietly on the gravestone. The air was sweet with the smell of grasses and vibrating with the high-treble midsummer chant of blackbird and thrush. He shut his eyes for a moment, breathing in the beauty, taking courage from its peace. Then he got to his feet and stood at the head of the avenue of elms to wait for Kalvert.

The gold braid on the all-white uniform gleamed in the sun. The tall figure, arrogant with confidence and power, walked unhesitatingly toward him, unsmiling, making no sign. When they were three feet apart, Kalvert stopped. They stood confronting each other. It was Dolby who spoke first. His voice was little more than a whisper.

'You killed her.'

He could not meet Kalvert's eyes. But he heard his reply.

'Yes, I killed her. Shall I tell you about it, Sergeant? You seem to have shown some initiative. You deserve to know part of the truth. I was her friend. That is prohibited by Regulation. She became my mistress. That is against the Law. We decided to get married. That is a serious crime. I killed her. That, as you earlier explained, is a felony. And what are you going to do about it, Sergeant?'

Dolby couldn't speak. Suddenly he took out the revolver. It seemed ridiculous to point it at Kalvert. He wasn't even sure that he would be able to fire it. But he held it close to his side and the curved stock fitted comfortably to his palm, giving him courage. He made himself meet Kalvert's eyes, and heard the Commissioner laugh.

'To kill a Normal is also against the Law. But it's something more. Capital murder, Dolby. Is that what you have in mind?'

Dolby spoke out of cracked lips, 'But why? *Why?*'

'I don't have to explain to you. But I'll try. Have you the imagination to understand that we might have loved each other, that I might have married her because it seemed a small risk for me and would give her pleasure, that I might have promised to kill her when her last symptoms began? Can you, Sergeant Dolby, enter into the mind of a girl like that? She was an Ipdic. And she was more alive in her condemned cell than you have ever been in your life. Female Ipdic PXN 07926431 found dead. Looks like murder. Remember how you reported it, Dolby? A felony. Something to be investigated. Against the Law. That's all it meant to you, isn't it?'

He had taken out his own revolver now. He held it easily, like a man casually dangling a familiar toy. He stood there, magnificent in the sunshine, the breeze lifting his black hair. He said quietly, 'Do you think I'd let any Law on earth keep me from the woman I loved?'

Dolby wanted to cry out that it hadn't been like that at all. That Kalvert didn't understand. That he, Dolby, had cared about the girl. But the contempt in those cold black eyes kept him silent. There was nothing they could say to each other. Nothing. And Kalvert would kill him.

The Squad would be here soon. Kalvert couldn't let him live to tell his story. He gazed with fascinated horror at the revolver held so easily, so confidently, in the Commissioner's hand. And he tightened the grip on his own, feeling with a shaking finger for the trigger.

The armored car roared up to the churchyard gate. The Squad were here. Kalvert lifted his revolver to replace it in the holster. Dolby, misunderstanding the gesture, whipped up his own gun and, closing his eyes, fired until the last cartridge was spent. Numbed by misery and panic, he didn't hear the shots or the thud of Kalvert's fall. The first sound to pierce his consciousness was a wild screaming and beating of wings as the terrified birds flew high. Then he was aware of an unnatural silence, and of an acrid smell tainting the summer air.

His right hand ached. It felt empty, slippery with sweat. He saw that he had dropped the gun. There was a long mournful cry of distress. It came from behind him. He turned and glimpsed the yellow-clad figure of the female Ipdic, hand to her mouth, watching him from the shadow of the church. Then she faded back into the dimness.

He dropped on his knees beside Kalvert. The torn arteries were pumping their blood onto the white tunic. The crimson stain burst open like a flower. Dolby took off his jacket with shaking hands and thrust it under Kalvert's head. He wanted to say he was sorry, to cry out like a child that he hadn't really meant it, that it was all a mistake.

Kalvert looked at him. Was there really pity in those dulling eyes? He was trying to speak. 'Poor Dolby! Your final error of judgment.'

The last word was hiccupped in a gush of blood. Kalvert turned his head away from Dolby and drew up his knees as if easing himself into sleep. And Dolby knew that it was too late to explain now, that there was no one there to hear him.

He stood up. The Squad were very close now, three of them, walking abreast, guns at hip, moving inexorably forward in the pool of their own shadows. And so he waited, all fear past, with Kalvert's body at his feet. And he thought for the first time of his daughter. Tessa, whom he had allowed to hide from him because that was the Law. Tessa, whom he had deserted and betrayed. Tessa, whom he had sought at last, but had found too late. Tessa, who had led him unwittingly to her lover and murderer. Tessa who would never have picked that Lady Orchid. Hadn't he taught her when she was a child that if you picked a wild orchid it can never bloom again?

A Terribly Strange Bed

WILKIE COLLINS

SHORTLY AFTER MY EDUCATION AT college was finished, I happened to be staying at Paris with an English friend. We were both young men then, and lived, I am afraid, rather a wild life, in the delightful city of our sojourn. One night we were idling about the neighbourhood of the Palais Royal, doubtful to what amusement we should next betake ourselves. My friend proposed a visit to Frascati's; but his suggestion was not to my taste. I knew Frascati's, as the French saying is, by heart; had lost and won plenty of five-franc pieces there, merely for amusement's sake, until it was amusement no longer, and was thoroughly tired, in fact, of all the ghastly respectabilities of such a social anomaly as a respectable gambling house. 'For Heaven's sake,' said I to my friend, 'let us go somewhere where we can see a little genuine, blackguard, poverty-stricken gaming, with no false gingerbread glitter thrown over it at all. Let us get away from fashionable Frascati's, to a house where they don't mind letting in a man with a ragged coat, or a man with no coat, ragged or otherwise.' – 'Very well,' said my friend, 'we needn't go out of the Palais Royal to find the sort of company you want. Here's the place just before us; as blackguard a place, by all report, as you could possibly wish to see.' In another minute we arrived at the door, and entered the house.

When we got upstairs, and had left our hats and sticks with the doorkeeper, we were admitted into the chief gambling-room. We did not find many people assembled there. But, few as the men were who looked up at us on our entrance, they were all types – lamentably true types – of their respective classes.

We had come to see blackguards; but these men were something worse. There is a comic side, more or less appreciable, in all blackguardism – here there was nothing but tragedy – mute, weird tragedy. The quiet in the room was horrible. The thin, haggard, long-haired young man, whose sunken eyes fiercely watched the turning up of the cards, never spoke; the flabby, fat-faced, pimply player, who pricked his piece of pasteboard perseveringly, to register how often black won, and how often red – never spoke; the dirty, wrinkled old man, with the vulture eyes and the darned greatcoat, who had lost his last *sou*, and still looked on desperately, after he could play no longer – never spoke. Even the voice of the croupier sounded as if it were strangely dulled and thickened in the atmosphere of the room. I had entered the place to laugh, but the spectacle before me was something to weep over. I soon found it necessary to take refuge in excitement from the depression of spirits which was fast stealing on me. Unfortunately I sought the nearest excitement, by going to the table, and beginning to play. Still more unfortunately, as the event will show, I won – won prodigiously; won incredibly; won at such a rate, that the regular players at the table crowded round me; and staring at my stakes with hungry, superstitious eyes, whispered to one another, that the English stranger was going to break the bank.

The game was *Rouge et Noir*. I had played at it in every city in Europe, without, however, the care or the wish to study the Theory of Chances – that philosopher's stone of all gamblers! And a gambler, in the strict sense of the word, I had never been. I was heart-whole from the corroding passion for play. My gaming was a mere idle amusement. I never resorted to it by necessity, because I never knew what it was to want money. I never practised it so incessantly as to lose more than I could afford, or to gain more than I could coolly pocket without being thrown off my balance by my good luck. In short, I had hitherto frequented gambling-tables – just as I frequented ballrooms and opera-houses – because they amused me, and because I had nothing better to do with my leisure hours.

But on this occasion it was very different – now, for the first time in my life, I felt what the passion for play really was. My success first bewildered, and then, in the most literal meaning of the word, intoxicated me. Incredible as it may appear, it is nevertheless true, that I only lost when I attempted to estimate chances, and played according to previous calculation. If I left everything to luck, and staked without any care or consideration, I was sure to win – to win in the face of every recognized probability in favour of the bank. At first, some of the men present ventured their money safely enough on my colour; but I speedily increased my stakes to sums which they dared not risk. One after another they left off playing, and breathlessly looked on at my game.

Still, time after time, I staked higher and higher, and still won. The excitement in the room rose to fever pitch. The silence was interrupted by a deep-muttered chorus of oaths and exclamations in different languages, every time the gold was shovelled across to my side of the table – even the imperturbable croupier dashed his rake on the floor in a (French) fury of astonishment at my success. But one man present preserved his self-possession; and that man was my friend. He came to my side, and whispering in English, begged me to leave the place, satisfied with what I had already gained. I must do him the justice to say that he repeated his warnings and entreaties several times, and only left me and went away, after I had rejected his advice (I was to all intents and purposes gambling-drunk) in terms which rendered it impossible for him to address me again that night.

Shortly after he had gone, a hoarse voice behind me cried: 'Permit me, my dear sir! – permit me to restore to their proper place two Napoleons which you have dropped. Wonderful luck, sir! I pledge you my word of honour, as an old soldier, in the course of my long experience in this sort of thing, I never saw such luck as yours! – never! Go on, sir – *Sacré mille bombes!* Go on boldly, and break the bank!'

I turned round and saw, nodding and smiling at me with inveterate civility, a tall man, dressed in a frogged and braided surtout.

If I had been in my senses, I should have considered him, personally, as being rather a suspicious specimen of an old soldier. He had goggling bloodshot eyes, mangy moustachios, and a broken nose. His voice betrayed a barrack-room intonation of the worst order, and he had the dirtiest pair of hands I ever saw – even in France. These little personal peculiarities exercised, however, no repelling influence on me. In the mad excitement, the reckless triumph of that moment, I was ready to 'fraternise' with anybody who encouraged me in my game. I accepted the old soldier's offered pinch of snuff; clapped him on the back, and swore he was the honestest fellow in the world – the most glorious relic of the Grand Army that I had ever met with. 'Go on!' cried my military friend, snapping his fingers in ecstasy, – 'Go on, and win! Break the bank – *Mille tonnerres!* my gallant English comrade, break the bank!'

And I *did* go on – went on at such a rate, that in another quarter of an hour the croupier called out: 'Gentlemen! the bank has discontinued for tonight.' All the notes, and all the gold in that 'bank,' now lay in a heap under my hands; the whole floating capital of the gambling house was waiting to pour into my pockets!

'Tie up the money in your pocket handkerchief, my worthy sir,' said the old soldier, as I wildly plunged my hands into my heap of gold. 'Tie it up, as we used to tie up a bit of dinner in the Grand Army; your winnings are too heavy for any breeches pockets that ever were sewed. There! that's it! – shovel them in, notes and all! *Crediê!* what luck! – Stop! another Napoleon on the floor! *Ah! Sacré petit polisson de Napoléon!* have I found thee at last? Now then, sir – two tight double knots each way with your honourable permission, and the money's safe. Feel it! feel it, fortunate sir! hard and round as a cannon ball – *Ah, bah!* if they had only fired such cannon balls at us at Austerlitz – *nom d'une pipe!* if they only had! And now, as an ancient grenadier, as an ex-brave of the French army, what remains for me to do? I ask what? Simply this: to entreat my valued English friend to drink a bottle of champagne with me, and toast the goddess Fortune in foaming goblets before we part!'

Excellent ex-brave! Convivial ancient grenadier! Champagne by all means! An English cheer for an old soldier! Hurrah! hurrah! Another English cheer for the goddess Fortune! Hurrah! hurrah! hurrah!

'Bravo! the Englishman; the amiable, gracious Englishman, in whose veins circulates the vivacious blood of France! Another glass? *Ah, bah!* – the bottle is empty! Never mind! *Vive le vin!* I, the old soldier, order another bottle, and half a pound of *Bon-bons* with it!'

'No, no, ex-brave; never – ancient grenadier! *Your* bottle last time; *my* bottle this. Behold it! Toast away! The French Army! – the great Napoleon! – the present company! the croupier! the honest croupier's wife and daughters – if he has any! the ladies generally! Everybody in the world!'

By the time the second bottle of champagne was emptied, I felt as if I had been drinking liquid fire – my brain seemed all aflame. No excess in wine had ever had this effect on me before in my life. Was it the result of a stimulant acting upon my system when I was in a highly excited state? Was my stomach in a particularly disordered condition? Or was the champagne amazingly strong?

'Ex-brave of the French Army!' cried I, in a mad state of exhilaration, '*I* am on fire! how are *you*? You have set me on fire! Do you hear, my hero of Austerlitz? Let us have a third bottle of champagne to put the flame out!'

The old soldier wagged his head, rolled his goggle eyes, until I expected to see them slip out of their sockets; placed his dirty forefinger by the side of his broken nose; solemnly ejaculated, 'Coffee!' and immediately ran off into an inner room.

The word pronounced by the eccentric veteran seemed to have a magical effect on the rest of the company present. With one accord they all rose to depart. Probably they had expected to profit by my intoxication; but finding that my new friend was benevolently bent on preventing me from getting dead drunk, had now abandoned all hope of thriving pleasantly on my winnings. Whatever their motive might be, at any rate they went away in a body. When the old soldier returned, and sat down again opposite to me at the table, we had the room to ourselves. I could see the croupier, in a sort of vestibule which opened out of it, eating his supper in solitude. The silence was now deeper than ever.

A sudden change, too, had come over the 'ex-brave.' He assumed a portentously solemn look; and when he spoke to me again, his speech was ornamented by no oaths, enforced by no finger-snapping, enlivened by no apostrophes or exclamations.

'Listen, my dear sir,' said he, in mysteriously confidential tones, 'listen, to an old soldier's advice. I have been to the mistress of the house (a very charming woman, with a genius for cookery!) to impress on her the necessity of making us some particularly strong and good coffee. You must drink this coffee in order to get rid of your little amiable exaltation of spirits before you think of going home – you *must*, my good and gracious friend! With all that money to take home tonight, it is a sacred duty to yourself to have your wits about you. You are known to be a winner to an enormous extent by several gentlemen present tonight, who, in a certain point of view, are very worthy and excellent fellows; but they are mortal men, my dear sir, and they have their amiable weaknesses! Need I say more? Ah, no, no! you understand me! Now, this is what you must do – send for a cabriolet when you feel quite well again – draw up all the windows when you get into it – and tell the driver to take you home only through the large and well-lighted thoroughfares. Do this; and you and your money will be safe. Do this; and tomorrow you will thank an old soldier for giving you a word of honest advice.'

Just as the ex-brave ended his oration in very lachrymose tones, the coffee came in, ready poured out in two cups. My attentive friend handed me one of the cups with a bow. I was parched with thirst, and drank it off at a draught. Almost instantly afterwards, I was seized with a fit of giddiness, and felt more completely intoxicated than ever. The room whirled round and round furiously; the old soldier seemed to be regularly bobbing up and down before me like the piston of a steam engine. I was half deafened by a violent singing in my ears; a feeling of utter bewilderment, helplessness, idiocy, overcame me. I rose from my chair, holding on by the table to keep my balance; and stammered out, that I felt dreadfully unwell – so unwell that I did not know how I was to get home.

'My dear friend,' answered the old soldier – and even his voice seemed to be bobbing up and down as he spoke – 'my dear friend, it would be madness to go home in *your* state; you would be sure to lose your money; you might be robbed and murdered with the greatest ease. *I* am going to sleep here: do *you* sleep here, too – they make up capital beds in this house – take one; sleep off the effects of the wine, and go home safely with your winnings tomorrow – tomorrow, in broad daylight.'

I had but two ideas left: one, that I must never let go hold of my handkerchief full of money; the other, that I must lie down somewhere immediately, and fall off into a comfortable sleep. So I agreed to the proposal about the bed, and took the offered arm of the old soldier, carrying my money with my disengaged hand. Preceded by the croupier, we passed along some passages and up a flight of stairs into the bedroom which I was to occupy. The ex-brave shook me warmly by the hand, proposed that we should breakfast together, and then, followed by the croupier, left me for the night.

I ran to the wash-hand stand; drank some of the water in my jug; poured the rest out, and plunged my face into it; then sat down in a chair and tried to compose myself. I soon felt better. The change for my lungs, from the fetid atmosphere of the gambling-room to the cool air of the apartment I now occupied; the almost equally refreshing change for my eyes, from the glaring gaslights of the 'Salon' to the dim, quiet flicker of one bedroom candle, aided wonderfully the restorative effects of cold water. The giddiness left me, and I began to feel a little like a reasonable being again. My first thought was of the risk of sleeping all night in a gambling-house; my second, of the still greater risk of trying to get out after the house was closed, and of going home alone at night, through the streets of Paris, with a large sum of money about me. I had slept in worse places than this on my travels; so I determined to lock, bolt, and barricade my door, and take my chance till the next morning.

Accordingly, I secured myself against all intrusion; looked under the bed, and into the cupboard; tried the fastening of the window; and then, satisfied that I had taken every proper precaution, pulled off my upper clothing, put my light, which was a dim one, on the hearth among a feathery litter of wood ashes, and got into bed, with the handkerchief full of money under my pillow.

I soon felt not only that I could not go to sleep, but that I could not even close my eyes. I was wide awake, and in a high fever. Every nerve in my body trembled – every one of my senses seemed to be preternaturally sharpened. I tossed and rolled, and tried every kind of position, and perseveringly sought out the cold corners of the bed, and all to no purpose. Now, I thrust my arms over the clothes; now, I poked them under the clothes, now, I violently shot my legs straight out down to the bottom of the bed; now, I convulsively coiled them up as near my chin as they would go; now, I shook out my crumpled pillow, changed it to the cool side, patted it flat, and lay down quietly on my back; now, I fiercely doubled it in two, set it up on end, thrust it against the board of the bed, and tried a sitting posture. Every effort was in vain; I groaned with vexation, as I felt that I was in for a sleepless night.

What could I do? I had no book to read. And yet, unless I found out some method of diverting my mind, I felt certain that I was in the condition to imagine all sorts of horrors; to rack my brain with forebodings of every possible and impossible danger; in short, to pass the night in suffering all conceivable varieties of nervous terror.

I raised myself on my elbow, and looked about the room – which was brightened by a lovely moonlight pouring straight through the window – to see if it contained any pictures or ornaments that I could at all clearly distinguish. While my eyes wandered from wall to wall, a remembrance of Le Maistre's delightful little book, *Voyage autour de ma Chambre*, occurred to me. I resolved to imitate the French author, and find occupation and amusement enough to relieve the tedium of my wakefulness, by making a mental inventory of every article of furniture I could see, and by following up to their sources the multitude of associations which even a chair, a table, or a wash-hand stand may be made to call forth.

In the nervous unsettled state of my mind at that moment, I found it much easier to make my inventory than to make my reflections, and thereupon soon gave up all hope of thinking in Le Maistre's fanciful track – or, indeed, of thinking at all. I looked about the room at the different articles of furniture, and did nothing more.

There was, first, the bed I was lying in; a four-post bed, of all things in the world to meet with in Paris! – yes, a thorough clumsy British four-poster, with the regular top lined with chintz – the regular fringed valance all round – the regular stifling unwholesome curtains, which I remembered having mechanically drawn back against the posts without particularly noticing the bed when I first got into the room. Then there was the marble topped wash-hand stand, from which the water I had spilt, in my hurry to pour it out, was still dripping, slowly and more slowly, on to the brick floor. Then two small chairs, with my coat, waistcoat, and trousers flung on them. Then a large elbow-chair covered with dirty white dimity, with my cravat and shirt collar thrown over the back. Then a chest of drawers with two of the brass handles off, and a tawdry, broken china inkstand placed on it by way of ornament for the top. Then the dressing table, adorned by a very small looking glass, and a very large pincushion. Then the window – an unusually large window. Then a dark old picture, which the feeble candle dimly showed me. It was the picture of a fellow in a high Spanish hat, crowned with a plume of towering feathers. A swarthy sinister ruffian, looking upward, shading his eyes with his hand, and looking intently upward – it might be at some tall gallows at which he was going to be hanged. At any rate, he had the appearance of thoroughly deserving it.

This picture put a kind of constraint upon me to look upward too – at the top of the bed. It was a gloomy and not an interesting object, and I looked back at the picture. I counted the feathers in the man's hat – they stood out in relief – three white, two green. I observed the crown of his hat, which was of a conical shape, according to the fashion supposed to have been favoured by Guido Fawkes. I wondered what he was looking up at. It couldn't be at the stars; such a desperado was neither astrologer nor astronomer. It must be at the high gallows, and he was going to be hanged presently. Would the executioner come into possession of his conical crowned hat and plume of feathers? I counted the feathers again – three white, two green.

While I still lingered over this very improving and intellectual employment, my thoughts insensibly began to wander. The moolight shining into the room reminded me of a certain moonlight night in England – the night after a picnic party in a Welsh valley. Every incident of the drive homeward, through lovely scenery, which the moonlight made lovelier than ever, came back to my remembrance, though I had never given the picnic a thought for years; though, if I had *tried* to recollect it, I could certainly have recalled little or nothing of that scene long past. Of all the wonderful faculties that help to tell us we are immortal, which speaks the sublime truth more eloquently than memory? Here was I, in a strange house of the most suspicious character, in a situation of uncertainty, and even of peril, which might seem to make the cool exercise of my recollection almost out of the question; nevertheless, remembering, quite involuntarily, places, people, conversations, minute circumstances of every kind, which I had thought forgotten for ever; which I could not possibly have recalled at will, even under the most favourable auspices. And what cause had produced in a moment the whole of this strange, complicated, mysterious effect? Nothing but some rays of moonlight shining in at my bedroom window.

I was still thinking of the picnic – of our merriment on the drive home – of the sentimental young lady who *would* quote *Childe Harold* because it was moonlight. I was absorbed by these past scenes and past amusements, when, in an instant, the thread on which my memories hung snapped asunder: my attention immediately came back to present things more vividly than ever, and I found myself, I neither knew why nor wherefore, looking hard at the picture again.

Looking for what?

Good God! the man had pulled his hat down on his brows! – No! the hat itself was gone! Where was the conical crown? Where the feathers – three white, two green? Not there! In place of the hat and feathers, what dusky object was it that now hid his forehead, his eyes, his shading hand?

Was the bed moving?

I turned on my back and looked up. Was I mad? drunk? dreaming? giddy again? or was the top of the bed really moving down – sinking slowly, regularly, silently, horribly, right down throughout the whole of its length and breadth – right down upon me, as I lay underneath?

My blood seemed to stand still. A deadly paralysing coldness stole all over me, as I turned my head round on the pillow, and determined to test whether the bed top was really moving or not, by keeping my eye on the man in the picture.

The next look in that direction was enough. The dull black, frowsy outline of the valance above me was within an inch of being parallel with his waist. I still looked breathlessly. And steadily, and slowly

– very slowly – I saw the figure, and the line of frame below the figure, vanish, as the valance moved down before it.

I am constitutionally, anything but timid. I have been on more than one occasion in peril of my life, and have not lost my self possession for an instant; but when the conviction first settled on my mind that the bed-top was really moving, was steadily and continuously sinking down upon me, I looked up shuddering, helpless, panic-stricken, beneath the hideous machinery for murder, which was advancing closer and closer to suffocate me where I lay.

I looked up, motionless, speechless, breathless. The candle, fully spent, went out; but the moonlight still brightened the room. Down and down, without pausing and without sounding, came the bed top, and still my panic-terror seemed to bind me faster and faster to the mattress on which I lay – down and down it sank, till the dusty odour from the lining of the canopy came stealing into my nostrils.

At that final moment the instinct of self-preservation startled me out of my trance, and I moved at last. There was just room for me to roll myself sideways off the bed. As I dropped noiselessly to the floor, the edge of the murderous canopy touched me on the shoulder.

Without stopping to draw my breath, without wiping the cold sweat from my face, I rose instantly on my knees to watch the bed-top. I was literally spellbound by it. If I had heard footsteps behind me, I could not have turned round; if a means of escape had been miraculously provided for me, I could not have moved to take advantage of it. The whole life in me was, at that moment, concentrated in my eyes.

It descended – the whole canopy, with the fringe round it, came down – down – close down; so close that there was not room now to squeeze my finger between the bed-top and the bed. I felt at the sides, and discovered that what had appeared to me from beneath to be the ordinary light canopy of a four-post bed, was in reality a thick, broad mattress, the substance of which was concealed by the valance and its fringe. I looked up and saw the four posts rising hideously bare. In the middle of the bed-top was a huge wooden screw that had evidently worked it down through a hole in the ceiling, just as ordinary presses are worked down on the substance selected for compression. The frightful apparatus moved without making the faintest noise. There had been no creaking as it came down; there was now not the faintest sound from the room above. Amid a dead and awful silence I beheld before me – in the 19th century, and in the civilised capital of France – such a machine for secret murder by suffocation as might have existed in the worst days of the Inquisition, in the lonely inns among the Hartz Mountains, in the mysterious tribunals of Westphalia! Still, as I looked on it, I could not move, I could hardly breathe, but I began to recover the power of thinking, and in a moment I discovered the murderous conspiracy framed against me in all its horror.

My cup of coffee had been drugged, and drugged too strongly. I had been saved from being smothered by having taken an overdose of some narcotic. How I had chafed and fretted at the fever-fit which had preserved my life by keeping me awake! How recklessly I had confided myself to the two wretches who had led me into this room, determined, for the sake of my winnings, to kill me in my sleep by the surest and most horrible contrivance for secretly accomplishing my destruction! How many men, winners like me, had slept, as I had proposed to sleep, in that bed, and had never been seen or heard of more! I shuddered at the bare idea of it.

But, ere long, all thought was again suspended by the sight of the murderous canopy moving once more. After it had remained on the bed – as nearly as I could guess – about ten minutes, it began to move up again. The villains who worked it from above evidently believed that their purpose was now accomplished. Slowly and silently, as it had descended, that horrible bed-top rose towards its former place. When it reached the upper extremities of the four posts, it reached the ceiling too. Neither hole nor screw could be seen; the bed became in appearance an ordinary bed again – the canopy an ordinary canopy – even to the most suspicious eyes.

Now, for the first time, I was able to move – to rise from my knees – to dress myself in my upper clothing – and to consider of how I should escape. If I betrayed, by the smallest noise, that the attempt to suffocate me had failed, I was certain to be murdered. Had I made any noise already? I listened intently, looking towards the door.

No! no footsteps in the passage outside – no sound of a tread, light or heavy, in the room above – absolute silence everywhere. Besides locking and bolting my door, I had moved an old wooden chest against it, which I had found under the bed. To remove this chest (my blood ran cold as I thought of what its contents *might* be!) without making some disturbance was impossible; and, moreover, to think of escaping through the house, now barred up for the night, was sheer insanity. Only one chance was left me – the window. I stole to it on tiptoe.

My bedroom was on the first floor, above an *entresol*, and looked into the back street. I raised my hand to open the window, knowing that on that action hung, by the merest hair's-breadth, my chance of safety. They keep vigilant watch in the House of Murder. If any part of the frame cracked, if the hinge creaked, I was a lost man! It must have occupied me at least five minutes, reckoning by time – five *hours*, reckoning by suspense – to open that window. I succeeded in doing it silently – in doing it with all the dexterity of a housebreaker – and then looked down into the street. To leap the distance beneath me would be almost certain destruction! Next, I looked round at the sides of the house. Down the left side ran a thick water-pipe – it passed close by the outer edge of the window. The moment I saw the pipe, I knew I was saved. My breath came and went freely for the first time since I had seen the canopy of the bed moving down upon me!

To some men the means of escape which I had discovered might have seemed difficult and dangerous enough – to *me* the prospect of slipping down the pipe into the street did not suggest even a thought of peril. I had always been accustomed, by the practice of gymnastics, to keep up my schoolboy powers as a daring and expert climber; and knew that my head, hands, and feet would serve me faithfully in any hazards of ascent or descent. I had already got one leg over the windowsill, when I remembered the handkerchief filled with money under my pillow. I could well have afforded to leave it behind me, but I was revengefully determined that the miscreants of the gambling-house should miss their plunder as well as their victim. So I went back to the bed and tied the heavy handkerchief at my back by my cravat.

Just as I had made it tight and fixed it in a comfortable place, I thought I heard a sound of breathing outside the door. The chill feeling of horror ran through me again as I listened. No! dead silence still in the passage – I had only heard the night air blowing softly into the room. The next moment I was on the windowsill – and the next I had a firm grip on the water-pipe with my hands and knees.

I slid down into the street easily and quietly, as I thought I should, and immediately set off at the top of my speed to a branch 'Prefecture' of Police, which I knew was situated in the immediate neighbour-hood. A 'Sub-prefect,' and several picked men among his subordinates, happened to be up, maturing, I believe, some scheme for discovering the perpetrator of a mysterious murder which all Paris was talking of just then. When I began my story, in a breathless hurry and in very bad French, I could see that the Sub-prefect suspected me of being a drunken Englishman who had robbed somebody; but he soon altered his opinion as I went on, and before I had anything like concluded, he shoved all the papers before him into a drawer, put on his hat, supplied me with another (for I was bareheaded), ordered a file of soldiers, desired his expert followers to get ready all sorts of tools for breaking open doors and ripping up brick flooring, and took my arm, in the most friendly and familiar manner possible, to lead me with him out of the house. I will venture to say, that when the Sub-prefect was a little boy, and was taken for the first time to the play, he was not half as much pleased as he was now at the job in prospect for him at the gambling house!

Away we went through the streets, the Sub-prefect cross-examining and congratulating me in the same breath as we marched at the head of our formidable *posse comitatus*. Sentinels were placed at the back and front of the house the moment we got to it; a tremendous battery of knocks was directed against the door; a light appeared at a window; I was told to conceal myself behind the police – then came more knocks, and a cry of 'Open in the name of the law!' At that terrible summons bolts and locks gave way before an invisible hand, and the moment after the Sub-prefect was in the passage, confronting a waiter half-dressed and ghastly pale. This was the short dialogue which immediately took place:

'We want to see the Englishman who is sleeping in this house!'

'He went away hours ago.'

'He did no such thing. His friend went away; *he* remained. Show us to his bedroom!'

'I swear to you, Monsieur le Sous-préfet, he is not here! he – '

'I swear to you, Monsieur le Garçon, he is. He slept here – he didn't find your bed comfortable – he came to us to complain of it – here he is among my men – and here am I ready to look for a flea or two in his bedstead. Renaudin! (calling to one of the subordinates, and pointing to the waiter) collar that man, and tie his hands behind him. Now, then, gentlemen, let us walk upstairs!'

Every man and woman in the house was secured – the 'Old Soldier' the first. Then I identified the bed in which I had slept, and then we went into the room above.

No object that was at all extraordinary appeared in any part of it. The Sub-prefect looked round the place, commanded everybody to be silent, stamped twice on the floor, called for a candle, looked attentively at the spot he had stamped on, and ordered the flooring there to be carefully taken up. This was done in no time. Lights were produced, and we saw a deep raftered cavity between the floor of this room and the ceiling of the room beneath. Through this cavity there ran perpendicularly a sort of case of iron thickly greased; and inside the case appeared the screw, which communicated with the bed-top below. Extra lengths of screw, freshly oiled; levers covered with felt; all the complete upper works of a heavy press – constructed with infernal ingenuity so as to join the fixtures below, and when taken to pieces again to go into the smallest possible compass – were next discovered and pulled out on the floor. After some little difficulty the Sub-prefect succeeded in putting the machinery together, and, leaving his men to work it, descended with me to the bedroom. The smothering canopy was then lowered, but not so noiselessly as I had seen it lowered. When I mentioned this to the Sub-prefect, his answer, simple as it was, had a terrible significance. 'My men,' said he, 'are working down the bed top for the first time – the men whose money you won were in better practice.'

We left the house in the sole possession of two police agents – every one of the inmates being removed to prison on the spot. The Sub-prefect, after taking down my' *procès-verbal'* in his office, returned with me to my hotel to get my passport. 'Do you think,' I asked, as I gave it to him, 'that any men have really been smothered in that bed, as they tried to smother *me?'*

'I have seen dozens of drowned men laid out at the Morgue,' answered the Sub-prefect, 'in whose pocket books were found letters, stating that they had committed suicide in the Seine, because they had lost everything at the gaming-table. Do I know how many of those men entered the same gambling-house that *you* entered? won as *you* won? took that bed as *you* took it? slept in it? were smothered in it? and were privately thrown into the river, with a letter of explanation written by the murderers and placed in their pocket-books? No man can say how many or how few have suffered the fate from which you have escaped. The people of the gambling-house kept their bedstead machinery a secret from *us* – even from the police! The dead kept the rest of the secret for them. Good night, or rather good morning, Monsieur Faulkner! Be at my office again at nine o'clock – in the meantime, *au revoir!'*

The rest of my story is soon told. I was examined and re-examined; the gambling-house was strictly searched all through from top to bottom; the prisoners were separately interrogated; and two of the less guilty among them made a confession. *I* discovered that the Old Soldier was the master of the gambling house – *justice* discovered that he had been drummed out of the army as a vagabond years ago; that he had been guilty of all sorts of villainies since; that he was in possession of stolen property, which the owners identified; and that he, the croupier, another accomplice, and the woman who had made my cup of coffee, were all in the secret of the bedstead. There appeared some reason to doubt whether the inferior persons attached to the house knew anything of the suffocating machinery; and they received the benefit of the doubt, by being treated simply as thieves and vagabonds. As for the Old Soldier and his two head-myrmidons, they went to the galleys; the woman who had drugged my coffee was imprisoned for I forget how many years; the regular attendants at the gambling-house were considered 'suspicious,' and placed under 'surveillance'; and I became, for one whole week (which is a long time), the head 'lion' in Parisian society. My adventure was drama-tised by three illustrious playmakers, but never saw theatrical day-light; for the censorship forbade the introduction on the stage of a correct copy of the gambling-house bedstead.

One good result was produced by my adventure, which any censorship must have approved – it cured me of ever again trying *Rouge et Noir* as an amusement. The sight of a green cloth, with packs of cards and heaps of money on it, will henceforth be for ever associated in my mind with the sight of a bed-canopy descending to suffocate me in the silence and darkness of the night.

The Landlady

ROALD DAHL

BILLY WEAVER HAD TRAVELLED down from London on the slow afternoon train, with a change at Reading on the way, and by the time he got to Bath it was about nine o'clock in the evening and the moon was coming up out of a clear starry sky over the houses opposite the station entrance. But the air was deadly cold and the wind was like a flat blade of ice on his cheeks.

'Excuse me,' he said, 'but is there a fairly cheap hotel not too far away from here?'

'Try The Bell and Dragon,' the porter answered, pointing down the road. 'They might take you in. It's about a quarter of a mile along on the other side.'

Billy thanked him and picked up his suitcase and set out to walk the quarter-mile to The Bell and Dragon. He had never been to Bath before. He didn't know anyone who lived there. But Mr Greenslade at the Head Office in London had told him it was a splendid town. 'Find your own lodgings,' he had said, 'and then go along and report to the Branch Manager as soon as you've got yourself settled.'

Billy was seventeen years old. He was wearing a new navy-blue overcoat, a new brown trilby hat, and a new brown suit, and he was feeling fine. He walked briskly down the street. He was trying to do everything briskly these days. Briskness, he had decided, was *the* one common characteristic of all successful businessmen. The big shots up at Head Office were absolutely fantastically brisk all the time. They were amazing.

There were no shops on this wide street that he was walking along, only a line of tall houses on each side, all of them identical. They had porches and pillars and four or five steps going up to their front doors, and it was obvious that once upon a time they had been very swanky residences. But now, even in the darkness, he could see that the paint was peeling from the woodwork on their doors and windows, and that the handsome white façades were cracked and blotchy from neglect.

Suddenly, in a downstairs window that was brilliantly illuminated by a street-lamp not six yards away, Billy caught sight of a printed notice propped up against the glass in one of the upper panes. It said BED AND BREAKFAST. There was a vase of yellow chrysanthemums, tall and beautiful, standing just underneath the notice.

He stopped walking. He moved a bit closer. Green curtains (some sort of velvety material) were hanging down on either side of the window. The chrysanthemums looked wonderful beside them. He went right up and peered through the glass into the room, and the first thing he saw was a bright fire burning in the hearth. On the carpet in front of the fire, a pretty little dachshund was curled up asleep with its nose tucked into its belly. The room itself, so far as he could see in the half-darkness, was filled with pleasant furniture. There was a baby-grand piano and a big sofa and several plump armchairs; and in one corner he spotted a large parrot in a cage. Animals were usually a good sign in a place like this, Billy told himself; and all in all, it looked to him as though it would be a pretty decent house to stay in. Certainly it would be more comfortable than The Bell and Dragon.

On the other hand, a pub would be more congenial than a boarding-house. There would be beer and darts in the evenings, and lots of people to talk to, and it would probably be a good bit cheaper, too. He had stayed a couple of nights in a pub once before and he had liked it. He had never stayed in any boarding-houses, and, to be perfectly honest, he was a tiny bit frightened of them. The name itself conjured up images of watery cabbage, rapacious landladies, and a powerful smell of kippers in the living-room.

After dithering about like this in the cold for two or three minutes, Billy decided that he would walk on and take a look at The Bell and Dragon before making up his mind. He turned to go.

And now a queer thing happened to him. He was in the act of stepping back and turning away from the window when all at once his eye was caught and held in the most peculiar manner by the small notice that was there. BED AND BREAKFAST, it said. BED AND BREAKFAST, BED AND BREAKFAST, BED AND BREAKFAST. Each word was like a large black eye staring at him through the glass, holding him, compelling him, forcing him to stay where he was and not to walk away from that house, and the next thing he knew, he was actually moving across from the window to the front door of the house, climbing the steps that led up to it, and reaching for the bell.

He pressed the bell. Far away in a back room he heard it ringing, and then *at once* – it must have been at once because he hadn't even had time to take his finger from the bell-button – the door swung open and a woman was standing there.

Normally you ring the bell and you have at least a half-minute's wait before the door opens. But this dame was like a jack-in-the-box. He pressed the bell – and out she popped! It made him jump.

She was about forty-five or fifty years old, and the moment she saw him, she gave him a warm welcoming smile.

'*Please* come in,' she said pleasantly. She stepped aside, holding the door wide open, and Billy found himself automatically starting forward. The compulsion or, more accurately, the desire to follow after her into that house was extraordinarily strong.

'I saw the notice in the window,' he said, holding himself back.

'Yes, I know.'

'I was wondering about a room.'

'It's *all* ready for you, my dear,' she said. She had a round pink face and very gentle blue eyes.

'I was on my way to The Bell and Dragon,' Billy told her. 'But the notice in your window just happened to catch my eye.'

'My dear boy,' she said, 'why don't you come in out of the cold?'

'How much do you charge?'

'Five and sixpence a night, including breakfast.'

It was fantastically cheap. It was less than half of what he had been willing to pay.

'If that is too much,' she added, 'then perhaps I can reduce it just a tiny bit. Do you desire an egg for breakfast? Eggs are expensive at the moment. It would be sixpence less without the egg.'

'Five and sixpence is fine,' he answered. 'I should like very much to stay here.'

'I knew you would. Do come in.'

She seemed terribly nice. She looked exactly like the mother of one's best school-friend welcoming one into the house to stay for the Christmas holidays. Billy took off his hat, and stepped over the threshold.

'Just hang it there,' she said, 'and let me help you with your coat.'

There were no other hats or coats in the hall. There were no umbrellas, no walking-sticks – nothing.

'We have it *all* to ourselves,' she said, smiling at him over her shoulder as she led the way upstairs. 'You see, it isn't very often I have the pleasure of taking a visitor into my little nest.'

The old girl is slightly dotty, Billy told himself. But at five and sixpence a night, who gives a damn about that? 'I should've thought you'd be simply swamped with applicants,' he said politely.

'Oh, I am, my dear, I am, of course I am. But the trouble is that I'm inclined to be just a teeny weeny bit choosy and particular – if you see what I mean.'

'Ah, yes.'

'But I'm always ready. Everything is always ready day and night in this house just on the off-chance that an acceptable young gentleman will come along. And it is such a pleasure, my dear, such a very great pleasure when now and again I open the door and I see someone standing there who is just *exactly* right.' She was halfway up the stairs, and she paused with one hand on the stair-rail, turning her head and smiling down at him with pale lips. 'Like you,' she added, and her blue eyes travelled slowly all the way down the length of Billy's body, to his feet, and then up again.

On the second-floor landing she said to him, 'This floor is mine.'

They climbed up another flight. 'And this one is *all* yours,' she said. 'Here's your room. I do hope you'll like it.' She took him into a small but charming front bedroom, switching on the light as she went in.

'The morning sun comes right in the window, Mr Perkins. It *is* Mr Perkins, isn't it?'

'No,' he said. 'It's Weaver.'

'Mr Weaver. How nice. I've put a water-bottle between the sheets to air them out, Mr Weaver. It's such a comfort to have a hot water-bottle in a strange bed with clean sheets, don't you agree? And you may light the gas fire at any time if you feel chilly.'

'Thank you,' Billy said. 'Thank you ever so much.' He noticed that the bedspread had been taken off the bed, and that the bedclothes had been neatly turned back on one side, all ready for someone to get in.

'I'm so glad you appeared,' she said, looking earnestly into his face. 'I was beginning to get worried.'

'That's all right,' Billy answered brightly. 'You mustn't worry about me.' He put his suitcase on the chair and started to open it.

'And what about supper, my dear? Did you manage to get anything to eat before you came here?'

'I'm not a bit hungry, thank you,' he said. 'I think I'll just go to bed as soon as possible because tomorrow I've got to get up rather early and report to the office.'

'Very well, then. I'll leave you now so that you can unpack. But before you go to bed, would you be kind enough to pop into the sittng-room on the ground floor and sign the book? Everyone has to do that because it's the law of the land, and we don't want to go breaking any laws at *this* stage in the proceedings, do we?' She gave him a little wave of the hand and went quickly out of the room and closed the door.

Now, the fact that his landlady appeared to be slightly off her rocker didn't worry Billy in the least. After all, she not only was harmless – there was no question about that – but she was also quite obviously a kind and generous soul. He guessed that she had probably lost a son in the war, or something like that, and had never gotten over it.

So a few minutes later, after unpacking his suitcase and washing his hands, he trotted downstairs to the ground floor and entered the living-room. His landlady wasn't there, but the fire was glowing in the hearth, and the little dachshund was still sleeping soundly in front of it. The room was wonderfully warm and cosy. I'm a lucky fellow, he thought, rubbing his hands. This is a bit of all right.

He found the guest-book lying open on the piano, so he took out his pen and wrote down his name and address. There were only two other entries above his on the page, and, as one always does with guest-books, he started to read them. One was a Christopher Mulholland from Cardiff. The other was Gregory W. Temple from Bristol.

That's funny, he thought suddenly. Christopher Mulholland. It rings a bell.

Now where on earth had he heard that rather unusual name before?

Was it a boy at school? No. Was it one of his sister's numerous young men, perhaps, or a friend of his father's. No, no, it wasn't any of those. He glanced down again at the book.

> *Christopher Mulholland*   *231 Cathedral Road, Cardiff*
> *Gregory W. Temple*   *27 Sycamore Drive, Bristol*

As a matter of fact, now he came to think of it, he wasn't at all sure that the second name didn't have almost as much of a familiar ring about it as the first.

'Gregory Temple?' he said aloud, searching his memory. 'Christopher Mulholland? . . .'

'Such charming boys,' a voice behind him answered, and he turned and saw his landlady sailing into the room with a large silver tea-tray in her hands. She was holding it well out in front of her, and rather high up, as though the tray were a pair of reins on a frisky horse.

'They sound somehow familiar,' he said.

'They do? How interesting.'

'I'm almost positive I've heard those names before somewhere. Isn't that odd? Maybe it was in the newspapers. They weren't famous in any way, were they? I mean famous cricketers or footballers or something like that?'

'Famous,' she said, setting the tea-tray down on the low table in front of the sofa. 'Oh no, I don't think they were famous. But they were incredibly handsome, both of them, I cam promise you that. They were tall and young and handsome, my dear, just exactly like you.'

Once more, Billy glanced down at the book. 'Look here,' he said noticing the dates. 'This last entry is over two years old.'

'It is?'

'Yes, indeed. And Christopher Mulholland's is nearly a year before that – more than *three years* ago.'

'Dear me,' she said, shaking her head and heaving a dainty little sigh. 'I would never have thought it. How time does fly away from us all, doesn't it, Mr Wilkins?'

'It's Weaver,' Billy said. 'W-e-a-v-e-r.'

'Oh, of course it is!' she cried, sitting down on the sofa. 'How silly of me. I do apologize. In one ear and out the other, that's me, Mr Weaver.'

'You know something?' Billy said. 'Something that's really quite extraordinary about all this?'

'No, dear, I don't.'

'Well, you see, both of these names – Mulholland and Temple – I not only seem to remember each one of them separately, so to speak, but somehow or other, in some peculiar way, they both appear to be sort of connected together as well. As though they were both

famous for the same sort of thing, if you see what I mean – like . . .
well . . . like Dempsey and Tunney, for example, or Churchill and
Roosevelt.'

'How amusing,' she said. 'But come over here now, dear, and sit
down beside me on the sofa and I'll give you a nice cup of tea and a
ginger biscuit before you go to bed.'

'You really shouldn't bother,' Billy said. 'I didn't mean you to do
anything like that.' He stood by the piano, watching her as she fussed
about with the cups and saucers. He noticed that she had small,
white, quickly moving hands, and red finger-nails.

'I'm almost positive it was in the newspapers I saw them,' Billy
said. 'I'll think of it in a second, I'm sure I will.'

There is nothing more tantalizing than a thing like this that lingers
just outside the borders of one's memory. He hated to give up.

'Now wait a minute,' he said. 'Wait just a minute. Mulholland . . .
Christopher Mulholland . . . wasn't *that* the name of the Eton
schoolboy who was on a walking-tour through the West Country,
and then all of a sudden . . .'

'Milk?' she said. 'And sugar?'

'Yes, please. And then all of a sudden . . .'

'Eton schoolboy?' she said. 'Oh no, my dear, that can't possibly be
right because *my* Mr Mulholland was certainly not an Eton schoolboy
when he came to me. He was a Cambridge undergraduate. Come
over here now and sit next to me and warm yourself in front of this
lovely fire. Come on. Your tea's all ready for you.' She patted the
empty place beside her on the sofa, and she sat there smiling at Billy
and waiting for him to come over.

He crossed the room slowly, and sat down on the edge of the sofa.
She placed his teacup on the table in front of him.

'*There* we are,' she said. 'How nice and cosy this is, isn't it?'

Billy started sipping his tea. She did the same. For half a minute
or so, neither of them spoke. But Billy knew that she was looking at
him. Her body was half turned toward him, and he could feel her
eyes resting on his face, watching him over the rim of her teacup.
Now and again, he caught a whiff of a peculiar smell that seemed to
emanate directly from her person. It was not in the least unpleasant,
and it reminded him – well, he wasn't quite sure what it reminded
him of. Pickled walnuts? New leather? Or was it the corridors of a
hospital?

At length, she said, 'Mr Mulholland was a great one for his tea.

Never in my life have I seen anyone drink as much tea as dear, sweet Mr Mulholland.'

'I suppose he left fairly recently,' Billy said. He was still puzzling his head about the two names. He was positive now that he had seen them in the newspapers – in the headlines.

'Left?' she said, arching her brows. 'But my dear boy, he never left. He's still here. Mr Temple is also here. They're on the fourth floor, both of them together.'

Billy set his cup down slowly on the table and stared at his landlady. She smiled back at him, and then she put out one of her white hands and patted him comfortingly on the knee. 'How old are you, my dear?' she asked.

'Seventeen.'

'Seventeen!' she cried. 'Oh, it's the perfect age! Mr Mulholland was also seventeen. But I think he was a trifle shorter than you are; in fact I'm sure he was, and his teeth weren't *quite* so white. You have the most beautiful teeth, Mr Weaver, did you know that?'

'They're not as good as they look,' Billy said. 'They've got simply masses of fillings in them at the back.'

'Mr Temple, of course, was a little older,' she said, ignoring his remark. 'He was actually twenty-eight. And yet I never would have guessed it if he hadn't told me, never in my whole life. There wasn't a *blemish* on his body.'

'A what?' Billy said.

'His skin was *just* like a baby's.'

There was a pause. Billy picked up his teacup and took another sip of his tea, then he set it down again gently in its saucer. He waited for her to say something else, but she seemed to have lapsed into another of her silences. He sat there staring straight ahead of him into the far corner of the room, biting his lower lip.

'That parrot,' he said at last. 'You know something? It had me completely fooled when I first saw it through the window. I could have sworn it was alive.'

'Alas, no longer.'

'It's most terribly clever the way it's been done,' he said. 'It doesn't look in the least bit dead. Who did it?'

'I did.'

'You did?'

'Of course,' she said. 'And have you met my little Basil as well?' She nodded towards the dachshund curled up so comfortably in front of the fire. Billy looked at it. And suddenly, he realized that this animal had all the time been just as silent and motionless as the parrot. He put out a hand and touched it gently on the top of its back. The back was hard and cold, and when he pushed the hair to one side with his fingers, he could see the skin underneath, greyish-black and dry and perfectly preserved.

'Good gracious me,' he said. 'How absolutely fascinating.' He turned away from the dog and stared with deep admiration at the little woman beside him on the sofa. 'It must be most awfully difficult to do a thing like that.'

'Not in the least,' she said. 'I stuff *all* my little pets myself when they pass away. Will you have another cup of tea?'

'No, thank you,' Billy said. The tea tasted faintly of bitter almonds, and he didn't much care for it.

'You did sign the book, didn't you?'

'Oh, yes.'

'That's good. Because later on, if I happen to forget what you were called, then I could always come down here and look it up. I still do that almost every day with Mr Mulholland and Mr. . . . Mr. . . .'

'Temple,' Billy said. 'Gregory Temple. Excuse my asking, but haven't there been *any* other guests here except them in the last two or three years?'

Holding her teacup high in one hand, inclining her head slightly to the left, she looked up at him out of the corners of her eyes and gave him another gentle little smile.

'No, my dear,' she said. 'Only you.'

Thrawn Janet

ROBERT LOUIS STEVENSON

THE REVEREND MURDOCH SOULIS was long minister of the moorland parish of Balweary, in the vale of Dule. A severe, bleak-faced old man, dreadful to his hearers, he dwelt in the last years of his life, without relative or servant or any human company, in the small and lonely manse under the Hanging Shaw. In spite of the iron composure of his features, his eye was wild, scared, and uncertain; and when he dwelt, in private admonitions, on the future of the impenitent, it seemed as if his eye pierced through the storms of time to the terrors of eternity. Many young persons, coming to prepare themselves against the season of the Holy Communion, were dreadfully affected by his talk. He had a sermon on 1st Peter, v. and 8th, 'The devil as a roaring lion,' on the Sunday after every seventeenth of August, and he was accustomed to surpass himself upon that text both by the appalling nature of the matter and the terror of his bearing in the pulpit. The children were frightened into fits, and the old looked more than usually oracular, and were, all that day, full of those hints that Hamlet deprecated. The manse itself, where it stood by the water of Dule among some thick trees, with the Shaw overhanging it on the one side, and on the other many cold, moorish hilltops rising toward the sky, had begun, at a very early period of Mr Soulis's ministry, to be avoided in the dusk hours by all who valued themselves upon their prudence; and guidmen sitting at the clachan alehouse shook their heads together at the thought of passing late by that uncanny neighbourhood. There was one spot, to be more particular, which was regarded with especial awe. The manse stood between the high road and the water of Dule, with a gable to each; its back was toward the kirktown of Balweary, nearly half a mile away; in front of it, a bare garden, hedged with thorn, occupied the land between the river and the road. The house was two stories high, with two large rooms on each. It opened not directly on the garden, but on a causewayed path, or passage, giving on the road on the one hand, and closed on the other by the tall willows and elders that bordered on the stream. And it was this strip of causeway that enjoyed among the young parishioners of Balweary so infamous a reputation. The minister walked there often after dark, sometimes groaning aloud in the instancy of his unspoken prayers; and when he was from home, and the manse door was locked, the more daring schoolboys ventured, with beating hearts, to 'follow my leader' across that legendary spot.

This atmosphere of terror, surrounding, as it did, a man of God of spotless character and orthodoxy, was a common cause of wonder and subject of inquiry among the few strangers who were led by chance or business into that unknown, outlying country. But many even of the people of the parish were ignorant of the strange events which had marked the first year of Mr Soulis's ministrations; and among those who were better informed, some were naturally reticent, and others shy of that particular topic. Now and again, only, one of the older folk would warm into courage over his third tumbler, and recount the cause of the minister's strange looks and solitary life.

Fifty years syne, when Mr Soulis cam' first into Ba'weary, he was still a young man – a callant, the folk said – fu' o' book learnin' and grand at the exposition, but, as was natural in sae young a man, wi' nae leevin' experience in religion. The younger sort were greatly taken wi' his gifts and his gab; but auld, concerned, serious men and women were moved even to prayer for the young man, whom they took to be a self-deceiver, and the parish that was like to be sae ill-supplied. It was before the days o' the moderates – weary fa' them; but ill things are like guid – they baith come bit by bit, a pickle at a time; and there were folk even then that said the Lord had left the college professors to their ain devices, an' the lads that went to study wi' them wad hae done mair and better sittin' in a peat-bog, like their forebears of the persecution, wi' a Bible under their oxter and a speerit o' prayer in their heart. There was nae doubt, onyway, but that Mr Soulis had been ower lang at the college. He was careful and troubled for mony things besides the ae thing needful. He had a feck o' books wi' him – mair than had ever been seen before in a' that presbytery; and a sair wark the carrier had wi' them, for they were a' like to have smoored in the Deil's Hag between this and Kilmackerlie. They were books o' divinity, to be sure, or so they ca'd them; but the serious were o' opinion there was little service for sae mony, when the hail o' God's Word would gang in the neuk of a plaid. Then he wad sit half the day and half the nicht forbye, which was scant decent – writin', nae less; and first, they were feared he wad read his sermons; and syne it proved he was writin' a book himsel', which was surely no fittin' for ane of his years an' sma' experience.

Onyway it behooved him to get an auld, decent wife to keep the manse for him an' see to his bit denners; and he was recommended to an auld limmer – Janet M'Clour, they ca'd her – and sae far left to himsel' as to be ower persuaded. There was mony advised him to the contrar, for Janet was mair than suspeckit by the best folk in Ba'weary. Lang or that, she had had a wean to a dragoon; she hadnae come forrit for maybe thretty year; and bairns had seen her mumblin' to hersel' up on Key's Loan in the gloamin', whilk was an unco time an' place for a God-fearin' woman. Howsoever, it was the laird himsel' that had first tauld the minister o' Janet; and in thae days he wad have gane a far gate to pleesure the laird. When folk tauld him that Janet was sib to the deil, it was a' superstition by his way of it; an' when they cast up the Bible to him an' the witch of Endor, he wad threep it doun their thrapples that thir days were a' gane by, and the deil was mercifully restrained.

Weel, when it got about the clachan that Janet M'Clour was to be servant at the manse, the folk were fair mad wi' her an' him thegether; and some o' the guidwives had nae better to dae than get round her door cheeks and chairge her wi' a' that was ken't again her, frae the sodger's bairn to John Tamson's twa kye. She was nae great speaker; folk usually let her gang her ain gate, an' she let them gang theirs, wi' neither Fair-guid-een nor Fair-guid-day; but when she buckled to she had a tongue to deave the miller. Up she got, an' there wasnae an auld story in Ba'weary but she gart somebody lowp for it that day; they couldnae say ae thing but she could say twa to it; till, at the hinder end, the guidwives up and claucht haud of her, and clawed the coats aff her back, and pu'd her doun the clachan to the water o' Dule, to see if she were a witch or no, soum or droun. The carline skirled till ye could hear her at the Hangin' Shaw, and she focht like ten; there was mony a guidwife bure the mark of her neist day, an' mony a lang day after; and just in the hettest o' the collieshangie, wha suld come up (for his sins) but the new minister.

'Women,' said he (and he had a grand voice), 'I charge you in the Lord's name to let her go.'

Janet ran to him – she was fair wud wi' terror – an' clang to him an' prayed him, for Christ's sake, save her frae the cummers; an' they, for their part, tauld him a' that was ken't, and maybe mair.

'Woman,' says he to Janet, 'is this true?'

'As the Lord sees me,' says she, 'as the Lord made me, no a word o't. Forbye the bairn,' says she. 'I've been a decent woman a' my days.'

'Will you,' says Mr Soulis, 'in the name of God, and before me, His unworthy minister, renounce the devil and his works?'

Weel, it wad appear that when he askit that, she gave a girn that fairly frichtit them that saw her, an' they could hear her teeth play dirl thegether in her chafts; but there was naething for it but the ae way or the ither; an' Janet lifted up her hand and renounced the deil before them a'.

'And now,' said Mr Soulis to the guidwives, 'home with ye, one and all, and pray to God for His forgiveness.'

And he gied Janet his arm, though she had little on her but a sark, and took her up the clachan to her ain door like a leddy of the land; an' her skreighin' and laughin' as was a scandal to be heard.

There were mony grave folk lang ower their prayers that nicht; but when the morn cam' there was sic a fear fell upon a' Ba'weary that the bairns hid theirsels, and even the men-folk stood and keekit frae their doors. For there was Janet comin' doun the clachan – her or her likeness, nane could tell – wi' her neck thrawn, and her heid on ae side, like a body that has been hangit, and a girn on her face like an unstreakit corp. By an' by they got used wi' it, and even speered at her to ken what was wrang; but frae that day forth she couldnae speak like a Christian woman, but slavered and played click wi' her teeth like a pair o' shears; and frae that day forth the name o' God cam' never on her lips. Whiles she wad try to say it, but it michtnae be. Them that kenned best said least; but they never gied that Thing the name o' Janet M'Clour; for the auld Janet, by their way o't, was in muckle hell that day. But the minister was neither to haud nor to bind; he preached about naething but the folks' cruelty that had gi'en her a stroke of the palsy; he skelpt the bairns that meddled her; and he had her up to the manse that same nicht and dwalled there a' his lane wi' her under the Hangin' Shaw.

Weel, time gaed by: and the idler sort commenced to think mair

lichtly o' that black business. The minister was weel thocht o'; he
was aye late at the writing, folk wad see his can'le doun by the Dule
water after twal' at e'en; and he seemed pleased wi' himsel' and
upsitten as at first, though a' body could see that he was dwining.
As for Janet she cam' an' she gaed; if she didnae speak muckle afore;
it was reason she should speak less then; she meddled naebody; but
she was an eldritch thing to see, an' nane wad hae mistrysted wi' her
for Ba'weary glebe. About the end o' July there cam' a spell o'
weather, the like o't never was in that countryside; it was lown an'
het an' heartless; the herds couldnae win up the Black Hill, the
bairns were ower weariet to play; an' yet it was gousty too, wi' claps
o' het wund that rumm'led in the glens, and bits o' shouers that
slockened naething. We aye thocht it but to thun'er on the morn;
but the morn cam', and the morn's morning, and it was aye the same
uncanny weather, sair on folks and bestial. Of a' that were the waur,
nane suffered like Mr Soulis; he could neither sleep nor eat, he tauld
his elders; an' when he wasnae writin' at his weary book, he wad be
stravaguin' ower a' the countryside like a man possessed, when a'
body else was blythe to keep caller ben the house.

Abune Hangin' Shaw, in the bield o' the Black Hill, there's a bit
inclosed grund wi' an iron yett; and it seems in the auld days, that
was the kirkyaird o' Ba'weary, and consecrated by the Papists before
the blessed licht shone upon the kingdom. It was a great howff o'
Mr Soulis's, onyway; there he would sit an' consider his sermons;
and indeed it's a bieldy bit. Weel, as he cam' ower the wast end o'
the Black Hill, ae day, he saw first twa, an' syne fower, an' syne
seeven corbie craws fleein' round an' round abune the auld kirkyaird.
They flew laigh and heavy, an' squawked to ither as they gaed; and
it was clear to Mr Soulis that something had put them frae their
ordinar. He wasnae easy fleyed, an' gaed straucht up to the wa's; an'
what suld he find there but a man, or the appearance of a man, sittin'
in the inside upon a grave. He was of a great stature, an' black as
hell, and his een were singular to see. Mr Soulis had heard tell o'
black men, mony's the time; but there was something unco about
this black man that daunted him. Het as he was, he took a kind o'
cauld grue in the marrow o' his banes; but up he spak for a' that; an'
says he: 'My friend, are you a stranger in this place?' The black man
answered never a word; he got upon his feet, an' begude to hirstle to
the wa' on the far side; but he aye lookit at the minister; an' the
minister stood an' lookit back, till a' in a meenute the black man

was over the wa' an' rinnin' for the bield o' the trees. Mr Soulis, he hardly kenned why, ran after him; but he was sair forjaskit wi' his walk an' the het, unhalesome weather; and rin as he likit, he got nae mair than a glisk o' the black man amang the birks, till he won doun to the foot o' the hillside, an' there he saw him ance mair, gaun, hap, step, an' lowp, ower Dule water to the manse.

Mr Soulis wasnae weel pleased that this fearsome gangrel suld mak' sae free wi' Ba'weary manse; an' he ran the harder, an', wet shoon, ower the burn, an' up the walk; but the deil a black man was there to see. He stepped out upon the road, but there was naebody there; he gaed a' ower the gairden, but na, nae black man. At the hinder end, and a bit feared as was but natural, he lifted the hasp and into the manse; and there was Janet M'Clour before his een, wi' her thrawn craig, and nane sae pleased to see him. And he aye minded sinsyne, when first he set his een upon her, he had the same cauld and deidly grue.

'Janet,' says he, 'have you seen a black man?'

'A black man?' quo' she. 'Save us a'! Ye're no wise, minister. There's nae black man in a' Ba'weary.'

But she didnae speak plain, ye maun understand; but yam-yammered, like a powney wi' the bit in its moo.

'Weel,' says he, 'Janet, if there was nae black man, I have spoken with the Accuser of the Brethren.'

And he sat down like ane wi' a fever, an' his teeth chittered in his heid.

'Hoots,' says she, 'think shame to yoursel', minister'; an' gied him a drap brandy that she keepit aye by her.

Syne Mr Soulis gaed into his study amang a' his books. It's a lang, laigh, mirk chalmer, perishin' cauld in winter, an' no very dry even in the tap o' the simmer, for the manse stands near the burn. Sae doun he sat, and thocht of a' that had come an' gane since he was in Ba'weary, an' his hame, an' the days when he was a bairn an' ran daffin' on the braes; and that black man aye ran in his heid like the owercome of a sang. Aye the mair he thocht, the mair he thocht o' the black man. He tried the prayer, an' the words wouldnae come to him; an' he tried, they say, to write at his book, but he couldnae mak' nae mair o' that. There was whiles he thocht the black man was at his oxter, an' the swat stood upon him cauld as well-water; and there was other whiles, when he cam' to himself' like a christened bairn and minded naething.

The upshot was that he gaed to the window an' stood glowrin' at Dule water. The trees are unco thick, an' the water lies deep an' black under the manse; an' there was Janet washin' the cla'es wi' her coats kilted. She had her back to the minister, an' he, for his pairt, hardly kenned what he was lookin' at. Syne she turned round an' shawed her face; Mr Soulis had the same cauld grue as twice that day afore, an' it was borne in upon him what folk said, that Janet was deid lang syne, an' this was a bogle in her clay cauld flesh. He drew back a pickle and he scanned her narrowly. She was tramp-trampin' in the cla'es, croonin' to hersel'; and eh! Gude guide us, but it was a fearsome face. Whiles she sang louder, but there was nae man born o' woman that could tell the words o' her sang; an' whiles she lookit side-lang doun, but there was naething there for her to look at. There gaed a scunner through the flesh upon his banes; and that was Heeven's advertisement. But Mr Soulis just blamed himsel', he said, to think sae ill of a puir, auld afflicted wife that hadnae a freend forby himsel'; and he put up a bit prayer for him and her, an' drank a little caller water – for his heart rose again the meat – an' gaed up to his naked bed in the gloaming.

That was a nicht that has never been forgotten in Ba'weary, the nicht o' the seeventeenth of August, seeventeen hun'er an' twal'. It had been het afore, as I hae said, but that nicht it was hetter than ever. The sun gaed doun amang unco-lookin' clouds; it fell as mirk as the pit; no a star, no a breath o' wund; ye couldnae see your han' before your face, and even the auld folk cuist the covers frae their beds and lay pechin' for their breath. Wi' a' that he had upon his mind, it was gey and unlikely Mr Soulis wad get muckle sleep. He lay an' he tummled; the gude, caller bed that he got into brunt his very banes; whiles he slept, and whiles he waukened; whiles he hèard the time o' nicht, and whiles a tyke youlin' up the muir, as if somebody was deid; whiles he thocht he heard bogles claverin' in his lug, an' whiles he saw spunkies in the room. He behooved, he judged, to be sick; an' sick he was – little he jaloosed the sickness.

At the hinder end, he got a clearness in his mind, sat up in his sark on the bedside, and fell thinkin' ance mair o' the black man an' Janet. He couldnae weel tell how – maybe it was the cauld to his feet – but it cam' in upon him wi' a spate that there was some connection between thir twa, an' that either or baith o' them were bogles. And just at that moment, in Janet's room, which was neist to his, there cam' a stramp o' feet as if men were wars'lin', an' then a loud bang; an' then a wund gaed reishling round the fower quarters of the house; an' then a' was aince mair as seelent as the grave.

Mr Soulis was feared for neither man nor deevil. He got his tinder box, an' lighted a can'le, an' made three steps o't ower to Janet's door. It was on the hasp, an' he pushed it open, an' keeked bauldly in. It was a big room, as big as the minister's ain, an' plenished wi' grand, auld, solid gear, for he had naething else. There was a fower-posted bed wi' auld tapestry; and a braw cabinet of aik, that was fu' o' the minister's divinity books, an' put there to be out o' the gate; an' a wheen duds o' Janet's lying here and there about the floor. But nae Janet could Mr Soulis see; nor ony sign of a contention. In he gaed (an' there's few that wad ha'e followed him) an' lookit a' round, an' listened. But there was naethin' to be heard, neither inside the manse nor in a' Ba'weary parish, an' naethin' to be seen but the muckle shadows turnin' round the can'le. An' then a' at aince, the minister's heart played dunt an' stood stock-still; an' a cauld wund blew amang the hairs o' his heid. Whaten a weary sicht was that for the puir man's een! For there was Janet hangin' frae a nail beside the auld aik cabinet: her heid aye lay on her shouther, her een were steeked, the tongue projekit frae her mouth, and her heels were twa feet clar abune the floor.

'God forgive us all!' thocht Mr Soulis; 'poor Janet's dead.'

He cam' a step nearer to the corp; an' then his heart fair whammled in his inside. For by what cantrip it wad ill-beseem a man to judge, she was hingin' fae a single nail an' by a single wursted thread for darnin' hose.

It's an awfu' thing to be your lane at nicht wi' siccan prodigies o' darkness; but Mr Soulis was strong in the Lord. He turned an' gaed his ways oot o' that room, and lockit the door ahint him; and step by step, doon the stairs, as heavy as leed; and set doon the can'le on the table at the stairfoot. He couldnae pray, he couldnae think, he was dreepin' wi' caul' swat, an' naething could he hear but the dunt-dunt-duntin' o' his ain heart. He micht maybe have stood there an hour, or maybe twa, he minded sae little; when a' o' a sudden he heard a laigh, uncanny steer upstairs; a foot gaed to an' fro in the cha'mer whaur the corp was hingin'; syne the door was opened, though he minded weel that he had lockit it; an' syne there was a step upon the landin', an' it seemed to him as if the corp was lookin' ower the rail and doun upon him whaur he stood.

He took up the can'le again (for he coudnae want the licht) and,

as saftly as ever he could, gaed straucht out o' the manse an' to the
far end o' the causeway. It was aye pitmirk; the flame o' the can'le,
when he set it on the grund, brunt steedy and clear as in a room;
naething moved, but the Dule water seepin' and sabbin' doon the
glen, an' yon unhaly footstep that cam' ploddin' doun the stairs inside
the manse. He kenned the foot ower weel, for it was Janet's; and at
ilka step that cam' a wee thing nearer, the cauld got deeper in his
vitals. He commended his soul to Him that made an' keepit him;
'and O Lord,' said he, 'give me strength this night to war against the
powers of evil.'

By this time the foot was comin' through the passage for the door;
he could hear a hand skirt alang the wa', as if the fearsome thing
was feelin' for its way. The saughs tossed an' maned thegether, a
lang sigh cam' ower the hills, the flame o' the can'le was blawn
aboot; an' there stood the corp of Thrawn Janet, wi' her grogram
goun an' her black mutch, wi' the heid aye upon the shouther, an'
the girn still upon the face o't – leevin', ye wad hae said – deid, as
Mr Soulis weel kenned – upon the threshold o' the manse.

It's a strange thing that the saul of man should be that thirled into
his perishable body; but the minister saw that, an' his heart didnae
break.

She didnae stand there lang; she began to move again an' cam'
slowly toward Mr Soulis whaur he stood under the saughs. A' the
life o' his body, a' the strength o' his speerit, wer glowerin' frae his
een. It seemed she was gaun to speak, but wanted words, an' made a
sign wi' the left hand. There cam' a clap o' wund, like a cat's fuff;
oot gaed the can'le, the saughs skrieghed like folk; an' Mr Soulis
kenned that, live or die, this was the end o't.

'Witch, beldam, devil!' he cried, 'I charge you, by the power of
God, begone – if you be dead, to the grave – if you be damned, to
hell.'

An' at that moment the Lord's ain hand out o' the Heevens struck
the Horror whaur it stood; the auld, deid, desecrated corp o' the
witchwife, sae lang keepit frae the grave and hirsled round by deils,
lowed up like a brunstane spunk and fell in ashes to the grund; the
thunder followed, peal on dirling peal, the rairing rain upon the back
o' that; and Mr Soulis lowped through the garden hedge, and ran,
wi' skelloch upon skelloch, for the clachan.

That same mornin', John Christie saw the Black Man pass the
Muckle Cairn as it was chappin' six; before eicht, he gaed by the

change-house at Knockdow; an' no lang after, Sandy M'Lellan saw him gaun linkin' doun the braes frae Kilmackerlie. There's little doubt it was him that dwalled sae lang in Janet's body; but he was awa' at last; and sinsyne the deil has never fashed us in Ba'weary.

But it was a sair dispensation for the minister; lang, lang he lay ravin' in his bed; and frae that hour to this, he was the man ye ken the day.

Something Special

IRIS MURDOCH

'WHY WOULDN'T YOU TAKE HIM NOW?' said Mrs Geary. She was setting the evening papers to rights on the counter.

Yvonne sat astride a chair in the middle of the shop. She had it tilting precariously and was rubbing her small head animal fashion on the wood of the back, while her long legs were braced to prevent herself from toppling over. In answer to the qeustion she said nothing.

'She's cross again,' said her uncle, who was standing at the door of the inner room.

'Who's she? She's the cat!' said Yvonne. She began to rock the chair violently to and fro.

'Don't be breaking down that chair,' said her mother. 'It's the last we have of the decent ones till the cane man is back. Why wouldn't you take him is what I asked.'

Close outside the shop the tram for Dublin came rattling by, darkening the scene for a moment and making little objects on the higher shelves jump and tinkle. It was a hot evening and the doors stood wide open to the dust of the street.

'Oh leave off, leave off!' said Yvonne. 'I don't *want* him, I don't *want* to marry. He's nothing special.'

'Nothing special is it?' said her uncle. 'He's a nice young man in a steady job and he wants to wed you and you no longer so young. Or would you be living all your life on your ma?'

'If you won't wed him you shouldn't be leading him up the garden,' said her mother, 'and leave breaking that chair.'

'Can't I be ordinary friends with a boy,' said Yvonne, 'without the pair of you being at me? I'm twenty-four and I know what I'm about.'

'You're twenty-four indeed,' said her mother, 'and there's Betty Nolan and Maureen Burke are married these three years and they in a lower form than you at school.'

'I'm not the like of those two,' said Yvonne.

'True for you!' said her mother.

'It's the women's magazines,' said her uncle, 'and the little novels she's for ever reading that are putting ideas in her head until she won't marry except it's the Sheik of Araby.'

'It's little enough she finds to do with her time,' said her mother, 'so that she's always in there in the little dark room, flat on her tum with her nose inside a novel till it's a wonder her two eyes aren't worn away in her head.'

'Can't I live my life as I please,' said Yvonne, 'since it's the only thing I have? It's that I can't see him as something special and I won't marry him if I can't.'

'He's one of the Chosen People,' said her uncle. 'Isn't that special enough?'

'Don't start on that thing again,' said her mother. 'Sam's a nice young fellow, and not like the run of the Jew-boys at all. He'd bring the children up Church of Ireland.'

'At that,' said her uncle, 'it's better than the other lot with the little priest after them the whole time and bobbing their hats at the chapel doors so you can't even have a peaceful ride on the tram. I've nothing against the Jews.'

'Our Lord was a Jew,' said Yvonne.

'Don't be saying bold things like that!' said her mother.

'Our Lord was the Son of God,' said her uncle, 'and that's neither Jew nor Greek.'

'Is it this evening the Christmas card man is coming?' said Yvonne.

'It is,' said her mother, 'though why they want to be bothering us with Christmas cards in the middle of summer I'm at a loss to know.'

'I'll wait by and see him,' said Yvonne. 'You always pick the dull ones.'

'I pick the ones that sell,' said her mother, 'and don't you be after hanging around acting the maggot when Sam comes, there's little enough room in there.'

'If you were married at least you'd be out of this,' said her uncle, 'and it isn't your ma you'd be sharing a bed with then, and you always complaining about the poky hole this place is.'

'It is a poky hole,' said Yvonne, 'but then I'd be in another poky hole some other place.'

'I'm tired telling you,' said her mother, 'you could get one of those new little houses off the Drumcondra Road. The man in Macmullan's shop knows the man that keeps the list.'

'I don't want a new little house,' said Yvonne. 'I tell you I don't see him right and that's that!'

'If you wait till you marry for love,' said her uncle, 'you'll wait ten years and then make a foolish match. You're not Greta Garbo and you're lucky there's a young fellow after you at all. Sensible people marry because they want to be in the married state and not because of feelings they have in their breasts.'

'She's still stuck on the English lad,' said her mother, 'the tall fellow, Tony Thingummy was his name.'

'I am not!' said Yvonne. 'Good riddance to bad rubbish!'

'I could not abide his voice,' said her uncle. 'He had his mouth all prissed up when he talked, like a man was acting in a play.'

'Isn't it the like of the bloody English to win the Sweep again this year?' said her mother.

'He brought me flowers,' said Yvonne.

'Flowers is it!' said her uncle. 'And singing little songs to you you said once!'

'He was a jaunty boy,' said her mother, 'and a fine slim thing with some pretty ways to him, but he's gone now. And you wait till you see what Sam'll bring you one of these days.'

'Ah, you're potty with that diamond ring story,' said her uncle. 'You'll turn the child's head on her. That fellow's as poor as we are.'

'There's nobody is as poor as we are,' said Yvonne.

'He's a hired man,' said her uncle. 'I don't deny he may get to have his own tailoring shop one day and be his own master. I can see that in him, that he's not a Jew for nothing. But he's no fancy worker now and he's poorly off.'

'Those ones are never poor,' said her mother. 'They just pretend to be so their own people won't be taking their bits of money off them.'

'It's near his time to come,' said Yvonne. 'Don't be talking about him when he comes in, it's not manners.'

'Listen who's mentioning manners!' said her uncle.

'You recall the time,' said her mother, 'we met him at poor Mr Stacey's sale and we went to Sullavan's bar after and he paid for two rounds?'

'He was for catching Yvonne's eye,' said her uncle, 'with flashing his wad round. I'll lay he had to walk home.'

'You're a fine one,' said her mother, 'and you telling me to encourage the child!'

'Did I ever say she should marry him for his money?' said her uncle.

'Well, you'll see,' said her mother. 'It's the custom of those ones. When they want to be engaged to a girl they suddenly bring the diamond ring out and the girl says yes.'

'If they do it's on hire from the pop shop,' said her uncle, 'and it's back in the window directly.'

'What's Julia Batey's ring then?' said her mother, 'and what's her name, young Polly's sister, who married Jews the pair of them, and it happened that way with both. One evening quite suddenly "I want to show you something" says he, and there was the ring and they were engaged from then. I tell you it's a custom.'

'Well, I hope you're right I'm sure,' said her uncle. 'It might be just the thing that would make up the grand young lady's mind. A diamond ring now, that would be something special, wouldn't it?'

'A diamond ring,' said Yvonne, 'would be a change at least.'

'Perhaps he'll have it with him this very night!' said her mother.

'I *don't* think!' said Yvonne.

'Where are you off to anyway?' said her mother.

'I haven't the faintest,' said Yvonne. 'Into town, I suppose.'

'You might go down the pier,' said her uncle, 'and see the mail boat out. That would be better for you than sitting in those stuffy bars or walking along the Liffey breathing the foul airs of the river, and coming home smelling of Guinness.'

'Besides, you know Sam likes the sea,' said her mother. 'He's been all day long dying of suffocation in that steamy room with the clothes press.'

'It's more fun in town,' said Yvonne. 'They've the decorations up for Ireland At Home. And I've been all day long dying of boredom in Kingstown.'

'It's well for you,' said her uncle, 'that it's Sam that pays!'

'And I don't like your going into those low places,' said her mother. 'That's not Sam's idea, I know, it's you. Sam's not one for sitting dreaming in a bar. That's another thing I like about him.'

'Kimball's have got a new saloon lounge,' said Yvonne, 'like a real drawing-room done up with flowers and those crystal lights. Maybe we'll go there.'

'You'll pay extra!' said her uncle.

'Let Sam worry about that!' said her mother. 'It's a relief they have those saloon lounges in the pubs nowadays where you can get away from the smell of porter and a lady can sit there without being taken for something else.'

'Here's the Christmas card man!' said Yvonne, and jumped up from her chair.

'Why, Mr Lynch,' said Mrs Geary, 'it's a pleasure to see you again, who'd think a whole year had gone by, it seems like yesterday you were here before.'

'Good evening, Mrs Geary,' said Mr Lynch, 'it's a blessing to see you looking so well, and Miss Geary and Mr O'Brien still with you. Change and decay in all around we see. I'm told poor Mrs Taylor at the place in Monkstown has passed on since now a year ago.'

'Yes, the poor old faggot,' said Mrs Geary, 'but after seventy years you can't complain, can you? The good Lord's lending it to you after that.'

'Our time is always on loan, Mrs Geary,' said Mr Lynch, 'and who knows when the great Creditor will call? We are as grass which today flourisheth and tomorrow it is cast into the oven.'

'We'll go through,' said Mrs Geary, 'and Mr O'Brien will mind the shop.'

Yvonne and her mother went into the inner room, followed by Mr Lynch. The inner room was very dark, lit only on the far side by a window of frosted glass that gave onto the kitchen. It had a bedroom smell of ancient fabrics and perspiration and dust. Mrs Geary turned on the light. The mountainous double bed with its great white quilt and brass knobs and rails, wherein she and her daughter slept, took up half of the room. A shiny horsehair sofa took up most of the other half, leaving space for a small velvet-topped table and three black chairs which stood in a row in front of the towering mantelshelf where photographs and brass animals rose in tiers to the ceiling. Mr Lynch opened his suitcase and began to spread out the Christmas cards on the faded red velvet.

'The robin and the snow go well,' said Mrs Geary, 'and the stage-coach is popular and the church lit up at night.'

'The traditional themes of Christmas-tide,' said Mr Lynch, 'have a universal appeal.'

'Oh look,' said Yvonne, 'that's the nicest one I've *ever* seen! Now that's really special.' She held it aloft. A frame of glossy golden cardboard enclosed a little square of white silk on which some roses were embroidered.

'That's a novelty,' said Mr Lynch, 'and comes a bit more expensive.'

'It's not like a true Christmas card, the fancy thing,' said Mrs Geary. 'I always think a nice picture and a nice verse is what you want. The sentiment is all.'

'Here's Sam,' said Mr O'Brien from the shop.

Sam came and stood in the doorway from the shop, frowning in the electric light. He was a short man, 'portly' Mr O'Brien called him, and he could hardly count as handsome. He had a pale moon-face and fugitive hands, but his eyes were dark, and his dark bushy head of hair was like the brave plume of a bird. He had his best suit on, which was a midnight blue with a grey stripe, and his tie was of light yellow silk.

'Come on in, Sam,' said Mrs Geary. 'Yvonne's been ready this long time. Mr Lynch, this is Mr Goldman.'

'How do you do?' they said.

'You're mighty smart tonight, Sam,' said Mrs Geary. 'Going to have a special evening?'

'We're choosing the Christmas cards,' said Yvonne. 'Have you got any with the ox and the ass on, Mr Lynch?'

'Here,' said Mr Lynch, 'we have the ox and the ass, and here we see our Lord lying in the manger, and His Mother by, and here the three Magi with their costly gifts, and here the angels coming to the poor shepherds by night, and here the star of glory that led them on. When Jesus was born in Bethlehem of Judaea in the days of Herod the King —'

'I still like this one best,' said Yvonne. 'Look, Sam, isn't that pretty?' She held up the card with the golden frame.

'You two be off now,' said Mrs Geary, 'and leave troubling Sam with these Christian things.'

'I don't mind,' said Sam. 'I always observe Christmas just as you do, Mrs Geary. I take it as a sort of emblem.'

'That's right,' said Mr Lynch. 'What after all divides us one from another? In My Father's house are many mansions. If it were not so I would have told you.'

'I'll just get my coat,' said Yvonne.

'Don't keep her out late, Sam,' said Mrs Geary. 'Good-bye now, and mind you have a really nice evening.'

'Abyssinia,' said Yvonne.

They left the cool musty air of the shop and emerged into the big warm perfumed summer dusk. Yvonne threw her head back, and pranced along in her high-heeled shoes, wearing the look of petulant intensity which she always affected for the benefit of Sam. She would not take his arm, and they went a little aimlessly down the street.

'Where shall we go?' said Sam.

'I don't mind,' she said.

'We might walk a bit by the sea,' said Sam, 'and sit on the rocks beyond the Baths.'

'It's too windy down there and I can't go on the rocks in these shoes.'

'Well, let's go into town.'

At that moment from the seaward side came a sonorous booming sound, very deep and sad. It came again, was sustained in a melancholy roar, and died slowly away.

'Ah, the mail boat!' said Sam. 'Let's just see it out, it's ages since I saw it out.'

They walked briskly as far as the Mariners' Church and turned along the front into the racing breeze. In the evening light the scene before them glowed like a coloured postcard. The mail boat had its lights on already, making pale, shifting reflections in the water which was still glossy with daylight. As they came nearer the boat began to move very slowly, and drew away from the big brown wooden quay revealing upon it the rows and rows of people left behind agitating their white handkerchiefs in the darkening air. The scene was utterly silent. A curly plume of black smoke gathered upon the metallic water, hid the ship for a moment, and then lifted to show it gliding away between the two lighthouses, whose beams were kindled at that very time, and into the open sea. Beyond it a large pale moon was rising over Howth Head.

'The moon hath raised her lamp above,' said Sam.

'I've seen the mail boat out a hundred times,' said Yvonne, 'and one day I'll be on it.'

'Would you like to go to England then?' said Sam.

Yvonne gave him a look of exaggerated scorn. 'Doesn't every Irish person with a soul in them want to go to England?' she said.

They walked more slowly back now, past the golden windows of Ross's Hotel to take the Dublin tram. By the time they had climbed the hill the ship was halfway toward the horizon, its trail of smoke taken up into the gathering night, and by the time they got off the tram at Nelson's Pillar the daylight was gone entirely.

'Now where would you like to go?' said Sam.

'Don't be eternally asking me that question!' she said. 'Just go somewhere yourself and I'll probably follow!'

Sam took her arm, which she let him hold this time, and walked her back toward O'Connell Bridge and along onto the quays. The Liffey flowed past them, oily and glistening, as black as Guinness, bound for Dublin Bay. It had not far to go now. Along the parapet at intervals, and hanging suspended from the iron tracery of the street lamps, were metal baskets full of flowers, while a banner hanging on the bridge announced in English and in Irish that Ireland was At Home to visitors. There was a mingled smell of garbage and pollen.

Sam turned her toward the river, and was for lingering there in a sentimental way, his arm creeping about her waist. The moon was risen now over the top of the houses. But Yvonne said firmly, 'You'll get your death with the smell of the drains here. Let's go to Kimball's place and try the new saloon lounge.'

They turned up the side street that led to Kimball's. It was a dirty, dark little street, but a blaze of light and a good deal of hubbub at the far end of it declared the whereabouts of that hostelry. The ordinary bar, which had formerly been the only one, was in the basement, while on the street level was Kimball's grocery store, and above this the saloon lounge before mentioned. From the well of the stairs below came an odour of men and drink and the tinkling of a piano and an uproar of male voices.

Sam and Yvonne turned aside and mounted a brightly lit carpeted stairway, which smelt strongly of new paint, and emerged into the lounge. The door shut itself quietly behind them. Here everything was still. Yvonne walked across the heavy carpet and sat down on a fat chintz sofa and arranged her dress. In the gilded mirror behind the bar she could see the reflection of Sam's face as he ordered a gin and lime for her and a draught Guinness for himself. For an instant she concentrated the glow of her imagination upon him; but could only notice that he leaned forward in an apologetic way to the barman, and how absurdly his small feet turned out as he stood there. He gave the order in a low voice, as if he were asking for something not quite nice at the chemist's. A few couples sat scattered about the room, huddled under the shaded lights, murmuring to each other.

When Sam came back with the drinks Yvonne said loudly, 'You'd think you were in a church here, not in a public-house!'

'Sssh!' said Sam. One or two people stared. Sam sat down close beside her on the sofa, trying to make himself drink. He edged nearer still, but curling into himself like a hedgehog so as to be as near as possible without giving offence. He put down his glass on the table and began laboriously in his mind the long search for words, for the simple words that would lead on to the more important ones. His pale stumpy hand caressed Yvonne's bony brown hand. Hers lay there listlessly in a way that was familiar to him. He squeezed it a little and tried to draw her back towards him, deeper into the sofa. So they sat there a while in silence, Sam searching and holding, and Yvonne stiff. The upholstered stillness around them was not good for their talk. The barman chinked a glass and everyone in the room jumped.

'This place gives me heart disease', said Yvonne. 'It's like a lot of dead people giving a party. Let's go and see what it's like downstairs. I've never been downstairs here.'

'It's not nice,' said Sam. 'Ladies don't go downstairs. Why not let's go back to Henry Street? There's the little coffee bar you liked once.'

'That was a silly place!' said Yvonne. 'I'm going downstairs anyway. You can do as you like.' She said this in a loud voice, and then got up and walked firmly toward the door. Sam, red with embarrassment, jumped up too, took a hasty pull at his drink, and followed her out. They descended into the street and took the iron staircase that led to the basement. The noise and the smell were stronger than before.

Yvonne hesitated halfway down. 'You'd better lead,' she said. Sam stumbled past her and pushed at the blackened door of the bar. He had never been down those stairs either.

They came out into a very big low-roofed room with white tiled walls and blazing unshaded lights. The floor was slimy with spilt drink and beery sawdust and the atmosphere was thick. The pounding repetitive beat of a piano, its melody absorbed into the continuous din of voices, was felt rather than heard. A great many men who were adhering to a circular bar in the centre, turned to stare at Yvonne as she entered. It looked at first as if no women were present, but as the haze shifted here and there it was possible to discern one or two lurking in the darkened alcoves.

'There *are* women here!' called Yvonne triumphantly.

'Not nice ones,' said Sam. 'What's your drink?' He hated being looked at.

'Whisky,' said Yvonne. She refused to sit down, but stood there swaying slightly and holding onto one of the ironwork pillars that

circled the bar. The men near by studied her with insolent appreciation and made remarks. She coloured a little, but stared straight in
front of her, bright-eyed.

It was not easy for poor Sam to get at the bar. The clients who
were standing in his way were in no hurry to move, though they
looked at him amiably enough. The bar-tender, an infernal version
of his upstairs colleague, pointedly served two later-comers first, and
then with ironic politeness handed Sam the drinks.

'Isn't this better than up there?' Yvonne shouted, seizing her glass
from him as he got back to her side.

'That's the stuff'll put the red neck on you!' observed a man with
a penetrating voice, who was standing close to Yvonne.

'Your mother something or other,' Sam shouted back, propelling
Yvonne fussily into a space in the middle of the floor, where he stood
holding tightly onto her arm.

She stopped trying to hear his voice and gave herself up to the
pleasure of being part of such a noisy crowded drunken scene. By
the time she had sipped the half of her whisky she was perceptibly
enjoying herself very much indeed. Upon the confused flood of noise
and movement she was now afloat.

After a short while there was something quite particular to watch:
a little scene which seemed to be developing on the near side of the
bar. Someone was waving his arms and shouting in an angry voice.
Whereon the publican in even higher tones was heard to cry, 'Just
raise your hand again, mister, and you're out in the street! Patsy, put
that gentleman out in the street!'

People crowded quickly forward from the alcoves to see the fun.
The piano stopped abruptly and the sound of voices became suddenly
jagged and harsh. A woman with a red carnation in her hair and an
overwhelming perfume came and stood beside Yvonne, her bare arm
touching the girl's sleeve. Yvonne could see at once that she was not
a nice sort of woman at all, and she removed herself from the contact.
The woman gave her a provoking stare.

'Time for us to make tracks,' said Sam to Yvonne.

'Ah shut up!' she said, looking past him with glowing eyes to
where the drama was unfolding.

A tall thin young fellow, the prey designate of Patsy, was swaying
to and fro, still flourishing his fist, and trying to make a statement,
intended no doubt as insult or vindication, but whose complexity
was such that he began it several times over without succeeding in

making himself clear. His antagonist, a thick man with a Cork accent, who accompanied these attempts with a continual sneering noise, suddenly gave him a violent jab in the stomach. The young man oscillated, and lurched back amid laughter, with a look of extreme surprise. To keep his balance he twisted dexterously about on his heel and found himself face to face with Yvonne.

'Ah!' said the young man. He stood there poised, frozen in the gesture of turning, with one hand outstretched ballet-wise, and slowly allowed a look of imbecile delight to transfigure his features. Another laugh went up.

'Ah!' said the young man. 'I thought the flowers were all falling, but here is a rose in the bud!' He seemed to have found his tongue.

The woman with the red carnation clapped Yvonne on the shoulder. 'Come along the little pet,' she cried, 'and give the kind gentleman a good answer!'

The thin young man turned upon her. 'You leave the young lady alone,' he shouted, 'she isn't your like!' And with that he darted out his hand and plucked the red carnation from the women's hair and thrust it with another lurch into the bosom of Yvonne's frock. There was a roar of applause.

Yvonne sprang away. The woman turned quick as a flash and slapped the young man in the face. But quicker still the woman's escort, a brown man with an arm like an ape, had snatched the flower back from where it hung at Yvonne's breast and given her a push which sent her flying back against the wall. There was a momentary delighted silence. People by now had climbed on chairs to get a better view, and tiers of grinning unshaven faces peered down through the haze. Yvonne was crimson. For a moment she leaned there rigid, as if pinned to the tiles. Then Sam had taken her by the hand and was leading her quickly out of the bar.

Before the heavy doors were shut again they heard the yell which followed them up into the street. 'It's safer upstairs, mister!' screamed a woman's voice.

When Yvonne got out onto the pavement she wrenched her hand away from Sam and began to run. She ran like a hare down the dark and ill-smelling street toward the open lamplight of the quays, and here Sam caught her up, leaning against the parapet of the river and drooping her head down and panting.

'Oh my dear darling, didn't –' Sam began to say; but he was interrupted. Out of the hazy darkness beyond the street lamps a third figure had emerged. It was the thin young man, also at a run. He gripped Sam by the arm.

'No offence, mister,' said the young man, 'no offence! It was a tribute, a sincere tribute, from one of Ireland's poets – a true poet, mister –' He stood there, still holding onto Sam with one hand, and staring wide-eyed at Yvonne, while the other hand fumbled in his coat pocket.

'That's all right,' said Sam. 'It wasn't your fault surely. We've just got to go now.' He began gently but vigorously to detach the clutching fingers from his arm.

The young man held on tight. 'If I could only find me bloody poem,' he said, 'a sincere tribute, a humble and sincere tribute, to one of the wonders of Nature, a beautiful woman is one of the wonders of Nature, a flower —'

'Yes, yes, all right,' said Sam. 'We don't mind, we've just got to go now to get our tram.'

'– fitting homage,' said the young man. 'Sweets to the sweet!' He let go abruptly of Sam and struck a graceful attitude. The post proving too difficult to maintain, he heeled over slowly against the edge of the quay and came into violent contact with one of the metal flower baskets.

'Did I mention flowers?' he cried. 'And here they are! Flowers for her, for a gift, for a tribute –' He plunged his fingers into the basket and brought out a handful of geraniums together with a great quantity of earth, all of which fell to the ground in a heap, partly engulfing Yvonne's shoes.

'Come on!' said Sam. But Yvonne had already turned and was walking away very fast, swinging her arms, and shaking her feet as she walked in order to get some of the earth out. Sam followed quickly after her, and the young man followed after Sam, still talking.

'What is her name?' he was crying in an aggrieved tone. 'What is her name, who makes rose petals rain from heaven, and with oh such eyes and lips, this was something that I spoke about in a poem –' And as they walked on, the three of them, in Indian file and with quickening pace in the direction of O'Connell Street, the young man plucked the flowers from the baskets and drew their stems through his fingers to gather tight handfuls of petals which he cast high over Sam's head so that they should rain down upon Yvonne.

'Now then, young fellow,' said the policeman, who suddenly materialized as the little procession neared O'Connell Bridge. 'Let me remind you it's public money is spent on those flowers you are defiling in a way renders you liable for prosecution.'

'Nature intended –' the young man began.

'That may well be,' said the policeman, 'and I intend to have you up for wilful and malicious damages.' The two figures converged. Sam and Yvonne drew away.

As they were passing Hannah's bookshop Sam caught up with her. Her face was stony. He began to ask her was she all right.

At first she would say nothing, but turned savagely away over the bridge in the direction of Westmoreland Street. Then she cried in a weary voice, 'Oh be silent, I've enough of this, just come to the tram.'

Sam raised his hands and then spread them out, opening the palms. For a while he trotted behind her in silence, his plume of black hair bobbing over his eyes. 'Yvonne,' he said then, 'don't go away yet. Let me just make you forget those things. You'll never pardon me if you go away with those things between us.'

Yvonne slowed her step and looked round at him sullenly. 'It isn't that anything matters,' she said, 'or that I'm surprised at all. It's that I thought it might be – a specially nice evening. More fool me and that's all!'

Sam's hands clasped themselves in front of him and then spread wide once more. He made her stop now and face him. They were well up the street. 'It can be still,' he said urgently, 'a special evening. Don't spoil it now by being cross. Wait a bit. It's not the last tram yet.'

Yvonne hesitated, and let Sam pull her limp arm through his. 'But where can we put ourselves at this hour?'

'Never you mind!' said Sam with a sudden confidence. 'You come along with me, and if you're a good girl there's something special I've got to show you.'

'Something – to show me?' said Yvonne. She let him lead her along in the direction of Grafton Street. As they turned the corner Sam boldly locked his fingers through hers and kneaded her thin hand in the palm of his own. She welcomed him with a very little pressure. So they walked the length of the street linked in a precarious and conscious hold. The dark mass of Stephen's Green was appearing now in front of them and they crossed the road towards it. A few people were gathered still in the golden glow outside the Shelbourne, but on the farther side of the square there was no one. Sam began to draw her along, slinking close beside the railings.

'I'm destroyed walking in these shoes,' said Yvonne. 'Where is the place you are going to?'

'Here it is,' said Sam. He stopped and pointed suddenly to a gap in the railings. 'There's a rail out and we can go through inside the garden.'

'It's not allowed,' said Yvonne, 'It's shut to the public now.'

'We're not the public, you and me,' said Sam. He put his feet boldly through the hole and ducked to the other side. Then with authority he pulled the girl in after him.

She gave a little cry, finding herself in a tangle of damp undergrowth. 'It's horrid in here, my stockings are tearing!'

'Give me your hands back,' said Sam. He took both her hands and half-lifted her out onto a dark lawn of grass. She took a few steps across its moist spongy surface and then felt the hard grit of the path underneath her feet. They emerged into bright moonlight beside the water. The big moon looked up at them from the lake, clear-cut and almost full, intensely bright.

'Oh dear!' said Yvonne, silenced for a moment by the ghostly radiance. They stood hand in hand looking into the black mirror of the lake, their long moon-shadows stretched out behind them.

Yvonne began to peer nervously about her. 'Sam,' she said in a whisper, 'I don't like this being here, someone'll find us, please let us go back —'

'I won't hurt you,' said Sam, whispering too in a caressing exultant tender whisper, 'I'll look after you, I'll always look after you. I just wanted to show you something nice.'

'Well —?' said Yvonne. She followed him a few steps as he moved, and looked up into his face.

'Here it is,' said Sam.

'Where?'

'Here, look —' He reached his hand towards a dark shape.

Yvonne recoiled from him violently. What seemed a monster was there in the darkness. Then she made out that there was a fallen tree lying right across the path beside the lake, its topmost branches just touching the water.

'What is it?' she said with revulsion.

'A fallen tree,' said Sam. 'I don't know what kind.'

Yvonne looked at him. She saw his two eyes gleam almost cat-like in the darkness in the light of the reflected moon, but they were not looking at her.

'But you were going to show me something.'

'Yes, this, the poor tree.'

Yvonne was dumb for a moment. Then she came choking into speech. 'This was it then you stopped me from the tram for and made me walk a mile for and tear my stockings, just a dirty rotten maggoty old tree!' Her voice rose higher and she hit out wildly with her hand, whipping a flurry of foliage across Sam's round moonlit face.

'But no,' said Sam, quite calmly now beside her, 'only see it, Yvonne, be quiet for a minute and see it. It's so beautiful, though indeed it's a sad thing for a tree to lie like this, all fresh with its green leaves on the ground, like a flower that's been picked. I know it's a sad thing. But come to me now and we'll be a pair of birds up in the branches.' He took her against her will and drew her to him among the rustling leaves which lay in a tall fan across the path. He kissed the girl very gently on the cheek.

Yvonne got free of his grasp and stumbled back, beating away the leafy twigs from her neck. 'Was this all?' she said with violence. 'Was this all that you wanted me to see? It's nothing, and I hate it. I hate your beastly tree and its dirt and the worms and beetles falling down inside my dress.' She began to cry.

Sam came out of the leaves and stood ruefully beside her, trying to get hold of her hand. 'I only wanted to please you,' he said. 'It's a sad thing to show you, I know, and not very exciting, but I thought it was beautiful, and —'

'I *hate* it,' said Yvonne, and began to run away from him across the grass, blubbering as she ran. She was before him at the hole in the railings, and he had to run after her as she hurried along the pavement, trailing a sort of bramble behind her from her skirt.

Now Sam's confidence was all gone. 'Yvonne,' he called, 'don't be holding it against me, Yvonne. I didn't mean —'

'Oh shut up!' said Yvonne.

'Don't be holding it against me.'

'Oh stop whingeing!' she said.

The tram for Dun Laoghaire came lurching into sight as Sam still followed after Yvonne, pawing at her arm and asking her to forgive him. Yvonne got onto the tram and without looking back at him climbed the stairs quickly to the top. Sam stood still on the pavement and was left behind, his two hands raised in the air in a gesture of dereliction.

her head under the sheet and began to slide her hips down toward the centre of the bed.

'You make me tired!' said her mother. 'Can you not tell me why at all?'

'No,' said Yvonne. 'It's a sad thing,' she added, 'oh, it's a sad thing!' She was silent then and would say no more.

All was quiet at last in the inner room and in the shop. There would be no more trams passing now until the following day. Yvonne Geary buried her face deep in the pillow, so deep that her mother should not be able to hear that she was just starting to cry. The long night was ahead.

The Stolen Bacillus

H.G. WELLS

'THIS AGAIN,' SAID THE BACTERIOLOGIST, slipping a glass slide under the microscope, 'is a preparation of the celebrated Bacillus of cholera – the cholera germ.'

The pale-faced man peered down the microscope. He was evidently not accustomed to that kind of thing, and held a limp white hand over his disengaged eye. 'I see very little,' he said.

'Touch this screw,' said the Bacteriologist; 'perhaps the microscope is out of focus for you. Eyes vary so much. Just the fraction of a turn this way or that.'

'Ah! now I see,' said the visitor. 'Not so very much to see after all. Little streaks and shreds of pink. And yet those little particles, those mere atomies, might multiply and devastate a city! Wonderful!'

He stood up, and releasing the glass slip from the microscope, held it in his hand towards the window. 'Scarcely visible,' he said, scrutinizing the preparation. He hesitated. 'Are these – alive? Are they dangerous now?'

'Those have been stained and killed,' said the Bacteriologist. 'I wish, for my own part, we could kill and stain every one of them in the universe.'

'I suppose,' the pale man said with a slight smile, 'that you scarcely care to have such things about you in the living – in the active state?'

'On the contrary, we are obliged to,' said the Bacteriologist. 'Here, for instance —' He walked across the room and took up one of several sealed tubes. 'Here is the living thing. This is a cultivation of the actual living disease bacteria.' He hesitated. 'Bottled cholera, so to speak.'

A slight gleam of satisfaction appeared momentarily in the face of the pale man. 'It's a deadly thing to have in your possession,' he said, devouring the little tube with his eyes. The Bacteriologist watched the morbid pleasure in his visitor's expression. This man, who had visited him that afternoon with a note of introduction from an old friend, interested him from the very contrast of their dispositions. The lank black hair and deep grey eyes, the haggard expression and nervous manner, the fitful yet keen interest of his visitor were a novel change from the phlegmatic deliberations of the ordinary scientific worker with whom the Bacteriologist chiefly associated. It was perhaps natural, with a hearer evidently so impressionable to the lethal nature of his topic, to take the most effective aspect of the matter.

He held the tube in his hand thoughtfully. 'Yes, here is the pestilence imprisoned. Only break such a little tube as this into a supply of drinking-water, say to these minute particles of life that one must needs stain and examine with the highest powers of the microscope even to see, and that one can neither smell nor taste – say to them, "Go forth, increase and multiply, and replenish the cisterns," and death – mysterious, untraceable death, death swift and terrible, death full of pain and indignity – would be released upon this city, and go hither and thither seeking his victims. Here he would take the husband from the wife, here the child from its mother, here the statesman from his duty, and here the toiler from his trouble. He would follow the water-mains, creeping along streets, picking out and punishing a house here and a house there where they did not boil their drinking-water, creeping into the wells of the mineral-water makers, getting washed into salad, and lying dormant in ices. He would wait ready to be drunk in the horse-troughs, and by unwary children in the public fountains. He would soak into the soil, to reappear in springs and wells at a thousand unexpected places. Once start him at the water supply, and before we could ring him in, and catch him again, he would have decimated the metropolis.'

He stopped abruptly. He had been told rhetoric was his weakness.

'But he is quite safe here, you know – quite safe.'

The pale-faced man nodded. His eyes shone. He cleared his throat. 'These Anarchist – rascals,' said he, 'are fools, blind fools – to use bombs when this kind of thing is attainable. I think –'

A gentle rap, a mere light touch of the fingernails was heard at the door. The Bacteriologist opened it. 'Just a minute, dear,' whispered his wife.

When he re-entered the laboratory his visitor was looking at his watch. 'I had no idea I had wasted an hour of your time,' he said. 'Twelve minutes to four. I ought to have left here by half-past three.

But your things were really too interesting. No, positively I cannot stop a moment longer. I have an engagement at four.'

He passed out of the room reiterating his thanks, and the Bacteriologist accompanied him to the door, and then returned thoughtfully along the passage to his laboratory. He was musing on the ethnology of his visitor. Certainly the man was not a Teutonic type nor a common Latin one. 'A morbid product, anyhow, I am afraid,' said the Bacteriologist to himself. 'How he gloated on those cultivations of disease-germs!' A disturbing thought struck him. He turned to the bench by the vapour-bath, and then very quickly to his writing-table. Then he felt hastily in his pockets, and then rushed to the door. 'I may have put it down on the hall table,' he said.

'Minnie!' he shouted hoarsely in the hall.

'Yes, dear,' came a remote voice.

'Had I anything in my hand when I spoke to you, dear, just now?' Pause.

'Nothing, dear, because I remember —'

'Blue ruin!' cried the Bacteriologist, and incontinently ran to the front door and down the steps of his house to the street.

Minnie, hearing the door slam violently, ran in alarm to the window. Down the street a slender man was getting into a cab. The Bacteriologist, hatless, and in his carpet slippers, was running and gesticulating wildly towards this group. One slipper came off, but he did not wait for it. 'He has gone *mad*!' said Minnie; 'it's that horrid science of his'; and, opening the window, would have called after him. The slender man, suddenly glancing round, seemed struck with the same idea of mental disorder. He pointed hastily to the Bacteriologist, said something to the cab-man, the apron of the cab slammed, the whip swished, the horse's feet clattered, and in a moment cab, and Bacteriologist hotly in pursuit, had receded up the vista of the roadway and disappeared round the corner.

Minnie remained straining out of the window for a minute. Then she drew her head back into the room again. She was dumbfounded. 'Of course he is eccentric,' she meditated. 'But running about London – in the height of the season, too – in his socks!' A happy thought struck her. She hastily put her bonnet on, seized his shoes, went into the hall, took down his hat and light overcoat from the pegs, emerged upon the doorstep, and hailed a cab that opportunely crawled by. 'Drive me up the road and round Havelock Crescent, and see if we can find a gentleman running about in a velveteen coat and no hat.'

'Velveteen coat, ma'am, and no 'at. Very good, ma'am.' And the cabman whipped up at once in the most matter-of-fact way, as if he drove to this address every day in his life.

Some few minutes later the little group of cabmen and loafers that collects round the cabmen's shelter at Haverstock Hill were startled by the passing of a cab with a ginger-coloured screw of a horse, driven furiously.

They were silent as it went by, and then as it receded – 'That's 'Arry 'Icks. Wot's *he* got?' said the stout gentleman known as Old Tootles.

'He's a-using his whip, he is, *to* rights,' said the ostler boy.

'Hullo!' said poor old Tommy Byles; 'here's another bloomin' loonatic. Blowed if there ain't.'

'It's old George,' said old Tootles, 'and he's drivin' a loonatic, *as* you say. Ain't he a-clawin' out of the keb? Wonder if he's after 'Arry 'Icks?'

The group round the cabmen's shelter became animated. Chorus: 'Go it, George!' 'It's a race!' 'You'll ketch 'em!' 'Whip up!'

'She's a goer, she is!' said the ostler boy.

'Strike me giddy!' cried old Tootles. 'Here! I'm a-goin' to begin in a minute. Here's another comin'. If all the kebs in Hampstead ain't gone mad this morning!'

'It's a fieldmale this time,' said the ostler boy.

'She's a followin' *him*,' said old Tootles. 'Usually the other way about.'

'What's she got in her 'and?'

'Looks like a 'igh 'at.'

'What a bloomin' lark it is! Three to one on old George,' said the ostler boy. 'Next!'

Minnie went by in a perfect roar of applause. She did not like it but she felt that she was doing her duty, and whirled on down Haverstock Hill and Camden Town High Street with her eyes ever intent on the animated back view of old George, who was driving her vagrant husband so incomprehensively away from her.

The man in the foremost cab sat crouched in the corner, his arms tightly folded, and the little tube that contained such vast possibilities of destruction gripped in his hand. His mood was a singular mixture of fear and exultation. Chiefly he was afraid of being caught before he could accomplish his purpose, but behind this was a vaguer but larger fear of the awfulness of his crime. But his exultation far exceeded his fear. No Anarchist before him had ever approached this conception of his. Ravachol, Vaillant, all those distinguished persons whose fame he had envied dwindled into insignificance beside him. He had only to make sure of the water supply, and break the little tube into a reservoir. How brilliantly he had planned it, forged the letter of introduction and got into the laboratory, and how brilliantly he had seized his opportunity! The world should hear of him at last. All those people who had sneered at him, neglected him, preferred other people to him, found his company undesirable, should consider him at last. Death, death, death! They had always treated him as a man of no importance. All the world had been in a conspiracy to keep him under. He would teach them yet what it is to isolate a man. What was this familiar street? Great Saint Andrew's Street, of course! How fared the chase? He craned out of the cab. The Bacteriologist was scarcely fifty yards behind. That was bad. He would be caught and stopped yet. He felt in his pocket for money, and found half-a-sovereign. This he thrust up through the trap in the top of the cab into the man's face. 'More,' he shouted, 'if only we get away.'

The money was snatched out of his hand. 'Right you are,' said the cabman, and the trap slammed, and the lash lay along the glistening side of the horse. The cab swayed, and the Anarchist, half-standing under the trap, put the hand containing the little glass tube upon the apron to preserve his balance. He felt the brittle thing crack, and the broken half of it rang upon the floor of the cab. He fell back into the seat with a curse, and stared dismally at the two or three drops of moisture on the apron.

He shuddered.

'Well! I suppose I shall be the first. *Phew!* Anyhow, I shall be a Martyr. That's something. But it is a filthy death, nevertheless. I wonder if it hurts as much as they say.'

Presently a thought occurred to him – he groped between his feet. A little drop was still in the broken end of the tube, and he drank that to make sure. It was better to make sure. At any rate, he would not fail.

Then it dawned upon him that there was no further need to escape the Bacteriologist. In Wellington Street he told the cabman to stop, and got out. He slipped on the step, and his head felt queer. It was rapid stuff this cholera poison. He waved his cabman out of existence, so to speak, and stood on the pavement with his arm folded upon his breast awaiting the arrival of the Bacteriologist. There was something tragic in his pose. The sense of imminent death gave him a certain dignity. He greeted his pursuer with a defiant laugh.

'Vive l'Anarchie! You are too late, my friend. I have drunk it. The cholera is abroad!'

The Bacteriologist from his cab beamed curiously at him through his spectacles. 'You have drunk it! An Anarchist! I see now.' He was about to say something more, and then checked himself. A smile hung in the corner of his mouth. He opened the apron of his cab as if to descend, at which the Anarchist waved him a dramatic farewell and strode off towards Waterloo Bridge, carefully jostling his infected body against as many people as possible. The Bacteriologist was so preoccupied with the vision of him that he scarcely manifested the slightest surprise at the appearance of Minnie upon the pavement with his hat and shoes and overcoat. 'Very good of you to bring my things,' he said, and remained lost in contemplation of the receding figure of the Anarchist.

'You had better get in,' he said, still staring. Minnie felt absolutely convinced now that he was mad, and directed the cabman home on her own responsibility. 'Put on my shoes? Certainly, dear,' said he, as the cab began to turn, and hid the strutting black figure, now small in the distance, from his eyes. Then suddenly something grotesque struck him, and he laughed. Then he remarked, 'It is really very serious, though.'

'You see, that man came to my house to see me, and he is an Anarchist. No – don't faint, or I cannot possibly tell you the rest. And I wanted to astonish him, not knowing he was an Anarchist, and took up a cultivation of that new species of Bacterium I was telling you of, that infest, and I think cause, the blue patches upon various monkeys; and like a fool, I said it was Asiatic cholera. And he ran away with it to poison the water of London, and he certainly might have made things look blue for this civilised city. And now he has swallowed it. Of course, I cannot say what will happen, but you know it turned that kitten blue, and the three puppies – in patches, and the sparrow – bright blue. But the bother is, I shall have all the trouble and expense of preparing some more.

'Put on my coat on this hot day! Why? Because we might meet Mrs Jabber. My dear, Mrs Jabber is not a draught. But why should I wear a coat on a hot day because of Mrs —? Oh! *very* well.'

Parthenope

REBECCA WEST

MY UNCLE ARTHUR HAD RED HAIR THAT lay close to his head in flat, circular curls, and a pointed red beard, and his blue-green eyes were at once penetrating and bemused. He was the object of mingled derision and respect in our family. He was a civil servant who had early attracted attention by his brilliance; but the chief of his department, like so many English civil servants, was an author in his spare time and, when he published a history of European literature, my uncle reviewed it in the leading weekly of the day, pointing out that large as was the number of works in the less familiar languages that his chief supposed to be written in prose, though in fact they were written in verse, it was not so large as the number of such works that he supposed to be written in verse, though in fact they were written in prose. He wrote without malice, simply thinking his chief would be glad to know. My uncle never connected this review with his subsequent failure to gain a promotion that had seemed certain, or to have the day as snug as civil servants usually had it in the 19th century. But in the course of time his chief died, and my uncle rose to be an important official. However, he did a Cabinet Minister much the same service he had rendered his chief, and he never received the title that normally went with his post.

So he seesawed through life, and I liked his company very much when he was an old man and I was a young girl, for it was full of surprises. When I asked him a question, I never knew if his answer would show that he knew far less than I did or far more; and though he was really quite old, for he was my father's elder by many years, he often made discoveries such as a schoolchild might make, and shared them with an enthusiasm as little adult. One day he gave me no peace till I had come with him to see the brightest field of buttercups he had ever found near London; it lay, solid gold, beside the great Jacobean mansion Ham House, by the River Thames. After we had admired it he took me to nearby Petersham Church, to see another treasure, the tomb of Captain Vancouver, who gave his name to the island; my uncle liked this tomb because he had spent some years of his boyhood in Canada and had been to Vancouver Island when it was hardly inhabited. Then we had tea in an inn garden, and it happened that the girl who waited on us was called away by the landlord as she set the china on the table. His voice came from the kitchen: 'Parthenope! Parthenope!' My uncle started, for no very good reason that I could see. There had been a time when many ships in the British Navy were called after characters in Greek history and mythology, male and female, and therefore many sailors' daughters had been given the names of nymphs and goddesses and Homeric princesses and heroines of Greek tragedy. The only strange thing was that it was a long time since British ships had been christened so poetically, and most of the women who had acquired these Classical names by this secondary interest were by now old or middle-aged, while our little waitress was very young. She had, as she told us when she came back, been called after a grandmother. But my uncle was plainly shaken by hearing those four syllables suddenly borne on the afternoon air. His thin hand plucked at the edge of the tablecloth, he cast down his eyes, his head began to nod and shake. He asked me if he had ever told me the story of the Admiral and his seven daughters, in a tone that suggested that he knew he had not and was still trying to make up his mind whether he wanted to tell it now. Indeed, he told me very little that day, though I was to hear the whole of it before he died.

The story began at the house of my grandmother's sister, Alice Darrell, and it could hardly have happened anywhere else. When her husband, an officer in the Indian Army, died of fever, her father-in-law had given her a house that he had recently and reluctantly inherited and could not sell because it was part of an entailed estate. He apologized for the gift, pleading justly that he could not afford to buy her another, and she accepted it bravely. But the house lay in a district that would strain anybody's bravery. To reach it, one travelled about eight miles out of London along the main Hammersmith Road, the dullest of highways, and then turned left and found something worse. For some forgotten reason, there had sprung up at this point a Hogarthian slum, as bad as anything in the East End, which turned into a brawling hell every Saturday night. Beyond this web of filthy hovels lay flatlands covered by orchards and farmlands and market gardens, among which there had been set down three or four large houses. There was nothing to recommend the site. The Thames was not far distant, and it was comprehensible enough that along its bank there had been built a line of fine houses. But at Alice Darrell's there was no view of the river, though it lay near enough to shroud the region in mist during the winter months. It was true that the gardens had an alluvial fertility, but even they did not give the pleasure they should have done, for the slum dwellers carried out periodical raids on the strawberry beds and raspberry canes and orchards.

These stranded houses had been built in Regency times and were beautiful, though disconcerting, because there was no reason why they should be there, and they were so oddly placed in relation to each other. They all opened off the same narrow road, and Aunt Alice's house, Currivel Lodge, which was the smallest of them, lay at the end of a drive, and there faced sideways, so that its upper windows looked straight down on the garden of the much bigger house beside it, as that had been built nearer the road. This meant that my grand-aunt could not sit on the pretty balcony outside her bedroom window without seeming to spy on her neighbours, so she never used it. But when my Uncle Arthur went to stay with her as a little boy, which was about a hundred years ago, nothing delighted him more than to shut himself in his bedroom and kneel on his window seat and do what his Aunt Alice could not bear to be suspected of doing.

Currivel Lodge should have been a dreary place for the child. There was nowhere to walk and nowhere to ride. There was no village where one could watch the blacksmith at his forge and the carpenter at his bench. In those days, nobody rowed on the Thames anywhere but at Oxford, unless they were watermen earning their living. There was little visiting, for it took a good hour to an hour and a half to drive to London, and my needy grand-aunt's horses were old crocks. Her children were all older than little Arthur. But he enjoyed his visit simply because of the hours he spent on that window seat. I know the setting of the scene on which he looked, since I often stayed in that house many years later; for of course my grand-aunt's family never left it. When the entail came to an end and the property could have been sold, there were the Zulu Wars, the South African War, the First World War, and all meant that the occupants were too busy or too troubled to move; and they were still living there when the house was swept away in a town-planning scheme during the 20s. What Arthur in his day and I in mine looked down on was a croquet lawn framed by trees, very tall trees – so tall and strong, my uncle said with approval, that though one could not see the river one knew that there must be one not far away. Born and reared in one of the wettest parts of Ireland, he regarded dry weather and a dry soil as the rest of us regard dry bread.

To the left of this lawn, seen through foliage, was a stone terrace overgrown with crimson and white roses. Behind the terrace rose the mellow red rectangle of a handsome Regency house with a green copper cupola rising from its roof. What my uncle saw there that was not there for me to see was a spectacle that gave him the same sort of enjoyment I was to get from the ballet *Les Sylphides*. When the weather was fine, it often happened that there would come down the broad stone steps of the terrace a number of princesses out of a fairy tale, each dressed in a different pale but bright colour. Sometimes there were as few as four of these princesses; occasionally there were as many as seven. Among the colours that my uncle thought he remembered them wearing were hyacinth blue, the green of the leaves of lilies of the valley, a silvery lilac that was almost grey, a transparent red that was like one's hand when one holds it up to a strong light, primrose yellow, a watery jade green, and a gentle orange. The dresses were made of muslin, and billowed in loops and swinging circles as their wearers' little feet carried them about in what was neither a dance nor the everyday motion of ordinary people. It was as if these lovely creatures were all parts of a brave and sensitive and melancholy being, and were at once confiding in each other about their griefs, which were their common grief, and giving each other reassurance.

Some carried croquet mallets and went on to the lawn and started to play, while the others sat down on benches to watch them. But sooner or later the players would pause and forget to make the next stroke, move toward each other and stand in a group, resting their mallets on the ground, and presently forget them and let them fall, as the spectators rose from their seats to join them in their exchange of confidences. Though they appeared in the garden as often as three times a week, they always seemed to have as much to say to one another as if they met but once a year; and they were always grave as they talked. There was a wildness about them; it was impossible to tell what they would do next; one might suddenly break away from the others and waltz round the lawn in the almost visible arms of an invisible partner; but when they talked they showed restraint; they did not weep, though what they said was so plainly sad, and they rarely laughed. What was true of them was true of all, for there seemed very little difference between them. All were golden-headed. The only one who could be told apart was the wearer of the lilac-grey dress. She was taller than the rest, and often stood aloof while they clustered together and swayed and spoke. Sometimes a woman in a black gown came down from the terrace and talked to this separate one.

The girls in the coloured dresses were the seven daughters of the Admiral who owned the house. My uncle saw him once, when he called on Alice Darrell to discuss with her arrangements for repairing the wall between their properties; a tall and handsome man with iron-grey hair, a probing, defensive gaze, and a mouth so sternly compressed that it was a straight line across his face. The call would never have been made had there not been business to discuss. The Admiral would have no social relations with his neighbours; nobody had ever been invited to his house. Nor, had such an invitation been sent, would Aunt Alice have accepted it, for she thought he treated his daughters abominably. She could not help smiling when she told her nephew their names, for they came straight off the Navy List: Andromeda, Cassandra, Clytie, Hera, Parthenope, Arethusa, and Persephone. But that was the only time she smiled when she spoke of them, for she thought they had been treated with actual cruelty, though not in the way that might have been supposed. They were not immured in this lonely house by a father who wanted to keep them to himself; their case was the very opposite.

The Admiral's daughters were, in effect, motherless. By Aunt Alice my Uncle Arthur was told that the Admiral's wife was an invalid and had to live in a mild climate in the west of England, but from the servants he learned that she was mad. Without a wife to soften him, the Admiral dealt with his daughters summarily by sending each of them, as she passed her seventeenth birthday, to be guided through the London season by his only sister, a wealthy woman with a house in Berkeley Square, and by giving each to the first man of reasonably respectable character who made her an offer of marriage. He would permit no delay, though his daughters, who had inheritances from a wealthy grandfather, as well as their beauty, would obviously have many suitors. These precipitate marriages were always against the brides' inclinations, for they had, strangely enough, no desire but to go on living in their lonely home.

'They are', Aunt Alice told her nephew, hesitating and looking troubled, 'oddly young for their ages. I know they are not old, and that they have lived a great deal alone, since their mother cannot be with them. But they are really very young for what they are.' They had yielded, it was said, only to the most brutal pressure exercised by their father. It astonished my uncle that all this was spoken of as something that had happened in the past. They did not look like grown-up ladies as they wandered in the garden, yet all but two were wives, and those two were betrothed, and some of them were already mothers. Parthenope, the one with most character, the one who had charge of the house in her father's absence, had married a North Country landowner who was reputed to be a millionaire. It was a pity that he was twice her age and had, by a dead wife, a son almost as old as she was, but such a fortune is a great comfort; and none of her sisters was without some measure of that same kind of consolation. Nevertheless, their discontent could be measured by the frequency with which they returned to the home of their childhood.

The first time my uncle visited Currivel Lodge, the Admiral's seven daughters were only a spectacle for his distant enjoyment. But one day during his second visit, a year later, his aunt asked him to deliver a note for Miss Parthenope at the house next door. Another section of the wall between the properties was in need of buttresses, and the builder had to have his orders. My uncle went up to his bedroom and smoothed his hair and washed his face, a thing he had never done before between morning and night of his own accord, and when he got to the Admiral's house he told the butler, falsely but without a tremor, that he had been told to give the note into Miss Parthenope's own hands. It did not matter to him that the butler looked annoyed at hearing this; too much was to stake. He followed the butler's offended back through several rooms full of fine furniture, which were very much like the rooms to which he was accustomed, but had a sleepy air, as if the windows were closed, though they were not. In one there were some dolls thrown down on the floor, though he had never heard that there were any children living in the house. In the last room, which opened on the stone terrace and its white and crimson roses, a woman in a black dress with a suggestion of a uniform about it was sitting at an embroidery frame. She stared at him as if he presented a greater problem than schoolboys usually do, and he recognized her as the dark figure he had seen talking with the tallest of the daughters in the garden.

She took the letter from him, and he saw that the opportunity he had seized was slipping out of his grasp, so he pretended to be younger and simpler than he was, and put on the Irish brogue, which he never used at home except when he was talking to the servants or the people on the farms, but which he had found charmed the English. 'May I not go out into the garden and see the young ladies?' he asked. 'I have watched them from my window, and they look so pretty.'

It worked. The woman smiled and said, 'You're from Ireland, aren't you?' and before he could answer she exclaimed, as if defying prohibitions of which she had long been weary, 'What is the harm? Yes, go out and give the note to Miss Parthenope yourself. You will know her – she is wearing grey and is the tallest.' When he got out on the terrace, he saw that all seven of the Admiral's daughters were on the lawn, and his heart was like a turning windmill as he went down the stone steps. Then one of the croquet players caught sight of him – the one who was wearing a red dress, just nearer flame colour than flesh. She dropped her mallet and cried, 'Oh, look, a little boy! A little red-haired boy!' and danced toward him, sometimes pausing and twirling right round, so that her skirts billowed out round her. Other voices took up the cry, and, cooing like pigeons, the croquet players closed in on him in a circle of unbelievable beauty. It was their complexions that he remembered in later life as the marvel that made them, among all the women he was ever to see, the non-pareils. Light lay on their skin as it lies on the petals of flowers, but it promised that it would never fade, that it would last forever, like a pearl. Yet even while he remarked their loveliness and was awed by it, he was disconcerted. They came so close, and it seemed as if they might do more than look at him and speak to him. It was as if a flock of birds had come down on him, and were fluttering and pecking about him; and they asked so many questions, in voices that chirped indefatigably and were sharper than the human note. 'Who are you?' 'You are Mrs Darrell's nephew?' 'Her brother's child or her sister's?' 'How old are you?' 'What is your name?' 'Why is your middle name Greatorex?' 'Oh, what lovely hair he has – true Titian! And those round curls like coins!' 'Have you sisters?' 'Have they hair like yours?' Their little hands darted out and touched his hands, his cheeks, his shoulders, briefly but not pleasantly. His flesh rose in goose pimples, as it did when a moth's wing brushed his face as he lay in bed in the dark. And while their feathery restlessness poked and cheeped at him, they looked at him with eyes almost as fixed as if they were blind and could not see him at all. Their eyes were immense and very bright and shaded by lashes longer than he had ever seen; but they were so light a grey that they were as colourless as clear water running over a bed of pebbles. He was glad when the woman in the black dress called from the terrace, 'Leave the boy alone!' He did not like anything about the Admiral's daughters, now he saw them at close range. Even their dresses, which had looked beautiful from a distance, repelled him. If a lady had been sitting to a portrait painter in the character of a wood nymph, she might have worn such draperies, but it was foolish to wear them in a garden, when there was nobody to see them. 'Leave the boy alone!' the woman in black called again. 'He has come with a letter for Parthenope.'

She had not been one of the circle. Now that the others fell back, my uncle saw her standing a little way off, biting her lip and knitting her brows, as if the scene disturbed her. There were other differences, beyond her height, that distinguished her from her sisters. While they were all that was most feminine, with tiny waists and hands and feet, she might have been a handsome and athletic boy dressed in woman's clothes for a school play. Only, of course, one knew quite well that she was not a boy. She stood erect, her arms hanging by her sides, smoothing back the muslin billows of her skirt, as if they were foolishness she would be glad to put behind her; and, indeed, she would have looked better in Greek dress. Like her sisters, she had golden hair, but hers was a whiter gold. As my uncle and she went toward each other, she smiled, and he was glad to see that her eyes were darker grey than her sisters', and were quick and glancing. He told her who he was, speaking honestly, not putting on a brogue to win her, and she smiled and held out her hand. It took her a little time to read the letter, and she frowned over it and held her forefinger to her lips, and bade him tell his aunt that she would send over an answer later in the day, after she had consulted her gardeners, and then she asked him if he would care to come into the house and drink some raspberry vinegar. As she led him across the lawn to the terrace, walking with long strides, he saw that her sisters were clustered in a group, staring up at a gutter high on the house, where a rook had perched, as if the bird were a great marvel. 'Should I say goodbye to the ladies?' he asked nervously, and Parthenope answered, 'No, they have forgotten you already.' However, one had not. The sister who wore the light-red dress ran after him, crying, 'Come back soon, little boy. Nobody ever comes into this garden except to steal our strawberries.'

Parthenope took him through the silent house, pausing in the room where the dolls lay on the floor to lift them up and shut them in a drawer, and they came to a dining-room, lined with pictures of great ships at war with stormy seas. There was no raspberry vinegar on the top of the sideboard – only decanters wearing labels marked with the names of adult drinks he was allowed only at Christmas and on his birthday, and then but one glass, and he always chose claret. So they opened the cupboard below, and sat down together on the carpet and peered into the darkness while he told her that he did not really want any but if it had gone astray he would be pleased to help her find it. But when the decanter turned up at the very back of the shelf (and they agreed that that was what always happened when one lost anything, and there was no doubt that objects can move) they both had a glass, talking meanwhile of what they liked to eat and drink. Like him, she hated boiled mutton, and she, too, liked goose better than turkey. When he had finished and the talk had slowed down, he rose and put his glass on the sideboard, and offered her a hand to help her up from the floor, but she did not need it; and he gave a last look round the room, so that he would not forget it. He asked her, 'Why is your chandelier tied up in a canvas bag? At home that only happens when the family is away.' She answered, 'Our family is away,' speaking so grimly that he said, 'I did not mean to ask a rude question.' She told him, 'You have not asked a rude question. What I meant was that all but two of us have our own homes, and those two will be leaving here soon.' It would not have been right to say that she spoke sadly. But her tone was empty of all it had held when they had talked about how much better chicken tastes when you eat it with your fingers when you are out shooting. He remembered all the sad things he had heard his aunt say about her family, the sadder things he had heard from the servants. He said, 'Why don't you come back with me and have tea with my aunt?' She said, smiling, 'She has not asked me.' And he said, 'Never think of that. We are not proper English, you know; we are from Ireland, and friends come in any time.' But she thanked him, sighing, so that he knew she would really have liked to come, and said that she must go back to her sisters. As the butler held the front door open for my uncle, she gave him a friendly slap across the shoulders, as an older boy might have done.

After that, my uncle never watched the Admiral's daughters again. If a glance told him that they were in the garden, he turned his back on the window. He had not liked those staring eyes that were colourless as water, and it troubled him that, though some of them had children, none had said, 'I have a boy, too, but he is much younger than you,' for mothers always said that. He remembered Parthenope so well that he could summon her to his mind when he wished, and he could not bear to see her with these women who made him feel uneasy, because he was sure that he and she felt alike, and therefore she must be in a perpetual state of unease. So when, the very day before he was to go back to Ireland, he looked out of his bedroom window and saw her alone on the lawn he threw up the sash and called to her; but she did not hear him.

She was absorbed in playing a game by herself, a game that he knew well. She was throwing a ball high into the air, then letting her arms drop by her sides, and waiting to the last, the very last moment, before stretching out a hand to catch it. It was a strange thing for a grown-up lady to be doing, but it did not distress him like the playground gambolling and chattering of her sisters. They had been like children as grown-ups like to think of them, silly and meaningless and mischievous. But she was being a child as children really are, sobered by all they have to put up with and glad to forget it in play. There was currently some danger that his own father was going to get a post in some foreign place and that the whole family would have to leave County Kerry for years and years; and when he and his brothers and sisters thought of this they would go and, each one apart, would play this very same game that Parthenope was playing.

He did not want to raise his voice in a shout, in case he was overheard by his aunt or his mother. They would not understand that, although Parthenope and he had met only once, they knew each other quite well. He got up from the window seat and went out of his room and down through the house and out into the garden. There was a ladder in the coach house, and he dragged it to the right part of the wall and propped it up and stopped it with stones, and climbed to the top and called 'Miss Parthenope!' When she saw him, she smiled and waved at him as if she really were glad to see him again.

'Where are your sisters?' he asked cautiously.

'They have all gone away. I am going home tomorrow.'

'So am I.'

'Are you glad?'

'Papa will be there,' he said, 'and my brothers and sisters, and Garrity the groom, and my pony.'

She asked him the names of his brothers and sisters, and how old they were, and where his home was; and he told her all these things and told her, too, that his father was always being sent all over the world, and that of late he and his brothers and sisters had heard talk that someday, and it might be soon, he would be sent to some foreign place for so long that they would have to go with him, and they didn't want this to happen; for, though they loved him and wanted to be near him, they loved County Kerry, too. At that, she stopped smiling and nodded her head, as if to say she knew how he must feel. 'But perhaps it won't happen,' he said, 'and then you must come and stay with us for the hunting.'

He thought of her in a riding-habit, and at that he noticed that she was wearing a dress such as his own mother might have worn – a dress of grey cloth, with a tight bodice and a stiffened skirt, ornamented with braid. He said, 'How funny to see you dressed like other ladies. Don't you usually wear that lilac-grey muslin dress?'

She shook her head. 'No. My sisters and I only wear those muslin dresses when we are together here. My sisters like them.'

'Don't you?' he said, for her tone had gone blank again.

'No,' she answered, 'not at all.'

He was glad to hear it, but it seemed horribly unfair that she should have to wear clothes she did not like, just because her sisters did; nothing of the sort happened in his own family. 'Then don't wear them!' he said passionately. 'You mustn't wear them! Not if you don't like them!'

'You're making your ladder wobble,' she said, laughing at him, 'and if you fall down I can't climb over the wall and pick you up.' She started across the lawn toward the house.

'Garrity says that you're lost if you let yourself be put upon,' he cried after her, his brogue coming back to him, but honestly, because he spoke to Garrity as Garrity spoke to him. He would have liked to have the power to make her do what she ought to do, and save her from all this foolishness.

'Goodbye, goodbye,' she called across the growing distance. 'Be a good boy, and come back to see us next year.'

'You will be here for sure?' he asked eagerly.

'Oh, yes,' she promised. 'We will always be back here for some time in the summer. My sisters would rather be here than anywhere in the world.'

'But do you like it yourself?' he asked angrily.

It was no use. She had run up the steps to the terrace.

My uncle did not come back the next year, because his fears were realized and his father was appointed to a post in Canada. But from his aunt's letters to his mother he learned that, even if he had returned to Currivel Lodge, he would not have seen Parthenope, for the Admiral sold the house later that year, as soon as his two remaining daughters went to the altar, which they did with even greater reluctance than their elder sisters. Alice Darrell's maid happened to be at the window one winter day and saw the two of them walking up and down the lawn, dressed in those strange, bright muslin gowns and wearing no mantles, though the river mist was thick, while they wept and wrung their hands. Aunt Alice felt that, even if the Admiral had felt obliged to bundle all his daughters into matrimony, he should at least not have sold the house, which was the one place where they could meet and have a little nursery happiness again.

In the course of time, Uncle Arthur came back to Ireland, and went to Trinity College, Dublin, and passed into the English Civil Service, and was sent to London. The first time he went back to Currivel Lodge, he stood at his bedroom window and stared out at the croquet lawn of the house next door, and it looked very much like other croquet lawns. Under the trees two men and two women were sitting round a tea table, all of them presenting the kind of appearance, more common then than now, that suggests that nothing untoward happens to the human race. It occurred to him that perhaps his boyish imagination had made a story out of nothing, but Aunt Alice gave him back his version intact. The Admiral had really hectored his daughters into early and undesired marriages, with the most brutal disregard for their feelings, and the daughters had really been very strange girls, given to running about the garden in a sort of fancy dress and behaving like children – all except Parthenope, who was quite remarkable. She had made her mark in society since then. Well, so they all had, in a way. Their photographs were always in the papers, at one time, and no wonder, they were so very pretty. But that seemed over now, and, indeed, they must all be out of their twenties by now, even the youngest. Parthenope's triumphs, however, had been more durable. It was said that Queen Victoria greatly approved of her, and she was often at Court.

My uncle always thought of Parthenope when he was dressing for any of the grander parties to which he was invited, and he soon found his way to the opera and ascertained which was her box, but she was never at the parties, and, unless she had changed out of all recognition, never in her box at Covent Garden either. My uncle did not wish to approach her, for he was a poor young man, far below her grandeur, and they had belonged to different generations; at the least, she was twelve years older than he was. But he would have liked to see her again. Soon, however, he received an intimation that that would not be possible. One morning at breakfast he unfolded his newspaper and folded it again almost immediately, having read a single paragraph, which told him that Parthenope had met a violent death.

He had failed to meet her at parties and to see her in her opera box because she had been spending the winter abroad, taking care of two of her sisters who had both been the victims of prolonged illness. Originally, they had settled at Nice, but had found it too urban, and had moved to a hotel at Grasse, where they spent some weeks. Then a friend had found them a pleasant villa at Hyères, and the party had started off from Grasse in two carriages. Parthenope and her sisters and a lady's maid had travelled in the first, and another maid and a courier had followed in the second. The second carriage had dropped far behind. Afterwards, the coachman remembered that he had been oddly delayed in leaving the inn where they had stopped for a midday meal; he had been told that a man was looking for him with a letter for his employers, and failing to find him had gone to a house some way down the village street. The coachman sought him but there was nobody there; and on his return to his horses he discovered that a harness strap was broken, and he had to mend it before they could resume their journey. After a sharp turn in the road, he had found himself driving into a felled tree trunk, and when the courier and the maid and the coachman got out they could see

Once upon the tram Yvonne shed no more tears. When she got back to Upper George's Street she fumbled in her bag for the latchkey, which she had not had for long, and let herself into the shop. It was very still in the shop. The familiar smell of wood and old paper made itself quietly known. Behind her the last cars and trams were rumbling by, and in the dark space in front of her was to be heard the heavy breathing of her mother, already sleeping in the inner room. But in the shop it was very silent and all the objects upon the shelves were alert and quiet like little listening animals. Yvonne stood quite still there for ten minutes, for nearly fifteen minutes. She had never stood still for so long in her whole life. Then she went through into the inner room on tiptoe and began to undress in the dark.

Her mother had taken up the deep centre of the bed as usual. When Yvonne put her knee upon the edge in order to get in, the whole structure groaned and rocked. Her mother woke up.

'It's you, is it?' said Yvonne's mother. 'I didn't hear you come in. Well, how did the evening go off? What did you do with yourselves?'

'Oh, nothing special,' said Yvonne. She thrust her long legs down under the clothes and reclined stiffly upon the high cold edge of the bed.

'You always say that,' said her mother, 'but you must have done something.'

'Nothing, I say,' said Yvonne.

'What did Sam have to show you?'

'Nothing, nothing,' she said.

'Don't keep repeating that word at me,' said her mother. 'Say something else, or has the cat got your tongue?'

'Did you get the Christmas cards with the roses on?' said Yvonne.

'I did not,' said her mother 'at tenpence the piece! Have you anything to say at all about your evening, or shall we go to sleep now?'

'Yes,' said Yvonne, 'I'm going to marry Sam.'

'Glory be to God!' said her mother. 'So he got you convinced.'

'He did not convince me,' said Yvonne, 'but I'm going to marry him now, I've decided.'

'You've decided, have you?' said her mother. 'Well, I'm glad of it. And why, may I ask, did your Majesty decide it just tonight?'

'For nothing,' said Yvonne, 'for nothing, for nothing.' She snuggled no sign of the first carriage. It was found some hours later, abandoned on a cart track running through a wood to a river. There was no trace of any of its occupants. Later that same day the maid crawled up to a farmhouse door. Before she collapsed, she was able to tell the story of an attack by masked men, who had, she thought, killed the three sisters outright because they refused to tell in which trunk their jewel cases were packed. She had escaped during the struggle, and while she was running away through the woods she had heard terrible prolonged screaming from the riverbank. As the river was in flood, there was no hope of recovering the bodies.

After my uncle had read all the accounts of the crime that appeared in the newspapers, and had listened to all he could hear from gossiping friends, there hung, framed on the wall of his mind, a romantic picture of a highway robbery, in the style of Salvator Rosa, with coal-black shadows and highlights white on hands lifted in imploration, and he felt no emotion whatsoever. When he had opened *The Times* at breakfast, his heart had stopped. But now he felt as if he had been stopped before an outmoded and conventional picture in a private gallery by a host who valued it too highly.

A year or so later, Alice Darrell mentioned to him an odd story she had heard. It appeared that Parthenope had been carrying a great deal more jewellery than would seem necessary for a woman travelling quietly with two invalid sisters. To be sure, she had not taken all the jewellery she possessed, but she had taken enough for the value to be estimated at fifty thousand pounds; and of this not a penny could be recovered, for it was uninsured. Her husband had left the matter for her to handle, because she had sold some old jewellery and had bought some to replace it just about the time that the policy should have been renewed, but she had failed to write the necessary letter to her lawyers till the very night before the journey to Hyères, and it was found, unposted, at the hotel in Grasse.

'Parthenope!' my uncle said. 'Let an insurance policy lapse! Parthenope! I'll not believe it.'

'That's just what I said,' Alice Darrell exclaimed. 'Any of the others, but not Parthenope. She had her hand on everything. Yet, of course, she may have changed. They are a queer family. There was the other one, you know – the one who disappeared. That was after the accident.'

It seemed that another sister – Hera, Aunt Alice thought it was –

had also suffered ill health, and had gone to France with a nurse, and one day her cloak and bonnet were found on the bank of a river.

'I wish that things turned out better,' Aunt Alice remarked sadly. 'They do sometimes, but not often enough.'

This was the only criticism of life he had ever heard her utter, though she had had a sad life, constantly losing the people she loved, to tropical diseases or to wars against obscure tribes that lacked even the interest of enmity. What she uttered now made him realise that she had indeed thought Parthenope remarkable, and he said, smiling, 'Why, we are making ourselves quite miserable about her, though all we know for sure is that she let an insurance policy lapse.'

He did not hear of the Admiral's daughters again until after a long space of time, during which he had many other things to think about: his career, which was alternately advanced by his brilliance and retarded by his abstracted candour; a long affair with a married woman older than himself, some others that were briefer; and his marriage, which, like his career, and for much the same reason, was neither a success nor a failure. One day when he was reading the papers at his club, he heard two men speaking of a friend who was distressed about his mother, whose behaviour had been strange since she had been left a widow. She had rejected the dower house and gone off to the Continent to travel by herself, and now refused to come back to see her family or to meet them abroad. The mother had an old Greek name, and so had a sister, who had got herself murdered for her jewels in the South of France. My uncle went on staring at his newspaper, but it was as if a door in his mind were swinging backward and forward on a broken hinge.

Many years later, when Aunt Alice was dead and my uncle was a middle-aged man, with children who were no longer children, he broke his journey home from a conference in Spain at a certain town in the south-west of France, for no other reason than that its name had always charmed him. But it proved to be a dull place, and as he sat down to breakfast at a café in the large and featureless station square it occurred to him to ask the waiter if there were not some smaller and pleasanter place in the neighbourhood where he could spend the rest of the day and night. The waiter said that, if Monsieur would take the horse-bus that started from the other side of the square in half an hour, it would take him to the village where he, the waiter, was born, and there he would find a good inn and a church that people came all the way from Paris to see. My uncle took his advice, and, because his night had been wakeful, he fell asleep almost as soon as the bus started. He woke suddenly to find that the journey had ended and he was in a village which was all that he had hoped it would be.

A broad, deliberate river, winding among low wooded hills, spread its blessings at this point through a circular patch of plain, a couple of miles or so across, which was studded with farm houses, each standing beside its deep green orchard. In the centre of this circle was a village that was no more than one long street, which looked very clean. The houses were built of stone that had been washed by the hill rains, and beside the road a brook flowed over a paved bed. There were bursts of red valerian growing from the cracks in the walls and in the yard-long bridges that crossed the brook. The street ended in a little square, where the church and the inn looked across cobblestones, shaded by pollarded limes, at the *mairie* and the post office. At the inn, my uncle took a room and slept for an hour or two in a bed smelling of the herbs with which the sheets had been washed. Then, as it was past noon, he went down to lunch, and ate some potato soup, a trout, some wood strawberries, and a slice of cheese. Afterward, he asked the landlord how soon the church would be open, and was told that he could open it himself when he chose. The priest and his housekeeper were away until vespers, and had left the church keys at the inn.

When he went to the church, it was a long time before he unlocked the door, for there was a beautiful tympanum in the porch, representing the Last Judgement. It was clearcut in more than one sense. There was no doubt who was saved and who was damned: there was a beatific smile on the faces of those walking in Paradise, which made it seem as if just there a shaft of sunlight had struck the dark stone. Also the edges of the carving, though the centuries had rubbed them down, showed a definition more positive than mere sharpness. Often my uncle played games when he was alone, and now he climbed on a wooden stool which was in the porch, and shut his eyes and felt the faces of the blessed, and pretended that he had been blind for a long time, and that the smiles of the blessed were striking into his darkness through his fingertips.

When he went into the church, he found, behind an oaken door, the steps that led to the top of the tower. He climbed up through darkness that was transfixed every few steps by thin shafts of light, dancing with dust coming through the eyelet windows, and he found that, though the tower was not very high, it gave a fine view of an amphitheatre of hills, green on their lower slopes with chestnut groves, banded higher with fir woods and bare turf, and crowned with shining rock. He marked some likely paths on the nearest hills, and then dropped his eyes to the village below, and looked down into the oblong garden of a house that seemed larger than the rest. At the farther end was the usual, pedantically neat French vegetable-garden; then there was a screen of espaliered fruit-trees; then there was a lawn framed in trees so tall and strong that it could have been guessed from them alone that not far away there was a river. The lawn was set with croquet hoops, and about them were wandering four figures in bright dresses – one hyacinth blue, one primrose yellow, one jade green, one clear light red. They all had croquet mallets in their hands, but they had turned from the game, and as my uncle watched them they drew together, resting their mallets on the ground. Some distance away, a woman in black, taller than the others, stood watching them.

When one of the croquet players let her mallet fall on the grass, and used her freed hands in a fluttering gesture, my uncle left the top of the tower and went down through the darkness and shafts of light and locked the church door behind him. In the corner of the square, he found what might have been the château of the village – one of those square and solid dwellings, noble out of proportion to their size, which many provincial French architects achieved in the 17th century. My uncle went through an iron gateway into a paved garden and found that the broad door of the house was open. He walked into the vestibule and paused, looking up the curved staircase. The pictures were as old as the house, and two had been framed to fit the recessed panels in which they hung. The place must have been bought as it stood. On the threshold of the corridor beyond, he paused again, for it smelled of damp stone, as all the back parts of his father's house in County Kerry did, at any time of the year but high summer. It struck him as a piece of good fortune for which he had never before been sufficiently grateful that he could go back to that house any time he pleased; he would be there again in a few weeks' time. He passed the open door of a kitchen, where two women were rattling dishes and pans and singing softly, and came to a closed door, which he stared at for a second before he turned the handle.

He found himself in a salon that ran across the whole breadth of the house, with three French windows opening on a stone terrace overlooking the garden. As he crossed it to the steps that led down to the lawn, he came close to a bird cage on a pole, and the scarlet parrot inside broke into screams. All the women on the lawn turned and saw him, and the tall woman in black called, 'Que voulez-vous, monsieur?' She had put her hand to her heart, and he was eager to reassure her, but could not think how, across that distance, to explain why he had come. So he continued to walk toward her, but could not reach her because the four others suddenly scampered toward him, crying 'Go away! Go away!' Their arms flapped like bats' wings, and their voices were cracked, but, under their white hair, their faces were unlined and their eyes were colourless as water. 'Go away!' shrilled the one in light red. 'We know you have come to steal our strawberries. Why may we not keep our own strawberries?' But the figure in black had come forward with long strides, and told them to go on with their game, and asked again, 'Que voulez-vous, monsieur?'

Her hair was grey now, and her mouth so sternly compressed that it was a straight line across her face. She reminded my uncle of a particular man -- her father, the Admiral – but she was not like a man, she was still a handsome and athletic boy, though a frost had fallen on him; and still it was strange that she should look like a boy, since she was also not male at all. My uncle found that now he was face to face with her it was just as difficult to explain to her why he had come. He said, 'I came to this village by chance this morning, and after I had luncheon at the inn I went to the top of the church tower, and looked down on the garden, and recognized you all. I came to tell you that if there is anything I can do for you I will do it. I am a civil servant who has quite a respectable career, and so I can hope that I might be efficient enough to help you, if you need it.'

'That is very kind,' she said, and paused, and it was as if she were holding a shell to her ear and listening to the voice of a distant sea. 'Very kind,' she repeated. 'But who are you?'

'I am the nephew of your neighbour, Mrs Darrell,' said my uncle. 'I brought you a letter from her, many years ago, when you were all in your garden.'

Her smile broke slowly. 'I remember you,' she said. 'You were a fatherly little boy. You gave me good advice from the top of a ladder. Why should you have found me here, I wonder? It can't be that, after all, there is some meaning in the things that happen. You had better come into the house and drink some of the cherry brandy we make here. I will get the cook to come out and watch them. I never leave them alone now.'

While she went to the kitchen, my uncle sat in the salon and noted that, for all its fine furniture and all its space and light, there was a feeling that the place was dusty, the same feeling that he had noticed in the Admiral's house long ago. It is the dust of another world, he thought with horror, and the housemaids of this world are helpless against it. It settles wherever these women live, and Parthenope must live with them.

When she came back, she was carrying a tray with a slender decanter and very tiny glasses. They sat sipping the cherry brandy in silence until she said, 'I did nothing wrong.' He looked at her in astonishment. Of course she had done nothing wrong. Wrong was what she did not do. But she continued gravely, 'When we all die, it will be found that the sum I got for the jewellery is intact. My stepson will not be a penny the worse off. Indeed, he is better off, for my husband has had my small inheritance long before it would have come to him if I had not done this.'

'I knew you would have done it honestly,' said my uncle. He hesitated. 'This is very strange. You see, I knew things about you which I had no reason to know. I knew you had not been murdered.'

Then my uncle had to think carefully. They were united by eternal bonds, but hardly knew each other, which was the reverse of what usually happened to men and women. But they might lapse into being strangers and nothing else if he showed disrespect to the faith by which she lived. He said only, 'Also I knew that what you were doing in looking after your family was terrible.'

She answered, 'Yes. How good it is to hear somebody say that it is terrible, and to be able to answer that it is. But I had to do it. I had to get my sisters away from their husbands. They were ashamed of them. They locked them up in the care of strangers. I saw their bruises.' My uncle caught his breath. 'Oh,' she said, desperately just, 'the people who looked after them did not mean to be cruel. But they were strangers; they did not know the way to handle my sisters. And their husbands were not all bad men either. And, even if they had been, I could not say a word against them, for they were cheated; my father cheated them. They were never told the truth about my mother. About my mother and half her family.' She raised her little glass of cherry brandy to her lips and nodded, to intimate that that was all she had to say, but words rushed out and she brought her glass down to her lap. 'I am not telling the truth. Their husbands cheated, too. . . . No, I am wrong. They did not cheat. But they failed to keep their bond. Still, there is no use talking about that.'

'What bond did your sisters' husbands not keep?' my uncle asked.

'They married my sisters because they were beautiful, and laughed easily, and could not understand figures. They might have considered that women who laugh easily might scream easily, and that, if figures meant nothing to them, words might mean nothing either, and that, if figures and words meant nothing to them, thoughts and feelings might mean nothing too. But these men had the impudence to feel a horror of my sisters.'

She rose, trembling, and told him that he must have a sweet biscuit with his cherry brandy, and that she would get him some; they were in a cupboard in the corner of the room. Over her shoulder, she cried, 'I cannot imagine you marrying a woman who was horrible because she was horrible, and then turning against her because she was horrible.' She went on setting some wafers out on a plate, and he stared at the back of her head, unable to imagine what was inside it, saying to himself, 'She realizes that they are horrible; there is no mitigation of her state.'

When she sat down again, she said, 'But it was my father's fault.'

'What was your father's fault?' he asked gently, when she did not go on.

'Why, he should not have made us marry; he should not have sold our house. My sisters were happy there, and all they asked was to be allowed to go on living there, like children.'

'Your father wanted his daughters to marry so that they would have someone to look after them when he was dead,' my uncle told her.

'I could have looked after them.'

'Come now,' said my uncle, 'you are not being fair. You are the same sort of person as your father. And you know quite well that if you were a man you would regard all women as incapable. You see, men of the better kind want to protect the women they love, and there is so much stupidity in the male nature and the circumstances of life are generally so confused that they end up thinking they must look after women because women cannot look after themselves. It is only very seldom that a man meets a woman so strong and wise that he cannot doubt her strength and wisdom, and realizes that his desire to protect her is really the same as his desire to gather her into his arms and partake of her glory.'

Moving slowly and precisely, he took out his cardcase and was about to give her one of his cards when a thought struck him. She must have the name of his family's house in County Kerry as well as his London address, and know that he went there at Christmas and at Easter, and in the summer too. She would be able to find him whenever she wanted him, since such bootblack service was all he could render her.

She read the card and said in an astonished whisper, 'Oh, how kind, how kind.' Then she rose and put it in a drawer in a *secrétaire*, which she locked with a key she took from a bag swinging from the belt of her hateful black gown. 'I have to lock up everything,' she said, wearily. 'They mean no harm, but sometimes they get at papers and tear them up.'

'What I have written on that card is for an emergency,' said my uncle. 'But what is there that I can do now? I do not like the thought of you sitting here in exile, among things that mean nothing to you. Can I not send you out something English – a piece of furniture, a picture, some china or glass? If I were in your place, I would long for something that reminded me of the houses where I had spent my childhood.'

'If you were in my place, you would not,' she said. 'You are very kind, but the thing that has happened to my family makes me not at all anxious to remember my childhood. We were all such pretty children. Everybody always spoke as if we were bound to be happy. And in those days nobody was frightened of Mamma – they only laughed at her, because she was such a goose. Then one thing followed another, and it became quite certain about Mamma, and then it became quite certain about the others; and now I cannot bear to think of the good times that went before. It is as if someone had known and was mocking us. But you may believe that it is wonderful for me to know that there is someone I can call on at any time. You see, I had supports, which are being taken away from me. You really have no idea how I got my sisters out here?'

My uncle shook his head. 'I only read what was in the newspapers and knew it was not true.'

'But you must have guessed I had helpers,' she said. 'There was the highway robbery to be arranged. All that was done by somebody who was English but had many connections in France, a man who was very fond of Arethusa. Arethusa is the one who spoke to you in the garden; she always wears red. This man was not like her husband; when she got worse and worse, he felt no horror for her, only pity. He has always been behind me, but he was far older than we were, and he died three years ago; and since then his lawyer in Paris has been a good friend, but now he is old, too, and I must expect him to go soon. I have made all arrangements for what is to happen to my sisters after my death. They will go to a convent near here, where the nuns are really kind, and we are preparing them for it. One or other of the nuns comes here every day to see my sisters, so that they will never have to be frightened by strange faces; and I think that, if my sisters go on getting worse at the same rate as at present, they will by then believe the nuns when they say that I have been obliged to go away and will come back presently. But till that time comes I will be very glad to have someone I can ask for advice. I can see that you are to be trusted. You are like the man who loved Arethusa. My poor Arethusa! Sometimes I think,' she said absently, 'that she might have been all right if it had been that man whom she had married. But no,' she cried, shaking herself awake, 'none of us should have married, not even me.'

'Why should you not have married?' asked my uncle. 'That the others should not I understand. But why not you? There is nothing wrong with you.'

'Is there not?' she asked. 'To leave my family and my home, to stage a sham highway robbery, and later to plot and lie, and lie and plot, in order to get my mad sisters to a garden I had once noted, in my travels, as something like the garden taken from them when they were young. There is an extravagance in the means my sanity took to rescue their madness that makes the one uncommonly like the other.'

'You must not think that,' my uncle told her. 'Your strange life forced strangeness on your actions, but you are not strange. You were moved by love; you had seen their bruises.'

'Yes, I had seen their bruises,' she agreed. 'But', she added, hesitantly, 'you are so kind that I must be honest with you. It was not only for the love of my sisters that I arranged this flight. It is also true that I could not bear my life. I was not wholly unselfish. You do not know what it is like to be a character in a tragedy. Something has happened which can only be explained by supposing that God hates you with merciless hatred, and nobody will admit it. The people nearest you stand round you saying that you must ignore this extraordinary event, you must – what were the words I was always hearing? – "keep your sense of proportion", "not brood on things". They do not understand that they are asking you to deny your experiences, which is to pretend that you do not exist and never have existed. And, as for the people who do not love you, they laugh. Our tragedy was so ridiculous that the laughter was quite loud. There were all sorts of really quite funny stories about the things my mother and sisters did before they were shut up. That is another terrible thing about being a character in a tragedy; at the same time you become a character in a farce. Do not deceive yourself,' she said, looking at him kindly and sadly. 'I am not a Classical heroine, I am not Iphigenia or Electra or Alcestis, I am the absurd Parthenope. There is no dignity in my life. For one thing, too much has happened to me. One calamity evokes sympathy; when two calamities call for it, some still comes, but less. Three calamities are felt to be too many, and when four are reported, or five, the thing is ludicrous. God has only to strike one again and again for one to become a clown. There is nothing about me which is not comical. Even my flight with my sisters has become a joke.' She sipped at her glass. 'My sisters' husbands and their families must by now have found out where we are. I do not think my husband ever did, or he would have come to see me. But there are many little indications that the others know, and keep their knowledge secret, rather than let loose so monstrous a scandal.'

'You say your husband would have to come to see you?' asked my uncle, wanting to make sure. 'But that must mean he loved you.'

At last the tears stood in her eyes. She said, her voice breaking, 'Oh, things might have gone very well with my husband and myself, if love had been possible for me. But of course it never was.'

'How wrong you are,' said my uncle. 'There could be nothing better for any man to have you as his wife. If you did not know that, your husband should have made you understand it.'

'No, no,' she said. 'The fault was not in my husband or myself. It was in love, which cannot do all that is claimed for it. Oh, I can see that it can work miracles, some miracles, but not all the miracles that are required before life can be tolerable. Listen: I love my sisters, but I dare not love them thoroughly. To love them as much as one can love would be to go to the edge of an abyss and lean over the edge, farther and farther, till one was bound to lose one's balance and fall into the blackness of that other world where they live. That is why I never dared let my husband love me fully. I was so much afraid that I might be an abyss, and if he understood me, if we lived in each other, he would be drawn down into my darkness.'

'But there is no darkness in you,' said my uncle, 'you are not an abyss, you are the solid rock.'

'Why do you think so well of me?' she wondered. 'Of course you are right to some extent – I am not the deep abyss I might be. But how could I be sure of that when I was young? Every night when I lay down in bed I examined my day for signs of folly. If I had lost my temper, if I had felt more joy than was reasonable, I was like one of a tuberculous family who has just heard herself cough. Only the years that had not then passed made me sure that I was unlike my sisters and, until I knew, I had to hold myself back. I could not let the fine man who was my husband be tempted into my father's fault.'

'What was your father's fault?' asked my uncle, for the second time since he had entered that room.

Again her disapproval was absolute, her eyes were like steel. But this time she answered at once, without a moment's hesitation: 'Why, he should not have loved my mother.'

'But you are talking like a child!' he exclaimed. 'You cannot blame anyone for loving anyone.'

'Did you ever see him?' she asked, her eyes blank because they were filled with a distant sight. 'Yes? You must have been only a boy, but surely you saw that he was remarkable. And he had a mind, he was a mathematician, he wrote a book on navigation that was thought brilliant; they asked him to lecture to the Royal Society. And one would have thought from his face that he was a giant of goodness and strength. How could such a man love such a woman as my mother? It was quite mad, the way he made us marry. How could he lean over the abyss of her mind and let himself be drawn down into that darkness?'

'Do not let your voice sink to a whisper like that,' my uncle begged her. 'It – it —'

'It frightens you,' she supplied.

'But have you', he pressed her, 'no feeling for your mother?'

'Oh, yes,' she said, her voice breaking. 'I loved my mother very much. But when she went down into the darkness I had to say goodbye to her or I could not have looked after my sisters.' It seemed as if she was going to weep, but she clung to her harshness and asked again, 'How could my father love such a woman?'

My uncle got up and knelt in front of her chair and took her trembling hands in his. 'There is no answer, so do not ask the question.'

'I must ask it,' she said. 'Surely it is blasphemy to admit that one can ask questions to which there are no answers. I must ask why my father leaned over the abyss of my mother's mind and threw himself into it, and dragged down victim after victim with him – not only dragging them down but manufacturing them for that sole purpose, calling them out of nothingness simply so that they could fall and fall. How could he do it? If there is not an answer —'

He put his hand over her lips. 'He cannot have known that she was mad when he begot his children.'

Her passion had spent itself in her question. She faintly smiled as she said, 'No, but I never liked the excuse that he and my sisters' husbands made for themselves. They all said that at first they had simply thought their wives were rather silly. I could not have loved someone whom I thought rather silly. Could you?'

'It is not what I have done,' said my uncle. 'May I have some more cherry brandy?'

'I am so glad you like it,' she said, suddenly happy. 'But you have given me the wrong glass to fill. This is mine.'

'I knew that,' he told her. 'I wanted to drink from your glass.'

'I would like to drink from yours,' she said, and for a little time they were silent. 'Tell me,' she asked meekly, as if now she had put herself in his hands, 'do you think it has been wrong for me to talk about what has happened to me? When I was at home they always said it was bad to brood over it.'

'What nonsense,' said my uncle. 'I am sure that it was one of the major misfortunes of Phèdre and Bérénice that they were unable to read Racine's clearheaded discussions of their miseries.'

'You are right,' said Parthenope. 'Oh, how kind Racine was to tragic people! He would not allow for a moment that they were comic. People at those courts must have giggled behind their hands at poor Bérénice, at poor Phèdre. But he ignored them. You are kind like Racine.' There was a tapping on the glass of the French window, and her face went grey. 'What has happened now? Oh, what has happened?' she murmured to herself. It was the cook who had tapped, and she was looking grave.

Parthenope went out and spoke with her for a minute, and then came back, and again the tears were standing in her eyes. 'I thought I might ask you to stay all day with me,' she said. 'I thought we might dine together. But my sisters cannot bear it that there is a stranger here. They are hiding in the raspberry canes, and you must have heard them screaming. Part of that noise comes from the parrot, but part from them. It sometimes takes hours to get them quiet. I cannot help it; you must go.'

He took both her hands and pressed them against his throat, and felt it swell as she muttered, 'Goodbye.'

But as he was going through the paved garden to the gateway he heard her call 'Stop! Stop!' and she was just behind him, her skirts lifted over her ankles so that she could take her long strides. 'The strangest thing,' she said, laughing. 'I have not told you the name by which I am known here.' She spelled it out to him as he wrote it down in his diary, and turned back toward the house, exclaiming, 'What a thing to forget!' But then she swung back again, suddenly pale, and said, 'But do not write to me. I am only giving you the name so that if I send you a message you will be able to answer it. But do not write to me.'

'Why not?' he asked indignantly. 'Why not?'

'You must not be involved in my life,' she said. 'There is a force outside the world that hates me and all my family. If you wrote to me too often it might hate you, too.'

'I would risk that,' he said, but she cried, covering her eyes, 'No, no, by being courageous you are threatening my last crumb of happiness. If you stay a stranger, I may be allowed to keep what I have of you. So do as I say.'

He made a resigned gesture, and they parted once more. But as she got to the door he called to her to stop and hurried back. 'I will not send you anything that will remind you of your home,' he said, 'but may I not send you a present from time to time – some stupid little thing that will not mean much but might amuse you for a minute or two?'

She hesitated but in the end nodded. 'A little present, a very little present,' she conceded. 'And not too often.' She smiled like the saved in the sculpture in the church, and slowly closed the door on him.

But when he was out in the square and walking toward the inn he heard her voice crying again 'Stop! Stop!' This time she came quite close to him and said, as if she were a child ashamed to admit to a fault, 'There is another thing that I would like to ask of you. You said that I might write to you if I wanted anything, and I know that you meant business things – the sort of advice men give women. But I wonder if your kindness goes beyond that; you are so very kind. I know all about most dreadful things in life, but I know nothing about death. Usually I think I will not mind leaving this world, but just now and then, if I wake up in the night, particularly in winter, when it is very cold, I am afraid that I may be frightened when I die.'

'I fear that, too, sometimes,' he said.

'It seems a pity, too, to leave this world, in spite of the dreadful things that happen in it,' she went on. 'There are things that nothing can spoil – the spring and the summer and the autumn.'

'And, indeed, the winter, too,' he said.

'Yes, the winter, too,' she said and looked up at the amphitheatre of hills round the village. 'You cannot think how beautiful it is here when the snow has fallen. But, of course, death may be just what one has been waiting for; it may explain everything. But, still, I may be frightened when it comes. So if I do not die suddenly, if I have warning of my death, would it be a great trouble for you to come and be with me for a little?'

'As I would like to be with you always, I would certainly want to be with you then,' he said. 'And, if I have notice of my death and you are free to travel, I will ask you to come to me.'

My uncle found that he did not want to go back to the inn just then, and he followed a road leading up to the foothills. There he climbed one of the paths he had remarked from the top of the church tower, and when he got to the bare rock, he sat down and looked at the village beneath him till the twilight fell. On his return to London, he painted a watercolour of the view of the valley as he recollected it, and pasted it in a book, which he kept by his bedside. From time to time, some object in the window of an antique shop or a jeweller's would bring Parthenope to his mind, and he would send it to her. The one that pleased him as most fitting was a gold ring in the form of two leaves, which was perhaps Saxon. She acknowledged these presents in brief letters; and delighted him that often her solemn purpose of brevity broke down and she added an unnecessary sentence or two, telling him of something that had brightened her days – of a strayed fawn she had found in her garden, or a prodigious crop of cherries, which had made her trees quite red. But after some years these letters stopped. When he took into account how old he was, and by how many years she had been the elder, he realized that probably she had died. He told himself that at least she had enjoyed the mercy of sudden death, and presently ceased to think of her. It was as if the memory of her were too large to fit inside his head; he felt actual physical pain when he tried to recollect her. This was the time when such things as the finest buttercup field near London and the tomb of Captain Vancouver seemed to be all that mattered to him. But from the day when he heard the girl at the inn called by the name of his Parthenope he again found it easy to think of her; and he told me about her very often during the five years that passed before his death.

Mortmain

GRAHAM GREENE

HOW WONDERFULLY SECURE AND peaceful a genuine marriage seemed to Carter, when he attained it at the age of forty-two. He even enjoyed every moment of the church service, except when he saw Josephine wiping away a tear as he conducted Julia down the aisle. It was typical of this new frank relationship that Josephine was there at all. He had no secrets from Julia; they had often talked together of his ten tormented years with Josephine, of her extravagant jealousy, of her well-timed hysterics. 'It was her insecurity,' Julia argued with understanding, and she was quite convinced that in a little while it would be possible to form a friendship with Josephine.

'I doubt it, darling.'

'Why? I can't help being fond of anyone who loved you.'

'It was a rather cruel love.'

'Perhaps at the end when she knew she was losing you, but darling, there *were* happy years.'

'Yes.' But he wanted to forget that he had ever loved anyone before Julia.

Her generosity sometimes staggered him. On the seventh day of their honeymoon, when they were drinking retsina in a little restaurant on the beach by Sunium, he accidentally took a letter from Josephine out of his pocket. It had arrived the day before and he had concealed it, for fear of hurting Julia. It was typical of Josephine that she could not leave him alone for the brief period of the honeymoon. Even her handwriting was now abhorrent to him – very neat, very small, in black ink the colour of her hair. Julia was platinum-fair. How had he ever thought that black hair was beautiful? Or been impatient to read letters in black ink?

'What's the letter, darling? I didn't know there had been a post.'

'It's from Josephine. It came yesterday.'

'But you haven't even opened it!' she exclaimed without a word of reproach.

'I don't want to think about her.'

'But, darling, she may be ill.'

'Not she.'

'Or in distress.'

'She earns more with her fashion-designs than I do with my stories.'

'Darling, let's be kind. We can afford to be. We are so happy.'

So he opened the letter. It was affectionate and uncomplaining and he read it with distaste.

Dear Philip, I didn't want to be a death's head at the reception, so I had no chance to say goodbye and wish you both the greatest possible happiness. I thought Julia looked terribly beautiful and so very, very young. You must look after her carefully. I know how well you can do that, Philip dear. When I saw her, I couldn't help wondering why you took such a long time to make up your mind to leave me. Silly Philip. It's much less painful to act quickly.

I don't suppose you are interested to hear about my activities now, but just in case you are worrying a little about me – you know what an old worrier you are – I want you to know that I'm working *very* hard at a whole series for – guess, the French *Vogue*. They are paying me a fortune in francs, and I simply have no time for unhappy thoughts. I've been back once – I hope you don't mind – to our apartment (slip of the tongue) because I'd lost a key sketch. I found it at the back of our communal drawer – the ideas-bank, do you remember? I thought I'd taken all my stuff away, but there it was between the leaves of the story you started that heavenly summer, and never finished, at Napoule. Now I'm rambling on when all I really wanted to say was: Be happy both of you. Love, Josephine.

Carter handed the letter to Julia and said, 'It could have been worse.'

'But would she like me to read it?'

'Oh, it's meant for both of us.' Again he thought how wonderful it was to have no secrets. There had been so many secrets during the last ten years, even innocent secrets, for fear of misunderstanding, of Josephine's rage or silence. Now he had no fear of anything at all: he could have trusted even a guilty secret to Julia's sympathy and comprehension. He said, 'I was a fool not to show you the letter yesterday. I'll never do anything like that again.' He tried to recall Spenser's line – ' . . . port after stormie seas.'

When Julia had finished reading the letter she said, 'I think she's a wonderful woman. How very, very sweet of her to write like that. You know I was – only now and then of course – just a little worried about her. After all *I* wouldn't like to lose you after ten years.'

When they were in the taxi going back to Athens she said, 'Were you very happy at Napoule?'

'Yes, I suppose so. I don't remember, it wasn't like this.'

With the antennae of a lover he could feel her moving away from him, though their shoulders still touched. The sun was bright on the road from Sunium, the warm sleepy loving siesta lay ahead, and yet . . . 'Is anything the matter, darling?' he asked.

'Not really . . . It's only . . . do you think one day you'll say the same about Athens as about Napoule? "I don't remember, it wasn't like this."'

'What a dear fool you are,' he said and kissed her. After that they played a little in the taxi going back to Athens, and when the streets began to unroll she sat up and combed her hair, 'You aren't really a cold man, are you?' she asked and he knew that all was right again. It was Josephine's fault that – momentarily – there had been a small division.

When they got out of bed to have dinner, she said, 'We must write to Josephine.'

'Oh, no!'

'Darling, I know how you feel, but really it was a wonderful letter.'

'A picture-postcard then.'

So they agreed on that.

Suddenly it was autumn when they arrived back in London – if not winter already, for there was ice in the rain falling on the tarmac, and they had quite forgotten how early the lights came on at home – passing Gillette and Lucozade and Smith's Crisps, and no view of the Parthenon anywhere. The BOAC posters seemed more than usually sad – 'BOAC takes you there and brings you back.'

'We'll put on all the electric fires as soon as we get in,' Carter said, 'and it will be warm in no time at all.' But when they opened the door of the apartment they found the fires were already alight. Little glows greeted them in the twilight from the depths of the living-room and the bedroom.

'Some fairy has done this,' Julia said.

'Not a fairy of any kind,' Carter said. He had already seen the envelope on the mantelpiece addressed in black ink to 'Mrs Carter'.

Dear Julia, you won't mind my calling you Julia, will you? I feel we have so much in common, having loved the same man. Today was so icy that I could not help thinking of how you two were returning from the sun and the warmth to a cold flat. (I know how cold the flat can be. I used to catch a chill every year when we came back from the south of France.) So I've done a very presumptuous thing. I've slipped in and put on the fires, but to show you that I'll never do such a thing again, I've hidden my key under the mat outside the front door. That's just in case your plane is held up in Rome or somewhere. I'll telephone the airport and if by some unlikely chance you haven't arrived, I'll come back and turn out the fires for safety (and economy! the rates are awful). Wishing you a very warm evening in your new home, love from Josephine.

    P.S. I did notice that the coffee jar was empty, so I've left a packet of Blue Mountain in the kitchen. It's the only coffee Philip really cares for.

'Well,' Julia said laughing, 'she does think of everything.'

    'I wish she'd just leave us alone,' Carter said.

    'We wouldn't be warm like this, and we wouldn't have any coffee for breakfast.'

    'I feel that she's lurking about the place and she'll walk in at any moment. Just when I'm kissing you.' He kissed Julia with one careful eye on the door.

    'You *are* a bit unfair, darling. After all, she's left her key under the mat.'

    'She might have had a duplicate made.'

    She closed his mouth with another kiss.

    'Have you noticed how erotic an aeroplane makes you after a few hours?' Carter asked.

    'Yes.'

    'I suppose it's the vibration.'

    'Let's do something about it, darling.'

    'I'll just look under the mat first. To make sure she wasn't lying.'

    He enjoyed marriage – so much that he blamed himself for not having married before, forgetting that in that case he would have been married to Josephine. He found Julia, who had no work of her own, almost miraculously available. There was no maid to mar their relationship with habits. As they were always together, at cocktail parties, in restaurants, at small dinner parties, they had only to meet each other's eyes . . . Julia soon earned the reputation of being delicate and easily tired, it occurred so often that they left a cocktail party after a quarter of an hour or abandoned a dinner after the coffee – 'Oh dear, I'm so sorry, such a vile headache, so stupid of me. Philip, you must stay . . .'

'Of course I'm not going to stay.'

Once they had a narrow escape from discovery on the stairs while they were laughing uncontrollably. Their host had followed them out to ask them to post a letter. Julia in the nick of time changed her laughter into what seemed to be a fit of hysterics. . . . Several weeks went by. It was a really successful marriage. . . . They liked – between whiles – to discuss its success, each attributing the main merit to the other. 'When I think you might have married Josephine,' Julia said. 'Why didn't you marry Josephine?'

'I suppose at the back of our minds we knew it wasn't going to be permanent.'

'Are we going to be permanent?'

'If we aren't, nothing will ever be.'

It was early in November that the timebombs began to go off. No doubt they had been planned to explode earlier, but Josephine had not taken into account the temporary change in his habits. Some weeks passed before he had occasion to open what they used to call the ideas-bank in the days of their closest companionship – the drawer in which he used to leave notes for stories, scraps of overheard dialogue and the like, and she would leave roughly sketched ideas for fashion advertisements.

Directly he opened the drawer he saw her letter. It was labelled heavily 'Top Secret' in black ink with a whimsically drawn exclamation mark in the form of a girl with big eyes (Josephine suffered in an elegant way from exophthalmic goitre) rising genie-like out of a bottle. He read the letter with extreme distaste:

Dear, you didn't expect to find me here, did you? But after ten years I can't not now and then say, Good-night or good-morning, how are you? Bless you. Lots of love (really and truly), Your Josephine.

The threat of 'now and then' was unmistakable. He slammed the drawer shut and said 'Damn' so loudly that Julia looked in. 'Whatever is it, darling?'

'Josephine again.'

She read the letter and said, 'You know, I can understand the way she feels. Poor Josephine. Are you tearing it up, darling?'

'What else do you expect me to do with it? Keep it for a collected edition of her letters?'

'It just seems a bit unkind.'

'Me unkind to *her*? Julia, you've no idea of the sort of life that we led those last years. I can show you scars: when she was in a rage she would stub her cigarettes *anywhere*.'

'She felt she was losing you, darling, and she got desperate. They are my fault really, those scars, every one of them.' He could see growing in her eyes that soft amused speculative look which always led to the same thing.

Only two days passed before the next timebomb went off. When they got up Julia said, 'We really ought to change the mattress. We both fall into a kind of hole in the middle.'

'I hadn't noticed.'

'Lots of people change the mattress every week.'

'Yes. Josephine always did.'

They stripped the bed and began to roll the mattress. Lying on the springs was a letter addressed to Julia. Carter saw it first and tried to push it out of sight, but Julia saw him.

'What's that?'

'Josephine, of course. There'll soon be too many letters for one volume. We shall have to get them properly edited at Yale like George Eliot's.'

'Darling, this is addressed to me. What were you planning to do with it?'

'Destroy it in secret.'

'I thought we were going to have no secrets.'

'I had counted without Josephine.'

For the first time she hesitated before opening the letter. 'It's certainly a bit bizarre to put a letter here. Do you think it got there accidentally?'

'Rather difficult, I should think.'

She read the letter and then gave it to him. She said with relief, 'Oh, she explains why. It's quite natural really.' He read:

Dear Julia, how I hope you are basking in a really Greek sun. Don't tell Philip (Oh, but of course you wouldn't have secrets yet) but I never really cared for the south of France. Always that mistral, drying the skin. I'm glad to think you are not suffering there. We always

planned to go to Greece when we could afford it, so I know Philip
will be happy. I came in today to find a sketch and then remembered
that the mattress hadn't been turned for at least a fortnight. We were
rather distracted, you know, the last weeks we were together. Anyway
I couldn't bear the thought of your coming back from the lotus islands
and finding bumps in your bed the first night, so I've turned it for
you. I'd advise you to turn it every week: otherwise a hole always
develops in the middle. By the way I've put up the winter curtains
and sent the summer ones to the cleaners at 153 Brompton Road. Love,
Josephine.

'If you remember, she wrote to me that Napoule had been heavenly,'
he said. 'The Yale editor will have to put in a cross-reference.'

'You *are* a bit cold-blooded,' Julia said. 'Darling, she's only trying
to be helpful. After all I never knew about the curtains or the
mattress.'

'I suppose you are going to write a long cosy letter in reply, full
of household chat.'

'She's been waiting weeks for an answer. This is an *ancient* letter.'

'And I wonder how many more ancient letters there are waiting
to pop out. By God, I'm going to search the flat through and through.
From attic to basement.'

'We don't have either.'

'You know very well what I mean.'

'I only know you are getting fussed in an exaggerated way. You
really behave as though you are frightened of Josephine.'

'Oh hell!'

Julia left the room abruptly and he tried to work. Later that day a
squib went off – nothing serious, but it didn't help his mood. He
wanted to find the dialling number for overseas telegrams and he
discovered inserted in volume one of the directory a complete list in
alphabetical order, typed on Josephine's machine on which O was
always blurred, a complete list of the numbers he most often required.
John Hughes, his oldest friend, came after Harrods; and there were
the nearest taxi-rank, the chemist's, the butcher's, the bank, the dry-
cleaners, the greengrocer's, the fishmonger's, his publisher and agent,
Elizabeth Arden's and local hairdressers' – marked in brackets ('For
J. please note, quite reliable and very inexpensive') – it was the first
time he noticed they had the same initials.

Julia, who saw him discover the list, said, 'The angel-woman.

We'll pin it up over the telephone. It's really terribly complete.'

'After the crack in her last letter I'd have expected her to include Cartier's.'

'Darling, it wasn't a crack. It was a bare statement of fact. If I hadn't a little money, we would have gone to the south of France too.'

'I suppose you think I married you to get to Greece.'

'Don't be an owl. You don't see Josephine clearly, that's all. You twist every kindness she does.'

'Kindness?'

'I expect it's the sense of guilt.'

After that he really began a search. He looked in cigarette-boxes, drawers, filing-cabinets, he went through all the pockets of the suits he had left behind, he opened the back of the television-cabinet, he lifted the lid of the lavatory-cistern, and even changed the roll of toiletpaper (it was quicker than unwinding the whole thing). Julia came to look at him, as he worked in the lavatory, without her usual sympathy. He tried the pelmets (who knew what they mightn't discover when next the curtains were sent for cleaning?), he took their dirty clothes out of the basket in case something had been overlooked at the bottom. He went on hands-and-knees through the kitchen to look under the gas-stove, and once, when he found a piece of paper wrapped around a pipe, he exclaimed in a kind of triumph, but it was nothing at all – a plumber's relic. The afternoon post rattled through the letter-box and Julia called to him from the hall – 'Oh, good, you never told me you took in the French *Vogue*.'

'I don't.'

'Sorry, there's a kind of Christmas card in another envelope. A subscription's been taken out for us by Miss Josephine Heckstall-Jones. I do call that sweet of her.'

'She's sold a series of drawings to them. I won't look at it.'

'Darling, you are being childish. Do you expect her to stop reading your books?'

'I only want to be left alone with you. Just for a few weeks. It's not so much to ask.'

'You're a bit of an egoist, darling.'

He felt quiet and tired that evening, but a little relieved in mind. His search had been very thorough. In the middle of dinner he had remembered the wedding-presents, still crated for lack of room, and insisted on making sure between the courses that they were still nailed down – he knew Josephine would never have used a screwdriver for fear of injuring her fingers, and she was terrified of hammers. The peace of a solitary evening at last descended on them: the delicious calm which they knew either of them could alter at any moment with a touch of the hand. Lovers cannot postpone as married people can. 'I am grown peaceful as old age tonight,' he quoted to her.

'Who wrote that?'

'Browning.'

'I don't know Browning. Read me some.'

He loved to read Browning aloud – he had a good voice for poetry, it was his small harmless Narcissism. 'Would you really like it?'

'Yes.'

'I used to read to Josephine,' he warned her.

'What do I care? We can't help doing *some* of the same things, can we, darling?'

'There is something I never read to Josephine. Even though I was in love with her, it wasn't suitable. We weren't – permanent.' He began:

> How well I know what I mean to do
>   When the long dark autumn-evenings come . . .

He was deeply moved by his own reading. He had never loved Julia so much as at this moment. Here was home – nothing else had been other than a caravan.

> . . . I will speak now,
>   No longer watch you as you sit
> Reading by firelight, that great brow
>   And the spirit-small hand propping it,
> Mutely, my heart knows how.

He rather wished that Julia had really been reading, but then of course she wouldn't have been listening to him with such adorable attention.

> . . . If two lives join, there is oft a scar.
>   They are one and one, with a shadowy third;
> One near one is too far.

He turned the page and there lay a sheet of paper (he would have discovered it at once, before reading, if she had put it in an envelope) with the black neat handwriting.

> Dearest Philip, only to say goodnight to you between the pages of your favourite book – and mine. We are so lucky to have ended in the way we have. With memories in common we shall for ever be a little in touch. Love, Josephine.

He flung the book and the paper on the floor. He said, 'The bitch. The bloody bitch.'

'I won't have you talk of her like that,' Julia said with surprising strength. She picked up the paper and read it.

'What's wrong with that?' she demanded. 'Do you hate memories? What's going to happen to our memories?'

'But don't you see the trick she's playing? Don't you understand? Are you an idiot, Julia?'

That night they lay in bed on opposite sides, not even touching with their feet. It was the first night since they had come home that they had not made love. Neither slept much. In the morning Carter found a letter in the most obvious place of all, which he had somehow neglected: between the leaves of the unused single-lined foolscap on which he always wrote his stories. It began, 'Darling, I'm sure you won't mind my using the old term . . .'

The Baby Party

F. SCOTT FITZGERALD

WHEN JOHN ANDROS FELT OLD HE FOUND solace in the thought of life continuing through his child. The dark trumpets of oblivion were less loud at the patter of his child's feet or at the sound of his child's voice babbling mad non sequiturs to him over the telephone. The latter incident occurred every afternoon at three when his wife called the office from the country, and he came to look forward to it as one of the vivid minutes of his day.

He was not physically old, but his life had been a series of struggles up a series of rugged hills, and here at thirty-eight having won his battles against ill-health and poverty he cherished less than the usual number of illusions. Even his feeling about his little girl was qualified. She had interrupted his rather intense love-affair with his wife, and she was the reason for their living in a surburban town, where they paid for country air with endless servant troubles and the weary merry-go-round of the commuting train.

It was little Ede as a definite piece of youth that chiefly interested him. He liked to take her on his lap and examine minutely her fragrant, downy scalp and her eyes with their irises of morning blue. Having paid this homage John was content that the nurse should take her away. After ten minutes the very vitality of the child irritated him; he was inclined to lose his temper when things were broken, and one Sunday afternoon when she had disrupted a bridge game by permanently hiding up the ace of spades, he had made a scene that had reduced his wife to tears.

This was absurd and John was ashamed of himself. It was inevitable that such things would happen, and it was impossible that little Ede should spend all her indoor hours in the nursery upstairs when she was becoming, as her mother said, more nearly a 'real person' every day.

She was two and a half, and this afternoon, for instance, she was going to a baby party. Grown-up Edith, her mother, had telephoned the information to the office, and little Ede had confirmed the business by shouting 'I yam going to a *pantry*!' into John's unsuspecting left ear.

'Drop in at the Markeys' when you get home, won't you, dear?' resumed her mother. 'It'll be funny. Ede's going to be all dressed up in her new pink dress —'

The conversation terminated abruptly with a squawk which indicated that the telephone had been pulled violently to the floor. John laughed and decided to get an early train out; the prospect of a baby party in someone else's house amused him.

'What a peach of a mess!' he thought humorously. 'A dozen mothers, and each one looking at nothing but her own child. All the babies breaking things and grabbing at the cake, and each mamma going home thinking about the subtle superiority of her own child to every other child there.'

He was in a good humour today – all the things in his life were going better than they had ever gone before. When he got off the train at his station he shook his head at an importunate taxi man, and began to walk up the long hill toward his house through the crisp December twilight. It was only six o'clock but the moon was out, shining with proud brilliance on the thin sugary snow that lay over the lawns.

As he walked along drawing his lungs full of cold air his happiness increased, and the idea of a baby party appealed to him more and more. He began to wonder how Ede compared to other children of her own age, and if the pink dress she was to wear was something radical and mature. Increasing his gait he came in sight of his own house, where the lights of a defunct Christmas tree still blossomed in the window, but he continued on past the walk. The party was at the Markeys' next door.

As he mounted the brick step and rang the bell he became aware of voices inside, and he was glad he was not too late. Then he raised his head and listened – the voices were not children's voices, but they were loud and pitched high with anger; there were at least three of them and one, which rose as he listened to a hysterical sob, he recognized immediately as his wife's.

'There's been some trouble,' he thought quickly.

Trying the door, he found it unlocked and pushed it open.

The baby party began at half past four, but Edith Andros, calculating shrewdly that the new dress would stand out more sensationally against vestments already rumpled, planned the arrival of herself and little Ede for five. When they appeared it was already a flourishing affair. Four baby girls and nine baby boys, each one curled and washed and dressed with all the care of a proud and jealous heart, were dancing to the music of a phonograph. Never more than two or three were dancing at once, but as all were continually in motion running to and from their mothers for encouragement, the general effect was the same.

As Edith and her daughter entered, the music was temporarily drowned out by a sustained chorus, consisting largely of the word *cute* and directed toward little Ede, who stood looking timidly about and fingering the edges of her pink dress. She was not kissed – this is the sanitary age – but she was passed along a row of mammas each one of whom said 'cu-u-ute' to her and held her pink little hand before passing her on to the next. After some encouragement and a few mild pushes she was absorbed into the dance, and became an active member of the party.

Edith stood near the door talking to Mrs Markey, and keeping one eye on the tiny figure in the pink dress. She did not care for Mrs Markey; she considered her both snippy and common, but John and Joe Markey were congenial and went in together on the commuting train every morning, so the two women kept up an elaborate pretense of warm amity. They were always reproaching each other for 'not coming to see me,' and they were always planning the kind of parties that began with 'You'll have to come to dinner with us soon, and we'll go in to the theater,' but never matured further.

'Little Ede looks perfectly darling,' said Mrs Markey, smiling and moistening her lips in a way that Edith found particularly repulsive. 'So *grown-up* – I can't *believe* it!'

Edith wondered if 'little Ede' referred to the fact that Billy Markey, though several months younger, weighed almost five pounds more. Accepting a cup of tea she took a seat with two other ladies on a divan and launched into the real business of the afternoon, which of course lay in relating the recent accomplishments and insouciances of her child.

An hour passed. Dancing palled and the babies took to sterner sport. They ran into the dining-room, rounded the big table, and essayed the kitchen door, from which they were rescued by an expeditionary force of mothers. Having been rounded up they immediately broke loose, and rushing back to the dining-room tried the familiar swinging door again. The word 'overheated' began to be used, and small white brows were dried with small white handkerchiefs. A general attempt to make the babies sit down began, but the babies squirmed off laps with peremptory cries of 'Down! Down!' and the rush into the fascinating dining-room began anew.

This phase of the party came to an end with the arrival of refreshments, a large cake with two candles, and saucers of vanilla ice cream. Billy Markey, a stout laughing baby with red hair and legs somewhat bowed, blew out the candles, and placed an experimental thumb on the white frosting. The refreshments were distributed, and the children ate, greedily but without confusion – they had behaved remarkably well all afternoon. They were modern babies who ate and slept at regular hours, so their dispositions were good, and their faces healthy and pink – such a peaceful party would not have been possible thirty years ago.

After the refreshments a gradual exodus began. Edith glanced anxiously at her watch – it was almost six, and John had not arrived. She wanted him to see Ede with the other children – to see how dignified and polite and intelligent she was, and how the only ice-cream spot on her dress was some that had dropped from her chin when she was joggled from behind.

'You're a darling,' she whispered to her child, drawing her suddenly against her knee. 'Do you know you're a darling? Do you *know* you're a darling?'

Ede laughed. 'Bow-wow,' she said suddenly.

'Bow-wow?' Edith looked around. 'There isn't any bow-wow.'

'Bow-wow,' repeated Ede. 'I want a bow-wow.'

Edith followed the small pointing finger.

'That isn't a bow-wow, dearest, that's a teddy-bear.'

'Bear?'

'Yes, that's a teddy-bear, and it belongs to Billy Markey. You don't want Billy Markey's teddy-bear, do you?'

Ede did want it.

She broke away from her mother and approached Billy Markey, who held the toy closely in his arms. Ede stood regarding him with inscrutable eyes, and Billy laughed.

Grown-up Edith looked at her watch again, this time impatiently.

The party had dwindled until, besides Ede and Billy, there were only two babies remaining – and one of the two remained only by virtue of having hidden himself under the dining-room table. It was selfish of John not to come. It showed so little pride in the child. Other fathers had come, half a dozen of them, to call for their wives, and they had stayed for a while and looked on.

There was a sudden wail. Ede had obtained Billy's teddy-bear by pulling it forcibly from his arms, and on Billy's attempt to recover it, she had pushed him casually to the floor.

'Why, Ede!' cried her mother, repressing an inclination to laugh.

Joe Markey, a handsome, broad-shouldered man of thirty-five, picked up his son and set him on his feet. 'You're a fine fellow,' he said jovially. 'Let a girl knock you over! You're a fine fellow.'

'Did he bump his head?' Mrs Markey returned anxiously from bowing the next to last remaining mother out the door.

'No-o-o-o,' exclaimed Markey. 'He bumped something else, didn't you, Billy? He bumped something else.'

Billy had so far forgotten the bump that he was already making an attempt to recover his property. He seized a leg of the bear which projected from Ede's enveloping arms and tugged at it but without success.

'No,' said Ede emphatically.

Suddenly, encouraged by the success of her former half-accidental manoeuver, Ede dropped the teddy-bear, placed her hands on Billy's shoulders and pushed him backward off his feet.

This time he landed less harmlessly; his head hit the bare floor just off the rug with a dull hollow sound, whereupon he drew in his breath and delivered an agonized yell.

Immediately the room was in confusion. With an exclamation Markey hurried to his son, but his wife was first to reach the injured baby and catch him up into her arms.

'Oh, *Billy*,' she cried, 'what a terrible bump! She ought to be spanked.'

Edith, who had rushed immediately to her daughter, heard this remark, and her lips came sharply together.

'Why, Ede,' she whispered perfunctorily, 'you bad girl!'

Ede put back her little head suddenly and laughed. It was a loud laugh, a triumphant laugh with victory in it and challenge and contempt. Unfortunately it was also an infectious laugh. Before her mother realized the delicacy of the situation, she too had laughed, an audible, distinct laugh not unlike the baby's, and partaking of the same overtones.

Then, as suddenly, she stopped.

Mrs Markey's face had grown red with anger, and Markey, who had been feeling the back of the baby's head with one finger, looked at her, frowning.

'It's swollen already,' he said with a note of reproof in his voice. 'I'll get some witch-hazel.'

But Mrs Markey had lost her temper. 'I don't see anything funny about a child being hurt!' she said in a trembling voice.

Little Ede meanwhile had been looking at her mother curiously. She noted that her own laugh had produced her mother's, and she wondered if the same cause would always produce the same effect. So she chose this moment to throw back her head and laugh again.

To her mother the additonal mirth added the final touch of hysteria to the situation. Pressing her handkerchief to her mouth she giggled irrepressibly. It was more than nervousness – she felt that in a peculiar way she was laughing with her child – they were laughing together.

It was in a way a defiance – those two against the world.

While Markey rushed upstairs to the bathroom for ointment, his wife was walking up and down rocking the yelling boy in her arms.

'Please go home!' she broke out suddenly. 'The child's badly hurt, and if you haven't the decency to be quiet, you'd better go home.'

'Very well,' said Edith, her own temper rising. 'I've never seen anyone make such a mountain out of –'

'Get out!' cried Mrs Markey frantically. 'There's the door, get out – I never want to see you in our house again. You or your brat either!'

Edith had taken her daughter's hand and was moving quickly toward the door, but at this remark she stopped and turned around, her face contracting with indignation.

'Don't you dare call her that!'

Mrs Markey did not answer but continued walking up and down, muttering to herself and to Billy in an inaudible voice.

Edith began to cry.

'I will get out!' she sobbed, 'I've never heard anybody so rude and c-common in my life. I'm glad your baby did get pushed down – he's nothing but a f-fat little fool anyhow.'

Joe Markey reached the foot of the stairs just in time to hear this remark.

'Why, Mrs Andros,' he said sharply, 'can't you see the child's hurt? You really ought to control yourself.'

'Control m-myself!' exclaimed Edith brokenly. 'You better ask her to c-control herself. I've never heard anybody so c-common in my life.'

'She's insulting me!' Mrs Markey was now livid with rage. 'Did you hear what she said, Joe? I wish you'd put her out. If she won't go, just take her by the shoulders and put her out!'

'Don't you dare touch me!' cried Edith. 'I'm going just as quick as I can find my c-coat!'

Blind with tears she took a step toward the hall. It was just at this moment that the door opened and John Andros walked anxiously in.

'John!' cried Edith, and fled to him wildly.

'What's the matter? Why, what's the matter?'

'They're – they're putting me out!' she wailed, collapsing against him. 'He'd just started to take me by the shoulders and put me out. I want my coat!'

'That's not true,' objected Markey hurriedly. 'Nobody's going to put you out.' He turned to John. 'Nobody's going to put her out,' he repeated. 'She's —'

'What do you mean "put her out"?' demanded John abruptly. 'What's all this talk, anyhow?'

'Oh, let's go!' cried Edith. 'I want to go. They're so *common*, John!'

'Look here!' Markey's face darkened. 'You've said that about enough. You're acting sort of crazy.'

'They called Ede a brat!'

For the second time that afternoon little Ede expressed emotion at an inopportune moment. Confused and frightened at the shouting voices, she began to cry, and her tears had the effect of conveying that she felt the insult in her heart.

'What's the idea of this?' broke out John. 'Do you insult your guests in your own house?'

'It seems to me it's your wife that's done the insulting!' answered Markey crisply. 'In fact, your baby there started all the trouble.'

John gave a contemptuous snort. 'Are you calling names at a little baby?' he inquired. 'That's fine manly business!'

'Don't talk to him, John,' insisted Edith. 'Find my coat!'

'You must be in a bad way,' went on John angrily, 'if you have to take out your temper on a helpless little baby.'

'I never heard anything so damn twisted in my life,' shouted Markey. 'If that wife of yours would shut her mouth for a minute —'

'Wait a minute! You're not talking to a woman and child now —'

There was an incidental interruption. Edith had been fumbling on a chair for her coat, and Mrs Markey had been watching her with hot angry eyes. Suddenly she laid Billy down on the sofa, where he immediately stopped crying and pulled himself upright, and coming into the hall she quickly found Edith's coat and handed it to her without a word. Then she went back to the sofa, picked up Billy, and rocking him in her arms looked again at Edith with hot, angry eyes. The interruption had taken less than half a minute.

'Your wife comes in here and begins shouting around about how common we are!' burst out Markey violently. 'Well, if we're so damn common, you'd better stay away! And, what's more, you'd better get out now!'

Again John gave a short, contemptuous laugh.

'You're not only common,' he returned, 'you're evidently an awful bully – when there's any helpless women and children around.' He felt for the knob and swung the door open. 'Come on, Edith.'

Taking up her daughter in her arms, his wife stepped outside and John, still looking contemptuously at Markey, started to follow.

'Wait a minute!' Markey took a step forward; he was trembling slightly, and two large veins on his temple were suddenly full of blood. 'You don't think you can get away with that, do you? With me?'

Without a word John walked out the door, leaving it open.

Edith, still weeping, had started for home. After following her with his eyes until she reached her own walk, John turned back toward the lighted doorway where Markey was slowly coming down the slippery steps. He took off his overcoat and hat, tossed them off the path onto the snow. Then, sliding a little on the iced walk, he took a step forward.

At the first blow, they both slipped and fell heavily to the sidewalk, half rising then, and again pulling each other to the ground. They found a better foothold in the thin snow to the side of the walk and rushed at each other, both swinging wildly and pressing out the snow into a pasty mud underfoot.

The street was deserted, and except for their short tired gasps and the padded sound as one or the other slipped down into the slushy mud, they fought in silence, clearly defined to each other by the full moonlight as well as by the amber glow that shone out of the open door. Several times they both slipped down together, and then for a while the conflict threshed about wildly on the lawn.

For ten, fifteen, twenty minutes they fought there senselessly in the moonlight. They had both taken off coats and vests at some silently agreed upon interval and now their shirts dripped from their backs in wet pulpy shreds. Both were torn and bleeding and so exhausted that they could stand only when by their position they mutually supported each other – the impact, the mere effort of a blow, would send them both to their hands and knees.

But it was not weariness that ended the business, and the very meaninglessness of the fight was a reason for not stopping. They stopped because once when they were straining at each other on the ground, they heard a man's footsteps coming along the sidewalk. They had rolled somehow into the shadow, and when they heard these footsteps they stopped fighting, stopped moving, stopped breathing, lay huddled together like two boys playing Indian until the footsteps had passed. Then, staggering to their feet, they looked at each other like two drunken men.

'I'll be damned if I'm going on with this any more,' cried Markey thickly.

'I'm not going on any more either,' said John Andros. 'I've had enough of this thing.'

Again they looked at each other, sulkily this time, as if each suspected the other of urging him to a renewal of the fight. Markey spat out a mouthful of blood from a cut lip; then he cursed softly, and picking up his coat and vest, shook off the snow from them in a surprised way, as if their comparative dampness was his only worry in the world.

'Want to come in and wash up?' he asked suddenly.

'No, thanks,' said John. 'I ought to be going home – my wife'll be worried.'

He too picked up his coat and vest and then his overcoat and hat. Soaking wet and dripping with perspiration, it seemed absurd that less than half an hour ago he had been wearing all these clothes.

'Well – good night,' he said hesitantly.

Suddenly they both walked toward each other and shook hands. It was no perfunctory handshake: John Andros's arm went around

Markey's shoulder, and he patted him softly on the back for a little while.

'No harm done,' he said brokenly.

'No – you?'

'No, no harm done.'

'Well,' said John Andros after a minute, 'I guess I'll say good-night.'

'Good night.'

Limping slightly and with his clothes over his arm, John Andros turned away. The moonlight was still bright as he left the dark patch of trampled ground and walked over the intervening lawn. Down at the station, half a mile away, he could hear the rumble of the seven o'clock train.

'But you must have been crazy,' cried Edith brokenly. 'I thought you were going to fix it all up there and shake hands. That's why I went away.'

'Did you want us to fix it up?'

'Of course not, I never want to see them again. But I thought of course that was what you were going to do.' She was touching the bruises on his neck and back with iodine as he sat placidly in a hot bath. 'I'm going to get the doctor,' she said insistently. 'You may be hurt internally.'

He shook his head. 'Not a chance,' he answered. 'I don't want this to get all over town.'

'I don't understand yet how it all happened.'

'Neither do I.' He smiled grimly. 'I guess these baby parties are pretty rough affairs.'

'Well, one thing —' suggested Edith hopefully, 'I'm certainly glad we have beefsteak in the house for tomorrow's dinner.'

'Why?'

'For your eye, of course. Do you know I came within an ace of ordering veal? Wasn't that the luckiest thing?'

Half an hour later, dressed except that his neck would accommodate no collar, John moved his limbs experimentally before the glass. 'I believe I'll get myself in better shape,' he said thoughtfully. 'I must be getting old.'

'You mean so that next time you can beat him?'

'I did beat him,' he announced. 'At least, I beat him as much as he beat me. And there isn't going to be any next time. Don't you go calling people common any more. If you get in any trouble, you just take your coat and go home. Understand?'

'Yes, dear,' she said meekly. 'I was very foolish and now I understand.'

Out in the hall, he paused abruptly by the baby's door.

'Is she asleep?'

'Sound asleep. But you can go in and peek at her – just to say good night.'

They tiptoed in and bent together over the bed. Little Ede, her cheeks flushed with health, her pink hands clasped tight together, was sleeping soundly in the cool, dark room. John reached over the railing of the bed and passed his hand lightly over the silken hair.

'She's asleep,' he murmured in a puzzled way.

'Naturally, after such an afternoon.'

'Miz Andros,' the colored maid's stage whisper floated in from the hall, 'Mr and Miz Markey downstairs an' want to see you. Mr Markey he's all cut up in pieces, ma'am. His face look like a roast beef. An' Miz Markey she 'pear mighty mad.'

'Why, what incomparable nerve!' exclaimed Edith. 'Just tell them we're not home. I wouldn't go down for anything in the world.'

'You most certainly will.' John's voice was hard and set.

'What?'

'You'll go down right now, and, what's more, whatever that other woman does, you'll apologize for what you said this afternoon. After that you don't ever have to see her again.'

'Why – John, I can't.'

'You've got to. And just remember that she probably hated to come over here just twice as much as you hate to go downstairs.'

'Aren't you coming? Do I have to go alone?'

'I'll be down – in just a minute.'

John Andros waited until she had closed the door behind her; then he reached over into the bed, and picking up his daughter, blankets and all, sat down in the rocking-chair holding her tightly in his arms. She moved a little, and he held his breath, but she was sleeping soundly, and in a moment she was resting quietly in the hollow of his elbow. Slowly he bent his head until his cheek was against her bright hair. 'Dear little girl,' he whispered. 'Dear little girl, dear little girl.'

John Andros knew at length what it was he had fought for so

savagely that evening. He had it now, he possessed it forever, and for some time he sat there rocking very slowly to and fro in the darkness.

The Reunion

MARGARET DRABBLE

THERE MUST HAVE BEEN A MOMENT at which she decided to go down the street and round the corner and into the café. She knew that: for she knew that at one point she was walking quite idly, quite innocently, with no recollection or association in her head but the dimmest faintest palest shadow of long long past knowledge, and that within ten yards, twenty yards perhaps of innocence, the distance of two frontages of those ancient crumbling small tall buildings, now so uniformly shoddy warehouses, she had made up her mind that she would go and have her lunch there, in that place where they had always had their lunch together. Or no, she said to herself, not even always (excusing herself, apologetic, already diminishing any possible significance of her act), they had not had their lunch there always, they had had it there merely occasionally, once a fortnight or so over that long and lovely year, and the first time that they had gone there had had no significance at all, for it was simply that, being in such an area, an area they did not know well, they had had lunch in the only place that they could find. And they had liked it there, and so they had gone back, because it was the kind of place where nobody would ever see them, where nobody that either of them knew would ever go, and yet at the same time not impossibly inconvenient, not so very far from Holborn, where they both had good reason from time to time to be. They had felt safe there, as safe as they could ever feel, yet at the same time aware that they had not allowed themselves to be driven into grotesque precautions. They had found it themselves so much by chance, and they did not think that anyone they knew could chance to walk that way.

And now, after so long, after a three year gap, she had found herself there and almost as it were upon the threshold, and at lunch time too. She was hungry. There is nothing more to it than that, she said to herself, as she found herself walking so instinctively towards

193

it. I happened to be near, and wanting my lunch, and the fact that I wanted my lunch merely reminded me of this place, and that I did curiously enough know it was here, and moreover that there is nowhere else possible within a five minutes walk. She had done enough walking she thought. she had never liked walking. it had been enough of a walk, from Old Street tube station to the place where they had made her new tooth. She ran her tongue over her new front tooth, reassuringly, and was slightly ashamed by the immense relief that she felt at being once more presentable, no longer disfigured by that humiliating gap. being beautiful, she had always made much of caring little for her beauty, and was always profoundly disturbed by the accidents which from time to time brought her face to face with her own vanity – by the inconvenient pimple, by the unperceived smudge on the cheek, by the heavy cold. And that lost tooth had been something of a test case, ever since she had had it knocked out, while still at school. Her dentist had made for her the most elaborate and delicate bridge, so that not even she herself would ever have to endure the sight of herself toothless, but the night before last she had fallen downstairs after a party and broken it. She had rung up her dentist in the morning, and made a dreadful fuss, and a special visit, and he had promised her a temporary plate to last her until he had made her a new elaborate and delicate bridge. and when he had told her the name of the place that she should go to collect the plate, she had noticed in herself a small, hardly noticeable flicker of recollection. He went on explaining to her, obliging yet irritable, 'You've got that then, Mrs Harvey, 82 St Luke's Street? You go to Old Street station, then turn right . . .' and she heard herself saying, 'Oh yes, St Luke's Street, that's just off Tunstall Square.' As though anybody might be expected to know about Tunstall Square. And he had agreed, without surprise, about its proximity to Tunstall Square, and then had continued to explain to her about the fact that he was doing her a special favour, and that she should suitably express her gratitude to the man at the works, in view of the shortness of the notice. and she had duly expressed it to the man at the works when he had handed her, ten minutes ago, her tooth, all wrapped up somewhat brutally she thought in a brown paper bag. She had been effusive, in her gratitude, and the man had looked at her biankly and said oh that was quite all right, no trouble at all.

And then she had come out, and walked along this street. And as she paused at the café door, she knew that she had been thinking of him and of that other year all the time, that she could not very well have avoided the thought of him, amongst so much familiar scenery. There they had sat in the car, and kissed and endlessly discussed the impossibility of kissing: there they had stood by that lamp-post, transfixed, unable to move. The pavement seemed still to bear the marks of their feet. And yet it was all so long ago, so thoroughly slaughtered and decayed. She did not care at all: it was two years since she had cared, more than two years since she had suffered, since she suffered more for the loss of him than for the old tedium of her life, and the old anxieties, which had existed before him, and which would exist forever, because they were what she was made of. Inadequacy, loneliness, panic, vanity, decay. These words she said to herself, because words consoled her.

Though she was not unhappy. She was content, she was occupied, she had got her tooth back, everything was under control, the evening would be fine, now that the horror and strain of pretending not to mind that one had a tooth missing had been so successfully averted. She had even quite enjoyed going to that odd place where they made teeth: it was the kind of place that she enjoyed seeing, and she would even be able to tell people about her panic about her tooth, now that the real panic was truly over. And perhaps in a way it made her almost happy, even a little happier than usual, to be back in this place, to find how thoroughly dead it all was, how most efficiently she had died. She saw no ghosts of him here: for a year after their parting she had seen him on every street corner, in every passing car, in shapes of head and hand and forms of movement, but now he was nowhere any more, not even here. For as long as she had imagined that she saw him, she had imagined that he had remembered: that those false ghosts had been in some way the projected shadows of his love: but now she knew that surely they had both forgotten. Remembering him, she thought that this was what she knew.

She pushed open the door and went in. It looked the same. Nothing had changed. She realized that she had been imagining that it must look different, had been preparing herself for heaven knows what ugly transformations and redecorations, but it looked the same. The sameness of it made her pause, took her breath away, though even as she stood there she said to herself, how foolish to imagine it takes my breath away, for I am breathing quite regularly, quite normally. It is simply that I have become, for an instant, aware of the fact that I am breathing.

She went to the side of the room that they had always favoured, the wall side, away from the door and the window, and sat on the corner table, where they had always sat when they.could with her back to the door. She sat there, and looked down at the red veined Formica table top, with its cluster of salt pot, pepper pot, mustard pot, sauce bottle, and ash tray: the salt pot was of thick-ribbed Perspex, and she remembered the exact common mounting scallops of its edges. She took it in her hand, and felt it. She did not often now lunch in places where such objects might be found. Then she looked up at the dark yellow ceiling, with its curiously useless trellis work hung with plastic lemons and bananas: and then at the wall, the wall papered as before in a strange delicate dirty flowered print, with paper badly cut, and joining badly at the seams, and broken up by protruding obsolescent functionless bits of woodwork, dating from former decorative schemes. On the wall hung the only thing that was different. It was a calendar, a gift from a garage, and the picture showed an Alpine hut in snowy mountains, for all that the month was May. In their day, the calendar had been one donated by a fruit juice firm, and they had seen it through three seasons; she recalled the anguish with which she had seen its leaves turn, more relentless even than those leaves falling so dreadfully and ominously from more natural trees, and she recalled the appalling photograph of their parting, which had portrayed an autumn evening in a country garden, with an old couple sitting by their creeper-covered door. They had both been insatiable, merciless deliverers of ultimatums, the one upon the other. And she had selected in her own soul this month, and one day of this month – the twenty-third, she knew it even now, the twenty-third – for her final, last, unalterable decision, and she had watched it come up upon them; she had sat at this table, or perhaps after all not at this one but at the one next to it, and she had said, 'Look, that's it, on the twenty-third, that's it, and I mean it this time.' She wondered if he had known that she had meant it: whether an indefinable resolution in her, so small that she did not herself trust it, had somehow communicated itself to him, so that he had known that for this one last time it was for real. Because he had taken her at her word. It was the first time that she had not relented, nor he persisted; each other time he had left her forever, a phone call had been enough to regain him, and each time she had left him, she had sat by the telephone biting her nails and waiting for it to ring. But this time he did not ring, and after a couple of days she ceased to leave the receiver off when nobody was looking. She said to herself from time to time, perhaps in those two days he rang, and rang repeatedly, rang every hour and found me perpetually engaged, and knew what I had done, and knew that at last I meant what I had said: but she knew that she would never never know, and that for her it was all the same if he once rung, or twenty times, or never even tried. It had happened, after so many false attempts, it had finally happened; preparations for death had been in a way like death itself, and she supposed that was why they must so incessantly have made them, more merciful to each other than they knew, for the experience of losing him, so often endured in imagination, had solidified from imagination into reality so slowly, with such obdurate slow accretions, that there was no point at which she said, Look, it is done and done for good. There had always seemed a point at which it might be undone. But not now, not now. She looked at the snowy hut upon the wall, at the icy mountains and the frozen glaciers, and she thought, Ah well, there was a point at which I feared we did not have it in us to part. And a kind of admiration for her past self possessed her, a respect for a woman who had been so thoroughly capable of so sizeable a renunciation.

The menu, when it was brought to her, had not altered much. She was glad of this, for without her glasses she doubted whether she would have made much of its faded violet overduplicated manuscript. Though she never knew why she bothered to read menus, for she always with unfailing regularity wherever she was ate the same lunch: she always had cheese omelette and chips. So she ordered her meal, and then sat back to wait. Usually, whenever left alone in a public place, she would read, and through habit she propped her book up against the sauce bottle and rested her eyes upon it, but she did not look at the words. Nor was she dwelling entirely upon the past, for a certain pleasurable anxiety about her evening's engagement was stealing most of her attention, and she found herself wondering whether she had adequately prepared her piece, and whether David Rathbone would offer to drive her home, and whether her hair would look all right, for the last time she had been on the television there had been a girl in the make-up place who had messed it about dreadfully, and cut bits off her fringe, and generally made her look like some quite other kind of person. And most of all, she wondered if she ought to wear her grey skirt. She was really worried about the grey skirt question: all the anxiety that had previously attached itself to the importance of getting her tooth in time had now transferred itself to the skirt, for although she liked it very much she was not at all sure that it was not just a very very little bit tight. If it wasn't, then it was perfect, for it was the kind of thing that she always looked marvellous in: but just supposing that it was? There was nobody in the whole world who could tell her, who could decide for her this delicate point: she had even asked her husband about it, the night before, and he had looked at it and nodded his head and said it looked lovely, and she knew exactly how much and how little that meant. There was nobody but herself with the finesse, with the information to decide such a point, and she could not decide; and she was just saying to herself, the very fact that I'm *worrying* about it must mean that it must be too tight after all, or the thought of its being too tight wouldn't have crossed my mind, would it? when she saw him.

What was really most shocking about it was the way that they noticed each other at exactly the same moment, simultaneously, without a chance of turning away or in any way managing the shock. They were both such managers, but this time they had not a chance. Their eyes met, and they both jerked, beyond hope of dissimulation.

'Oh Christ,' he said, after a second or two, and stood there and went on looking at her.

And she felt at such a loss, sitting there with her book propped up against the tomato ketchup, and her head full of skirts and false teeth, and she said, hurriedly, throwing away what might after all to such as her have been really quite a moment, 'Oh Lord, oh well, since you're there, do sit down, I mean you might as well sit down!' and she moved up the small two-seater bench, pushing her bag along, losing a shoe, for she had kicked them off under the table, inelegantly dragging her jacket out of his way, closing up her book with a rapid snap, averting her eyes, confused, deprecating, unable to look.

And he sat down by her, and then said quite suddenly and intimately, as though perfectly at home with her after so many years of silence, as though perfectly confident that she would share whatever he might have to think or say.

'Oh Lord, my darling, what a dreadful dreadful surprise, I don't think I shall ever ever recover.'

'Oh, I don't know,' she said, as though she too had discovered exactly where she was. 'Oh, I don't know. One gets over these things quite quickly. I feel better already, don't you?'

'Why, yes, I suppose I do,' he said. 'I feel better now I'm sitting down, thought I was going to faint, standing there and looking at you.'

'Well,' she said, 'it wasn't quite a fair test of me, was it, because after all I was sitting down already. I mean, nobody ever fainted sitting down, surely?'

'Oh, I'm sure it has been done,' he said. 'If you'd fainted, I'd have had to put your head between your knees. And God knows how we'd have managed that at one of these tables. I'd forgotten how cramped it all was. But we used to like that, I suppose, didn't we?'

'Yes, I suppose we did,' she said.

'Even though you didn't faint,' he said, 'didn't you feel some sort of slight tremor? Surely you must have done?'

'It's hard to tell,' she said, 'when one's sitting down. It isn't a fair test. Even of tremors.'

'No,' he said, 'no.'

Then they were silent for a moment or two, and then she said, very precisely and carefully, offering her first generous signal of intended retreat,

'I suppose that what *is* odd, really, is that we haven't come across one another before?'

'Oh, I don't know,' he said, with equal, disappointing neutrality. 'Where would we have met? It's not as though we ever belonged to what you might call the same world.'

'No,' she said, 'no, I suppose not.'

'Have you ever been back here before?' he asked.

'No, never,' she said. 'Have you?'

'Yes,' he said. 'Yes, I have. And if you had been back, you might have seen me. I looked for you.'

'You're lying,' she said quickly, elated, looking at him for the first time since he had sat down by her, and then looking away quickly, horrified by the dangerous and appalling proximity of his head, but keeping nevertheless her nerve, being more or less sure that he was in fact lying.

'No, I'm not,' he said. 'I came here, and looked for you. I was sure that you would come.'

'It's a safe lie,' she said, 'like all your lies. A lie I could never catch you out in. Unless I really had been here, looking for you, and simply hadn't wanted to admit it.'

'And even then,' he said, 'we might merely have missed each other.'

'Yes,' she conceded.

'But,' he said with conviction, 'you weren't here at all. I know you weren't here. I was here, I came, but you didn't. You were faithless, weren't you, my darling?'

'Faithless?'

'You forgot me quicker than I forgot you, didn't you? When you had so promised to remember.'

'Oh,' she said, wondering if she should admit so much, but unable to resist the ominous luxury of admission, 'oh, I didn't forget you.'

'Didn't you? How long did you remember me for?'

'Oh, how can one say? she said. 'After all, there are degrees of remembrance.'

'Tell me,' he said, 'tell me. What harm can it do, to tell me now?'

She moved a little on the seat, away from him, but settling at the same time into a more comfortable pose of confidence: because she wanted to tell him, she had been waiting for years to tell him.

'I suffered quite horribly,' she said. 'Really quite horribly. That's what you want to hear, isn't it?'

'Of course it is,' he said.

'Oh, I really did,' she said. 'I can't tell you. I cried, all the time, for weeks. For a month. For at least a month. And whenever the phone went, I started, I jumped, like a fool, as though I'd been shot. It was pathetic, it was ludicrous. In the end I had to invent some bloody silly story about waiting for a call about a job, though what job could ever have got anyone in such a state I can hardly imagine, and each time I answered and it wasn't you I could hardly speak, I could somehow hardly make the effort to speak. It's odd how people don't notice when one doesn't reply. I would stand there listening, and they would go on talking, and sometimes I would say yes or no, as I waited for them to ring off, and when they did ring off I don't think they'd even noticed. And then I would sit down and cry. Is that what you want me to say?'

'I want to hear it,' he said, 'but it can't, it can't be true.'

'It's as true as that you came to this place to look for me,' she said.

'I did come,' he said.

'And I did weep,' she said.

'Did you ever try to ring me?' he asked, then, unable to resist.

'No!' she said with some pride. 'No, not once. I never tried, not once. I'd said I wouldn't, and I didn't.'

'I rang you, once,' he said.

'You didn't,' she said, 'you didn't,' and became aware at that instant that her knees under the table were trembling; they were, quite unmistakably.

'I did,' he said. 'It was just over a year ago, and we'd just got back from a party, about three in the morning it was, and I rang you. But you didn't answer. He answered.'

'Oh God,' she said, 'oh God. It's true, it's true, it's not a lie, because I remember it. Oliver said it was burglars. A Friday night. Wasn't it a Friday night?'

'Yes,' he said, 'my darling darling, it was. Did you know it might have been me?'

'I didn't think it could have been you,' she said. 'Not you, after so long a time. But I thought of you. When the phone rang and woke us, I thought of you, and when Oliver said there was no answer, I thought of you. Oh my darling, I can't tell you how I've had to stop myself ringing you, how I've sat there by the phone and lifted the receiver and dialled the first numbers of your number, and then stopped, and not let myself do it, and the receiver would be dripping with sweat when I put it down, but I stopped myself, I did stop myself. That was good of me wasn't it?'

'Oh,' he said, 'if you knew how I'd wanted you to ring.'

'I did write to you once,' she said. 'But I couldn't bring myself to post it. But I'll tell you what I did, I typed out an envelope to you, and I put one of those circulars from that absurd Poetry Club of mine into it, and I sent it off to you, because I thought that at least it might create in you a passing thought of me. And I liked the thought of something from my house reaching your house. Though perhaps she threw it away before it even got to you.'

'I remember it,' he said. 'I did think of you. But I didn't think you sent it, because the post mark was Croydon.'

'Oh,' she said, weakly. 'You got it. You did get it. Oh Lord, how alarmingly faithful we have both been.'

'Did you expect us not to be? We swore that we would be. Oh look, my darling here's your lunch, are you still eating cheese omelettes every day, now that really *is* what I call alarming consistency. And I haven't even ordered. What shall I have, what about some Moussaka, I always used to like that, it was always rather nice, in its own disgusting way. One Moussaka, please.'

'I *like* cheese omelettes,' she said. 'And after all, I don't see why one shouldn't have the same lunch every day. I mean, most people always have the same breakfast, don't they. Nobody complains when people go on eating toast and marmalade, do they?'

'I wasn't complaining,' he said. 'I was just remarking. I like your habits, I always did. You don't think I've changed, do you?'

'How should I know?' she said, and ate her first mouthful. Then she put down her knife and fork, and said, reflectively, 'You know, from my point of view at least, the whole business was quite unnecessary. What I mean is, Oliver hadn't the faintest suspicion. The thought of you had never even crossed his mind. Which, considering how ludicrously careless we were, is quite astonishing. We could have carried on forever, and he'd never have known. He was far too preoccupied himself with his own affairs to notice. I got it all out of him in the end, and I forgave him very nicely, and do you know what he said at the end of it all, at the end of all my forgiveness? He said that he'd had his suspicions that I'd been carrying on at the time with Robert Bennington. Have you ever heard of such a thing? I was so horrified by the very idea that I flew into a terrible rage and defended myself so vehemently that I quite frightened him. I mean to say, Robert, what a choice that would have been, what a ghastly mistake that would have been. I was never so offended in my life. What a pleasure it was, all that virtuous indignation, it was like getting rid of three years guilt, I can't tell you what a relief it was.'

'Robert Bennington,' he said, 'Robert Bennington. Who was he? Was he that tall fellow in films, with that fat wife?'

'Oh,' she said, 'he's nobody, just nobody, I mean he's quite nice, but as for anyone thinking him more than quite nice . . .', and she noticed as she spoke that her voice had taken on, somehow, as with age-old habit, those provocative, defensive tones in which they would always discuss others, other people, the stray characters with which they would decorate from time to time their charmed and passionate dialogue and she knew that he, in reply, would use that note of confident and yet in some way truly, dreadfully suspicious jealousy.

'I seem to remember,' he said, sure enough, 'that Robert Bennington took you out to the cinema one evening, when Oliver was in Ireland. That was him, wasn't it?'

'You remember everything,' she said.

'And you said that you thought of me when you were in the cinema, but you didn't, I know you didn't,' he said.

'Oh, I did, I did,' she protested. 'I thought of you everywhere, and what better place to think of you than in the cinema, especially when with a dull fellow like Robert?'

'I thought you said he was quite nice,' he said, and she started to say 'Yes, he is quite nice,' and then instead she started to laugh, and said,

'You are absurd, darling, it was Oliver that introduced that Robert motif, there's no need for *you* to start on it, especially so long after the event, I mean any concern you might now feel would be well and truly irrelevant.'

'After what event?' he said, incurable.

'No event, there wasn't any event,' she said, 'the whole point of the story was that Oliver had got it so wrong, so pointlessly wrong, I mean suspecting Robert instead of you . . .'

'It's no good,' he said, 'whatever you say, I simply can't prevent myself feeling annoyed that anyone might have had any reason for thinking that you were in love with anyone but me . . .' and then, the word love being mentioned, that final syllable, they were both reduced to silence, and they sat there, still, in their ridiculous proximity, until she managed to take another mouthful of her omelette.

'You know,' he said, when the movement of her jaws had sufficiently disrupted the connection, 'all those continual threats of separation, that was really corrupt, you know, that was as bad as nagging. I feel bad about it now, looking back. Don't you?'

'How do you mean, bad about it?' she said.

'I feel we ought to have been able to do better than that. Though come to think of it, it was you that did nearly all the threatening. Every time I saw you, you said it was for the last time. Every time. And I must have seen you six days in every week for over a year. You can't have meant it, each time.'

'I did mean it,' she said. 'I did mean it. Though each time I stopped meaning it and fixed up the next time to see you, I felt that of course I hadn't meant it. By then again I did mean it, because I finally did it. Didn't I?'

'You mean we did it,' he said. 'You couldn't have done it without my help. If I'd rung you, if I'd written to you, it would have started all over again.'

'Do you really think so?' she said, sadly, without malice, without recrimination. 'Yes, I suppose you might be right. I could never decide whether I could do it on my own or not. Evidently I couldn't. It takes two to part, just as it takes two to love.'

'It was corrupt, though,' he said, 'to make ourselves live under that perpetual threat.'

'Yes,' she said, 'but remember how lovely it was, how horribly lovely, each time that one relented. Each time one said I'll never see you again, all right I'll meet you tomorrow in the usual place at half past one. It was lovely.'

'Lovely but wicked,' he said.

'Oh, that sensation,' she said, 'that sensation of defeat, that was so lovely, every time, every time you touched me, every time I saw you ... and I felt so sure, so entirely sure that what you felt was what I felt, that you were as weak as me, and as capable of enduring such ghastly self-inflicted wounds ... Lord, we were so alike, and to think that when I first knew you I couldn't think of anything to say to you at all, I thought you came from another world, that we had nothing in common at all nothing at all except, well, except you know what, I feel it would be dangerous even to mention it, even now. Oh darling, what a disaster, our being so alike.'

'It was that that made it so hard,' he said. 'The reverse of the irresistible force and unbreakable object principle, whatever that might be.'

'Two objects most infinitely breakable, perhaps,' she said.

'I liked it though,' he said. 'I liked it, breaking up together. Better than having it done to one, better than doing it.'

'Better?'

'Perhaps even after all less corrupt,' he said.

'Yes, but more seriously incurable,' she said. And silence threatening to fall once more, she said quickly. 'Anyway, tell me what you're doing round here. I mean to say, one has to have some reason, for coming to a place like this.'

'I told you,' he said, 'I was looking for you.'

'You *are* a liar,' she said, smiling, amazed that she still even here could allow herself to be amused: indeed, could not prevent herself from smiling.

'What are you doing here then?' he said.

'Oh, I had a perfectly good reason,' she said, 'perfectly good, though rather embarrassing, I don't know if I'll tell you, but I suppose I will. You know that false front tooth? Well yesterday morning I lost it, and I've got to be on a television thing tonight, and the thought of being without a tooth was so alarming so I went to my dentist and he made them make me a new one, and I had to come round here to the warehouse to pick it up.'

'Have you got it in?'

'Yes,' she said, and turned to face him, smiling, lifting her upper lip. 'Look, there it is.'

'Do you mean,' he said, 'that if you'd had lunch *before* collecting your tooth, I would at least have seen you without it in?'

'Theoretically,' she said, 'but it wouldn't in fact have been possible, because how could I ever have had my lunch in a public place without my front tooth?'

'I'd hardly call this a public place,' he said. 'What a vain woman you are. You always were.'

'I don't see anything wrong with vanity,' she said. 'And look, if you really want to see me without my tooth, there you are,' and she took it out, and turned to him, and showed him.

'You look lovely,' he said. 'You look like a school child. You look like my daughter, she's got three missing at the moment.'

'You still haven't told me what you're doing here,' she said, putting her plate back again. 'I bet you haven't got as good a reason as me. Mine is entirely convincing, don't you think? I mean, where else could I have lunch? I think my reason clears me entirely of any suspicion of any kind, don't you?'

'Any suspicion of sentiment?'

'That's what I meant.'

He thought for a moment, and then he said,

'I had to call on a man about my Income Tax. Look, here's his address,' And he got an envelope out of his pocket and showed her.

'Ah,' she said.

'You see,' he said.

'See what?' she said.

'I came here on purpose,' he said. 'To think of you. I could have had lunch at lots of places between London Wall and here.'

'Yes, I suppose so,' she said, 'but you always were rather conservative about eating places. Suspicious, almost. You didn't come here because of me, you came here because it's the only place you know about.'

'It comes to the same thing,' he said.

'No, it doesn't,' she said, firmly. She felt creeping upon her the familiar illusion of control, created as always before by a concentration upon trivialities, which could no longer even momentarily disguise the gravity of any outcome: and she reflected that their conversations had always so closely followed the patterns of their dialogues in bed, and that these idle points of concentration were like those frivolous, delaying gestures in which she would turn aside, in which he would lie still and stare at the ceiling, hardly touching her, not daring, as he said, to touch her, and thus merely deferring, in their own studiously developed amorous dialectic, the inevitable: and thinking this, and able to live only in the deferment, for now there was no inevitability, no outcome that she could see, she said, eating her last chip,

'And how are your children?'

'They're fine,' he said, 'fine. Saul got into Grammar School, and starts next year. We were pleased about that. What about yours?'

'Oh, they're all right too. I've had some dreadful nights with Laura recently, I must say I thought I was through with all that, I mean the child's five now, but she says she can't sleep and has these dreadful nightmares, so she's been every night in my bed for the last fortnight. It's wearing me out. Then in the morning she just laughs. And then at night it starts all over again. She doesn't kick, she's not as bony and awful as Fred used to be, it's just that I can't sleep with anyone else in the bed.'

'What does Oliver say?' he asked, and she said, without thinking, having said it so often to others,

'Oh, I don't sleep with Oliver any more,' and realizing as she said it precisely what she had said, wondering how she could have made such a mistake, and wondering how to get out of it. But fortunately at that instant his Moussaka arrived, and the depositing of the plate and the redeployment of cutlery made it unnecessary to pursue the subject. Though once it had become unnecessary, she regretted the subject's disappearance: and she thought of saying what was no less than the truth, what was the truth itself: she thought of saying that she had slept with nobody since she had slept with him, that for three years she had slept alone, and was quite prepared to sleep alone forever. But she was not sure, not entirely sure that he would want to hear it, and she knew that such a remark once made could never be retracted, so she said nothing.

He stared at his Moussaka, at the browned yellow crust.

'It looks all right,' he said, and took a mouthful, and chewed it, and then he put his fork down and said, 'Oh Lord, oh Lord, what a Proustian experience. I can't believe it. I can't believe that I'm sitting here with you. It tastes of you, that stuff, oh God it reminds me of you. You look so beautiful, you look so lovely, my darling, Oh God I loved you so much. I really loved you, do you believe me that I really loved you?'

'I haven't slept with anyone,' she said, 'since I last slept with you.'

'Oh darling,' he said: and she could feel herself fainting and sighing away, drifting downwards on that fatefully descending eddying spiral, like Paulo and Francesca in hell, helpless, the mutually entwined drifting fall of all true lovers, unresisting, finally unresisting, as though three years of solitude had been nothing but a pause, nothing but a long breath before this final acknowledgement of nature, damnation and destiny; she turned towards him, and said, 'Oh my darling, I love you, what can I do, I love you,' and he with the same breath said, 'I love you, I all the time love you, I want you,' and they kissed there, their faces already so close that little inclination was needed, they kissed there above the Moussaka and chips, because they believed in such things, because that was what they believed in, because, like disastrous romantics, they habitually connived with fate by remembering the names of restaurants and the streets they had once walked along as lovers. Those who forget, forget, he said to her later: and those who do not forget will meet again.

The Dead

JAMES JOYCE

LILY, THE CARETAKER'S DAUGHTER, was literally run off her feet. Hardly
had she brought one gentleman into the little pantry behind the
office on the ground floor and helped him off with his overcoat, than
the wheezy hall-door bell clanged again and she had to scamper along
the bare hallway to let in another guest. It was well for her she had
not to attend to the ladies also. But Miss Kate and Miss Julia had
thought of that and had converted the bathroom upstairs into a ladies'
dressing-room. Miss Kate and Miss Julia were there, gossiping and
laughing and fussing, walking after each other to the head of the
stairs, peering down over the banisters and calling down to Lily to
ask her who had come.

It was always a great affair, the Misses Morkan's annual dance.
Everybody who knew them came to it, members of the family, old
friends of the family, the members of Julia's choir, any of Kate's
pupils that were grown up enough, and even some of Mary Jane's
pupils too. Never once had it fallen flat. For years and years it had
gone off in splendid style, as long as anyone could remember; ever
since Kate and Julia, after the death of their brother Pat, had left the
house in Stoney Batter and taken Mary Jane, their only niece, to live
with them in the dark, gaunt house on Usher's Island, the upper
part of which they had rented from Mr Fulham, the corn-factor on
the ground floor. That was a good thirty years ago if it was a day.
Mary Jane, who was then a little girl in short clothes, was now the
main prop of the household, for she had the organ in Haddington
Road. She had been through the Academy and gave a pupils' concert
every year in the upper room of the Antient Concert Rooms. Many
of her pupils belonged to the better-class families on the Kingstown
and Dalkey line. Old as they were, her aunts also did their share.
Julia, though she was quite grey, was still the leading soprano in
Adam and Eve's, and Kate, being too feeble to go about much, gave

music lessons to beginners on the old square piano in the back room. Lily, the caretaker's daughter, did housemaid's work for them. Though their life was modest, they believed in eating well; the best of everything: diamond-bone sirloins, three-shilling tea and the best bottled stout. But Lily seldom made a mistake in the orders, so that she got on well with her three mistresses. They were fussy, that was all. But the only thing they would not stand was back answers.

Of course, they had good reason to be fussy on such a night. And then it was long after ten o'clock and yet there was no sign of Gabriel and his wife. Besides they were dreadfully afraid that Freddy Malins might turn up screwed. They would not wish for worlds that any of Mary Jane's pupils should see him under the influence; and when he was like that it was sometimes very hard to manage him. Freddy Malins always came late, but they wondered what could be keeping Gabriel: and that was what brought them every two minutes to the banisters to ask Lily had Gabriel or Freddy come.

'O, Mr Conroy,' said Lily to Gabriel when she opened the door for him, 'Miss Kate and Miss Julia thought you were never coming. Good night, Mrs Conroy.'

'I'll engage they did,' said Gabriel, 'but they forget that my wife here takes three mortal hours to dress herself.'

He stood on the mat, scraping the snow from his goloshes, while Lily led his wife to the foot of the stairs and called out:

'Miss Kate, here's Mrs Conroy.'

Kate and Julia came toddling down the dark stairs at once. Both of them kissed Gabriel's wife, said she must be perished alive, and asked was Gabriel with her.

'Here I am as right as the mail, Aunt Kate! Go on up. I'll follow,' called out Gabriel from the dark.

He continued scraping his feet vigorously while the three women went upstairs, laughing, to the ladies' dressing-room. A light fringe of snow lay like a cape on the shoulders of his overcoat and like toecaps on the toes of his goloshes; and, as the buttons of his overcoat slipped with a squeaking noise through the snow-stiffened frieze, a cold, fragrant air from out-of-doors escaped from crevices and folds.

'Is it snowing again, Mr Conroy?' asked Lily.

She had preceded him into the pantry to help him off with his overcoat. Gabriel smiled at the three syllables she had given his surname and glanced at her. She was a slim, growing girl, pale in complexion and with hay-coloured hair. The gas in the pantry made her look still paler. Gabriel had known her when she was a child and used to sit on the lowest step nursing a rag doll.

'Yes, Lily,' he answered, 'and I think we're in for a night of it.'

He looked up at the pantry ceiling, which was shaking with the stamping and shuffling of feet on the floor above, listened for a moment to the piano and then glanced at the girl, who was folding his overcoat carefully at the end of a shelf.

'Tell me, Lily,' he said in a friendly tone, 'do you still go to school?'

'O no, sir,' she answered. 'I'm done schooling this year and more.'

'O, then,' said Gabriel gaily, 'I suppose we'll be going to your wedding one of these fine days with your young man, eh?'

The girl glanced back at him over her shoulder and said with great bitterness:

'The men that is now is only all palaver and what they can get out of you.'

Gabriel coloured, as if he felt he had made a mistake, and, without looking at her, kicked off his goloshes and flicked actively with his muffler at his patent-leather shoes.

He was a stout, tallish young man. The high colour of his cheeks pushed upwards even to his forehead, where it scattered itself in a few formless patches of pale red; and on his hairless face there scintillated restlessly the polished lenses and the bright gilt rims of the glasses which screened his delicate and restless eyes. His glossy black hair was parted in the middle and brushed in a long curve behind his ears where it curled slightly beneath the groove left by his hat.

When he had flicked lustre into his shoes he stood up and pulled his waistcoat down more tightly on his plump body. Then he took a coin rapidly from his pocket.

'O Lily,' he said, thrusting it into her hands, 'it's Christmas-time, isn't it? Just . . . here's a little . . .'

He walked rapidly towards the door.

'O no, sir!' cried the girl, following him. 'Really, sir, I wouldn't take it.'

'Christmas-time! Christmas-time!' said Gabriel, almost trotting to the stairs and waving his hand to her in deprecation.

The girl, seeing that he had gained the stairs, called out after him:

'Well, thank you, sir.'

He waited outside the drawing-room door until the waltz should finish, listening to the skirts that swept against it and to the shuffling of feet. He was still discomposed by the girl's bitter and sudden retort. It had cast a gloom over him which he tried to dispel by arranging his cuffs and the bows of his tie. He then took from his waistcoat pocket a little paper and glanced at the headings he had made for his speech. He was undecided about the lines from Robert Browning, for he feared they would be above the heads of his hearers. Some quotation that they would recognize from Shakespeare or from the Melodies would be better. The indelicate clacking of the men's heels and the shuffling of their soles reminded him that their grade of culture differed from his. He would only make himself ridiculous by quoting poetry to them which they could not understand. They would think that he was airing his superior education. He would fail with them just as he had failed with the girl in the pantry. He had taken up a wrong tone. His whole speech was a mistake from first to last, an utter failure.

Just then his aunts and his wife came out of the ladies' dressing-room. His aunts were two small, plainly dressed old women. Aunt Julia was an inch or so the taller. Her hair, drawn low over the tops of her ears, was grey; and grey also, with darker shadows, was her large flaccid face. Though she was stout in build and stood erect, her slow eyes and parted lips gave her the appearance of a woman who did not know where she was or where she was going. Aunt Kate was more vivacious. Her face, healthier than her sister's, was all puckers and creases, like a shrivelled red apple, and her hair, braided in the same old-fashioned way, had not lost its ripe nut colour.

They both kissed Gabriel frankly. He was their favourite nephew, the son of their dead elder sister, Ellen, who had married T.J. Conroy of the Port and Docks.

'Gretta tells me you're not going to take a cab back to Monkstown tonight, Gabriel,' said Aunt Kate.

'No,' said Gabriel, turning to his wife, 'we had quite enough of that last year, hadn't we? Don't you remember, Aunt Kate, what a cold Gretta got out of it? Cab windows rattling all the way, and the east wind blowing in after we passed Merrion. Very jolly it was. Gretta caught a dreadful cold.'

Aunt Kate frowned severely and nodded her head at every word.

'Quite right, Gabriel, quite right,' she said. 'You can't be too careful.'

'But as for Gretta there,' said Gabriel, 'she'd walk home in the snow if she were let.'

Mrs Conroy laughed.

'Don't mind him, Aunt Kate,' she said. 'He's really an awful bother, what with green shades for Tom's eyes at night and making him do the dumb-bells, and forcing Eva to eat the stirabout. The poor child! And she simply hates the sight of it!... O, but you'll never guess what he makes me wear now!'

She broke out into a peal of laughter and glanced at her husband, whose admiring and happy eyes had been wandering from her dress to her face and hair. The two aunts laughed heartily, too, for Gabriel's solicitude was a standing joke with them.

'Goloshes!' said Mrs Conroy. 'That's the latest. Whenever it's wet underfoot I must put on my goloshes. Tonight even, he wanted me to put them on, but I wouldn't. The next thing he'll buy me will be a diving suit.'

Gabriel laughed nervously and patted his tie reassuringly, while Aunt Kate nearly doubled herself, so heartily did she enjoy the joke. The smile soon faded from Aunt Julia's face and her mirthless eyes were directed towards her nephew's face. After a pause she asked:

'And what are goloshes, Gabriel?'

'Goloshes, Julia!' exclaimed her sister. 'Goodness me, don't you know what goloshes are? You wear them over your... over your boots, Gretta, isn't it?'

'Yes,' said Mrs Conroy. 'Gutta-percha things. We both have a pair now. Gabriel says everyone wears them on the Continent.'

'O, on the Continent,' murmured Aunt Julia, nodding her head slowly.

Gabriel knitted his brows and said, as if he were slightly angered:

'It's nothing very wonderful, but Gretta thinks it very funny, because she says the word reminds her of Christy Minstrels.'

'But tell me, Gabriel,' said Aunt Kate, with brisk tact. 'Of course, you've seen about the room. Gretta was saying...'

'O, the room is all right,' replied Gabriel. 'I've taken one in the Gresham.'

'To be sure,' said Aunt Kate, 'by far the best thing to do. And the children, Gretta, you're not anxious about them?'

'O, for one night,' said Mrs Conroy. 'Besides, Bessie will look after them.'

'To be sure,' said Aunt Kate again. 'What a comfort it is to have a girl like that, one you can depend on! There's that Lily, I'm sure I don't know what has come over her lately. She's not the girl she was at all.'

Gabriel was about to ask his aunt some questions on this point, but she broke off suddenly to gaze after her sister, who had wandered down the stairs and was craning her neck over the banisters.

'Now, I ask you,' she said almost testily, 'where is Julia going? Julia! Julia! Where are you going?'

Julia, who had gone half-way down one flight, came back and announced blandly:

'Here's Freddy.'

At the same moment a clapping of hands and a final flourish of the pianist told that the waltz had ended. The drawing-room door was opened from within and some couples came out. Aunt Kate drew Gabriel aside hurriedly and whispered into his ear:

'Slip down, Gabriel, like a good fellow and see if he's all right, and don't let him up if he's screwed. I'm sure he's screwed. I'm sure he is.'

Gabriel went to the stairs and listened over the banisters. He could hear two persons talking in the pantry. Then he recognized Freddy Malins' laugh. He went down the stairs noisily.

'It's such a relief,' said Aunt Kate to Mrs Conroy, 'that Gabriel is here. I always feel easier in my mind when he's here . . . Julia, there's Miss Daly and Miss Power will take some refreshment. Thanks for your beautiful waltz, Miss Daly. It made lovely time.'

A tall wizen-faced man, with a stiff grizzled moustache and swarthy skin, who was passing out with his partner, said:

'And may we have some refreshment, too, Miss Morkan?'

'Julia,' said Aunt Kate summarily, 'and here's Mr Browne and Miss Furlong. Take them in, Julia, with Miss Daly and Miss Power.'

'I'm the man for the ladies,' said Mr Browne, pursing his lips until his moustache bristled, and smiling in all his wrinkles. 'You know, Miss Morkan, the reason they are so fond of me is –'

He did not finish his sentence, but, seeing that Aunt Kate was out of earshot, at once led the three young ladies into the back room. The middle of the room was occupied by two square tables placed end to end, and on these Aunt Julia and the caretaker were straightening and smoothing a large cloth. On the sideboard were arrayed dishes and plates, and glasses and bundles of knives and forks and spoons. The top of the closed square piano served also as a sideboard for viands and sweets. At a smaller sideboard in one corner two young men were standing, drinking hop-bitters.

Mr Browne led his charges thither and invited them all, in jest, to some ladies' punch, hot, strong, and sweet. As they said they never took anything strong, he opened three bottles of lemonade for them. Then he asked one of the young men to move aside, and, taking hold of the decanter, filled out for himself a goodly measure of whisky. The young men eyed him respectfully while he took a trial sip.

'God help me,' he said, smiling, 'it's the doctor's orders.'

His wizened face broke into a broader smile, and the three young ladies laughed in musical echo to his pleasantry, swaying their bodies to and fro, with nervous jerks of their shoulders. The boldest said:

'O, now, Mr Browne, I'm sure the doctor never ordered anything of the kind.'

Mr Browne took another sip of his whisky and said, with sidling mimicry:

'Well, you see, I'm the famous Mrs Cassidy, who is reported to have said: "Now, Mary Grimes, if I don't take it, make me take it, for I feel I want it."'

His hot face had leaned forward a little too confidentially and he had assumed a very low Dublin accent, so that the young ladies, with one instinct, received his speech in silence. Miss Furlong, who was one of Mary Jane's pupils, asked Miss Daly what was the name of the pretty waltz she had played; and Mr Browne, seeing that he was ignored, turned promptly to the two young men, who were more appreciative.

A red-faced young woman, dressed in pansy, came into the room, excitedly clapping her hands and crying:

'Quadrilles! Quadrilles!'

Close on her heels came Aunt Kate, crying:

'Two gentlemen and three ladies, Mary Jane!'

'O, here's Mr Bergin and Mr Kerrigan,' said Mary Jane. 'Mr Kerrigan, will you take Miss Power? Miss Furlong, may I get you a partner, Mr Bergin. O, that'll just do now.'

'Three ladies, Mary Jane,' said Aunt Kate.

The two young gentlemen asked the ladies if they might have the pleasure, and Mary Jane turned to Miss Daly.

'O, Miss Daly, you're really awfully good, after playing for the last two dances, but really we're so short of ladies tonight.'

'I don't mind in the least, Miss Morkan.'

'But I've a nice partner for you, Mr Bartell D'Arcy, the tenor. I'll get him to sing later on. All Dublin is raving about him.'

'Lovely voice, lovely voice!' said Aunt Kate.

As the piano had twice begun the prelude to the first figure Mary Jane led her recruits quickly from the room. They had hardly gone when Aunt Julia wandered slowly into the room, looking behind her at something.

'What is the matter, Julia?' asked Aunt Kate anxiously. 'Who is it?'

Julia, who was carrying in a column of table-napkins, turned to her sister and said, simply, as if the question had surprised her:

'It's only Freddy, Kate, and Gabriel with him.'

In fact, right behind her Gabriel could be seen piloting Freddy Malins across the landing. The latter, a young man of about forty, was of Gabriel's size and build, with very round shoulders. His face was fleshy and pallid, touched with colour only at the thick hanging lobes of his ears and at the wide wings of his nose. He had coarse features, a blunt nose, a convex and receding brow, tumid and protruded lips. His heavy-lidded eyes and the disorder of his scanty hair made him look sleepy. He was laughing heartily in a high key at a story which he had been telling Gabriel on the stairs and at the same time rubbing the knuckles of his left fist backwards and forwards into his left eye.

'Good evening, Freddy,' said Aunt Julia.

Freddy Malins bade the Misses Morkan good evening in what seemed an off-hand fashion by reason of the habitual catch in his voice and then, seeing that Mr Browne was grinning at him from the sideboard, crossed the room on rather shaky legs and began to repeat in an undertone the story he had just told to Gabriel.

'He's not so bad, is he?' said Aunt Kate to Gabriel.

Gabriel's brows were dark, but he raised them quickly and answered:

'O, no, hardly noticeable.'

'Now, isn't he a terrible fellow!' she said. 'And his poor mother made him take the pledge on New Year's Eve. But come on, Gabriel, into the drawing-room.'

Before leaving the room with Gabriel she signalled to Mr Browne by frowning and shaking her forefinger in warning to and fro. Mr Browne nodded in answer and, when she had gone, said to Freddy Malins:

'Now, then, Teddy, I'm going to fill you out a good glass of lemonade just to buck you up.'

Freddy Malins, who was nearing the climax of his story, waved the offer aside impatiently, but Mr Browne, having first called Freddy Malins' attention to a disarray in his dress, filled out and handed him a full glass of lemonade. Freddy Malins' left hand accepted the glass mechanically, his right hand being engaged in the mechanical readjustment of his dress. Mr Browne, whose face was once more wrinkling with mirth, poured out for himself a glass of whisky while Freddy Malins exploded, before he had well reached the climax of his story, in a kink of high-pitched bronchitic laughter and, setting down his untasted and overflowing glass, began to run the knuckles of his left fist backwards and forwards into his left eye, repeating words of his last phrase as well as his fit of laughter would allow him.

Gabriel could not listen while Mary Jane was playing her Academy piece, full of runs and difficult passages, to the hushed drawing-room. He liked music, but the piece she was playing had no melody for him and he doubted whether it had any melody for the other listeners, though they had begged Mary Jane to play something. Four young men, who had come from the refreshment-room to stand in the doorway at the sound of the piano, had gone away quietly in couples after a few minutes. The only persons who seemed to follow the music were Mary Jane herself, her hands racing along the keyboard or lifted from it at the pauses like those of a priestess in momentary imprecation, and Aunt Kate standing at her elbow to turn the page.

Gabriel's eyes, irritated by the floor, which glittered with beeswax under the heavy chandelier, wandered to the wall above the piano. A picture of the balcony scene in *Romeo and Juliet* hung there and beside it was a picture of the two murdered princes in the Tower which Aunt Julia had worked in red, blue, and brown wools when she was a girl. Probably in the school they had gone to as girls that kind of work had been taught for one year. His mother had worked for him as a birthday present a waistcoat of purple tabinet, with little foxes' heads upon it, lined with brown satin and having round mulberry buttons. It was strange that his mother had had no musical talent, though Aunt Kate used to call her the brains carrier of the Morkan family. Both she and Julia had always seemed a little proud of their serious and matronly sister. Her photograph stood before the pier-glass. She had an open book on her knees and was pointing out something in it to Constantine who, dressed in a man-o'-war suit, lay at her feet. It was she who had chosen the names of her sons, for she was very sensible of the dignity of family life. Thanks to her, Constantine was now senior curate in Balbriggan and, thanks to her, Gabriel himself had taken his degree in the Royal University. A shadow passed over his face as he remembered her sullen opposition to his marriage. Some slighting phrases she had used still rankled in his memory; once she had spoken of Gretta as being country cute and that was not true of Gretta at all. It was Gretta who had nursed her during all her last long illness in their house at Monkstown.

He knew that Mary Jane must be near the end of her piece, for she was playing again the opening melody with runs of scales after every bar, and while he waited for the end the resentment died down in his heart. The piece ended with a trill of octaves in the treble and a final deep octave in the bass. Great applause greeted Mary Jane as, blushing and rolling up her music nervously, she escaped from the room. The most vigorous clapping came from the four young men in the doorway who had gone away to the refreshment-room at the beginning of the piece but had come back when the piano had stopped.

Lancers were arranged. Gabriel found himself partnered with Miss Ivors. She was a frank-mannered, talkative young lady, with a freckled face and prominent brown eyes. She did not wear a low-cut bodice, and the large brooch which was fixed in the front of her collar bore on it an Irish device and motto.

When they had taken their places she said abruptly:

'I have a crow to pluck with you.'

'With me?' said Gabriel.

She nodded her head gravely.

'What is it?' asked Gabriel, smiling at her solemn manner.

'Who is G.C.?' answered Miss Ivors, turning her eyes upon him.

Gabriel coloured and was about to knit his brows, as if he did not understand, when she said bluntly:

'O, innocent Amy! I have found out that you write for *The Daily Express*. Now, aren't you ashamed of yourself?'

'Why should I be ashamed of myself?' asked Gabriel, blinking his eyes and trying to smile.

'Well, I'm ashamed of you,' said Miss Ivors frankly. 'To say you'd write for a paper like that. I didn't think you were a West Briton.'

A look of perplexity appeared on Gabriel's face. It was true that he wrote a literary column every Wednesday in *The Daily Express*, for which he was paid fifteen shillings. But that did not make him a West Briton surely. The books he received for review were almost more welcome than the paltry cheque. He loved to feel the covers and turn over the pages of newly printed books. Nearly every day when his teaching in the college was ended he used to wander down the quays to the second-hand booksellers, to Hickey's on Bachelor's Walk, to Webb's or Massey's on Aston's Quay, or to O'Clohissey's in the by-street. He did not know how to meet her charge. He wanted to say that literature was above politics. But they were friends of many years' standing and their careers had been parallel, first at the University and then as teachers: he could not risk a grandiose phrase with her. He continued blinking his eyes and trying to smile and murmured lamely that he saw nothing political in writing reviews of books.

When their turn to cross had come he was still perplexed and inattentive. Miss Ivors promptly took his hand in a warm grasp and said in a soft friendly tone:

'Of course, I was only joking. Come, we cross now.'

When they were together again she spoke of the University question and Gabriel felt more at ease. A friend of hers had shown her his review of Browning's poems. That was how she had found out the secret: but she liked the review immensely. Then she said suddenly:

'O, Mr Conroy, will you come for an excursion to the Aran Isles this summer? We're going to stay there a whole month. It will be splendid out in the Atlantic. You ought to come. Mr Clancy is coming, and Mr Kilkelly and Kathleen Kearney. It would be splendid for Gretta too if she'd come. She's from Connacht, isn't she?'

'Her people are,' said Gabriel shortly.

'But you will come, won't you?' said Miss Ivors, laying her warm hand eagerly on his arm.

'The fact is,' said Gabriel, 'I have just arranged to go –'

'Go where?' asked Miss Ivors.

'Well, you know, every year I go for a cycling tour with some fellows and so –'

'But where?' asked Miss Ivors.

'Well, we usually go to France or Belgium or perhaps Germany,' said Gabriel awkwardly.

'And why do you go to France and Belgium,' said Miss Ivors, 'instead of visiting your own land?'

'Well,' said Gabriel, 'it's partly to keep in touch with the languages and partly for a change.'

'And haven't you your own language to keep in touch with – Irish?' asked Miss Ivors.

'Well,' said Gabriel, 'if it comes to that, you know, Irish is not my language.'

Their neighbours had turned to listen to the cross-examination. Gabriel glanced right and left nervously and tried to keep his good humour under the ordeal, which was making a blush invade his forehead.

'And haven't you your own land to visit,' continued Miss Ivors, 'that you know nothing of, your own people, and your own country?'

'O, to tell you the truth,' retored Gabriel suddenly, 'I'm sick of my own country, sick of it!'

'Why?' asked Miss Ivors.

Gabriel did not answer, for his retort had heated him.

'Why?' repeated Miss Ivors.

They had to go visiting together and, as he had not answered her, Miss Ivors said warmly:

'Of course, you've no answer.'

Gabriel tried to cover his agitation by taking part in the dance with great energy. He avoided her eyes, for he had seen a sour expression on her face. But when they met in the long chain he was surprised to feel his hand firmly pressed. She looked at him from under her brows for a moment quizzically until he smiled. Then, just as the chain was about to start again, she stood on tiptoe and whispered into his ear:

'West Briton!'

When the lancers were over Gabriel went away to a remote corner of the room where Freddy Malins' mother was sitting. She was a stout, feeble old woman with white hair. Her voice had a catch in it like her son's and she stuttered slightly. She had been told that Freddy had come and that he was nearly all right. Gabriel asked her whether she had had a good crossing. She lived with her married daughter in Glasgow and came to Dublin on a visit once a year. She answered placidly that she had had a beautiful crossing and that the captain had been most attentive to her. She spoke also of the beautiful house her daughter kept in Glasgow, and of all the friends they had there. While her tongue rambled on Gabriel tried to banish from his mind all memory of the unpleasant incident with Miss Ivors. Of course the girl, or woman, or whatever she was, was an enthusiast, but there was a time for all things. Perhaps he ought not to have answered her like that. But she had no right to call him a West Briton before people, even in joke. She had tried to make him ridiculous before people, heckling him and staring at him with her rabbit's eyes.

He saw his wife making her way towards him through the waltzing couples. When she reached him she said into his ear:

'Gabriel, Aunt Kate wants to know won't you carve the goose as usual. Miss Daly will carve the ham and I'll do the pudding.'

'All right,' said Gabriel.

'She's sending in the younger ones first as soon as this waltz is over so that we'll have the table to ourselves.'

'Were you dancing?' asked Gabriel.

'Of course I was. Didn't you see me? What row had you with Molly Ivors?'

'No row. Why? Did she say so?'

'Something like that. I'm trying to get that Mr D'Arcy to sing. He's full of conceit, I think.'

'There was no row,' said Gabriel moodily, 'only she wanted me to go for a trip to the west of Ireland and I said I wouldn't.'

His wife clasped her hands excitedly and gave a little jump.

'O, do go, Gabriel,' she cried. 'I'd love to see Galway again.'

'You can go if you like,' said Gabriel coldly.

She looked at him for a moment, then turned to Mrs Malins and said:

'There's a nice husband for you, Mrs Malins.'

While she was threading her way back across the room Mrs Malins, without adverting to the interruption, went on to tell Gabriel what beautiful places there were in Scotland and beautiful scenery. Her son-in-law brought them every year to the lakes and they used to go fishing. Her son-in-law was a splendid fisher. One day he caught a beautiful big fish and the man in the hotel cooked it for their dinner.

Gabriel hardly heard what she said. Now that supper was coming near he began to think again about his speech and about the quotation. When he saw Freddy Malins coming across the room to visit his mother Gabriel left the chair free for him and retired into the embrasure of the window. The room had already cleared and from the back room came the clatter of plates and knives. Those who still remained in the drawing-room seemed tired of dancing and were conversing quietly in little groups. Gabriel's warm, trembling fingers tapped the cold pane of the window. How cool it must be outside! How pleasant it would be to walk out alone, first along by the river and then through the park! The snow would be lying on the branches of the trees and forming a bright cap on the top of the Wellington Monument. How much more pleasant it would be there than at the supper-table!

He ran over the headings of his speech: Irish hospitality, sad memories, the Three Graces, Paris, the quotation from Browning. He repeated to himself a phrase he had written in his review: 'One feels that one is listening to a thought-tormented music.' Miss Ivors had praised the review. Was she sincere? Had she really any life of her own behind all her propagandism? There had never been any ill-feeling between them until that night. It unnerved him to think that she would be at the supper-table, looking up at him, while he spoke, with her critical quizzing eyes. Perhaps she would not be sorry to see him fail in his speech. An idea came into his mind and gave him courage. He would say, alluding to Aunt Kate and Aunt Julia: 'Ladies and Gentlemen, the generation which is now on the wane among us may have had its faults, but for my part I think it had certain qualities of hospitality, of humour, of humanity, which the new and very serious and hyper-educated generation that is growing up around us seems to me to lack.' Very good: that was one for Miss Ivors. What did he care that his aunts were only two ignorant old women?

A murmur in the room attracted his attention. Mr Browne was advancing from the door, gallantly escorting Aunt Julia, who leaned upon his arm, smiling and hanging her head. An irregular musketry of applause escorted her also as far as the piano and then, as Mary Jane seated herself on the stool, and Aunt Julia, no longer smiling, half turned so as to pitch her voice fairly in the room, gradually ceased. Gabriel recognized the prelude. It was that of an old song of Aunt Julia's – 'Arrayed for the Bridal'. Her voice, strong and clear in tone, attacked with great spirit the runs which embellish the air, and though she sang very rapidly she did not miss even the smallest of the grace notes. To follow the voice, without looking at the singer's face, was to feel and share the excitement of swift and secure flight.

Gabriel applauded loudly with all the others at the close of the song, and loud applause was borne in from the invisible supper-table. It sounded so genuine that a little colour struggled into Aunt Julia's face as she bent to replace in the music-stand the old leather-bound songbook that had her initials on the cover. Freddy Malins, who had listened with his head perched sideways to hear her better, was still applauding when everyone else had ceased and talking animatedly to his mother, who nodded her head gravely and slowly in acquiescence. At last, when he could clap no more, he stood up suddenly and hurried across the room to Aunt Julia whose hand he seized and held in both his hands, shaking it when words failed him or the catch in his voice proved too much for him.

'I was just telling my mother,' he said, 'I never heard you sing so well, never. No, I never heard your voice so good as it is tonight. Now! Would you believe that now? That's the truth. Upon my word and honour that's the truth. I never heard your voice sound so fresh and so . . . so clear and fresh, never.'

Aunt Julia smiled broadly and murmured something about compliments as she released her hand from his grasp. Mr Browne extended his open hand towards her and said to those who were near him in the manner of a showman introducing a prodigy to an audience:

'Miss Julia Morkan, my latest discovery!'

He was laughing very heartily at this himself when Freddy Malins turned to him and said:

'Well, Browne, if you're serious you might make a worse discovery. All I can say is I never heard her sing half so well as long as I am coming here. And that's the honest truth.'

'Neither did I,' said Mr Browne. 'I think her voice has greatly improved.'

Aunt Julia shrugged her shoulders and said with meek pride:

'Thirty years ago I hadn't a bad voice as voices go.'

'I often told Julia,' said Aunt Kate emphatically, 'that she was simply thrown away in that choir. But she never would be said by me.'

She turned as if to appeal to the good sense of the others against a refractory child, while Aunt Julia gazed in front of her, a vague smile of reminiscence playing on her face.

'No,' continued Aunt Kate, 'she wouldn't be said or led by anyone, slaving there in that choir night and day, night and day. Six o'clock on Christmas morning! And all for what?'

'Well, isn't it for the honour of God, Aunt Kate?' asked Mary Jane, twisting round on the piano-stool and smiling.

Aunt Kate turned fiercely on her niece and said:

'I know all about the honour of God, Mary Jane, but I think it's not at all honourable for the Pope to turn out the women out of the choirs that have slaved there all their lives and put little whipper-snappers of boys over their heads. I suppose it is for the good of the Church, if the Pope does it. But it's not just, Mary Jane, and it's not right.'

She had worked herself into a passion and would have continued in defence of her sister, for it was a sore subject with her, but Mary Jane, seeing that all the dancers had come back, intervened pacifically.

'Now, Aunt Kate, you're giving scandal to Mr Browne, who is of the other persuasion.'

Aunt Kate turned to Mr Browne, who was grinning at this allusion to his religion, and said hastily:

'O, I don't question the Pope's being right. I'm only a stupid old woman and I wouldn't presume to do such a thing. But there's such a thing as common everyday politeness and gratitude. And if I were in Julia's place I'd tell that Father Healey straight up to his face . . .'

'And besides, Aunt Kate,' said Mary Jane, 'we really are all hungry and when we are hungry we are all very quarrelsome.'

'And when we are thirsty we are also quarrelsome,' added Mr Browne.

'So that we had better go to supper,' said Mary Jane, 'and finish the discussion afterwards.'

On the landing outside the drawing-room Gabriel found his wife and Mary Jane trying to persuade Miss Ivors to stay for supper. But Miss Ivors, who had put on her hat and was buttoning her cloak, would not stay. She did not feel in the least hungry and she had already overstayed her time.

'But only for ten minutes, Molly,' said Mrs Conroy. 'That won't delay you.'

'To take a pick itself,' said Mary Jane, 'after all your dancing.'

'I really couldn't,' said Miss Ivors.

'I am afraid you didn't enjoy yourself at all,' said Mary Jane hopelessly.

'Ever so much, I assure you,' said Miss Ivors, 'but you really must let me run off now.'

'But how can you get home?' asked Mrs Conroy.

'O, it's only two steps up the quay.'

Gabriel hesitated a moment and said:

'If you will allow me, Miss Ivors, I'll see you home if you are really obliged to go.'

But Miss Ivors broke away from them.

'I won't hear of it,' she cried. 'For goodness' sake go in to your suppers and don't mind me. I'm quite well able to take care of myself.'

'Well, you're the comical girl, Molly,' said Mrs Conroy frankly.

'*Beannacht libh*,' cried Miss Ivors, with a laugh, as she ran down the staircase.

Mary Jane gazed after her, a moody puzzled expression on her face, while Mrs Conroy leaned over the banisters to listen for the hall-door. Gabriel asked himself was he the cause of her abrupt departure. But she did not seem to be in ill humour – she had gone away laughing. He stared blankly down the staircase.

At the moment Aunt Kate came toddling out of the supper-room, almost wringing her hands in despair.

'Where is Gabriel?' she cried. 'Where on earth is Gabriel?' There's everyone waiting in there, stage to let, and nobody to carve the goose!'

'Here I am, Aunt Kate!' cried Gabriel, with sudden animation, 'ready to carve a flock of geese, if necessary.'

A fat brown goose lay at one end of the table, and at the other end, on a bed of creased paper strewn with sprigs of parsley, lay a great ham, stripped of its outer skin and peppered over with crust crumbs, a neat paper frill round its shin, and beside this was a round of spiced beef. Between these rival ends ran parallel lines of side-dishes: two little minsters of jelly, red and yellow; a shallow dish full of blocks of blancmange and red jam, a large green leaf-shaped dish with a stalk-shaped handle, on which lay bunches of purple raisins and peeled almonds, a companion dish on which lay a solid rectangle of Smyrna figs, a dish of custard topped with grated nutmeg, a small bowl full of chocolates and sweets wrapped in gold and silver papers and a glass vase in which stood some tall celery stalks. In the centre of the table there stood, as sentries to a fruit-stand which upheld a pyramid of oranges and American apples, two squat old-fashioned decanters of cut glass, one containing port and the other dark sherry. On the closed square piano a pudding in a huge yellow dish lay in waiting, and behind it were three squads of bottles of stout and ale and minerals drawn up according to the colours of their uniforms, the first two black, with brown and red labels, the third and smallest squad white, with transverse green sashes.

Gabriel took his seat boldly at the head of the table and, having looked to the edge of the carver, plunged his fork firmly into the goose. He felt quite at ease now, for he was an expert carver and liked nothing better than to find himself at the head of a well-laden table.

'Miss Furlong, what shall I send you?' he asked. 'A wing or a slice of the breast?'

'Just a small slice of the breast.'

'Miss Higgins, what for you?'

'O, anything at all, Mr Conroy.'

While Gabriel and Miss Daly exchanged plates of goose and plates of ham and spiced beef, Lily went from guest to guest with a dish of hot floury potatoes wrapped in a white napkin. This was Mary Jane's idea and she had also suggested apple sauce for the goose, but Aunt Kate had said that plain roast goose without any apple sauce had always been good enough for her and she hoped she might never eat worse. Mary Jane waited on her pupils and saw that they got the best slices, and Aunt Kate and Aunt Julia opened and carried across from the piano bottles of stout and ale for the gentlemen and bottles of minerals for the ladies. There was a great deal of confusion and laughter and noise, the noise of orders and counter-orders, of knives and forks, of corks and glass-stoppers. Gabriel began to carve second helpings as soon as he had finished the first round without serving himself. Everyone protested loudly, so that he compromised by taking a long draught of stout, for he had found the carving hot work. Mary Jane settled down quietly to her supper, but Aunt Kate and Aunt Julia were still toddling round the table, walking on each other's heels, getting in each other's way and giving each other unheeded orders. Mr Browne begged of them to sit down and eat their suppers and so did Gabriel, but they said there was time enough, so that, at last, Freddy Malins stood up and, capturing Aunt Kate, plumped her down on her chair amid general laughter.

When everyone had been well served Gabriel said, smiling:

'Now, if anyone wants a little more of what vulgar people call stuffing let him or her speak.'

A chorus of voices invited him to begin his own supper, and Lily came forward with three potatoes which she had reserved for him.

'Very well,' said Gabriel amiably, as he took another preparatory draught, 'kindly forget my existence, ladies and gentlemen, for a few minutes.'

He set to his supper and took no part in the conversation with which the table covered Lily's removal of the plates. The subject of talk was the opera company which was then at the Theatre Royal. Mr Bartell D'Arcy, the tenor, a dark-complexioned young man with a smart moustache, praised very highly the leading contralto of the company, but Miss Furlong thought she had a rather vulgar style of production. Freddy Malins said there was a Negro chieftain singing in the second part of the Gaiety pantomime who had one of the finest tenor voices he had ever heard.

'Have you heard him?' he asked Mr Bartell D'Arcy across the table.

'No,' answered Mr Bartell D'Arcy carelessly.

'Because,' Freddy Malins explained, 'now I'd be curious to hear your opinion of him. I think he has a grand voice.'

'It takes Teddy to find out the really good things,' said Mr Browne familiarly to the table.

'And why couldn't he have a voice too?' asked Freddy Malins sharply. 'Is it because he's only a black?'

Nobody answered this question and Mary Jane led the table back to the legitimate opera. One of her pupils had given her a pass for *Mignon*. Of course it was very fine, she said, but it made her think of poor Georgina Burns. Mr Browne could go back farther still, to the old Italian companies that used to come to Dublin – Tietjens, Ilma de Murzka, Campanini, the great Trebelli, Giuglini, Ravelli, Aramburo. Those were the days, he said, when there was something like singing to be heard in Dublin. He told too of how the top gallery of the old Royal used to be packed night after night, of how one night an Italian tenor had sung five encores to 'Let me like a Soldier fall', introducing a high C every time, and of how the gallery boys would sometimes in their enthusiasm unyoke the horses from the carriage of some great *prima donna* and pull her themselves through the streets to her hotel. Why did they never play the grand old operas now, he asked, *Dinorah*, *Lucrezia Borgia*? Because they could not get the voices to sing them: that was why.

'O, well,' said Mr Bartell D'Arcy, 'I presume there are as good singers today as there were then.'

'Where are they?' asked Mr Browne defiantly.

'In London, Paris, Milan,' said Mr Bartell D'Arcy warmly. 'I suppose Caruso, for example, is quite as good, if not better than any of the men you have mentioned.'

'Maybe so,' said Mr Browne. 'But I may tell you I doubt it strongly.'

'O, I'd give anything to hear Caruso sing,' said Mary Jane.

'For me,' said Aunt Kate, who had been picking a bone, 'there was only one tenor. To please me, I mean. But I suppose none of you ever heard of him.'

'Who was he, Miss Morkan?' asked Mr Bartell D'Arcy politely.

'His name,' said Aunt Kate, 'was Parkinson. I heard him when he was in his prime and I think he had then the purest tenor voice that was ever put into a man's throat.'

'Strange,' said Mr Bartell D'Arcy. 'I never even heard of him.'

'Yes, yes, Miss Morkan is right,' said Mr Browne. 'I remember hearing old Parkinson, but he's too far back for me.'

'A beautiful, pure, sweet, mellow English tenor,' said Aunt Kate with enthusiasm.

Gabriel having finished, the huge pudding was transferred to the table. The clatter of forks and spoons began again. Gabriel's wife served out spoonfuls of the pudding and passed the plates down the table. Midway down they were held up by Mary Jane, who replenished them with raspberry or orange jelly or with blancmange and jam. The pudding was of Aunt Julia's making, and she received praise for it from all quarters. She herself said that it was not quite brown enough.

'Well, I hope, Miss Morkan,' said Mr Browne, 'that I'm brown enough for you because, you know, I'm all Brown.'

All the gentlemen, except Gabriel, ate some of the pudding out of compliment to Aunt Julia. As Gabriel never ate sweets the celery had been left for him. Freddy Malins also took a stalk of celery and ate it with his pudding. He had been told that celery was a capital thing for the blood and he was just then under doctor's care. Mrs Malins, who had been silent all through the supper, said that her son was going down to Mount Melleray in a week or so. The table then spoke of Mount Melleray, how bracing the air was down there, how hospitable the monks were and how they never asked for a penny-piece from their guests.

'And do you mean to say,' asked Mr Browne incredulously, 'that a chap can go down there and put up there as if it were a hotel and live on the fat of the land and then come away without paying anything?'

'O, most people give some donation to the monastery when they leave,' said Mary Jane.

'I wish we had an institution like that in our Church,' said Mr Browne candidly.

He was astonished to hear that the monks never spoke, got up at two in the morning and slept in their coffins. He asked what they did it for.

'That's the rule of the order,' said Aunt Kate firmly.

'Yes, but why?' asked Mr Browne.

Aunt Kate repeated that it was the rule, that was all. Mr Browne still seemed not to understand. Freddy Malins explained to him, as best he could, that the monks were trying to make up for the sins committed by all the sinners in the outside world. The explanation was not very clear, for Mr Browne grinned and said:

'I like that idea very much, but wouldn't a comfortable spring bed do them as well as a coffin?'

'The coffin,' said Mary Jane, 'is to remind them of their last end.'

As the subject had grown lugubrious it was buried in a silence of the table, during which Mrs Malins could be heard saying to her neighbour in an indistinct undertone:

'They are very good men, the monks, very pious men.'

The raisins and almonds and figs and apples and oranges and chocolates and sweets were now passed about the table, and Aunt Julia invited all the guests to have either port or sherry. At first Mr Bartell D'Arcy refused to take either, but one of his neighbours nudged him and whispered something to him, upon which he allowed his glass to be filled. Gradually as the last glasses were being filled the conversation ceased. A pause followed, broken only by the noise of the wine and by unsettling of chairs. The Misses Morkan, all three, looked down at the tablecloth. Someone coughed once or twice, and then a few gentlemen patted the table gently as a signal for silence. The silence came and Gabriel pushed back his chair and stood up.

The patting at once grew louder in encouragement and then ceased altogether. Gabriel leaned his ten trembling fingers on the tablecloth and smiled nervously at the company. Meeting a row of upturned faces he raised his eyes to the chandelier. The piano was playing a waltz tune and he could hear the skirts sweeping against the drawing-room door. People, perhaps, were standing in the snow on the quay outside, gazing up at the lighted windows and listening to the waltz music. The air was pure there. In the distance lay the park, where the trees were weighted with snow. The Wellington Monument wore a gleaming cap of snow that flashed westwards over the white field of Fifteen Acres.

He began:

'Ladies and Gentlemen,

'It has fallen to my lot this evening, as in years past, to perform a very pleasing task, but a task for which I am afraid my poor powers as a speaker are all too inadequate.'

'No, no!' said Mr Browne.

'But, however that may be, I can only ask you tonight to take the will for the deed, and to lend me your attention for a few moments while I endeavour to express to you in words what my feelings are on this occasion.

'Ladies and Gentlemen, it is not the first time that we have gathered together under this hospitable roof, around this hospitable board. It is not the first time that we have been the recipients – or perhaps, I had better say, the victims – of the hospitality of certain good ladies.'

He made a circle in the air with his arm and paused. Everyone laughed or smiled at Aunt Kate and Aunt Julia and Mary Jane, who all turned crimson with pleasure. Gabriel went on more boldly:

'I feel more strongly with every recurring year that our country has no tradition which does it so much honour and which it should guard so jealously as that of its hospitality. It is a tradition that is unique as far as my experience goes (and I have visited not a few places abroad) among the modern nations. Some would say, perhaps, that with us it is rather a failing than anything to be boasted of. But granted even that, it is, to my mind, a princely failing, and one that I trust will long be cultivated among us. Of one thing, at least, I am sure. As long as this one roof shelters the good ladies aforesaid – and I wish from my heart it may do so for many and many a long year to come – the tradition of genuine warm-hearted courteous Irish hospitality, which our forefathers have handed down to us and which we must hand down to our descendants, is still alive among us.'

A hearty murmur of assent ran round the table. It shot through Gabriel's mind that Miss Ivors was not there and that she had gone away discourteously: and he said with confidence in himself:

'Ladies and Gentlemen,

'A new generation is growing up in our midst, a generation actuated by new ideas and new principles. It is serious and enthusiastic for these new ideas and its enthusiasm, even when it is misdirected, is, I believe, in the main sincere. But we are living in a sceptical and, if I may use the phrase, a thought-tormented age: and sometimes I fear that this new generation, educated or hyper-educated as it is, will lack those qualities of humanity, of hospitality, of kindly humour which belonged to an older day. Listening tonight to the names of all those great singers of the past it seemed to me, I must confess, that we were living in a less spacious age. Those days might, without exaggeration, be called spacious days: and if they are gone beyond recall, let us hope, at least, that in gatherings such as this we shall still speak of them with pride and affection, still cherish in our hearts the memory of those dead and gone great ones whose fame the world will not willingly let die.'

'Hear, hear!' said Mr Browne loudly.

'But yet,' continued Gabriel, his voice falling into a softer inflection, 'there are always in gatherings such as this sadder thoughts that will recur to our minds: thoughts of the past, of youth, of changes, of absent faces that we miss here tonight. Our path through life is strewn with many such sad memories: and were we to brood upon them always we could not find the heart to go on bravely with our work among the living. We have all of us living duties and living affections which claim, and rightly claim, our strenuous endeavours.

'Therefore, I will not linger on the past. I will not let any gloomy moralizing intrude upon us here tonight. Here we are gathered together for a brief moment from the bustle and rush of our everyday routine. We are met here as friends, in the spirit of good-fellowship, as colleagues, also, to a certain extent, in the true spirit of *camaraderie*, and as the guests of – what shall I call them? – the Three Graces of the Dublin musical world.'

The table burst into applause and laughter at this allusion. Aunt Julia vainly asked each of her neighbours in turn to tell her what Gabriel had said.

'He says we are the Three Graces, Aunt Julia,' said Mary Jane.

Aunt Julia did not understand, but she looked up, smiling, at Gabriel, who continued in the same vein:

'Ladies and Gentlemen,

'I will not attempt to play tonight the part that Paris played on another occasion. I will not attempt to choose between them. The task would be an invidious one and one beyond my poor powers. For when I view them in turn, whether it be our chief hostess herself, whose good heart, whose too good heart, has become a byword with all who know her; or her sister, who seems to be gifted with perennial youth and whose singing must have been a surprise and a revelation to us all tonight; or, last but not least, when I consider our youngest hostess, talented, cheerful, hardworking and the best of nieces, I confess, Ladies and Gentlemen, that I do not know to which of them I should award the prize.'

Gabriel glanced down at his aunts and, seeing the large smile on Aunt Julia's face and the tears which had risen to Aunt Kate's eyes, hastened to his close. He raised his glass of port gallantly, while every member of the company fingered a glass expectantly, and said loudly:

'Let us toast them all three together. Let us drink to their health, wealth, long life, happiness, and prosperity and may they long continue to hold the proud and self-won position which they hold in their profession and the position of honour and affection which they hold in our hearts.'

All the guests stood up, glass in hand, and turning towards the three seated ladies, sang in unison, with Mr Browne as leader:

> *For they are jolly gay fellows,*
> *For they are jolly gay fellows,*
> *For they are jolly gay fellows,*
> *Which nobody can deny.*

Aunt Kate was making frank use of her handkerchief and even Aunt Julia seemed moved. Freddy Malins beat time with his pudding-fork and the singers turned towards one another, as if in melodious conference, while they sang with emphasis:

> *Unless he tells a lie,*
> *Unless he tells a lie.*

Then, turning once more towards their hostesses, they sang:

> *For they are jolly gay fellows,*
> *For they are jolly gay fellows,*
> *For they are jolly gay fellows,*
> *Which nobody can deny.*

The acclamation which followed was taken up beyond the door of the supper room by many of the other guests and renewed time after time, Freddy Malins acting as officer with his fork on high.

The piercing morning air came into the hall where they were standing so that Aunt Kate said:

'Close the door, somebody. Mrs Malins will get her death of cold.'

'Browne is out there, Aunt Kate,' said Mary Jane.

'Browne is everywhere,' said Aunt Kate, lowering her voice.

Mary Jane laughed at her tone.

'Really,' she said archly, 'he is very attentive.'

'He has been laid on here like the gas,' said Aunt Kate in the same tone, 'all during the Christmas.'

She laughed herself this time good-humouredly and then added quickly:

'But tell him to come in, Mary Jane, and close the door. I hope to goodness he didn't hear me.'

At that moment the hall-door was opened and Mr Browne came in from the doorstep, laughing as if his heart would break. He was dressed in a long green overcoat with mock astrakhan cuffs and collar and wore on his head an oval fur cap. He pointed down the snow-covered quay from where the sound of shrill prolonged whistling was borne in.

'Teddy will have all the cabs in Dublin out,' he said.

Gabriel advanced from the little pantry behind the office, struggling into his overcoat and, looking round the hall, said:

'Gretta not down yet?'

'She's getting on her things, Gabriel,' said Aunt Kate.

'Who's playing up there?' asked Gabriel.

'Nobody. They're all gone.'

'O no, Aunt Kate,' said Mary Jane. 'Bartell D'Arcy and Miss O'Callaghan aren't gone yet.'

'Someone is fooling at the piano anyhow,' said Gabriel.

Mary Jane glanced at Gabriel and Mr Browne and said with a shiver:

'It makes me feel cold to look at you two gentlemen muffled up like that. I wouldn't like to face your journey home at this hour.'

'I'd like nothing better this minute,' said Mr Browne stoutly, 'than a rattling fine walk in the country or a fast drive with a good spanking goer between the shafts.'

'We used to have a very good horse and trap at home,' said Aunt Julia, sadly.

'The never-to-be-forgotten Johnny,' said Mary Jane, laughing.

Aunt Kate and Gabriel laughed too.

'Why, what was wonderful about Johnny?' asked Mr Browne.

'The late lamented Patrick Morkan, our grandfather, that is,' explained Gabriel, 'commonly known in his later years as the old gentleman, was a glue-boiler.'

'O, now, Gabriel,' said Aunt Kate, laughing, 'he had a starch mill.'

'Well, glue or starch,' said Gabriel, 'the old gentleman had a horse by the name of Johnny. And Johnny used to work in the old gentleman's mill, walking round and round in order to drive the mill. That was all very well; but now comes the tragic part about Johnny. One fine day the old gentleman thought he'd like to drive out with the quality to a military review in the park.'

'The Lord have mercy on his soul,' said Aunt Kate, compassionately.

'Amen,' said Gabriel. 'So the old gentleman, as I said, harnessed Johnny and put on his very best tall hat and his very best stock collar and drove out in grand style from his ancestral mansion somewhere near Back Lane, I think.'

Everyone laughed, even Mrs Malins, at Gabriel's manner, and Aunt Kate said:

'O, now, Gabriel, he didn't live in Back Lane, really. Only the mill was there.'

'Out from the mansion of his forefathers,' continued Gabriel, 'he drove with Johnny. And everthing went on beautifully until Johnny came in sight of King Billy's statue: and whether he fell in love with the horse King Billy sits on or whether he thought he was back again in the mill, anyway he began to walk round the statue.'

Gabriel paced in a circle round the hall in his goloshes amid the laughter of the others.

'Round and round he went,' said Gabriel, 'and the old gentleman, who was a very pompous old gentleman, was highly indignant. "Go on, sir! What do you mean, sir? Johnny! Johnny! Most extraordinary conduct! Can't understand the horse!"'

The peals of laughter which followed Gabriel's imitation of the incident were interrupted by a resounding knock at the hall door. Mary Jane ran to open it and let in Freddy Malins. Freddy Malins, with his hat well back on his head and his shoulders humped with cold, was puffing and steaming after his exertions.

'I could only get one cab,' he said.

'O, we'll find another along the quay,' said Gabriel.

'Yes,' said Aunt Kate. 'Better not keep Mrs Malins standing in the draught.'

Mrs Malins was helped down the front steps by her son and Mr Browne and, after many manoeuvres, hoisted into the cab. Freddy

Malins clambered in after her and spent a long time settling her on the seat, Mr Browne helping him with advice. At last she was settled comfortably and Freddy Malins invited Mr Browne into the cab. There was a good deal of confused talk, and then Mr Browne got into the cab. The cabman settled his rug over his knees, and bent down for the address. The confusion grew greater and the cabman was directed differently by Freddy Malins and Mr Browne, each of whom had his head out through a window of the cab. The difficulty was to know where to drop Mr Browne along the route, and Aunt Kate, Aunt Julia, and Mary Jane helped the discussion from the doorstep with cross-directions and contradictions and abundance of laughter. As for Freddy Malins he was speechless with laughter. He popped his head in and out of the window every moment to the great danger of his hat, and told his mother how the discussion was progressing, till at last Mr Browne shouted to the bewildered cabman above the din of everybody's laughter:

'Do you know Trinity College?'

'Yes, sir,' said the cabman.

'Well, drive bang up against Trinity College gates,' said Mr Browne, 'and then we'll tell you where to go. You understand now?'

'Yes, sir,' said the cabman.

'Make like a bird for Trinity College.'

'Right, sir,' said the cabman.

The horse was whipped up and the cab rattled off along the quay amid a chorus of laughter and adieux.

Gabriel had not gone to the door with the others. He was in a dark part of the hall gazing up the staircase. A woman was standing near the top of the first flight, in the shadow also. He could not see her face but he could see the terracotta and salmon-pink panels of her skirt which the shadow made appear black and white. It was his wife. She was leaning on the banisters, listening to something. Gabriel was surprised at her stillness and strained his ear to listen also. But he could hear little save the noise of laughter and dispute on the front steps, a few chords struck on the piano and a few notes of a man's voice singing.

He stood still in the gloom of the hall, trying to catch the air that the voice was singing and gazing up at his wife. There was grace and mystery in her attitude as if she were a symbol of something. He asked himself what is a woman standing on the stairs in the shadow, listening to distant music, a symbol of. If he were a painter he would paint her in that attitude. Her blue felt hat would show off the bronze of her hair against the darkness and the dark panels of her skirt would show off the light ones. *Distant Music* he would call the picture if he were a painter.

The hall-door was closed, and Aunt Kate, Aunt Julia, and Mary Jane came down the hall, still laughing.

'Well, isn't Freddy terrible?' said Mary Jane. 'He's really terrible.'

Gabriel said nothing, but pointed up the stairs towards where his wife was standing. Now that the hall-door was closed the voice and the piano could be heard more clearly. Gabriel held up his hand for them to be silent. The song seemed to be in the old Irish tonality and the singer seemed uncertain both of his words and of his voice. The voice, made plaintive by distance and by the singer's hoarseness, faintly illuminated the cadence of the air with words expressing grief:

> O, *the rain falls on my heavy locks*
> *And the dew wets my skin,*
> *My babe lies cold . . .*

'O,' exclaimed Mary Jane. 'It's Bartell D'Arcy singing, and he wouldn't sing all the night. O, I'll get him to sing a song before he goes.'

'O, do, Mary Jane,' said Aunt Kate.

Mary Jane brushed past the others and ran to the staircase, but before she reached it the singing stopped and the piano was closed abruptly.

'O, what a pity! she cried. 'Is he coming down, Gretta?'

Gabriel heard his wife answer yes and saw her come down towards them. A few steps behind her were Mr Bartell D'Arcy and Miss O'Callaghan.

'O, Mr D'Arcy,' cried Mary Jane, 'it's downright mean of you to break off like that when we were all in raptures listening to you.'

'I have been at him all the evening,' said Miss O'Callaghan, 'and Mrs Conroy, too, and he told us he had a dreadful cold and couldn't sing.'

'O, Mr D'Arcy,' said Aunt Kate, 'now that was a great fib to tell.'

'Can't you see that I'm as hoarse as a crow?' said Mr D'Arcy roughly.

He went into the pantry hastily and put on his overcoat. The others, taken back by his rude speech, could find nothing to say.

Aunt Kate wrinkled her brows and made signs to the others to drop the subject. Mr D'Arcy stood swathing his neck carefully and frowning.

'It's the weather,' said Aunt Julia, after a pause.

'Yes, everybody has colds,' said Aunt Kate readily, 'everybody.'

'They say,' said Mary Jane, 'we haven't had snow like it for thirty years, and I read this morning in the newspapers that the snow is general·all over Ireland.'

'I love the look of snow,' said Aunt Julia sadly.

'So do I,' said Miss O'Callaghan. 'I think Christmas is never really Christmas unless we have the snow on the ground.'

'But poor Mr D'Arcy doesn't like the snow,' said Aunt Kate, smiling.

Mr D'Arcy came from the pantry, fully swathed and buttoned, and in a repentant tone told them the history of his cold. Everyone gave him advice and said it was a great pity and urged him to be very careful of his throat in the night air. Gabriel watched his wife, who did not join in the conversation. She was standing right under the dusty fanlight and the flame of the gas lit up the rich bronze of her hair, which he had seen her drying at the fire a few days before. She was in the same attitude and seemed unaware of the talk about her. At last she turned towards them and Gabriel saw that there was colour on her cheeks and that her eyes were shining. A sudden tide of joy went leaping out of his heart.

'Mr D'Arcy,' she said, 'what is the name of that song you were singing?'

'It's called "The Lass of Aughrim",' said Mr D'Arcy, 'but I couldn't remember it properly. Why? Do you know it?'

'"The Lass of Aughrim",' she repeated. 'I couldn't think of the name.'

'It's a very nice air,' said Mary Jane. 'I'm sorry you were not in voice tonight.'

'Now, Mary Jane,' said Aunt Kate, 'don't annoy Mr D'Arcy. I won't have him annoyed.'

Seeing that all were ready to start she shepherded them to the door, where good night was said:

'Well, good night, Aunt Kate, and thanks for the pleasant evening.'

'Good night, Gabriel. Good night, Gretta!'

'Good night, Aunt Kate, and thanks ever so much. Good night, Aunt Julia.'

'O, good night, Gretta, I didn't see you.'
'Good night, Mr D'Arcy. Good night, Miss O'Callaghan.'
'Good night, Miss Morkan.'
'Good night, again.'
'Good night, all. Safe home.'
'Good night. Good night.'

The morning was still dark. A dull, yellow light brooded over the houses and the river; and the sky seemed to be descending. It was slushy underfoot, and only streaks and patches of snow lay on the roofs, on the parapets of the quay and on the area railings. The lamps were still burning redly in the murky air and, across the river, the palace of the Four Courts stood out menacingly against the heavy sky.

She was walking on before him with Mr Bartell D'Arcy, her shoes in a brown parcel tucked under one arm and her hands holding her skirt up from the slush. She had no longer any grace of attitude, but Gabriel's eyes were still bright with happiness. The blood went bounding along his veins and the thoughts went rioting through his brain, proud, joyful, tender, valorous.

She was walking on before him so lightly and so erect that he longed to run after her noiselessly, catch her by the shoulders and say something foolish and affectionate into her ear. She seemed to him so frail that he longed to defend her against something and then to be alone with her. Moments of their secret life together burst like stars upon his memory. A heliotrope envelope was lying beside his breakfast-cup and he was caressing it with his hand. Birds were twittering in the ivy and the sunny web of the curtain was shimmering along the floor: he could not eat for happiness. They were standing on the crowded platform and he was placing a ticket inside the warm palm of her glove. He was standing with her in the cold, looking in through a grated window at a man making bottles in a roaring furnace. It was very cold. Her face, fragrant in the cold air, was quite close to his, and suddenly he called out to the man at the furnace:

'Is the fire hot, sir?'

But the man could not hear with the noise of the furnace. It was just as well. He might have answered rudely.

A wave of yet more tender joy escaped from his heart and went coursing in warm flood along his arteries. Like the tender fire of stars moments of their life together, that no one knew of or would ever know of, broke upon and illumined his memory. He longed to recall to her those moments, to make her forget the years of their dull existence together and remember only their moments of ecstasy. For the years, he felt, had not quenched his soul or hers. Their children, his writing, her household cares had not quenched all their souls' tender fire. In one letter that he had written to her then he had said: 'Why is it that words like these seem to me so dull and cold? Is it because there is no word tender enough to be your name?'

Like distant music these words that he had written years before were borne towards him from the past. He longed to be alone with her. When the others had gone away, when he and she were in the room in their hotel, then they would be alone together. He would call her softly:

'Gretta!'

Perhaps she would not hear at once: she would be undressing. Then something in his voice would strike her. She would turn and look at him . . .

At the corner of Winetavern Street they met a cab. He was glad of its rattling noise as it saved him from conversation. She was looking out of the window and seemed tired. The others spoke only a few words, pointing out some building or street. The horse galloped along wearily under the murky morning sky, dragging his old rattling box after his heels, and Gabriel was again in a cab with her, galloping to catch the boat, galloping to their honeymoon.

As the cab drove across O'Connell Bridge Miss O'Callaghan said:

'They say you never cross O'Connell Bridge without seeing a white horse.'

'I see a white man this time,' said Gabriel.

'Where?' asked Mr Bartell D'Arcy.

Gabriel pointed to the statue, on which lay patches of snow. Then he nodded familiarly to it and waved his hand.

'Good night, Dan,' he said gaily.

When the cab drew up before the hotel, Gabriel jumped out and, in spite of Mr Bartell D'Arcy's protest, paid the driver. He gave the man a shilling over his fare. The man saluted and said:

'A prosperous New Year to you, sir.'

'The same to you,' said Gabriel cordially.

She leaned for a moment on his arm in getting out of the cab and while standing at the kerb-stone, bidding the others good night. She leaned lightly on his arm, as lightly as when she had danced with him a few hours before. He had felt proud and happy then, happy that she was his, proud of her grace and wifely carriage. But now, after the kindling again of so many memories, the first touch of her body, musical and strange and perfumed, sent through him a keen pang of lust. Under cover of her silence he pressed her arm closely to his side, and, as they stood at the hotel door, he felt that they had escaped from their lives and duties, escaped from home and friends and run away together with wild and radiant hearts to a new adventure.

An old man was dozing in a great hooded chair in the hall. He lit a candle in the office and went before them to the stairs. They followed him in silence, their feet falling in soft thuds on the thickly carpeted stairs. She mounted the stairs behind the porter, her head bowed in the ascent, her frail shoulders curved as with a burden, her skirt girt tightly about her. He could have flung his arms about her hips and held her still, for his arms were trembling with desire to seize her and only the stress of his nails against the palms of his hands held the wild impulse of his body in check. The porter halted on the stairs to settle his guttering candle. They halted, too, on the steps below him. In the silence Gabriel could hear the falling of molten wax into the tray and the thumping of his own heart against his ribs.

The porter led them along a corridor and opened a door. Then he set his unstable candle down on a toilet-table and asked at what hour they were to be called in the morning.

'Eight,' said Gabriel.

The porter pointed to the tap of the electric-light and began a muttered apology, but Gabriel cut him short.

'We don't want any light. We have light enough from the street. And I say,' he added, pointing to the candle, 'you might remove that handsome article, like a good man.'

The porter took up his candle again, but slowly, for he was surprised by such a novel idea. Then he mumbled good night and went out. Gabriel shot the lock to.

A ghastly light from the street lamp lay in a long shaft from one window to the door. Gabriel threw his overcoat and hat on a couch and crossed the room towards the window. He looked down into the street in order that his emotion might calm a little. Then he turned and leaned against a chest of drawers with his back to the light. She had taken off her hat and cloak and was standing before a large swinging mirror, unhooking her waist. Gabriel paused for a few moments, watching her, and then said:

'Gretta!'

She turned away from the mirror slowly and walked along the shaft of light towards him. Her face looked so serious and weary that the words would not pass Gabriel's lips. No, it was not the moment yet.

'You looked tired,' he said.

'I am a little,' she answered.

'You don't feel ill or weak?'

'No, tired: that's all.'

She went on to the window and stood there, looking out. Gabriel waited again and then, fearing that diffidence was about to conquer him, he said abruptly:

'By the way, Gretta!'

'What is it?'

'You know that poor fellow Malins?' he said quickly.

'Yes. What about him?'

'Well, poor fellow, he's a decent sort of chap, after all,' continued Gabriel in a false voice. 'He gave me back that sovereign I lent him, and I didn't expect it, really. It's a pity he wouldn't keep away from that Browne, because he's not a bad fellow, really.'

He was trembling now with annoyance. Why did she seem so abstracted? He did not know how he could begin. Was she annoyed, too, about something? If she would only turn to him or come to him of her own accord! To take her as she was would be brutal. No, he must see some ardour in her eyes first. He longed to be master of her strange mood.

'When did you lend him the pound?' she asked, after a pause.

Gabriel strove to restrain himself from breaking out into brutal language about the sottish Malins and his pound. He longed to cry to her from his soul, to crush her body against his, to overmaster her. But he said:

'O, at Christmas, when he opened that little Christmas-card shop, in Henry Street.'

He was in such a fever of rage and desire that he did not hear her come from the window. She stood before him for an instant, looking at him strangely. Then, suddenly raising herself on tiptoe and resting her hands lightly on his shoulders, she kissed him.

'You are a very generous person, Gabriel,' she said.

Gabriel, trembling with delight at her sudden kiss and at the quaintness of her phrase, put his hands on her hair and began smoothing it back, scarcely touching it with his fingers. The washing had made it fine and brilliant. His heart was brimming over with happiness. Just when he was wishing for it she had come to him of her own accord. Perhaps her thoughts had been running with his. Perhaps she had felt the impetuous desire that was in him, and then the yielding mood had come upon her. Now that she had fallen to him so easily, he wondered why he had been so diffident.

He stood, holding her head between his hands. Then, slipping one arm swiftly about her body and drawing her towards him, he said softly:

'Gretta, dear, what are you thinking about?'

She did not answer nor yield wholly to his arm. He said again, softly:

'Tell me what it is, Gretta. I think I know what is the matter. Do I know?'

She did not answer at once. Then she said in an outburst of tears:

'O, I am thinking about that song, "The Lass of Aughrim".'

She broke loose from him and ran to the bed and, throwing her arms across the bed-rail, hid her face. Gabriel stood stock-still for a moment in astonishment and then followed her. As he passed in the way of the cheval-glass he caught sight of himself in full length, his broad, well-filled shirt-front, the face whose expression always puzzled him when he saw it in a mirror, and his glimmering gilt-rimmed eyeglasses. He halted a few paces from her and said:

'What about the song? Why does that make you cry?'

She raised her head from her arms and dried her eyes with the back of her hand like a child. A kinder note than he had intended went into his voice.

'Why, Gretta?' he asked.

'I am thinking about a person long ago who used to sing that song.'

'And who was the person long ago?' asked Gabriel, smiling.

'It was a person I used to know in Galway when I was living with my grandmother,' she said.

The smile passed away from Gabriel's face. A dull anger began to gather again at the back of his mind and the dull fires of his lust began to glow angrily in his veins.

'Someone you were in love with?' he asked ironically.

'It was a young boy I used to know,' she answered, 'named Michael

Furey. He used to sing that song, "The Lass of Aughrim". He was very delicate.'

Gabriel was silent. He did not wish her to think that he was interested in this delicate boy.

'I can see him so plainly,' she said, after a moment. 'Such eyes as he had: big, dark eyes! And such an expression in them – an expression!'

'O, then, you were in love with him?' said Gabriel.

'I used to go out walking with him,' she said, 'when I was in Galway.'

A thought flew across Gabriel's mind.

'Perhaps that was why you wanted to go to Galway with that Ivors girl?' he said coldly.

She looked at him and asked in surprise:

'What for?'

Her eyes made Gabriel feel awkward. He shrugged his shoulders and said:

'How do I know? To see him, perhaps.'

She looked away from him along the shaft of light towards the window in silence.

'He is dead,' she said at length. 'He died when he was only seventeen. Isn't it a terrible thing to die so young as that?'

'What was he?' asked Gabriel, still ironically.

'He was in the gasworks,' she said.

Gabriel felt humiliated by the failure of his irony and by the evocation of this figure from the dead, a boy in the gasworks. While he had been full of memories of their secret life together, full of tenderness and joy and desire, she had been comparing him in her mind with another. A shameful consciousness of his own person assailed him. He saw himself as a ludicrous figure, acting as a penny-boy for his aunts, a nervous, well-meaning sentimentalist, orating to vulgarians and idealizing his own clownish lusts, the pitiable fatuous fellow he had caught a glimpse of in the mirror. Instinctively he turned his back more to the light lest she might see the shame that burned upon his forehead.

He tried to keep up his tone of cold interrogation, but his voice when he spoke was humble and indifferent.

'I suppose you were in love with this Michael Furey, Gretta,' he said.

'I was great with him at that time,' she said.

Her voice was veiled and sad. Gabriel, feeling now how vain it would be to try to lead her whither he had purposed, caressed one of her hands and said, also sadly:

'And what did he die of so young, Gretta? Consumption, was it?'

'I think he died for me,' she answered.

A vague terror seized Gabriel at this answer, as if, at that hour when he had hoped to triumph, some impalpable and vindictive being was coming against him, gathering forces against him in its vague world. But he shook himself free of it with an effort of reason and continued to caress her hand. He did not question her again, for he felt that she would tell him of herself. Her hand was warm and moist: it did not respond to his touch, but he continued to caress it just as he had caressed her first letter to him that spring morning.

'It was in the winter,' she said, 'about the beginning of the winter when I was going to leave my grandmother's and come up here to the convent. And he was ill at the time in his lodgings in Galway and wouldn't be let out, and his people in Oughterard were written to. He was in decline, they said, or something like that. I never knew rightly.'

She paused for a moment and sighed.

'Poor fellow,' she said. 'He was very fond of me and he was such a gentle boy. We used to go out together, walking, you know, Gabriel, like the way they do in the country. He was going to study singing only for his health. He had a very good voice, poor Michael Furey.'

'Well; and then?' asked Gabriel.

'And then when it came to the time for me to leave Galway and come up to the convent he was much worse and I wouldn't be let see him, so I wrote him a letter saying I was going up to Dublin and would be back in the summer, and hoping he would be better then.'

She paused for a moment to get her voice under control, and then went on:

'Then the night before I left, I was in my grandmother's house in Nuns' Island, packing up, and I heard gravel thrown up against the window. The window was so wet I couldn't see, so I ran downstairs as I was and slipped out the back into the garden and there was the poor fellow at the end of the garden, shivering.'

'And did you not tell him to go back?' asked Gabriel.

'I implored of him to go home at once and told him he would get his death in the rain. But he said he did not want to live. I can see his eyes as well as well! He was standing at the end of the wall where there was a tree.'

'And did he go home?' asked Gabriel.

'Yes, he went home. And when I was only a week in the convent he died and he was buried in Oughterard, where his people came from. O, the day I heard that, that he was dead!'

She stopped, choking with sobs, and, overcome by emotion, flung herself face downward on the bed, sobbing in the quilt. Gabriel held her hand for a moment longer, irresolutely, and then, shy of intruding on her grief, let it fall gently and walked quietly to the window.

She was fast asleep.

Gabriel, leaning on his elbow, looked for a few moments unresentfully on her tangled hair and half-open mouth, listening to her deep-drawn breath. So she had had that romance in her life: a man had died for her sake. It hardly pained him now to think how poor a part he, her husband, had played in her life. He watched her while she slept, as though he and she had never lived together as man and wife. His curious eyes rested long upon her face and on her hair: and, as he thought of what she must have been then, in that time of her first girlish beauty, a strange, friendly pity for her entered his soul. He did not like to say even to himself that her face was no longer beautiful, but he knew that it was no longer the face for which Michael Furey had braved death.

Perhaps she had not told him all the story. His eyes moved to the chair over which she had thrown some of her clothes. A petticoat string dangled to the floor. One boot stood upright, its limp upper fallen down: the fellow of it lay upon its side. He wondered at his riot of emotions of an hour before. From what had it proceeded? From his aunt's supper, from his own foolish speech, from the wine and dancing, the merry-making when saying good night in the hall, the pleasure of the walk along the river in the snow. Poor Aunt Julia! She, too, would soon be a shade with the shade of Patrick Morkan and his horse. He had caught that haggard look upon her face for a moment when she was singing 'Arrayed for the Bridal'. Soon, perhaps, he would be sitting in that same drawing-room, dressed in black, his silk hat on his knees. The blinds would be drawn down and Aunt Kate would be sitting beside him, crying and blowing her nose and telling him how Julia had died. He would cast about in his mind for some words that might console her, and would find only lame and useless ones. Yes, yes: that would happen very soon.

The air of the room chilled his shoulders. He stretched himself cautiously along under the sheets and lay down beside his wife. One by one, they were all becoming shades. Better pass boldly into that other world, in the full glory of some passion, than fade and wither dismally with age. He thought of how she who lay beside him had locked in her heart for so many years that image of her lover's eyes when he had told her that he did not wish to live.

Generous tears filled Gabriel's eyes. He had never felt like that himself towards any woman, but he knew that such a feeling must be love. The tears gathered more thickly in his eyes and in the partial darkness he imagined he saw the form of a young man standing under a dripping tree. Other forms were near. His soul had approached that region where dwell the vast hosts of the dead. He was conscious of, but could not apprehend, their wayward and flickering existence. His own identity was fading out into a grey impalpable world: the solid world itself, which these dead had one time reared and lived in, was dissolving and dwindling.

A few light taps upon the pane made him turn to the window. It had begun to snow again. He watched sleepily the flakes, silver and dark, falling obliquely against the lamplight. The time had come for him to set out on his journey westward. Yes, the newspapers were right: snow was general all over Ireland. It was falling on every part of the dark central plain, on the treeless hills, falling softly upon the Bog of Allen and, farther westward, softly falling into the dark mutinous Shannon waves. It was falling, too, upon every part of the lonely churchyard on the hill where Michael Furey lay buried. It lay thickly drifted on the crooked crosses and headstones, on the spears of the little gate, on the barren thorns. His soul swooned slowly as he heard the snow falling faintly through the universe and faintly falling, like the descent of their last end, upon all the living and the dead.

The Blood of the Lamb

BERNICE RUBENS

WHEN YOU SEE A WOMAN IN HER FORTIES, who, since you have known her, has always worn jeans, sandals and sweaters, the dampers that soft-pedal the passing of the year, when you see that same woman wearing a fur coat, you know that her mother has died.

So you compose your face as you see her coming towards you, ruling out anticipation, preparing for surprise, and you wait for her to inform you.

'Hullo, Rose. How are you?'

'Not so good. My mother died last week.'

'Oh, I'm sorry,' Now take your eyes off the coat that screams inheritance, but where can you look that isn't suddenly Persian Lamb? Even Rose's hair has caught its black curly texture.

'Hence the coat,' Rose is saying in apology.

'It's nice,' you say, the hypocrite you are. What's nice about Persian Lamb? A bequest fur, exclusively. Who in their right mind would buy it pristine off the ewe? A hand-me-down, rifled from a moth-balled wardrobe before the grass has time to grow. Then you notice the diamond earrings and your eye goes naturally to the fingers, and sure enough, the matching rings are there too. Poor Rose. She tucks in her ears and her hands, but only into the collar and muff of the lamb.

'Come back for a coffee,' she says, and you know that her familiar bedsitter, lined with books and records, now blushes for the invasion of alien silver and linen.

'The place is in a bit of a mess,' Rose is saying, her key in the door. Rose's place was always in a mess, but she'd never apologized for it. You didn't apologize for books strewn on the floor, records out of their sleeves, and a desk cluttered with ash, paper and files. It was your own mess, and you had made it, and it spoke of the work and the living of which you were not ashamed. But the mess that Rose was apologizing for was none of her making. It spoke not one syllable of her way of life. It was another's intrusion, another's chaos.

There was hardly room to open the door, and you had to go in singly, picking your way over chests of linen, cabinets of silver, the cluttered savings of another's mistaken priorities.

'What can I do with it all,' Rose is saying, but not asking, because you know that she is just stating a problem that she dares not solve. And you, being logical, sensible, and insensitive, say, 'Sell it,' and you look at her face and you see a friendship dying. You cover up, make the coffee, threading your way through the effects to the kitchen.

'She had a miserable life,' Rose is saying, huddled in her mother's lamb. 'Wouldn't spend a penny of herself. Saved, invested. Here it all is. And she did it for me. She was a good mother.' This last in almost a whisper, with too little confidence in its truth to spread it abroad.

'You were a good daughter,' you say, because it seems a natural corollary. Though you knew bloody well that Mrs Feigal was a rotten mother, that nothing Rose ever said or did was quite good enough, that everything merited her constant disapproval. That she had driven her own long-suffering husband to an early grave with her interminable expectations, and that for the length of her bitter widowhood, she had kept Rose by her, in the same bedroom even, and in at ten every night or she would want to know why, and who is this new feller of yours, what's his business, and you haven't got a better dress, and must you always wear the glasses? Until Rose was pushing thirty, and looking around, and hearing the dull thunder of the years nudging her limbs, in one wild moment of sanity, she stuffed some carrier-bags, and without blessing, left her mother's house.

That had been ten years ago, ten years since her mother had threatened a heart-attack, ten years since that heart-attack had refused to oblige, till in the end, it was bitterness and a consuming rage that carried her off; the old lady had simply died of anger. And still, from her seething grave, she refused to let Rose go, hanging on by the not-so-thin thread of Persian Lamb, shrouding her with the best linen and the blackmail of EPNS. Well, it takes two to tango, you tell yourself, but that only obtains when both partners are alive. Rose should have stopped dancing while her mother's stubborn heart still beat. What point now in such advice, when the rhythm had so taken you over that a partner was redundant.

You pour the coffee, and wish to God Rose woud take off the coat, but she wraps it round her as if it gives her some sick comfort. 'Why don't you take it off?' you practically shout at her. 'And diamond earrings look silly during the day.' You throw away what's left of your poor discretion, because you don't want to see your friend chain herself to what can now only be the future. She fingers the fur, as if to annoy you. 'I wish your mother the best of health, but one day, you may be in the same position as I.'

And that's precisely why you're shouting at her, because you too fear the lamb, and may your dear mother live for ever but there's no harm in a dress rehearsal if the authentic set is handed to you on a plate. Different location, it's true, but the dialogue's the same. You make a mental note to ring your mother that evening, after six o'clock, the cheap-rate time, not for your own thrift, but for hers, who would take offence at anyone's extravagance on her behalf.

'What can I do?' Rose is still saying.

'You can do one of two things,' you say, and hope that when your time comes, please God, not too soon, she, Rose will be the sensible one. 'You can keep it, or you can sell it. If you keep it, you'll have to find a bigger flat to accommodate it all. And a posher place it'll have to be to live up to it. Or you sell it, and you use the money for the things you've always wanted. Travel, for instance.'

Rose shudders at your insulting logic. 'She never travelled,' she is saying. 'Southend, maybe, once or twice in her life. She was saving it for me.'

Then you lose your cool, and you say, knowing that Rose is the end of the line, and now too unnaturally old to prolong it, you say, 'And who are *you* saving it for?' but all that succeeds in doing is to remind her of the barrenness of her own life, and the tears begin to flow. You get up to comfort her, climbing over the linen chest between you. And you slip, and the coffee upsets, and runs over the chest, seeping through the cracks onto the virgin linen inside. Rose leaps up like a panther and tears the chest open, winces at the trickle of coffee that slithers over the embroidered sheets and tablecloths, a gentle waterfall with the destructive force of a Niagara.

'Look what you've done,' she whimpers, crouching like a skinflint over his pile. And you look at her and marvel at how quickly the rot can set in.

'I'll go,' you say, doing yourself more of a favour than her, for you want to get out of there, back to your furless, linenless dwelling, and you pray to God that whatever the price, your own mother will live for ever.

You're back in your own bed-sitter, and you're dialling furiously – to hell with the cheap rate – and your heart is beating while she doesn't answer, and you pray she is there and well, and when at last you hear her martyred and long-suffering 'Hullo', you are not surprised at the overwhelming love that invades you.

'Momma?'

'Oh my God, what's the matter?'

'Nothing, Momma, nothing at all. Just phoning to say hello.'

'At this time of day? So much money you have?' And at the sound of her familiar disapproval, you feel at peace and back in battle, and you thank God that she lives to irritate you so.

'I just felt like talking to you.'

'I thought a husband at least you've found,' she is saying. 'Only for such a reason should you behave like a Rothschild.'

'But how are you?' you insist.

'I'm not complaining,' she is saying, complaining all the time, 'though if I saw you settled down in my life time, believe you me, I shouldn't have such aggravation.'

'How's your back?' you say, easing her into specifics.

'Not so good, but I'm not complaining,' and you know she's not complaining because in the middle of the day, at twenty pence a minute, it's cheaper to be well and without detail.

'You should go on a holiday,' you say. 'Go to America to see the family.'

'Holidays,' she sneers, 'who can afford holidays?' and you can see the solid Georgian silver shrieking behind her in the cabinet, and you know it could take her round the world a dozen times.

'You still going to Paris?' she asks joylessly.

'I have to go to a Teachers' conference,' you say, not daring to suggest for one moment that you might be going for pleasure.

'All right, so when you come back, perhaps I'll go to America,' she says, as if one of you has to stay at home to look after England.

'Look after yourself, Momma,' you say.

'Who else should look after me?' But you pass that one over, and tell her you'll ring her later in the week, and she tells you to do it after six o'clock, for nothing is that important, living or dying, that cannot wait to be told till the cut-price hour.

'I love you, Momma,' you hear yourself saying, and you hear her silence and know she is smiling.

'You're a good daughter to me.'

'And you're a good mother,' you mouth, and as you put the phone down, you pray to God, that whatever the price, your mother's senility, her irritations, her possessiveness, her stubbornness, her pride, whatever it costs, please God, do what You will with me, but save me from the lamb.

You let a few days pass before you call on Rose again, and when you do, it takes her some time to open the door. Through the glass pane, you can see her fumblings, and you hear the cries of locks and chains. There was a time, you remember, when Rose's door was always open, and casual coffee-drinkers dropped in and out. Now the hassle of opening up the place as if it were some museum precluded the casual visitor, and even you begin to doubt whether you will call again. She opens the door gingerly, and asks you inside, warning your hands off the wires that lead down from the door and touch off the burglar alarm. You feel suddenly as if you've come to the wrong place, and when you enter the living room, you look for traces of your friend. Where are the records and the books, even the desk and the papers that throbbed through the years of Rose. Quiet now, the pulse gone from the room, stilled by the bird's eye maple table, and its linen cloth, numbed by the cabinet of silver, wholly anaesthetised by inheritance.

'Where are your books?' you say.

'I sold them.'

'Where do you work? Where's the desk?'

'Given it up,' she says. 'I have enough to live on, thanks to my dear mother, God rest her soul.'

What's this? you ask yourself. This 'dear mother' bit, this 'God rest her soul'? Where did she pick up this middle-aged obsequious phraseology, she, who only a while ago was in monosyllabic and fearless jeans? And you have to face the truth, that when Rose's mother died, it was Rose, who, by her own and helpless choice, was buried.

'Shall I make coffee?' you say, more for old times' sake.

But no. Sit down. Rose will make it, like any good hostess, but now it takes hours to prepare, with respect to the Crown Derby and the side-plates, and embroidered serviettes, for God's sake, and Rose with her manicured little finger curled round the bone-china handle. And you long to go back to your Woolworth mugs, and the freedom of your comparative poverty.

'How is your mother?' Rose is saying, and you know that her question has nothing to do with concern.

'Immortal,' you say viciously.

You get up to go, but she presses you to another cake, and suddenly you can't bear the lace d'oyly, and the silver fork, and all the monogrammed paraphernalia that has nothing to do with your old and loved friend, and you scream to yourself, 'I'm not an orphan yet. I cannot live like this.'

Rose sees you out coldly, with much locking of doors behind, and you know that she resents you because you are still a daughter.

Small comfort in that, for you know too, and with an absolute and trembling certainty, that sooner or later, when the lamb comes to colonise you, Rose will be your friend again.

Suffer the Little Children

STEPHEN KING

MISS SIDLEY WAS HER NAME, AND TEACHING was her game.

She was a small woman who had to reach on tiptoes to write on the highest level of the blackboard, which she was doing now. Behind her, none of the children giggled or whispered or munched on secret sweets held in cupped hands. They knew Miss Sidley too well. Miss Sidley knew instinctively who was chewing gum at the back of the room, who had a beanshooter in his pocket, who wanted to go to the bathroom to trade baseball cards rather than use the facilities. Like God, she seemed to know everything all at once.

She was greying, and the brace she wore to support her failing back was lined clearly against her print dress. Small, constantly suffering, gimlet-eyed woman. But they feared her. Her tongue was a school-yard legend. The eyes, when turned on a giggler or a whisperer, could turn the stoutest knees to water.

Now, writing the day's list of spelling words on the slate, she reflected that the success of her long teaching career could be summed and checked and proven by this one everyday action. She could turn her back on her pupils in confidence.

'Vacation,' she said, pronouncing the word as she wrote it in her firm, no-nonsense script. 'Edward, you will please use the word *vacation* in a sentence.'

'I went on a vacation to New York City,' Edward piped. Then, as Miss Sidley had taught, he repeated the word carefully. 'Vay-cay-shun.'

'Very good, Edward.' She began the next word.

She had her little tricks, of course; success, she firmly believed, depended as much upon taking note of little things as it did upon the big ones. She applied the principle constantly in the classroom, and it never failed.

'Jane,' she said quietly.

Jane, who had been furtively perusing her Reader, looked up guiltily.

'Close that book right now, please.' The book shut; Jane looked pale, hating eyes at Miss Sidley's back. 'And you will stay for fifteen minutes after the final bell.'

Jane's lips trembled. 'Yes, Miss Sidley.'

One of her little tricks was the careful use of her glasses. The whole class was reflected to her in their thick lenses and she had always been thinly amused by their guilty frightened faces when she caught them at their nasty little games.

Now she saw a phantomish, distorted Robert in the first row wrinkle his nose. She did not speak. Robert would hang himself if given just a little more rope.

'Tomorrow,' she pronounced clearly. 'Robert, you will please use the word tomorrow in a sentence.' Robert frowned over the problem. The classroom was hushed and sleepy in the late September sun. The electric clock over the door buzzed a rumour of three o'clock dismissal just a half-hour away and the only thing that kept young heads from drowsing over their spellers was the silent, ominous threat of Miss Sidley's back.

'I am waiting, Robert.'

'Tomorrow a bad thing will happen,' Robert said. The words were perfectly innocuous, but Miss Sidley, with the seventh sense that all strict disciplinarians have, could sense a double meaning.

'Too-mor-row,' Robert finished. His hands were folded neatly on the desk, and he wrinkled his nose again. He also smiled a tiny side-of-the-mouth smile. Miss Sidley was suddenly unaccountably sure Robert knew her little trick with the glasses.

Very well.

She began to write the next word with no comment of commendation for Robert, letting her straight body speak its own message. She watched carefully with one eye. Soon Robert would stick out his tongue or make that disgusting finger gesture, just to see if she really knew what he was doing. Then he would be punished.

The reflection was small, ghostly, and distorted. And she had all but the barest corner of her eye on the word she was writing.

Robert changed.

She caught just a corner of it, just a frightening glimpse of Robert's face changing into something . . . different.

She whirled around, face white, barely noticing the protesting stab of pain in her back.

Robert looked at her blandly, questioningly. His hands were neatly folded. The first signs of an afternoon cowlick showed at the back of his head. He did not look frightened.

I have imagined it, she thought. I was looking for something, and when there was nothing, I just made something up. However —

'Robert?' she asked. She had meant to be authoritative; the unspoken demand for confession. It did not come out that way.

'Yes, Miss Sidley?' His eyes were a very dark brown, like the mud at the bottom of a slow-running stream.

'Nothing.'

She turned back to the board and a little whisper ran through the class.

'Be *quiet!*' her voice snapped. She turned again and faced them. 'Another sound and we will all stay after school with Jane!' She addressed the whole class, but looked particularly at Robert. He looked back with a child-like I-didn't-do-it innocence.

She turned to the board and began to write, not looking out of the corners of her glasses. The last half-hour dragged, and it seemed that Robert gave her a strange look on the way out. A look that said, *we have a secret, don't we?*

It wouldn't get out of her mind.

It seemed to be stuck like a tiny string of roast beef between two molars, a small thing, actually, but feeling as big as a cinderblock.

She sat down to her solitary dinner at five, poached eggs on toast, still thinking about it. She knew she was getting older and accepted the knowledge calmly. She was not going to be one of those old lady schoolteachers dragged kicking and screaming from their classrooms at the age of retirement. They reminded her of gamblers emotionally unable to leave the tables while they were losing. But *she* was not losing. She had always been a winner.

She looked down at her poached egg.

Hadn't she?

She thought of the well-scrubbed faces in her third grade classroom, and found Robert's face superimposed over them.

She got up and switched on a light.

Later, just before dropping off to sleep, Robert's face floated in front of her, smiling unpleasantly in the darkness behind her lids. The face began to change —

But before she saw exactly what it was changing into, she dropped off to sleep.

Miss Sidley spent an unrestful night and the next day her temper was short. She waited, almost hoped for a whisperer, a giggler, or perhaps even a note-passer. But the class was quiet – very quiet. They all stared at her unresponsively, and it seemed that she could feel the weight of their eyes on her like blind, crawling ants.

Now stop! she told herself sternly. She paused, controlling an urge to bite her lip. She was acting like a skittish girl just out of Seminary.

Again the day seemed to drag, and she believed she was more relieved than her charges when the dismissal bell rang. The children lined up in orderly rows at the door, boys and girls by height, hands dutifully linked.

'Dismissed,' she said, and listened sourly as they shrieked down the hall and into the bright sunlight.

What was it? It was bulbous. It shimmered and it changed and it stared at me, yes, stared and grinned and it wasn't a child at all. It was old and it was evil and —

'Miss Sidley?'

Her head jerked up; a little *oh!* hiccupped involuntarily from her throat.

It was Mr Hanning. He smiled apologetically. 'Didn't mean to disturb you.'

'Quite all right,' she said, more curtly than she had intended. What had she been thinking? What was wrong with her?

'Would you mind checking the paper towels in the girls' lavatory?'

'Surely.' She got up, placing her hands against the small of her back.

Mr Hanning looked at her sympathetically. Save it, she thought. The old maid is not amused. Or even interested.

She brushed by Mr Hanning and started down the hall to the girls' lavatory. A capering group of small boys, carrying scratched and pitted baseball equipment, grew silent at the sight of her and leaked out the door, where their cries began again.

Miss Sidley looked after them resentfully, reflecting that children had been different in her day. Not more polite – children have never had time for that – and not exactly more respectful of their elders; it was a kind of hypocrisy that had never been there before. A smiling quietness around adults that had never been there before. A kind of quiet contempt that was upsetting and unnerving. As if they were . . .

Hiding behind masks.

She pushed the thought away and went into the lavatory.

It was a small, tiled room with frosted glass windows, shaped like an L. The toilets were ranged along one bar, the sinks along both sides of the shorter bar.

As she checked along the paper towel containers, she caught a glimpse of her face in one of the mirrors and was startled into looking at it more closely.

God.

There was a look that hadn't been there two days before, a frightened, watching look. With sudden shock she realized that the tiny, blurred reflection in her glasses coupled with Robert's pale, respectful face had gotten inside her and was festering.

The door opened and she heard two girls come in, giggling secretly about something. She was about to turn the corner and walk out past them when she heard her own name. She turned back to the washbowls and began checking the towel holders again.

'And then he —'

Soft giggles.

'She knows, but —'

More giggles, soft and sticky as melting soap.

'Miss Sidley is —'

Stop it! Stop that noise!

By moving slightly she could see their shadows, made fuzzy and ill-defined by the diffuse light filtering through the frosted windows, holding on to each other with girlish glee.

Another thought crawled up out of her mind.

They knew she was there.

Yes, they did, the little bitches. They knew.

She would shake them. Shake them until their teeth rattled and their giggles turned to wails and she would make them admit that they knew, they knew, they —

The shadows changed.

They seemed to elongate, to flow like dripping tallow, taking on strange, hunched shapes that made Miss Sidley cringe back against the porcelain washstands, her heart swelling in her chest.

But they went on giggling.

The voices changed, no longer girlish, now sexless and soulless, and quite, quite evil. A slow, turgid sound of mindless humour that flowed around the corner to her like river mud.

She stared at the hunched shadows and suddenly screamed at them. The scream went on and on, swelling in her head until it attained a pitch of lunacy. And then she fainted. The giggling, like the laughter of demons, followed her down into darkness.

She could not, of course, tell them the truth.

Miss Sidley knew this even as she opened her eyes and looked up at the anxious faces of Mr Hanning and Mrs Crossen. Mrs Crossen was holding a bottle of sharp smelling stuff under her nose. Mr Hanning turned around and told the two little girls who were looking curiously at Miss Sidley to go on home now, please.

They both smiled at her, slow, we-have-a-secret smiles, and went out.

Very well. She would keep their secret. For a while. She would not have people thinking her insane. She would not have them thinking that the first feelers of senility had touched her early. She would play their game. Until she could expose their nastiness and rip it out. By the roots.

'I'm afraid I slipped,' she said calmly, sitting up and ignoring the excruciating pain in her back. 'A patch of wetness.'

'This is awful,' Mr Hanning said. 'Terrible. Are you —'

'Did the fall hurt your back, Emily?' Mrs Crossen interrupted. Mr Hanning looked at her gratefully.

Miss Sidley got up, her spine screaming in her body.

'No,' she said. 'In fact, something seems to have snapped back into place. It actually feels better.'

'We can send for a —' Mr Hanning began.

'No physician necessary. I'll just go on home.' Miss Sidley smiled at him coolly.

'I'll get you a taxi.'

'I always take the bus,' Miss Sidley said. She walked out.

Mr Hanning sighed and looked at Mrs Crossen. 'She *does* seem more like herself —'

The next day Miss Sidley kept Robert after school. He did nothing, so she simply accused him falsely. She felt no qualms; he was a monster, not a little boy. And she would make him admit it.

Her back was in agony. She realized Robert knew; he expected that would help him. But it wouldn't. That was another of her little advantages. Her back had been a constant pain to her for the last twelve years, and there had been times when it had been this bad – well, almost as bad – as this.

She closed the door, shutting the two of them in.

For a moment she stood still, training her gaze on Robert. She waited for him to drop his eyes. He didn't. He gazed back at her, and presently a little smile began to play around the corners of his mouth.

'Why are you smiling, Robert?' she asked softly.

'I don't know.' Robert went on smiling.

'Tell me, please, Robert.'

Robert said nothing. He went on smiling.

The outside sounds of children at play were far off, distant, dreamy. Only the hypnotic buzz of the wall clock was real.

'There's quite a few of us,' Robert said suddenly, as if he were commenting on the weather.

It was Miss Sidley's turn to be silent.

'Eleven right here in this school.' Robert went on smiling his small smile.

Quite evil, she thought, amazed. Very, incredibly evil.

'Please don't lie,' she said clearly. 'Lies only make things worse.'

Robert's smile grew wider; it became vulpine. 'Do you want to see me change, Miss Sidley?' he asked. 'Would you like to see it right out?'

Miss Sidley felt a nameless chill. 'Go away,' she said curtly. 'And bring your mother and father to school with you tomorrow. We'll get this business straightened out.' There. On solid ground again. She waited for his face to crumble, waited for the tears and the pleas to relent.

Robert's smile grew wider. He showed his teeth. 'It will be just like Show and Tell, won't it, Miss Sidley? Robert – the *other* Robert – he liked Show and Tell. He's still hiding 'way, 'way down in my head.' The smile curled at the corners of his mouth like charring paper. 'Sometimes he runs around ... it itches. He wants me to let him out.'

'Go away,' Miss Sidley said numbly. The buzzing of the clock seemed very loud.

Robert changed.

His face suddenly ran together like melting wax, the eyes flattening and spreading like knife-struck egg yolks, nose widening and yawning, mouth disappearing. The head elongated, and the hair was suddenly not hair but straggling, twitching growths.

Robert began to chuckle.

The slow, cavernous sound came from what had been his nose,

but the nose was eating into the lower half of his face, nostrils meeting and merging into a central blackness like a huge, shouting mouth.

Robert got up, still chuckling, and behind it all she could see the last shattered remains of the other Robert, howling in maniac terror, screeching to be let out.

She ran.

She fled screaming down the corridor, and the few late-leaving pupils turned to look at her with large and uncomprehending eyes.

Mr Hanning jerked open his door and looked out just as Miss Sidley plunged through the wide glass front doors, a wild, waving scarecrow silhouetted against the bright September sky.

He ran after her, Adam's apple bobbing convulsively 'Miss Sidley! *Miss Sidley!*'

Robert came out of the classroom and watched curiously.

Miss Sidley neither heard nor saw. She clattered down the walk and across the sidewalk and into the streets with her screams trailing behind her like banners. There was a huge, blatting horn and then the bus was looming over her, the bus driver's face a plaster mask of fear. Air brakes whined and hissed like dragons in flight.

Miss Sidley fell, and the huge wheels shuddered to a smoking stop just eight inches from her frail, brace-armoured body. She lay shuddering in the pavement, hearing the crowd gather around her.

She turned over and the children were staring down at her. They were ringed in a tight little circle, like mourners around an open grave. And at the head of the grave was Robert, his little face sober and solemn, ready to read the death rites and shovel the first spade of dirt over her face.

From far away, the bus driver's shaken babble: ' . . . crazy or somethin' . . . my God, another half a foot . . .'

Miss Sidley stared numbly at the children. Their shadows covered her and blocked out the sun. Their faces were impassive. Some of them were smiling little secret smiles, and Miss Sidley knew that soon she would begin to scream again.

Then Mr Hanning broke their tight noose and shooed them away.

Miss Sidley began to sob weakly.

She did not go back to her third grade for a month. She told Mr Hanning calmly that she had not been feeling herself, and Mr Hanning suggested that she go to a reputable, ah, doctor, and discuss the matter with him. Miss Sidley agreed that this was the only sensible and rational course. She also said that if the school board wished her resignation she would tender it immediately, although it would hurt her very much. Mr Hanning, looking uncomfortable, said he doubted if that would be necessary.

The upshot of the matter was that Miss Sidley went back to her class in late October, once again ready to play the game and now knowing how to play it.

For the first week she let things go on as ever. It seemed the whole class now regarded her with hostile, shielded eyes. Robert smiled distantly at her from his first-row seat, and she did not have the courage to take him to task.

Once, while on playground duty, Robert walked over to her, holding a dodgem ball, smiling. 'There's more of us now,' he said. 'Lots, lots more.' A girl on the jungle gym looked across the playground at them and smiled, as if she had heard.

Miss Sidley smiled serenely, refusing to remember the face changing, mutating: 'Why, Robert, whatever do you mean?'

But Robert only continued smiling and went back to his game. Miss Sidley knew the time had come.

She brought the gun to school in her handbag.

It had been her brother Jim's. He had taken it from a dead German shortly after the Battle of the Bulge. Jim had been gone ten years now. She had not opened the box that held the gun in more years than that, but when she did it was still there, gleaming dully. The four clips of shells were still in the box, too, and she loaded carefully the way Jim had showed her once.

She smiled pleasantly at her class; at Robert in particular. Robert smiled back and she could see the murky alienness swimming just below his skin, muddy, full of filth.

She never cared wondering just what was impersonating Robert, but she wished she knew if the real Robert was still inside. She did not wish to be a murderess. She decided that the real Robert must have died or gone insane, living inside the dirty, crawling thing that had chuckled at her in the classroom and sent her screaming into the street. So even if he was still alive, putting him out of his misery would be a mercy.

'Today we're going to have a Test,' Miss Sidley said.

The class did not groan or shift apprehensively; they merely looked at her. She could feel their eyes, like weights. Heavy, smothering.

'It's a very special Test. I will call you down to the mimeographing room one by one and give you your Test. Then you may have a candy and go home for the day. Won't that be nice?'

They smiled empty smiles and said nothing.

'Robert, will you come first?'

Robert got up, smiling his little smile. He wrinkled his nose quite openly at her. 'Yes, Miss Sidley.'

Miss Sidley took her bag and they went down the empty, echoing corridor together, past the sleepy buzz of reciting classes coming from behind closed doors.

The mimeograph room was at the far end of the hall, past the lavatories. It had been soundproofed two years ago; the big machine was very old and very noisy.

Miss Sidley closed the door behind them and locked it.

'No one can hear you,' she said calmly. She took the gun from her bag. 'You or the gun.'

Robert smiled innocently. 'There are lots of us, though. Lots more than here.' He put one small scrubbed hand on the paper-tray of the mimeograph machine. 'Would you like to see me change, Miss Sidley?'

Before she could speak, the change began. Robert's face began to melt and shimmer into the grotesqueness beneath, and Miss Sidley shot him. Once. In the head.

He fell back against the paper-lined shelves and slid down to the floor, a little dead boy with a round black hole above the right eye.

He looked very pathetic.

Miss Sidley stood over him, breathing hard. Her scrawny cheeks were livid.

The huddled figure didn't move.

It was human.

It was Robert.

No!

It was all in your mind, Emily. All in your mind.

No! No, no, *no!*

She went back up to the room and began to lead them down, one by one. She killed twelve of them and would have killed them all if Mrs Crossen hadn't come down for a package of composition paper.

Mrs Crossen's eyes got very big; one hand crept up and clutched her mouth. She began to scream and she was still screaming when Miss Sidley reached her and put a hand on her shoulder. 'It had to be done, Margaret,' she said sadly to the screaming Mrs Crossen. 'It's terrible, but it had to. They are all monsters. I found out.'

Mrs Crossen stared at the gay-clothed little bodies scattered around the mimeograph and continued to scream.

The little girl whose hand Miss Sidley was holding began to cry steadily and monotonously.

'Change,' Miss Sidley said. 'Change for Mrs Crossen. Show her it had to be done.'

The girl continued to weep uncomprehendingly.

'Damn you, *change!*' Miss Sidley screamed. 'Dirty bitch, dirty, crawling, filthy unnatural *bitch!* Change! God damn you, *change!*' She raised the gun. The little girl cringed, and then Mrs Crossen was on her like a cat, and Miss Sidley's back gave way.

No trial.

The papers screamed for a trial, bereaved parents swore hysterical oaths against Miss Sidley, and the city sat back on its haunches in numb shock —

— Twelve children!

The State Legislature called for more stringent teacher examination tests, Summer Street School closed for a week of mourning, and Miss Sidley went quietly to an antiseptic madhouse in the next state. She was put in deep analysis, given the most modern drugs, introduced into daily work-therapy sessions. A year later, under strictly controlled conditions, Miss Sidley was put in an experimental encounter-therapy situation.

Buddy Jenkins was his name, psychiatry was his game.

He sat behind a one-way glass with a clipboard, looking into a room which had been outfitted as a nursery. On the far wall, the cow was jumping over the moon and the mouse was halfway up the clock. Miss Sidley sat in her wheelchair with a story book, surrounded by a group of soft, trusting, totally mindless retarded children. They smiled at her and drooled and touched her with small wet fingers while attendants at the next window watched for the first sign of an aggressive move.

For a time Buddy thought she responded well. She read aloud, stroked a girl's head, picked up a small boy when he fell over a toy block. Then she seemed to see something which disturbed her; a frown creased her brow and she looked away from the children.

'Take me away, please,' Miss Sidley said, softly and tonelessly, to no one in particular.

And so they took her away. Buddy Jenkins watched the children watch her go, their eyes wide and empty, but somehow deep. One smiled, and another put his fingers in his mouth slyly. Two little girls clutched each other and giggled.

That night Miss Sidley cut her throat with a bit of broken mirror-glass, and Buddy Jenkins began to watch the children.

The New Girlfriend

RUTH RENDELL

'You know what we did last time?' he said.

She had waited for this for weeks. 'Yes?'

'I wondered if you'd like to do it again.'

She longed to but she didn't want to sound too keen. 'Why not?'

'How about Friday afternoon then? I've got the day off and Angie always goes to her sister's on Friday.'

'Not *always*, David.' She giggled.

He also laughed a little. 'She will this week. Do you think we could use your car? Angie'll take ours.'

'Of course. I'll come for you about two, shall I?'

'I'll open the garage doors and you can drive straight in. Oh, and Chris, could you fix it to get back a bit later? I'd love it if we could have the whole evening together.'

'I'll try,' she said, and then, 'I'm sure I can fix it. I'll tell Graham I'm going out with my new girl friend.'

He said good-bye and that he would see her on Friday. Christine put the receiver back. She had almost given up expecting a call from him. But there must have been a grain of hope still, for she had never left the receiver off the way she used to.

The last time she had done that was on a Thursday three weeks before, the day she had gone round to Angie's and found David there alone. Christine had got into the habit of taking the phone off the hook during the middle part of the day to avoid getting calls for the Midland Bank. Her number and the Midland Bank's differed by only one digit. Most days she took the receiver off at nine-thirty and put it back at three-thirty. On Thursday afternoons she nearly always went round to see Angie and never bothered to phone first.

Christine knew Angie's husband quite well. If she stayed a bit later on Thursdays she saw him when he came home from work. Sometimes she and Graham and Angie and David went out together as a foursome. She knew that David, like Graham, was a salesman or sales executive, as Graham always described himself, and she guessed from her friend's lifestyle that David was rather more successful at it. She had never found him particularly attractive, for, although he was quite tall, he had something of a girlish look and very fair wavy hair.

Graham was a heavily-built, very dark man with a swarthy skin. He had to shave twice a day. Christine had started going out with him when she was fifteen and they had got married on her eighteenth birthday. She had never really known any other men at all intimately and now if she ever found herself alone with a man she felt awkward and apprehensive. The truth was that she was afraid a man might make an advance to her and the thought of that frightened her very much. For a long while she carried a penknife in her handbag in case she should need to defend herself. One evening, after they had been out with a colleague of Graham's and had had a few drinks, she told Graham about this fear of hers.

He said she was silly but he seemed rather pleased.

'When you went off to talk to those people and I was left with John I felt like that. I felt terribly nervous. I didn't know how to talk to him.'

Graham roared with laughter. 'You don't mean you thought old John was going to make a pass at you in the middle of a crowded restaurant?'

'I don't know,' Christine said. 'I never know what they'll do.'

'So long as you're not afraid of what I'll do,' said Graham, beginning to kiss her, 'that's all that matters.'

There was no point in telling him now, ten years too late, that she was afraid of what he did and always had been. Of course she had got used to it, she wasn't actually terrified, she was resigned and sometimes even quite cheerful about it. David was the only man she had ever been alone with when it felt all right.

That first time, that Thursday when Angie had gone to her sister's and hadn't been able to get through on the phone and tell Christine not to come, that time it had been fine. And afterwards she had felt happy and carefree, though what had happened with David took on the colouring of a dream next day. It wasn't really believable. Early on he had said:

'Will you tell Angie?'

'Not if you don't want me to.'

'I think it would upset her, Chris. It might even wreck our marriage. You see . . .' He had hesitated. 'You see, that was the first time I – I mean, anyone ever . . .' And he had looked into her eyes. 'Thank God it was you.'

The following Thursday she had gone round to see Angie as usual. In the meantime there had been no word from David. She stayed late in order to see him, beginning to feel a little sick with apprehension, her heart beating hard when he came in.

He looked quite different from how he had when she had found him sitting at the table reading, the radio on. He was wearing a grey flannel suit and a grey striped tie. When Angie went out of the room and for a minute she was alone with him, she felt a flicker of that old wariness that was the forerunner of her fear. He was getting her a drink. She looked up and met his eyes and it was all right again. He gave her a conspiratorial smile, laying a finger on his lips.

'I'll give you a ring,' he had whispered.

She had to wait two more weeks. During that time she went twice to Angie's and twice Angie came to her. She and Graham and Angie and David went out as a foursome and while Graham was fetching drinks and Angie was in the Ladies, David looked at her and smiled and lightly touched her foot with his foot under the table.

'I'll phone you. I haven't forgotten.'

It was a Wednesday when he finally did phone. Next day Christine told Graham she had made a new friend, a girl she had met at work. She would be going out somewhere with this new friend on Friday and she wouldn't be back till eleven. She was desperately afraid he would want the car – it was *his* car or his firm's – but it so happened he would be in the office that day and would go by train. Telling him these lies didn't make her feel guilty. It wasn't as if this were some sordid affair, it was quite different.

When Friday came she dressed with great care. Normally, to go round to Angie's, she would have worn jeans and a teeshirt with a sweater over it. That was what she had on the first time she found herself alone with David. She put on a skirt and blouse and her black velvet jacket. She took the heated rollers out of her hair and brushed it into curls down on her shoulders. There was never much money to spend on clothes. The mortgage on the house took up a third of what Graham earned and half what she earned at her part-time job. But she could run to a pair of sheer black tights to go with the highest-heeled shoes she'd got, her black pumps.

The doors of Angie and David's garage were wide open and their car was gone. Christine turned into their driveway, drove into the garage and closed the doors behind her. A door at the back of the garage led into the yard and garden. The kitchen door was unlocked as it had been that Thursday three weeks before and always was on Thursday afternoons. She opened the door and walked in.

'Is that you, Chris?'

The voice sounded very male. She needed to be reassured by the sight of him. She went into the hall as he came down the stairs.

'You look lovely,' he said.

'So do you.'

He was wearing a suit. It was of navy silk with a pattern of pink and white flowers. The skirt was very short, the jacket clinched into his waist with a wide navy patent belt. The long golden hair fell to his shoulders, he was heavily made-up and this time he had painted his fingernails. He looked far more beautiful than he had that first time.

Then, three weeks before, the sound of her entry drowned in loud music from the radio, she had come upon this girl sitting at the table reading *Vogue*. For a moment she had thought it must be David's sister. She had forgotten Angie had said David was an only child. The girl had long fair hair and was wearing a red summer dress with white spots on it, white sandals and around her neck a string of white beads. When Christine saw that it was not a girl but David himself she didn't know what to do.

He stared at her in silence and without moving and then he switched off the radio. Christine said the silliest and least relevant thing.

'What are you doing home at this time?'

That made him smile. 'I'd finished so I took the rest of the day off. I should have locked the back door. Now you're here you may as well sit down.'

She sat down. She couldn't take her eyes off him. He didn't look like a man dressed up as a girl, he looked like a girl and a much prettier one than she or Angie. 'Does Angie know?'

He shook his head.

'But why do you do it?' she burst out and she looked about the room, Angie's small, rather untidy living room, at the radio, the *Vogue* magazine. 'What do you get out of it?' Something came back to her from an article she had read. 'Did your mother dress you as a girl when you were little?'

'I don't know,' he said. 'Maybe. I don't remember. I don't want to *be* a girl. I just want to dress up as one sometimes.'

The first shock of it was past and she began to feel easier with him. It wasn't as if there was anything grotesque about the way he looked. The very last thing he reminded her of was one of those female impersonators. A curious thought came into her head, that it was *nicer*, somehow more civilised, to be a woman and that if only all men were more like women ... That was silly, of course, it couldn't be.

'And it's enough for you just to dress up and be here on your own?'

He was silent for a moment. Then, 'Since you ask, what I'd really like would be to go out like this and ...' He paused, looking at her, ' ... and be seen by lots of people, that's what I'd like. I've never had the nerve for that.'

The bold idea expressed itself without her having to give it a moment's thought. She wanted to do it. She was beginning to tremble with excitement.

'Let's go out then, you and I. Let's go out now. I'll put my car in your garage and you can get into it so the people next door don't see and then we'll go somewhere. Let's do that, David, shall we?'

She wondered afterwards why she had enjoyed it so much. What had it been, after all, as far as anyone else knew but two girls walking on Hampstead Heath? If Angie had suggested that the two of them do it she would have thought it a poor way of spending the afternoon. But with David ... She hadn't even minded that of the two of them he was infinitely the better dressed, taller, better-looking, more graceful. She didn't mind now as he came down the stairs and stood in front of her.

'Where shall we go?'

'Not the Heath this time,' he said. 'Let's go shopping.'

He bought a blouse in one of the big stores. Christine went into the changing room with him when he tried it on. They walked about in Hyde Park. Later on they had dinner and Christine noted that they were the only two women in the restaurant dining together.

'I'm grateful to you,' David said. He put his hand over hers on the table.

'I enjoy it,' she said. 'It's so – crazy. I really love it. You'd better not do that, had you? There's a man over there giving a funny look.'

'Women hold hands,' he said.

'Only *those* sort of women. David, we could do this every Friday you don't have to work.'

'Why not?' he said.

There was nothing to feel guilty about. She wasn't harming Angie and she wasn't being disloyal to Graham. All she was doing was going on innocent outings with another girl. Graham wasn't interested in her new friend, he didn't even ask her name. Christine came to long for Fridays, especially for the moment when she let herself into Angie's house and saw David coming down the stairs and for the moment when they stepped out of the car in some public place and the first eyes were turned on him. They went to Holland Park, they went to the zoo, to Kew Gardens. They went to the cinema and a man sitting next to David put his hand on his knee. David loved that, it was a triumph for him, but Christine whispered they must change their seats and they did.

When they parted at the end of an evening he kissed her gently on the lips. He smelt of *Alliage* or *Je Reviens* or *Opium*. During the afternoon they usually went into one of the big stores and sprayed themselves out of the tester bottles.

Angie's mother lived in the north of England. When she had to convalesce after an operation Angie went up there to look after her. She expected to be away two weeks and the second weekend of her absence Graham had to go to Brussels with the sales manager.

'We could go away somewhere for the weekend,' David said.

'Graham's sure to phone,' Christine said.

'One night then. Just for the Saturday night. You can tell him you're going out with your new girlfriend and you're going to be late.'

'All right.'

It worried her that she had no nice clothes to wear. David had a small but exquisite wardrobe of suits and dresses, shoes and scarves and beautiful underclothes. He kept them in a cupboard in his office to which only he had a key and he secreted items home and back again in his briefcase. Christine hated the idea of going away for the night in her grey flannel skirt and white silk blouse and that velvet jacket while David wore his Zandra Rhodes dress. In a burst of recklessness she spent all of two weeks' wages on a linen suit.

They went in David's car. He had made the arrangements and

Christine had expected they would be going to a motel twenty miles outside London. She hadn't thought it would matter much to David where they went. But he surprised her by his choice of an hotel that was a three-hundred-year-old house on the Suffolk coast.

'If we're going to do it,' he said, 'we may as well do it in style.'

She felt very comfortable with him, very happy. She tried to imagine what it would have felt like going to spend a night in an hotel with a man, a lover. If the person sitting next to her were dressed, not in a black and white printed silk dress and scarlet jacket but in a man's suit with shirt and tie. If the face it gave her so much pleasure to look at were not powdered and rouged and mascara'd but rough and already showing beard growth. She couldn't imagine it. Or, rather, she could only think how in that case she would have jumped out of the car at the first red traffic lights.

They had single rooms next door to each other. The rooms were very small but Christine could see that a double might have been awkward for David who must at some point – though she didn't care to think of this – have to shave and strip down to being what he really was.

He came in and sat on her bed while she unpacked her nightdress and spare pair of shoes.

'This is fun, isn't it?'

She nodded, squinting into the mirror, working on her eyelids with a little brush. David always did his eyes beautifully. She turned round and smiled at him.

'Let's go down and have a drink.'

The dining room, the bar, the lounge were all low-ceilinged timbered rooms with carved wood on the walls David said was called linenfold panelling. There were old maps and pictures of men hunting in gilt frames and copper bowls full of roses. Long windows were thrown open on to a terrace. The sun was still high in the sky and it was very warm. While Christine sat on the terrace in the sunshine David went off to get their drinks. When he came back to their table he had a man with him, a thickset paunchy man of about forty who was carrying a tray with four glasses on it.

'This is Ted,' David said.

'Delighted to meet you,' Ted said. 'I've asked my friend to join us. I hope you don't mind.'

She had to say she didn't. David looked at her and from his look she could tell he had deliberately picked Ted up.

'But why did you?' she said to him afterwards. 'Why did you want to? You told me you didn't really like it when that man put his hand on you in the cinema.'

'That was so physical. This is just a laugh. You don't suppose I'd let them touch me, do you?'

Ted and Peter had the next table to theirs at dinner. Christine was silent and standoffish but David flirted with them. Ted kept leaning across and whispering to him and David giggled and smiled. You could see he was enjoying himself tremendously. Christine knew they would ask her and David to go out with them after dinner and she began to be afraid. Suppose David got carried away by the excitement of it, the 'fun', and went off somewhere with Ted, leaving her and Peter alone together? Peter had a red face and a black moustache and beard and a wart with black hairs growing out of it on his left cheek. She and David were eating steak and the waiter had brought them sharp pointed steak knives. She hadn't used hers. The steak was very tender. When no one was looking she slipped the steak knife into her bag.

Ted and Peter were still drinking coffee and brandies when David got up quite abruptly and said, 'Coming?' to Christine.

'I suppose you've arranged to meet them later?' Christine said as soon as they were out of the dining room.

David looked at her. His scarlet-painted lips parted into a wide smile. He laughed.

'I turned them down.'

'Did you *really*?'

'I could tell you hated the idea. Besides, we want to be alone, don't we? I know I want to be alone with you.'

She nearly shouted his name so that everyone could hear, the relief was so great. She controlled herself but she was trembling. 'Of course I want to be alone with you,' she said.

She put her arm in his. It wasn't uncommon, after all, for girls to walk along with linked arms. Men turned to look at David and one of them whistled. She knew it must be David the whistle was directed at because he looked so beautiful with his long golden hair and high-heeled red sandals. They walked along the sea front, along the little low promenade. It was too warm even at eight-thirty to wear a coat. There were a lot of people about but not crowds for the place was too select to attract crowds. They walked to the end of the pier. They had a drink in the Ship Inn and another in the Fishermen's Arms.

A man tried to pick David up in the Fishermen's Arms but this time he was cold and distant.

'I'd like to put my arm round you,' he said as they were walking back, 'but I suppose that wouldn't do, though it is dark.'

'Better not,' said Christine. She said suddenly, 'This has been the best evening of my life.'

He looked at her. 'You really mean that?'

She nodded. 'Absolutely the best.'

They came into the hotel. 'I'm going to get them to send us up a couple of drinks. To my room. Is that okay?'

She sat on the bed. David went into the bathroom. To do his face, she thought, maybe to shave before he let the man with the drinks see him. There was a knock at the door and a waiter came in with a tray on which were two long glasses of something or other with fruit and leaves floating in it, two pink table napkins, two olives on sticks and two peppermint creams wrapped up in green paper.

Christine tasted one of the drinks. She ate an olive. She opened her handbag and took out a mirror and a lipstick and painted her lips. David came out of the bathroom. He had taken off the golden wig and washed his face. He hadn't shaved, there was a pale stubble showing on his chin and cheeks. His legs and feet were bare and he was wearing a very masculine robe made of navy blue towelling. She tried to hide her disappointment.

'You've changed,' she said brightly.

He shrugged. 'There are limits.'

He raised his glass and she raised her glass and he said:

'To us!'

The beginnings of a feeling of panic came over her. Suddenly he was so evidently a man. She edged a little way along the mattress.

'I wish we had the whole weekend.'

She nodded nervously. She was aware her body had started a faint trembling. He had noticed it too. Sometimes before he had noticed how emotion made her tremble.

'Chris,' he said.

She sat passive and afraid.

'I'm not really like a woman, Chris. I just play at that sometimes for fun. You know that, don't you?' The hand that touched her smelt of nail varnish remover. There were hairs on the wrist she had never noticed before. 'I'm falling in love with you,' he said 'And you feel the same, don't you?'

She couldn't speak. He took her by the shoulders. He brought his mouth up to hers and put his arms round her and began kissing her. His skin felt abrasive and a smell as male as Graham's came off his body. She shook and shuddered. He pushed her down on the bed and his hands began undressing her, his mouth still on hers and his body heavy on top of her.

She felt behind her, put her hand into the open handbag and pulled out the knife. Because she could feel his heart beating steadily against her right breast she knew where to stab and she stabbed again and again. The bright red heart's blood spurted over her clothes and the bed and the two peppermint creams on the tray.

Odour of Chrysanthemums

D.H. LAWRENCE

THE SMALL LOCOMOTIVE ENGINE, Number 4, came clanking, stumbling down from Selston with seven full wagons. It appeared round the corner with loud threats of speed, but the colt that it startled from among the gorse, which still flickered indistinctly in the raw afternoon, out-distanced it at a canter. A woman, walking up the railway line to Underwood, drew back into the hedge, held her basket aside, and watched the footplate of the engine advancing. The trucks thumped heavily past, one by one, with slow inevitable movements, as she stood insignificantly trapped between the jolting black wagons and the hedge; then they curved away towards the coppice where the withered oak leaves dropped noiselessly, while the birds, pulling at the scarlet hips beside the track, made off into the dusk that had already crept into the spinney. In the open, the smoke from the engine sank and cleaved to the rough grass. The fields were dreary and forsaken, and in the marshy strip that led to the whimsey, a reedy pit-pond, the fowls had already abandoned their run among the alders, to roost in the tarred fowl-house. The pit bank looked up beyond the pond, flames like red sores licking its ashy sides, in the afternoon's stagnant light. Just beyond rose the tapering chimneys and the clumsy black headstocks of Brinsley Colliery. The two wheels were spinning fast up against the sky, and the winding engine rapped out its little spasms. The miners were being turned up.

The engine whistled as it came into the wide bay of railway lines beside the colliery, where rows of trucks stood in harbour.

Miners, single, trailing and in groups, passed like shadows diverging home. At the edge of the ribbed level of sidings squat a low cottage, three steps down from the cinder track. A large bony vine clutched at the house, as if to claw down the tiled roof. Round the bricked yard grew a few wintry primroses. Beyond, the long garden sloped down to a bush-covered brook course. There were some twiggy apple trees, wintercrack trees, and ragged cabbages. Beside the path hung dishevelled pink chrysanthemums, like pink cloths hung on bushes. A woman came stooping out of the felt-covered fowlhouse, half-way down the garden. She closed and padlocked the door, then drew herself erect, having brushed some bits from her white apron.

She was a tall woman of imperious mien, handsome, with definite black eyebrows. Her smooth black hair was parted exactly. For a few moments she stood steadily watching the miners as they passed along the railway; then she turned towards the brook course. Her face was calm and set, her mouth was closed with disillusionment. After a moment she called:

'John!' There was no answer. She waited, and then said distinctly: 'Where are you?'

'Here!' replied a child's sulky voice from among the bushes. The woman looked piercingly through the dusk.

'Are you at that brook?' she asked sternly.

For answer the child showed himself before the raspberry-canes that rose like whips. He was a small, sturdy boy of five. He stood quite still, defiantly.

'Oh!' said the mother, conciliated. 'I thought you were down at that wet brook – and you remember what I told you –'

The boy did not move or answer.

'Come, come on in,' she said more gently, 'it's getting dark. There's your grandfather's engine coming down the line!'

The lad advanced slowly, with resentful, taciturn movement. He was dressed in trousers and waistcoat of cloth that was too thick and hard for the size of the garments. They were evidently cut down from a man's clothes.

As they went slowly towards the house he tore at the ragged wisps of chrysanthemums and dropped the petals in handfuls along the path.

'Don't do that – it does look nasty,' said his mother. He refrained, and she, suddenly pitiful, broke off a twig with three or four wan flowers and held them against her face. When mother and son reached the yard her hand hesitated, and instead of laying the flower aside, she pushed it in her apron-band. The mother and son stood at the foot of the three steps looking across the bay of lines at the passing home of the miners. The trundle of the small train was imminent. Suddenly the engine loomed past the house and came to a stop opposite the gate.

The engine-driver, a short man with round grey beard, leaned out of the cab high above the woman.

'Have you got a cup of tea?' he said in a cheery, hearty fashion.

It was her father. She went in, saying she would mash. Directly, she returned.

'I didn't come to see you on Sunday,' began the little grey-bearded man.

'I didn't expect you,' said his daughter.

The engine-driver winced; then, reassuming his cheery, airy manner, he said:

'Oh, have you heard then? Well, and what do you think –'

'I think it is soon enough,' she replied.

At her brief censure the little man made an impatient gesture, and said coaxingly, yet with dangerous coldness:

'Well, what's a man to do? It's no sort of life for a man of my years, to sit at my own hearth like a stranger. And if I'm going to marry again it may as well be soon as late – what does it matter to anybody?'

The woman did not reply, but turned and went into the house. The man in the engine-cab stood assertive, till she returned with a cup of tea and a piece of bread and butter on a plate. She went up the steps and stood near the footplate of the hissing engine.

'You needn't 'a' brought me bread an' butter,' said her father. 'But a cup of tea' – he sipped appreciatively – 'it's very nice.' He sipped for a moment or two, then: 'I hear as Walter's got another bout on,' he said.

'When hasn't he? said the woman bitterly.

'I heerd tell of him in the "Lord Nelson" braggin' as he was going to spend that b— afore he went: half a sovereign that was.'

'When?' asked the woman.

'A' Sat'day night – I know that's true.'

'Very likely,' she laughed bitterly. 'He gives me twenty-three shillings.'

'Aye, it's a nice thing, when a man can do nothing with his money but make a beast of himself!' said the grey-whiskered man. The woman turned her head away. Her father swallowed the last of his tea and handed her the cup.

'Aye,' he sighed, wiping his mouth. 'It's a settler, it is –'

He put his hand on the lever. The little engine strained and groaned, and the train rumbled towards the crossing. The woman again looked across the metals. Darkness was settling over the spaces of the railway and trucks: the miners, in grey sombre groups, were still passing home. The winding engine pulsed hurriedly, with brief pauses. Elizabeth Bates looked at the dreary flow of men, then she went indoors. Her husband did not come.

The kitchen was small and full of firelight; red coals piled glowing up the chimney mouth. All the life of the room seemed in the white, warm hearth and the steel fender reflecting the red fire. The cloth was laid for tea; cups glinted in the shadows. At the back, where the lowest stairs protruded into the room, the boy sat struggling with a knife and a piece of white wood. He was almost hidden in the shadow. It was half-past four. They had but to await the father's coming to begin tea. As the mother watched her son's sullen little struggle with the wood, she saw herself in his silence and pertinacity; she saw the father in her child's indifference to all but himself. She seemed to be occupied by her husband. He had probably gone past his home, slunk past his own door, to drink before he came in, while his dinner spoiled and wasted in waiting. She glanced at the clock, then took the potatoes to strain them in the yard. The garden and fields beyond the brook were closed in uncertain darkness. When she rose with the saucepan, leaving the drain steaming into the night behind her, she saw the yellow lamps were lit along the high road that went up the hill away beyond the space of the railway lines and the field.

Then again she watched the men trooping home, fewer now and fewer.

Indoors the fire was sinking and the room was dark red. The woman put her saucepan on the hob, and set a batter-pudding near the mouth of the oven. Then she stood unmoving. Directly, gratefully, came quick young steps to the door. Something hung on the latch a moment, then a little girl entered and began pulling off her outdoor things, dragging a mass of curls, just ripening from gold to brown, over her eyes with her hat.

Her mother chid her for coming late from school, and said she would have to keep her at home the dark winter days.

'Why, mother, it's hardly a bit dark yet. The lamp's not lighted, and my father's not home.'

'No, he isn't. But it's a quarter to five! Did you see anything of him?'

The child became serious. She looked at her mother with large, wistful blue eyes.

'No, mother, I've never seen him. Why? Has he come up an' gone past, to Old Brinsley? He hasn't, mother, 'cos I never saw him.'

'He'd watch that,' said the mother bitterly, 'he'd take care as you didn't see him. But you may depend upon it, he's seated in the "Prince o' Wales". He wouldn't be this late.'

The girl looked at her mother piteously.

'Let's have our teas, mother, should we?' said she.

The mother called John to table. She opened the door once more and looked out across the darkness of the lines. All was deserted: she could not hear the winding-engines.

'Perhaps,' she said to herself, 'he's stopped to get some ripping done.'

They sat down to tea. John, at the end of the table near the door, was almost lost in the darkness. Their faces were hidden from each other. The girl crouched against the fender slowly moving a thick piece of bread before the fire. The lad, his face a dusky mark on the shadow, sat watching her who was transfigured in the red glow.

'I do think it's beautiful to look in the fire,' said the child.

'Do you?' said her mother. 'Why?'

'It's so red, and full of little caves – and it feels so nice, and you can fair smell it.'

'It'll want mending directly,' replied her mother, 'and then if your father comes he'll carry on and say there never is a fire when a man comes home sweating from the pit. A public-house is always warm enough.'

There was silence till the boy said complainingly: 'Make haste, our Annie.'

'Well, I am doing! I can't make the fire do it no faster, can I?'

'She keeps wafflin' it about so's to make 'er slow,' grumbled the boy.

'Don't have such an evil imagination, child,' replied the mother.

Soon the room was busy in the darkness with the crisp sound of crunching. The mother ate very little. She drank her tea determinedly, and sat thinking. When she rose her anger was evident in the stern unbending of her head. She looked at the pudding in the fender, and broke out:

'It is a scandalous thing as a man can't even come home to his dinner! If it's crozzled up to a cinder I don't see why I should care.

Past his very door to get to a public-house, and here I sit with his dinner waiting for him — '

She went out. As she dropped piece after piece of coal on the red fire, the shadows fell on the walls, till the room was almost in total darkness.

'I canna see,' grumbled the invisible John. In spite of herself, the mother laughed.

'You know the way to your mouth,' she said. She set the dust-pan outside the door. When she came again like a shadow on the hearth, the lad repeated, complaining sulkily:

'I canna see.'

'Good gracious!' cried the mother irritably, 'you're as bad as your father if it's a bit dusk!'

Nevertheless, she took a paper spill from a sheaf on the mantelpiece and proceeded to light the lamp that hung from the ceiling in the middle of the room. As she reached up, her figure displayed itself just rounding with maternity.

'Oh, mother —!' exclaimed the girl.

'What?' said the woman, suspended in the act of putting the lamp-glass over the flame. The copper reflector shone handsomely on her, as she stood with uplifted arm, turning to face her daughter.

'You've got a flower in your apron!' said the child, in a little rapture at this unusual event.

'Goodness me!' exclaimed the woman, relieved. 'One would think the house was afire.' She replaced the glass and waited a moment before turning up the wick. A pale shadow was seen floating vaguely on the floor.

'Let me smell!' said the child, still rapturously, coming forward and putting her face to her mother's waist.

'Go along, silly!' said the mother, turning up the lamp. The light revealed their suspense so that the woman felt it almost unbearable. Annie was still bending at her waist. Irritably, the mother took the flowers out from her apron-band.

'Oh, mother – don't take them out!' Annie cried catching her hand and trying to replace the sprig.

'Such nonsense!' said the mother, turning away. The child put the pale chrysanthemums to her lips, murmuring:

'Don't they smell beautiful!'

Her mother gave a short laugh.

'No,' she said, 'not to me. It was chrysanthemums when I married him, and chrysanthemums when you were born, and the first time they ever brought him home drunk, he'd got brown chrysanthemums in his button-hole.'

She looked at the children. Their eyes and their parted lips were wondering. The mother sat rocking in silence for some time. Then she looked at the clock.

'Twenty minutes to six!' In a tone of fine bitter carelessness she continued: 'Eh, he'll not come now till they bring him. There he'll stick! But he needn't come rolling in here in his pit-dirt, for *I* won't wash him. He can lie on the floor — Eh, what a fool I've been, what a fool! And this is what I came here for, to this dirty hole, rats and all, for him to slink past his very door. Twice last week – he's begun now—' She silenced herself, and rose to clear the table.

While for an hour or more the children played, subduedly intent, fertile of imagination, united in fear of the mother's wrath, and in dread of their father's home-coming, Mrs Bates sat in her rocking-chair making a 'singlet' of thick cream-coloured flannel, which gave a dull wounded sound as she tore off the grey edge. She worked at her sewing with energy, listening to the children, and her anger wearied itself, lay down to rest, opening its eyes from time to time and steadily watching, its ears raised to listen. Sometimes even her anger quailed and shrank, and the mother suspended her sewing, tracing the footsteps that thudded along the sleepers outside; she would lift her head sharply to bid the children 'hush', but she recovered herself in time, and the footsteps went past the gate, and the children were not flung out of their play-world.

But at last Annie sighed, and gave in. She glanced at her wagon of slippers, and loathed the game. She turned plaintively to her mother.

'Mother!' – but she was inarticulate.

John crept out like a frog from under the sofa. His mother glanced up.

'Yes,' she said, 'just look at those shirt-sleeves!'

The boy held them out to survey them, saying nothing. Then somebody called in a hoarse voice away down the line, and suspense bristled in the room, till two people had gone by outside, talking.

'It is time for bed,' said the mother.

'My father hasn't come,' wailed Annie plaintively. But her mother was primed with courage.

'Never mind. They'll bring him when he does come – like a log.' She meant there would be no scene. 'And he may sleep on the floor till he wakes himself. I know he'll not go to work to-morrow after this!'

The children had their hands and faces wiped with a flannel. They were very quiet. When they had put on their nightdresses, they said their prayers, the boy mumbling. The mother looked down at them, at the brown silken bush of intertwining curls in the nape of the girl's neck, at the little black head of the lad, and her heart burst with anger at their father, who caused all three such distress. The children hid their faces in her skirts for comfort.

When Mrs Bates came down, the room was strangely empty, with a tension of expectancy. She took up her sewing and stitched for some time without raising her head. Meantime her anger was tinged with fear.

The clock struck eight and she rose suddenly, dropping her sewing on her chair. She went to the stair-foot door, opened it, listening. Then she went out, locking the door behind her.

Something scuffled in the yard, and she started, though she knew it was only the rats with which the place was over-run. The night was very dark. In the great bay of railway lines, bulked with trucks, there was no trace of light, only away back she could see a few yellow lamps at the pit-top, and the red smear of the burning pit-bank on the night. She hurried along the edge of the track, then, crossing the converging lines, came to the stile by the white gates, whence she emerged on the road. Then the fear which had led her shrank. People were walking up to New Brinsley; she saw the lights in the houses; twenty yards farther on were the broad windows of the 'Prince of Wales', very warm and bright, and the loud voices of men could be heard distinctly. What a fool she had been to imagine that anything had happened to him! He was merely drinking over there at the 'Prince of Wales'. She faltered. She had never yet been to fetch him, and she never would go. So she continued her walk towards the long straggling line of houses, standing back on the highway. She entered a passage between the dwellings.

'Mr Rigley? – Yes! Did you want him? No, he's not in at this minute.'

The raw-boned woman leaned forward from her dark scullery and peered at the other, upon whom fell a dim light through the blind of the kitchen window.

'Is it Mrs Bates?' She asked in a tone tinged with respect.

'Yes. I wondered if your Master was at home. Mine hasn't come yet.'

''Asn't e! Oh, Jack's been 'ome an' 'ad 'is dinner an' gone out. 'E's just gone for 'alf an hour afore bed-time. Did you call at the "Prince of Wales"?'

'No —'

'No, you didn't like —! It's not very nice.' The other woman was indulgent. There was an awkward pause. 'Jack never said nothing about – about your Master,' she said.

'No! – I expect he's stuck in there!'

Elizabeth Bates said this bitterly, and with recklessness. She knew that the woman across the yard was standing at her door listening, but she did not care. As she turned:

'Stop a minute! I'll just go an' ask Jack if 'e knows anythink,' said Mrs Rigley.

'Oh no – I wouldn't like to put —!'

'Yes, I will, if you'll just step inside an' see as th' childer doesn't come downstairs and set theirselves afire.'

Elizabeth Bates, murmuring a remonstrance, stepped inside. The other woman apologized for the state of the room.

The kitchen needed apology. There were little frocks and trousers and childish undergarments on the squab and on the floor, and a litter of playthings everywhere. On the black American cloth of the table were pieces of bread and cake, crusts, slops, and a teapot with cold tea.

'Eh, ours is just as bad,' said Elizabeth Bates, looking at the woman, not at the house. Mrs Rigley put a shawl over her head and hurried out, saying:

'I shanna be a minute.'

The other sat, noting with faint disapproval the general untidiness of the room. Then she fell to counting the shoes of various sizes scattered over the floor. There were twelve. She sighed and said to herself: 'No wonder!' – glancing at the litter. There came the scratching of two pairs of feet on the yard, and the Rigleys entered. Elizabeth Bates rose. Rigley was a big man, with very large bones. His head looked particularly bony. Across his temple was a blue scar, caused by a wound got in the pit, a wound in which the coal-dust remained blue like tattooing.

''Asna 'e come whoam yit?' asked the man, without any form of greeting, but with deference and sympathy. 'I couldn'a say wheer he is – 'e's non ower theer!' – he jerked his head to signify the 'Prince of Wales'.

"E's 'appen gone up to th' "Yew",' said Mrs Rigley.

There was another pause. Rigley had evidently something to get off his mind:

'Ah left 'im finishin' a stint,' he began. 'Loose-all 'ad bin gone about ten minutes when we com'n away, an' I shouted: "Are ter comin', Walt?" an' 'e said: "Go on, Ah shanna be but a'ef a minnit," so we com'n ter th' bottom, me an' Bowers, thinkin' as 'e wor just behint, an' 'ud come up i' the next bantle —'

He stood perplexed, as if answering a charge of deserting his mate.

Elizabeth Bates, now again certain of disaster, hastened to reassure him:

'I expect 'e's gone up to th' "Yew Tree", as you say. It's not the first time. I've fretted myself into a fever before now. He'll come home when they carry him.'

'Ay, isn't it too bad!' deplored the other woman.

'I'll just step up to Dick's an' see if 'e is theer,' offered the man, afraid of appearing alarmed, afraid of taking liberties.

'Oh, I wouldn't think of bothering you that far,' said Elizabeth Bates, with emphasis, but he knew she was glad of his offer.

As they stumbled up the entry, Elizabeth Bates heard Rigley's wife run across the yard and open her neighbour's door. At this, suddenly all the blood in her body seemed to switch away from her heart.

'Mind!' warned Rigley. 'Ah've said many a time as Ah'd fill up them ruts in this entry, sumb'dy 'll be breakin' their legs yit.'

She recovered herself and walked quickly along with the miner.

'I don't like leaving the children in bed, and nobody in the house,' she said.

'No, you dunna!' he replied courteously. They were soon at the gate of the cottage.

'Well, I shanna be many minnits. Dunna you be frettin' now, 'e'll be all right,' said the butty.

'Thank you very much, Mr Rigley,' she replied.

'You're welcome!' he stammered, moving away. 'I shanna be many minnits.'

The house was quiet. Elizabeth Bates took off her hat and shawl, and rolled back the rug. When she had finished, she sat down. It was a few minutes past nine. She was startled by the rapid chuff of the winding-engine at the pit, and the sharp whirr of the brakes on the rope as it desended. Again she felt the painful sweep of blood, and she put her hand to her side, saying aloud: 'Good gracious! – it's only the nine o'clock deputy going down,' rebuking herself.

She sat still, listening. Half an hour of this, and she was wearied out.

'What am I working myself up like this for?' she said pitiably to herself. 'I s'll only be doing myself some damage.'

She took out her sewing again.

At a quarter to ten there were footsteps. One person! She watched for the door to open. It was an elderly woman, in a black bonnet and a black woollen shawl – his mother. She was about sixty years old, pale, with blue eyes, and her face all wrinkled and lamentable. She shut the door and turned to her daughter-in-law peevishly.

'Eh, Lizzie, whatever shall we do, whatever shall we do!' she cried.

Elizabeth drew back a little, sharply.

'What is it, mother?' she said.

The elder woman seated herself on the sofa.

'I don't know, child, I can't tell you!' – she shook her head slowly. Elizabeth sat watching her, anxious and vexed.

'I don't know,' replied the grandmother, sighing very deeply. 'There's no end to my troubles, there isn't. The things I've gone through, I'm sure it's enough —!' She wept without wiping her eyes, the tears running.

'But, mother,' interrupted Elizabeth, 'what do you mean? What is it?'

The grandmother slowly wiped her eyes. The fountains of her tears were stopped by Elizabeth's directness. She wiped her eyes slowly.

'Poor child! Eh, you poor thing!' she moaned. 'I don't know what we're going to do, I don't – and you as you are – it's a thing, it is indeed!'

Elizabeth waited.

'Is he dead?' she asked, and at the words her heart swung violently, though she felt a slight flush of shame at the ultimate extravagance of the question. Her words sufficiently frightened the old lady, almost brought her to herself.

'Don't say so, Elizabeth! We'll hope it's not as bad as that; no, may the Lord spare us that, Elizabeth. Jack Rigley came just as I was sittin' down to a glass afore going to bed, an' 'e said: '''Appen you'll go down th' line, Mrs Bates. Walt's had an accident. 'Appen you'll go an' sit wi' 'er till we can get him home." I hadn't time to ask him a word afore he was gone. An' I put my bonnet on an' come straight down, Lizzie. I thought to myself: "Eh, that poor blessed child, if anybody should come an' tell her of a sudden, there's no knowin' what'll 'appen to 'er." You mustn't let it upset you, Lizzie – or you know what to expect. How long is it, six months – or is it five, Lizzie? Ay!' – the old woman shook her head – 'time slips on, it slips on! Ay!'

Elizabeth's thoughts were busy elsewhere. If he was killed – would she be able to manage on the little pension and what she could earn? – she counted up rapidly. If he was hurt – they wouldn't take him to the hospital – how tiresome he would be to nurse! – but perhaps she'd be able to get him away from the drink and his hateful ways. She would – while he was ill. The tears offered to come to her eyes at the picture. But what sentimental luxury was this she was beginning? She turned to consider the children. At any rate she was absolutely necessary for them. They were her business.

'Ay!' repeated the old woman, 'it seems but a week or two since he brought me his first wages. Ah – he was a good lad, Elizabeth, he was, in his way. I don't know why he got to be such a trouble, I don't. He was a happy lad at home, only full of spirits. But there's no mistake he's been a handful of trouble, he has! I hope the Lord'll spare him to mend his ways. I hope so, I hope so. You've had a sight o' trouble with him, Elizabeth, you have indeed. But he was a jolly enough lad wi' me, he was, I can assure you. I don't know how it is. . . .'

The old woman continued to muse aloud, a monotonous irritating sound, while Elizabeth thought concentratedly, startled once, when she heard the winding-engine chuff quickly, and the brakes skirr with a shriek. Then she heard the engine more slowly, and the brakes made no sound. The old woman did not notice. Elizabeth waited in suspense. The mother-in-law talked, with lapses into silence.

'But he wasn't your son, Lizzie, an' it makes a difference. Whatever he was, I remember him when he was little, an' I learned to understand him and to make allowances. You've got to make allowances for them –'

It was half-past ten, and the old woman was saying: 'But it's trouble from beginning to end; you're never too old for trouble, never too old for that –' when the gate banged back, and there were heavy feet on the steps.

'I'll go, Lizzie, let me go,' cried the old woman, rising. But Elizabeth was at the door. It was a man in pit-clothes.

'They're bringin' 'im, Missis,' he said. Elizabeth's heart halted a moment. Then it surged on again, almost suffocating her.

'Is he – is it bad?' she asked.

The man turned away, looking at the darkness:

'The doctor says 'e'd been dead hours. 'E saw 'im i' th' lamp-cabin.'

The old woman, who stood just behind Elizabeth, dropped into a chair, and folded her hands crying: 'Oh, my boy, my boy!'

'Hush!' said Elizabeth, with a sharp twitch of a frown. 'Be still, mother, don't waken th' children: I wouldn't have them down for anything!'

The old woman moaned softly, rocking herself. The man wwas drawing away. Elizabeth took a step forward.

'How was it?' she asked.

'Well, I couldn't say for sure,' the man replied, very ill at ease. ''E wor finishin' a stint an' th' butties 'ad gone, an' a lot o' stuff come down atop 'n 'im.'

'And crushed him?' cried the widow, with a shudder.

'No,' said the man, 'it fell at th' back of 'im. 'E wor under th' face, an' it niver touched 'im. It shut 'im in. It seems 'e wor smothered.'

Elizabeth shrank back. She heard the old woman behind her cry:

'What? – what did 'e say it was?'

The man replied, more loudly: ''E wor smothered!'

Then the old woman wailed aloud, and this relieved Elizabeth.

'Oh, mother,' she said, putting her hand on the old woman, 'don't waken th' children, don't waken th' children.'

She wept a little, unknowing, while the old mother rocked herself and moaned. Elizabeth remembered that they were bringing him home, and she must be ready. 'They'll lay him in the parlour.' she said to herself, standing a moment pale and perplexed.

Then she lighted a candle and went into the tiny room. The air was cold and damp, but she could not make a fire, there was no fireplace. She set down the candle and looked round. The candlelight glittered on the lustre-glasses, on two vases that held some of the pink chrysanthemums, and on the dark mahogany. There was a cold, deathly smell of chrysanthemums in the room. Elizabeth stood looking at the flowers. She turned away, and calculated whether there would be room to lay him on the floor, between the couch and the chiffonier. She pushed the chairs aside. There would be room to lay him down and to step round him. Then she fetched the old red tablecloth, and another old cloth, spreading them down to save her bit of carpet. She shivered on leaving the parlour; so, from the dresser drawer she took a clean shirt and put it at the fire to air. All the time her mother-in-law was rocking herself in the chair and moaning.

'You'll have to move from there, mother,' said Elizabeth. 'They'll be bringing him in. Come in the rocker.'

The old mother rose mechanically, and seated herself by the fire, continuing to lament. Elizabeth went into the pantry for another candle, and there, in the little pent-house under naked tiles, she heard them coming. She stood still in the pantry doorway, listening. She heard them pass the end of the house, and come awkwardly down the three steps, a jumble of shuffling footsteps and muttering voices. The old woman was silent. The men were in the yard.

Then Elizabeth heard Matthews, the manager of the pit, say: 'You go in first, Jim. Mind!'

The door came open, and the two women saw a collier backing into the room, holding one end of a stretcher, on which they could see the nailed pit-boots of the dead man. The two carriers halted, the man at the head stooping to the lintel of the door.

'Wheer will you have him?' asked the manager, a short, white-bearded man.

Elizabeth roused herself and came from the pantry carrying the unlighted candle.

'In the parlour,' she said.

'In there, Jim!' pointed the manager, and the carriers backed round into the tiny room. The coat with which they had covered the body fell off as they awkwardly turned through the two doorways, and the women saw their man, naked to the waist, lying stripped for work. The old woman began to moan in a low voice of horror.

'Lay th' stretcher at th' side,' snapped the manager, 'an' put 'im on th' cloths. Mind now, mind! Look you now —!'

One of the men had knocked off a vase of chrysanthemums. He stared awkwardly, then they set down the stretcher. Elizabeth did not look at her husband. As soon as she could get in the room, she went and picked up the broken vase and the flowers.

'Wait a minute!' she said.

The three men waited in silence while she mopped up the water with a duster.

'Eh, what a job, what a job, to be sure!' the manager was saying, rubbing his brow with trouble and perplexity. 'Never knew such a thing in my life, never! He'd no business to ha' been left. I never knew such a thing in my life! Fell over him clean as a whistle, an' shut him in. Not four feet of space, there wasn't – yet it scarce bruised him.'

He looked down at the dead man, lying prone, half naked, all grimed with coal-dust.

'"'Sphyxiated," the doctor said. It *is* the most terrible job I've ever known. Seems as if it was done o' purpose. Clean over him, an' shut 'im in, like a mouse-trap' – he made a sharp, descending gesture with his hand.

The colliers standing by jerked aside their heads in hopeless comment.

The horror of the thing bristled upon them all.

Then they heard the girl's voice upstairs calling shrilly: 'Mother, mother – who is it? Mother, who is it?'

Elizabeth hurried to the foot of the stairs and opened the door:

'Go to sleep!' She commanded sharply. 'What are you shouting about? Go to sleep at once – there's nothing —'

Then she began to mount the stairs. They could hear her on the boards, and on the plaster floor of the little bedroom. They could hear her distinctly:

'What's the matter now? – what's the matter with you, silly thing?' – her voice was much agitated, with an unreal gentleness.

'I thought it was some men come,' said the plaintive voice of the child. 'Has he come?'

'Yes, they've brought him. There's nothing to make a fuss about. Go to sleep now, like a good child.'

They could hear her voice in the bedroom, they waited whilst she covered the children under the bedclothes.

'Is he drunk?' asked the girl, timidly, faintly.

'No! No – he's not! He's asleep.'

'Is he asleep downstairs?'

'Yes – and don't make a noise.'

There was silence for a moment, then the men heard the frightened child again:

'What's that noise?'

'It's nothing, I tell you, what are you bothering for?'

The noise was the grandmother moaning. She was oblivious of

everything, sitting on her chair rocking and moaning. The manager put his hand on her arm and bade her 'Sh – sh!!'

The old woman opened her eyes and looked at him. She was shocked by this interruption, and seemed to wonder.

'What time is it?' the plaintive thin voice of the child, sinking back unhappily into sleep, asked this last question.

'Ten o'clock,' answered the mother more softly. Then she must have bent down and kissed the children.

Matthews beckoned to the men to come away. They put on their caps and took up the stretcher. Stepping over the body, they tiptoed out of the house. None of them spoke till they were far from the wakeful children.

When Elizabeth came down she found her mother alone on the parlour floor, leaning over the dead man, the tears dropping on him.

'We must lay him out,' the wife said. She put on the kettle, then returning knelt at the feet, and began to unfasten the knotted leather laces. The room was clammy and dim with only one candle, so that she had to bend her face almost to the floor. At last she got off the heavy boots and put them away.

'You must help me now,' she whispered to the old woman. Together they stripped the man.

When they arose, saw him lying in the naïve dignity of death, the women stood arrested in fear and respect. For a few moments they remained still, looking down, the old mother whimpering. Elizabeth felt countermanded. She saw him, how utterly inviolable he lay in himself. She had nothing to do with him. She could not accept it. Stooping, she laid her hand on him, in claim. He was still warm, for the mine was hot where he had died. His mother had his face between her hands, and was murmuring incoherently. The old tears fell in succession as drops from wet leaves; the mother was not weeping, merely her tears flowed. Elizabeth embraced the body of her husband, with cheek and lips. She seemed to be listening, inquiring, trying to get some connection. But she could not. She was driven away. He was impregnable.

She rose, went into the kitchen, where she poured warm water into a bowl, brought soap and flannel and a soft towel.

'I must wash him,' she said.

Then the old mother rose stiffly, and watched Elizabeth as she carefully washed his face, carefully brushing the big blond moustache from his mouth with the flannel. She was afraid with a bottomless fear, so she ministered to him. The old woman, jealous, said:

'Let me wipe him!' – and she kneeled on the other side drying slowly as Elizabeth washed, her big black bonnet sometimes brushing the dark head of her daughter-in-law. They worked thus in silence for a long time. They never forgot it was death, and the touch of the man's dead body gave them strange emotions, different in each of the women; a great dread possessed them both, the mother felt the lie was given to her womb, she was denied; the wife felt utter isolation of the human soul, the child within her was a weight apart from her.

At last it was finished. He was a man of handsome body, and his face showed no traces of drink. He was blond, full-fleshed, with fine limbs. But he was dead.

'Bless him,' whispered his mother, looking always at his face, and speaking out of sheer terror. 'Dear lad – bless him!' She spoke in a faint, sibilant ecstasy of fear and mother love.

Elizabeth sank down again to the floor, and put her face against his neck, and trembled and shuddered. But she had to draw away again. He was dead, and her living flesh had no place against his. A great dread and weariness held her: she was so unavailing. Her life was gone like this.

'White as milk he is, clear as a twelve-month baby, bless him, the darling!' the old mother murmured to herself. 'Not a mark on him, clear and clean and white, beautiful as ever a child was made,' she murmured with pride. Elizabeth kept her face hidden.

'He went peaceful, Lizzie – peaceful as sleep. Isn't he beautiful, the lamb? Ay – he must ha' made his peace, Lizzie. 'Appen he made it all right, Lizzie, shut in there. He'd have time. He wouldn't look like this if he hadn't made his peace. The lamb, the dear lamb. Eh, but he had a hearty laugh. I loved to hear it. He had the heartiest laugh, Lizzie, as a lad —'

Elizabeth looked up. The man's mouth was fallen back, slightly open under the cover of the moustache. The eyes, half shut, did not show glazed in the obscurity. Life with its smoky burning gone from him, had left him apart and utterly alien to her. And she knew what a stranger he was to her. In her womb was ice of fear, because of this separate stranger with whom she had been living as one flesh. Was this what it all meant – utter, intact separateness, obscured by heat of living? In dread she turned her face away. The fact was too deadly.

There had been nothing between them, and yet they had come together, exchanging their nakedness repeatedly. Each time he had taken her, they had been two isolated beings, far apart as now. He was no more responsible than she. The child was like ice in her womb. For as she looked at the dead man, her mind, cold and detached, said clearly: 'Who am I? What have I been doing? I have been fighting a husband who did not exist. *He* existed all the time. What wrong have I done? What was that I have been living with? There lies the reality, this man'. And her soul died in her for fear: she knew she had never seen him, and he had never seen her, they had met in the dark and had fought in the dark, not knowing whom they met nor whom they fought. And now she saw, and turned silent in seeing. For she had been wrong. She had said he was something he was not; she had felt familiar with him. Whereas he was apart all the while, living as she never lived, feeling as she never felt.

In fear and shame she looked at his naked body, that she had known falsely. And he was the father of her children. Her soul was torn from her body and stood apart. She looked at his naked body and was ashamed, as if she had denied it. After all, it was itself. It seemed awful to her. She looked at his face, and she turned her own face to the wall. For his look was other than hers, his way was not her way. She had denied him what he was – she saw it now. She had refused him as himself. And this had been her life, and his life. She was grateful to death, which restored the truth. And she knew she was not dead.

And all the while her heart was bursting with grief and pity for him. What had he suffered? What stretch of horror for this helpless man! She was rigid with agony. She had not been able to help him. He had been cruelly injured, this naked man, this other being, and she could make no reparation. There were the children – but the children belonged to life. This dead man had nothing to do with them. He and she were only channels through which life had flowed to issue in the children. She was a mother – but how awful she knew it now to have been a wife. And he, dead now, how awful he must have felt it to be a husband. She felt that in the next world he would be a stranger to her. If they met, there in the beyond, they would only be ashamed of what had been before. The children had come, for some mysterious reason, out of both of them. But the children did not unite them. Now he was dead, she knew how eternally he was apart from her, how eternally he had nothing more to do with her. She saw this episode of her life closed. They had denied each other in life. Now he had withdrawn. An anguish came over her. It was finished then: it had become hopeless between them long before he died. Yet he had been her husband. But how little!

'Have you got his shirt, 'Lizabeth?'

Elizabeth turned without answering, though she strove to weep and behave as her mother-in-law expected. But she could not, she was silenced. She went into the kitchen and returned with the garment.

'It is aired,' she said, grasping the cotton shirt here and there to try. She was almost ashamed to handle him; what right had she or anyone to lay hands on him; but her touch was humble on his body. It was hard work to clothe him. He was so heavy and inert. A terrible dread gripped her all the while: that he could be so heavy and utterly inert, unresponsive, apart. The horror of the distance between them was almost too much for her – it was so infinite a gap she must look across.

At last it was finished. They covered him with a sheet and left him lying, with his face bound. And she fastened the door of the little parlour, lest the children should see what was lying there. Then, with peace sunk heavy on her heart, she went about making tidy the kitchen. She knew she submitted to life, which was her immediate master. But from death, her ultimate master, she winced with fear and shame.

Mysterious Kôr

ELIZABETH BOWEN

FULL MOONLIGHT DRENCHED THE city and searched it; there was not a niche left to stand in. The effect was remorseless: London looked like the moon's capital – shallow, cratered, extinct. It was late, but not yet midnight; now the buses had stopped the polished roads and streets in this region sent for minutes together a ghostly unbroken reflection up. The soaring new flats and the crouching old shops and houses looked equally brittle under the moon, which blazed in windows that looked its way. The futility of the black-out became laughable: from the sky, presumably, you could see every slate in the roofs, every whited kerb, every contour of the naked winter flowerbeds in the park; and the lake, with its shining twists and tree-darkened islands would be a landmark for miles, yes, miles, overhead.

However, the sky, in whose glassiness floated no clouds but only opaque balloons, remained glassy-silent. The Germans no longer came by the full moon. Something more immaterial seemed to threaten, and to be keeping people at home. This day between days, this extra tax, was perhaps more than senses and nerves could bear. People stayed indoors with a fervour that could be felt: the buildings strained with battened-down human life, but not a beam, not a voice, not a note from a radio escaped. Now and then under streets and buildings the earth rumbled: the Underground sounded loudest at this time.

Outside the now gateless gates of the park, the road coming downhill from the north-west turned south and became a street, down whose perspective the traffic lights went through their unmeaning performance of changing colour. From the promontory of pavement outside the gates you saw at once up the road and down the street: from behind where you stood, between the gateposts, appeared the lesser strangements of grass and water and trees. At this point, at this moment, three French soldiers, directed to a hostel they could not find, stopped singing to listen derisively to the water-birds wakened up by the moon. Next, two wardens coming off duty emerged from their post and crossed the road diagonally, each with an elbow cupped inside a slung-on tin hat. The wardens turned their faces, mauve in the moonlight, towards the Frenchmen with no expression at all. The two sets of steps died in opposite directions, and, the birds subsiding, nothing was heard or seen until, a little way down the street, a trickle of people came out of the Underground, around the anti-panic brick wall. These all disappeared quickly, in an abashed way, or as though dissolved in the street by some white acid, but for a girl and a soldier who, by their way of walking, seemed to have no destination but each other and to be not quite certain even of that. Blotted into one shadow, he tall, she little, these two proceeded towards the park. They looked in, but did not go in; they stood there debating without speaking. Then, as though a command from the street behind them had been received by their synchronized bodies, they faced round to look back the way they had come.

His look up the height of a building made his head drop back, and she saw his eyeballs glitter. She slid her hand from his sleeve, stepped to the edge of the pavement and said: 'Mysterious Kôr.'

'What is?' he said, not quite collecting himself.

'This is –

> Mysterious Kôr thy walls forsaken stand,
> Thy lonely towers beneath a lonely moon –

– this is Kôr.'

'Why,' he said, 'it's years since I've thought of that.'

She said: 'I think of it all the time –

> Not in the waste beyond the swamps and sand,
> The fever-haunted forest and lagoon,
> Mysterious Kôr thy walls –

– a completely forsaken city, as high as cliffs and as white as bones, with no history —'

'But something must once have happened: why had it been forsaken?'

'How could anyone tell you when there's nobody there?'

'Nobody there since how long?'

'Thousands of years.'

'In that case, it would have fallen down.'

'No, not Kôr,' she said with immediate authority. 'Kôr's altogether

different; it's very strong; there is not a crack in it anywhere for a
weed to grow in; the corners of stones and the monuments might
have been cut yesterday, and the stairs and arches are built to support
themselves.'

'You know all about it,' he said, looking at her.

'I know, I know all about it.'

'What, since you read that book?'

'Oh, I didn't get much from that; I just got the name. I knew that
must be the right name; it's like a cry.'

'Most like the cry of a crow to me.' He reflected, then said: 'But
the poem begins with "Not" – " Not in the waste beyond the swamps
and sand — " And it goes on, as I remember, to prove Kôr's not really
anywhere. When a poem says there's no such place — '

'What it tries to say doesn't matter: I see what it makes me see.
Anyhow, that was written some time ago, at that time when they
thought they had got everything taped, because the whole world had
been explored, even the middle of Africa. Every thing and place had
been found and marked on some map: so what wasn't marked on
any map couldn't be there at all. So *they* thought: that was why he
wrote the poem. "The world is disenchanted," it goes on. That was
what set me off hating civilization.'

'Well, cheer up,' he said, 'there isn't much of it left.'

'Oh, yes, I cheered up some time ago. This war shows we've by
no means come to the end. If you can blow whole places out of
existence, you can blow whole places into it. I don't see why not.
They say we can't say what's come out since the bombing started.
By the time we've come to the end, Kôr may be the one city left:
the abiding city. I should laugh.'

'No, you wouldn't,' he said sharply, 'You wouldn't – at least, I
hope not. I hope you don't know what you're saying – does the moon
make you funny?'

'Don't be cross about Kôr; please don't, Arthur,' she said.

'I thought girls thought about people.'

'What, these days?' she said. 'Think about people? How can anyone
think about people? How can anyone think about people if they've
got any heart? I don't know how other girls manage: I always think
about Kôr.'

'Not about me?' he said. When she did not at once answer, he
turned her hand over, in anguish, inside his grasp. 'Because I'm not
there when you want me – is that my fault?'

'But to think about Kôr *is* to think about you and me.'

'In that dead place?'

'No, ours – we'd be alone there.'

Tightening his thumb on her palm while he thought this over, he looked behind them, around them, above them – even up at the sky. He said finally: 'But we're alone here.'

'That was why I said "Mysterious Kôr".'

'What, you mean we're there now, that here's there, that now's then? . . . *I* don't mind,' he added, letting out as a laugh the sigh he had been holding in for some time. 'You ought to know the place, and for all I could tell you we might be anywhere: I often do have it, this funny feeling, the first minute or two when I've come up out of the Underground. Well, well: join the Army and see the world.' He nodded towards the perspective of traffic lights and said, a shade craftily: 'What are those, then?'

Having caught the quickest possible breath, she replied: 'Inexhaustible gases; they bored through to them and lit them as they came up; by changing colour they show the changing of minutes; in Kôr there is no sort of other time.'

'You've got the moon, though: that can't help making months.'

'Oh, and the sun, of course; but those two could do what they liked; we should not have to calculate when they'd come or go.'

'We might not have to,' he said, 'but I bet I should.'

'I should not mind what you did, so long as you never said, "What next?"'

'I don't know about "next", but I do know what we'd do first.'

'What, Arthur?'

'Populate Kôr.'

She said: 'I suppose it would be all right if our children were to marry each other?'

But her voice faded out; she had been reminded that they were homeless on this his first night of leave. They were, that was to say, in London without any hope of any place of their own. Pepita shared a two-roomed flatlet with a girl-friend, in a bystreet off the Regent's Park Road, and towards this they must make their half-hearted way. Arthur was to have the sitting-room divan, usually occupied by Pepita, while she herself had half of her girl-friend's bed. There was really no room for a third, and least of all for a man, in those small rooms packed with furniture and the two girls' belongings: Pepita tried to be grateful for her friend Callie's forbearance – but how could she be, when it had not occurred to Callie that she would do better to be away tonight? She was more slow-witted than narrow-minded – but Pepita felt she owed a kind of ruin to her. Callie, not yet known to be home later than ten, would be now waiting up, in her housecoat, to welcome Arthur. That would mean three-sided chat, drinking cocoa, then turning in: that would be that, and that would be all. That was London, this war – they were lucky to have a roof – London, full enough before the Americans came. Not a place: they would even grudge you sharing a grave – that was what even married couples complained. Whereas in Kôr . . .

In Kôr. . . . Like glass, the illusion shattered: a car hummed like a hornet towards them, veered, showed its scarlet tail-light, streaked away up the road. A woman edged round a front door and along the area railings timidly called her cat; meanwhile a clock near, then another set further back in the dazzling distance, set about striking midnight. Pepita, feeling Arthur release her arm with an abruptness that was the inverse of passion, shivered; whereat he asked brusquely: 'Cold? Well, which way? – we'd better be getting on.'

Callie was no longer waiting up. Hours ago she had set out the three cups and saucers, the tins of cocoa and household milk and, on the gas-ring, brought the kettle to just short of the boil. She had turned open Arthur's bed, the living-room divan, in the neat inviting way she had learnt at home – then, with a modest impulse, replaced the cover. She had, as Pepita foresaw, been wearing her cretonne house-coat, the nearest thing to a hostess gown that she had; she had already brushed her hair for the night, rebraided it, bound the braids in a coronet round her head. Both lights and the wireless had been on, to make the room both look and sound gay: all alone, she had come to that peak moment at which company should arrive – but so seldom does. From then on she felt welcome beginning to wither in her, a flower of the heart that had bloomed too early. There she had sat like an image, facing the three cold cups, on the edge of the bed to be occupied by an unknown man.

Callie's innocence and her still unsought-out state had brought her to take a proprietary pride in Arthur; this was all the stronger, perhaps, because they had not yet met. Sharing the flat with Pepita, this last year, she had been content with reflecting heat of love. It was not, surprisingly, that Pepita seemed very happy – there were times when she was palpably on the rack, and this was not what

Callie could understand. 'Surely you owe it to Arthur,' she would then say 'to keep cheerful? So long as you love each other — '. Callie's calm brow glowed – one might say that it glowed in place of her friend's; she became the guardian of that ideality which for Pepita was constantly lost to view. It was true, with the sudden prospect of Arthur's leave, things had come nearer to earth: he became a proposition, and she would have been as glad if he could have slept somewhere else. Physically shy, a brotherless virgin, Callie shrank from sharing this flat with a young man. In this flat you could hear everything: what was once a three-windowed Victorian drawing-room had been partitioned, by very thin walls, into kitchenette, living-room, Callie's bedroom. The living room was in the centre; the two others open off it. What was once the conservatory, half a flight down, was now converted into a draughty bathroom, shared with somebody else on the girls' floor. The flat, for these days, was cheap – even so, it was Callie, earning more than Pepita, who paid the greater part of the rent: it thus became up to her, more or less, to express goodwill as to Arthur's making a third. 'Why, it will be lovely to have him here,' Callie said. Pepita accepted the good will without much grace – but then, had she ever much grace to spare? – she was as restlessly secretive, as self-centred, as a little half-grown black cat. Next came a puzzling moment: Pepita seemed to be hinting that Callie should fix herself up somewhere else. 'But where would I go?' Callie marvelled when this was at last borne in on her. 'You know what London's like now. And, anyway' – here she laughed, but hers was a forehead that coloured as easily as it glowed – 'it wouldn't be proper, would it, me going off and leaving just you and Arthur; I don't know what your mother would say to me. No, we may be a little squashed, but we'll make things ever so homey. I shall not mind playing gooseberry, really, dear'.

But the hominess by now was evaporating, as Pepita and Arthur still and still did not come. At half-past ten, in obedience to the rule of the house, Callie was obliged to turn off the wireless, whereupon silence out of the stepless street began seeping into the slighted room. Callie recollected the fuel target and turned off her dear little table lamp, gaily painted with spots to make it look like a toadstool, thereby leaving only the hanging light. She laid her hand on the kettle, to find it gone cold again and sigh for the wasted gas if not for her wasted thought. Where are they? Cold crept up her out of the kettle; she went to bed.

Callie's bed lay along the wall under the window: she did not like sleeping so close up under glass, but the clearance that must be left for the opening of door and cupboards made this the only possible place. Now she got in and lay rigidly on the bed's inner side, under the hanging hems of the window curtains, training her limbs not to stray to what would be Pepita's half. This sharing of her bed with another body would not be the least of her sacrifice to the lovers' love; tonight would be the first night – or at least, since she was an infant – that Callie had slept with anyone. Child of a sheltered middle-class household, she had kept physical distances all her life. Already repugnance and shyness ran through her limbs; she was preyed upon by some more obscure trouble than the expectation that she might not sleep. As to *that*, Pepita was restless; her tossings on the divan, her broken-off exclamations and blurred pleas had been to be heard, most nights, through the dividing wall.

Callie knew, as though from a vision, that Arthur would sleep soundly, with assurance and majesty. Did they not all say, too, that a soldier sleeps like a log? With awe she pictured, asleep, the face that she had not yet, awake, seen – Arthur's man's eyelids, cheekbones and set mouth turned up to the darkened ceiling. Wanting to savour darkness herself, Callie reached out and put off her bedside lamp.

At once she knew that something was happening – outdoors, in the street, the whole of London, the world. An advance, an extraordinary movement was silently taking place; blue-white beams overflowed from it, silting, dropping round the edges of the muffling black-out curtains. When, starting up, she knocked a fold of the curtain, a beam like a mouse ran across her bed. A searchlight, the most powerful of all time, might have been turned full and steady upon her defended window; finding flaws in the black-out stuff, it made veins and stars. Once gained by this idea of pressure she could not lie down again; she sat tautly, drawn-up knees touching her breasts, and asked herself if there were anything she should do. She parted the curtains, opened them slowly wider, looked out – and was face to face with the moon.

Below the moon, the houses opposite her window blazed black in transparent shadow; and something – was it a coin or a ring – glittered half-way across the chalk-white street. Light marched in past her face, and she turned to see where it went: out stood the curves and garlands of the great white marble Victorian mantelpiece of that lost drawing-room; out stood, in the photographs turned her way, the thoughts with which her parents had faced the camera, and the humble puzzlement of her two dogs at home. Of silver brocade, just faintly purpled with roses, became her housecoat hanging over the chair. And the moon did more: it exonerated and beautified the lateness of the lovers' return. No wonder, she said to herself, no wonder – if this was the world they walked in, if this was whom they were with. Having drunk in the white explanation, Callie lay down again. Her half of the bed was in shadow, but she allowed one hand to lie, blanched, in what would be Pepita's place. She lay and looked at the hand until it was no longer her own.

Callie woke to the sound of Pepita's key in the latch. But no voices? What had happened? Then she heard Arthur's step. She heard his unslung equipment dropped with a weary, dull sound, and the plonk of his tin hat on a wooden chair. 'Ssssh-sssh!' Pepita exclaimed, 'she *might* be asleep!'

Then at last Arthur's voice: 'But I thought you said —'

'I'm not asleep; I'm just coming!' Callie called out with rapture, leaping out from her form in shadow into the moonlight, zipping on her enchanted housecoat over her nightdress, kicking her shoes on, and pinning in place, with a trembling firmness, her plaits in their coronet round her head. Between these movements of hers she heard not another sound. Had she only dreamed they were there? Her heart beat: she stepped through the living-room, shutting her door behind her.

Pepita and Arthur stood the other side of the table; they gave the impression of being lined up. Their faces, at different levels – for Pepita's rough, dark head came only an inch above Arthur's khaki shoulder – were alike in abstention from any kind of expression; as though spiritually, they both still refused to be here. Their features looked faint, weathered – was this the work of the moon? Pepita said at once: 'I suppose we are very late?'

'I don't wonder,' Callie said, 'on this lovely night.'

Arthur had not raised his eyes; he was looking at the three cups. Pepita now suddenly jogged his elbow, saying, 'Arthur, wake up; say something; this is Callie – well, Callie, this is Arthur, of course.'

'Why, yes, of course this is Arthur,' returned Callie, whose candid eyes since she entered had not left Arthur's face. Perceiving that Arthur did not know what to do, she advanced round the table to shake hands with him. He looked up, she looked down, for the first time: she rather beheld than felt his red-brown grip on what still seemed her glove of moonlight. 'Welcome, Arthur', she said. 'I'm so glad to meet you at last, I hope you will be comfortable in the flat.'

'It's been kind of you,' he said after consideration.

'Please do not feel that,' said Callie. 'This is Pepita's home, too, and we both hope – don't we, Pepita? – that you'll regard it as yours. Please feel free to do just as you like. I am sorry it is so small.'

'Oh, I don't know,' Arthur said, as though hypnotized; 'it seems a nice little place.'

Pepita, meanwhile, glowered and turned away.

Arthur continued to wonder, though he had once been told, how these two unalike girls had come to set up together – Pepita so small, except for her too-big head, compact of childish brusqueness and of unchildish passion, and Callie, so sedate, waxy and tall – an unlit candle. Yes, she was like one of those candles on sale outside a church; there could be something votive even in her demeanour. She was unconscious that her good manners, those of an old-fashioned country doctor's daughter, were putting the other two at a disadvantage. He found himself touched by the grave good faith with which Callie was wearing that tartish housecoat, above which her face kept the glaze of sleep; and, as she knelt to relight the gas ring under the kettle, he marked the strong, delicate arch of one bare foot, disappearing into the arty green shoe. Pepita was now too near him ever again to be seen as he now saw Callie – in a sense, he never *had* seen Pepita for the first time: she had not been, and still sometimes was not, his type. No, he had not thought of her twice; he had not remembered her until he began to remember her with passion. You might say he had not seen Pepita coming: their love had been a collision in the dark.

Callie, determined to get this over, knelt back and said: 'Would Arthur like to wash his hands?' When they had heard him stumble down the half-flight of stairs, she said to Pepita: 'Yes, I was so glad you had the moon'.

'Why?' said Pepita. She added: 'There was too much of it.'

'You're tired. Arthur looks tired, too.'

'How would you know? He's used to marching about. But it's all this having no place to go.'

'But, Pepita, you —'

But at this point Arthur came back: from the door he noticed the wireless, and went direct to it. 'Nothing much on now, I suppose?' he doubtfully said.

'No, you see it's past midnight; we're off the air. And, anyway, in this house they don't like the wireless late. By the same token,' went on Callie, friendlily smiling, 'I'm afraid I must ask you, Arthur, to take your boots off, unless, of course, you mean to stay sitting down. The people below us —'

Pepita flung off, saying something under her breath, but Arthur, remarking, 'No, I don't mind,' both sat down and began to take off his boots. Pausing, glancing to left and right at the divan's fresh cotton spread, he said: 'It's all right is it, for me to sit on this?'

'That's my bed,' said Pepita, 'You are to sleep in it.'

Callie then made the cocoa, after which they turned in. Preliminary trips to the bathroom having been worked out, Callie was first to retire, shutting the door behind her so that Pepita and Arthur might kiss each other good-night. When Pepita joined her, it was without knocking: Pepita stood still in the moon and began to tug off her clothes. Glancing with hate at the bed, she asked: 'Which side?'

'I expect you'd like the outside.'

'What are you standing about for?'

'I don't really know: as I'm inside I'd better get in first.'

'Then why not get in?'

When they had settled rigidly, side by side, Callie asked: 'Do you think Arthur's got all he wants?'

Pepita jerked her head up. 'We can't sleep in all this moon.'

'Why, you don't believe the moon does things, actually?'

'Well, it couldn't hope to make some of us *much* more screwy.'

Callie closed the curtains, then said: 'What do you mean? And – didn't you hear? – I asked if Arthur's got all he wants.'

'That's what I meant – have you got a screw loose, really?'

'Pepita, I won't stay here if you're going to be like this.'

'In that case, you had better go in with Arthur.'

'What about me?' Arthur loudly said through the wall, 'I can hear practically all you girls are saying.'

They were both startled – rather that than abashed. Arthur, alone in there, had thrown off the ligatures of his social manner: his voice held the whole authority of his sex – he was impatient, sleepy, and he belonged to no one.

'Sorry,' the girls said in unison. Then Pepita laughed soundlessly, making their bed shake, till to stop herself she bit the back of her hand, and this movement made her elbow strike Callie's cheek. 'Sorry,' she had to whisper. No answer: Pepita fingered her elbow and found, yes, it was quite true, it was wet. 'Look, shut up crying, Callie: what have I done?'

Callie rolled right round, in order to press her forehead closely under the window, into the curtains, against the wall. Her weeping continued to be soundless: now and then, unable to reach her handkerchief, she staunched her eyes with a curtain, disturbing slivers of moon. Pepita gave up marvelling, and soon slept: at least there is something in being dog-tired.

A clock struck four as Callie woke up again – but something else had made her open her swollen eyelids. Arthur, stumbling about on his padded feet, could be heard next door attempting to make no noise. Inevitably, he bumped the edge of the table. Callie sat up: by her side Pepita lay like a mummy rolled half over, in forbidding, tenacious sleep. Arthur groaned, Callie caught a breath, climbed lightly over Pepita, felt for her torch on the mantelpiece, stopped to listen again. Arthur groaned again: Callie, with movements soundless as they were certain, opened the door and slipped through to the living-room. 'What's the matter?' she whispered. 'Are you ill?'

'No; I just got a cigarette. Did I wake you up?'

'But you groaned.'

'I'm sorry; I'd no idea.'

'But do you often?'

'I've no idea, really, I tell you,' Arthur repeated. The air of the room was dense with his presence, overhung by tobacco. He must be sitting on the edge of his bed, wrapped up in his overcoat – she could smell the coat, and each time he pulled on the cigarette his features appeared down there, in the fleeting, dull reddish glow. 'Where are you?' he said. 'Show a light.'

Her nervous touch on her torch, like a reflex to what he said, made it flicker up for a second. 'I am just by the door; Pepita's asleep; I'd better go back to bed.'

'Listen. Do you two get on each other's nerves?'

'Not till tonight,' said Callie, watching the uncertain swoops of the cigarette as he reached across to the ashtray on the edge of the table. Shifting her bare feet patiently, she added: 'You don't see us as we usually are.'

'She's a girl who shows things in funny ways – I expect she feels bad at our putting you out like this – I know I do. But then we'd got no choice, had we?'

'It is really I who am putting you out,' said Callie.

'Well, that can't be helped either, can it? You had the right to stay in your own place. If there'd been more time, we might have gone to the country, though I still don't see where we'd have gone there. It's one harder when you're not married, unless you've got the money. Smoke?'

'No, thank you. Well, if you're all right, I'll go back to bed.'

'I'm glad she's asleep – funny the way she sleeps, isn't it? You can't help wondering where she is. You haven't got a boy, have you, just at present?'

'No. I've never had one.'

'I'm not sure in one way you're not better off. I can see there's not so much in it for a girl these days. It makes me feel cruel the way I unsettle her; I don't know how much it's me myself or how much it's something the matter that I can't help. How are any of us to know how things could have been? They forget war's not just only war; it's years out of people's lives that they've never had before and won't have again. Do you think she's fanciful?'

'Who, Pepita?'

'It's enough to make her – tonight was the pay-off. We couldn't get near any movie or any place for sitting; you had to fight into the bars, and she hates the staring in bars, and with all that milling about, every street we went, they kept knocking her even off my arm. So then we took the tube to that park down there, but the place was as bad as daylight, let alone it was cold. We hadn't the nerve – well, that's nothing to do with you.'

'I don't mind.'

'Or else you don't understand. Se we began to play – we were off in Kôr.'

'Core of what?'

'Mysterious Kôr – ghost city.'

'Where?'

'You may ask. But I could have sworn she saw it, and from the way she saw it I saw it, too. A game's a game, but what's a hallucination? You begin by laughing, then it gets in you and you can't laugh it off. I tell you, I woke up just now not knowing where I'd been; and I had to get up and feel round this table before I even knew where I was. It wasn't till then that I thought of a cigarette. Now I see why she sleeps like that, if that's where she goes.'

'But she is just as often restless; I often hear her.'

'Then she doesn't always make it. Perhaps it takes me, in some way — Well, I can't see any harm: when two people have got no place, why not want Kôr, as a start? There are no restrictions on wanting, at any rate.'

'But, oh, Arthur, can't wanting want what's human?'

He yawned. 'To be human's to be at a dead loss.' Stopping yawning, he ground out his cigarette: the china tray skidded at the edge of the table. 'Bring that light here a moment – that is, will you? I think I've messed ash all over these sheets of hers.'

Callie advanced with the torch alight, but at arm's length: now and then her thumb made the beam wobble. She watched the lit-up inside of Arthur's hand as he brushed the sheet; and once he looked up to see her white-nightgowned figure curving above and away from him, behind the arc of light. 'What's that swinging?'

'One of my plaits of hair. Shall I open the window wider?'

'What, to let the smoke out? Go on. And how's your moon?'

'Mine?' Marvelling over this, as the first sign that Arthur remembered that she was Callie, she uncovered the window, pushed up the sash, then after a minute said: 'Not so strong.'

Indeed, the moon's power over London and the imagination had now declined. The siege of light had relaxed; the search was over; the street had a look of survival and no more. Whatever had glittered there, coin or ring, was now invisible or had gone. To Callie it seemed likely that there would never be such a moon again; and on the whole she felt this was for the best. Feeling air reach in like a tired arm round her body, she dropped the curtains against it and returned to her own room.

Back by her bed, she listened: Pepita's breathing still had the regular sound of sleep. At the other side of the wall the divan creaked as Arthur stretched himself out again. Having felt ahead of her lightly, to make sure her half was empty, Callie climbed over Pepita and got in. A certain amount of warmth had travelled between the sheets from Pepita's flank, and in this Callie extended her sword-cold body: she tried to compose her limbs; even they quivered after Arthur's words in the dark, words to the dark. The loss of her own mysterious expectation, of her love for love, was a small thing beside the war's total of unlived lives. Suddenly Pepita flung out one hand: its back knocked Callie lightly across the face.

Pepita had now turned over and lay with her face up. The hand that had struck Callie must have lain over the other, which grasped the pyjama collar. Her eyes, in the dark, might have been either shut or open, but nothing made her frown more or less steadily: it became certain, after another moment, that Pepita's act of justice had been unconscious. She still lay, as she had lain, in an avid dream, of which Arthur had been the source, of which Arthur was not the end. With him she looked this way, that way, down the wide, void, pure streets, between statues, pillars and shadows, through archways and colonnades. With him she went up the stairs down which nothing but moon came; with him trod the ermine dust of the endless halls, stood on terraces, mounted the extreme tower, looked down on the statued squares, the wide, void, pure streets. He was the password, but not the answer: it was to Kôr's finality that she turned.

The Adventure of the Speckled Band

SIR ARTHUR CONAN DOYLE

IN GLANCING OVER MY NOTES OF THE seventy-odd cases in which I have during the last eight years studied the methods of my friend Sherlock Holmes, I find many tragic, some comic, a large number merely strange, but none commonplace; for, working as he did rather for the love of his art than for the acquirement of wealth, he refused to associate himself with any investigation which did not tend towards the unusual, and even the fantastic. Of all these varied cases, however, I cannot recall any which presented more singular features than that which was associated with the well-known Surrey family of the Roylotts of Stoke Moran. The events in question occurred in the early days of my association with Holmes, when we were sharing rooms as bachelors, in Baker Street. It is possible that I might have placed them upon record before, but a promise of secrecy was made at the time, from which I have only been freed during the last month by the untimely death of the lady to whom the pledge was given. It is perhaps as well that the facts should now come to light, for I have reasons to know there are widespread rumours as to the death of Dr Grimesby Roylott which tend to make the matter even more terrible than the truth.

It was early in April, in the year '83, that I woke one morning to find Sherlock Holmes standing, fully dressed, by the side of my bed. He was a late riser as a rule, and, as the clock on the mantelpiece showed me that it was only a quarter past seven, I blinked up at him in some surprise, and perhaps just a little resentment, for I was myself regular in my habits.

'Very sorry to knock you up, Watson,' said he, 'but it's the common lot this morning. Mrs Hudson has been knocked up, she retorted upon me, and I on you.'

'What is it, then? A fire?'

'No, a client. It seems that a young lady has arrived in a considerable state of excitement, who insists upon seeing me. She is waiting now in the sitting-room. Now, when young ladies wander about the Metropolis at this hour of the morning, and knock sleepy people up out of their beds, I presume that it is something very pressing which they have to communicate. Should it prove to be an interesting case, you would, I am sure, wish to follow it from the outset. I thought at any rate that I should call you, and give you the chance.'

'My dear fellow, I would not miss it for anything.'

I had no keener pleasure than in following Holmes in his professional investigations, and in admiring the rapid deductions, as swift as intuitions, and yet always founded on a logical basis, with which he unravelled the problems which were submitted to him. I rapidly threw on my clothes, and was ready in a few minutes to accompany my friend down to the sitting-room. A lady dressed in black and heavily veiled, who had been sitting in the window, rose as we entered.

'Good morning, madam,' said Holmes cheerily. 'My name is Sherlock Holmes. This is my intimate friend and associate, Dr Watson, before whom you can speak as freely as before myself. Ha, I am glad to see that Mrs Hudson has had the good sense to light the fire. Pray draw up to it, and I shall order you a cup of hot coffee, for I observe that you are shivering.'

'It is not cold which makes me shiver,' said the woman in a low voice, changing her seat as requested.

'What then?'

'It is fear, Mr Holmes. It is terror,' She raised her veil as she spoke, and we could see that she was indeed in a pitiable state of agitation, her face all drawn and grey, with restless, frightened eyes, like those of some hunted animal. Her features and figure were those of a woman of thirty, but her hair was shot with premature grey, and her expression was weary and haggard. Sherlock Holmes ran her over with one of his quick, all-comprehensive glances.

'You must not fear,' said he soothingly, bending forward and patting her forearm. 'We shall soon set matters right, I have no doubt. You have come in by train this morning, I see.'

'You know me, then?'

'No, but I observe the second half of a return ticket in the palm of your left glove. You must have started early, and yet you had a good drive in a dog-cart, along heavy roads, before you reached the station.'

The lady gave a violent start, and stared in bewilderment at my companion.

'There is no mystery, my dear madam,' said he, smiling. 'The left arm of your jacket is spattered with mud in no less than seven places. The marks are perfectly fresh. There is no vehicle save a dog-cart which throws up mud in that way, and then only when you sit on the left-hand side of the driver.'

'Whatever your reasons may be, you are perfectly correct,' said she. 'I started from home before six, reached Leatherhead at twenty past, and came in by the first train to Waterloo. Sir, I can stand this strain no longer, I shall go mad if it continues, I have no one to turn to – none, save only one, who cares for me, and he, poor fellow, can be of little aid. I have heard of you, Mr Holmes; I have heard of you from Mrs Farintosh, whom you helped in the hour of her sore need. It was from her that I had your address. Oh, sir, do you think you could help me too, and at least throw a little light through the dense darkness which surrounds me? At present it is out of my power to reward you for your services, but in a month or two I shall be married, with the control of my own income, and then at least you shall not find me ungrateful.'

Holmes turned to his desk, and unlocking it, drew out a small casebook which he consulted.

'Farintosh,' said he. 'Ah, yes, I recall the case; it was concerned with an opal tiara. I think it was before your time, Watson. I can only say, madam, that I shall be happy to devote the same care to your case as I did to that of your friend. As to reward, my profession is its reward; but you are at liberty to defray whatever expenses I may be put to, at the time which suits you best. And now I beg that you will lay before us everything that may help us in forming an opinion upon the matter.'

'Alas!' replied our visitor. 'The horror of my situation lies in the fact that my fears are so vague, and my suspicions depend so entirely upon small points, which might seem trivial to another, that even he to whom of all others I have a right to look for help and advice looks upon all that I tell him about it as the fancies of a nervous woman. He does not say so, but I can read it from his soothing answers and averted eyes. But I have heard, Mr Holmes, that you can see deeply into the manifold wickedness of the human heart. You may advise me how to walk amid the dangers which encompass me.'

'I am all attention, madam.'

'My name is Helen Stoner, and I am living with my stepfather, who is the last survivor of one of the oldest Saxon families in England, the Roylotts of Stoke Moran, on the western border of Surrey.'

Holmes nodded his head. 'The name is familiar to me,' said he.

'The family was at one time among the richest in England, and the estate extended over the borders into Berkshire in the north, and Hampshire in the west. In the last century, however, four successive heirs were of a dissolute and wasteful disposition, and the family ruin was eventually completed by a gambler, in the days of the Regency. Nothing was left, save a few acres of ground and the two-hundred-year-old house, which is itself crushed under a heavy mortgage. The last squire dragged out his existence there, living the horrible life of an aristocratic pauper; but his only son, my stepfather, seeing that he must adapt himself to the new conditions, obtained an advance from a relative, which enabled him to take a medical degree, and went out to Calcutta, where, by his professional skill and his force of character, he established a large practice. In a fit of anger, however, caused by some robberies which had been perpetrated in the house, he beat his native butler to death, and narrowly escaped a capital sentence. As it was, he suffered a long term of imprisonment, and afterwards returned to England a morose and disappointed man.

'When Dr Roylott was in India he married my mother, Mrs Stoner, the young widow of Major-General Stoner, of the Bengal Artillery. My sister Julia and I were twins, and we were only two years old at the time of my mother's remarriage. She had a considerable sum of money, not less than a thousand a year, and this she bequeathed to Dr Roylott entirely whilst we resided with him, with a provision that a certain annual sum should be allowed to each of us in the event of our marriage. Shortly after our return to England my mother died – she was killed eight years ago in a railway accident near Crewe. Dr Roylott then abandoned his attempts to establish himself in practice in London, and took us to live with him in the ancestral house at Stoke Moran. The money which my mother had left was enough for all our wants, and there seemed no obstacle to our happiness.

'But a terrible change came over our stepfather about this time. Instead of making friends and exchanging visits with our neighbours, who had at first been overjoyed to see a Roylott of Stoke Moran back in the old family seat, he shut himself up in his house, and seldom came out save to indulge in ferocious quarrels with whoever might cross his path. Violence of temper approaching to mania has been hereditary in the men of the family, and in my stepfather's case it had, I believe, been intensified by his long residence in the tropics. A series of disgraceful brawls took place, two of which ended in the police-court, until at last he became the terror of the village and the folks would fly at his approach, for he is a man of immense strength, and absolutely uncontrollable in his anger.

'Last week he hurled the local backsmith over a parapet into a stream, and it was only by paying over all the money that I could gather together that I was able to avert another public exposure. He had no friends at all save the wandering gipsies, and he would give these vagabonds leave to encamp upon the few acres of bramble-covered land which represent the family estate, and would accept in return the hospitality of their tents, wandering away with them sometimes for weeks on end. He has a passion also for Indian animals, which are sent over to him by a correspondent, and he has at this moment a cheetah and a baboon, which wander freely over his grounds, and are feared by the villagers almost as much as their master.

'You can imagine from what I say that my poor sister Julia and I had no great pleasure in our lives. No servant would stay with us, and for a long time we did all the work of our house. She was but thirty at the time of her death, and yet her hair had already begun to whiten, even as mine has.'

'Your sister is dead, then?'

'She died just two years ago, and it is of her death that I wish to speak to you. You can understand that, living the life which I desribed, we were little likely to see anyone of our own age and position. We had, however, an aunt, my mother's maiden sister, Miss Honoria Westphail, who lives near Harrow, and we were occasionally allowed to pay short visits at this lady's house. Julia went there at Christmas two years ago, and met there a half-pay Major of Marines, to whom she became engaged. My stepfather learned of the engagement when my sister returned, and offered no objection to the marriage; but within a fortnight of the day which had been fixed for the wedding, the terrible event occurred which has deprived me of my only companion.'

Sherlock Holmes had been leaning back in his chair with his eyes closed, and his head sunk in a cushion, but he half-opened his lids now, and glanced across at his visitor.

'Pray be precise as to details,' said he.

'It is easy for me to be so, for every event of that dreadful time is seared into my memory. The manor house is, as I have already said, very old, and only one wing is now inhabited. The bedrooms in this wing are on the ground floor, the sitting-rooms being in the central block of the buildings. Of these bedrooms, the first is Dr Roylott's, the second my sister's, and the third my own. There is no communication between them, but they all open out into the same corridor. Do I make myself plain?'

'Perfectly so.'

'The windows of the three rooms open out upon the lawn. The fatal night Dr Roylott had gone to his room early, though we knew that he had not retired to rest, for my sister was troubled by the smell of the strong Indian cigars which it was his custom to smoke. She left her room, therefore, and came into mine, where she sat for some time, chatting about her approaching wedding. At eleven o'clock she rose to leave me, but she paused at the door and looked back.

'"Tell me, Helen," said she, "have you ever heard anyone whistle in the dead of the night?"

'"Never," said I.

'"I suppose that you could not possibly whistle yourself in your sleep?"

'"Certainly not. But why?"

'"Because during the last few nights I have always, about three in the morning, heard a low clear whistle. I am a light sleeper, and it has awakened me. I cannot tell where it came from – perhaps from the next room, perhaps from the lawn. I thought that I would just ask you whether you had heard it."

'"No, I have not. It must be those wretched gipsies in the plantation."

'"Very likely. And yet if it were on the lawn I wonder that you did not hear it also."

'"Ah, but I sleep more heavily than you."

'"Well, it is of no great consequence at any rate," she smiled back at me, closed my door, and a few moments later I heard her key turn in the lock.'

'Indeed,' said Holmes. 'Was it your custom always to lock yourselves in at night?'

'Always.'

'And why?'

'I think that I mentioned to you that the Doctor kept a cheetah and a baboon. We had no feeling of security unless our doors were locked.'

'Quite so. Pray proceed with your statement.'

'I could not sleep that night. A vague feeling of impending misfortune impressed me. My sister and I, you will recollect, were twins, and you know how subtle are the links which bind two souls which are so closely allied. It was a wild night. The wind was howling outside, and the rain was beating and splashing against the windows. Suddenly, amidst all the hubbub of the gale, there burst forth the wild scream of a terrified woman. I knew that it was my sister's voice. I sprang from my bed, wrapped a shawl round me, and rushed into the corridor. As I opened my door I seemed to hear a low whistle, such as my sister described, and a few moments later a clanging sound, as if a mass of metal had fallen. As I ran down the passage my sister's door was unlocked, and revolved slowly upon its hinges. I stared at it horror-stricken, not knowing what was about to issue from it. By the light of the corridor lamp I saw my sister appear at the opening, her face blanched with terror, her hands groping for help, her whole figure swaying to and fro like that of a drunkard. I ran to her and threw my arms around her, but at that moment her knees seemed to give way and she fell to the ground. She writhed as one who is in terrible pain, and her limbs were dreadfully convulsed. At first I thought that she had not recognized me, but as I bent over her she suddenly shrieked out in a voice which I shall never forget, "O, my God! Helen! It was the band! The speckled band!" There was something else which she would fain have said, and she stabbed with her finger into the air in the direction of the Doctor's room, but a fresh convulsion seized her and choked her words. I rushed out, calling loudly for my stepfather, and I met him hastening from his room in his dressing-gown. When he reached my sister's side she was unconscious, and though he poured brandy down her throat, and sent for medical aid from the village, all efforts were in vain, for she slowly sank and died without having recovered her consciousness. Such was the dreadful end of my beloved sister.'

'One moment,' said Holmes; 'are you sure about this whistle and metallic sound? Could you swear to it?'

'That was what the county coroner asked me at the inquiry. It is my strong impression that I heard it, and yet among the crash of the gale, and the creaking of an old house, I may possibly have been deceived.'

'Was your sister dressed?'

'No, she was in her nightdress. In her right hand was found the charred stump of a match, and in her left a match-box.'

'Showing that she had struck a light and looked about her when the alarm took place. That is important. And what conclusions did the coroner come to?'

'He investigated the case with great care, for Dr Roylott's conduct had long been notorious in the county, but he was unable to find any satisfactory cause of death. My evidence showed that the door had been fastened upon the inner side, and the windows were blocked by old fashioned shutters with broad iron bars, which were secured every night. The walls were carefully sounded, and were shown to be quite solid all round, and the flooring was also thoroughly examined, with the same result. The chimney is wide, but is barred up by four large staples. It is certain, therefore, that my sister was quite alone when she met her end. Besides, there were no marks of any violence upon her.'

'How about poison?'

'The doctors examined her for it, but without success.'

'What do you think that this unfortunate lady died of, then?'

'It is my belief that she died of pure fear and nervous shock, though what is was which frightened her I cannot imagine.'

'Were there gipsies in the plantation at the time?'

'Yes, there are nearly always some there.'

'Ah, and what did you gather from this allusion to a band – a speckled band?'

'Sometimes I have thought that it was merely the wild talk of delirium, sometimes that it may have referred to some band of people, perhaps to these very gipsies in the plantation. I do not know whether the spotted handkerchiefs which so many of them wear over their heads might have suggested the strange adjective which she used.'

Holmes shook his head like a man who is far from being satisfied.

'These are very deep waters,' said he: 'pray go on with your narrative.'

'Two years have passed since then, and my life has been until lately lonelier than ever. A month ago, however, a dear friend, whom I have known for many years, has done me the honour to ask my hand in marriage. His name is Armitage – Percy Armitage – the second son of Mr Armitage, of Crane Water, near Reading. My stepfather has offered no opposition to the match, and we are to be married in the course of the spring. Two days ago some repairs were started in the west wing of the building, and my bedroom wall has been pierced, so that I have had to move into the chamber in which my sister died, and to sleep in the very bed in which she slept. Imagine, then, my thrill of terror when last night, as I lay awake, thinking over her terrible fate, I suddenly heard in the silence of the night the low whistle which had been the herald of her own death. I sprang up and lit the lamp, but nothing was to be seen in the room. I was too shaken to go to bed again, however, so I dressed, and as soon as it was daylight I slipped down, got a dog-cart at the Crown Inn, which is opposite, and drove to Leatherhead, from whence I have come on this morning, with the one object of seeing you and asking your advice.'

'You have done wisely,' said my friend. 'But have you told me all?'

'Yes, all.'

'Miss Roylott, you have not. You are screening your stepfather.'

'Why, what do you mean?'

For answer Holmes pushed back the frill of black lace which fringed the hand that lay upon our visitor's knee. Five little livid spots, the marks of four fingers and a thumb, were printed upon the white wrist.

'You have been cruelly used,' said Holmes.

The lady coloured deeply, and covered over her injured wrist. 'He is a hard man,' she said, 'and perhaps he hardly knows his own strength.'

There was a long silence, during which Holmes leaned his chin upon his hands and stared into the crackling fire.

'This is very deep business, ' he said at last. 'There are a thousand details which I should desire to know before I decide upon our course of action. Yet we have not a moment to lose. It we were to come to Stoke Moran today, would it be possible for us to see over these rooms without the knowledge of your stepfather?'

'As it happens, he spoke of coming into town today upon some important business. It is probable that he will be away all day, and that there would be nothing to disturb you. We have a housekeeper now, but she is old and foolish, and I could easily get her out of the way.'

'Excellent. You are not averse to this trip, Watson?'

'By no means.'

'Then we shall both come. What are you going to do yourself?'

'I have one or two things which I would wish to do now that I am in town. But I shall return by the twelve o'clock train, so as to be there in time for your coming.'

'And you may expect us early in the afternoon. I have myself some small business matters to attend to. Will you not wait and breakfast?'

'No, I must go. My heart is lightened already since I have confided my trouble to you. I shall look forward to seeing you again this afternoon.' She dropped her thick black veil over her face, and glided from the room.

'And what do you think of it all, Watson?' asked Sherlock Holmes, leaning back in his chair.

'It seems to me to be a most dark and sinister business.'

'Dark enough and sinister enough.'

'Yet if the lady is correct in saying that the flooring and walls are sound, and that the door, window and chimney are impassable, then her sister must have been undoubtedly alone when she met her mysterious end.'

'What becomes, then, of these nocturnal whistles, and what of the very peculiar words of the dying woman?'

'I cannot think.'

'When you combine the ideas of whistles at night, the presence of a band of gipsies who are on intimate terms with this old doctor, the fact that we have every reason to believe that the doctor has an interest in preventing his stepdaughter's marriage, the dying allusion to a band, and finally, the fact that Miss Helen Stoner heard a metallic clang, which might have been caused by one of these metal bars which secured the shutters falling back into its place, I think there is good ground to think that the mystery may be cleared along these lines.'

'But what, then, did the gipsies do?'

'I cannot imagine.'

'I see many objections to any such a theory.'

'And so do I. It is precisely for that reason that we are going to Stoke Moran this day. I want to see whether the objections are fatal, or if they may be explained away. But what, in the name of the devil!'

The ejaculation had been drawn from my companion by the fact that our door had been suddenly dashed open, and that a huge man framed himself in the aperture. His costume was a peculiar mixture of the professional and of the agricultural, having a black top hat, a long frock-coat, and a pair of high gaiters, with a hunting-crop swinging in his hand. So tall was he that his hat actually brushed the cross-bar of the doorway, and his breadth seemed to span it across from side to side. A large face, seared with a thousand wrinkles, burned yellow with the sun and marked with every evil passion, was turned from one to the other of us, while his deep-set, bile-shot eyes, and the high, thin, fleshless nose gave him somewhat the resemblance to a fierce old bird of prey.

'Which of you is Holmes?' asked this apparition.

'My name, sir, but you have the advantage of me,' said my companion quietly.

'I am Dr Grimesby Roylott, of Stoke Moran.'

'Indeed, Doctor,' said Holmes blandly. 'Pray take a seat.'

'I will do nothing of the kind. My stepdaughter has been here. I have traced her. What has she been saying to you?'

'It is a little cold for the time of the year,' said Holmes.

'What has she been saying to you?' screamed the old man furiously.

'But I have heard that the crocuses promise well,' continued my companion imperturbably.

'Ha! You put me off, do you?' said our new visitor, taking a step forward, and shaking his hunting-crop. 'I know you, you scoundrel! I have heard of you before. You are Holmes the meddler.'

My friend smiled.

'Holmes the busybody!'

His smile broadened.

'Holmes the Scotland-yard Jack-in-office.'

Holmes chuckled heartily. 'Your conversation is most entertaining,' said he. 'When you go out close the door, for there is a decided draught.'

'I will go when I have had my say. Don't you dare meddle with my affairs. I know that Miss Stoner has been here – I traced her! I am a dangerous man to fall foul of! See here.' He stepped swiftly forward, seized the poker, and bent it into a curve with his huge brown hands.

'See that you keep yourself out of my grip,' he snarled, and, hurling the twisted poker into the fireplace, he strode out of the room.

'He seems a very amiable person,' said Holmes, laughing. 'I am not quite so bulky, but if he had remained I might have shown him that my grip was not much more feeble than his own.' As he spoke he picked up the steel poker, and with a sudden effort straightened it out again.

'Fancy his having the insolence to confound me with the official detective force! This incident gives zest to our investigation, however, and I only trust that our little friend will not suffer from her imprudence in allowing this brute to trace her. And now, Watson, we shall order breakfast, and afterwards I shall walk down to Doctors' Commons, where I hope to get some data which may help us in this matter.'

It was nearly one o'clock when Sherlock Holmes returned from his excursion. He held in his hand a sheet of blue paper, scrawled over with notes and figures.

'I have seen the will of the deceased wife,' said he. 'To determine its exact meaning I have been obliged to work out the present prices of the investments with which it is concerned. The total income, which at the time of the wife's death was little short of £1,100, is now through the fall in agricultural prices not more than £750. Each daughter can claim an income of £250, in case of marriage. It is evident, therefore, that if both girls had married this beauty would have had a mere pittance, while even one of them would cripple him to a serious extent. My morning's work has not been wasted, since it has proved that he has the very strongest motives for standing in the way of anything of the sort. And now, Watson, this is too serious for dawdling, especially as the old man is aware that we are interesting ourselves in his affairs, so if you are ready we shall call a cab and drive to Waterloo. I should be very much obliged if you would slip your revolver into your pocket. An Eley's No. 2 is an excellent argument with gentlemen who can twist steel pokers into knots. That and a tooth-brush are, I think, all that we need.'

At Waterloo we were fortunate in catching a train for Leatherhead, where we hired a trap at the station inn, and drove for four or five miles through the lovely Surrey lanes. It was a perfect day, with a bright sun and a few fleecy clouds in the heavens. The trees and wayside hedges were just throwing out their first green shoots, and the air was full of the pleasant smell of the moist earth. To me at least there was a strange contrast between the sweet promise of the spring and this sinister quest upon which we were engaged. My companion sat in front of the trap, his arms folded, his hat pulled down over his eyes, and his chin sunk upon his breast, buried in the deepest thought. Suddenly, however, he started, tapped me on the shoulder, and pointed over the meadows.

'Look there!' said he.

A heavily-timbered park stretched up in a gentle slope, thickening into a grove at the highest point. From amidst the branches there jutted out the grey gables and high rooftree of a very old mansion.

'Stoke Moran?' said he.

'Yes, sir, that be the house of Dr Grimesby Roylott,' remarked the driver.

'There is some building going on there,' said Holmes; 'that is where we are going.'

'There's the village,' said the driver, pointing to a cluster of roofs some distance to the left; 'but if you want to get to the house, you'll find it shorter to go over this stile, and so by the foot-path over the fields. There it is, where the lady is walking.'

'And the lady, I fancy, is Miss Stoner,' observed Holmes, shading his eyes. 'Yes, I think we had better do as you suggest.'

We got off, paid our fare, and the trap rattled back on its way to Leatherhead.

'I thought it as well,' said Holmes, as we climbed the stile, 'that this fellow should think we had come here as architects, or on some definite business. It may stop his gossip. Good afternoon, Miss Stoner. You see that we have been as good as our word.'

Our client of the morning had hurried forward to meet us with a face which spoke her joy. 'I have been waiting so eagerly for you,' she cried, shaking hands with us warmly. 'All has turned out splendidly. Dr Roylott has gone to town, and it is unlikely that he will be back before evening.'

'We have had the pleasure of making the Doctor's acquaintance,' said Holmes, and in a few words he sketched out what had occurred. Miss Stoner turned white to the lips as she listened.

'Good heavens!' she cried, 'he has followed me, then.'

'So it appears!'

'He is so cunning that I never know when I am safe from him. What will he say when he returns?'

'He must guard himself, for he may find that there is someone more cunning than himself upon his track. You must lock yourself from him tonight. If he is violent, we shall take you away to your aunt's at Harrow. Now, we must make the best use of our time, so kindly take us at once to the rooms which we are to examine.'

The building was of grey, lichen-blotched stone, with a high central portion, and two curving wings, like the claws of a crab, thrown out on each side. In one of these wings the windows were broken, and blocked with wooden boards, while the roof was partly caved in, a picture of ruin. The central portion was in little better repair, but the right-hand block was comparatively modern, and the blinds in the windows, with the blue smoke curling up from the chimneys, showed that this was where the family resided. Some scaffolding had been erected against the end wall, and the stonework had been broken into, but there were no signs of any workmen at the moment of our visit. Holmes walked slowly up and down the ill-trimmed lawn, and examined with deep attention the outsides of the windows.

'This, I take it, belongs to the room in which you used to sleep, the centre one to your sister's, and the one next to the main building to Dr Roylott's chamber?'

'Exactly so. But I am now sleeping in the middle one.'

'Pending the alterations, as I understand. By the way, there does not seem to be any pressing need for repairs at the end wall.'

'There were none. I believe that it was an excuse to move me from my room.'

'Ah! that is suggestive. Now, on the other side of this narrow wing runs the corridor from which these three rooms open. There are windows in it, of course?'

'Yes, but very small ones. Too narrow for anyone to pass through.'

'As you both locked your doors at night, your rooms were unapproachable from that side. Now, would you have the kindness to go into your room, and to bar your shutters.'

Miss Stoner did so, and Holmes, after a careful examination through the open window, endeavoured in every way to force the shutter open, but without success. There was no slit through which a knife could be passed to raise the bar. Then with his lens he tested the hinges, but they were of solid iron, built firmly into the massive masonry. 'Hum!' said he, scratching his chin in some perplexity, 'my theory certainly presents some difficulty. No one could pass these shutters if they were bolted. Well, we shall see if the inside throws any light upon the matter.'

A small side-door led into the white-washed corridor from which the three bedrooms opened. Holmes refused to examine the third chamber, so we passed at once to the second, that in which Miss Stoner was now sleeping, and in which her sister had met her fate. It was a homely little room, with a low ceiling and a gaping fire-place, after the fashion of old country houses. A brown chest of drawers stood in one corner, a narrow white-counterpaned bed in another, and a dressing-table on the left-hand side of the window. These articles, with two small wickerwork chairs, made up all the furniture in the room, save for a square of Wilton carpet in the centre. The boards round and the panelling of the walls were brown, worm-eaten oak, so old and discoloured that it may have dated from the original building of the house. Holmes drew one of the chairs into a corner and sat silent, while his eyes travelled round and round and up and down, taking in every detail of the apartment.

'Where does that bell communicate with?' he asked at last, pointing to a thick bell-rope which hung down beside the bed, the tassel actually lying upon the pillow.

'It goes to the housekeeper's room.'

'It looks newer than the other things?'

'Yes, it was only put there a couple of years ago.'

'Your sister asked for it, I suppose?'

'No, I never heard of her using it. We used always to get what we wanted for ourselves.'

'Indeed, it seemed unnecessary to put so nice a bell-pull there. You will excuse me for a few minutes while I satisfy myself as to this floor.' He threw himself down upon his face with his lens in his hand, and crawled swiftly backwards and forwards, examining minutely the cracks between the boards. Then he did the same with the woodwork with which the chamber was panelled. Finally he walked over to the bed and spent some time in staring at it, and in running his eye up and down the wall. Finally he took the bell-rope in his hand and gave it a brisk tug.

'Why, it's a dummy,' said he.

'Won't it ring?'

'No, it is not even attached to a wire. This is very interesting. You can see now that is is fastened to a hook just above where the little opening of the ventilator is.'

'How very absurd! I never noticed that before.'

'Very strange!' muttered Holmes, pulling at the rope. 'There are one or two very singular points about this room. For example, what a fool a builder must be to open a ventilator in another room, when, with the same trouble, he might have communicated with the outside air!'

'That is also quite modern,' said the lady.

'Done about the same time as the bell-rope,' remarked Holmes'

'Yes, there were several little changes carried out about that time.'

'They seem to have been of a most interesting character – dummy bell-ropes, and ventilators which do not ventilate. With your permission, Miss Stoner, we shall now carry our researches into the inner apartment.'

Dr Grimesby Roylott's chamber was larger than that of his step-daughter, but was as plainly furnished. A camp bed, a small wooden shelf full of books, mostly of a technical character, an arm chair beside the bed, a plain wooden chair against the wall, a round table, and a large iron safe were the principal things which met the eye. Holmes walked slowly round and examined each and all of them with the keenest interest.

'What's in here?' he asked, tapping the safe.

'My stepfather's business papers.'

'Oh! you have seen inside, then!'

'Only once, some years ago. I remember that it was full of papers.'

'There isn't a cat in it, for example?'

'No. What a strange idea!'

'Well, look at this!' He took up a small saucer of milk which stood on the top of it.

'No; we don't keep a cat. But there is a cheetah and a baboon.'

'Ah, yes, of course! Well, a cheetah is just a big cat, and yet a saucer of milk does not go very far in satisfying its wants, I dare say. There is one point which I should wish to determine.' He squatted down in front of the wooden chair, and examined the seat of it with the greatest attention.

'Thank you. That is quite settled,' said he, rising and putting his lens in his pocket. 'Hullo! here is something interesting!'

The object which had caught his eye was a small dog lash hung on one corner of the bed. The lash, however, was curled upon itself, and tied so as to make a loop of whipcord.

'What do you make of that, Watson?'

'It's a common enough lash. But I don't know why it should be tied.'

'That is not quite so common, is it? Ah, me! it's a wicked world, and when a clever man turns his brain to crime it is the worst of all. I think that I have seen enough now, Miss Stoner, and, with your permission, we shall walk out upon the lawn.'

I had never seen my friend's face so grim or his brow so dark, as it was when we turned from the scene of this investigation. We had walked several times up and down the lawn, neither Miss Stoner nor myself liking to break in upon his thoughts before he roused himself from his reverie.

'It is very essential, Miss Stoner,' said he, 'that you should absolutely follow my advice in every respect.'

'I shall most certainly do so.'

'The matter is too serious for any hesitation. Your life may depend upon your compliance.'

'I assure you that I am in your hands.'

'In the first place, both my friend and I must spend the night in your room.'

Both Miss Stoner and I gazed at him in astonishment.

'Yes, it must be so. Let me explain. I believe that that is the village inn over there?'

'Yes, that is the "Crown."'

'Very good. Your windows would be visible from there?'

'Certainly.'

'You must confine yourself to your room, on pretence of a headache, when your stepfather comes back. Then when you hear him retire for the night, you must open the shutters of your window, undo the hasp, put your lamp there as a signal to us, and then withdraw with everything which you are likely to want into the room which you used to occupy. I have no doubt that, in spite of the repairs, you could manage there for one night.'

'Oh, yes, easily.'

'The rest you will leave in our hands.'

'But what will you do?'

'We shall spend the night in your room, and we shall investigate the cause of this noise which has disturbed you.'

'I believe, Mr Holmes, that you have already made up your mind,' said Miss Stoner, laying her hand upon my companion's sleeve.

'Perhaps I have.'

'Then for pity's sake tell me what was the cause of my sister's death.'

'I should prefer to have clearer proofs before I speak.'

'You can at least tell me whether my own thought is correct, and if she died from some sudden fright.'

'No, I do not think so. I think that there was probably some more tangible cause. And now, Miss Stoner, we must leave you, for if Dr Roylott returned and saw us, our journey would be in vain. Goodbye, and be brave, for if you will do what I have told you, you may rest assured that we shall soon drive away the danger that threatens you.'

Sherlock Holmes and I had no difficulty in engaging a bedroom and sitting-room at the Crown Inn. They were on the upper floor, and from our window we could command a view of the avenue gate, and of the inhabited wing of Stoke Moran manor house. At dusk we saw Dr Grimesby Roylott drive past, his huge form looming up beside the little figure of the lad who drove him. The boy had some slight difficulty in undoing the heavy iron gates, and we heard the hoarse roar of the Doctor's voice, and saw the fury with which he shook his clenched fists at him. The trap drove on, and a few minutes later we saw a sudden light spring up among the trees as the lamp was lit in one of the sitting-rooms.

'Do you know, Watson,' said Holmes, as we sat together in the gathering darkness, 'I have really some scruples as to taking you tonight. There is a distinct element of danger.'

'Can I be of assistance?'

'Your presence might be invaluable.'

'Then I shall certainly come.'

'It is very kind of you.'

'You speak of danger. You have evidently seen more in these rooms than was visible to me.'

'No, but I fancy that I may have deduced a little more. I imagine that you saw all that I did.'

'I saw nothing remarkable save the bell-rope, and what purpose that could answer I confess is more than I can imagine.'

'You saw the ventilator, too?'

'Yes, but I do not think that it is such a very unusual thing to have a small opening between two rooms. It was so small that a rat could hardly pass through.'

'I knew that we should find a ventilator before ever we came to Stoke Moran.'

'My dear Holmes!'

'Oh, yes, I did. You remember in her statement she said that her sister could smell Dr Roylott's cigar. Now, of course, that suggests at once that there must be a communication between the two rooms. It could only be a small one, or it would have been remarked upon at the coroner's inquiry. I deduced a ventilator.'

'But what harm can there be in that?'

'Well, there is at least a curious coincidence of dates. A ventilator is made, a cord is hung, and a lady who sleeps in the bed dies. Does not that strike you?'

'I cannot as yet see any connection.'

'Did you observe anything very peculiar about that bed?'

'No.'

'It was clamped to the floor. Did you ever see a bed fastened like that before?'

'I cannot say that I have'

'The lady could not move her bed. It must always be in the same relative position to the ventilator and to the rope – for so we may call it, since it was clearly never meant for a bell-pull.'

'Holmes,' I cried, 'I seem to see dimly what you are hitting at. We are only just in time to prevent some subtle and horrible crime.'

'Subtle enough and horrible enough. When a doctor does go wrong he is the first of criminals. He has nerve and he has knowledge. Palmer and Pritchard were among the heads of their profession. This man strikes even deeper, but I think, Watson, that we shall be able to strike deeper still. But we shall have horrors enough before the night is over: for goodness' sake let us have a quiet pipe, and turn our minds for a few hours to something more cheerful.'

About nine o'clock the light among the trees was extinguished, and all was dark in the direction of the manor house. Two hours passed slowly away, and then suddenly, just at the stroke of eleven, a single bright light shone out right in front of us.

'That is our signal,' said Holmes, springing to his feet; 'it comes from the middle window.'

As we passed out he exchanged a few words with the landlord, explaining that we were going on a late visit to an acquaintance, and that it was possible that we might spend the night there. A moment later we were out on the dark road, a chill wind blowing in our faces, and one yellow light twinkling in front of us through the gloom to guide us on our sombre errand.

There was little difficulty in entering the grounds, for unrepaired breaches gaped in the old park wall. Making our way among the trees, we reached the lawn, crossed it, and were about to enter through the window, when out from a clump of laurel bushes there darted what seemed to be a hideous and distorted child, who threw itself on the grass with writhing limbs, and then ran swiftly across the lawn into the darkness.

'My God!' I whispered, 'did you see it?'

Holmes was for the moment as startled as I. His hand closed like a vice upon my wrist in his agitation. Then he broke into a low laugh, and put his lips to my ear.

'It is a nice household,' he murmured, 'that is the baboon.'

I had forgotten the strange pets which the Doctor affected. There was a cheetah, too; perhaps we might find it upon our shoulders at any moment. I confess that I felt easier in my mind when, after following Holmes's example and slipping off my shoes, I found myself inside the bedroom. My companion noiselessly closed the shutters, moved the lamp on to the table, and cast his eyes round the room. All was as we had seen it in the day-time. Then, creeping up to me and making a trumpet of his hand, he whispered into my ear again so gently that it was all that I could do to distinguish the words:

'The least sound would be fatal to our plans.'

I nodded to show that I had heard.

'We must sit without a light. He would see it through the ventilator.'

I nodded again.

'Do not go to sleep; your very life may depend upon it. Have your pistol ready in case we should need it. I will sit on the side of the bed, and you in that chair.'

I took out my revolver and laid it on the corner of the table.

Holmes had brought up a long thin cane, and this he placed upon the bed beside him. By it he laid the box of matches, and the stump of a candle. Then he turned down the lamp and we were left in darkness.

How shall I ever forget that dreadful vigil! I could not hear a sound, not even the drawing of a breath, and yet I knew that my companion sat open-eyed, within a few feet of me, in the same state of nervous tension in which I was myself. The shutters cut off the least ray of light, and we waited in absolute darkness. From outside came the occasional cry of a night-bird, and once at our very window a long drawn, cat-like whine, which told us that the cheetah was indeed at liberty. Far away we could hear the deep tones of the parish clock, which boomed out every quarter of an hour. How long they seemed, those quarters! Twelve o'clock, and one, and two, and three, and still we sat waiting silently for whatever might befall.

Suddenly there was the momentary gleam of light up in the direction of the ventilator, which vanished immediately, about was succeeded by a strong smell of burning oil and heated metal. Someone in the next room had lit a dark lantern. I heard a gentle sound of movement, and then all was silent once more, though the smell grew stronger. For half an hour I sat with straining ears. Then suddenly another sound became audible – a very gentle, soothing sound, like that of a small jet of steam escaping continually from a kettle. The instant that we heard it, Holmes sprang from the bed, struck a match, and lashed furiously with his cane at the bell-pull.

'You see it, Watson?' he yelled. 'You see it?'

But I saw nothing. At the moment when Holmes struck the light I heard a low, clear whistle, but the sudden glare flashing into my weary eyes made it impossible for me to tell what it was at which my friend lashed so savagely. I could, however, see that his face was deadly pale, and filled with horror and loathing.

He had ceased to strike, and was gazing up at the ventilator, when suddenly there broke from the silence of the night the most horrible cry to which I have ever listened. It swelled up louder and louder, a hoarse yell of pain and fear and anger all mingled in the one dreadful shriek. They say that away down in the village, and even in the distant parsonage, that cry raised the sleepers from their beds. It struck cold to our hearts, and I stood gazing at Holmes, and he at me, until the last echoes of it had died away into the silence from which it rose.

'What can it mean?' I gasped.

'It means that it is all over,' Holmes answered. 'And perhaps, after all, it is for the best. Take your pistol and we shall enter Dr Roylott's room.'

With a grave face he lit the lamp, and led the way down the corridor. Twice he struck at the chamber door without any reply from within. Then he turned the handle and entered, I at his heels, with the cocked pistol in my hand.

It was a singular sight which met our eyes. On the table stood a dark lantern with the shutter half open, throwing a brilliant beam of light upon the iron safe, the door of which was ajar. Beside this table, on the wooden chair, sat Dr Grimesby Roylott, clad in a long grey dressing-gown, his bare ankles protruding beneath, and his feet thrust into red heelless Turkish slippers. Across his lap lay the short stock with the long lash which we had noticed during the day. His chin was cocked upwards, and his eyes were fixed in a dreadful rigid stare at the corner of the ceiling. Round his brow he had a peculiar yellow band, with brownish speckles, which seemed to be bound tightly round his head. As we entered he made neither sound nor motion.

'The band! the speckled band!' whispered Holmes.

I took a step forward, In an instant his strange headgear began to move, and there reared itself from among his hair the squat diamond-shaped head and puffed neck of a loathsome serpent.

'It was a swamp adder!' cried Holmes – 'the deadliest snake in India. He has died within ten seconds of being bitten. Violence does, in truth recoil upon the violent, and the schemer falls into the pit which he digs for another. Let us thrust this creature back into its den, and we can then remove Miss Stoner to some place of shelter, and let the county police know what has happened.'

As he spake he drew the dog whip swiftly from the dead man's lap, and throwing the noose round the reptile's neck, he drew it from its horrid perch, and carrying it at arm's length, threw it into the iron safe, which he closed upon it.

Such are the true facts of the death of Dr Grimesby Roylott, of Stoke Moran. It is not necessary that I should prolong a narrative which has already run to too great a length, by telling how we broke the sad news to the terrified girl, how we conveyed her by the morning train to the care of her good aunt at Harrow, of how the slow process of official inquiry came to the conclusion that the doctor met his fate while indiscreetly playing with a dangerous pet. The little which I had yet to learn of the case was told me by Sherlock Holmes as we travelled back next day.

'I had,' said he, 'come to an entirely erroneous conclusion, which shows, my dear Watson, how dangerous it always is to reason from insufficient data. The presence of the gipsies, and the use of the word "band," which was used by the poor girl, no doubt, to explain the appearance which she had caught a horrid glimpse of by the light of her match, were sufficient to put me upon an entirely wrong scent. I can only claim the merit that I instantly reconsidered my position when, however, it became clear to me that whatever danger threatened an occupant of the room could not come either from the window or the door. My attention was speedily drawn, as I have already remarked to you, to this ventilator, and to the bell-rope which hung down to the bed. The discovery that this was a dummy, and that the bed was clamped to the floor, instantly gave rise to the suspicion that the rope was there as a bridge for something passing through the hole, and coming to the bed. The idea of a snake instantly occurred to me, and when I coupled it with my knowledge that the Doctor was furnished with a supply of creatures from India, I felt that I was probably on the right track. The idea of using a form of poison which could not possibly be discovered by any chemical test was just such a one as would occur to a clever and ruthless man who had had an Eastern training. The rapidity with which such a poison would take effect would also, from his point of view, be an advantage. It would be a sharp-eyed coroner indeed who could distinguish the two little dark punctures which would show where the poison fangs had done their work. Then I thought of the whistle. Of course, he must recall the snake before the morning light revealed it to the victim. He had trained it, probably by the use of the milk which we saw, to return to him when summoned. He wuld put it through the ventilator at the hour that he thought best, with the certainty that it would crawl down the rope, and land on the bed. It might or might not bite the occupant, perhaps she might escape every night for a week, but sooner or later she must fall a victim.

'I had come to these conclusions before ever I had entered his room. An inspection of his chair showed me that he had been in the habit of standing on it, which, of course, would be necessary in order that he should reach the ventilator. The sight of the safe, the saucer of milk, and the loop of whipcord was enough to finally dispel any doubts which may have remained. The metallic clang heard by Miss Stoner was obviously caused by her father hastily closing the door of his safe upon its terrible occupant. Having once made up my mind, you know the steps which I took in order to put the matter to the proof. I heard the creature hiss, as I have no doubt that you did also, and I instantly lit the light and attacked it.'

'With the result of driving it through the ventilator.'

'And also with the result of causing it to turn upon its master at the other side. Some of the blows of my cane came home, and roused its snakish temper, so that it flew upon the first person it saw. In this way I am no doubt indirectly responsible for Dr Grimesby Roylott's death, and I cannot say that it is likely to weigh very heavily upon my conscience.'

Strictly from Hunger

S.J. PERELMAN

YES I WAS EXCITED, AND SMALL WONDER. What boy wouldn't be, boarding a huge, mysterious, puffing steam train for golden California? As Mamma adjusted my reefer and strapped on my leggings, I almost burst with impatience. Grinning redcaps lifted my luggage into the compartment and spat on it. Mamma began to weep into a small pillow case she had brought along for the purpose.

'Oh, son, I wish you hadn't become a scenario writer!' she sniffled.

'Aw, now, Moms,' I comforted her, 'it's no worse than playing the piano in a call-house.' She essayed a brave little smile, and, reaching into her reticule, produced a flat package which she pressed into my hands. For a moment I was puzzled, then I cried out with glee.

'Jelly sandwiches! Oh, Moms!'

'Eat them all, boy o' mine,' she told me, 'they're good for boys with hollow little legs.' Tenderly she pinned to my lapel the green tag reading 'To Plushnik Productions, Hollywood, California.' The whistle shrilled and in a moment I was chugging out of Grand Central's dreaming spires followed only by the anguished cries of relatives who would now have to go to work. I had chugged only a few feet when I realized that I had left without the train, so I had to run back and wait for it to start.

As we sped along the glorious fever spots of the Hudson I decided to make a tour of inspection. To my surprise I found that I was in the only passenger car of the train; the other cars were simply dummies snipped out of cardboard and painted to simulate coaches. Even 'passengers' had been cunningly drawn in coloured crayons in the 'window', as well as ragged tramps clinging to the blinds below and drinking Jamaica ginger. With a rueful smile I returned to my seat and gorged myself on jelly sandwiches.

At Buffalo the two other passengers and I discovered to our horror that the conductor had been left behind. We finally decided to divide up his duties; I punched the tickets, the old lady opposite me wore a conductor's hat and locked the washroom as we came into stations, and the young man who looked as if his feet were not mates consulted a Hamilton watch frequently. But we missed the conductor's earthy conversation and it was not until we had exchanged several questionable stories that we began to forget our loss.

A flicker of interest served to shorten the trip. At Fort Snodgrass, Ohio, two young and extremely polite road-agents boarded the train and rifled us of our belongings. They explained that they were modern Robin Hoods and were stealing from the poor to give to the rich. They had intended to rape all the women and depart for Sherwood Forest, but when I told them that Sherwood Forest as well as the women were in England, their chagrin was comical in the extreme. They declined my invitation to stay and take a chance on the train's pool, declaring that the engineer had fixed the run and would fleece us, and got off at South Bend with every good wish.

The weather is always capricious in the Middle West, and although it was midsummer, the worst blizzard in Chicago's history greeted us on our arrival. The streets were crowded with thousands of newsreel cameramen trying to photograph one another bucking the storm on the Lake Front. It was a novel idea for the newsreels and I wished them well. With only two hours in Chicago I would be unable to see the city, and the thought drew me into a state of composure. I noted with pleasure that a fresh coat of grime had been given to the Dearborn Street station, though I was hardly vain enough to believe that it had anything to do with my visit. There was the usual ten-minute wait while the porters withdrew with my portable typewriter to a side room and flailed it with hammers, and at last I was aboard the 'Sachem', crack train of the B.B.D. & O. lines.

It was as if I had suddenly been transported into another world. 'General Crook', in whom I was to make my home for the next three days, and his two neighbours, 'Lake Tahoe' and 'Chief Malomai', were everything that the word 'Pullman' implies; they were Pullmans. Uncle Eben, in charge of 'General Crook', informed me that the experiment of air-cooling the cars had been so successful that the road intended trying to heat them next winter.

'Ah suttinly looks fo'd to dem roastin' ears Ah's gwine have next winter he, he, he!' he chuckled, rubbing soot into my hat.

The conductor told me he had been riding on trains for so long that he had begun to smell like one, and sure enough, two brakemen waved their lanterns at him that night and tried to tempt him down a siding in Kansas City. We became good friends and it came as something of a blow when I heard next morning that he had fallen off the train during the night. The fireman said that we had circled about for and hour trying to find him but that it had been impossible to lower a boat because we did not carry a boat.

The run was marked by only one incident out of the ordinary. I had ordered breaded veal cutlet the first evening, and my waiter, poking his head into the kitchen, had repeated the order. The cook, unfortunately, understood him to say '*dreaded* veal cutlet', and resenting the slur, sprang at the waiter with drawn razor. In a few seconds I was the only living remnant of the shambles, and at Topeka I was compelled to wait until a new shambles was hooked on and I proceeded with dinner.

It seemed only a scant week or ten days before we were pulling into Los Angeles. I had grown so attached to my porter that I made him give me lock of his hair. I wonder if he still has the ten-cent piece I gave him? There was a gleam in his eye which could only have been insanity as he leaned over me. Ah, Uncle Eben, faithful old retainer, where are you now? Gone to what obscure ossuary? If this should chance to meet your kindly gaze, drop me a line care of *Variety*, won't you? They know what to do with it.

The violet hush of twilight was descending over Los Angeles as my hostess, Violet Hush, and I left the suburbs headed toward Hollywood. In the distance a glow of huge piles of burning motion-picture scripts lit up the sky. The crisp tang of frying writers and directors whetted my appetite. How good it was to be alive, I thought, inhaling deep lungfuls of carbon monoxide. Suddenly our powerful Gatti-Gazazza slid to a stop in the traffic.

'What is it, Jenkin?' Violet called anxiously through the speaking-tube to the chauffeur (played by Lyle Talbot).

A *suttee* was in progress by the roadside, he said – did we wish to see it? Quickly Violet and I elbowed our way through the crowd. An enormous funeral pyre composed of thousands of feet of film and scripts, drenched with Chanel Number Five, awaited the torch of Jack Holt, who was to act as master of ceremonies. In a few terse words Violet explained this unusual custom borrowed from the Hindus and never paid for. The worst disgrace that can befall a producer is an unkind notice from a New York reviewer. When this happens, the producer becomes a pariah in Hollywood. He is shunned by his friends, thrown into bankruptcy, and like a Japanese electing hara-kiri, he commits *suttee*. A great bonfire is made of the film, and the luckless producer, followed by directors, actors, technicians, and the producer's wives, immolate themselves. Only the scenario writers are exempt. These are tied between the tails of two spirited Caucasian ponies, which are then driven off in opposite directions. The custom is called 'a conference'.

Violet and I watched the scene breathlessly. Near us, Harry Cohn, head of Columbia Studios, was being rubbed with huck towels preparatory to throwing himself into the flames. He was nonchalantly smoking a Rocky Ford five-center, and the man's courage drew a tear to the eye of even the most callous. Weeping relatives besought him to eschew his design, but he stood adamant. Adamant Eve, his plucky secretary, was being rubbed with crash towels preparatory to flinging herself into Cohn's embers. Assistant directors busily prepared spears, war bonnets and bags of pemmican which the Great Chief would need on his trip to the 'Happy Hunting Grounds'. Wampas and beads to placate the Great Spirit (played by Will Hays) were piled high about the stoical tribesman.

Suddenly Jack Holt (played by Edmund Lowe) raised his hand for silence. The moment had come. With bowed head Holt made a simple invocation couched in one-syllable words so that even the executives might understand. Throwing his five-center to a group of autograph-hunters, the great man poised himself for the fatal leap. But from off-scene came the strident clatter of coconut shells, and James Agee, Filmdom's fearless critic, wearing the uniform of a confederate guerrilla and the whiskers of General Beauregard, galloped in on a foam-flecked pinto. It was he whose mocking review had sent Cohn into Coventry. It was a dramatic moment as the two stood pitted against each other – Cohn against Agee, the Blue against the Grey. But with true Southern gallantry Agee was the first to extend the hand of friendship.

'Ah reckon it was an unworthy slur, suh,' he said in manly tones. 'Ah-all thought you-all's pictuah was lousy but it opened at the Rialto to sensational grosses, an' Ah-all 'pologizes. Heah, have a yam.' And he drew a yam from his tunic. Not to be outdone in hospitality, Cohn drew a yam from his tunic, and soon they were exchanging yams and laughing over the old days.

When Violet and I finally stole away to our waiting motor, we felt that we were somehow nearer to each other. I snuggled luxuriously into the buffalo lap-robe Violet had provided against the treacherous night air and gazed out at the gleaming neon lights. Soon we would be in Beverly Hills, and already the quaint native women were swarming alongside in their punts urging us to buy their cunning beadwork and mangoes. Occasionally I threw a handful of coppers to the Negro boys, who dived for them joyfully. The innocent squeals of the policemen as the small blackamoors pinched them were irresistible. Unable to resist them, Violet and I were soon pinching each other till our skins glowed. Violet was good to the touch, with a firm fleshy texture like a winesap or pippin. It seemed but a moment before we were sliding under the porte-cochère of her home, a magnificent rambling structure of beaver-board patterned after an Italian ropewalk of the sixteenth century. It had recently been re-modelled by a family of wrens who had introduced chewing-gum into the left wing, and only three or four obscure Saxon words could do it justice.

I was barely warming my hands in front of the fire and watching Jimmy Fidler turn on a spit when my presence on the Pacific Slope made itself felt. The news of my arrival had thrown international financial centres into an uproar, and sheaves of wires, cables, phone messages and even corn began piling up. An ugly rumour that I might reorganize the motion-picture industry was being bruited about in the world's commodity markets. My brokers, Whitelipped & Trembling, were beside themselves. The New York Stock Exchange was begging them for assurances of stability, and Threadneedle Street awaited my next move with drumming pulses. Film shares ricocheted sharply, although wools and meats were sluggish, if not downright sullen. To the reporters who flocked around me I laughingly disclaimed that this was a business trip. I was simply a scenario writer to whom the idea of work was abhorrent. A few words murmured into the transatlantic telephone, the lift of an eyebrow here, the shrug of a shoulder there, and equilibrium was soon restored. I washed sparsely, curled my moustache with a heated hairpin, flicked a drop of Sheik Lure on my lapel, and rejoined my hostess.

After a copious dinner, melting-eyed beauties in lacy black under-things fought each other to serve my kümmel. A hurried apology, and I was curled up in bed with the Autumn, 1927, issue of *The Yale Review*. Halfway through an exciting symposium on St Thomas

Aquinas' indebtedness to Professors Whitehead and Spengler, I suddenly detected a stowaway blonde under the bed. Turning a deaf ear to her heartrending entreaties and burning glances, I sent her packing. Then I treated my face to a feast of skin food, buried my head in the pillow and went bye-bye.

Hollywood Boulevard! I rolled the rich syllables over on my tongue and thirstily drank in the beauty of the scene before me. On all sides nattily attired boulevarders clad in rich stuffs strolled nonchalantly, inhaling cubebs and exchanging epigrams stolen from Martial and Wilde. Thousands of scantily draped but none the less appetizing extra girls milled past me, their mouths a scarlet wound and their eyes clearly defined in their faces. Their voluptuous curves set my blood on fire, and as I made my way down Mammary Lane, a strange thought began to invade my brain: I realized that I had not eaten breakfast yet. In a Chinese eatery cunningly built in the shape of an old shoe I managed to assuage the inner man with a chopped glove salad topped off with frosted cocoa. Charming platinum-haired hostesses in red pyjamas and peaked caps added a note of colour to the surroundings, whilst a gypsy orchestra played selections from Victor Herbert's operettas on musical saws. It was a bit of old Vienna come to life, and the sun was a red ball in the heavens before I realized with a start that I had promised to report at the Plushnick Studios.

Commandeering a taxicab, I arrived at the studio just in time to witness the impressive ceremony of changing the guard. In the central parade ground, on a snowy white charger, sat Max Plushnick, resplendent in a producer's uniform, his chest glittering with first mortgage liens, amortizations, and estoppels. His personal guard, composed of picked vice-presidents of the Chase National Bank, was drawn up stiffly about him in a hollow square.

But the occasion was not a happy one. A writer had been caught trying to create an adult picture. The drums rolled dismally, and the writer, his head sunk on his chest, was led out amid a ghastly silence. With the aid of a small step-ladder Plushnick slid lightly from his steed. Sternly he ripped the epaulettes and buttons from the traitor's tunic, broke his sword across his knee, and in a few harsh words demoted him to the mail department.

'And now,' began Plushnick, 'I further condemn you to eat ...'

'No, no!' screamed the poor wretch, falling to his knees and embracing Plushnick's jack boots, 'not that, not that!'

'Stand up, man,' ordered Plushnick, his lip curling. 'I condemn you to eat in the studio restaurant for ten days and may God have mercy on your soul.' The awful words rang out on the still evening air and even Plushnick's hardened old mercenaries shuddered. The heartrending cries of the unfortunate were drowned in the boom of the sunset gun.

In the wardrobe department I was photographed, fingerprinted, and measured for the smock and Windsor tie which was to be my uniform. A nameless fear clutched at my heart as two impressive turnkeys herded me down a corridor to my supervisor's office. For what seemed hours we waited in an ante-room. Then my serial number was called, the leg-irons were struck off, and I was shoved through a door into the presence of Diana ffrench-Mamoulian.

How to describe what followed? Diana ffrench-Mamoulian was accustomed to having her way with writers, and my long lashes and peachblow mouth seemed to whip her to insensate desire. In vain, time and again, I tried to bring her attention back to the story we were discussing, only to find her gem-encrusted fingers straying through my hair. When our interview was over, her cynical attempt to 'date me up' made every fibre of my being cry out in revolt.

'P-please,' I stammered, my face burning, 'I – I wish you wouldn't . . . I'm engaged to a Tri Kappa at Goucher —'

'Just one kiss,' she pleaded, her breath hot against my neck. In desperation I granted her boon, knowing full well that my weak defences were crumbling before the onslaught of this love tigree. Finally she allowed me to leave, but only after I had promised to dine at her penthouse apartment and have an intimate chat about the script. The basket of slave bracelets and marzipan I found awaiting me on my return home made me realize to what lengths Diana would go.

I was radiant that night in blue velvet tails and a boutonniere of diamonds from Cartier's, my eyes starry and the merest hint of cologne at my ear-lobes. An inscrutable Oriental served the Lucullan repast and my *vis-à-vis* was as effervescent as the wine

'Have a bit of wine, darling?' queried Diana solicitously, indicating the roast Long Island aeroplane with apple-sauce, I tried to turn our conversation from the personal note, but Diana would have none of it. Soon we were exchanging gay bantam over the mellow Vouvray, laughing as we dipped fastidious fingers into the Crisco parfait for which Diana was famous. Our meal finished, we sauntered into the rumpus room and Diana turned on the radio. With a savage snarl the radio turned on her and we slid over the waxed floor in the intricate maze of the jackdaw strut. Without quite knowing why, I found myself hesitating before the plate of liqueur candies Diana was pressing on me.

'I don't think I should – really, I'm a trifle faint —'

'Oh, come on,' she urged masterfully, 'After all, you're old enough to be your father – I mean I'm old enough to be my mother. . . .' She stuffed a brandy bonbon between my clenched teeth. Before long I was eating them thirstily, reeling about the room and shouting snatches of coarse drunken doggerel. My brain was on fire, I tell you. Through the haze I saw Diana ffrench-Mamoulian, her nostrils dilated, groping for me. My scream of terror only egged her on, overturning chairs and tables in her bestial pursuit. With superhuman talons she tore off my collar and suspenders, I sank to my knees, choked with sobs, hanging on to my last shirt-stud like a drowning man. Her Svengali eyes were slowly hypnotizing me; I fought like a wounded bird – and then, blissful unconsciousness.

When I came to, the Oriental servant and Diana were battling in the centre of the floor. As I watched, Yen Shee Gow drove a well-aimed blow to her mid-section, followed it with a right cross to the jaw. Diana staggered and rolled under a table. Before my astonished eyes John Chinaman stripped the mask from his face and revealed the features of Blanche Almonds, a little seamstress I had long wooed unsuccessfully in New York. Gently she bathed my temples with Florida water and explained how she had followed me, suspecting Diana ffrench-Mamoulian's intentions. I let her rain kisses over my face and lay back in her arms as beaming Ivan tucked us in and cracked his whip over the prancing bays. In a few seconds our sleigh was skimming over the hard crust toward Port Arthur and freedom, leaving Plushnick's discomfited officers gnashing one another's teeth. The wintry Siberian moon glowed over the tundras, drenching my hair with moonbeams for Blanche to kiss away. And so, across the silvery steppes amid the howling of wolves, we rode into a new destiny, purified in the crucible that men call Hollywood.

Kiss Me Again, Stranger

DAPHNE DU MAURIER

I LOOKED AROUND FOR A BIT, AFTER LEAVING the army and before settling down, and then I found myself a job up Hampstead way, in a garage it was, at the bottom of Haverstock Hill near Chalk Farm, and it suited me fine. I'd always been one for tinkering with engines, and in REME that was my work and I was trained to it – it had always come easy to me, anything mechanical.

My idea of having a good time was to lie on my back in my greasy overalls under a car's belly, or a lorry's with a spanner in my hand, working on some old bolt or screw, with the smell of oil about me, and someone starting up an engine, and the other chaps around clattering their tools and whistling. I never minded the smell or the dirt. As my old Mum used to say when I'd be that way as a kid, mucking about with a grease can, 'It won't hurt him, it's clean dirt,' and so it is, with engines.

The boss at the garage was a good fellow, easy-going, cheerful, and he saw I was keen on my work. He wasn't much of a mechanic himself, so he gave me the repair jobs, which was what I liked.

I didn't live with my old Mum – she was too far off, over Shepperton way, and I saw no point in spending half the day getting to and from my work. I like to be handy, have it on the spot, as it were. So I had a bedroom with a couple called Thompson, only about ten minutes' walk away from the garage. Nice people, they were. He was in the shoe business, cobbler I suppose he'd be called, and Mrs Thompson cooked the meals and kept the house for him over the shop. I used to eat with them, breakfast and supper – we always had a cooked supper – and being the only lodger I was treated as family.

I'm one for routine. I like to get on with my job, and then when the day's work's over settle down to a paper and a smoke and a bit of music on the wireless, variety or something of the sort, and then turn in early. I never had much use for girls, not even when I was doing my time in the army. I was out in the Middle East, too, Port Said and that.

No, I was happy enough living with the Thompsons, carrying on much the same day after day, until that one night, when it happened. Nothing's been the same since. Nor ever will be. I don't know . . .

The Thompsons had gone to see their married daughter up at Highgate. They asked me if I'd like to go along, but somehow I didn't fancy barging in, so instead of staying home alone after leaving the garage I went down to the picture palace, and taking a look at the poster saw it was cowboy and Indian stuff – there was a picture of a cowboy sticking a knife into the Indian's guts. I like that – proper baby I am for westerns – so I paid my one and twopence and went inside. I handed my slip of paper to the usherette and said, 'Back row, please,' because I like sitting far back and leaning my head against the board.

Well, then I saw her. They dress the girls up no end in some of these places, velvet tams and all, making them proper guys. They hadn't made a guy out of this one, though. She had copper hair, pageboy style I think they call it, and blue eyes, the kind that look shortsighted but see further than you think, and go dark by night, nearly black, and her mouth was sulky-looking, as if she was fed up, and it would take someone giving her the world to make her smile. She hadn't freckles, nor a milky skin, but warmer than that, more like a peach, and natural too. She was small and slim, and her velvet coat – blue it was – fitted her close, and the cap on the back of her head showed up her copper hair.

I bought a programme – not that I wanted one, but to delay going in through the curtain – and I said to her, 'What's the picture like?'

She didn't look at me. She just went on staring into nothing, at the opposite wall. 'The knifing's amateur,' she said, 'but you can always sleep.'

I couldn't help laughing. I could see she was serious though. She wasn't trying to have me on or anything.

'That's no advertisement,' I said. 'What if the manager heard you?'

Then she looked at me. She turned those blue eyes in my direction, still fed-up they were, not interested, but there was something in them I'd not seen before, and I've never seen it since, a kind of laziness like someone waking from a long dream and glad to find you there. Cat's eyes have that gleam sometimes, when you stroke them, and they purr and curl themselves into a ball and let you do anything you want. She looked at me this way a moment, and there was a smile lurking somewhere behind her mouth if you gave it a chance, and tearing my slip of paper in half she said, 'I'm not paid to advertise. I'm paid to look like this and lure you inside.'

She drew aside the curtains and flashed her torch in the darkness. I couldn't see a thing. It was pitch black, like it always is at first until you get used to it and begin to make out the shapes of the other people sitting there, but there were two great heads on the screen and some chap saying to the other, 'If you don't come clean I'll put a bullet through you,' and somebody broke a pane of glass and a woman screamed.

'Looks all right to me,' I said, and began groping for somewhere to sit.

She said, 'This isn't the picture, it's the trailer for next week,' and she flicked on her torch and showed me a seat in the back row, one away from the gangway.

I sat through the advertisements and the news reel, and then some chap came and played the organ, and the colours of the curtains over the screen went purple and gold and green – funny, I suppose they think they have to give you your money's worth – and looking around I saw the house was half empty – and I guessed the girl had been right, the big picture wasn't going to be much, and that's why nobody much was there.

Just before the hall went dark again she came sauntering down the aisle. She had a tray of ice-creams, but she didn't even bother to call them out and try and sell them. She could have been walking in her sleep, so when she went up the other aisle I beckoned to her.

'Got a sixpenny one?' I said.

She looked at me. I might have been something dead under her feet, and then she must have recognized me, because that half smile came back again, and the lazy look in the eye, and she walked round the back of the seats to me.

'Wafer or cornet?' she said.

I didn't want either, to tell the truth. I just wanted to buy something from her and keep her talking.

'Which do you recommend?' I asked.

She shrugged her shoulders. 'Cornets last longer,' she said, and put one in my hand before I had time to give her my choice.

'How about one for you too?' I said.

'No thanks,' she said, 'I saw them made.'

And she walked off, and the place went dark, and there I was sitting with a great sixpenny cornet in my hand looking a fool. The damn thing slopped all over the edge of the holder, spilling on to my shirt, and I had to ram the frozen stuff into my mouth as quick as I could for fear it would all go on my knees, and I turned sideways, because someone came and sat in the empty seat beside the gangway.

I finished it at last, and cleaned myself up with my pocket handkerchief, and then concentrated on the story flashing across the screen. It was a western all right, carts lumbering over prairies, and a train full of bullion being held to ransom, and the heroine in breeches one moment and full evening dress the next. That's the way pictures should be, not a bit like real life at all; but as I watched the story I began to notice the whiff of scent in the air, and I didn't know what it was or where it came from, but it was there just the same. There was a man to the right of me, and on my left were two empty seats, and it certainly wasn't the people in front, and I couldn't keep turning round and sniffing.

I'm not a great one for liking scent. It's too often cheap and nasty, but this was different. There was nothing stale about it, or stuffy, or strong; it was like the flowers they sell up in the West End in the big flower shops before you get them on the barrows – three bob a bloom sort of touch, rich chaps buy them for actresses and such – and it was so darn good, the smell of it there, in that murky old picture palace full of cigarette smoke, that it nearly drove me mad.

At last I turned right round in my seat, and I spotted where it came from. It came from the girl, the usherette; she was leaning on the back board behind me, her arms folded across it.

Don't fidget,' she said. 'You're wasting one and twopence. Watch the screen.'

But not out loud, so that anyone could hear. In a whisper, for me alone. I couldn't help laughing to myself. The cheek of it! I knew where the scent came from now, and somehow it made me enjoy the picture more. It was as though she was beside me in one of the empty seats and we were looking at the story together.

When it was over, and the lights went on, I saw I'd sat through the last showing and it was nearly ten. Everyone was clearing off for the night. So I waited a bit, and then she came down with her torch and started squinting under the seats to see if anybody had dropped a glove or a purse, the way they do and only remember about afterwards when they get home, and she took no more notice of me than if I'd been a rag which no one would bother to pick up.

I stood up in the back row, alone – the house was clear now – and when she came to me she said, 'Move over, you're blocking the gangway,' and flashed about with her torch, but there was nothing there, only an empty packet of Player's which the cleaners would throw away in the morning. Then she straightened herself and looked me up and down, and taking off the ridiculous cap from the back of her head that suited her so well she fanned herself with it and said, 'Sleeping here tonight?', and then went off, whistling under her breath, and disappeared through the curtains.

It was proper maddening. I'd never been taken so much with a girl in my life. I went into the vestibule after her, but she had gone through the door to the back, behind the box-office place, and the commissionaire chap was already getting the doors to and fixing them for the night. I went out and stood in the street and waited. I felt a bit of a fool, because the odds were that she would come out with a bunch of others, the way girls do. There was the one who had sold me my ticket, and I dare say there were other usherettes up in the balcony, and perhaps a cloak-room attendant too, and they'd all be giggling together, and I wouldn't have the nerve to go up to her.

In a few minutes, though, she came swinging out of the place alone. She had a mac on, belted, and her hands in her pockets, and she had no hat. She walked straight up the street, and she didn't look to right or left of her. I followed, scared that she would turn round and see me off, but she went on walking, fast and direct, staring straight in front of her, and as she moved her copper page-boy hair swung with her shoulders.

Presently she hesitated, then crossed over and stood waiting for a bus. There was a queue of four or five people, so she didn't see me join the queue, and when the bus came she climbed on to it, ahead of the others, and I climbed too, without the slightest notion where it was going, and I couldn't have cared less. Up the stairs she went with me after her, and settled herself in the back seat, yawning, and closed her eyes.

I sat myself down beside her nervous as a kitten, the point being that I never did that sort of thing as a rule and expected a rocket, and when the conductor stumped up and asked for fares I said, 'Two sixpennies, please,' because I reckoned she would never be going the whole distance and this would be bound to cover her fare and mine too.

He raised his eyebrows – they like to think themselves smart, some of these fellows – and he said, 'Look out for the bumps when the driver changes gear. He's only just passed his test.' And he went down the stairs chuckling, telling himself he was no end of a wag, no doubt.

The sound of his voice woke the girl, and she looked at me out of her sleepy eyes, and looked too at the tickets in my hand – she must have seen by the colour they were sixpennies – and she smiled, the first real smile I had got out of her that evening, and said without any sort of surprise, 'Hullo, stranger.'

I took out a cigarette, to put myself at ease, and offered her one, but she wouldn't take it. She just closed her eyes again, to settle herself to sleep. Then, seeing there was no one else to notice up on the top deck, only an Air Force chap in the front slopped over a newspaper, I put out my hand and pulled her head down on my shoulder, and got my arm round her, snug and comfortable, thinking of course she'd throw it off and blast me to hell. She didn't, though. She gave a sort of laugh to herself, and settled down as if she might have been in an armchair, and she said, 'It's not every night I get a free ride and a free pillow. Wake me at the bottom of the hill, before we get to the cemetery.'

I didn't know what hill she meant, or what cemetery, but I wasn't going to wake her, not me. I had paid for two sixpennies, and I was darn well going to get value for my money.

So we sat there together, jogging along in the bus, very close and very pleasant, and I thought to myself that it was a lot more fun than sitting at home in the bed-sit reading the football news, or spending an evening up Highgate at Mr and Mrs Thompson's daughter's place.

Presently I got more daring, and let my head lean against hers, and tightened up my arm a bit, not too obvious-like, but nicely. Anyone coming up the stairs to the top deck would have taken us for a courting couple.

Then, after we had had about fourpenny-worth, I got anxious. The old bus wouldn't be turning round and going back again, when we reached the sixpenny limit; it would pack up for the night, we'd have come to the terminus. And there we'd be, the girl and I, stuck out somewhere at the back of beyond, with no return bus, and I'd got about six bob in my pocket and no more. Six bob would never pay for a taxi, not with a tip and all. Besides, there probably wouldn't be any taxis going.

What a fool I'd been not to come out with more money. It was silly, perhaps, to let it worry me, but I'd acted on impulse right from the start, and if only I'd known how the evening was going to turn out I'd have had my wallet filled. It wasn't often I went out with a girl, and I hate a fellow who can't do the thing in style. Proper slap-up do at the Corner House – they're good these days with that help-yourself service – and if she had a fancy for something stronger than coffee or orangeade, well, of course as late as this it wasn't much use, but nearer home I knew where to go. There was a pub where my boss went, and you paid for your gin and kept it there, and could go in and have a drink from your bottle when you felt like it. They have the same sort of racket at the posh night clubs up West, I'm told, but they make you pay through the nose for it.

Anyway, here I was riding a bus to the Lord knows where, with my girl beside me – I called her 'my girl' just as if she really was and we were courting – and bless me if I had the money to take her home. I began to fidget about, from sheer nerves, and I fumbled in one pocket after another, in case by a piece of luck I should come across a half-crown, or even a ten bob note I had forgotten all about, and I suppose I disturbed her with all this, because she suddenly pulled my ear and said, 'Stop rocking the boat.'

Well, I mean to say . . . It just got me. I can't explain why. She held my ear a moment before she pulled it like as though she were feeling the skin and liked it, and then she just gave it a lazy tug. It's the kind of thing anyone would do to a child, and the way she said it, as if she had known me for years and we were out picnicking together, 'Stop rocking the boat.' Chummy, matey, yet better than either.

'Look here,' I said, 'I'm awfully sorry, I've been and done a darn silly thing. I took tickets to the terminus because I wanted to sit beside you, and when we get there we'll be turned out of the bus, and it will be miles from anywhere, and I've only got six bob in my pocket.'

'You've got legs, haven't you?' she said.

'What d'you mean, I've got legs?'

'They're meant to walk on. Mine were,' she answered.

Then I knew it didn't matter, and she wasn't angry either, and the evening was going to be all right. I cheered up in a second, and gave her a squeeze, just to show her I appreciated her being such a sport – most girls would have torn me to shreds – and I said, 'We haven't passed a cemetery, as far as I know. Does it matter very much?'

'Oh, there'll be others,' she said, 'I'm not particular.'

I didn't know what to make of that. I thought she wanted to get out at the cemetery stopping point because it was her nearest stop for home, like the way you say, 'Put me down at Woolworth's' if you live handy. I puzzled over it for a bit, and then I said, 'How do you mean, there'll be others? It's not a thing you see often along a bus route.'

'I was speaking in general terms,' she answered. 'Don't bother to talk, I like you silent best.'

It wasn't a slap on the face, the way she said it. Fact was, I knew what she meant. Talking's all very pleasant with people like Mr and Mrs Thompson, over supper, and you say how the day has gone, and one of you reads a bit out of the paper, and the other says, 'Fancy, there now,' and so it goes on in bits and pieces until one of you yawns, and somebody says, 'Who's for bed?' Or it's nice enough with a chap like the boss, having a cuppa mid-morning, or about three when there's nothing doing, 'I tell you what I think, those blokes in the government are making a mess of things, no better than the last lot,' and then we'll be interrupted with someone coming to fill up with petrol. And I like talking to my old Mum when I go and see her, which I don't do often enough, and she tells me how she spanked my bottom when I was a kid, and I sit on the kitchen table like I did then, and she bakes rock cakes and gives me peel, saying 'You always were one for peel.' That's talk, that's conversation.

But I didn't want to talk to my girl. I just wanted to keep my arm round her the way I was doing, and rest my chin against her head, and that's what she meant when she said she liked me silent. I liked it too.

One last thing bothered me a bit, and that was whether I could kiss her before the bus stopped and we were turned out at the terminus. I mean, putting an arm round a girl is one thing, and kissing her is another. It takes a little time as a rule to warm up. You start off with a long evening ahead of you, and by the time you've been to a picture or a concert, and then had something to eat and to drink, well, you've got yourselves acquainted, and it's the usual thing to end up with a bit of kissing and a cuddle, the girls expect it. Truth to tell, I was never much of a one for kissing. There was a girl I walked out with back home, before I went into the army, and she was quite a good sort, I liked her. But her teeth were a bit prominent, and even if you shut your eyes and tried to forget who it was you were kissing, well, you knew it was her, and there was nothing to it. Good old Doris from next door. But the opposite kind are even worse, the ones that grab you and nearly eat you. You come across plenty of them, when you're in uniform. They're much too eager, and they muss you about, and you get the feeling they can't wait for a chap to get busy about them. I don't mind saying it used to make me sick. Put me dead off, and that's a fact. I suppose I was born fussy. I don't know.

But now, this evening in the bus, it was all quite different. I don't know what it was about the girl – the sleepy eyes, and the copper hair, and somehow not seeming to care if I was there yet liking me at the same time; I hadn't found anything like this before. So I said to myself, 'Now, shall I risk it, or shall I wait?', and I knew, from the way the driver was going and the conductor was whistling below and saying 'good-night' to the people getting off, that the final stop couldn't be far away; and my heart began to thump under my coat, and my neck grew hot below the collar – darn silly, only a kiss you know, she couldn't kill me – and then ... It was like diving off a spring-board. I thought, 'Here goes,' and I bent down, and turned her face to me, and lifted her chin with my hand, and kissed her good and proper.

Well, if I was poetical, I'd say what happened then was a revelation. But I'm not poetical, and I can only say that she kissed me back, and it lasted a long time, and it wasn't a bit like Doris.

Then the bus stopped with a jerk, and the conductor called out in a sing-song voice. 'All out, please.' Frankly, I could have wrung his neck.

She gave me a kick on the ankle. 'Come on, move,' she said, and I stumbled from my seat and racketed down the stairs, she following behind, and there we were, standing in a street. It was beginning to rain too, not badly but just enough to make you notice and want to turn up the collar of your coat, and we were right at the end of a great wide street, with deserted unlighted shops on either side, the end of the world it looked to me, and sure enough there was a hill over to the left, and at the bottom of the hill a cemetery. I could see the railings and the white tombstones behind, and it stretched a long way, nearly half way up the hill. There were acres of it.

'God darn it,' I said, 'is this the place you meant?'

'Could be' she said, looking over her shoulder vaguely, and then she took my arm. 'What about a cup of coffee first?' she said.

First . . .? I wondered if she meant before the long trudge home, or was this home? It didn't really matter. It wasn't much after eleven. And I could do with a cup of coffee, and a sandwich too. There was a stall across the road, and they hadn't shut up shop.

We walked over to it, and the driver was there too, and the conductor, and the Air Force fellow who had been up in front on the top deck. They were ordering cups of teas and sandwiches, and we had the same, only coffee. They cut them tasty at the stalls, the sandwiches, I've noticed it before, nothing stingy about it, good slices of ham between thick white bread, and the coffee is piping hot, full cups too, good value, and I thought to myself, 'Six bob will see this lot all right.'

I noticed my girl looking at the Air Force chap, sort of thoughtful-like, as though she might have seen him before, and he looked at her too. I couldn't blame him for that. I didn't mind either; when you're out with a girl it gives you a kind of pride if other chaps notice her. And you couldn't miss this one. Not my girl.

Then she turned her back on him, deliberate, and leant with her elbows on the stall, sipping her hot coffee, and I stood beside her doing the same. We weren't stuck up or anything, we were pleasant and polite enough, saying good evening all round, but anyone could tell that we were together, the girl and I, we were on our own. I liked that. Funny, it did something to me inside, gave me a protective feeling. For all they knew we might have been a married couple on our way home.

They were chaffing a bit, the other three and the chap serving the sandwiches and tea, but we didn't join in.

'You want to watch out, in that uniform,' said the conductor to the Air Force fellow, 'or you'll end up like those others. It's late too, to be out on your own.'

They all started laughing. I didn't quite see the point, but I supposed it was a joke.

'I've been awake a long time,' said the Air Force fellow. 'I know a bad lot when I see one.'

'That's what the others said, I shouldn't wonder,' remarked the driver, 'and we know what happened to them. Makes you shudder. But why pick on the Air Force, that's what I want to know?'

'It's the colour of our uniform,' said the fellow. 'You can spot it in the dark.'

They went on laughing in that way. I lighted up a cigarette, but my girl wouldn't have one.

'I blame the war for all that's gone wrong with the women,' said the coffee-stall bloke, wiping a cup and hanging it up behind. 'Turned a lot of them balmy, in my opinion. They don't know the difference between right or wrong.'

"Tisn't that, it's sport that's the trouble,' said the conductor. 'Develops their muscles and that, what weren't never meant to be developed. Take my two youngsters, f'r instance. The girl can knock the boy down any time, she's a proper little bully. Makes you think.'

'That's right,' agreed the driver, 'equality of the sexes, they call it, don't they? It's the vote that did it. We ought never to have given them the vote.'

'Garn,' said the Air Force chap, 'giving them the vote didn't turn the women balmy. They've always been the same, under the skin. The people out East know how to treat 'em. They keep 'em shut up, out there. That's the answer. Then you don't get any trouble.'

'I don't know what my old woman would say if I tried to shut her up,' said the driver. And they all started laughing again.

My girl plucked at my sleeve and I saw she had finished her coffee. She motioned with her head towards the street.

'Want to go home?' I said.

Silly. I somehow wanted the others to believe we were going home. She didn't answer. She just went striding off, her hands in the pockets of her mac. I said good-night and followed her, but not before I noticed the Air Force fellow staring after her over his cup of tea.

She walked off along the street, and it was still raining, dreary somehow, made you want to be sitting over a fire somewhere snug, and when she had crossed the street, and had come to the railings outside the cemetery she stopped, and looked up at me, and smiled.

'What now?' I said.

'Tomb-stones are flat,' she said, 'sometimes.'

'What if they are?' I asked, bewildered-like.

'You can lie down on them,' she said.

She turned and strolled along, looking at the railings, and then she came to one that was bent wide, and the next beside it broken, and she glanced up at me and smiled again.

'It's always the same,' she said. 'You're bound to find a gap if you look long enough.'

She was through that gap in the railings as quick as a knife through butter. You could have knocked me flat.

'Here, hold on,' I said, 'I'm not as small as you.'

But she was off and away, wandering among the graves. I got through the gap, puffing and blowing a bit, and then I looked around, and bless me if she wasn't lying on a long flat gravestone, with her arms under her head and her eyes closed.

Well, I wasn't expecting anything. I mean, it had been in my mind to see her home and that. Date her up for the next evening. Of course, seeing as it was late, we could have stopped a bit when we came to the doorway of her place. She needn't have gone in right away. But lying there on the gravestone wasn't hardly natural.

I sat down, and took her hand.

'You'll get wet lying there,' I said. Feeble, but I didn't know what else to say.

'I'm used to that,' she said.

She opened her eyes and looked at me. There was a street light not far away, outside the railings, so it wasn't all that dark, and anyway in spite of the rain the night wasn't pitch black, more murky somehow. I wish I knew how to tell you about her eyes, but I'm not one for fancy talk. You know how a luminous watch shines in the dark. I've got one myself. When you wake up in the night, there it is on your wrist, like a friend. Somehow my girl's eyes shone like that, but they were lovely too. And they weren't lazy cat's eyes any more. They were loving and gentle, and they were sad, too, all at the same time.

'Used to lying in the rain?' I said.

'Brought up to it,' she answered. 'They gave us a name in the shelters. The dead-end kids, they used to call us, in the war days.'

'Weren't you never evacuated?' I asked.

'Not me,' she said. 'I never could stop any place. I always came back.'

'Parents living?'

'No. Both of them killed by the bomb that smashed my home.' She didn't speak tragic-like. Just ordinary.

'Bad luck,' I said.

She didn't answer that one. And I sat there, holding her hand, wanting to take her home.

'You been on your job some time, at the picture-house?' I asked.

'About three weeks,' she said. 'I don't stop anywhere long. I'll be moving on again soon.'

'Why's that?'

'Restless,' she said.

She put up her hands suddenly and took my face and held it. It was gentle the way she did it, not as you'd think.

'You've got a good kind face. I like it,' she said to me.

It was queer. The way she said it made me feel daft and soft, not sort of excited like I had been in the bus, and I thought to myself, well, maybe this is it. I've found a girl at last I really want. But not for an evening, casual. For going steady.

'Got a bloke?' I asked.

'No,' she said.

'I mean, regular.'

'No, never.'

It was a funny line of talk to be having in a cemetery, and she lying there like some figure carved on the old tomb-stone.

'I haven't got a girl either,' I said. 'Never think about it, the way other chaps do. Faddy, I guess. And then I'm keen on my job. Work in a garage, mechanic you know, repairs, anything that's going. Good pay. I've saved a bit, besides what I send my old Mum. I live in digs. Nice people, Mr and Mrs Thompson, and my boss at the garage is a nice chap too. I've never been lonely, and I'm not lonely now. But since I've seen you, it's made me think. You know, it's not going to be the same any more.'

She never interrupted once, and somehow it was like speaking my thoughts aloud.

'Going home to the Thompsons is all very pleasant and nice,' I said, 'and you couldn't wish for kinder people. Good grub too, and we chat a bit after supper, and listen to the wireless. But d'you know, what I want now is different. I want to come along and fetch you from the cinema, when the programme's over, and you'd be standing there by the curtains, seeing the people out, and you'd give me a bit of a wink to show me you'd be going through to change your clothes and I could wait for you. And then you'd come out into the street, like you did to-night, but you wouldn't go off on your own, you'd take my arm, and if you didn't want to wear your coat I'd carry it

for you, or a parcel maybe, or whatever you had. Then we'd go off
to the Corner House or some place for supper, handy. We'd have a
table reserved – they'd know us, the waitresses and them; they'd
keep back something special, just for us.'

I could picture it too, clear as anything. The table with the ticket
on 'Reserved.' The waitress nodding at us, 'Got curried eggs tonight.'
And we going through to get our trays, and my girl acting like she
didn't know me, and me laughing to myself.

'D'you see what I mean?' I said to her. 'It's not just being friends,
it's more than that.'

I don't know if she heard. She lay there looking up at me, touching
my ear and my chin in that funny, gentle way. You'd say she was
sorry for me.

'I'd like to buy you things,' I said, 'flowers sometimes. It's nice to
see a girl with a flower tucked in her dress, it looks clean and fresh.
And for special occasions, birthdays, Christmas, and that, something
you'd seen in a shop window, and wanted, but hadn't liked to go in
and ask the price. A brooch perhaps, or a bracelet, something pretty.
And I'd go in and get it when you weren't with me, and it'd cost
much more than my week's pay, but I wouldn't mind.'

I could see the expression on her face, opening the parcel. And
she'd put it on, what I'd bought, and we'd go out together, and she'd
be dressed up a bit for the purpose, nothing glaring I don't mean, but
something that took the eye. You know, saucy.

'It's not fair to talk about getting married,' I said, 'not in these
days, when everything's uncertain. A fellow doesn't mind the uncertainty, but it's hard on a girl. Cooped up in a couple of rooms maybe,
and queueing and rations and all. They like their freedom, and being
in a job, and not being tied down, the same as us. But it's nonsense
the way they were talking back in the coffee stall just now. About
girls not being the same as in the old days, and the war to blame. As
for the way they treat them out East – I've seen some of it. I suppose
that fellow meant to be funny, they're all smart Alicks in the Air
Force, but it was a silly line of talk, I thought.'

She dropped her hands to her side and closed her eyes. It was
getting quite wet there on the tomb-stone. I was worried for her,
though she had her mac of course, but her legs and feet were damp
in her thin stockings and shoes.

'You weren't ever in the Air Force, were you?' she said.

Queer. Her voice had gone quite hard. Sharp, and different. Like as if she was anxious about something, scared even.

'Not me,' I said, 'I served my time with REME. Proper lot they were. No swank, no nonsense. You know where you are with them.'

'I'm glad', she said. 'You're good and kind. I'm glad.'

I wondered if she'd known some fellow in the RAF who had let her down. They're a wild crowd, the ones I've come across. And I remembered the way she'd looked at the boy drinking his tea at the stall. Reflective, somehow. As if she was thinking back. I couldn't expect her not to have been around a bit, with her looks, and then brought up to play about the shelters, without parents, like she said. But I didn't want to think of her being hurt by anyone.

'Why, what's wrong with them?' I said. 'What's the RAF done to you?'

'They smashed my home,' she said.

'That was the Germans, not our fellows.'

'It's all the same, they're killers, aren't they?' she said.

I looked down at her, lying on the tomb-stone, and her voice wasn't hard any more, like when she'd asked me if I'd been in the Air Force, but it was tired, and sad, and oddly lonely, and it did something queer to my stomach, right in the pit of it, so that I wanted to do the darndest silliest thing and take her home with me, back to where I lived with Mr and Mrs Thompson, and say to Mrs Thompson – she was a kind old soul, she wouldn't mind – 'Look, this is my girl. Look after her.' Then I'd known she'd be safe, she'd be all right, nobody could do anything to hurt her. That was the thing I was afraid of suddenly, that someone would come along and hurt my girl.

I bent down and put my arms round her and lifted her up close.

'Listen,' I said, 'it's raining hard. I'm going to take you home. You'll catch your death, lying here on the wet stone.'

'No,' she said, her hands on my shoulders, 'Nobody ever sees me home. You're going back where you belong, alone.'

'I won't leave you here,' I said.

'Yes, that's what I want you to do. If you refuse I shall be angry. You wouldn't want that, would you?'

I stared at her, puzzled. And her face was queer in the murky old light there, whiter than before, but it was beautiful, Jesus Christ, it was beautiful. That's blasphemy. But I can't say it no other way.

'What do you want me to do?' I asked.

'I want you to go and leave me here, and not look back,' she said, 'like someone dreaming, sleep-walking, they call it. Go back walking through the rain. It will take you hours. It doesn't matter, you're young and strong and you've got long legs. Go back to your room, wherever it is, and get into bed, and go to sleep, and wake and have your breakfast in the morning, and go off to work, the same as you always do.'

'What about you?'

'Never mind about me. Just go.'

'Can I call for you at the cinema tomorrow night? Can it be like what I was telling you, you know . . . going steady?'

She didn't answer. She only smiled. She sat quite still, looking in my face, and then she closed her eyes and threw back her head and said, 'Kiss me again, stranger.'

I left her, like she said. I didn't look back. I climbed through the railings of the cemetery, out on to the road. No one seemed to be about, and the coffee stall by the stop had closed down, the boards were up.

I started walking the way the bus had brought us. The road was straight, going on for ever. A High Street it must have been. There were shops on either side, and it was right away north-east of London, nowhere I'd ever been before. I was proper lost, but it didn't seem to matter. I felt like a sleep-walker, just as she said.

I kept thinking of her all the time. There was nothing else, only her face in front of me as I walked. They had a word for it in the army, when a girl gets a fellow that way, so he can't see straight or hear right or know what he's doing; and I thought it a lot of cock, or it only happened to drunks, and now I knew it was true and it had happened to me. I wasn't going to worry any more about how she'd get home; she'd told me not to, and she must have lived handy, she'd never have ridden out so far else, though it was funny such a way from her work. But maybe in time she'd tell me more, bit by bit. I wouldn't drag it from her. I had one thing fixed in my mind, and that was to pick her up the next evening from the picture palace. It was firm and set, and nothing would budge me from that. The hours in between would just be a blank for me until ten p.m. came round.

I went on walking in the rain, and presently a lorry came along and I thumbed a lift, and the driver took me a good part of the way before he had to turn left in the other direction, and so I got down and walked again, and it must have been close on three when I got home.

I would have felt bad, in an ordinary way, knocking up Mr Thompson to let me in, and it had never happened before either, but I was all lit up inside from loving my girl, and I didn't seem to mind. He came down at last and opened the door. I had to ring several times before he heard, and there he was, grey with sleep, poor old chap, his pyjamas all crumpled from the bed.

'Whatever happened to you?' he said. 'We've been worried, the wife and me. We thought you'd been knocked down, run over. We came back here and found the house empty and your supper not touched.'

'I went to the pictures,' I said.

'The pictures?' He stared up at me, in the passage-way. 'The pictures stop at ten o'clock.'

'I know,' I said, 'I went walking after that. Sorry. Goodnight.'

And I climbed up the stairs to my room, leaving the old chap muttering to himself and bolting the door, and I heard Mrs Thompson calling from her bedroom, 'What is it? Is it him? Is he come home?'

I'd put them to trouble and to worry, and I ought to have gone in there and then and apologized, but I couldn't somehow, it wouldn't have come right; so I shut my door and threw off my clothes and got into bed, and it was like as if she was with me still, my girl, in the darkness.

They were a bit quiet at breakfast the next morning, Mr and Mrs Thompson. They didn't look at me. Mrs Thompson gave me my kipper without a word, and he went on looking at his newspaper.

I ate my breakfast, and then I said, 'I hope you had a nice evening up at Highgate?', and Mrs Thompson, with her mouth a bit tight, she said, 'Very pleasant, thank you, we were home by ten,' and gave a little sniff and poured Mr Thompson out another cup of tea.

We went on being quiet, no one saying a word, and then Mrs Thompson said, 'Will you be in to supper this evening?' and I said, 'No, I don't think so. I'm meeting a friend,' and then I saw the old chap look at me over his spectacles.

'If you're going to be late,' he said, 'we'd best take the key for you.'

Then he went on reading his paper. You could tell they were proper hurt that I didn't tell them anything, or say where I was going.

I went off to work, and we were busy at the garage that day, one job after the other came along, and any other time I wouldn't have minded. I liked a full day and often worked overtime, but today I wanted to get away before the shops closed; I hadn't thought about anything else since the idea came into my head.

It was getting on for half-past four, and the boss came to me and said, 'I promised the doctor he'd have his Austin this evening, I said you'd be through with it by seven-thirty. That's O.K., isn't it?'

My heart sank. I'd counted on getting off early, because of what I wanted to do. Then I thought quickly that if the boss let me off now, and I went out to the shop before it closed, and came back again to do the job on the Austin, it would be all right, so I said, 'I don't mind working a bit of overtime, but I'd like to slip out now, for half-an-hour, if you're going to be here. There's something I want to buy before the shops shut.'

He told me that suited him, so I took off my overalls and washed and got my coat and I went off to the line of shops down at the bottom of Haverstock Hill. I knew the one I wanted. It was a jeweller's, where Mr Thompson used to take his clock to be repaired, and it wasn't a place where they sold trash at all, but good stuff, solid silver frames and that, and cutlery.

There were rings, of course, and a few fancy bangles, but I didn't like the look of them. All the girls in the NAAFI used to wear bangles with charms on them, quite common it was, and I went on staring in at the window and then I spotted it, right at the back.

It was a brooch. Quite small, not much bigger than your thumbnail, but with a nice blue stone on it and a pin at the back, and it was shaped like a heart. That was what got me, the shape. I stared at it a bit, and there wasn't a ticket to it, which meant it would cost a bit, but I went in and asked to have a look at it. The jeweller got it out of the window for me, and he gave it a bit of a polish and turned it this way and that, and I saw it pinned on my girl, showing up nice on her frock or her jumper, and I knew this was it.

'I'll take it,' I said, and then asked him the price.

I swallowed a bit when he told me, but I took out my wallet and counted the notes, and he put the heart in a box wrapped up careful with cotton wool, and made a neat package of it, tied with fancy string. I knew I'd have to get an advance from the boss before I went off work that evening, but he was a good chap and I was certain he'd give it to me.

I stood outside the jeweller's, with the packet for my girl safe in my breast pocket, and I heard the church clock strike a quarter to five. There was time to slip down to the cinema and make sure she understood about the date for the evening, and then I'd beat it fast up the road and get back to the garage, and I'd have the Austin done by the time the doctor wanted it.

When I got to the cinema my heart was beating like a sledge-hammer and I could hardly swallow. I kept picturing to myself how she'd look, standing there by the curtains going in, with that velvet jacket and the cap on the back of her head.

There was a bit of a queue outside, and I saw they'd changed the programme. The poster of the western had gone, with the cowboy throwing a knife in the Indian's guts, and they had instead a lot of girls dancing, and some chap prancing in front of them with a walking-stick. It was a musical.

I went in, and didn't go near the box office but looked straight to the curtains, where she'd be. There was an usherette there all right, but it wasn't her. This was a great tall girl, who looked silly in the clothes, and she was trying to do two things at once – tear off the slips of tickets as the people went past, and hang on to her torch at the same time.

I waited a moment. Perhaps they'd switched over positions and my girl had gone up to the circle. When the last lot had got in through the curtains and there was a pause and she was free, I went up to her and I said, 'Excuse me, do you know where I could have a word with the other young lady?'

She looked at me. 'What other young lady?'

'The one who was here last night, with copper hair.' I said.

She looked at me closer then, suspicious-like.

'She hasn't shown up today,' she said. 'I'm taking her place.'

'Not shown up?'

'No. And it's funny you should ask. You're not the only one. The police was here not long ago. They had a word with the manager, and the commissionaire too, and no one's said anything to me yet, but I think there's been trouble.'

My heart beat different then. Not excited, bad. Like when someone's ill, took to hospital, sudden.

'The police?' I said. 'What were they here for?'

'I told you, I don't know,' she answered, 'but it was something to do with her, and the manager went with them to the police station, and he hasn't come back yet. This way, please, circle on the left, stalls to the right.'

I just stood there, not knowing what to do. It was like as if the floor had been knocked away from under me.

The tall girl tore another slip of a ticket and then she said to me, over her shoulder, 'Was she a friend of yours?'

'Sort of,' I said. I didn't know what to say.

'Well, if you ask me, she was queer in the head, and it wouldn't surprise me if she'd done away with herself and they'd found her dead. No, ice-creams served in the interval, after the news reel.'

I went out and stood in the street. The queue was growing for the cheaper seats, and there were children too, talking, excited. I brushed past them and started walking up the street, and I felt sick inside, queer. Something had happened to my girl. I knew it now. That was why she had wanted to get rid of me last night, and for me not to see her home. She was going to do herself in, there in the cemetery. That's why she talked funny and looked so white, and now they'd found her, lying there on the gravestone by the railings.

If I hadn't gone away and left her she'd have been all right. If I'd stayed with her just five minutes longer, coaxing her, I'd have got her round to my way of thinking and seen her home, standing no nonsense, and she'd be at the picture palace now, showing the people to their seats.

It might be it wasn't as bad as what I feared. It might be she was found wandering, lost her memory and got picked up by the police and taken off, and then they found out where she worked and that, and now the police wanted to check up with the manager at the cinema to see if it was so. If I went down to the police station and asked them there, maybe they'd tell me what had happened, and I could say she was my girl, we were walking out, and it wouldn't matter if she didn't recognize me even, I'd stick to the story. I couldn't let down my boss, I had to get that job done on the Austin, but afterwards, when I'd finished, I could go down to the police station.

All the heart had gone out of me, and I went back to the garage hardly knowing what I was doing, and for the first time ever the smell of the place turned my stomach, the oil and the grease, and there was a chap roaring up his engine, before backing out his car, and a great cloud of smoke coming from his exhaust, filling the workshop with stink.

I went and got my overalls, and put them on, and fetched the tools, and started on the Austin, and all the time I was wondering what it was that had happened to my girl, if she was down at the police station, lost and lonely, or if she was lying somewhere ... dead. I kept seeing her face all the time like it was last night.

It took me an hour and a half, not more, to get the Austin ready for the road, filled up with petrol and all, and I had her facing outwards to the street for the owner to drive out, but I was all in by then, dead tired, and the sweat pouring down my face. I had a bit of a wash and put on my coat, and I felt the package in the breast-pocket. I took it out and looked at it, done so neat with the fancy ribbon, and I put it back again, and I hadn't noticed the boss come in – I was standing with my back to the door.

'Did you get what you want?' he said, cheerful-like and smiling.

He was a good chap, never out of temper, and we got along well.

'Yes,' I said.

But I didn't want to talk about it. I told him the job was done and the Austin was ready to drive away. I went to the office with him so that he could note down the work done, and the overtime, and he offered me a fag from the packet lying on his desk beside the evening paper.

'I see Lady Luck won the three-thirty,' he said. 'I'm a couple of quid up this week.'

He was entering my work in his ledger, to keep the pay-roll right.

'Good for you,' I said.

'Only backed it for a place, like a clot,' he said. 'She was twenty-five to one. Still, it's all in the game.'

I didn't answer. I'm not one for drinking, but I needed one bad, just then. I mopped my forehead with my handkerchief. I wished he'd get on with the figures, and say good night, and let me go.

'Another poor devil's had it,' he said. 'That's the third now in three weeks, ripped right up the guts, same as the others. He died in hospital this morning. Looks like there's a hoodoo on the RAF.'

'What was it, flying jets?' I asked.

'Jets?' he said. 'No, damn it, murder. Sliced up the belly, poor sod. Don't you ever read the papers? It's the third one in three weeks, done identical, all Air Force fellows, and each time they've found 'em near a graveyard or a cemetery. I was saying just now, to that chap who came in for petrol, it's not only men who go off their rockers and turn sex maniacs, but women too. They'll get this one all right though, you see. It says in the paper they've got a line on her, and expect an arrest shortly. About time too, before another poor blighter cops it.'

He shut up his ledger and stuck his pencil behind his ear.

'Like a drink?' he said. 'I've got a bottle of gin in the cupboard.'

'No,' I said, 'no, thanks very much. I've . . . I've got a date.'

'That's right,' he said smiling, 'enjoy yourself.'

I walked down the street and bought an evening paper. It was like what he said about the murder. They had it on the front page. They said it must have happened about two a.m. Young fellow in the Air Force, in north-east London. He had managed to stagger to a call-box and get through to the police, and they found him there on the floor of the box when they arrived.

He made a statement in the ambulance before he died. He said a girl called to him, and he followed her, and he thought it was just a bit of lovemaking – he'd seen her with another fellow drinking coffee at a stall a little while before – and he thought she'd thrown this other fellow over and had taken a fancy to him, and then she got him, he said, right in the guts.

It said in the paper that he had given the police a full description of her, and it said also that the police would be glad if the man who had been seen with the girl earlier in the evening would come forward to help in identification.

I didn't want the paper any more. I threw it away. I walked about the streets till I was tired, and when I guessed Mr and Mrs Thompson had gone to bed I went home, and groped for the key they'd left on a piece of string hanging inside the letterbox, and I let myself in and went upstairs to my room.

Mrs Thompson had turned down the bed and put a Thermos of tea for me, thoughtful-like, and the evening paper, the late edition.

They'd got her. About three o'clock in the afternoon. I didn't read the writing, nor the name nor anything. I sat down on my bed, and took up the paper, and there was my girl staring up at me from the front page.

Then I took the package from my coat and undid it, and threw away the wrapper and the fancy string, and sat there looking down at the little heart I held in my hand.

The Dancing-Partner

JEROME K. JEROME

'THIS STORY,' COMMENCED MACSHAUGNASSY, 'comes from Furtwangen, a small town in the Black Forest. There lived there a very wonderful old fellow named Nicholau Geibel. His business was the making of mechanical toys, at which work he had aquired an almost European reputation. He made rabbits that would emerge from the heart of a cabbage, flop their ears, smooth their whiskers, and disappear again; cats that would wash their faces, and mew so naturally that dogs would mistake them for real cats, and fly at them; dolls, with phonographs concealed within them, that would raise their hats and say, "Good morning; how do you do?" and some that would even sing a song.

'But he was something more than a mere mechanic; he was an artist. His work was with him a hobby, almost a passion. His shop was filled with all manner of strange things that never would, or could, be sold, things he had made for the pure love of making them. He had contrived a mechanical donkey that would trot for two hours by means of stored electricity, and trot, too, much faster than the live article, and with less need for exertion on the part of the driver; a bird that would shoot up into the air, fly round and round in a circle, and drop to earth at the exact spot from where it started, a skeleton that, supported by an upright iron bar, would dance a hornpipe; a life-size lady doll that could play the fiddle; and a gentleman with a hollow inside who could smoke a pipe and drink more lager beer than any three average German students put together, which is saying much.

'Indeed, it was the belief of the town that old Geibel could make a man capable of doing everything that a respectable man need want to do. One day he made a man who did too much, and it came about in this way.

'Young Doctor Follen had a baby, and the baby had a birthday. Its

361

first birthday put Doctor Follen's household into somewhat of a flurry, but on the occasion of its second birthday, Mrs Doctor Follen gave a ball in honour of the event. Old Geibel and his daughter Olga were among the guests.

'During the afternoon of the next day some three or four of Olga's bosom friends, who had also been present at the ball, dropped in to have a chat about it. They naturally fell to discussing the men, and to criticizing their dancing. Old Geibel was in the room, but he appeared to be absorbed in his newspaper, and the girls took no notice of him.

'"There seem to be fewer men who can dance at every ball you go to," said one of the girls.

'"Yes, and don't the ones who can, give themselves airs," said another, "they make quite a favour of asking you."

'"And how stupidly they talk," added a third. "They always say exactly the same things: 'How charming you are looking tonight.' 'Do you often go to Vienna? Oh, you should, it's delightful.' 'What a charming dress you have on.' 'What a warm day it has been.' 'Do you like Wagner?' I do wish they'd think of something new."

'"Oh, I never mind how they talk," said a fourth. "If a man dances well he may be a fool for all I care."

'"He generally is," slipped in a thin girl, rather spitefully.

'"I go to a ball to dance," continued the previous speaker, not noticing the interruption. "All I ask of a partner is that he shall hold me firmly, take me round steadily, and not get tired before I do."

'"A clockwork figure would be the thing for you," said the girl who had interrupted.

'"Bravo!" cried one of the others, clapping her hands, "what a capital idea!"

'"What's a capital idea?" they asked.

'"Why, a clockwork dancer, or, better still, one that would go by electricity and never run down."

'The girls took up the idea with enthusiasm.

'"Oh, what a lovely partner he would make," said one; "he would never kick you, or tread on your toes."

'"Or tear your dress," said another.

'"Or get out of step."

'"Or get giddy and lean on you."

'"And he would never want to mop his face with his handkerchief. I do hate to see a man do that after every dance."

'"And wouldn't want to spend the whole evening in the supper-room."

'"Why, with a phonograph inside him to grind out all the stock remarks, you would not be able to tell him from a real man," said the girl who had first suggested the idea.

'"Oh yes, you would," said the thin girl, "he would be so much nicer."

'Old Geibel had laid down his paper, and was listening with both his ears. On one of the girls glancing in his direction, however, he hurriedly hid himself again behind it.

'After the girls were gone, he went into his workshop, where Olga heard him walking up and down, and every now and then chuckling to himself; and that night he talked to her a good deal about dancing and dancing men – asked what they usually said and did – what dances were most popular – what steps were gone through, with many other questions bearing on the subject.

'Then for a couple of weeks he kept much to his factory, and was very thoughtful and busy, though prone at unexpected moments to break into a quiet low laugh, as if enjoying a joke that nobody else knew of.

'A month later another ball took place in Furtwangen. On this occasion it was given by old Wenzel, the wealthy timber merchant, to celebrate his niece's betrothal, and Geibel and his daughter were again among the invited.

'When the hour arrived to set out, Olga sought her father. Not finding him in the house, she tapped at the door of his workshop. He appeared in his shirt-sleeves, looking hot but radiant.

'"Don't wait for me," he said, "you go on. I'll follow you. I've got something to finish."

'As she turned to obey he called after her. "Tell them I'm going to bring a young man with me – such a nice young man, and an excellent dancer. All the girls will like him." Then he laughed and closed the door.

'Her father generally kept his doings secret from everybody, but she had a pretty shrewd suspicion of what he had been planning, and so, to a certain extent, was able to prepare the guests for what was coming. Anticipation ran high, and the arrival of the famous mechanist was eagerly awaited.

'At length the sound of wheels was heard outside, followed by a great commotion in the passage, and old Wenzel himself, his jolly face red with excitement and suppressed laughter, burst into the room and announced in stentorian tones:

"'Herr Geibel – and a friend."

'Herr Geibel and his "friend" entered, greeted with shouts of laughter and applause, and advanced to the centre of the room.

"'Allow me, ladies and gentlemen," said Herr Geibel, "to introduce you to my friend, Lieutenant Fritz. Fritz, my dear fellow, bow to the ladies and gentlemen."

'Geibel placed his hand encouragingly on Fritz's shoulder, and the lieutenant bowed low, accompanying the action with a harsh clicking noise in his throat, unpleasantly suggestive of a death rattle. But that was only a detail.

"'He walks a little stiffly" (old Geibel took his arm and walked him forward a few steps. He certainly did walk stiffly), "but then walking is not his forte. He is essentially a dancing man. I have only been able to teach him the waltz as yet, but at that he is faultless. Come, which of you ladies may I introduce him to as a partner? He keeps perfect time; he never gets tired; he won't kick you or tread on your dress; he will hold you as firmly as you like, and go as quickly or as slowly as you please; he never gets giddy; and he is full of conversation. Come, speak up for yourself, my boy."

'The old gentleman twisted one of the buttons at the back of his coat, and immediately Fritz opened his mouth, and in thin tones that appeared to proceed from the back of his head, remarked suddenly, "May I have the pleasure?" and then shut his mouth again with a snap.

'That Lieutenant Fritz had made a strong impression on the company was undoubted, yet none of the girls seemed inclined to dance with him. They looked askance at his waxen face, with its staring eyes and fixed smile, and shuddered. At last old Geibel came to the girl who had conceived the idea.

"'It is your own suggestion, carried out to the letter," said Geibel, "an electric dancer. You owe it to the gentleman to give him a trial."

'She was a bright, saucy little girl, fond of a frolic. Her host added his entreaties, and she consented.

'Herr Geibel fixed the figure to her. Its right arm was screwed round her waist, and held her firmly; its delicately jointed left hand was made to fasten itself upon her right. The old toy-maker showed her how to regulate its speed, and how to stop it, and release her.

'"It will take you round in a complete circle," he explained, "be careful that no one knocks against you, and alters its course."

'The music struck up. Old Geibel put the current in motion, and Annette and her strange partner began to dance.

'For a while everyone stood watching them. The figure performed its purpose admirably. Keeping perfect time and step, and holding its little partner tight clasped in an unyielding embrace, it revolved steadily, pouring forth at the same time a constant flow of squeaky conversation, broken by brief intervals of grinding silence.

'"How charming you are looking tonight," it remarked in its thin, faraway voice. "What a lovely day it has been. Do you like dancing? How well our steps agree. You will give me another, won't you? Oh, don't be so cruel. What a charming gown you have on. Isn't waltzing delightful? I could go on dancing for ever – with you. Have you had supper?"

'As she grew more familiar with the uncanny creature, the girl's nervousness wore off, and she entered into the fun of the thing.

'"Oh, he's just lovely," she cried, laughing, "I could go on dancing with him all my life."

'Couple after couple now joined them, and soon all the dancers in the room were whirling round behind them. Nicholau Geibel stood looking on, beaming with childish delight at his success.

'Old Wenzel approached him, and whispered something in his ear. Geibel laughed and nodded, and the two worked their way quietly towards the door.

'"This is the young people's house tonight," said Wenzel, so soon as they were outside; "you and I will have a quiet pipe and a glass of hock, over in the counting-house."

'Meanwhile the dancing grew more fast and furious. Little Annette loosened the screw regulating her partner's rate of progress, and the figure flew round with her, swifter and swifter. Couple after couple dropped out exhausted, but they only went the faster, till at length they remained dancing alone.

'Madder and madder became the waltz. The music lagged behind: the musicians, unable to keep pace, ceased, and sat staring. The younger guests applauded, but the older faces began to grow anxious.

'"Hadn't you better stop, dear?" said one of the women. "You'll make yourself so tired."

'But Annette did not answer.

"'I believe she's fainted," cried out a girl who had caught sight of her face as it was swept by.

'One of the men sprang forward and clutched at the figure, but its impetus threw him down on to the floor, where its steel-cased feet laid bare his cheek. The thing evidently did not intend to part with its prize easily.

'Had anyone retained a cool head, the figure, one cannot help thinking, might easily have been stopped. Two or three men acting in concert might have lifted it bodily off the floor, or have jabbed it into a corner. But few human heads are capable of remaining cool under excitement. Those who are not present think how stupid must have been those who were; those who are reflect afterwards how simple it would have been to do this, that, or the other, if only they had thought of it at the time.

'The women grew hysterical. The men shouted contradictory directions to one another. Two of them made a bungling rush at the figure, which had the result of forcing it out of its orbit in the centre of the room, and sending it crashing against the walls and furniture. A stream of blood showed itself down the girl's white frock, and followed her along the floor. The affair was becoming horrible. The women rushed screaming from the room. The men followed them.

'One sensible suggestion was made: "Find Geibel – fetch Geibel."

'No one had noticed him leave the room, no one knew where he was. A party went in search of him. The others, too unnerved to go back into the ball-room, crowded outside the door and listened. They could hear the steady whir of the wheels upon the polished floor as the thing spun round and round; the dull thud as every now and again it dashed itself and its burden against some opposing object and ricocheted off in a new direction.

'And everlastingly it talked in that thin ghostly voice, repeating over and over the same formula: "How charming you are looking tonight. What a lovely day it has been. Oh, don't be so cruel. I could go on dancing for ever – with you. Have you had supper?"

'Of course they sought for Geibel everywhere but where he was. They looked in every room in the house, then they rushed off in a body to his own place, and spent precious minutes in waking up his deaf old housekeeper. At last it occurred to one of the party that Wenzel was missing also, and then the idea of the counting-house across the yard presented itself to them, and there they found him.

'He rose up, very pale, and followed them; and he and old Wenzel forced their way through the crowd of guests gathered outside, and entered the room, and locked the door behind them.

'From within there came the muffled sound of low voices and quick steps, followed by a confused scuffling noise, then silence, then the low voices again.

'After a time the door opened, and those near it pressed forward to enter, but old Wenzel's broad shoulders barred the way.

'"I want you – and you, Bekler," he said, addressing a couple of the older men. His voice was calm, but his face was deadly white. "The rest of you, please go – get the women away as quickly as you can."

'From that day old Nicholau Geibel confined himself to the making of mechanical rabbits, and cats that mewed and washed their faces.'

The Viscountess
and the Short-Haired Girl

ROBERT GRAVES

TWENTY-FIVE YEARS AGO, MASTER Toni, the squat, bald, dark-eyed, muscular, smiling proprietor of our village garage, invited me to dinner on his Saint's Day. The fiesta of San Antonio, which falls on January 17th, is always marked in Majorcan villages by the priest's rather hilarious aspersion with holy water of as many asses, mules, sheep-dogs and motor-cars as his parishioners may care to bring along to the Church door; and by a bonfire, lighted on the previous evening, which around midnight has usually died down low enough for *buñuelos* – a sort of doughnut – to be fried over the embers. On this occasion, the fire being still alive after morning mass, Master Toni's wife Doña Isabel sent her children with shovels to salvage lumps of glowing charcoal for the brazier under our dinner table. The main dish was missel-thrushes stewed in cabbage-leaves, with snails, octopus and saffron rice. We also ate smoked ham; slices of outsized radish; the first pickled black olives of the season; Minorcan sheep-cheese; fig-bread; ordinary bread; and plenty of Binisalem red wine. I remember the missel-thrushes, because a German lady had been enraged to see a pile of them heaped on the garage floor that morning. 'How dare you massacre our beautiful German songbirds?' she screamed.

'Señora,' Master Toni answered, 'your German songbirds are ill-educated; they come to steal the olives. Olives are our main source of wealth: olives, and figs – figs such as I often watched you steal from my trees as you went down the path by our house this last September.'

Missel-thrushes are caught by a method once known as 'bat-fowling' in England, but now, I believe, extinct there. Two men station themselves a few paces apart, in one of the broad alleys down which the thrushes fly from their roosts among evergreen oaks near the mountain top. The bat-fowlers stretch across the alley a length of fishing-net lashed to two very long canes, held upright. At dawn, the first coveys of thrushes, known as *tordos d'auba*, descend on the olive groves and find themselves entangled in the net. Both canes are simultaneously flung forward and downward, after which the bat-fowlers wring the necks of whatever birds have been caught underneath. At about eight o'clock down flies a smaller wave of thrushes, known as *tordos de gran dia*; then no more can be expected until the *tordos de vispera*, or evening thrushes. Bat-fowling is one of the few sports in which the villagers engage. A mountain terraced steeply all the way up from the sea provides no level space large enough for a football field, or even a tennis court; and since 1906, when a passing traveller had his eye knocked out by a sling-stone flung by young Mateo of the Painted House – he had mischievously aimed at the man's pipe – the ancient Balearic sling has been officially banned even for rabbit-hunting.

Anyhow, Master Toni, having made merry on the Eve of San Antonio, and eaten quantities of *buñuelos*, had returned home for a couple of hours' sleep, then started off at five o'clock to catch *tordos d'auba* for our dinner. But along came the sexton, in overcoat and slippers, to say that his sister, Maria the Spaghetti-maker, was desperately ill again and that the Doctor must be fetched at once from Sóller. So Master Toni climbed into his antiquated Studebaker; and by the time the Doctor had attended to Maria (on her deathbed these past fifteen years) and been driven back to Sóller, only the despised *tordos de gran dia* were left to hunt. Nevertheless, Master Toni and a certain Sentiá Dog-beadle, the village odd-job man, managed between them to bag two dozen – a remarkable catch that year. And very good they tasted.

Perhaps I should explain that Maria Spaghetti-maker had never made any spaghetti; it was her great-grandmother who plied the trade, but the nickname persisted in the female line. There is now a grown-up grand-daughter who holds it, though she only sews gloves. Similarly, the timorous and greedy Sentiá Dog-beadle inherited his nickname from an ancestor whose task had been to keep stray dogs from taking sanctuary on hot days in the cool of Palma Cathedral. 'Sentiá' is short for Sebastian. There are almost too many things which need explanation, once one begins to tell stories about our village.

After dinner, over the coffee and brandy, I found it easy to swear that I had never eaten so well, or so much, in all my life.

'Not even in Piccadilly, Don Roberto?' asked Master Toni shrewdly.

'Certainly not, I assure you!'

'Well, Damián the Coachman, Sentiá Dog-beadle and I ate pretty well there, during our famous stay at the Regent *Palacio* Hotel.'

'Why have you never told me of this visit to London?'

'I am a busy man, you are a busy man. I have saved up the long history of the Viscountess and the Short-haired Girl for this fiesta.'

Here then is Master Toni's story, as I wrote it down that same evening. Respecting his inability to manage an initial *St, Sc, Sp* or *Sm* without an anticipatory *e,* I prefixed one to all the proper names which demanded it. Let that *e* stay as a convenient reminder of the estory-teller's Espanishness.

The Viscountess and The Short-Haired Girl

It all began one day in August when two gentlemen, both wearing black coats and striped trousers – hardly suitable clothes for the weather, which was of a barbarous heat – drove up in a very fine taxi from Palma and stopped at my garage. The chauffeur, who knew me, asked whether they might have a private word in my ear. 'At the gentlemen's service,' I answered, 'unless they are trying to sell me something. I am excessively short of money this month.'

One of the gentlemen, who could speak Spanish, heard what I said. He was a little game-cock of a man, and had a habit of tilting his head on one side inquiringly, as poultry often do. From his black mushroom hat, I judged him to be less important than the other, who wore a black silk stove-pipe hat. 'Then let me congratulate you, Don Antonio,' he said. 'My friend here, Mr P.P. Jonés, will soon remedy your financial straits. If you listen to his proposal, he will fill your pockets with silver *duros.* My own name is Charley Estrutt, at your service.'

'He does not require me to violate the Law?' I asked.

Mr Estrutt translated this question to Mr Jonés, who resembled a large, well-cured ham. Mr Jonés shook his head violently, saying: 'On the contrary!' – a phrase which I understood, the word 'contrary' being identical in our Majorcan idiom, though we sound it differently.

I asked them both upstairs, to take a coffee. They accepted, and when we had emptied our cups I waited until they should come to the point, after all Mr Estrutt's compliments on the beauty and tranquillity of our village. When he continued silent, I said boldly: 'By your gold watch-chains and your reticence, gentlemen, I judge you to be lawyers; and your black clothes indicate that you are here on business, not on a vacation. The labels on your brief-cases say "London". Therefore, since this village has had the honour of welcoming only one compatriot of yours during the past twelve months, that is to say a certain young girl with hair cut short like a boy's, who stayed for a week in May at the Hotel Bonsol with a tall foreigner from God knows where, may I conclude that your business somehow concerns her?'

Mr Estrutt's face lighted up. He said: 'You are very intelligent, Don Antonio! That is almost precisely the case, though Señor Jonés alone is a lawyer. In effect, he represents the short-haired girl's disconsolate mother, recently widowed.'

I asked: 'And your profession, Señor? Would it be inconvenient to divulge it?'

Mr Estrutt smiled. 'No inconvenience at all,' he said. 'I used to be an inspector in our Metropolitan Police force. I am now retired, and have become a private detective employed by rich people to conduct delicate inquiries. The remuneration is better.'

I went on: 'By the formality of Mr Jonés's appearance, he must be a lawyer of great importance?'

Mr Estrutt whistled. 'He never accepts less than fifty thousand pesetas a week for a case! The fact is that the disconsolate mother in question reeks of money. Her father was a multi-millionaire from Chile: I worked for the family once; an illegitimate son of his happened to be blackmailing him.'

I remarked: 'One recognizes your accent as South American.'

He blushed a little: 'Yes, yes,' he said, 'you Spaniards despise South Americans for their abuse of your ancient tongue.'

Since Mr Charley Estrutt seemed a pleasant enough man, for all the ridiculous black mushroom-hat balanced on his knee. I assured him that here in Majorca we speak coarser dialect of Spanish than the Chileans. Our talk proceeded in this inconclusive manner until Mr Jonés, who did not understand a word, looked at his big gold watch and made some observation to Mr Estrutt. Clearly, the moment had come to discuss business. I told myself: 'These people can pay well. I shall certainly not accept the first price they offer – for whatever it is that they require of me.'

Mr Estrutt now put forward his proposal. He explained that the short-haired girl, a minor, having run away from a French convent where she was being educated, had been brutally kidnapped by a Bulgarian artist. The pair had, with great difficulty, been traced to our village. The disconsolate Viscountess, her mother, wished to collect sufficient sworn evidence about the tragedy to incarcerate this Bulgarian heretic for life. Yet scandal must be avoided at all costs, and therefore the Spanish police had not been invited to assist. Well, if I and two friends of mine could testify before an English judge to the Bulgarian's having dragged the wretched girl to our Hotel Bonsol, and there committed an offence against her, the unfortunate entanglement could be legally proved, and the criminal punished.

Mr Jonés, so Mr Estrutt told me, knew that I had conveyed the couple in my taxi from the mole at Palma to the Hotel Bonsol; that a certain Sebastián Vivés (meaning Sentiá Dog-beadle) had carried their bags up to a bedroom at the said hotel; and that Damián Frau, meaning 'Damián the Coachman', the hotelkeeper, had brought them breakfast in bed, on a tray, the next morning. Mr Jonés hoped that we would kindly visit London in a month's time, to avenge the honour of a noble English house, more particularly because the disconsolate Viscountess was a very devout Catholic; he had heard of our Majorcan zeal for the sanctity of a Catholic home.

I replied: 'Speaking between ourselves, Mr Estrutt, the short-haired girl seemed to be in no way acting under duress; in fact, on our journey from Palma she was embracing and caressing the heretic – as I could not help seeing in my driving mirror – with every appearance of genuine enjoyment.'

Imagine my surprise, when Mr Estrutt winked at me (but with the eye hidden from Mr Jonés) and answered: 'Don Antonio, in England our young girls have been completely demoralized by the excitements of the recent war. Moreover, the poor child may have feared that, unless she caressed him in public, he would ill treat her most cruelly once they were alone.'

To be brief, the terms offered us three witnesses for a visit to London were twenty pesetas a day, besides travelling expenses, bed, board, laundry, wine, cigars, and anything else within reason that we might need, not omitting sight-seeing excursions; and another five hundred pesetas each, if we gave our evidence in a way that convinced the Judge. He also asked, would I be kind enough to repeat this offer to my friends, Don Sebastián and Don Damián?

I wanted to know how long we should be away, and Mr Estrutt estimated that we should be home again within three weeks. My reply was that we should answer yes or no after a night's reflection; but Mr Jonés urged us to sign a contract that same night. He intended to catch the Barcelona boat.

Well, I left the Englishmen at my house while I went to the Bonsol and took Damián for a little stroll. 'You are a knowledgeable man,' I said, 'and acquainted with the ways of the rich. I have been invited to visit London as witness in a kidnapping case. Now, for a commission of this sort, are twenty pesetas a day, all found, sufficient? I shall be away for about three weeks.'

Damián stopped, gazed at me in wonder, spat with emphasis, and said: 'Ka, man, you would be a fool to refuse! Myself, I would gladly go without pay – if only to escape from this dull hole and see grand civilization again.'

Damián, you must understand, had earned his nickname himself as coachman to the President of the Argentine Republic, and still remembered those days of glory. He added: 'But what in the Devil's name, has the kidnapping case to do with you?'

'Patience, friend,' said I. 'First advise me whether the fee is correct in principle.'

He considered the matter. Then he spat again and said: 'In principle, Toni, you should insist upon thirty pesetas a day. The English, as a rule, allow fifty per cent for bargaining where Spaniards are concerned.'

'And five hundred pesetas on top of that!'

'A tidy sum, by God! I wish I had the chance to earn so much by a three weeks' holiday.'

'Then be joyful, Damián! You are invited too!'

He took this for a joke, but when he heard my story he threw his hat so high into the air that it sailed over the terrace down the valley and into the torrent, and was not found again.

We went off together at once and acquainted Sentiá with his luck. As Sentiá was earning hardly five pesetas a day, a casual labourer's wage at that time, his eyes truly bulged with greed. Yet we had to pour a deal of *coñac* down his throat before we could persuade him to join us. Never having left the island in his life, Sentiá cherished a tremendous fear of being drowned by a tempest at sea. Finally, however, he agreed; and after Damián and I had won the extra ten pesetas a day from Mr Jonés, without a struggle, we took Sentiá along to the Mayor, who was the local Justice of the Peace, and persuaded him to witness the amended contract. In effect, we all signed the document, which had been prepared by a Spanish notary. Sentiá scrawled his name and rubric with a trembling hand, saying: 'God grant that this be not my death warrant!'

Nobody from our village had ever seen the shores of England, and it seemed a great thing for us three to be the first. Naturally, our wives did not favour the adventure, unless they could come too; is that not so, Isabel? But Mr Estrutt declared that such an arrangement would be most unwise, even if we cared to pay those extra passages and expenses out of what we should earn. Then Sentiá's wife created a scandal. She called us fools for not asking fifty pesetas a day, and a thousand at the close, Mr Jonés having agreed to our demand so readily. She knew in her heart, she shrieked, that I had been bribed by the Englishmen to keep the payment low. But Isabel here, and Damián's wife, Angela, told her to be silent, since the offer was a handsome one and the document had now been securely signed.

Nothing more. After promising to write frequently, and making our wives promise to behave themselves during our absence and keep the children in good order, we declared, hands on heart, that we should never have dreamed of leaving the village even for three weeks, were the preservation of a Catholic home not at stake. Indeed, the women of this island are hardly less zealous in this matter than Mr Estrutt suggested; and I doubt whether any of the three concerned would have let us go for the money alone. I learned later that, while we were away, Isabel here spent half her days in church, praying for my safety and for the spiritual consolation of the unhappy widow.

Well, you have made that journey more than once, Don Roberto, so it is nothing new to you, but for me it was tremendous once we had crossed the frontier into France! It seemed a miracle that within half a mile of country the aspect of so many things could suddenly change: the clothes, the language, the uniforms, the telegraph-poles, the colour of the mail-boxes, the very shape and taste of the bread!

Mr Estrutt had fetched us by taxi from the village in order to shepherd us through the customs, the passport inspections, and other troubles. He seemed a very different man, once he had emerged from the shadow of the serious Mr Jonés: being dressed now in a cream-coloured gaberdine suit, a hard straw hat with a canary-yellow ribbon, and carrying a gold-headed cane. He also began to tell us jokes of the sort we call 'green'. He arrived at my house somewhat fatigued, having spent the previous night at the Bar Macarena. Perhaps you know the Macarena? If so, you will consider it no small feat that he escaped alive from those gipsies and even contrived to preserve his wallet, his pearl tie-pin, and his gold-headed cane. The Metropolitan Police must be a race of lions.

We embarked on the night-boat to Barcelona, and the tears streamed down our wives' faces as they waved us goodbye from the quay; and I confess that, for a moment, I wondered whether my decision had been a prudent one. As for Sentiá, he was in a lamentable condition, and Mr Estrutt made him swallow a tablet which rapidly put him to sleep.

As soon as we were clear of Palma harbour, Mr Estrutt invited Damián and me to join him in the Bar. Over a *coñac*, he said: 'Boys, presently I shall go to the cabin to restore my loss of sleep, but first let me be honest with you. That kidnapping story, you must understand, is a work of fantasy. The old Viscountess and I thought it out together as a means of convincing your wives that it was their duty to let you go. Moreover, we decided that we should say no word about it to Mr Jonés. Though an intelligent lawyer, he is insular and highly moral, and would never practise a little deception even to assist a good cause.'

'Well, then for God's sake tell us the truth at once!' Damián demanded fiercely.

'The truth,' he replied, 'is that this old witch of a Viscountess lost her husband, the Viscount, three months ago – he fell from the balcony of their bedroom at the Hotel Esplendido, Cannes, and perhaps it truly was an accident – who can say? But no matter! The widow is now enamoured of a retired officer in the King's Bodyguard; and this officer, whose profession is to direct a pack of foxhounds, possesses a large estate, but little money to maintain it – only a mountain of gambling debts. In fact, he is willing to marry the old trout, who is not bad-looking by candle light, if one places the candle well behind her and wears sunglasses. The sole bar to their union has been his young wife, an actress, who married him not long ago, thinking he was rich but, finding that he had cheated her, now considers herself free to take what consolation she can find in the company of others. Yet she carefully covers her tracks when she goes hunting – hunting men, not foxes, of course. She is good looking, you agree?'

Since Mr Estrutt was clearly referring to the short-haired girl, Damián and I pronounced that, yes, she was a delicious morsel, though a little thin perhaps, and her eyes of too pallid a blue.

Mr Estrutt went on. 'So you see, boys, that your testimony will be most valuable to the Viscountess. If the foxhunting officer wins his decree of divorce from the short-haired girl, the Viscountess can then marry him, having paid all the expenses of the trial. Now, this is how I enter the story. Last May, the short-haired girl was invited to stay with her elder sister at Tossa on the Costa Brava; but when the Viscountess sent me there in July to make inquiries, I found after only a single morning at Tossa the girl had crossed over to Majorca at the side of the Bulgarian artist, whom she had met on the Paris train. I discreetly followed their tracks and obtained your names, without visiting your village, from a friendly corporal of Coastguards. With such information I went back to London, where Mr Jonés resolved to make the Viscountess pay a capital sum for his corroboration of my story. I should add that other acts of adultery are charged against the short-haired girl; but this is the only one which Mr Jonés at present dares to bring into Court. Well, boys, do you forgive me for the lies I told you?'

I laughed. 'Ka, man, it is all the same to Damián and me,' I said, 'so long as we are paid according to our contract.'

Mr Estrutt slapped my back and cried: 'I like your spirit, Toni, if I may call you that? And you must call me Charley, as everyone else does who is anyone at all! Now, another thing. When you asked for those extra ten pesetas a day, I informed Mr Jonés that, being staunch Catholics, you were dead against the marriage of divorced persons, and must therefore obtain at least thirty pesetas in all before testifying in a matter that so little interested you. Now I have said enough; but I wager that we will enjoy a wonderful time in London. By the bye, you must not let my lovesick old baggage of a Viscountess know that I have given you the true story; and it would be well, surely, not to let the good Sentiá into our secret, either. It might unsettle his ideas about me.'

Then we refilled our glasses and toasted the Viscountess, the late Viscount, the short-haired girl, the foxhunting officer, Mr P.P. Jonés and the Judge, together with many other persons more remotely connected with the affair, in a multitude of *coñacs*. Mr Estrutt did not restore his loss of sleep during that particular night.

Despite our excesses we reached port safely, and later ate a grand meal at the Hotel *Palacio* of Barcelona, with lobster mayonnaise, French wines, and everything of the best. Sentiá Dog-beadle, feeling much embarrassed by the elegant ambience, opened his mouth only a little when he introduced food and kept his enormous red hands under the table while not using them. But Damián gloried in this brief return to the high life he had enjoyed at the Presidential Palace of Buenos Aires, and recounted more about his past than I should ever have believed, though we had known each other twenty years or longer.

After a night spent on a train with very narrow beds, we came to Paris and were taken in a taxi to the Gare du Nord. At once Mr Estrutt said: 'Boys, will you do me a great favour? I am off into the city. Please wait for me in the restaurant yonder, order what food and drink may be convenient, but be careful to enter into conversation with no one at all! My orders from the Viscountess are never to leave you out of my sight. I shall be back in time to catch our train.'

Damián asked: 'What is this great favour worth to us, Don Charley?'

He answered: 'If you protect me, Damián, I shall protect you. Is that not sufficient?'

Since Mr Estrutt had all the money and our tickets, his answer could not fail to satisfy Damián. Yet it was embarrasing that two Palma businessmen whom I knew by sight should enter the Station Restaurant and greet me. I gazed blankly at them and pretended to be German. I even turned to Damián, saying: *'Heute ist Sonntag!'* which was all the German I knew. Damián, who is quick-witted enough, shook his head and answered: *'Donnerwetter!'* which was all the German *he* knew. The two Palma men sat down at a table in the far corner, and from there stared at us. We three dared not talk to one another in our own language until they had gone out again. The food, by the way, was not good.

This was two o'clock. Our train to Calais would depart at six o'clock; but four o'clock had passed, and five, and half past five, and a quarter to six, and still there we sat. At ten minutes to six, Damián said: 'I like this very little. What can have happened to Mr Estrutt?'

'Patience!' said I. 'He's a good fellow and will keep his word.'

But Sentiá grew more and more nervous. He cried out that we should never have come: we have been decoyed to Paris for some business of the Devil, he said – to be sold in slavery to the Moors, it might be. Had he not been plagued by a black foreboding on the day of the contract?

We made no reply. At last Damián stood up: 'Well', he said, 'let us put on our overcoats and have everything ready. Mr Estrutt will, I have no doubt, appear mathematically at the last moment.'

Even as he spoke, Mr Estrutt burst into the restaurant, paid our small bill with a single large banknote, and rushed us off to the platform. We caught the Calais train with thirty seconds to spare.

'My God, that was close!' exclaimed Mr Estrutt, sinking into his seat. 'Nevertheless, I found what I went out to find!'

Damián asked: 'Was it a nice tender chicken?'

Mr Estrutt took the joke in good part. 'Alas, no,' he answered, 'this was serious business, not gastronomic pleasure. You shall hear about it one day. But I thank you very much for your great patience, boys! Now, what about a game of cards?' So we played *truc* until we reached Calais.

Contrary to all we had heard, the English Channel was as smooth as glass, and on the other side we found an altogether different country again, green and beautiful! Though it was already autumn, the sun shone without pause all the time we spent there. I cannot imagine why Spaniards call the English climate a bad one. At Dover, a huge Rolls-Royce limousine took us by road to London, in which we drove for hours, it seemed, through a wilderness of streets, and across the river *Tamesis*. Finally we came to Piccadilly Circus with its fantastic coloured signs, and its hurrying crowds. Close by stood the Regent *Palacio* Hotel, where a private suite awaited us on the first floor, complete with two bathrooms, a dining room, and every comfort in the world, including waiters to wait on us and a barber to shave us every day after breakfast!

Mr Estrutt was a humorous man. On the next morning he took Damián and me aside, and said: 'When the old hen enters to greet you, do not omit to condole with her on the fate of her poor daughter. The more profuse your condolences, the more it will disturb her conscience because of the kidnapping fiction; and the less carefully will she examine our expense account. Flatter her, too! I should have explained that we occupy this private suite owing to her fear of your making contact with the general public. I myself suggested that, were the short-haired girl's lawyer to hear of your presence here, he would surely try to impress the true story upon you; with the result that you might not wish to testify. It is a situation very useful for us. We shall play on these fears of hers, and enjoy a marvellous life together; and I shall never (in theory) let you stray from my sight.'

Scarcely had he spoken, when the Viscountess herself came through the door, wearing a fur-coat of black sable-skins, a black hat, and black gloves. She also kept a black-edged handkerchief pressed to her black eyes. After welcoming us in fluent Spanish, broken by many sobs, she thanked us from the bottom of a mother's heart for our readiness to rescue her daughter from that criminal Bulgarian heretic – whom the police, thanks be to the Virgin of Guadalupe! now held in safe custody. Sentiá wept too, and Damián assured her that he also had suffered a like tragic sorrow – his own daughter having once been decoyed away from home by an English Lord, ruined and cast aside like an old glove. Damián, as you know, is childless; and can lie without a tremor of his wicked face, which resembles carved mahogany. This tale impressed even Mr Estrutt, who patted Damián on the back and said in admiration: 'I wonder, Señor Frau, that your heart ever permitted you to forgive the English aristocracy. It must be ruled by a very pious spirit.'

A comedy, in short! For myself, I told the Viscountess that only so great a distress as hers could have persuaded me to abandon my island, my wife and my children, and venture to this unknown, this most terrifying city. The Viscountess, still occupied with her handkerchief, replied that only a Spaniard could have spoken so nobly. She was no less devout a Catholic than I, she declared, and God and the Virgin would bring the righteous cause to triumph.

I spoke what came into my mind. 'The Bulgarian heretic looked a veritable ruffian,' I said. 'Let us hope that they hang him high! Imagine any well-nurtured girl trusting herself to the beast! Yet that your poor daughter did so, must surely be a sign of her formidable innocence ... But what surprises me in this painful affair is, how you, Señora Viscountess, can be her mother – you do not look half old enough!'

'I married very young,' she explained, drying her eyes again.

When she went away, we opened the windows in order to drive out the strong perfume of violets and sandalwood which she had left behind.

The trial was postponed for a fortnight, because of some legal complication; we should now be absent for another three weeks at least, but none of us cared a tassel. On Mr Estrutt's advice, however, we told Mr Jonés that our business would surely go to ruin in our absence, and that we should need fifty pesetas a day, and one thousand at the close. The Viscountess was delighted to meet our demands, and we were delighted to sign a new contract. Never in my life had I earned so much money for nothing at all!

Mr Estrutt, I should tell you, had that same enormous Rolls-Royce limousine at his disposal whenever we wished to take an outing. He showed us the principal sights of London: the Tower and the Tower Bridge, and the Historical Waxworks, and the Museum of Animals and Birds, and the Docks, and the wonderful Botanical Gardens where one enters a tropical palm-house and nearly dies of the heat! Also the Law Courts, where we would soon give evidence, and many other places; with *cinés* or music-halls nearly every evening.

Mr Estrutt also took us to visit his wives, first explaining to Sentiá that polygamy was customary among the Metropolitan Police force. Two of these wives lived in different parts of London – each occupying a small red brick house with a flower garden. We Majorcans sat in the sunny garden drinking beer and smoking cigarettes, while Mr Estrutt went upstairs to talk family affairs with his wife. Each wife also had a little boy, with whom we played, throwing a ball about on the lawn. We next met a third wife, who had a big house near Brighton. She seemed very rich, though not nearly so beautiful as the other two. The rich one gave us whisky and cigars, while we Majorcans sat on the lawn and played with a poodle dog. Mr Estrutt afterwards showed us a new gold cigarette lighter, his birthday present from this lady. The fourth wife, however, who lived many kilometres to the north of London, was old, ugly and ill-tempered. To judge from her curt greeting to Mr Estrutt, she must have been the head wife. Or so Damián said, who had seen similar behaviour in Moorish families while doing his military service at Melilla; the head-wife was invariably jealous and spiteful.

One day Mr Estrutt took me aside and said: 'Toni, my friend, I think we need a little change. I have no complaint to make against the *Palacio*, but even the best hotel grows wearisome after three weeks. Nor should I wish my old clothes-rack of a Viscountess to think that I have forgotten the serious task that she has imposed on me. Be prepared, therefore, to move at midnight; but, as usual, not a word to Sentiá!'

That night, Sentiá retired at about eleven o'clock and was soon snoring. Then Mr Estrutt telephoned the Viscountess, speaking in tones of great seriousness. Damián and I heard her frightened voice ring high through the apparatus. Mr Estrutt answered: 'Yes, yes, yes, my lady!' several times. He told her, I believe, that though a Spanish-speaking waiter had been bribed by the short-haired girl's lawyer to provide us with the true story, his own prompt appearance fortunately interrupted the conversation as soon as it started. The Viscountess urgently begged Mr Estrutt to remove us to another hotel at once.

We packed our bags and woke Sentiá. Damián said: 'Lad, we are in great danger! The Bulgarian heretic has discovered us. Pack for your life!'

The Rolls-Royce limousine was waiting at the hotel door when we emerged. The Viscountess sat inside, very nervous, and wearing a purple scarf pulled over her face so that she might not be recognized. Mr Estrutt agreed that no time should be lost, and the chauffeur drove off without delay. We purred away at great velocity, but the Viscountess felt certain that we were being pursued. She ordered the chauffeur to dodge down side-streets at random, twisting and turning until we had shaken off the pursuit. The chauffeur obeyed but, however wild his course, she continued to peer through the rear window and cry: 'There it is! The same car again!' Sentiá, sweating with terror, kept crossing himself and asking: 'Do you think they will kill us?'

After an hour of this foolishness we reached open country. The chauffeur backed the Rolls-Royce down a lane, and turned off its lights. We sat in the darkness for another hour, while a stream of cars raced by. When at last the Viscountess was confident that she had cheated our pursuers, we turned back by devious ways, and at two o'clock in the morning found a new private suite awaiting us in the Estrand *Palacio* Hotel (hardly a kilometre distant from the Regent *Palacio*) where, for secrecy, we were admitted by the service door. Strange, was it not, that each of the hotels we visited on our journey was named the *Palacio*? But poor Sentiá had died a hundred deaths that night!

We wrote home once every week to say we were well, that business prospered, and that we trusted all would end normally; adding those graceful concluding phrases which one learns at school. Our families replied in the same manner, though more religiously. Nothing of importance had happened to the village during our absence, except that a great thunderstorm had torn many branches from my olive grove, and caused the walls of three terraces to collapse.

One day Mr Estrutt asked me: 'My friend, do you still enjoy this life?'

I answered: 'Enormously! Only think! under this new contract I shall soon have gained enough money for the purchase of a fine American car; giving my old Studebaker in partial payment. A just reward for all my hard labours! But, Don Charley, in one thing you have deceived us!'

'How deceived you?' he asked with surprise.

'Well,' I answered, 'you have fed us nobly, you have given us good beds, good drinks, and admirable Havana cigars, you have taken us often to the *ciné* and the music-halls and once, even, to the Opera, besides showing us the famous sights of London . . . But you have not ministered to other pressing needs of ours! That is, as we say in Majorca, like asking children to view the confectioner's shop, but buying them no caramels. Though we are all good Catholics, none of us happens to be a monk!'

(How fortunate, Don Roberto, that at this particular stage of my story Isabel has gone off, to wash the dishes, I suppose, and feed the hens; otherwise I should have been forced to omit the subsequent incident. In any case, I must keep it short.)

Well, Mr Estrutt understood me before the words were well out of my mouth. 'If there is nothing else, my friend Toni, this can readily be arranged,' said he, 'but I had feared to make any suggestion that might offend your sensibilities. Not being members of the Metropolitan Police force, I thought you might consider yourselves less free in certain respects than I am. Very well, I shall at once telephone to an associate of mine who orders such matters. I promise that you will have no further cause to complain of having been deceived.'

He kept his word. That night after coffee, we heard a soft knocking at the door and in walked three beautiful smiling blondes, all wearing the tightest of silk dresses. Mr Estrutt at once made the necessary introductions, taking care to give us fictitious names. Then he uncorked a prodigiously large bottle of champagne and filled seven glasses. I quickly engaged the attention of the leading young lady, and Damián was not far behind me in securing the second. But Sentiá, who, as usual, had not been informed of the arrangement, sat perplexed and paralysed, goggling like a great moribund fish, when he saw the two young ladies perch on our knees. The third had addressed herself to Mr Estrutt, who explained, however, that the shy gentleman in the corner was her chosen sweetheart; he himself would merely be our interpreter. Although disappointed, she flung herself on Sentiá with a fine pretence of enthusiasm. Sentiá leaped up, knocking over his chair, and retreated to the bathroom; but the determined girl thrust her foot between the door and the jamb, calling on Mr Estrutt for help. Mr Estrutt pushed the door open, and when she had entered, locked it behind her.

I shall say no more than that Damiań and I needed no interpreter ... But, Lord, how ashamed of himself Sentiá was afterwards, and how we laughed! Of one thing we could be sure; once safely home again, he would never reveal one word of the proceedings, not even in the confessional!

The Viscountess came to visit us the next morning, with her usual tale of how God and the Virgin would uphold the right, and how greatly she appreciated our chivalrous defence of her Catholic home. Then, noticing suddenly how ill at ease Sentiá appeared to be, she laid a black-gloved hand on his shoulder to comfort him. 'My poor fellow,' she cried, 'you must miss your wife deeply!'

At that, Sentiá Dog-beadle wept like a little child. Fearful that he would make some foolish remark, I hastened to say: 'Yes, my lady, Sebastian here misses his Joana terribly, not having expected to be away so many weeks. Nor is he the only one of us who suffers. Don Damián and I are equally sensitive; but, for the sake of your unfortunate daughter, we try to suppress our misery.'

The Viscountess promised that we should never regret our visit, and charitably dabbed Sentiá's eyes with her scented black lace handkerchief. But even that did not console him!

Two days later, the divorce case began. Mr Estrutt sat with us in the Law Court and explained in a whisper who was who, and what was happening. The foxhunter had presented four or five charges of adultery in respect of the short-haired girl, but Mr Jonés·and his squadron of lawyers chose from them only those two that seemed easiest to prove; namely, the affair with the Bulgarian artist at Damián's hotel, and an earlier affair in Paris with a rich Escottish manufacturer named Simon Macwilly. Mr Macwilly was married and, shocked to find himself cited as co-respondent in this case, had agreed to pay the short-haired girl's defence, so as to protect himself against the complaints of his wife.

It appears that an official of the British Embassy at Paris had lent Mr Macwilly his apartment during a temporary absence, and that the short-haired girl passed the night there with Mr Macwilly. This Embassy official, however, did not wish to be accused of pandering to his friend's vices, and when Mr Estrutt and Mr Jonés went to make inquiries of him, immediately sent his two servants away into the country, thus preventing them from becoming witnesses. The only relevant evidence could now come from a taxi driver who had conducted the couple, with their bags, to the door of the apartment; and this would, perhaps, be found insufficient. Yet Mr Estrutt, by studying the calendar, reckoned that the short-haired girl must have spent another night somewhere in Paris, after vacating the Embassy official's apartment. Therefore, during our long wait at the Gare du Nord, he had persuaded his friends among the French Police to scrutinize the registers of certain hotels. Sure enough, they found a small hotel on the left bank of the *Sena* where Mr Macwilly had signed the register for himself and Mrs Macwilly on the night in question. The French hotelkeeper and his wife demanded an expense fee which Mr Jonés thought excessive, but which they refused to make less; to give the required evidence, they said, might injure their establishment's name for discretion. The Viscountess, however, would pay almost anything for this testimony, and an agreement was reached.

The charge of having committed adultery with Mr Macwilly was heard first. Now, on the previous afternoon the advocate, a King's Councillor, had explained to us just what questions he would ask, and how we should reply. This drama we rehearsed over and over again with the help of an interpreter; but Sentiá Dog-beadle proved so slow at learning his lesson that the advocate cried impatiently: 'Man, man, I hardly dare call you as a witness; for fear you may ruin our case! Your companions have far greater agility of mind.' We implored Sentiá to gather his wits, since three thousand pesetas hung on our satisfying the Judge; but he seemed like a lost man.

'You will be called next, boys!' Mr Estrutt warned us, as the first witness appeared and took the oath on a large Bible, which he kissed. Sentiá went whiter than a sheet at the warning, and began crossing himself like a madman. I felt uneasy myself, though with little cause, being now word-perfect in my lesson.

To be brief: the French hotelkeepers identified the short-haired girl, who was now wearing black in competition with the Viscountess, and swore to her presence at their establishment that night, in company with the fat, bald man who signed the register as Simon

Macwilly. The couple had engaged two bedrooms with a communicating door, the key of which was on the short-haired girl's side.

When summoned to give evidence herself, the short-haired girl admitted having spent a night in that hotel, but strongly denied the charge of adultery. Mr Macwilly, she said, was liable to heart attacks and, as his only reliable friend in Paris, she had wished to be at hand to attend him if he were taken ill during the hours of darkness. Our advocate put it to her that misconduct had certainly taken place between them. She pretended to be outraged and cried: 'Misconduct, why, that is ridiculous! Mr Macwilly is an ancient man of sixty!'

It was a grave error in tactics. At once our advocate addressed the Judge (who was wearing an enormous wig, I did not ask why). Having observed the Judge's angry expression when the short-haired girl implied that, at sixty, a man is ancient and altogether spent, he said very shrewdly: 'My Lord, I shall call no more witnesses; but let my plea rest upon the evidence you have now heard.' For this Judge had not only just celebrated his sixtieth birthday: he had emphasized it by a third marriage!

Mr Estrutt had difficulty in repressing his joy when he heard these words spoken. He clapped Sentiá on the shoulder and whispered in his ear: 'My lad, you are saved!' Then he similarly told Damián and me: 'You also are saved. You will not be required to give evidence after all.'

Damián flew into a temper and asked in a loud voice: 'What of my thousand pesetas? I am being robbed. Why should I not give evidence?'

The Judge glared at Damián in great anger, calling for order in Court.

Mr Estrutt whispered: 'You madman, of course you will be paid!'

At that, Damián subsided, muttering.

We listened to the Judge's summing-up, and his decision that he could not believe the story told by this shameless young woman, and doubted whether anyone else present could believe it either. Then he praised our advocate for his great restraint in not pressing the second charge, and thus perhaps exposing the wretched woman as a common prostitute – since two proved charges of adultery, she must be aware, would under English Law earn her that disgraceful appellation!

In brief, he granted the divorce, and ordered the short-haired girl to pay all the legal costs of the case. Her advocate did not appeal from this decision, and so the case ended . . .

But this is not quite the end of my story. When the Judge and all the fashionable spectators had dispersed, there remained in Court only ourselves, the French hotelkeeper and his wife, several lawyers and their clerks, some ushers, the short-haired girl and the Viscountess. The costs of the case having been paid by Mr Macwilly's lawyers, the Viscountess came running up with eyes that shone like stars, and kissed us each in turn on both cheeks, including Mr Estrutt. She cried: 'God and the Virgin have listened to my prayers!'

It then amused me to say: 'Heartiest congratulations, my lady. Yet your poor daughter there seems quite overcome by distress. Perhaps she grieves for the fate of that Bulgarian heretic? Or could it be that she fears you will never forgive her?'

'Indeed, friend!' she cried. 'How stupid I am! I must make my peace with her at once.'

She hurried across to the short-haired girl, followed by Mr Estrutt, who was a most inquisitive man. He heard her say: 'My dear girl, you put up a very good fight, I must admit, and I do not wish to triumph over your misery, having suffered this sort of trouble myself once. What do you propose to do now?'

The short-haired girl smiled back at her faintly and replied: 'How can I tell? I have lost everything! Though Mr Macwilly has paid the costs of the case, his wife would never agree to a divorce, even if I consented to marry him, which I have no intention of doing. Boris is the man I love. Yet I have not a copper to call my own, and neither has Boris.'

The Viscountess kissed her on the forehead. 'My poor innocent,' she said, cooing like a pigeon. 'You should never have chosen an artist as your prospective husband, and really, were you not rather imprudent to tease the old Judge as you did? How much money would put you right with the world again?'

The short-haired girl thought for a moment. Then she said slowly: 'I fear I could hardly manage with less than ten thousand pounds. Boris and I might start some business with that, I suppose.'

'Let me make it twenty thousand!' cried the Viscountess in a burst of commiseration, producing her cheque book and a gold fountain pen. She signed the cheque then and there.

We Majorcans, too, profited from her generosity to the extent of still another thousand pesetas each; and six months later, we heard that she had married her foxhunter. On the very same day, but in a different city, the short-haired girl was united with the Bulgarian artist. They bought a *pensión* near San Sebastian, which is now very luxurious and always crowded; so Mr Estrutt recently informed me on a picture postcard. He wrote that his wife had accompanied him to San Sebastian for a holiday, and that he wished Damián Frau and I could have been present to share their fun. He did not specify which wife; but perhaps he had recently married a fifth, unknown to us, with the money that the Viscountess paid him.

You may wonder, as we all did, why the Viscountess, however fabulously rich, wasted so much money on the case when, by offering the short-haired girl twenty thousand pounds before the trial, she might have persuaded her not to defend the action. Well, the answer, supplied by Mr Estrutt, was that Mr P.P. Jonés advised against this course, which would have been a crime known as 'collusion,' and therefore in conflict with his high moral principles. Besides, why should he deprive himself of an excessively profitable legal case? Again, the short-haired girl prided herself on having shown such prudence that no charge could possibly be proved against her; but she had not reckoned with a detective of the experience and perspicacity possessed by my friend, Mr Charley Estrutt!

Suspicion

DOROTHY L. SAYERS

AS THE ATMOSPHERE OF THE RAILWAY carriage thickened with tobacco smoke, Mr Mummery became increasingly aware that his breakfast had not agreed with him.

There could have been nothing wrong with the breakfast itself. Brown bread, rich in vitamin content, as advised by the *Morning Star*'s health expert; bacon fried to a delicious crispness; eggs just nicely set; coffee made as only Mrs Sutton knew how to make it. Mrs Sutton had been a real find, and that was something to be thankful for. For Ethel, since her nervous breakdown in the summer, had really not been fit to wrestle with the untrained girls who had come and gone in tempestuous succession. It took very little to upset Ethel nowadays, poor child. Mr Mummery, trying hard to ignore his growing internal discomfort, hoped he was not in for an illness. Apart from the trouble it would cause at the office, it would worry Ethel terribly, and Mr Mummery would cheerfully have laid down his rather uninteresting little life to spare Ethel a moment's uneasiness.

He slipped a digestive tablet into his mouth – he had taken lately to carrying a few tablets about with him – and opened his paper. There did not seem to be very much news. A question had been asked in the House about government typewriters. The Prince of Wales had smilingly opened an all-British exhibition of footwear. A further split had occurred in the Liberal Party. The police were still looking for the woman who was supposed to have poisoned a family in Lincoln. Two girls had been trapped in a burning factory. A film star had obtained her fourth decree nisi.

At Paragon Station, Mr Mummery descended and took a tram. The internal discomfort was taking the form of a definite nausea. Happily he contrived to reach his office before the worst occurred. He was seated at his desk, pale but in control of himself, when his partner came breezing in. "Morning, Mummery,' said Mr Brookes in his loud tones, adding inevitably, 'Cold enough for you?'

'Quite,' replied Mr Mummery. 'Unpleasantly raw, in fact.'

'Beastly, beastly,' said Mr Brookes. 'Your bulbs all in?'

'Not quite all,' confessed Mr Mummery. 'As a matter of fact I haven't been feeling — '

'Pity,' interrupted his partner. 'Great pity. Ought to get 'em in early. Mine were in last week. My little place will be a picture in the spring. For a town garden, that is. You're lucky, living in the country. Find it better than Hull, I expect, eh? Though we get plenty of fresh air up in the avenues. How's the missus?'

'Thank you, she's very much better.'

'Glad to hear that, very glad. Hope we shall have her about again this winter as usual. Can't do without her in the Drama Society, you know. By Jove! I shan't forget her acting last year in *Romance*. She and young Welbeck positively brought the house down, didn't they? The Welbecks were asking after her only yesterday.'

'Thank you, yes. I hope she will soon be able to take up her social activities again. But the doctor says she mustn't overdo it. No worry, he says – that's the important thing. She is to go easy and not rush about or undertake too much.'

'Quite right, quite right. Worry's the devil and all. I cut out worrying years ago and look at me! Fit as a fiddle, for all I shan't see fifty again. *You're* not looking altogether the thing, by the way.'

'A touch of dyspepsia,' said Mr Mummery. 'Nothing much. Chill on the liver, that's what I put it down to.'

'That's what it is,' said Mr Brookes, seizing his opportunity. 'Is life worth living? It depends upon the liver. Ha, ha! Well now, well now – we must do a spot of work, I suppose. Where's that lease of Ferraby's?'

Mr Mummery, who did not feel at his conversational best that morning, rather welcomed this suggestion, and for half an hour was allowed to proceed in peace with the duties of an estate agent. Presently, however, Mr Brookes burst into speech again.

'By the way,' he said abruptly, 'I suppose your wife doesn't know of a good cook, does she?'

'Well, no,' replied Mr Mummery. 'They aren't so easy to find nowadays. In fact, we've only just got suited ourselves. But why? Surely your old Cookie isn't leaving you?'

'Good lord, no!' Mr Brookes laughed heartily. 'It would take an earthquake to shake off old Cookie. No. It's for the Philipsons. Their girl's getting married. That's the worst of girls. I said to Philipson, "You mind what you're doing," I said. "Get somebody you know something about, or you may find yourself landed with this poisoning woman – what's her name – Andrews. Don't want to be sending wreaths to your funeral yet awhile," I said. He laughed, but it's no laughing matter and so I told him. What we pay the police for I simply don't know. Nearly a month now, and they can't seem to lay hands on the woman. All they say is, they think she's hanging about the neighbourhood and "may seek a situation as cook". As cook! Now I ask you!'

'You don't think she committed suicide, then?' sugested Mr Mummery.

'Suicide my foot!' retorted Mr Brookes coarsely. 'Don't you believe it, my boy. That coat found in the river was all eyewash. *They* don't commit suicide, that sort don't.'

'What sort?'

'Those arsenic maniacs. They're too damned careful of their own skins. Cunning as weasels, that's what they are. It's only to be hoped they'll manage to catch her before she tries her hand on anybody else. As I told Philipson –'

'You think Mrs Andrews did it, then?'

'Did it? Of course she did it. It's plain as the nose on your face. Looked after her old father, and he died suddenly – left her a bit of money, too. Then she keeps house for an elderly gentleman, and *he* dies suddenly. Now there's this husband and wife – man dies and woman taken very ill, of arsenic poisoning. Cook runs away, and you ask, did she do it? I don't mind betting that when they dig up the father and the other old bird they'll find *them* bung-full of arsenic, too. Once that sort gets started, they don't stop. Grows on 'em, as you might say.'

'I suppose it does,' said Mr Mummery. He picked up his paper again and studied the photographs of the missing woman. 'She looks harmless enough,' he remarked. 'Rather a nice, motherly-looking kind of woman.'

'She's got a bad mouth,' pronounced Mr Brookes. He had a theory that character showed in the mouth. 'I wouldn't trust that woman an inch.'

As the day went on, Mr Mummery felt better. He was rather nervous about his lunch, choosing carefully a little boiled fish and custard pudding and being particular not to rush about immediately after the meal. To his great relief, the fish and custard remained where they were put, and he was not visited by that tiresome pain which had become almost habitual in the last fortnight. By the end of the day he became quite lighthearted. The bogey of illness and doctor's bills ceased to haunt him. He bought a bunch of bronze chrysanthemums to carry home to Ethel, and it was with a feeling of pleasant anticipation that he left the train and walked up the garden path of Mon Abri.

He was a little dashed by not finding his wife in the sitting room. Still clutching the bunch of chrysanthemums he pattered down the passage and pushed open the kitchen door.

Nobody was there but the cook. She was sitting at the table with her back to him, and started up almost guiltily as he approached.

'Lor' sir,' she said, 'you give me quite a start. I didn't hear the front door go.'

'Where is Mrs Mummery? Not feeling bad again, is she?'

'Well, sir, she's got a bit of a headache, poor lamb. I made her lay down and took her up a nice cup o' tea at half past four. I think she's dozing nicely now.'

'Dear, dear,' said Mr Mummery.

'It was turning out the dining room done it, if you ask me,' said Mrs Sutton. "Now, don't you overdo yourself ma'am," I says to her, but you know how she is, sir. She gets that restless, she can't abear to be doing nothing.'

'I know,' said Mr Mummery. 'It's not your fault, Mrs Sutton. I'm sure you look after us both admirably. I'll just run up and have a peep at her. I won't disturb her if she's asleep. By the way, what are we having for dinner?'

'Well, I *had* made a nice steak and kidney pie,' said Mrs Sutton, in accents suggesting that she would readily turn it into a pumpkin or a coach-and-four if it was not approved of.

'Oh!' said Mr Mummery. 'Pastry? Well, I —'

'You'll find it beautiful and light,' protested the cook, whisking open the oven door for Mr Mummery to see. 'And it's made with butter, sir, you having said that you found lard indigestible.'

'Thank you, thank you,' said Mr Mummery. 'I'm sure it will be most excellent. I haven't been feeling altogether the thing just lately, and lard does not seem to suit me nowadays.'

'Well, it don't suit some people, and that's a fact,' agreed Mrs Sutton. 'I shouldn't wonder if you've got a bit of a chill on the liver. I'm sure this weather is enough to upset anybody.' She bustled to the table and cleared away the picture paper which she had been reading.

'Perhaps the mistress would like her dinner sent up to her?' she suggested.

Mr Mummery said he would go and see, and tiptoed his way upstairs.

Ethel was lying snuggled under the eiderdown and looked very small and fragile in the big double bed. She stirred as he came in and smiled up at him. 'Hullo, darling!' said Mr Mummery.

'Hullo! You back? I must have been asleep. I got tired and headachy, and Mrs Sutton packed me off upstairs.'

'You've been doing too much, sweetheart,' said her husband, taking her hand in his and sitting down on the edge of the bed.

'Yes – it was naughty of me. What lovely flowers, Harold. All for me?'

'All for you, Tiddleywinks,' said Mr Mummery tenderly. 'Don't I deserve something for that?' Mrs Mummery smiled, and Mr Mummery took his reward several times over.

'That's quite enough, you sentimental old thing,' said Mrs Mummery. 'Run away, now, I'm going to get up.'

'Much better go to bed, my precious, and let Mrs Sutton send your dinner up,' said her husband.

Ethel protested, but he was firm with her. If she didn't take care of herself, she wouldn't be allowed to go to the Drama Society meetings. And everybody was so anxious to have her back. The Welbecks had been asking after her and saying that they really couldn't get on without her.

'Did they?' said Ethel with some animation. 'It's very sweet of them to want me. Well, perhaps I'll go to bed after all. And how has my old hubby been all day?'

'Not too bad, not too bad.'

'No more tummyaches?'

'Well, just a *little* tummyache. But it's quite gone now. Nothing for Tiddleywinks to worry about.'

Mr Mummery experienced no more distressing symptoms the next day or the next. Following the advice of the newspaper expert, he took to drinking orange juice, and was delighted with the results of the treatment. On Thursday, however, he was taken so ill in the night that Ethel was alarmed and insisted on sending for the doctor. The doctor felt his pulse and looked at his tongue and appeared to take the matter lightly. An inquiry into what he had been eating elicited the fact that dinner had consisted of pigs' trotters, followed by a milk pudding, and that, before retiring, Mr Mummery had consumed a large glass of orange juice, according to his new regime.

'There's your trouble,' said Dr Griffiths cheerfully. 'Orange juice is an excellent thing, and so are trotters, but not in combination. Pig and oranges together are extraordinarily bad for the liver. I don't know why they should be, but there's no doubt that they are. Now I'll send you round a little prescription and you stick to slops for a day or two and keep off pork. And don't you worry about him, Mrs Mummery, he's as sound as a trout. *You're* the one we've got to look after. I don't want to see those black rings under the eyes, you know. Disturbed night, of course – yes. Taking your tonic regularly? That's right. Well, don't be alarmed about your hubby. We'll soon have him out and about again.'

The prophecy was fulfilled, but not immediately. Mr Mummery, though confining his diet to baby food, bread and milk, and beef tea skilfully prepared by Mrs Sutton and brought to his bedside by Ethel, remained very seedy all through Friday, and was only able to stagger rather shakily downstairs on Saturday afternoon. He had evidently suffered a 'thorough upset'. However, he was able to attend to a few papers which Brookes had sent down from the office for his signature, and to deal with the household books. Ethel was not a businesswoman, and Mr Mummery always ran over the accounts with her. Having settled up with the butcher, the baker, the dairy and the coal merchant, Mr Mummery looked up inquiringly. 'Anything more, darling?'

'Well, there's Mrs Sutton. This is the end of her month, you know.'

'So it is. Well, you're quite satisfied with her, aren't you, darling?'

'Yes, rather – aren't you? She's a good cook, and a sweet, motherly old thing, too. Don't you think it was a real brainwave of mine, engaging her like that, on the spot?'

'I do, indeed,' said Mr Mummery.

'It was a perfect providence, her turning up like that, just after that wretched Janet had gone off without even giving notice. I was in absolute *despair*. It was a little bit of a gamble, of course, taking her without any references, but naturally, if she'd been looking after a widowed mother, you couldn't expect her to give references.'

'N-no,' said Mr Mummery. At the time he had felt uneasy about the matter, though he had not liked to say much because, of course, they simply had to have somebody. And the experiment had justified itself so triumphantly in practice that one couldn't say much about it now. He had once rather tentatively suggested writing to the clergyman of Mrs Sutton's parish but, as Ethel had said, the clergyman wouldn't have been able to tell them anything about cooking, and cooking, after all, was the chief point.

Mr Mummery counted out the month's money.

'And by the way, my dear,' he said, 'you might just mention to Mrs Sutton that if she *must* read the morning paper before I come down, I should be obliged if she would fold it neatly afterwards.'

'What an old fussbox you are, darling,' said his wife.

Mr Mummery sighed. He could not explain that it was somehow important that the morning paper should come to him fresh and prim, like a virgin. Women did not feel these things.

On Sunday, Mr Mummery felt very much better – quite his old self, in fact. He enjoyed the *News of the World* over breakfast in bed, reading the murders rather carefully. Mr Mummery got quite a lot of pleasure out of murders – they gave him an agreeable thrill of vicarious adventure, for naturally, they were matters quite remote from daily life in the outskirts of Hull. He noticed that Brookes had been perfectly right. Mrs Andrews' father and former employer had been 'dug up' and had, indeed, proved to be 'bung-full' of arsenic.

He came downstairs for dinner – roast sirloin, with the potatoes done under the meat and Yorkshire pudding of delicious lightness, and an apple tart to follow. After three days of invalid diet, it was delightful to savour the crisp fat and underdone lean. He ate moderately, but with a sensuous enjoyment. Ethel, on the other hand, seemed a little lacking in appetite, but then, she had never been a great meat eater. She was fastidious and, besides, she was (quite unnecessarily) afraid of getting fat.

It was a fine afternoon, and at three o'clock, when he was quite certain that the roast beef was 'settling' properly, it occurred to Mr Mummery that it would be a good thing to put the rest of those bulbs in. He slipped on his old gardening coat and wandered out to the potting shed. Here he picked up a bag of tulips and a trowel, and then, remembering that he was wearing his good trousers, decided that it would be wise to take a mat to kneel on. When had he had the mat last? He could not recollect, but he rather fancied he had put it away in the corner under the potting shelf. Stooping down, he felt about in the dark among the flowerpots. Yes, there it was, but there was a tin of something in the way. He lifted the tin carefully out. Of course, yes – the remains of the weed killer.

Mr Mummery glanced at the pink label, printed in staring letters with the legend: ARSENICAL WEED KILLER. *POISON*, and observed, with a mild feeling of excitement, that it was the same brand of stuff that had been associated with Mrs Andrews' latest victim. He was rather pleased about it. It gave him a sensation of being remotely but definitely in touch with important events. Then he noticed, with surprise and a little annoyance, that the stopper had been put in quite loosely.

'However'd I come to leave it like that?' he grunted. 'Shouldn't wonder if all the goodness has gone off.' He removed the stopper and squinted into the can, which appeared to be half full. Then he rammed the thing home again, giving it a sharp thump with the handle of the trowel for better security. After that he washed his hands carefully at the scullery tap, for he did not believe in taking risks.

He was a trifle disconcerted, when he came in after planting the tulips, to find visitors in the sitting room. He was always pleased to see Mrs Welbeck and her son, but he would rather have had warning, so that he could have scrubbed the garden mould out of his nails more thoroughly. Not that Mrs Welbeck appeared to notice. She was a talkative woman and paid little attention to anything but her own conversation. Much to Mr Mummery's annoyance, she chose to prattle about the Lincoln poisoning case. A most unsuitable subject for the tea table, thought Mr Mummery, at the best of times. His own 'upset' was vivid enough in his memory to make him queasy over the discussion of medical symptoms, and besides, this kind of talk was not good enough for Ethel. After all, the poisoner was still supposed to be in the neighbourhood. It was enough to make even a strong nerved woman uneasy. A glance at Ethel showed him that she was looking quite white and tremulous. He must stop Mrs Welbeck somehow, or there would be a repetition of one of the old dreadful, hysterical scenes. He broke into the conversation with violent abruptness. 'Those forsythia cuttings, Mrs Welbeck,' he said.

'Now is just about the time to take them. If you care to come down the garden I will get them for you.'

He saw a relieved glance pass between Ethel and young Welbeck. Evidently the boy understood the situation and was chafing at his mother's tactlessness. Mrs Welbeck, brought up all standing, gasped slightly and then veered off with obliging readiness on the new tack. She accompanied her host down the garden and chattered cheerfully about horticulture while he selected and trimmed the cuttings. She complimented Mr Mummery on the immaculacy of his gravel paths. 'I simply *cannot* keep the weeds down,' she said.

Mr Mummery mentioned the weed killer and praised its efficacy.

'That stuff!' Mrs Welbeck stared at him. Then she shuddered. 'I wouldn't have it in my place for a thousand pounds,' she said, with emphasis.

Mr Mummery smiled. 'Oh, we keep it well away from the house,' he said. 'Even if I were a careless sort of person —'

He broke off. The recollection of the loosened stopper had come to him suddenly, and it was as though, deep down in his mind, some obscure assembling of ideas had taken place. He left it at that, and went into the kitchen to fetch a newspaper to wrap up the cuttings.

Their approach to the house had evidently been seen from the sitting-room window, for when they entered, young Welbeck was already on his feet and holding Ethel's hand in the act of saying good-bye. He manoeuvred his mother out of the house with tactful promptness and Mr Mummery returned to the kitchen to clear up the newspapers he had fished out of the drawer. To clear them up and to examine them more closely. Something had struck him about them, which he wanted to verify. He turned them over very carefully, sheet by sheet. Yes – he had been right. Every portrait of Mrs Andrews, every paragraph and line about the Lincoln poisoning case, had been carefully cut out.

Mr Mummery sat down by the kitchen fire. He felt as though he needed warmth. There seemed to be a curious cold lump of something at the pit of his stomach – something that he was chary of investigating.

He tried to recall the appearance of Mrs Andrews as shown in the newspaper photographs, but he had not a good visual memory. He remembered having remarked to Brookes that it was a 'motherly' face. Then he tried counting up the time since the disappearance. Nearly a month, Brookes had said – and that was a week ago. Must be over a month now. A month. He had just paid Mrs Sutton her month's money.

Ethel! was the thought that hammered at the door of his brain. At all costs, he must cope with this monstrous suspicion on his own. He must spare her any shock or anxiety. And he must be sure of his ground. To dismiss the only decent cook they had ever had out of sheer, unfounded panic, would be wanton cruelty to both women. If he did it at all, it would have to be done arbitrarily, preposterously – he could not suggest horrors to Ethel. However it was done, there would be trouble. Ethel would not understand and he dared not tell her.

But if by any chance there was anything in this ghastly doubt – how could he expose Ethel to the appalling danger of having the woman in the house a moment longer? He thought of the family at Lincoln – the husband dead, the wife escaped by a miracle with her life. Was not any shock, any risk, better than that?

Mr Mummery felt suddenly very lonely and tired. His illness had taken it out of him. Those illnesses – they had begun, when? Three weeks ago he had had the first attack. Yes, but then he had always been rather subject to gastric troubles. Bilious attacks. Not so violent, perhaps, as these last, but undoubted bilious attacks.

He pulled himself together and went, rather heavily, into the sitting room. Ethel was tucked up in a corner of the chesterfield.

'Tired, darling?'

'Yes, a little.'

'That woman has worn you out with talking. She oughtn't to talk so much.'

'No.' Her head shifted wearily in the cushions. 'All about that horrible case. I don't like hearing about such things.'

'Of course not. Still, when a thing like that happens in the neighbourhood, people will gossip and talk. It would be a relief if they caught the woman. One doesn't like to think – '

'I don't want to think of anything so hateful. She must be a horrible creature.'

'Horrible. Brookes was saying the other day – '

'I don't want to hear what he said. I don't want to hear about it at all. I want to be quiet. I want to be quiet!'

He recognized the note of rising hysteria. 'Tiddleywinks shall be quiet. Don't worry, darling. We won't talk about horrors.'

No. It would not do to talk about them.

Ethel went to bed early. It was understood that on Sundays Mr Mummery should sit up till Mrs Sutton came in. Ethel was a little anxious about this, but he assured her that he felt quite strong enough. In body, indeed, he did; it was his mind that felt weak and confused. He had decided to make a casual remark about the mutilated newspapers – just to see what Mrs Sutton would say.

He allowed himself the usual indulgence of a whisky and soda as he sat waiting. At a quarter to ten he heard the familiar click of the garden gate. Footsteps passed up the gravel – squeak, squeak, to the back door. Then the sound of the latch, the shutting of the door, the rattle of the bolts being shot home. Then a pause. Mrs Sutton would be taking off her hat. The moment was coming. The step sounded in the passage. The door opened. Mrs Sutton in her neat black dress stood on the threshold. He was aware of a reluctance to face her. Then he looked up. A plump-faced woman, her eyes obscured by thick horn-rimmed spectacles. Was there, perhaps, something hard about the mouth? Or was it just that she had lost most of her front teeth?

'Would you be requiring anything tonight, sir, before I go up?'

'No, thank you, Mrs Sutton.'

'I hope you are feeling better, sir.' Her eager interest in his health seemed to him almost sinister, but the eyes, behind the thick glasses, were inscrutable.

'Quite better, thank you, Mrs Sutton.'

'Mrs Mummery is not indisposed, is she, sir? Should I take her up a glass of hot milk or anything?'

'No, thank you, no.' He spoke hurriedly, and fancied that she looked disappointed.

'Very well, sir. Good night, sir.'

'Good night. Oh! by the way, Mrs Sutton —'

'Yes, sir?'

'Oh, nothing,' said Mr Mummery, 'nothing.'

Next morning Mr Mummery opened his paper eagerly. He would have been glad to learn that an arrest had been made over the weekend. But there was no news for him. The chairman of a trust company had blown out his brains, and the headlines were all occupied with tales about lost millions and ruined shareholders. Both in his own paper and in those he purchased on the way to the office, the Lincoln poisoning tragedy had been relegated to an obscure paragraph on a back page, which informed him that the police were still baffled.

The next few days were the most uncomfortable that Mr Mummery had ever spent. He developed a habit of coming down early in the morning and prowling about the kitchen. This made Ethel nervous, but Mrs Sutton offered no remark. She watched him tolerantly, even, he thought, with something like amusement. After all, it was ridiculous. What was the use of supervising the breakfast, when he had to be out of the house every day between half past nine and six?

At the office, Brookes rallied him on the frequency with which he rang up Ethel. Mr Mummery paid no attention. It was reassuring to hear her voice and to know that she was safe and well.

Nothing happened, and by the following Thursday he began to think that he had been a fool. He came home late that night. Brookes had persuaded him to go with him to a little bachelor dinner for a friend who was about to get married. He left the others at eleven o'clock, however, refusing to make a night of it. The household was in bed when he got back but a note from Mrs Sutton lay on the table, informing him that there was cocoa for him in the kitchen, ready for hotting up. He hotted it up accordingly in the little saucepan where it stood. There was just one good cupful.

He sipped it thoughtfully, standing by the kitchen stove. After the first sip, he put the cup down. Was it his fancy, or was there something queer about the taste? He sipped it again, rolling it upon his tongue. It seemed to him to have a faint tang, metallic and unpleasant. In a sudden dread he ran out to the scullery and spat the mouthful into the sink.

After this, he stood quite still for a moment or two. Then, with a curious deliberation, as though his movements had been dictated to him, he fetched an empty medicine bottle from the pantry shelf, rinsed it under the tap and tipped the contents of the cup carefully into it. He slipped the bottle into his coat pocket and moved on tiptoe to the back door. The bolts were difficult to draw without noise, but he managed it at last. Still on tiptoe, he stole across the garden to the potting shed. Stooping down, he struck a match. He knew exactly where he had left the tin of weed killer, under the shelf behind the pots at the back. Cautiously he lifted it out. The match flared up and burnt his fingers, but before he could light another his sense of touch had told him what he wanted to know. The stopper was loose again.

Panic seized Mr Mummery, standing there in the earthy-smelling shed, in his dress suit and overcoat, holding the tin in one hand and the matchbox in the other. He wanted very badly to run and tell somebody what he had discovered.

Instead, he replaced the tin exactly where he had found it and went back to the house. As he crossed the garden again, he noticed a light in Mrs Sutton's bedroom. This terrified him more than anything which had gone before. Was she watching him? Ethel's window was dark. If she had drunk anything deadly there would be lights everywhere, movements, calls for the doctor, just as when he himself had been attacked. Attacked – that was the right word.

Still with the same odd presence of mind and precision, he went in, washed out the utensils and made a second brew of cocoa, which he left standing in the saucepan. He crept quietly to his bedroom. Ethel's voice greeted him on the threshold.

'How late you are, Harold. Naughty old boy! Have a good time?'

'Not bad. You all right, darling?'

'Quite all right. Did Mrs Sutton leave something hot for you? She said she would.'

'Yes, but I wasn't thirsty.'

Ethel laughed. 'Oh! it was *that* sort of party, was it?'

Mr Mummery did not attempt any denials. He undressed and got into bed and clutched his wife to him as though defying death and hell to take her from him. Next morning he would act. He thanked God that he was not too late.

Mr Dimthorpe, the chemist, was a great friend of Mr Mummery's. They had often sat together in the untidy little shop of Spring Bank and exchanged views on greenfly and clubroot. Mr Mummery told his story frankly to Mr Dimthorpe and handed over the bottle of cocoa. Mr Dimthorpe congratulated him on his prudence and intelligence. 'I will have it ready for you by this evening,' he said, 'and if it's what you think it is, then we shall have a clear case on which to take action.'

Mr Mummery thanked him, and was extremely vague and inattentive at business all day. But that hardly mattered, for Mr Brookes, who had seen the party through to a riotous end in the small hours, was in no very observant mood. At half past four, Mr Mummery shut up his desk decisively and announced that he was off early, he had a call to make. Mr Dimthorpe was ready for him.

'No doubt about it,' he said. 'I used the Marsh test. It's a heavy dose – no wonder you tasted it. There must be four or five grains of pure arsenic in that bottle. Look, here's the test tube. You can see the mirror for yourself.'

Mr Mummery gazed at the little glass tube with its ominous purple-black stain.

'Will you ring up the police from here?' asked the chemist.

'No,' said Mr Mummery. 'No – I want to get home. God knows what's happening there. And I've only just time to catch my train.'

'All right,' said Mr Dimthorpe. 'Leave it to me. I'll ring them up for you.'

The local train was not fast enough for Mr Mummery. Ethel – poisoned – dying – dead – Ethel – poisoned – dying – dead – the wheels drummed in his ears. He almost ran out of the station and along the road. A car was standing at his door. He saw it from the end of the street and broke into a gallop. It had happened already. The doctor was there. Fool, murderer that he was, to have left things so late.

Then, while he was still a hundred and fifty yards off, he saw the front door open. A man came out followed by Ethel herself. The visitor got into his car and was driven away. Ethel went in again. She was safe – safe! He could hardly control himself to hang up his hat and coat and go in looking reasonably calm. His wife had returned to the armchair by the fire and greeted him in some surprise. There were tea things on the table.

'Back early, aren't you?'

'Yes – business was slack. Somebody been to tea?'

'Yes, young Welbeck. About the arrangements for the Drama Society.' She spoke briefly but with an undertone of excitement.

A qualm came over Mr Mummery. Would a guest be any protection? His face must have shown his feelings, for Ethel stared at him in amazement.

'What's the matter, Harold, you look so queer?'

'Darling,' said Mr Mummery, 'there's something I want to tell you about.' He sat down and took her hand in his. 'Something a little unpleasant, I'm afraid –'

'Oh, ma'am!' The cook was in the doorway.

'I beg your pardon, sir – I didn't know you was in. Will you be taking tea or can I clear away? And oh, ma'am, there was a young man at the fishmonger's and he's just come from Grimsby and they've caught that dreadful woman – that Mrs Andrews. Isn't it a good thing? It's worritted me dreadful to think she was going about like that, but they've caught her. Taken a job as housekeeper she had to two elderly ladies and they found the wicked poison on her. Girl as spotted her will get a reward. I been keeping my eyes open for her, but it's at Grimsby she was all the time.'

Mr Mummery clutched at the arm of his chair. It had all been a mad mistake then. He wanted to shout or cry. He wanted to apologize to this foolish, pleasant, excited woman. All a mistake.

But there had been the cocoa. Mr Dimthorpe. The Marsh test. Five grains of arsenic. Who, then —?

He glanced around at his wife, and in her eyes he saw something that he had never seen before . . .

Pig-Hoo-o-o-o-ey!

P.G. WODEHOUSE

THANKS TO THE PUBLICITY GIVEN to the matter by *The Bridgnorth, Shifnal, and Albrighton Argus* (with which is incorporated *The Wheat-Growers' Intelligence and Stock Breeders' Gazetteer*), the whole world today knows that the silver medal in the Fat Pigs class at the eighty-seventh annual Shropshire Agricultural Show was won by the Earl of Emsworth's black Berkshire sow, Empress of Blandings.

Very few people, however, are aware how near that splendid animal came to missing the coveted honour.

Now it can be told.

This brief chapter of Secret History may be said to have begun on the night of the eighteenth of July, when George Cyril Wellbeloved (twenty-nine), pig-man in the employ of Lord Emsworth, was arrested by Police-Constable Evans of Market Blandings for being drunk and disorderly in the tap-room of the Goat and Feathers. On July the nineteenth, after first offering to apologize, then explaining that it had been his birthday, and finally attempting to prove an alibi, George Cyril was very properly jugged for fourteen days without the option of a fine.

On July the twentieth, Empress of Blandings, always hitherto a hearty and even boisterous feeder, for the first time on record declined all nourishment. And on the morning of July the twenty-first, the veterinary surgeon called in to diagnose and deal with this strange asceticism, was compelled to confess to Lord Emsworth that the thing was beyond his professional skill.

Let us just see, before proceeding, that we have got these dates correct:

July 18. – Birthday Orgy of Cyril Wellbeloved.
July 19. – Incarceration of Ditto.
July 20. – Pig Lays off the Vitamins.

July 21. – Veterinary Surgeon Baffled.
Right.

The effect of the veterinary surgeon's announcement on Lord Emsworth was overwhelming. As a rule, the wear and tear of our complex modern life left this vague and amiable peer unscathed. So long as he had sunshine, regular meals, and complete freedom from the society of his younger son Frederick, he was placidly happy. But there were chinks in his armour, and one of these had been pierced this morning. Dazed by the news he stood at the window of the great library of Blandings Castle, looking out with unseeing eyes.

As he stood there, the door opened. Lord Emsworth turned; and having blinked once or twice, as was his habit when confronted suddenly with anything, recognized in the handsome and imperious looking woman who had entered, his sister, Lady Constance Keeble. Her demeanour, like his own, betrayed the deepest agitation.

'Clarence,' she cried, 'an awful thing has happened!'

Lord Emsworth nodded dully. 'I know. He's just told me.'

'What! Has he been here?'

'Only this moment left.'

'Why did you let him go? You must have known I would want to see him.'

'What good would that have done?'

'I could at least have assured him of my sympathy,' said Lady Constance stiffly.

'Yes, I suppose you could,' said Lord Emsworth, having considered the point. 'Not that he deserves any sympathy. The man's an ass.'

'Nothing of the kind. A most intelligent young man, as young men go.'

'Young? Would you call him young? Fifty, I should have said, if a day.'

'Are you out of your senses? Heacham fifty?'

'Not Heacham. Smithers.'

As frequently happened to her when in conversation with her brother, Lady Constance experienced a swimming sensation.

'Will you kindly tell me, Clarence, in a few simple words, what you imagine we are talking about?'

'I'm talking about Smithers. Empress of Blandings is refusing her food, and Smithers says he can't do anything about it. And he calls himself a vet!'

'Then you haven't heard? Clarence, a dreadful thing has happened. Angela has broken off her engagement to Heacham.'

'And the Agricultural Show on Wednesday week!'

'What on earth has that got to do with it?' demanded Lady Constance, feeling a recurrence of the swimming sensation.

'What has it got to do with it?' said Lord Emsworth warmly. 'My champion sow, with less than ten days to prepare herself for a most searching examination in competition with all the finest pigs in the county, starts refusing her food —'

'Will you stop maundering on about your insufferable pig and give your attention to something that really matters? I tell you that Angela – your niece Angela – has broken off her engagement to Lord Heacham and expresses her intention of marrying that hopeless ne'er-do-well, James Belford.'

'The son of Old Belford, the parson?'

'Yes.'

'She can't. He's in America.'

'He is not in America. He is in London.'

'No,' said Lord Emsworth, shaking his head sagely. 'You're wrong. I remember meeting his father two years ago out on the road by Meeker's twenty-acre field, and he distinctly told me the boy was sailing for America next day. He must be there by this time.'

'Can't you understand? He's come back.'

'Oh? Come back? I see. Come *back*?'

'You know there was once a silly sentimental sort of affair between him and Angela; but a year after he left she became engaged to Heacham and I thought the whole thing was over and done with. And now it seems she met this young man Belford when she was in London last week, and it has started all over again. She tells me she has written to Heacham and broken the engagement.'

There was a silence. Brother and sister remained for a space plunged in thought. Lord Emsworth was the first to speak.

'We've tried acorns,' he said. 'We've tried skim milk. And we've tried potato peel. But, no, she won't touch them.'

Conscious of two eyes raising blisters on his sensitive skin, he came to himself with a start.

'Absurd! Ridiculous! Preposterous!' he said, hurriedly. 'Breaking the engagement? Pooh! Tush! What nonsense! I'll have a word with that young man. If he thinks he can go about the place playing fast and loose with my niece and jilting her without so much as a —'

'Clarence!'

Lord Emsworth blinked. Something appeared to be wrong, but he could not imagine what. It seemed to him that in his last speech he had struck just the right note – strong, forceful, dignified.

'Eh?'

'It is Angela who has broken the engagement.'

'Oh, Angela?'

'She is infatuated with this man Belford. And the point is, what are we to do about it?'

Lord Emsworth reflected.

'Take a strong line,' he said firmly. 'Stand no nonsense. Don't send 'em a wedding present.'

There is no doubt that, given time, Lady Constance would have found and uttered some adequately corrosive comment on this imbecile suggestion; but even as she was swelling preparatory to giving tongue, the door opened and a girl came in.

She was a pretty girl, with fair hair and blue eyes which in their softer moments probably reminded all sorts of people of twin lagoons slumbering beneath a southern sky. This, however, was not one of those moments. To Lord Emsworth, as they met his, they looked like something out of an oxyacetylene blow pipe; and, as far as he was capable of being disturbed by anything that was not his younger son Frederick, he was disturbed. Angela, it seemed to him, was upset about something; and he was sorry. He liked Angela.

To ease a tense situation, he said:

'Angela, my dear, do you know anything about pigs?'

The girl laughed. One of those sharp, bitter laughs which are so unpleasant just after breakfast.

'Yes, I do. You're one.'

'Me?'

'Yes, you. Aunt Constance says that, if I marry Jimmy, you won't let me have my money.'

'Money? Money?' Lord Emsworth was mildly puzzled. 'What money? You never lent me any money.'

Lady Constance's feelings found vent in a sound like an overheated radiator.

'I believe this absent-mindedness of yours is nothing but a ridiculous pose, Clarence. You know perfectly well that when poor Jane died she left you Angela's trustee.'

'And I can't touch my money without your consent till I'm twenty-five.'

'Well, how old are you?'

'Twenty-one.'

'Then what are you worrying about?' asked Lord Emsworth, surprised. 'No need to worry about it for another four years. God bless my soul, the money is quite safe. It is in excellent securities.'

Angela stamped her foot. An unladylike action, but how much better than kicking an uncle with it, as her lower nature prompted.

'I have told Angela,' explained Lady Constance, 'that, while we naturally cannot force her to marry Lord Heacham, we can at least keep her money from being squandered by this wastrel on whom she proposes to throw herself away.'

'He isn't a wastrel. He's got quite enough money to marry me on, but he wants some capital to buy a partnership in a —'

'He is a wastrel. Wasn't he sent abroad because —'

'That was two years ago. And since then —'

'My dear Angela, you may argue until —'

'I'm not arguing. I'm simply saying that I'm going to marry Jimmy, if we both have to starve in the gutter.'

'What gutter?' asked his lordship, wrenching his errant mind away from thoughts of acorns.

'Any gutter.'

'Now, please listen to me, Angela.'

It seemed to Lord Emsworth that there was a frightful amount of conversation going on. He had the sensation of having become a mere bit of flotsam upon a tossing sea of female voices. Both his sister and his niece appeared to have much to say, and they were saying it simultaneously and *fortissimo*. He looked wistfully at the door.

It was smoothly done. A twist of the handle, and he was beyond those voices where there was peace. Galloping gaily down the stairs, he charged out into the sunshine.

His gaiety was not long-lived. Free at last to concentrate itself on the really serious issues of life, his mind grew sombre and grim. Once more there descended upon him the cloud which had been oppressing his soul before all this Heacham-Angela-Belford business began. Each step that took him nearer to the sty where the ailing Empress resided seemed a heavier step than the last. He reached the sty; and, draping himself over the rails, peered moodily at the vast expanse of pig within.

For, even though she had been doing a bit of dieting of late, Empress of Blandings was far from being an ill-nourished animal. She resembled a captive balloon with ears and a tail, and was as nearly circular as a pig can be without bursting. Nevertheless, Lord Emsworth, as he regarded her, mourned and would not be comforted. A few more square meals under her belt, and no pig in all Shropshire could have held its head up in the Empress's presence. And now, just for lack of those few meals, the supreme animal would probably be relegated to the mean obscurity of an 'Honourably Mentioned'. It was bitter, bitter.

He became aware that somebody was speaking to him; and, turning, perceived a solemn young man in riding breeches.

'I say,' said the young man.

Lord Emsworth, though he would have preferred solitude, was relieved to find that the intruder was at least one of his own sex. Women are apt to stray off into side-issues, but men are practical and can be relied on to stick to the fundamentals. Besides, young Heacham probably kept pigs himself and might have a useful hint or two up his sleeve.

'I say, I've just ridden over to see if there was anything I could do about this fearful business.'

'Uncommonly kind and thoughtful of you, my dear fellow,' said Lord Emsworth, touched. 'I fear things look very black.'

'It's an absolute mystery to me.'

'To me, too.'

'I mean to say, she was all right last week.'

'She was all right as late as the day before yesterday.'

'Seemed quite cheery and chirpy and all that.'

'Entirely so.'

'And then this happens – out of a blue sky, as you might say.'

'Exactly. It is insoluble. We have done everything possible to tempt her appetite.'

'Her appetite? Is Angela ill?'

'Angela? No, I fancy not. She seemed perfectly well a few minutes ago.'

'You've seen her this morning, then? Did you say anything about this fearful business?'

'No. She was speaking about some money.'

'It's all so dashed unexpected.'

'Like a bolt from the blue,' agreed Lord Emsworth. 'Such a thing has never happened before. I fear the worst. According to the Wolff-Lehmann feeding standards, a pig, if in health, should consume daily nourishment amounting to fifty-seven thousand eight hundred calories, these to consist of proteins four pounds five ounces, carbohydrates twenty-five pounds —'

'What has that got to do with Angela?'

'Angela?'

'I came to find out why Angela has broken off our engagement.'

Lord Emsworth marshalled his thoughts. He had a misty idea that he had heard something mentioned about that. It came back to him.

'Ah, yes, of course. She has broken off the engagement, hasn't she? I believe it is because she is in love with someone else. Yes, now that I recollect, that was distinctly stated. The whole thing comes back to me quite clearly. Angela has decided to marry someone else. I knew there was some satisfactory explanation. Tell me, my dear fellow, what are your views on linseed meal.'

'What do you mean, linseed meal?'

'Why, linseed meal,' said Lord Emsworth, not being able to find a better definition. 'As a food for pigs.'

'Oh, curse all pigs!'

'What!' There was a sort of astounded horror in Lord Emsworth's voice. He had never been particularly fond of young Heacham, for he was not a man who took much to his juniors, but he had not supposed him capable of anarchistic sentiments like this.

'What did you say?'

'I said, "Curse all pigs!" You keep talking about pigs. I'm not interested in pigs. I don't want to discuss pigs. Blast and damn every pig in existence!'

Lord Emsworth watched him, as he strode away, with an emotion that was partly indignation and partly relief – indignation that a landowner and a fellow son of Shropshire could have brought himself to utter such words, and relief that one capable of such utterance was not going to marry into his family. He had always in his woollen-headed way been very fond of his niece Angela, and it was nice to think that the child had such solid good sense and so much cool discernment. Many girls of her age would have been carried away by the glamour of young Heacham's position and wealth; but she, divining with an intuition beyond her years that he was unsound on the subject of pigs, had drawn back while there was still time and refused to marry him.

A pleasant glow suffused Lord Emsworth's bosom, to be frozen out a few moments later as he perceived his sister Constance bearing down upon him. Lady Constance was a beautiful woman, but there were times when the charm of her face was marred by a rather curious expression; and from nursery days onward his lordship had learned that this expression meant trouble. She was wearing it now.

'Clarence,' she said, 'I have had enough of this nonsense of Angela and young Belford. The thing cannot be allowed to go drifting on. You must catch the two o'clock train to London.'

'What! Why?'

'You must see this man Belford and tell him that, if Angela insists on marrying him, she will not have a penny for four years. I shall be greatly surprised if that piece of information does not put an end to the whole business.'

Lord Emsworth scratched meditatively at the Empress's tank-like back. A mutinous expression was on his mild face.

'Don't see why she shouldn't marry the fellow,' he mumbled.

'Marry James Belford?'

'I don't see why not. Seems fond of him and all that.'

'You never have had a grain of sense in your head, Clarence. Angela is going to marry Heacham.'

'Can't stand that man. All wrong about pigs.'

'Clarence, I don't wish to have any more discussion and argument. You will go to London on the two o'clock train. You will see Mr Belford. And you will tell him about Angela's money. Is that quite clear?'

'Oh, all right,' said his lordship moodily. 'All right, all right.'

The emotions of the Earl of Emsworth, as he sat next day facing his luncheon-guest, James Bartholomew Belford, across a table in the main dining room of the Senior Conservative Club, were not of the liveliest and most agreeable. It was bad enough to be in London at all on such a day of golden sunshine. To be charged, while there, with the task of blighting the romance of two young people for whom he entertained a warm regard was unpleasant to a degree.

For, now that he had given the matter thought, Lord Emsworth recalled that he had always liked this boy Belford. A pleasant lad, with, he remembered now, a healthy fondness for that rural existence which so appealed to himself. By no means the sort of fellow who, in the very presence and hearing of Empress of Blandings, would have spoken disparagingly and with oaths of pigs as a class. It occurred to Lord Emsworth, as it has occurred to so many people, that the distribution of money in this world is all wrong. Why should a man like pig-despising Heacham have a rent roll that ran into the tens of thousands, while this very deserving youngster had nothing?

These thoughts not only saddened Lord Emsworth – they embarrassed him. He hated unpleasantness, and it was suddenly borne in upon him that, after he had broken the news that Angela's bit of capital was locked up and not likely to get loose, conversation with his young friend during the remainder of lunch would tend to be somewhat difficult.

He made up his mind to postpone the revelation. During the meal, he decided, he would chat pleasantly of this and that; and then, later, while bidding his guest goodbye, he would spring the thing on him suddenly and dive back into the recesses of the club.

Considerably cheered at having solved a delicate problem with such adroitness, he started to prattle.

'The gardens at Blandings,' he said, 'are looking particularly attractive this summer. My head-gardener, Angus McAllister, is a man with whom I do not always find myself seeing eye to eye, notably in the matter of hollyhocks, on which I consider his views subversive to a degree; but there is no denying that he understands roses. The rose garden —'

'How well I remember that rose garden,' said James Belford, sighing slightly and helping himself to brussels sprouts. 'It was there that Angela and I used to meet on summer mornings.'

Lord Emsworth blinked. This was not an encouraging start, but the Emsworths were a fighting clan. He had another try.

'I have seldom seen such a blaze of colour as was to be witnessed there during the month of June. Both McAllister and I adopted a very strong policy with the slugs and plant lice, with the result that the place was a mass of flourishing Damasks and Ayrshires and —'

'Properly to appreciate roses,' said James Belford, 'you want to see them as a setting for a girl like Angela. With her fair hair gleaming against the green leaves she makes a rose garden seem a veritable Paradise.'

'No doubt,' said Lord Emsworth. 'No doubt. I am glad you liked my rose garden. At Blandings, of course, we have the natural advantage of loamy soil, rich in plant food and humus; but, as I often say to McAllister, and on this point we have never had the slightest disagreement, loamy soil by itself is not enough. You must have manure. If every autumn a liberal mulch of stable manure is spread upon the beds and the coarser parts removed in the spring before the annual forking —'

'Angela tells me,' said James Belford, 'that you have forbidden our marriage.'

Lord Emsworth choked dismally over his chicken. Directness of this kind, he told himself with a pang of self-pity, was the sort of thing young Englishmen picked up in America. Diplomatic circumlocution flourished only in a more leisurely civilization, and in those energetic and forceful surroundings you learned to Talk Quick and Do It Now, and all sorts of uncomfortable things.

'Er – well, yes, now you mention it, I believe some informal decision of that nature was arrived at. You see, my dear fellow, my sister Constance feels rather strongly —'

'I understand. I suppose she thinks I'm a sort of prodigal.'

'No, no, my dear fellow. She never said that. Wastrel was the term she employed.'

'Well, perhaps I did start out in business on those lines. But you can take it from me that when you find yourself employed on a farm in Nebraska belonging to an applejack-nourished patriarch with strong views on work and a good vocabulary, you soon develop a certain liveliness.'

'Are you employed on a farm?'

'I was employed on a farm.'

'Pigs?' said Lord Emsworth in a low, eager voice.

'Among other things.'

Lord Emsworth gulped. His fingers clutched at the tablecloth.

'Then perhaps, my dear fellow, you can give me some advice. For the last two days my prize sow, Empress of Blandings, has declined nourishment. And the Agricultural Show is on Wednesday week. I am distracted with anxiety.'

James Belford frowned thoughtfully.

'What does your pig-man say about it?'

'My pig-man was sent to prison two days ago. Two days!' For the first time the significance of the coincidence struck him. 'You don't think that can have anything to do with the animal's loss of appetite?'

'Certainly. I imagine she is missing him and pining away because he isn't there.'

Lord Emsworth was surprised. He had only a distant acquaintance with George Cyril Wellbeloved, but from what he had seen of him he had not credited him with this fatal allure.

'She probably misses his afternoon call.'

Again his lordship found himself perplexed. He had had no notion that pigs were such sticklers for the formalities of social life.

'His call?'

'He must have had some special call that he used when he wanted her to come to dinner. One of the first things you learn on a farm is hog-calling. Pigs are temperamental. Omit to call them, and they'll starve rather than put on the nose-bag. Call them right, and they will follow you to the ends of the earth with their mouths watering.'

'God bless my soul! Fancy that.'

'A fact, I assure you. These calls vary in different parts of America. In Wisconsin, for example, the words "Poig, Poig, Poig" bring home – in both the literal and the figurative sense – the bacon. In Illinois, I believe they call "Burp, Burp, Burp," while in Iowa the phrase "Kus, Kus, Kus" is preferred. Proceeding to Minnesota, we find "Peega, Peega, Peega," or alternatively, "Oink, Oink, Oink," whereas in Milwaukee, so largely inhabited by those of German descent, you will hear the good old Teuton "Komm Schweine, Komm Schweine." Oh, yes, there are all sorts of pig-calls, from the Massachusetts. "Phew, Phew, Phew" to the "Loo-ey, Loo-ey, Loo-ey" of Ohio, not counting various local devices such as beating on tin cans with axes or rattling pebbles in a suitcase. I knew a man out in Nebraska who used to call his pigs by tapping on the edge of the trough with his wooden leg.'

'Did he, indeed?'

'But a most unfortunate thing happened. One evening, hearing a woodpecker at the top of a tree, they started shinning up it; and when the man came out he found them all lying there in a circle with their necks broken.'

'This is no time for joking,' said Lord Emsworth, pained.

'I'm not joking. Solid fact. Ask anybody out there.'

Lord Emsworth placed a hand to his throbbing forehead.

'But if there is this wide variety, we have no means of knowing which call Wellbeloved . . .'

'Ah,' said James Belford, 'but wait. I haven't told you all. There is a master-word.'

'A what?'

'Most people don't know it, but I had it straight from the lips of Fred Patzel, the hog-calling champion of the Western States. What a man! I've known him to bring pork chops leaping from their plates. He informed me that, no matter whether an animal had been trained to answer to the Illinois "Burp" or the Minnesota "Oink", it will always give immediate service in response to this magic combination of syllables. It is to the pig world what the Masonic grip is to the human. "Oink" in Illinois or "Burp" in Minnesota, and the animal merely raises its eyebrows and stares coldly. But go to either State and call "Pig-hoo-oo-ey!" . . .'

The expression on Lord Emsworth's face was that of a drowning man who sees a lifeline.

'Is that the master-word of which you spoke?'

'That's it.'

'Pig —?'

' – hoo-oo-ey.'

'Pig-hoo-o-o-ey.'

'You haven't got it right. The first syllable should be short and staccato, the second long and rising into a falsetto, high but true.'

'Pig-hoo-o-o-ey.'

'Pig-hoo-o-o-ey.'

'Pig-hoo-o-o-ey!' yodelled Lord Emsworth, flinging his head back and giving tongue in a high, penetrating tenor which caused ninety-three Senior Conservatives, lunching in the vicinity, to congeal into living statues of alarm and disapproval.

'More body to the "hoo,"' advised James Belford.

'Pig-hoo-o-o-ey!'

The Senior Conservative Club is one of the few places in London where lunchers are not accustomed to getting music with their meals. White-whiskered financiers gazed bleakly at bald-headed politicians, as if asking silently what was to be done about this. Bald-headed politicians stared back at white-whiskered financiers, replying in the language of the eye that they did not know. The general sentiment prevailing was a vague determination to write to the Committee about it.

'Pig-hoo-o-o-ey!' carolled Lord Emsworth. And, as he did so, his eye fell on the clock over the mantelpiece. Its hands pointed to twenty minutes to two.

He started convulsively. The best train in the day for Market Blandings was the one which left Paddington station at two sharp. After that there was nothing till the five-five.

He was not a man who often thought; but, when he did, to think was with him to act. A moment later he was scudding over the carpet, making for the door that led to the broad staircase.

Throughout the room which he had left, the decision to write in strong terms to the Committee was now universal; but from the mind, such as it was, of Lord Emsworth the past, with the single exception of the word 'Pig-hoo-o-o-o-ey!' had been completely blotted.

Whispering the magic syllables, he sped to the cloakroom and retrieved his hat. Murmuring them over and over again, he sprang into a cab. He was still repeating them as the train moved out of the station; and he would doubtless have gone on repeating them all the way to Market Blandings, had he not, as was his invariable practice when travelling by rail, fallen asleep after the first ten minutes of the journey.

The stopping of the train at Swindon Junction woke him with a start. He sat up, wondering, after his usual fashion on these occasions, who and where he was. Memory returned to him, but a memory that was, alas, incomplete. He remembered his name. He remembered that he was on his way home from a visit to London. But what it was that you said to a pig when inviting it to drop in for a bite of dinner he had completely forgotten.

It was the opinion of Lady Constance Keeble, expressed verbally during dinner in the brief intervals when they were alone, and by means of silent telepathy when Beach, the butler, was adding his dignified presence to the proceedings, that her brother Clarence, in his expedition to London to put matters plainly to James Belford, had made an outstanding idiot of himself.

There had been no need whatever to invite the man Belford to lunch; but, having invited him to lunch, to leave him sitting, without having clearly stated that Angela would have no money for four years, was the act of a congenital imbecile. Lady Constance had been aware ever since their childhood days that her brother had about as much sense as a —

Here Beach entered, superintending the bringing-in of the savoury, and she had been obliged to suspend her remarks.

This sort of conversation is never agreeable to a sensitive man, and his lordship had removed himself from the danger zone as soon as he could manage it. He was now seated in the library, sipping port and straining a brain which nature had never intended for hard exercise in an effort to bring back that word of magic of which his unfortunate habit of sleeping in trains had robbed him.

'Pig —'

He could remember as far as that; but of what avail was a single syllable? Besides, weak as his memory was, he could recall that the whole gist or nub of the thing lay in the syllable that followed. The 'pig' was a mere preliminary.

Lord Emsworth finished his port and got up. He felt restless, stifled. The summer night seemed to call him like some silver-voiced swineherd calling to his pig. Possibly, he thought, a breath of fresh air might stimulate his brain cells. He wandered downstairs; and, having dug a shocking old slouch hat out of the cupboard where he hid it to keep his sister Constance from impounding and burning it, he strode heavily out into the garden.

He was pottering aimlessly to and fro in the parts adjacent to the rear of the castle when there appeared in his path a slender female form. He recognized it without pleasure. Any unbiased judge would have said that his niece Angela, standing there in the soft pale light, looked like some dainty spirit of the Moon. Lord Emsworth was not an unbiased judge. To him Angela merely looked like Trouble. The march of civilization has given the modern girl a vocabulary and an ability to use it which her grandmother never had. Lord Emsworth would not have minded meeting Angela's grandmother a bit.

'Is that you, my dear?' he said nervously.

'Yes.'

'I didn't see you at dinner.'

'I didn't want any dinner. The food would have choked me. I can't eat.'

'It's precisely the same with my pig,' said his lordship. 'Young Belford tells me —'

Into Angela's queenly disdain there flashed a sudden animation.

'Have you seen Jimmy? What did he say?'

'That's just what I can't remember. It began with the word "Pig" —'

'But after he had finished talking about you, I mean. Didn't he say anything about coming down here?'

'Not that I remember.'

'I expect you weren't listening. You've got a very annoying habit, Uncle Clarence,' said Angela maternally, 'of switching your mind off and just going blah when people are talking to you. It gets you very much disliked on all sides. Didn't Jimmy say anything about me?'

'I fancy so. Yes, I am nearly sure he did.'

'Well, what?'

'I cannot remember.'

There was a sharp clicking noise in the darkness. It was caused by Angela's upper front teeth meeting her lower front teeth; and was followed by a sort of wordless exclamation. It seemed only too plain that the love and respect which a niece should have for an uncle were in the present instance at a very low ebb.

'I wish you wouldn't do that,' said Lord Emsworth plaintively.

'Do what?'

'Make clicking noises at me.'

'I will make clicking noises at you. You know perfectly well, Uncle Clarence, that you are behaving like a bohunkus.'

'A what?'

'A bohunkus,' explained his niece coldly, 'is a very inferior sort of worm. Not the kind that you see on lawns, which you can respect, but a really degraded species.'

'I wish you would go in, my dear,' said Lord Emsworth. 'The night air may give you a chill.'

'I won't go in. I came out here to look at the moon and think of Jimmy. What are you doing out here, if it comes to that?'

'I came here to think. I am greatly exercised about my pig, Empress of Blandings. For two days she has refused her food, and young Belford says she will not eat until she hears the proper call or cry. He very kindly taught it to me, but unfortunately I have forgotten it.'

'I wonder you had the nerve to ask Jimmy to teach you pig-calls, considering the way you're treating him.'

'But —'

'Like a leper, or something. And all I can say is that, if you remember this call of his, and it makes the Empress eat, you ought to be ashamed of yourself if you still refuse to let me marry him.'

'My dear,' said Lord Emsworth earnestly, 'if through young Belford's instrumentality Empress of Blandings is induced to take nourishment once more, there is nothing I will refuse him – nothing.'

'Honour bright?'

'I give you my solemn word.'

'You won't let Aunt Constance bully you out of it?'

Lord Emsworth drew himself up.

'Certainly not,' he said proudly. 'I am always ready to listen to your Aunt Constance's views, but there are certain matters where I claim the right to act according to my own judgement.' He paused and stood musing. 'It began with the word "Pig" – '

From somewhere near at hand music made itself heard. The servants' hall, its day's labours ended, was refreshing itself with the housekeeper's gramophone. To Lord Emsworth the strains were merely an additional annoyance. He was not fond of music. It reminded him of his younger son Frederick, a flat but persevering songster both in and out of the bath.

'Yes, I can distinctly recall as much as that. Pig – Pig – '

'WHO – '

Lord Emsworth leaped in the air. It was as if an electric shock had been applied to his person.

'WHO stole my heart away?' howled the gramophone. 'WHO – ?'

The peace of the summer night was shattered by a triumphant shout.

'Pig-HOO-o-o-o-ey!'

A window opened. A large, bald head appeared. A dignified voice spoke.

'Who is there? Who is making that noise?'

'Beach!' cried Lord Emsworth. 'Come out here at once.'

'Very good, your lordship.'

And presently the beautiful night was made still more lovely by the added attraction of the butler's presence.

'Beach, listen to this.'

'Very good, your lordship.'

'Pig-hoo-o-o-o-ey!'

'Very good, your lordship.'

'Now, you do it.'

'I, your lordship?'

'Yes. It's a way you call pigs.'

'I do not call pigs, your lordship,' said the butler coldly.

'What do you want Beach to do it for?' asked Angela.

'Two heads are better than one. If we both learn it, it will not matter should I forget it again.'

'By jove, yes! Come on, Beach. Push it over the thorax,' urged the girl eagerly. 'You don't know it, but this is a matter of life and death. At-a-boy, Beach! Inflate the lungs and go to it.'

It had been the butler's intention, prefacing his remarks with the statement that he had been in service at the castle for eighteen years, to explain frigidly to Lord Emsworth that it was not his place to stand in the moonlight practising pig-calls. If, he would have gone on to add, his lordship saw the matter from a different angle, then it was his, Beach's, painful duty to tender his resignation, to become effective one month from that day.

But the intervention of Angela made this impossible to a man of chivalry and heart. A paternal fondness for the girl, dating from the days when he had stooped to enacting – and very convincingly, too, for his was a figure that lent itself to the impersonation – the role of a hippopotamus for her childish amusement, checked the words he would have uttered. She was looking at him with bright eyes, and even the rendering of pig-noises seemed a small sacrifice to make for her sake.

'Very good, your lordship,' he said in a low voice, his face pale and set in the moonlight. 'I shall endeavour to give satisfaction. I would merely advance the suggestion, your lordship, that we move a few steps farther away from the vicinity of the servants' hall. If I were to be overheard by any of the lower domestics, it would weaken my position as a disciplinary force.'

'What chumps we are!' cried Angela, inspired. 'The place to do it is outside the Empress's sty. Then, if it works, we'll see it working.'

Lord Emsworth found this a little abstruse, but after a moment he got it.

'Angela,' he said, 'you are a very intelligent girl. Where you get your brains from, I don't know. Not from my side of the family.'

The bijou residence of the Empress of Blandings looked very snug and attractive in the moonlight. But beneath even the beautiful things of life there is always an underlying sadness. This was supplied in the present instance by a long, low trough, only too plainly full to the brim of succulent mash and acorns. The fast, obviously, was still in progress.

The sty stood some considerable distance from the castle walls, so that there had been ample opportunity for Lord Emsworth to rehearse his little company during the journey. By the time they had ranged themselves against the rails, his two assistants were letter-perfect.

'Now,' said his lordship.

There floated out upon the summer night a strange composite sound that sent the birds roosting in the trees above shooting off their perches like rockets. Angela's clear soprano rang out like the voice of the village blacksmith's daughter. Lord Emsworth contributed a reedy tenor. And the bass notes of Beach probably did more to startle the birds than any other one item in the programme.

They paused and listened. Inside the Empress's boudoir there sounded the movement of a heavy body. There was an inquiring grunt. The next moment the sacking that covered the doorway was pushed aside, and the noble animal emerged.

'Now!' said Lord Emsworth again.

Once more that musical cry shattered the silence of the night. But it brought no responsive movement from Empress of Blandings. She stood there motionless, her nose elevated, her ears hanging down, her eyes everywhere but on the trough where, by rights, she should now have been digging in and getting hers. A chill disappointment crept over Lord Emsworth, to be succeeded by a gust of petulant anger.

'I might have known it,' he said bitterly. 'That young scoundrel was deceiving me. He was playing a joke on me.'

'He wasn't,' cried Angela indignantly. 'Was he, Beach?'

'Not knowing the circumstances, Miss, I cannot venture an opinion.'

'Well, why has it no effect?' demanded Lord Emsworth.

'You can't expect it to work right away. We've got her stirred up, haven't we? She's thinking it over, isn't she? Once more will do the trick. Ready, Beach?'

'Quite ready, miss.'

'Then when I say three. And this time, Uncle Clarence, do please for goodness' sake not yowl like you did before. It was enough to put any pig off. Let it come out quite easily and gracefully. Now, then. One, two – three!'

The echoes died away. And as they did so a voice spoke.

'Community singing?'

'Jimmy!' cried Angela, whisking round.

'Hullo, Angela. Hullo, Lord Emsworth. Hullo, Beach.'

'Good evening, sir. Happy to see you once more.'

'Thanks. I'm spending a few days at the Vicarage with my father. I got down here by the five-five.'

Lord Emsworth cut peevishly in upon these civilities.

'Young man,' he said, 'what do you mean by telling me that my pig would respond to that cry? It does nothing of the kind.'

'You can't have done it right.'

'I did it precisely as you instructed me. I had had, moreover, the assistance of Beach here and my niece Angela — '

'Let's hear a sample.'

Lord Emsworth cleared his throat. 'Pig-hoo-o-o-o-ey!'

James Belford shook his head.

'Nothing like it,' he said. 'You want to begin the "Hoo" in a low minor of two quarter notes in four-four time. From this build gradually to a higher note, until at last the voice is soaring in full crescendo, reaching F sharp on the natural scale and dwelling for two retarded half-notes, then breaking into a shower of accidental grace-notes.'

'God bless my soul!' said Lord Emsworth, appalled. 'I shall never be able to do it.'

'Jimmy will do it for you,' said Angela. 'Now that he's engaged to me, he'll be one of the family and always popping about here. He can do it every day till the show is over.'

James Belford nodded.

'I think that would be the wisest plan. It is doubtful if an amateur could ever produce real results. You need a voice that has been trained on the open prairie and that has gathered richness and strength from competing with tornadoes. You need a manly, wind-scorched voice with a suggestion in it of the crackling of corn husks and the whisper of evening breezes in the fodder. Like this!'

Resting his hands on the rail before him, James Belford swelled before their eyes like a young balloon. The muscles on his cheekbones stood out, his forehead became corrugated, his ears seemed to shimmer. Then, at the very height of the tension, he let it go like, as the poet beautifully puts it, the sound of a great Amen.

'Pig-HOOOOO-OOO-OOO-O-O-ey!'

They looked at him, awed. Slowly, fading off across hill and dale, the vast bellow died away. And suddenly, as it died, another, softer sound succeeded it. A sort of gulpy, gurgly, plobby, squishy, woffle-some sound, like a thousand eager men drinking soup in a foreign restaurant. And, as he heard it, Lord Emsworth uttered a cry of rapture.

The Empress was feeding.

The Fathers' Daughters

MURIEL SPARK

SHE LEFT THE OLD MAN IN HIS DECKCHAIR on the front, having first adjusted the umbrella awning with her own hand, and with her own hand, put his panama hat at a comfortable angle. The beach attendant had been sulky, but she didn't see why one should lay out tips only for adjusting an umbrella and a panama hat. Since the introduction of the new franc it was impossible to tip less than a franc. There seemed to be a conspiracy all along the coast to hide the lesser coins from the visitors, and one could only find franc pieces in one's purse, and one had to be careful not to embarrass Father, and one . . .

She hurried along the Rue Paradis, keeping in the hot shade, among all the old, old smells of Nice, not only garlic wafting from the cafés, and of the hot invisible air itself, but the smells from her memory, from thirty-five summers at Nice in apartments of long ago, Father's summer salon, Father's friends' children, Father's friends, writers, young artists dating back five years at Nice, six, nine years; and then, before the war, twenty years ago – when we were at Nice, do you remember, Father? Do you remember the pension on the Boulevard Victor Hugo when we were rather poor? Do you remember the Americans at the Negresco in 1937 – how changed, how demure they are now! Do you remember, Father, how in the old days we disliked the thick carpets – at least, you disliked them, and what you dislike, I dislike, isn't it so, Father?

Yes, Dora, we don't care for luxury. Comfort, yes, but luxury, no.

I doubt if we can afford to stay at an hotel on the front this year, Father.

What's that? What's that you say?

I said I doubt if we ought to stay on the front this year, Father; the Promenade des Anglais is becoming very trippery. Remember you disliked the thick carpets . . .

Yes, yes, of course.

Of course, and so we'll go, I suggest, to a little place I've found on the Boulevard Gambetta, and if we don't like that there's a very good place on the Boulevard Victor Hugo. Within our means, Father, modest and . . .

What's that you say?

I said it wasn't a vulgar place, Father.

Ah. No.

And so I'll just drop them a note and book a couple of bedrooms. They may be small, but the food . . .

Facing the sea, Dora.

They are all very vulgar places facing the sea, Father. Very distracting. No peace at all. Times have changed, you know.

Ah. Well, I leave it to you, dear. Tell them I desire a large room, suitable for entertaining. Spare no expense, Dora.

Oh, of course not, Father.

And I hope to God we've won the lottery, she thought, as she hurried up the little street to the lottery kiosk. Someone's got to win it out of the whole of France. The dark skinned blonde at the lottery kiosk took an interest in Dora, who came so regularly each morning rather than buy a newspaper to see the results. She leaned over the ticket, holding her card of numbers, comparing it with Dora's ticket, with an expression of earnest sympathy.

'No luck,' Dora said.

'Try again tomorrow,' said the woman. 'One never knows. Life is a lottery . . .'

Dora smiled as one who must either smile or weep. On her way back to the sea front she thought, tomorrow I will buy five hundred francs' worth. Then she thought, no, no, I'd better not, I may run short of francs and have to take Father home before time. Dora, the food here is inferior. – I know, Father, but it's the same everywhere in France now, times have changed. – I think we should move to another hotel, Dora. – The others are all very expensive, Father. – What's that? What's that you say? – There are no other rooms available, Father, because of the tourists, these days.

The brown legs of lovely young men and girls passed her as she approached the sea. I ought to appreciate every minute of this, she thought, it may be the last time. This thoroughly blue sea, these brown limbs, these white teeth and innocent inane tongues, these palm trees – all this is what we are paying for.

'Everything all right, Father?'

'Where have you been, dear?'

'Only for a walk round the back streets to smell the savours.'

'Dora, you are a chip off the old block. What did you see?'

'Brown limbs, white teeth, men in shirt sleeves behind café windows, playing cards with green bottles in front of them.'

'Good – you see everything with my eyes, Dora.'

'Heat, smell, brown legs – it's what we are paying for, Father.'

'Dora, you are becoming vulgar, if you don't mind my saying so. The eye of the true artist doesn't see life in the way of goods paid for. The world is ours. It is our birthright. We take it without payment.'

'I'm not an artist like you, Father. Let me move the umbrella – you mustn't get too much sun.'

'Times have changed,' he said, glancing along the pebble beach, 'the young men today have no interest in life.'

She knew what her father meant. All along the beach, the young men playing with the air, girls, the sun; they were coming in from the sea, shaking the water from their heads; they were walking over the pebbles, then splashing into the water; they were taking an interest in their environment with every pore of their skin, as Father would have said in younger days when he was writing his books. What he meant, now, when he said, 'the young men today have no interest in life' was that his young disciples, his admirers, had all gone, they were grown old and preoccupied, and had not been replaced. The last young man to seek out Father had been a bloodless-looking youth – not that one judged by appearances – who had called about seven years ago at their house in Essex. Father had made the most of him, giving up many of his mornings to sitting in the library talking about books with the young man, about life and the old days. But this, the last of Father's disciples, had left after two weeks with a promise to send them the article he was going to write about Father and his works. Indeed he had sent a letter: 'Dear Henry Castlemaine, – Words cannot express my admiration . . .' After that they had heard no more. Dora was not really sorry. He was a poor specimen compared with the men who, in earlier days, used to visit Father. Dora in her late teens could have married one of three or four vigorous members of the Henry Castlemaine set, but she had not done so because of her widowed father and his needs as a public figure; and now she sometimes felt it would have served Father better if she had married, because of Father – one could have contributed from a husband's income, perhaps, to his declining years.

Dora said, 'We must be going back to the hotel for lunch.'

'Let us lunch somewhere else. The food there is . . .'

She helped her father from the deck-chair and, turning to the sea, took a grateful breath of the warm blue breeze. A young man, coming up from the sea, shook his head blindly and splashed her with water; then noticing what he had done he said – turning and catching her by the arm – 'Oh, I'm so sorry.' He spoke in English, was an Englishman, and she knew already how unmistakably she was an Englishwoman. 'All right,' she said, with a quick little laugh. The father was fumbling with his stick, the incident had passed, was immediately forgotten by Dora as she took his arm and propelled him across the wide hot boulevard where the white-suited policemen held up the impetuous traffic. 'How would you like to be arrested by one of those, Dora?' He gave his deep short laugh and looked down at her. 'I'd love it, Father.' Perhaps he wouldn't insist on lunching elsewhere. If only they could reach the hotel, it would be all right; Father would be too exhausted to insist. But already he was saying, 'Let's find somewhere for lunch.'

'Well, we've paid for it at the hotel, Father.'

'Don't be vulgar, my love.'

In the following March, when Dora met Ben Donadieu for the first time, she had the feeling she had seen him somewhere before, she knew not where. Later, she told him of this, but he could not recall having seen her. But this sense of having seen him somewhere remained with Dora all her life. She came to believe she had met him in a former existence. In fact, it was on the beach at Nice that she had seen him, when he came up among the pebbles from the sea, and shook his hair, wetting her, and took her arm, apologizing.

'Don't be vulgar, my love. The hotel food is appalling. Not French at all.'

'It's the same all over France, Father, these days.'

There used to be a restaurant – what was its name? – in one of those little streets behind the Casino. Let's go there. All the writers go there.'

'Not any more, Father.'

'Well, so much the better. Let's go there in any case. What's the name of the place? – Anyway, come on, I could go there blindfold. All the writers used to go . . .'

She laughed, because, after all, he was sweet. As she walked with him towards the Casino she did not say – Not any more, Father, do the writers go there. The writers don't come to Nice, not those of moderate means. But there's one writer here this year, Father, called Kenneth Hope, whom you haven't heard about. He uses our beach, and I've seen him once – a shy, thin, middle-aged man. But he won't speak to anyone. He writes wonderfully, Father. I've read his novels, they open windows in the mind that have been bricked up for a hundred years. I have read *The Inventors*, which made great fame and fortune for him. It is about the inventors of patent gadgets, what lives they lead, how their minds apply themselves to invention and to love, and you would think, while you were reading *The Inventors*, that the place they live in was dominated by inventors. He has that magic, Father – he can make you believe anything. Dora did not say this, for her father had done great work too, and deserved a revival. His name was revered, his books were not greatly spoken of, they were not read. He would not understand the fame of Kenneth Hope. Father's novels were about the individual consciences of men and women, no one could do the individual conscience like Father. 'Here we are, Father – this is the place, isn't it?'

'No, Dora, it's further along.'

'Oh, but that's the Tumbril; it's wildly expensive.'

'Really, darling!'

She decided to plead the heat, and to order only a slice of melon for lunch with a glass of her father's wine. Both tall and slim, they entered the restaurant. Her hair was drawn back, the bones of her face were good, her eyes were small and fixed ready for humour, for she had decided to be a spinster and do it properly; she looked forty-six and she did not look forty-six; her skin was dry; her mouth was thin, and was growing thinner with the worry about money. The father looked eighty years old, as he was. Thirty years ago people used to turn round and say, as he passed, 'That's Henry Castlemaine.'

Ben lay on his stomach on his mattress on the beach enclosure. Carmelita Hope lay on her mattress, next to him. They were eating rolls and cheese and drinking white wine which the beach attendant had brought to them from the café. Carmelita's tan was like a perfect garment, drawn skin-tight over her body. Since leaving school she had been in numerous jobs behind the scenes of film and television studios. Now she was out of a job again. She thought of marrying

Ben, he was so entirely different from all the other men of her acquaintance, he was joyful and he was serious. He was also good looking; he was half French, brought up in England. And an interesting age, thirty-one. He was a school teacher, but Father could probably get him a job in advertising or publishing. Father could do a lot of things for them both if only he would exert himself. Perhaps if she got married he would exert himself.

'Did you see your father at all yesterday, Carmelita?'

'No; as a matter of fact he's driven up the coast. I think he's gone to stay at some villa on the Italian border.'

'I should like to see more of him,' said Ben. 'And have a talk with him. I've never really had a chance to have a talk with him.'

'He's awfully shy,' said Carmelita, 'with my friends.'

Sometimes she felt a stab of dissatisfaction when Ben talked about her father. Ben had read all his books through and through – that seemed rather obsessive to Carmelita, reading books a second time and a third, as if one's memory was defective. It seemed to her that Ben loved her only because she was Kenneth Hope's daughter, and then, again, it seemed to her that this couldn't be so, for Ben wasn't attracted by money and success. Carmelita knew lots of daughters of famous men, and they were beset by suitors who were keen on their fathers' money and success. But it was the books that Ben liked about her father.

'He never interferes with me,' she said. 'He's rather good that way.'

'I would like to have a long talk with him,' Ben said.

'What about? – He doesn't like talking about his work.'

'No, but a man like that. I would like to know his mind.'

'What about my mind?'

'You've got a lovely mind. Full of pleasant laziness. No guile.' He drew his forefinger from her knee to her ankle. She was wearing a pink bikini. She was very pretty and had hoped to become a starlet before her eighteenth birthday. Now she was very close to twenty-one and was thinking of marrying Ben instead, and was relieved that she no longer wanted to be an actress. He had lasted longer than any other boyfriend. She had often found a boy exciting at first but usually went off him quite soon. Ben was an intellectual, and intellectuals, say what you like, seemed to last longer than anyone else. There was more in them to find out about. One was always discovering new things – she supposed it was Father's blood in her that drew her towards the cultivated type, like Ben.

He was staying at a tiny hotel in a back street near the old quay. The entrance was dark, but the room itself was right at the top of the house, with a little balcony. Carmelita was staying with friends at a villa. She spent a lot of time in Ben's room, and sometimes slept there. It was turning out to be a remarkably happy summer.

'You won't see much of Father,' she said, 'if we get married. He works and sees nobody. When he doesn't write he goes away. Perhaps he'll get married again and —'

'That's all right,' he said, 'I don't want to marry your father.'

Dora Castlemaine had several diplomas for elocution which she had never put to use. She got a part-time job, after the Christmas holidays that year, in Basil Street Grammar School in London, and her job was to try to reform the more pronounced Cockney accents of the more promising boys into a near-standard English. Her father was amazed.

'Money, money, you are always talking about money. Let us run up debts. One is nobody without debts.'

'One's credit is limited, Father. Don't be an old goose.'

'Have you consulted Waite?' Waite was the publisher's young man who looked after the Castlemaine royalties, diminishing year by year.

'We've drawn more than our due for the present.'

'Well, it's a bore, you going out to teach.'

'It may be a bore to you,' she said at last, 'but it isn't for me.'

'Dora, do you really mean you want to go to this job in London?'

'Yes, I want to. I'm looking forward to it.'

He didn't believe her. But he said, 'I suppose I'm a bit of a burden on you, Dora, these days. Perhaps I ought to go off and die.'

'Like Oates at the South Pole,' Dora commented.

He looked at her and she looked at him. They were shrewd in their love for each other.

She was the only woman teacher in the school, with hardly the status of a teacher. She had her own corner of the common room and, anxious to reassure the men that she had no intention of intruding upon them, would, during free periods, spread out on the table one of the weekly journals and study it intently, only looking up to say good morning or good afternoon to the masters who came in with piles of exercise books under their arms. Dora had no exercise books to correct, she was something apart, a reformer of vowel sounds. One of the masters, and then another, made conversation with her during morning break, when she passed round the sugar for the coffee. Some were in their early thirties. The ginger-moustached science master was not long graduated from Cambridge. Nobody said to her, as intelligent young men had done as late as fifteen years ago, 'Are you any relation, Miss Castlemaine, to Henry Castlemaine the writer?'

Ben walked with Carmelita under the trees of Lincoln's Inn Fields in the spring of the year, after school, and watched the children at their games. They were a beautiful couple. Carmelita was doing secretarial work in the City. Her father was in Morocco, having first taken them out to dinner to celebrate their engagement.

Ben said, 'There's a woman at the school, teaching elocution.'

'Oh?' said Carmelita. She was jumpy, because since her father's departure for Morocco Ben had given a new turn to their relationship. He would not let her stay overnight in his flat in Bayswater, not even at the weekends. He said it would be nice, perhaps, to practise restraint until they were married in the summer, and that would give them something to look forward to. 'And I'm interested to see,' said Ben, 'what we mean to each other without sex.'

This made her understand how greatly she had become obsessed with him. She thought perhaps he was practising a form of cruelty to intensify her obsession. In fact, he did want to see what they meant to each other without sex.

She called at his flat unexpectedly and found him reading, with piles of other books set out on the table as if waiting to be read.

She accused him: You only want to get rid of me so that you can read your books.

'The fourth form is reading Trollope,' he explained, pointing to a novel of Trollope's among the pile.

'But you aren't studying Trollope just now.'

He had been reading a life of James Joyce. He banged it down and said, 'I've been reading all my life, and you won't stop me, Carmelita.'

She sat down. 'I don't want to stop you,' she said.

'I know,' he said.

'We aren't getting on at all well without sex,' she said, and on that occasion stayed the night.

He was writing an essay on her father. She wished that her father had taken more interest in it. Father had taken them out to dinner with his party face, smiling and boyish. Carmelita had seen him otherwise – in his acute dejection, when he seemed hardly able to endure the light of day.

'What's the matter, Father?'

'There's a comedy of errors going on inside me, Carmelita.' He sat at his desk most of the day while he was in these moods, doing nothing. Then, during the night, he would perhaps start writing, and sleep all the next morning, and gradually in the following days the weight would pass.

'There's a man on the phone wants you, Father – an interview.'

'Tell him I'm in the Middle East.'

'What did you think of Ben, Father?'

'A terribly nice man, Carmelita. You've made the right choice, I think.'

'An intellectual – I do like them best, you know.'

'I'd say he was the student type. Always will be.'

'He wants to write an essay about you, Father. He's absolutely mad about your books.'

'Yes.'

'I mean, couldn't you help him, Father? Couldn't you talk to him about your work, you know?'

'Oh, God, Carmelita. It would be easier to write the bloody essay myself.'

'All right, all right. I was only asking.'

'I don't want any disciples, Carmelita. They give me the creeps.'

'Yes, yes, all right. I know you're an artist, Father, there's no need to show off your temperament. I only wanted you to help Ben. I only . . .'

I only, she thought as she walked in Lincoln's Inn Fields with Ben, wanted him to help me. I should have said, 'I want you to talk more to Ben, to help me.' And Father would have said, 'How do you mean?' And I would have said, 'I don't know, quite.' And he would have said, 'Well, if you don't know what you mean, how the hell do I?'

Ben was saying, 'There's a woman at the school, teaching elocution.'

'Oh?' said Carmelita jumpily.

'A Miss Castlemaine. She's been there four months, and I only found out today that she's the daughter of Henry Castlemaine.'

'But he's dead!' said Carmelita.

'Well, I thought so too. But apparently he isn't dead, he's very much alive in a house in Essex.'

'How old is Miss Castlemaine?' said Carmelita.

'Middle-aged. Middle forties. Perhaps late forties. She's a nice woman, a classic English spinster. She teaches the boys to say "How now brown cow." You could imagine her doing wood-engravings in the Cotswolds. I only found out today —'

'You might manage to get invited to meet him, with any luck,' Carmelita said.

'Yes, she said I must come and see him, perhaps for a weekend. Miss Castlemaine is going to arrange it. She was awfully friendly when she found I was a Castlemaine admirer. A lot of people must think he's dead. Of course, his work belongs to a past world, but it's wonderful. Do you know *The Pebbled Shore?* – that's an early one.'

'No, but I've read *Sin of Substance*, I think. It —'

'You mean *The Sinner and the Substance*. Oh, it has fine things in it. Castlemaine's due for a revival.'

Carmelita felt a sharp stab of anger with her father, and then a kind of despair which was not as yet entirely familiar to her, although already she wondered if this was how Father felt in his great depressions when he sat all day, staring and enduring, and all night miraculously wrote the ache out of his system in prose of harsh merriment.

Helplessly, she said, 'Castlemaine's novels aren't as good as Father's, are they?'

'Oh, there's no comparison. Castlemaine is quite different. You can't say one type is *better* than another – goodness me!' He was looking academically towards the chimney stacks of Lincoln's Inn. This was the look in which she loved him most. After all, she thought, the Castlemaines might make everything easier for both of us.

'Father, it's really absurd. A difference of sixteen years . . . People will say —'

'Don't be vulgar, Dora dear. What does it matter what people say? Mere age makes no difference when there's a true affinity, a marriage of true minds.'

'Ben and I have a lot in common.'

'I know it,' he said, and sat a little higher in his chair.

'I shall be able to give up my job, Father, and spend my time here with you again. I never really wanted that job. And you are so much better in health now . . .'

'I know.'

'And Ben will be here in the evenings and the weekends. You get on well with Ben, don't you?'

'A remarkably fine man, Dora. He'll go far. He's perceptive.'

'He's keen to revive your work.'

'I know. He should give up that job, as I told him, and devote himself entirely to literary studies. A born essayist.'

'Oh, Father, he'll have to keep his job for the meantime, anyhow. We'll need the money. It will help us all; we —'

'What's that? What's that you say?'

'I said he finds work in the grammar school stimulating, Father.'

'Do you love the man?'

'It's difficult to say, at my age, Father.'

'To me, you both seem children. Do you love him?'

'I feel,' she said, 'that I have known him much longer than I have. Sometimes I think I've known him all my life. I'm sure we have met before, perhaps even in a former existence. That's the decisive factor. There's something of *destiny* about my marrying Ben; do you know what I mean?'

'Yes, I think I do.'

'He was engaged, last year for a short time, to marry quite a young girl,' she said. 'The daughter of a novelist called Kenneth Hope. Have you heard of him, Father?'

'Vaguely,' he said. 'Ben,' he said, 'is a born disciple.'

She looked at him and he looked at her, shrewd in their love for each other.

The Signalman

CHARLES DICKENS

'HALLOA! BELOW THERE!'

When he heard a voice thus calling to him, he was standing at the door of his box, with a flag in his hand, furled round its short pole. One would have thought, considering the nature of the ground, that he could not have doubted from what quarter the voice came; but, instead of looking up to where I stood on the top of the steep cutting nearly over his head, he turned himself about and looked down the Line. There was something remarkable in his manner of doing so, though I could not have said for my life, what. But, I know it was remarkable enough to attract my notice, even though his figure was foreshortened and shadowed, down in the deep trench, and mine was high above him, so steeped in the glow of an angry sunset that I had shaded my eyes with my hand before I saw him at all.

'Halloa! Below!'

From looking down the Line, he turned himself about again, and, raising his eyes, saw my figure high above him.

'Is there any path by which I can come down and speak to you?'

He looked up at me without replying, and I looked down at him without pressing him too soon with a repetition of my idle question. Just then, there came a vague vibration in the earth and air, quickly changing into a violent pulsation, and an oncoming rush that caused me to start back, as though it had force to draw me down. When such vapour as rose to my height from this rapid train, had passed me and was skimming away over the landscape, I looked down again, and saw him refurling the flag he had shown while the train went by.

I repeated my inquiry. After a pause, during which he seemed to regard me with fixed attention, he motioned with his rolled-up flag towards a point on my level, some two or three hundred yards distant. I called down to him, 'All right!' and made for that point. There, by dint of looking closely about me, I found a rough zigzag descending path notched out: which I followed.

The cutting was extremely deep, and unusually precipitate. It was made through a clammy stone that became oozier and wetter as I went down. For these reasons, I found the way long enough to give me time to recall a singular air of reluctance or compulsion with which he had pointed out the path.

When I came down low enough upon the zigzag descent, to see him again, I saw that he was standing between the rails on the way by which the train had lately passed, in an attitude as if he were waiting for me to appear. He had his left hand at his chin, and that left elbow rested on his right hand crossed over his breast. His attitude was one of such expectation and watchfulness, that I stopped a moment, wondering at it.

I resumed my downward way, and, stepping out upon the level of the railroad and drawing nearer to him, saw that he was a dark sallow man, with a dark beard and rather heavy eyebrows. His post was in as solitary and dismal a place as ever I saw. On either side, a dripping-wet wall of jagged stone, excluding all view but a strip of sky; the perspective one way, only a crooked prolongation of this great dungeon; the shorter perspective in the other direction, terminating in a gloomy red light, and the gloomier entrance to a black tunnel, in whose massive architecture there was a barbarous, depressing, and forbidding air. So little sunlight ever found its way to this spot, that it had an earthy deadly smell; and so much cold wind rushed through it, that it struck chill to me, as if I had left the natural world.

Before he stirred, I was near enough to him to have touched him. Not even then removing his eyes from mine, he stepped back one step, and lifted his hand.

This was a lonesome post to occupy (I said), and it had riveted my attention when I looked down from up yonder. A visitor was a rarity, I should suppose; not an unwelcome rarity, I hoped? In me, he merely saw a man who had been shut up within narrow limits all his life, and who, being at last set free, had a newly-awakened interest in these great works. To such purpose I spoke to him; but I am far from sure of the terms I used, for, besides that I am not happy in opening any conversation, there was something in the man that daunted me.

He directed a most curious look towards the red light near the tunnel's mouth, and looked all about it, as if something were missing from it, and then looked at me.

That light was part of his charge? Was it not?

He answered in a low voice: 'Don't you know it is?'

The monstrous thought came into my mind as I perused the fixed eyes and the saturnine face, that this was a spirit, not a man. I have speculated since, whether there may have been infection in his mind.

In my turn, I stepped back. But in making the action, I detected in his eyes some latent fear of me. This put the monstrous thought to flight.

'You look at me,' I said, forcing a smile, 'as if you had a dread of me.'

'I was doubtful,' he returned, 'whether I had seen you before.'

'Where?'

He pointed to the red light he had looked at.

'There?' I said.

Intently watchful of me, he replied (but without sound), Yes.

'My good fellow, what should I do there? However, be that as it may, I never was there, you may swear.'

'I think I may,' he rejoined. 'Yes. I am sure I may.'

His manner cleared, like my own. He replied to my remarks with readiness, and in well-chosen words. Had he much to do there? Yes; that was to say, he had enough responsibility to bear; but exactness and watchfulness were what was required of him, and of actual work – manual labour – he had next to none. To change that signal, to trim those lights, and to turn this iron handle now and then, was all he had to do under that head. Regarding those many long and lonely hours of which I seemed to make so much, he could only say that the routine of his life had shaped itself into that form, and he had grown used to it. He had taught himself a language down here – if only to know it by sight, and to have formed his own crude ideas of its pronunciation, could be called learning it. He had also worked at fractions and decimals, and tried a little algebra; but he was, and had been as a boy, a poor hand at figures. Was it necessary for him when on duty, always to remain in that channel of damp air, and could he never rise into the sunshine from between those high stone walls? Why, that depended upon times and circumstances. Under some conditions there would be less upon the Line than under others, and the same held good as to certain hours of the day and night. In bright weather, he did choose occasions for getting a little above these lower shadows; but, being at all times liable to be called by his electric bell, and at such times listening for it with redoubled anxiety, the relief was less than I would suppose.

He took me into his box, where there was a fire, a desk for an official book in which he had to make certain entries, a telegraphic instrument with its dial face and needles, and the little bell of which he had spoken. On my trusting that he would excuse the remark that had he been well educated, and (I hoped I might say without offence), perhaps educated above that station, he observed that instances of slight incongruity in such-wise would rarely be found wanting among large bodies of men; that he had heard it was so in workhouses, in the police force, even in that last desperate resource, the army; and that he knew it was so, more or less, in any great railway staff. He had been when young (if I could believe it, sitting in that hut; he scarcely could), a student of natural philosophy, and had attended lectures; but he had run wild, misused his opportunities, gone down, and never risen again. He had no complaint to offer about that. He had made his bed, and he lay upon it. It was far too late to make another.

All that I have here condensed, he said in a quiet manner, with his grave dark regards divided between me and the fire. He threw in the word 'Sir', from time to time, and especially when he referred to his youth: as though to request me to understand that he claimed to be nothing but what I found him. He was several times interrupted by the little bell, and had to read off messages, and send replies. Once, he had to stand without the door, and display a flag as a train passed, and make some verbal communication to the driver. In the discharge of his duties I observed him to be remarkably exact and vigilant, breaking off his discourse at a syllable, and remaining silent until what he had to do was done.

In a word, I should have set this man down as one of the safest of men to be employed in that capacity, but for the circumstance that while he was speaking to me he twice broke off with a fallen colour, turned his face towards the little bell when it did NOT ring, opened the door of the hut (which was kept shut to exclude the unhealthy damp), and looked out towards the red light near the mouth of the tunnel. On both of those occasions, he came back to the fire with the inexplicable air upon him which I had remarked, without being able to define, when we were so far asunder.

Said I when I rose to leave him: 'You almost make me think that I have met with a contented man.'

(I am afraid I must acknowledge that I said it to lead him on.)

'I believe I used to be so,' he rejoined, in the low voice in which he had first spoken; 'but I am troubled, sir, I am troubled.'

He would have recalled the words if he could. He had said them, however, and I took them up quickly.

'With what? What is your trouble?'

'It is very difficult to impart, sir. It is very, very difficult to speak of. If ever you make me another visit, I will try to tell you.'

'But I expressly intend to make you another visit. Say, when shall it be?'

'I go off early in the morning, and I shall be on again at ten tomorrow night, sir.'

'I will come at eleven.'

He thanked me, and went out at the door with me. 'I'll show my white light, sir,' he said, in his peculiar low voice, 'till you have found the way up. When you have found it, don't call out! And when you are at the top, don't call out!'

His manner seemed to make the place strike colder to me, but I said no more than 'Very well.'

'And when you come down tomorrow night, don't call out! Let me ask you a parting question. What made you cry "Halloa! Below there!" tonight?'

'Heaven knows,' said I. 'I cried something to that effect —'

'Not to that effect, sir. Those were the very words. I know them well.'

'Admit those were the very words. I said them, no doubt, because I saw you below.'

'For no other reason?'

'What other reason could I possibly have!'

'You have no feeling that they were conveyed to you in any supernatural way?'

'No.'

He wished me good night, and held up his light. I walked by the side of the down Line of rails (with a very disagreeable sensation of a train coming behind me), until I found the path. It was easier to mount than to descend, and I got back to my inn without any adventure.

Punctual to my appointment, I placed my foot on the first notch of the zigzag next night, as the distant clocks were striking eleven. He was waiting for me at the bottom, with his white light on. 'I have not called out,' I said, when we came close together; 'may I speak now?' 'By all means, sir.' 'Good night then, and here's my hand.' 'Good night, sir, and here's mine.' With that, we walked side by side to his box, entered it, closed the door, and sat down by the fire.

'I have made up my mind, sir,' he began, bending forward as soon as we were seated, and speaking in a tone but a little above a whisper, 'that you shall not have to ask me twice what troubles me. I took you for some one else yesterday evening. That troubles me.'

'That mistake?'

'No. That some one else.'

'Who is it?'

'I don't know.'

'Like me?'

'I don't know. I never saw the face. The left arm is across the face, and the right arm is waved. Violently waved. This way.'

I followed his action with my eyes, and it was the action of an arm gesticulating with the utmost passion and vehemence: 'For God's sake clear the way!'

'One moonlight night,' said the man, 'I was sitting here, when I heard a voice cry "Halloa! Below there!" I started up, looked from that door, and saw this Some one else standing by the red light near the tunnel, waving as I just showed you. The voice seemed hoarse with shouting, and it cried, "Look out! Look out!" And then again "Halloa! Below there! Look out!" I caught up my lamp, turned it on red, and ran towards the figure, calling, "What's wrong? What has happened? Where?" It stood just outside the blackness of the tunnel. I advanced so close upon it that I wondered at its keeping the sleeve across its eyes. I ran right up at it, and had my hand stretched out to pull the sleeve away, when it was gone.'

'Into the tunnel,' said I.

'No. I ran on into the tunnel, five hundred yards. I stopped and held my lamp above my head, and saw the figures of the measured distance, and saw the wet stains stealing down the walls and trickling through the arch. I ran out again, faster than I had run in (for I had a mortal abhorrence of the place upon me), and I looked all round the red light with my own red light, and I went up the iron ladder to the gallery atop of it, and I came down again, and ran back here. I telegraphed both ways: "An alarm has been given. Is anything wrong?" The answer came back, both ways: "All well."'

Resisting the slow touch of a frozen finger tracing out my spine,

I showed him how that this figure must be a deception of his sense of sight, and how that figures, originating in disease of the delicate nerves that minister to the function of the eye, were known to have often troubled patients, some of whom had become conscious of the nature of their affliction, and had even proved it by experiments upon themselves. 'As to an imaginary cry,' said I, 'do but listen for a moment to the wind in this unnatural valley while we speak so low, and to the wild harp it makes of the telegraph wires!'

That was all very well, he returned, after we had sat listening for a while, he who so often passed long winter nights there, alone and watching. But he would beg to remark that he had not finished.

I asked his pardon, and he slowly added these words, touching my arm:

'Within six hours after the Appearance, the memorable accident on this Line happened, and within ten hours the dead and wounded were brought along through the tunnel over the spot where the figure had stood.'

A disagreeable shudder crept over me, but I did my best against it. It was not to be denied, I rejoined, that this was a remarkable coincidence, calculated deeply to impress his mind. But, it was unquestionable that remarkable coincidences did continually occur, and they must be taken into account in dealing with such a subject. Though to be sure I must admit, I added (for I thought I saw that he was going to bring the objection to bear upon me), men of common sense did not allow much for coincidences in making the ordinary calculations of life.

He again begged to remark that he had not finished.

I again begged his pardon for being betrayed into interruptions.

'This,' he said, again laying his hand upon my arm, and glancing over his shoulder with hollow eyes, 'was just a year ago. Six or seven months passed, and I had recovered from the surprise and shock, when one morning, as the day was breaking, I, standing at that door, looked towards the red light, and saw the spectre again.' He stopped, with a fixed look at me.

'Did it cry out?'

'No. It was silent.'

'Did it wave its arm?'

'No. It leaned against the shaft of the light, with both hands before the face. Like this.'

Once more, I followed his action with my eyes. It was an action of mourning. I have seen such an attitude in stone figures on tombs.

'Did you go up to it?'

'I came in and sat down, partly to collect my thoughts, partly because it had turned me faint. When I went to the door again, daylight was above me, and the ghost was gone.'

'But nothing followed? Nothing came of this?'

He touched me on the arm with his forefinger twice or thrice, giving a ghastly nod each time:

'That very day, as a train came out of the tunnel, I noticed, at a carriage window on my side, what looked like a confusion of hands and heads, and something waved. I saw it, just in time to signal the driver, Stop! He shut off, and put his brake on, but the train drifted past here a hundred and fifty yards or more. I ran after it, and, as I went along, heard terrible screams and cries. A beautiful young lady had died instantaneously in one of the compartments, and was brought in here, and laid down on this floor between us.'

Involuntarily, I pushed my chair back, as I looked from the boards at which he pointed, to himself.

'True, sir. True. Precisely as it happened, so I tell it you.'

I could think of nothing to say, to any purpose, and my mouth was very dry. The wind and the wires took up the story with a long lamenting wail.

He resumed. 'Now, sir, mark this, and judge how my mind is troubled. The spectre came back, a week ago. Ever since, it has been there, now and again, by fits and starts.'

'At the light?'

'At the Danger-light.'

'What does it seem to do?'

He repeated, if possible with increased passion and vehemence, that former gesticulation of 'For God's sake clear the way!'

Then, he went on. 'I have no peace or rest for it. It calls to me, for many minutes together, in an agonized manner, "Below there! Look out! Look out!" It stands waving to me. It rings my little bell —'

I caught at that. 'Did it ring your bell yesterday evening when I was here, and you went to the door?'

'Twice.'

'Why, see,' said I, 'how your imagination misleads you. My eyes were on the bell, and my ears were open to the bell, and if I am a living man, it did NOT ring at those times. No, nor at any other time, except when it was rung in the natural course of physical things by the station communicating with you.'

He shook his head. 'I have never made a mistake as to that, yet, sir. I have never confused the spectre's ring with the man's. The ghost's ring is a strange vibration in the bell that it derives from nothing else, and I have not asserted that the bell stirs to the eye. I don't wonder that you have failed to hear it. But *I* heard it.'

'And did the spectre seem to be there, when you looked out?'

'It WAS there.'

'Both times?'

He repeated firmly: 'Both times.'

'Will you come to the door with me, and look for it now?'

He bit his underlip as though he were somewhat unwilling, but arose. I opened the door, and stood on the step, while he stood in the doorway. There, was the Danger-light. There, was the dismal mouth of the tunnel. There, were the high wet stone walls of the cutting. There, were the stars above them.

'Do you see it?' I asked him, taking particular note of his face. His eyes were prominent and strained; but not very much more so, perhaps, than my own had been when I had directed them earnestly towards the same spot.

'No,' he answered. 'It is not there.'

'Agreed,' said I.

We went in again, shut the door, and resumed our seats. I was thinking how best to improve this advantage, if it might be called one, when he took up the conversation in such a matter of course way, so assuming that there could be no serious question of fact between us, that I felt myself in the weakest of positions.

'By this time you will fully understand, sir,' he said, 'that what troubles me so dreadfully, is the question, What does the spectre mean?'

I was not sure, I told him, that I did fully understand.

'What is its warning against?' he said, ruminating, with his eyes on the fire, and only by times turning them on me. 'What is the danger? Where is the danger? There is danger overhanging, some-where on the Line. Some dreadful calamity will happen. It is not to be doubted this third time, after what has gone before. But surely this is a cruel haunting of *me*. What can *I* do!'

He pulled out his handkerchief, and wiped the drops from his heated forehead.

'If I telegraph Danger, on either side of me, or on both, I can give no reason for it,' he went on, wiping the palms of his hands. 'I should get into trouble, and do no good. They would think I was mad. This is the way it would work: Message: "Danger! Take care!" Answer: "What Danger! Where?" Message: "Don't know. But for God's sake take care!" They would displace me. What else could they do?'

His pain of mind was most pitiable to see. It was the mental torture of a conscientious man, oppressed beyond endurance by an unintelligible responsibility involving life.

'When it first stood under the Danger-light,' he went on, putting his dark hair back from his head, and drawing his hands outward across and across his temples in an extremity of feverish distress, 'why not tell me where that accident was to happen – if it must happen? Why not tell me how it could be averted – if it could have been averted? When on its second coming it hid its face, why not tell me instead: "She is going to die. Let them keep her at home"? If it came, on those two occasions, only to show me that its warnings were true, and so to prepare me for the third, why not warn me plainly now? And I, Lord help me! A mere poor signalman on this solitary station! Why not go to somebody with credit to be believed, and power to act!'

When I saw him in this state, I saw that for the poor man's sake, as well as for the public safety, what I had to do for the time was, to compose his mind. Therefore, setting aside all question of reality or unreality between us, I represented to him that whoever thoroughly discharged his duty, must do well, and that at least it was his comfort that he understood his duty, though he did not understand these confounding Appearances. In this effort I succeeded far better than in an attempt to reason him out of his conviction. He became calm; the occupations incidental to his post as the night advanced, began to make large demands on his attention; and I left him at two in the morning. I had offered to stay through the night, but he would not hear of it.

That I more than once looked back at the red light as I ascended the pathway, that I did not like the red light, and that I should have slept but poorly if my bed had been under it, I see no reason to conceal. Nor, did I like the two sequences of the accident and the dead girl. I see no reason to conceal that, either.

But, what ran most in my thoughts was the consideration how ought I to act, having become the recipient of this disclosure? I had proved the man to be intelligent, vigilant, painstaking, and exact; but how long might he remain so, in his state of mind? Though in a subordinate position, still he held a most important trust, and would I (for instance) like to stake my own life on the chances of his continuing to execute it with precision?

Unable to overcome a feeling that there would be something treacherous in my communicating what he had told me, to his superiors in the Company, without first being plain with himself and proposing a middle course to him, I ultimately resolved to offer to accompany him (otherwise keeping his secret for the present) to the wisest medical practitioner we could hear of in those parts, and to take his opinion. A change in his time of duty would come round next night, he had apprised me, and he would be off an hour or two after sunrise, and on again soon after sunset. I had appointed to return accordingly.

Next evening was a lovely evening, and I walked out early to enjoy it. The sun was not yet quite down when I traversed the field path near the top of the deep cutting. I would extend my walk for an hour, I said to myself, half an hour on and half an hour back, and it would then be time to go to my signalman's box.

Before pursuing my stroll, I stepped to the brink, and mechanically looked down, from the point from which I had first seen him. I cannot describe the thrill that seized upon me, when, close at the mouth of the tunnel, I saw the appearance of a man, with his left sleeve across his eyes, passionately waving his right arm.

The nameless horror that oppressed me, passed in a moment, for in a moment I saw this appearance of a man was a man indeed, and that there was a little group of other men standing at a short distance, to whom he seemed to be rehearsing the gesture he made. The Danger-light was not yet lighted. Against its shaft, a little low hut, entirely new to me, had been made of some wooden supports and tarpaulin. It looked no bigger than a bed.

With an irresistible sense that something was wrong – with a flashing self-reproachful fear that fatal mischief had come of my leaving the man there, and causing no one to be sent to overlook or correct what he did – I descended the notched path with all the speed I could make.

'What is the matter?' I asked the men.

'Signalman killed this morning, sir.'

'Not the man belonging to that box?'

'Yes, sir.'

'Not the man I know?'

'You will recognize him, sir, if you knew him,' said the man who spoke for the others, solemnly uncovering his own head and raising an end of the tarpaulin, 'for his face is quite composed.'

'O! how did this happen, how did this happen?' I asked, turning from one to another as the hut closed in again.

'He was cut down by an engine, sir. No man in England knew his work better. But somehow he was not clear of the outer rail. It was just at broad day. He had struck the light, and had the lamp in his hand. As the engine came out of the tunnel, his back was towards her, and she cut him down. That man drove her, and was showing how it happened. Show the gentleman, Tom.'

The man, who wore a rough dark dress, stepped back to his former place at the mouth of the tunnel.

'Coming round the curve in the tunnel, sir,' he said, 'I saw him at the end, like as if I saw him down a perspective-glass. There was no time to check speed, and I knew him to be very careful. As he didn't seem to take heed of the whistle, I shut it off when we were running down upon him, and called to him as loud as I could call.'

'What did you say?'

'I said, Below there! Look out! Look out! For God's sake clear the way!'

I started.

'Ah! it was a dreadful time, sir. I never left off calling to him. I put this arm before my eyes, not to see, and I waved this arm to the last; but it was no use.'

Without prolonging the narrative to dwell on any one of its curious circumstances more than on any other, I may, in closing it, point out the coincidence that the warning of the Engine-Driver included, not only the words which the unfortunate Signalman had repeated to me as haunting him, but also the words which I myself – not he – had attached, and that only in my own mind, to the gesticulation he had imitated.

Doctor Zeit

ANTONIA FRASER

'I'M BEING PURSUED BY THIS FACE,' she thought. 'This old face. I'm frightened. I'll have to do something.'

The first time Nola saw the face she was in the underground, on the moving stairs coming up to the Tottenham Court Road. The last leg of the journey. Nola always felt like a seal coming up for air at Tottenham Court Road tube with its double staircase. She began to breathe deeply as she reached the top. Nola was not particularly strong and she felt she needed all the air she could get before she reached the British Museum, and the somewhat airless atmosphere of its Reading Room.

Nola had been working for the past two years on a study of seventeenth-century family life. She still had a long way to go. From time to time she told her publisher, lightly, that twentieth-century family life came first. Which meant the house in Islington with the lovely wooden polished floors, kitchen often full of healthy foods, large country-style garden – all of them rivals for her attention with the British Museum.

And, of course, there were Denis and Johnnie. Denis was Nola's husband and Johnnie was her son. To Nola, privately, they were the perfect family unit. She had no wish for another child. Denis protected Nola – he was much older than her – and Nola protected Johnnie. Indeed, when she thought about Johnnie's small but perfectly male body, Nola imagined that she felt the same joy that Denis often told her he felt in her youth, her beauty (because of the difference in their ages, he said, to him she would always look young, no matter how the years passed).

On her route to and from the British Museum, Nola's favourite thoughts were of the two of them. She was meditating on Johnnie and how perfect he was, and how in a way she wished he could stay five years old forever, so gay, so ebullient, so amusing, so much her little boy . . . when she felt a slight tug on her long skirt. Nola turned round. The staircase was not particularly crowded – it was after ten o'clock and the workers had vanished to their offices. Several steps below her a woman with a very old face was smiling at her. At least Nola thought at the time that she was a woman, but she was so very old, judging from her face at least, that she had already reached that stage of asexuality of appearance which makes it difficult to tell the inhabitants of male and female geriatric wards apart.

Nola had certainly never seen the woman before in her life. Nola presumed therefore that she had dropped something. But her bag was standing neatly intact on the step above her. She checked it, looked round again, missed the old woman completely, found the top of the staircase claiming her attention, searched for her ticket and forgot the incident.

The second time that Nola saw the face, it was definitely on a man. On him – that was how she instinctively put it to herself because despite the fact that the face was exactly the same as the previous face, old, really old, seamily wrinkled flesh hanging round the jowls, wispy hair, she got the odd impression that she was not seeing the same person so much as the same face.

On this occasion she saw the face and its bearer standing on the platform of Tottenham Court Road tube station as her train drew in. She had a quick uncomfortable flash of recognition and the face – the man rather – seemed to feel likewise because he gave a little salute with his hand. The other hand held a stick. When Nola got off the train, he was gone. He had presumably entered the train elsewhere where it was less crowded.

The third occasion she saw the face was more disturbing. It was Johnnie's half term. Nola had a choice of staying at home with him or taking him along with her, since Denis was, of course, at the office. She decided to take him on a visit to the British Museum. Not into the Reading Room, of course; that was out of the question, perish the thought of introducing rumbustious Johnnie into such a sanctum even if it had been permitted. But she did think it would be rather pleasant to show Johnnie some of the sights, the Elgin Marbles, vast sphinxes, statues, the sort of thing that an intelligent five year old would find quite stimulating to the imagination without precisely understanding them. And she would point to the door of the Reading Room, perhaps, and call it 'Mum's office'. Johnnie knew about offices. He had visited Denis' office on several occasions. When Denis returned in the evening, Johnnie used to chant: 'Backfromtheoffice' as if it was all one word. They set off early so as to be back for Johnnie's lunch.

But Johnnie and Nola never got as far as the British Museum. At Tottenham Court Road station ('This is where Mum comes to work in the morning'), the most awful thing happened. Johnnie disappeared. One moment he was holding Nola's hand, the next moment there was a sharp tug and he was gone. Through the pressing crowd, he vanished completely. Nola was distraught, sick with fear.

'Johnnie, Johnnie,' she screamed, turning round and trying to battle her way against the incoming crowd.

She struggled back finally onto the platform from whence they had come. And saw two things. Johnnie, tearful, holding the hand of a black Underground Inspector, who was bending down and trying to comfort him. For a split second she also saw that face, that old face. She would know it anywhere. But this time on quite a young and sturdy body: she had the impression of jeans, a tee-shirt. The man, woman, whatever it was, smiled and vanished down the far exit to the other line.

Johnnie, sobbing, seemed to expect Nola to punish him. In self-defence he talked of a horrible old man with a nasty smell pulling him away.

'I couldn't help it. He was much stronger than me,' he kept saying.

'Darling, we're going straight home,' was all Nola could bring herself to reply.

When she told Denis about it in the evening – an edited version not mentioning the previous encounters with the face – he said quite sharply:

'Wasn't it rather silly to take a kid to the BM in the first place? I mean, you can go there as much as you like when he's at school. I shouldn't think it would have been quite his cup of tea if you had got there. He's still at the playground stage if you ask me.'

Nola, feeling guilty, forbore to mention her plan of showing the door of 'Mum's office'. Denis was right. Johnnie had not yet reached the sightseeing stage: she was the one who did not want him to grow up too fast, and now she was trying to force the pace.

The fourth, fifth and sixth times Nola saw the face were in and around Islington when she was shopping or on her way to fetch Johnnie from school. On each occasion the face smiled at her. Johnnie was right: it was definitely an old man. The impression of a youthful body and jeans that day must have been part of her general distraction at losing the child. The truth was, she told herself, that he was just a rather mad old man who happened to live in Islington and filled in the time leering at young women . . . Perfectly harmless if unpleasant. Nola pulled herself up: not *totally* harmless, if her theory was correct. The old man had tried to kidnap Johnnie. No, that was really going much too far in the other direction. Kidnap was far too strong a word. Denis had been quite right when he pointed out that Johnnie was only a child, had been known to wriggle his hand free under other circumstances.

'Probably just didn't want to go to the BM,' said Denis with a smile. He worried a little all the same – not about Johnnie but about Nola. Nola, of all the women he knew, was the most conscientious mother. And wife. And then there was her book. And her health. Health, which was never strong and could too easily lead to nervousness and collapse if Nola overstretched herself. However, Denis and Nola had agreed long ago when they first married never to refer to Nola's condition and to live their lives exactly as if it did not exist. So Denis decided to say nothing more on this occasion, only to watch Nola more carefully in future. At least he could try and see that she did not overdo the British Museum stuff.

But, of course, Nola's projected book had to have its place in her life, along with the house and the garden and the creative kitchen and Denis and Johnnie. The idea had originated as a post-graduate thesis suggested by Nola's tutor, who had a high opinion of her work. It was a task to which marriage to Denis and the birth of Johnnie put an end. Only temporarily, however. Nola got back to it once Johnnie went to nursery school. And it was really much more fun doing it in terms of a proper book, being her own mistress as it were, without the inevitable restraints of the structure of a thesis. Besides which she no longer needed a grant to support herself while working on it.

'You're my grant,' she told Denis. 'And a very nice grant too.'

If Nola's progress was slow – school holidays were an interruption – at least it was steady. And she never found any difficulty in picking up her work again where she had left off: the mere entry into the atmosphere of the Reading Room, airless as it might be, transported her. It was in its own way like a Secret Garden to which Nola – and admittedly five hundred others – had the key.

So it was fantastically upsetting one morning, as she arrived later than her schedule, to see the face, sitting three along from the seat she usually occupied. Not in her seat, thank God, that would have been too much; might have persuaded her she was seeing an apparition, a sort of doppelganger, an aged version of herself – but she wasn't seeing an apparition, she knew that. This old woman – and she was definitely a woman this time – was real. What was more, as Nola flung down her bag on her seat, the woman with the old face got up and shuffled off in the direction of the North Library. The old face did not smile, Nola noticed, there was a nasty set grumpy look about it, the mouth above the hanging dewlaps. On the whole, however, Nola preferred this air of crossness even anger to the original leer. Besides which the old woman had left her books behind on the table. Nola could see them lying there.

Now was her chance to find out a little more about her pursuer. With a feeling of determination, Nola strode down the row of desks and picked up the book lying open. She nearly dropped it with surprise. It was Levin Schucking's *Puritan Family*. It was a comparatively new book which had come out since Nola began working on her subject and Nola had made quite a bit of use of it herself. She did not know why she was so surprised at the sight of it on the old woman's desk. It was a most disagreeable sensation.

Still more disagreeable, was the discovery that the other four books on the desk were all pertaining to the subject of women and marriage in the seventeenth-century – or as you might put it, seventeenth-century family life. Some of them were quite obscure.

Nola took a decision. She put in a slip for Schucking's book, and duly got her slip returned with the scribbled information on the back that it was 'Out to another reader': she could not quite read it but the name looked like Zett. Nola went to the centre desk and explained her problem.

'The old lady who has it out was sitting quite close to me as a matter of fact. But she went out an hour ago and hasn't returned. So I wondered if I could just check something . . .'

'Name?' said the man behind the desk with professional politeness but without interest.

'Zett, it looks like, or Zelt.'

The man's face clouded.

'Oh dear. Old Mrs Zeit. Or rather Frau Doktor Zeit as she prefers to be called. Oh dear. Well, I'll see what I can do when she comes back.'

'Is she – er?' Nola pursued delicately, prompting, not finishing the sentence. The man grinned and raised his eyebrows. She saw that he was quite young.

'Shall we say that she's a little difficult?' he said. 'We get them in here. Delusions of persecution. Probably a refugee from somewhere. She thinks everyone is trying to steal her researches from her before she can write her book – '

'And her book is on – ?'

The young man took thought.

'Seventeenth-century family life,' he answered. 'Something like that.'

He was surprised when Nola, who had seemed such a pleasant person, turned on her heel abruptly and marched out of the Reading Room. Actually Nola was going to the Ladies because she felt dizzy. And when she came back she just collected her bag and left. Frau Doktor Zeit was not there. All the same, she knew she could not do any work that day.

This was the point at which Nola thought: 'I'm being pursued by this face. This old face. I'm frightened. I shall have to do something.'

She told Denis that she had discovered an old woman in the Reading Room who was working on exactly the same subject as herself – and for a book, too; she felt that it was a catastrophe. That was as far as Nola could bring herself to relate recent events for the time being. If Denis were sympathetic – and she knew he would be – she could probably nerve herself to discuss the face itself thereafter.

'Don't go to the British Museum, darling, for a bit,' said Denis immediately. 'You've had a shock. I can see that. Not that some old crone is really going to write a book and steal your thunder. Not a chance. Your book will be terrific when it comes out, never fear. But the truth is you've been overdoing it lately. A rest – here at home – will freshen you up. Work twice as hard when you get back to it.'

'I've got so much to get through,' Nola began rather desperately. Denis soothed her. 'Darling, I know.'

'But the time's passing – '

'There's plenty of time. For one thing Johnnie won't be a baby forever. He won't need fetching and carrying from school forever.'

'And I suppose you're going to grow out of needing a hot dinner at night,' said Nola wryly.

'Exactly,' Denis beamed. 'My teeth will soon fall out. Then I shan't be able to eat anything but cereal. That means you won't have to cook at all.'

Nola looked worried again. 'Don't talk like that,' she begged. 'On top of everything else. You know I can't bear to think of you getting old.'

It was the solitary hang-up she had about the disparity in their ages. She could not bear a mention of such things, even a light reflexion like the fact that Denis would be sixty-five and retiring when Johnnie was twenty one and going out to work, caused her to shiver.

'Now Nola,' said Denis, taking her in his arms. 'You really are out to upset yourself, aren't you? As for me, I'm in the pink of health. I had the firm's annual medical check-up today. I forgot to tell you with all this going on. I'm A1. OK the doctor told me. The physique of a young man. Not so the doctor himself, I must say. Talking of the old, this was the oldest fellow I have ever seen. I thought I must have made a mistake when I stepped into the consulting room. He looked just like a tortoise.'

'A man with a very old face?' Nola asked carefully, after a pause.

'That's right. He might have been Methuselah himself. But he gave me a clean bill of health. Wait a moment, darling. I'm crazy. You *know* him. When I said goodbye, he asked me to give you his love. You and Johnnie. But especially you. He's an Austrian. Doctor Zeit, I think his name was – Why darling.'

As Denis held Nola, he felt her go slack and heavy in his arms. She had fainted.

'It was nothing,' said Nola a minute later when she found herself sitting on the sofa. 'Just one of my turns. Don't fuss me. You promised.' She saw Denis' anxious face leaning over her and went on: 'Don't *worry* . . .' It was like when they were first married. Her one concern was to reassure him about her.

But Denis did worry. Despite Nola's protests, he insisted on putting her to bed for the rest of the evening. In return, he promised not to fuss her too much the next day.

Nevertheless, Nola did not even try to go to the British Museum. She did not feel up to it. And she kept Johnnie at home, too, although Denis did not know that till later. He generally left for the office before Johnnie went to school. All the same Nola was determined not to waste the day entirely. She pondered between the rival claims of kitchen and garden. A day cooking for the deep freeze? Or a day really tidying up the garden before the onset of winter? In the end the garden won, because Nola had to admit that the garden was showing signs of positive neglect whereas the kitchen wasn't. When Denis telephoned her later that morning, ostensibly to consult her about an invitation, Nola told him:

'By the way, I'm clearing up the garden. It's rather fun.'

'Just the ticket.' Denis managed to sound delighted. 'It's a beautiful day for it too. I walked half the way to the office.'

Nola dug a little, created a pile of rubbish and finally went indoors with the laudable intention of doing to the airing cupboard what she had just done for the garden. She was upstairs on a ladder, reaching for the back of the cupboard when she heard the front door bell ring. Nola hesitated and looked at Johnnie.

'Johnnie, could you?'

''Course I could,' he said contemptuously. Later Johnnie shouted something up the stairs about the garden. Nola was rather puzzled. She ought really to go down – but Johnnie had panted back up the stairs again.

'Daddy sent someone to do the garden for you. So I let him through the back door,' he said importantly.

'Oh I see.' Nola was taken aback and suddenly rather chilled. Hadn't she been going to do the garden herself? Denis was treating her like a baby again, not wanting her to strain herself.

Presently Nola looked out of the window and saw the gardener's back. He was wearing jeans and to her surprise he appeared to be wielding a scythe. She looked again. Yes, it was definitely a scythe. In their garden and at this time of year! What was Denis thinking of?

Johnnie was in his room, playing with his little cars in the window seat. Nola gave him a quick glance and then clattered down the stairs and into the garden.

'Excuse me,' she said in a voice of authority. 'What are you doing with that scythe?' The young man stood up and turned round. He was still holding his scythe as he moved towards Nola. His voice was quite young and musical when he replied:

'I'm caring for your garden. Don't worry. I shall be here to care for it after you are gone.'

But his face was an old face, a familiar face.

Johnnie, looking out of the window, saw his mother fall down and lie still. Later he described to his father exactly the man who had come to do the garden, the man with the scythe, in jeans, but a man with a terribly old face. He told his father that the man with the terribly old face had cut down his mother with his scythe. But that was nonsense, of course; a child's reaction to shock. There was not a mark on Nola's body.

Identity Crisis

MICHAEL FRAYN

'THIS IS MR GOLDWASSER, YOUR Majesty,' said Riddle, as Nobbs shook hands with Haugh.

'No, no, no,' smiled Mrs Plushkov with exasperating patience. 'That's not Goldwasser, Riddle. That's Riddle.'

'For crying out loud,' snarled Riddle. 'He *can't* be. Goldwasser's Riddle.'

'But my dear Riddle, you forget that Riddle is Plushkov.'

Everyone was standing in the lobby, glaring at each other, or leaning hopelessly against the walls and staring dully at the floor. The whole staff of the Institute was tired and cross. They had been in the corridors all week, rehearsing for the Official Opening, and they all had that dreary, crushed feeling in their intestines that comes from standing around for a long time without knowing exactly what one is supposed to be doing.

What they were trying to do was to time the various sections of the visit against a stop watch, since the Coordinating Committee was advised by the Sub Committee on Timing that these occasions always had to be rehearsed down to the last second. But it was not easy. The 'Balmoral' scissors, the jewelled switch, the gas fired golden taper, and all the rest of the equipment had not yet arrived from the Empire Ceremonial Supply Company, and there was still no apparatus of any sort in the new wing itself. The missing links were replaced by a variety of more or less unsatisfactory substitutes and hypotheses, as were all the official guests whose hands would have to be shaken on the day, and one or two of the senior staff, like Nunn and Macintosh, who were impressive enough not to be argued with when they said they were too busy to attend. So, for the sake of rehearsals, Rowe was Vulgurian, Riddle was Nunn, and Goldwasser was Macintosh, which meant that Plushkov had to be Riddle and Haugh Goldwasser.

No, Riddle had to be Goldwasser, and . . . or was it Rowe who was Goldwasser?

The only point on which everyone was clear was that the principle deficiency, the Queen herself, was being supplied by Nobbs. He was not an ideal surrogate sovereign, or even a willing one, but when the Joint Committee for Understudying had appealed to Heads of Departments to spare someone for the job, Goldwasser had spared Nobbs before anyone else could think.

Now Goldwasser was regretting his generosity. It was bad enough to have Nobbs about the laboratory all day, humping his resentful bag of ill-articulated bones back and forth, catching the corners of desks with his thighs and knocking them slightly out of line. But to spend his days shaking Nobbs's limp hand over and over again, and calling him 'Ma'am', was less agreeable still. As the rehearsals wore on, Goldwasser became increasingly concerned about the hand's remarkable limpness. So far as Goldwasser could tell, it was not exactly a natural limpness. Nobbs kept his hand limp when he shook hands because he had read that the firm grasp he had affected as an adolescent to create the impression of strong character was merely an affectation designed to create the impression of a strong character. But then Nobbs wore a beard because he had read that since it was generally believed that only men with weak chins wore beards, no one with a weak chin would wear a beard for fear of being thought to have a weak chin; therefore, it could be deduced that anyone who wore a beard had in fact a strong chin; and in this way Nobbs grew a beard to hide his weak chin. Or so Goldwasser believed. Altogether there was something about Nobbs that was two-faced – or not so much two-faced as three-faced, with one face watching the other two.

'Let's go right back to the beginning,' said Mrs Plushkov. 'Opening positions, please, everyone.'

There was a weary groan. Goldwasser felt his crushed intestines pack down a little farther.

'Jellicoe,' said Mrs Plushkov to the janitor as they all trooped outside into the forecourt, 'don't slam the car door this time until Nobbs is well clear of it. Remember, you've got seven seconds before she – he – Nobbs is supposed to be on his feet on the pavement. Now, is One ready? Let's take it from – *now*.'

Jellicoe stepped forward and opened an imaginary car door. Nobbs lurched out of the imaginary car.

'Steady, Nobbs,' said Mrs Plushkov.

'Good afternoon,' said Chiddingfold, and led Nobbs across to the guard of honour of laboratory technicians.

'Stop!' cried Mrs Plushkov.

There was a general sigh. Jellicoe took out a pocket mirror and began to examine his moustache. Nobbs sat down on the edge of the pavement. Goldwasser tried to shuffle part of his weight on to a narrow ornamental ledge. He knew what the delay was. The Conversation Committee had gone into emergency session yet again. They would be discussing whether Chiddingfold should be asked to elaborate his greeting with a few conversational remarks. There was a faction which favoured the Director's making some comment on the weather. There was another faction which felt that any comment on the weather would present difficulties in timing, since the exact text could not be decided upon until the day, and that some remarks about the royal car would be preferable. 'How many miles to the gallon do you get out of her, Ma'am?' was thought to be the most generally acceptable. But finally the committee would face up to the impossibility of putting any of this to Chiddingfold, and would vote to postpone a decision until the next meeting. Goldwasser gazed hopelessly at a patch of ground about one foot square just in front of his shoes.

'Let's go on again, please,' said Mrs Plushkov. 'From where we stopped.'

Nobbs shambled across to the guard of honour of laboratory technicians.

'For inspection,' shouted the Senior Laboratory Technician, 'port – slide rules!'

'Up, two, three,' called Mrs Plushkov. 'In, two, three. Ragged, very ragged.'

Nobbs barged along the ranks, treading on the right marker's toe, and knocking another man's slide rule out of his hands.

'Steady, Nobbs,' said Mrs Plushkov.

'Ease – cursors!' shouted the Senior Laboratory Technician.

'Three seconds under,' said Mrs Plushkov. 'You were cutting the corners, Nobbs.'

Nobbs lumbered across to the foot of the steps, received a bouquet from Chiddingfold's small daughter, deputized for by Miss Fram, and reeled on into the lobby to meet the assembled staff and guests.

'Stop!' cried Mrs Plushkov. 'Nomenclature Committee around me, please!'

Goldwasser subsided weakly against a wall. The Nomenclature Committee was his fault. In a lighthearted moment one day he had suggested that calling Nobbs 'Your Majesty' might strictly speaking constitute an act of sedition, and within two days the question was being urgently debated throughout the thirty-seven committees. Almost everyone agreed that a seditious interpretation could be put upon the usage, and that to continue using it might open the Institute to the possibility of prosecution or blackmail. But the practical problem was what to call Nobbs if not Her Majesty. It would be ridiculous, everyone said, to expect people to bow and curtsy to him and call him Nobbs. The original smile had scarcely faded from Goldwasser's face before the Nomenclature Committee had been set up, to compose a formula which would both command respect and correspond more closely to the realities of Nobbs's situation. Various working parties and study groups had so far produced:

Your Humility
Your Servitude
Your Ordinariness
Your Humanity
Your Anonymity
Your Proxyship
Your Beardedness
Your Nobbs
Your Principal Research Assistantship

Once more, Goldwasser knew, the decision would have to be postponed.

'Carry on from where we were,' shouted Mrs Plushkov. 'Go on calling Nobbs "Your Majesty" for today. Let me once again ask everyone to use his discretion, and not to talk about this outside the Institute.'

Hands were shaken, at five seconds per hand, then off went everyone on the tour of the establishment, at two feet per second. Into a department. Meet typical Research Assistant (Grade One) and look at typical computer (12 seconds). Ask typical question about computer (say, 5 seconds). Get typical answer (15 seconds). Express appreciation of work done (say, 4 seconds).

On down corridor, at two feet per second, up stairs at two seconds per stair, and into next department. Meet typical Research Assistant

(Grade Two) and ask typical personal question (say, 10 seconds). Get typically modest answer (1 second). Comment on pleasantness of view out of window (say, 5 seconds). Deputy Director explains how fortunate Institute is in this respect (31 seconds). Adds polite joke (3 seconds). Laughter (26 seconds). Public amazement at how informal and charming Nobbs is (4 seconds). Out, striking ill-articulated Nobbs thigh against table and bringing down three files, a bottle of ink, and 140 loose sheets of foolscap manuscript. Recriminations all round (20 minutes).

For Goldwasser the afternoon began to go by in a dream. It was interrupted momentarily when he was caught a sharp blow on the side of the head with a window pole which was being used as a substitute for the golden taper to light a flame of undying remembrance to those who fell in the Luddite riots. At another point he was conscious of a limp hand being thrust authoritatively into his, and a well-known voice saying 'Wakey wakey, mate.' And there were a few moments of wonderful sitting down when the Special Purposes Committee met to consider once again whether time should be allowed for Nobbs to powder his nose.

Then they were in the new wing, and Rowe, deputizing for Macintosh, was showing Nobbs all the equipment so far installed, which consisted of several office tables and a number of chairs. Almost the last thing Goldwasser was conscious of was Rowe reading off a piece of paper.

'And this is a table, ma'am. What in essence it consists of is a horizontal rectilinear plane surface maintained by four vertical columnar supports, which we call legs. The tables in the laboratory, ma'am, are as advanced in design as one will find anywhere in the world.'

Which was how, when everybody else was standing up for the National Anthem, Goldwasser came to be lying on the floor, sprawling face downwards with great casualness. Nunn, who was keeping an eye on various security aspects from a discreet distance, was not surprised. The case against Goldwasser was open and closed already; he would be in no position to demonstrate his feelings about the National Anthem on the day.

What Nunn was really worrying about now was Nobbs's thighs. The more he saw of them in action the less he liked them. Were they a secret weapon in the pay of Goldwasser? They didn't appear to be in the pay of Nobbs. He watched them intently as they knocked things off desks and split chairs they came up against. They appeared to pursue their programme of sabotage and disruption quite independently of Nobbs.

Of course, they might be *unconscious* agents of Goldwasser's. It was possible that Nobbs had been brainwashed by Goldwasser without knowing about it. But then so might anyone else in the room. Such things could happen. Nobody who was in security was likely to underestimate what could be done these days with brainwashing techniques. For all Nunn knew, he might have been brainwashed himself. He might well be an unconscious agent of Goldwasser's. His whole campaign against Goldwasser might be the result of a post-hypnotic suggestion implanted by Goldwasser himself. Indeed, his very realization that he might be acting under Goldwasser's orders, even as Goldwasser took his ease down there on the floor, might itself be a response engineered by Goldwasser.

As soon as the anthem was over he retired to his room and brooded for a long time over a favourite niblick. These were deep waters he was fishing, and in deep waters, there was nothing to do but keep one's eye on the ball and wait for an opening. He took a nap to clear his head and was awakened, greatly refreshed, by the sound of the Director collapsing heavily into his chair in the office next door after finishing the day's rehearsals. The Director, when he went in to see him, looked surprisingly old and tired, and Nunn spent nearly an hour trying to cheer him up by telling him the full medical histories of everyone who had dropped dead while running the marathon.

The Canterville Ghost

OSCAR WILDE

1

WHEN MR HIRAM B. OTIS, THE American minister, bought Canterville Chase, everyone told him he was doing a very foolish thing, as there was no doubt at all that the place was haunted. Indeed, Lord Canterville himself, who was a man of the most punctilious honour, had felt it his duty to mention the fact to Mr Otis, when they came to discuss terms.

'We have not cared to live in the place ourselves,' said Lord Canterville, 'since my grand-aunt, the Dowager Duchess of Bolton, was frightened into a fit, from which she never really recovered, by two skeleton hands being placed on her shoulders as she was dressing for dinner, and I feel bound to tell you, Mr Otis, that the ghost has been seen by several living members of my family, as well as by the rector of the parish, the Rev Augustus Dampier, who is a fellow of King's College, Cambridge. After the unfortunate accident to the Duchess, none of our younger servants would stay with us, and Lady Canterville often got very little sleep at night, in consequence of the mysterious noises that came from the corridor and the library.'

'My lord,' answered the Minister, 'I will take the furniture and the ghost at a valuation. I come from a modern country, where we have everything that money can buy; and with all our spry young fellows painting the Old World red, and carrying off your best actresses and prima-donnas, I reckon that if there were such a thing as a ghost in Europe, we'd have it at home in a very short time in one of our public museums, or on the road as a show.'

'I fear that the ghost exists,' said Lord Canterville, smiling, 'though it may have resisted the overtures of your enterprising impresarios. It has been well known for three centuries, since 1584 in fact, and always makes its appearance before the death of any member of our family.'

'Well, so does the family doctor for that matter, Lord Canterville.

But there is no such thing, sir, as a ghost, and I guess the laws of nature are not going to be suspended for the British aristocracy.'

'You are certainly very natural in America,' answered Lord Canterville, who did not quite understand Mr Otis's last observation, 'and if you don't mind a ghost in the house, it is all right. Only you must remember I warned you.'

A few weeks after this, the purchase was completed, and at the close of the season the Minister and his family went down to Canterville Chase. Mrs Otis, who, as Miss Lucretia R Tappan, of West 53rd Street, had been a celebrated New York belle, was now a very handsome middle-aged woman, with fine eyes, and a superb profile. Many American ladies on leaving their native land adopt an appearance of chronic ill-health, under the impression that it is a form of European refinement, but Mrs Otis had never fallen into this error. She had a magnificent constitution, and a really wonderful amount of animal spirits. Indeed, in many respects, she was quite English, and was an excellent example of the fact that we have really everything in common with America nowadays, except, of course, language. Her eldest son, christened Washington by his parents in a moment of patriotism, which he never ceased to regret, was a fair-haired, rather good-looking young man, who had qualified himself for American diplomacy by leading the German at the Newport Casino for three successive seasons, and even in London was well known as an excellent dancer. Gardenias and the peerage were his only weaknesses. Otherwise he was extremely sensible. Miss Virginia E. Otis was a little girl of fifteen, lithe and lovely as a fawn, and with a fine freedom in her large blue eyes. She was a wonderful amazon, and had once raced old Lord Bilton on her pony twice round the park, winning by a length and a half, just in front of Achilles statue, to the huge delight of the young Duke of Cheshire, who proposed to her on the spot, and was sent back to Eton that very night by his guardians, in floods of tears. After Virginia came the twins, who were usually called 'The Stars and Stripes' as they were always getting swished. They were delightful boys, and with the exception of the worthy Minister the only true republicans of the family.

As Canterville Chase is seven miles from Ascot, the nearest railway station, Mr Otis had telegraphed for a waggonette to meet them, and they started on their drive in high spirits. It was a lovely July evening, and the air was delicate with the scent of the pinewoods. Now and then they heard a wood pigeon brooding over its own sweet voice, or saw, deep in the rustling fern, the burnished breast of the pheasant. Little squirrels peered at them from the beech trees as they went by, and the rabbits scudded away through the brushwood and over the mossy knolls, with their tails in the air. As they entered the avenue of Canterville Chase, however, the sky became suddenly overcast with clouds, a curious stillness seemed to hold the atmosphere, a great flight of rooks passed silently over their heads, and, before they reached the house, some big drops of rain had fallen.

Standing on the steps to receive them was an old woman, neatly dressed in black silk, with a white cap and apron. This was Mrs Umney, the housekeeper, whom Mrs Otis, at Lady Canterville's earnest request, had consented to keep on in her former position. She made them each a low curtsey as they alighted, and said in a quaint, old-fashioned manner, 'I bid you welcome to Canterville Chase.' Following her, they passed through the fine Tudor hall into the library, a long, low room, panelled in black oak, at the end of which was a large stained-glass window. Here they found tea laid out for them, and, after taking off their wraps, they sat down and began to look round, while Mrs Umney waited on them.

Suddenly Mrs Otis caught sight of a dull red stain on the floor just by the fireplace and, quite unconscious of what it really signified, said to Mrs Umney, 'I am afraid something has been spilt there.'

'Yes, madam,' replied the old housekeeper in a low voice, 'blood has been spilt on that spot.'

'How horrid,' cried Mrs Otis; 'I don't at all care for bloodstains in a sitting room. It must be removed at once.'

The old woman smiled, and answered in the same low, mysterious voice, 'It is the blood of Lady Eleanore de Canterville, who was murdered on that very spot by her own husband, Sir Simon de Canterville, in 1575. Sir Simon survived her nine years, and disappeared suddenly under very mysterious circumstances. His body has never been discovered, but his guilty spirit still haunts the Chase. The bloodstain has been much admired by tourists and others, and cannot be removed.'

'That is all nonsense,' cried Washington Otis; 'Pinkerton's Champion Stain Remover and Paragon Detergent will clean it up in no time,' and before the terrified housekeeper could interfere he had fallen upon his knees, and was rapidly scouring the floor with a small stick of what looked like a black cosmetic. In a few moments no trace of the bloodstain could be seen.

'I knew Pinkerton would do it,' he exclaimed triumphantly, as he looked round at his admiring family; but no sooner had he said these words than a terrible flash of lightning lit up the sombre room, a fearful peal of thunder made them all start to their feet, and Mrs Umney fainted.

'What a monstrous climate!' said the American Minister calmly, as he lit a long cheroot. 'I guess the old country is so overpopulated that they have not enough decent weather for everybody. I have always been of opinion that emigration is the only thing for England.'

'My dear Hiram,' cried Mrs Otis, 'what can we do with a woman who faints?'

'Charge it to her like breakages,' answered the Minister; 'she won't faint after that'; and in a few moments Mrs Umney certainly came to. There was no doubt, however, that she was extremely upset, and she sternly warned Mr Otis to beware of some trouble coming to the house.

'I have seen things with my own eyes, sir,' she said, 'that would make any Christian's hair stand on end, and many and many a night I have not closed my eyes in sleep for the awful things that are done here.' Mr Otis, however, and his wife warmly assured the honest soul that they were not afraid of ghosts, and, after invoking the blessings of Providence on her new master and mistress, and making arrangements for an increase of salary, the old housekeeper tottered off to her own room.

2

The storm raged fiercely all that night, but nothing of particular note occurred. The next morning, however, when they came down to breakfast, they found the terrible stain of blood once again on the floor. 'I don't think it can be the fault of the Paragon Detergent,' said Washington, 'for I have tried it with everything. It must be the ghost.' He accordingly rubbed out the stain a second time, but the second morning it appeared again. The third morning also it was there, though the library had been locked up at night by Mr Otis himself, and the key carried upstairs. The whole family were now quite interested; Mr Otis began to suspect that he had been too dogmatic in his denial of the existence of ghosts, Mrs Otis expressed her intention of joining the Psychical Society, and Washington prepared a long letter to Messrs Myers and Podmore on the subject of the Permanence of Sanguineous Stains when connected with crime. That night all doubts about the objective existence of phantasmata were removed for ever.

The day had been warm and sunny; and, in the cool of the evening, the whole family went out for a drive. They did not return home till nine o'clock, when they had a light supper. The conversation in no way turned upon ghosts, so there were not even those primary conditions of receptive expectation which so often precede the presentation of psychical phenomena. The subjects discussed, as I have since learned from Mr Otis, were merely such as form the ordinary conversation of cultured Americans of the better class, such as the immense superiority of Miss Fanny Davenport over Sarah Bernhardt as an actress; the difficulty of obtaining green corn, buckwheat cakes, and hominy, even in the best English houses; the importance of Boston in the development of the world-soul; the advantages of the baggage check system in railway travelling; and the sweetness of the New York accent as compared to the London drawl. No mention at all was made of the supernatural, nor was Sir Simon de Canterville alluded to in any way. At eleven o'clock the family retired and by half past all the lights were out. Some time after, Mr Otis was awakened by a curious noise in the corridor, outside his room. It sounded like the clank of metal, and seemed to be coming nearer every moment. He got up at once, struck a match, and looked at the time. It was exactly one o'clock. He was quite calm, and felt his pulse, which was not at all feverish. The strange noise still continued, and with it he heard distinctly the sound of footsteps. He put on his slippers, took a small oblong phial out of his dressing case, and opened the door. Right in front of him he saw, in the wan moonlight, an old man of terrible aspect. His eyes were as red as burning coals; long grey hair fell over his shoulders in matted coils; his garments, which were of antique cut, were soiled and ragged, and from his wrists and ankles hung heavy manacles and rusty gyves.

'My dear sir,' said Mr Otis, 'I really must insist on your oiling those chains, and have brought you for that purpose a small bottle of the Tammany Rising Sun Lubricator. It is said to be completely efficacious upon one application, and there are several testimonials to that effect on the wrapper from some of our most eminent native divines. I shall leave it here for you by the bedroom candles, and will be happy to supply you with more should you require it.' With these words the United States Minister laid the bottle down on a marble table, and, closing his door, retired to rest.

For a moment the Canterville ghost stood quite motionless in natural indignation; then, dashing the bottle violently upon the polished floor, he fled down the corridor, uttering hollow groans, and emitting a ghastly green light. Just, however, as he reached the top of the great oak staircase, a door was flung open, two little white robed figures appeared, and a large pillow whizzed past his head! There was evidently no time to be lost, so, hastily adopting the Fourth Dimension of Space as a means of escape, he vanished through the wainscoting, and the house became quite quiet.

On reaching a small secret chamber in the left wing, he leaned up against a moonbeam to recover his breath, and began to try and realize his position. Never, in a brilliant and uninterrupted career of three hundred years, had he been so grossly insulted. He thought of the Dowager Duchess, whom he had frightened into a fit as she stood before the glass in her lace and diamonds; of the four housemaids, who had gone off into hysterics when he merely grinned at them through the curtains of one of the spare bedrooms; of the rector of the parish, whose candle he had blown out as he was coming late one night from the library, and who had been under the care of Sir William Gull ever since, a perfect martyr to nervous disorders; and of old Madame de Tremouillac, who, having wakened up one morning early and seen a skeleton seated in an armchair by the fire reading her diary had been confined to her bed for six weeks with an attack of brain fever, and, on her recovery, had become reconciled to the Church, and had broken off her connection with that notorious sceptic Monsieur de Voltaire. He remembered the terrible night when the wicked Lord Canterville was found choking in his dressing-room, with the knave of diamonds halfway down his throat, and confessed, just before he died, that he had cheated Charles James Fox out of £50,000 at Crockford's by means of that very card, and swore that the ghost had made him swallow it. All his great achievements came back to him again, from the butler who had shot himself in the pantry because he had seen a green hand tapping at the window pane, to the beautiful Lady Stutfield, who was always obliged to wear a black velvet band round her throat to hide the mark of five fingers burnt upon her white skin, and who drowned herself at last in the carp-pond at the end of the King's Walk. With the enthusiastic egotism of the true artist he went over his most celebrated performances, and smiled bitterly to himself as he recalled to mind his last appearance as 'Red Ruben, or the Strangled Babe,' his *début* as 'Gaunt Gideon, the Blood-sucker of Bexley Moor,' and the *furore* he had excited one lonely June evening by merely playing ninepins with his own bones upon the lawn tennis ground. And after all this, some wretched modern Americans were to come and offer him the Rising Sun Lubricator, and throw pillows at his head! It was quite unbearable. Besides, no ghosts in history had ever been treated in this manner. Accordingly, he determined to have vengeance, and remained till daylight in an attitude of deep thought.

3

The next morning when the Otis family met at breakfast, they discussed the ghost at some length. The United States Minister was naturally a little annoyed to find that his present had not been accepted. 'I have no wish,' he said, 'to do the ghost any personal injury, and I must say that, considering the length of time he has been in the house, I don't think it is at all polite to throw pillows at him' – a very just remark, at which, I am sorry to say, the twins burst into shouts of laughter. 'Upon the other hand,' he continued, 'if he really declines to use the Rising Sun Lubricator, we shall have to take his chains from him. It would be quite impossible to sleep, with such a noise going on outside the bedrooms.'

For the rest of the week, however, they were undisturbed, the only thing that excited any attention being the continual renewal of the bloodstain on the library floor. This certainly was very strange, as the door was always locked at night by Mr Otis, and the windows kept closely barred. The chameleon-like colour, also, of the stain excited a good deal of comment. Some mornings it was a dull (almost Indian) red, then it would be vermilion, then a rich purple, and once when they came down for family prayers, according to the simple rites of the Free American Reformed Episcopalian Church, they found it a bright emerald green. These kaleidoscopic changes naturally amused the party very much, and bets on the subject were freely made every evening. The only person who did not enter into the joke was little Virginia, who, for some unexplained reason, was always a good deal distressed at the sight of the bloodstain, and very nearly cried the morning it was emerald green.

The second appearance of the ghost was on Sunday night. Shortly after they had gone to bed they were suddenly alarmed by a fearful crash in the hall. Rushing downstairs, they found that a large suit of old armour had become detached from its stand, and had fallen on the stone floor, while, seated in a high-backed chair, was the Canterville ghost, rubbing his knees with an expression of acute agony on his face. The twins, having brought their peashooters with them, at once discharged two pellets on him, with that accuracy of aim which can only be attained by long and careful practice on a writing-master, while the United States Minister covered him with his revolver, and called upon him, in accordance with Californian etiquette, to hold up his hands! The ghost started up with a wild shriek of rage, and swept through them like a mist, extinguishing Washington Otis's candle as he passed, and so leaving them all in total darkness. On reaching the top of the staircase he recovered himself, and determined to give his celebrated peal of demoniac laughter. This he had on more than one occasion found extremely useful. It was said to have turned Lord Raker's wig grey in a single night, and had certainly made three of Lady Canterville's French governesses give warning before their month was up. He accordingly laughed his most horrible laugh, till the old vaulted roof rang and rang again, but hardly had the fearful echo died away when a door opened, and Mrs Otis came out in a light blue dressing gown. 'I am afraid you are far from well,' she said, 'and have brought you a bottle of Dr Dobell's tincture. If it is indigestion, you will find it a most excellent remedy.' The ghost glared at her in fury, and began at once to make preparations for turning himself into a large black dog, an accomplishment for which he was justly renowned, and to which the family doctor always attributed the permanent idiocy of Lord Canterville's uncle, the Hon Thomas Horton. The sound of approaching footsteps, however, made him hesitate in his fell purpose, so he contented himself with becoming faintly phosphorescent, and vanished with a deep church-yard groan, just as the twins had come up to him.

On reaching his room he entirely broke down, and became a prey to the most violent agitation. The vulgarity of the twins, and the gross materialism of Mrs Otis, were naturally extremely annoying, but what really distressed him most was, that he had been unable to wear the suit of mail. He had hoped that even modern Americans would be thrilled by the sight of a Spectre In Armour, if for no more sensible reason, at least out of respect for their national poet

Longfellow, over whose graceful and attractive poetry he himself had whiled away many a weary hour when the Cantervilles were up in town. Besides, it was his own suit. He had worn it with success at the Kenilworth tournament, and had been highly complimented on it by no less a person than the Virgin Queen herself. Yet when he had put it on, he had been completely overpowered by the weight of the huge breastplate and steel casque, and had fallen heavily on the stone pavement, barking both his knees severely, and bruising the knuckles of his right hand.

For some days after this he was extremely ill, and hardly stirred out of his room at all, except to keep the bloodstain in proper repair. However, by taking great care of himself, he recovered, and resolved to make a third attempt to frighten the United States Minister and his family. He selected Friday, the 17th of August, for his appearance, and spent most of that day in looking over his wardrobe, ultimately deciding in favour of a large slouched hat with a red feather, a winding-sheet frilled at the wrists and neck, and a rusty dagger. Towards evening a violent storm of rain came on, and the wind was so high that all the windows and doors in the old house shook and rattled. In fact, it was just such weather as he loved. His plan of action was this. He was to make his way quietly to Washington Otis's room, gibber at him from the foot of the bed, and stab himself three times in the throat to the sound of slow music. He bore Washington a special grudge, being quite aware that it was he who was in the habit of removing the famous Canterville bloodstain, by means of Pinkerton's Paragon Detergent. Having reduced the reckless and foolhardy youth to a condition of abject terror, he was then to proceed to the room occupied by the United States Minister and his wife, and there to place a clammy hand on Mrs Otis's forehead, while he hissed into her trembling husband's ear the awful secrets of the charnel-house. With regard to little Virginia, he had not quite made up his mind. She had never insulted him in any way, and was pretty and gentle. A few hollow groans from the wardrobe, he thought, would be more than sufficient, or, if that failed to wake her, he might grabble at the counterpane with palsy-twitching fingers. As for the twins, he was quite determined to teach them a lesson. The first thing to be done was, of course, to sit upon their chests, so as to produce the stifling sensation of nightmare. Then, as their beds were quite close to each other, to stand between them in the form of a green, icy-cold corpse, till they became paralysed with fear, and finally, to throw off the winding-sheet, and crawl round the room, with white bleached bones and one rolling eyeball, in the character of 'Dumb Daniel, or the Suicide's Skeleton,' a *rôle* in which he had on more than one occasion produced a great effect, and which he considered quite equal to his famous part of 'Martin the Maniac, or the Masked Mystery.'

At half past ten he heard the family going to bed. For some time he was disturbed by wild shrieks of laughter from the twins, who, with the light-hearted gaiety of schoolboys, were evidently amusing themselves before they retired to rest, but at a quarter-past eleven all was still, and, as midnight sounded, he sallied forth. The owl beat against the window panes, the raven croaked from the old yew tree, and the wind wandered moaning round the house like a lost soul; but the Otis family slept unconscious of their doom, and high above the rain and storm he could hear the steady snoring of the Minister for the United States. He stepped stealthily out of the wainscoting, with an evil smile on his cruel, wrinkled mouth, and the moon hid her face in a cloud as he stole past the great oriel window, where his own arms and those of his murdered wife were blazoned in azure and gold. On and on he glided, like an evil shadow, the very darkness seeming to loathe him as he passed. Once he thought he heard something call, and stopped; but it was only the baying of a dog from the Red Farm, and he went on, muttering strange sixteenth-century curses, and ever and anon brandishing the rusty dagger in the midnight air. Finally he reached the corner of the passage that led to luckless Washington's room. For a moment he paused there, the wind blowing his long grey locks about his head, and twisting into grotesque and fantastic folds the nameless horror of the dead man's shroud. Then the clock struck the quarter, and he felt the time was come. He chuckled to himself, and turned the corner; but no sooner had he done so, than, with a piteous wail of terror, he fell back, and hid his blanched face in his long, bony hands. Right in front of him was standing a horrible spectre, motionless as a carven image, and monstrous as a madman's dream! Its head was bald and burnished; its face round, and fat, and white; and hideous laughter seemed to have writhed its features into an eternal grin. From the eyes streamed rays of scarlet light, the mouth was a wide well of fire, and a hideous garment, like to his own, swathed with its silent snows the Titan form. On its breast was a placard with strange writing in antique characters, some scroll of shame it seemed, some record of wild sins, some awful calendar of crime, and, with its right hand, it bore aloft a falchion of gleaming steel.

Never having seen a ghost before, he naturally was terribly frightened, and, after a second hasty glance at the awful phantom, he fled back to his room, tripping up in his long winding-sheet as he sped down the corridor, and finally dropping the rusty dagger into the Minister's jack-boots, where it was found in the morning by the butler. Once in the privacy of his own apartment, he flung himself down on a small pallet-bed and hid his face under the clothes. After a time, however, the brave old Canterville spirit asserted itself, and he determined to go and speak to the other ghost as soon as it was daylight. Accordingly, just as the dawn was touching the hills with silver, he returned towards the spot where he had first laid eyes on the grisly phantom, feeling that, after all, two ghosts were better than one, and that, by the aid of his new friend, he might safely grapple with the twins. On reaching the spot, however, a terrible sight met his gaze. Something had evidently happened to the spectre, for the light had entirely faded from its hollow eyes, the gleaming falchion had fallen from its hand, and it was leaning up against the wall in a strained and uncomfortable attitude. He rushed forward and seized it in his arms, when, to his horror, the head slipped off and rolled on the floor, the body assumed a recumbent posture, and he found himself clasping a white dimity bed curtain, with a sweeping brush, a kitchen cleaver, and a hollow turnip lying at his feet! Unable to understand this curious transformation, he clutched the placard with feverish haste, and there, in the grey morning light, he read these fearful words:-

> **YE OTIS GHOSTE.**
> Ye Onlie True and Originale Spook.
> Beware of Ye Imitationes.
> All others are Counterfeite.

The whole thing flashed across him. He had been tricked, foiled and outwitted! The old Canterville look came into his eyes; he ground his toothless gums together; and, raising his withered hands high above his head, swore, according to the picturesque phraseology of the antique school, that when Chanticleer had sounded twice his merry horn, deeds of blood would be wrought, and Murder walk abroad with silent feet.

Hardly had he finished this awful oath when, from the red-tiled roof of a distant homestead, a cock crew. He laughed a long, low, bitter laugh, and waited. Hour after hour he waited, but the cock, for some strange reason, did not crow again. Finally, at half past seven, the arrival of the housemaids made him give up his fearful vigil, and he stalked back to his room, thinking of his vain hope and baffled purpose. There he consulted several books of ancient chivalry, of which he was exceedingly fond, and found that, on every occasion on which his oath had been used, Chanticleer had always crowed a second time. 'Perdition seize the naughty fowl,' he muttered, 'I have seen the day when, with my stout spear, I would have run him through the gorge, and made him crow for me an 'twere in death!' He then retired to a comfortable lead coffin, and stayed there till evening.

4

The next day the ghost was very weak and tired. The terrible excitement of the last four weeks was beginning to have its effect. His nerves were completely shattered and he started at the slightest noise. For five days he kept his room, and at last made up his mind to give up the point of the bloodstain on the library floor. If the Otis family did not want it, they clearly did not deserve it. They were evidently people on a low, material plane of existence, and quite incapable of appreciating the symbolic value of sensuous phenomena. The question of phantasmic apparitions, and the development of astral bodies, was of course quite a different matter, and really not under his control. It was his solemn duty to appear in the corridor once a week, and to gibber from the large oriel window on the first and third Wednesday in every month, and he did not see how he could honourably escape from his obligations. It is quite true that his life had been very evil, but, upon the other hand, he was most conscientious in all things connected with the supernatural. For the next three Saturdays, accordingly, he traversed the corridor as usual between midnight and three o'clock, taking every possible precaution against being either heard or seen. He removed his boots, trod as lightly as possible on the old worm-eaten boards, wore a large black velvet cloak, and was careful to use the Rising Sun Lubricator for oiling his chains. I am bound to acknowledge that it was with a good deal of difficulty that he brought himself to adopt this last mode of protection. However, one night, while the family were at dinner, he slipped into Mr Otis's bedroom and carried off the bottle. He felt a little humiliated at first, but afterwards was sensible enough to see that there was a great deal to be said for the invention, and, to a certain degree, it served his purpose. Still, in spite of everything, he was not left unmolested. Strings were continually being stretched across the corridor, over which he tripped in the dark, and on one occasion, while dressed for the part of 'Black Isaac, or the Huntsman of Hogley Woods,' he met with a severe fall, through treading on a butter-slide, which the twins had constructed from the entrance of the Tapestry Chamber to the top of the oak staircase. This last insult so enraged him, that he resolved to make one final effort to assert his dignity and social position, and determined to visit the insolent young Etonians the next night in his celebrated character of 'Reckless Rupert, or the Headless Earl.'

He had not appeared in this disguise for more than seventy years; in fact, not since he had so frightened pretty Lady Barbara Modish by means of it, that she suddenly broke off her engagement with the present Lord Canterville's grandfather, and ran away to Gretna Green with handsome Jack Castleton, declaring that nothing in the world would induce her to marry into a family that allowed such a horrible phantom to walk up and down the terrace at twilight. Poor Jack was afterwards shot in a duel by Lord Canterville on Wandsworth Common, and Lady Barbara died of a broken heart at Tunbridge Wells before the year was out, so, in every way, it had been a great success. It was, however, an extremely difficult 'make-up,' if I may use such a theatrical expression in connection with one of the greatest mysteries of the supernatural, or, to employ a more scientific term, the higher-natural world, and it took him fully three hours to make his preparations. At last everything was ready, and he was very pleased with his appearance. The big leather riding-boots that went with the dress were just a little too large for him, and he could only find one of the two horse pistols, but, on the whole, he was quite satisfied, and at a quarter past one he glided out of the wainscoting and crept down the corridor. On reaching the room occupied by the twins, which I should mention was called the Blue Bed Chamber, on account of the colour of its hangings, he found the door just ajar. Wishing to make an effective entrance, he flung it wide open, when a heavy jug of water fell right down on him, wetting him to the skin, and just missing his left shoulder by a couple of inches. At the same moment he heard stifled shrieks of laughter proceeding from the four-post bed. The shock to his nervous system was so great that he fled back to his room as hard as he could go, and the next day he was laid up with a severe cold. The only thing that at all consoled him in the whole affair was the fact that he had not brought his head with him, for, had he done so, the consequences might have been very serious.

He now gave up all hope of ever frightening this rude American family, and contented himself, as a rule, with creeping about the passages in list slippers, with a thick red muffler round his throat for fear of draughts, and a small arquebuse, in case he should be attacked by the twins. The final blow he received occurred on the 19th of September. He had gone downstairs to the great entrance-hall, feeling sure that there, at any rate, he would be quite unmolested, and was amusing himself by making satirical remarks on the large Saroni photographs of the United States Minister and his wife, which had now taken the place of the Canterville family pictures. He was simply but neatly clad in a long shroud, spotted with churchyard mould, had tied up his jaw with a strip of yellow linen, and carried a small lantern and a sexton's spade. In fact, he was dressed for the character of 'Jonas the Graveless, or the Corpse-Snatcher of Chertsey Barn,' one of his most remarkable impersonations, and one which the Cantervilles had every reason to remember, as it was the real origin of their quarrel with their neighbour, Lord Rufford. It was about a quarter past two o'clock in the morning, and, as far as he could ascertain, no one was stirring. As he was strolling towards the library, however, to see if there were any traces left of the bloodstain, suddenly there leaped out on him from a dark corner two figures, who waved their arms wildly above their heads, and shrieked out 'BOO!' in his ear.

Seized with a panic, which, under the circumstances, was only natural, he rushed for the staircase, but found Washington Otis waiting for him there with the big garden syringe; and being thus hemmed in by his enemies on every side, and driven almost to bay, he vanished into the great iron stove, which, fortunately for him, was not lit, and had to make his way home through the flues and chimneys, arriving at his own room in a terrible state of dirt, disorder, and despair.

After this he was not seen again on any nocturnal expedition. The twins lay in wait for him on several occasions, and strewed the passages with nutshells every night to the great annoyance of their parents and the servants, but it was of no avail. It was quite evident that his feelings were so wounded that he would not appear. Mr Otis consequently resumed his great work on the history of the Democratic Party, on which he had been engaged for some years; Mrs Otis organized a wonderful clambake, which amazed the whole country; the boys took to lacrosse, euchre, poker, and other American national games; and Virginia rode about the lanes on her pony, accompanied by the young Duke of Cheshire, who had come to spend the last week of his holidays at Canterville Chase. It was generally assumed that the ghost had gone away, and, in fact, Mr Otis wrote a letter to that effect to Lord Canterville, who, in reply, expressed his great pleasure at the news, and sent his best congratulations to the Minister's worthy wife.

The Otises, however, were deceived, for the ghost was still in the house, and though now almost an invalid, was by no means ready to let matters rest, particularly as he heard that among the guests was the young Duke of Cheshire, whose grand-uncle, Lord Francis Stilton, had once bet a hundred guineas with Colonel Carbury that he would play dice with the Canterville ghost, and was found the next morning lying on the floor of the card room in such a helpless paralytic state, that though he lived on to a great age, he was never able to say anything again but 'Double Sixes.' The story was well known at the time, though, of course, out of respect to the feelings of the two noble families, every attempt was made to hush it up; and a full account of all the circumstances connected with it will be found in the third volume of Lord Tattle's *Recollections of the Prince Regent and his Friends*. The ghost, then, was naturally very anxious to show that he had not lost his influence over the Stiltons, with whom indeed, he was distantly connected, his own first cousin having been married *en secondes noces*[1] to the Sieur de Bulkeley, from whom, as every one

---

[1] For the second time.

knows, the Dukes of Cheshire are lineally descended. Accordingly, he made arrangements for appearing to Virginia's little lover in his celebrated impersonation of 'The Vampire Monk, or, the Bloodless Benedictine,' a performance so horrible that when old Lady Startup saw it, which she did on one fatal New Year's Eve, in the year 1764, she went off into the most piercing shrieks, which culminated in violent apoplexy, and died in three days, after disinheriting the Cantervilles, who were her nearest relations, and leaving all her money to her London apothecary. At the last moment, however, his terror of the twins prevented his leaving his room, and the little Duke slept in peace under the great feathered canopy in the Royal Bedchamber, and dreamed of Virginia.

5

A few days after this, Virginia and her curly-haired cavalier went out riding on Brockley meadows, where she tore her habit so badly in getting through a hedge, that, on her return home, she made up her mind to go up by the back staircase so as not to be seen. As she was running past the Tapestry Chamber, the door of which happened to be opened, she fancied she saw some one inside, and thinking it was her mother's maid, who sometimes used to bring her work there, looked in to ask her to mend her habit. To her immense surprise, however, it was the Canterville Ghost himself! He was sitting by the window, watching the ruined gold of the yellow trees fly through the air, and the red leaves dancing madly down the long avenue. His head was leaning on his hand, and his whole attitude was one of extreme depression. Indeed, so forlorn, and so much out of repair did he look, that little Virginia, whose first idea had been to run away and lock herself in her room, was filled with pity, and determined to try and comfort him. So light was her footfall, and so deep his melancholy, that he was not aware of her presence till she spoke to him.

'I am so sorry for you,' she said, 'but my brothers are going back to Eton tomorrow, and then, if you behave yourself, no one will annoy you.'

'It is absurd asking me to behave myself,' he answered, looking round in astonishment at the pretty little girl who had ventured to address him', 'quite absurd. I must rattle my chains, and groan through keyholes, and walk about at night, if that is what you mean. It is my only reason for existing.'

'It is no reason at all for existing, and you know you have been very wicked. Mrs Umney told us, the first day we arrived here, that you had killed your wife.'

'Well, I quite admit it,' said the Ghost petulantly, 'but it was a purely family matter, and concerned no one else.'

'It is very wrong to kill any one,' said Virginia, who at times had a sweet Puritan gravity, caught from some old New England ancestor.

'Oh, I hate the cheap severity of abstract ethics! My wife was very plain, never had my ruffs properly starched, and knew nothing about cookery. Why, there was a buck I had shot in Hogley Woods, a magnificent pricket, and do you know how she had it sent up to table? However, it is no matter now, for it is all over, and I don't think it was very nice of her brothers to starve me to death, though I did kill her.'

'Starve you to death? Oh, Mr Ghost, I mean Sir Simon, are you hungry? I have a sandwich in my case. Would you like it?'

'No, thank you, I never eat anything now; but it is very kind of you, all the same, and you are much nicer than the rest of your horrid, rude, vulgar, dishonest family.'

'Stop!' cried Virginia, stamping her foot, 'it is you who are rude, and horrid, and vulgar; and as for dishonesty, you know you stole the paints out of my box to try and furbish up that ridiculous blood-stain in the library. First you took all my reds, including the vermilion, and I couldn't do any more sunsets, then you took the emerald-green and the chrome-yellow, and finally I had nothing left but indigo and Chinese white, and could only do moonlight scenes, which are always depressing to look at, and not at all easy to paint. I never told on you, though I was very much annoyed, and it was most ridiculous, the whole thing; for who ever heard of emerald-green blood?'

'Well, really,' said the Ghost, rather meekly, 'what was I to do? It is a very difficult thing to get real blood nowadays, and, as your brother began it all with his Paragon Detergent, I certainly saw no reason why I should not have your paints. As for colour, that is always a matter of taste: the Cantervilles have blue blood, for instance, the very bluest in England; but I know you Americans don't care for things of this kind.'

'You know nothing about it, and the best thing you can do is to emigrate and improve your mind. My father will be only too happy to give you a free passage, and though there is a heavy duty on spirits of every kind, there will be no difficulty about the Custom House, as the officers are all Democrats. Once in New York, you are sure to be a great success. I know lots of people there who would give a hundred thousand dollars to have a grandfather, and much more than that to have a family Ghost.'

'I don't think I should like America.'

'I suppose because we have no ruins and no curiosities,' said Virginia satirically.

'No ruins! no curiosities!' answered the Ghost; 'you have your navy and your manners.'

'Good evening; I will go and ask papa to get the twins an extra week's holiday.'

'Please don't go, Miss Virginia,' he cried; 'I am so lonely and so unhappy, and I really don't know what to do. I want to go to sleep and I cannot.'

'That's quite absurd! You have merely to go to bed and blow out the candle. It is very difficult sometimes to keep awake, especially at church, but there is no difficulty at all about sleeping. Why, even babies know how to do that, and they are not very clever.'

'I have not slept for three hundred years,' he said sadly, and Virginia's beautiful blue eyes opened in wonder; 'for three hundred years I have not slept, and I am so tired.'

Virginia grew quite grave, and her little lips trembled like rose-leaves. She came towards him, and kneeling down at his side, looked up into his old withered face.

'Poor, poor Ghost,' she murmured; 'have you no place where you can sleep?'

'Far away beyond the pine-woods,' he answered, in a low dreamy voice, 'there is a little garden. There the grass grows long and deep, there are the great white stars of the hemlock flower, there the nightingale sings all night long. All night long he sings, and the cold, crystal moon looks down, and the yew tree spreads out its giant arms over the sleepers.'

Virginia's eyes grew dim with tears, and she hid her face in her hands.

'You mean the Garden of Death,' she whispered.

'Yes, Death. Death must be so beautiful. To lie in the soft brown earth, with the grasses waving above one's head, and listen to silence. To have no yesterday, and no tomorrow. To forget time, to forgive life, to be at peace. You can help me. You can open for me the portals of Death's House, for Love is always with you, and Love is stronger than Death is.'

Virginia trembled, a cold shiver ran through her, and for a few moments there was silence. She felt as if she was in a terrible dream.

Then the Ghost spoke again, and his voice sounded like the sighing of the wind.

'Have you ever read the old prophecy on the library window?'

'Oh, often,' cried the little girl, looking up; 'I know it quite well. It is painted in curious black letters, and it is difficult to read. There are only six lines:

> When a golden girl can win
> Prayer from out the lips of sin,
> When the barren almond bears,
> And a little child gives away its tears,
> Then shall all the house be still
> And peace come to Canterville.

But I don't know what they mean.'

'They mean,' he said sadly, 'that you must weep for me for my sins, because I have no tears, and pray with me for my soul, because I have no faith, and then, if you have always been sweet, and good, and gentle, the Angel of Death will have mercy on me. You will see fearful shapes in darkness, and wicked voices will whisper in your ear, but they will not harm you, for against the purity of a little child the powers of Hell cannot prevail.'

Virginia made no answer, and the Ghost wrung his hands in wild despair as he looked down at her bowed golden head. Suddenly she stood up, very pale, and with a strange light in her eyes. 'I am not afraid,' she said firmly, 'and I will ask the Angel to have mercy on you.'

He rose from his seat with a faint cry of joy, and taking her hand bent over it with old-fashioned grace and kissed it. His fingers were as cold as ice, and his lips burned like fire, but Virginia did not falter, as he led her across the dusky room. On the faded green tapestry were broidered little huntsmen. They blew their tasselled horns and with their tiny hands waved to her to go back. 'Go back! little Virginia,' they cried, 'go back!' but the Ghost clutched her hand more tightly, and she shut her eyes against them. Horrible animals with lizard tails, and goggle eyes, blinked at her from the carven chimney-piece, and murmured 'Beware! little Virginia, beware! we may never see you again,' but the Ghost glided on more swiftly, and Virginia did not listen. When they reached the end of the room he stopped, and muttered some words she could not understand. She opened her eyes, and saw the wall slowly fading away like a mist, and a great black cavern in front of her. A bitter cold wind swept round them, and she felt something pulling at her dress. 'Quick, quick,' cried the Ghost, 'or it will be too late,' and, in a moment, the wainscoting had closed behind them, and the Tapestry Chamber was empty.

6

About ten minutes later, the bell rang for tea, and, as Virginia did not come down, Mrs Otis sent up one of the footmen to tell her. After a little time he returned and said that he could not find Miss Virginia anywhere. As she was in the habit of going out to the garden every evening to get flowers for the dinner-table, Mrs Otis was not at all alarmed at first, but when six o'clock struck, and Virginia did not appear, she became really agitated, and sent the boys out to look for her, while she herself and Mr Otis searched every room in the house. At half-past six the boys came back and said that they could find no trace of their sister anywhere. There were all now in the greatest state of excitement, and did not know what to do, when Mr Otis suddenly remembered that, some few days before, he had given a band of gypsies permission to camp in the park. He accordingly at once set off for Blackfell Hollow, where he knew they were, accompanied by his eldest son and two of the farm servants. The little Duke of Cheshire, who was perfectly frantic with anxiety, begged hard to be allowed to go too, but Mr Otis would not allow him, as he was afraid there might be a scuffle. On arriving at the spot, however, he found that the gypsies had gone, and it was evident that their departure had been rather sudden, as the fire was still burning, and some plates were lying on the grass. Having sent off Washington and the two men to scour the district, he ran home, and despatched telegrams to all the police inspectors in the country, telling them to look out for a little girl who had been kidnapped by tramps or gypsies. He then ordered his horse to be brought round, and, after insisting on his wife and the three boys sitting down to dinner, rode off down the Ascot Road with a groom. He had hardly, however, gone a couple of miles when he heard somebody galloping after him, and, looking round, saw the little Duke coming up on his pony, with his face very flushed and no hat. 'I'm awfully sorry, Mr Otis,' gasped out the boy, 'but I can't eat any dinner as long as Virginia is lost. Please, don't be angry with me; if you had let us be engaged last year, there would never have been all this trouble. You won't send me back, will you? I can't go! I won't go!'

The Minister could not help smiling at the handsome young scapegrace, and was a good deal touched at his devotion to Virginia, so leaning down from his horse, he patted him kindly on the shoulders, and said, 'Well, Cecil, if you won't go back I suppose you must come with me, but I must get you a hat at Ascot.'

'Oh, bother my hat! I want Virginia!' cried the little Duke, laughing, and they galloped on to the railway station. There Mr Otis inquired of the station-master if any one answering the description of Virginia had been seen on the platform, but could get no news of her. The station-master, however, wired up and down the line, and assured him that a strict watch would be kept for her, and, after having bought a hat for the little Duke from a linen draper, who was just putting up his shutters, Mr Otis rode off to Bexley, a village about four miles away, which he was told was a well-known haunt of the gypsies, as there was a large common next to it. Here they roused up the rural policeman, but could get no information from him, and, after riding all over the common, they turned their horses' heads homewards, and reached the Chase about eleven o'clock, dead-tired and almost heartbroken. They found Washington and the twins waiting for them at the gate-house with lanterns, as the avenue was very dark. Not the slightest trace of Virginia had been discovered. The gypsies had been caught on Broxley meadows, but she was not with them, and they had explained their sudden departure by saying that they had mistaken the date of Chorton Fair, and had gone off in a hurry for fear they might be late. Indeed, they had been quite distressed at hearing of Virginia's disappearance, as they were very grateful to Mr Otis for having allowed them to camp in his park, and four of their number had stayed behind to help in the search. The carp-pond had been dragged, and the whole Chase thoroughly gone over, but without any result. It was evident that, for that night at any rate, Virginia was lost to them; and it was in a state of the deepest depression that Mr Otis and the boys walked up to the house, the groom following behind with the two horses and the pony. In the hall they found a group of frightened servants, and lying on a sofa in the library was poor Mrs Otis, almost out of her mind with terror and anxiety, and having her forehead bathed with eau-de-Cologne by the old housekeeper. Mr Otis at once insisted on her having something to eat, and ordered up supper for the whole party. It was a melancholy meal, as hardly any one spoke, and even the twins were awestruck and subdued, as they were very fond of their sister. When they had finished, Mr Otis, in spite of the entreaties of the little Duke, ordered them all to bed, saying that nothing more could be done that night, and that he would telegraph in the morning to Scotland Yard for some detectives to be sent down immediately. Just as they were passing out of the dining room, midnight began to boom from the clock tower, and when the last stroke sounded they heard a crash and a sudden shrill cry; a dreadful peal of thunder shook the house, a strain of unearthly music floated through the air, a panel at the top of the staircase flew back with a loud noise, and out on the landing, looking very pale and white, with a little casket in her hand, stepped Virginia. In a moment they had all rushed up to her. Mrs Otis clasped her passionately in her arms, the Duke smothered her with violent kisses, and the twins executed a wild war-dance round the group.

'Good heavens! child, where have you been?' said Mr Otis, rather angrily, thinking that she had been playing some foolish trick on them. 'Cecil and I have been riding all over the country looking for you, and your mother has been frightened to death. You must never play these practical jokes any more.'

'Except on the Ghost! except on the Ghost!' shrieked the twins, as they capered about.

'My own darling, thank God you are found; you must never leave my side again,' murmured Mrs Otis, as she kissed the trembling child, and smoothed the tangled gold of her hair.

'Papa,' said Virginia quietly, 'I have been with the Ghost. He is dead, and you must come and see him. He had been very wicked, but he was really sorry for all that he had done, and he gave me this box of beautiful jewels before he died.'

The whole family gazed at her in mute astonishment, but she was quite grave and serious; and, turning round, she led them through the opening in the wainscoting down a narrow secret corridor, Washington following with a lighted candle, which he had caught up from the table. Finally, they came to a great oak door, studded with rusty nails. When Virginia touched it, it swung back on its heavy hinges, and they found themselves in a little low room, with a vaulted ceiling, and one tiny grated window. Imbedded in the wall was a huge iron ring, and chained to it was a gaunt skeleton, that was stretched out at full length on the stone floor, and seemed to be trying to grasp with its long fleshless fingers an old-fashioned trencher and ewer, that were placed just out of its reach. The jug had evidently been once filled with water, as it was covered inside with green mould. There was nothing on the trencher but a pile of dust. Virginia knelt down beside the skeleton, and, folding her little hands together, began to pray silently, while the rest of the party looked on in wonder at the terrible tragedy whose secret was now disclosed to them.

'Hallo!' suddenly exclaimed one of the twins, who had been looking out of the window to try and discover in what wing of the house the room was situated. 'Hallo! the old withered almond-tree has blossomed. I can see the flowers quite plainly in the moonlight.'

'God has forgiven him,' said Virginia gravely, as she rose to her feet, and a beautiful light seemed to illuminate her face.

'What an angel you are!' cried the young Duke, and he put his arm round her neck and kissed her.

7

Four days after these curious incidents a funeral started from Canterville Chase at about eleven o'clock at night. The hearse was drawn by eight black horses, each of which carried on its head a great tuft of nodding ostrich plumes, and the leaden coffin was covered by a rich purple pall, on which was embroidered in gold the Canterville coat-of-arms. By the side of the hearse and the coaches walked the servants with lighted torches, and the whole procession was wonderfully impressive. Lord Canterville was the chief mourner, having come up specially from Wales to attend the funeral, and sat in the first carriage along with little Virginia. Then came the United States Minister and his wife, then Washington and the three boys, and in the last carriage was Mrs Umney. It was generally felt that, as she had been frightened by the ghost for more than fifty years of her life, she had a right to see the last of him. A deep grave had been dug in the corner of the churchyard, just under the old yew-tree, and the service was read in the most impressive manner by the Rev Augustus Dampier. When the ceremony was over the servants, according to an old custom observed in the Canterville family, extinguished their torches, and, as the coffin was being lowered into the grave, Virginia stepped forward and laid on it a large cross made of white and pink almond-blossoms. As she did so, the moon came out from behind a cloud, and flooded with its silent silver the little churchyard, and from a distant copse a nightingale began to sing. She thought of the ghost's description of the Garden of Death, her eyes became dim with tears, and she hardly spoke a word during the drive home.

The next morning, before Lord Canterville went up to town, Mr Otis had an interview with him on the subject of the jewels the ghost had given to Virginia. They were perfectly magnificent, especially a certain ruby necklace with old Venetian setting, which was really a superb specimen of sixteenth-century work, and their value was so great that Mr Otis felt considerable scruples about allowing his daughter to accept them.

'My Lord,' he said, 'I know that in this country mortmain is held to apply to trinkets as well as to land, and it is quite clear to me that these jewels are, or should be, heirlooms in your family. I must beg you, accordingly, to take them to London with you, and to regard them simply as a portion of your property which has been restored to you under certain strange conditions. As for my daughter, she is merely a child, and has as yet, I am glad to say, but little interest in such appurtenances of idle luxury. I am also informed by Mrs Otis, who, I may say, is no mean authority upon Art – having had the privilege of spending several winters in Boston when she was a girl – that these gems are of great monetary worth, and if offered for sale would fetch a tall price. Under these circumstances, Lord Canterville,

I feel sure that you will recognize how impossible it would be for me to allow them to remain in the possession of any member of my family; and, indeed, all such vain gauds and toys, however suitable or necessary to the dignity of the British aristocracy, would be completely out of place among those who have been brought up on the severe, and I believe immortal, principles of republican simplicity. Perhaps I should mention that Virginia is very anxious that you should allow her to retain the box as a memento of your unfortunate but misguided ancestor. As it is extremely old, and consequently a good deal out of repair, you may perhaps think fit to comply with her request. For my own part, I confess I am a good deal surprised to find a child of mine expressing sympathy with mediævalism in any form, and can only account for it by the fact that Virginia was born in one of your London suburbs shortly after Mrs Otis had returned from a trip to Athens.'

Lord Canterville listened very gravely to the worthy Minister's speech, pulling his grey moustache now and then to hide an involuntary smile, and when Mr Otis had ended, he shook him cordially by the hand, and said, 'My dear sir, your charming little daughter rendered my unlucky ancestor, Sir Simon, a very important service, and I and my family are much indebted to her for her marvellous courage and pluck. The jewels are clearly hers, and, egad, I believe that if I were heartless enough to take them from her, the wicked old fellow would be out of his grave in a fortnight, leading me the devil of a life. As for their being heirlooms, nothing is an heirloom that is not so mentioned in a will or legal document, and the existence of these jewels has been quite unknown. I assure you I have no more claim on them than your butler, and when Miss Virginia grows up I daresay she will be pleased to have pretty things to wear. Besides, you forget, Mr Otis, that you took the furniture and the ghost at a valuation, and anything that belonged to the ghost passed at once into your possession, as, whatever activity Sir Simon may have shown in the corridor at night, in point of law he was really dead, and you acquired his property by purchase.'

Mr Otis was a good deal distressed at Lord Canterville's refusal, and begged him to reconsider his decision, but the good natured peer was quite firm, and finally induced the Minister to allow his daughter to retain the present the ghost had given her, and when, in the spring of 1890, the young Duchess of Cheshire was presented at the Queen's first drawing-room on the occasion of her marriage, her jewels were the universal theme of admiration. For Virginia received the coronet, which is the reward of all good little American girls, and was married to her boy lover as soon as he came of age. They were both so charming, and they loved each other so much, that every one was delighted at the match, except the old Marchioness of Dumbleton, who had tried to catch the Duke for one of her seven unmarried daughters, and had given no less than three expensive dinner parties for that purpose, and, strange to say, Mr Otis himself. Mr Otis was extremely fond of the young Duke personally, but, theoretically, he objected to titles, and, to use his own words, 'was not without apprehension lest, amid the enervating influences of a pleasure-loving aristocracy, the true principles of republican simplicity should be forgotten'. His objections, however, were completely overruled, and I believe that when he walked up the aisle of St George's, Hanover Square, with his daughter leaning on his arm, there was not a prouder man in the whole length and breadth of England.

The Duke and Duchess, after the honeymoon was over, went down to Canterville Chase, and on the day after their arrival they walked over in the afternoon to the lonely churchyard by the pine-woods. There had been a great deal of difficulty at first about the inscription on Sir Simon's tombstone, but finally it had been decided to engrave on it simply the initials of the old gentleman's name, and the verse from the library window. The Duchess had brought with her some lovely roses, which she strewed upon the grave, and after they had stood by it for some time they strolled into the ruined chancel of the old abbey. There the Duchess sat down on a fallen pillar, while her husband lay at her feet smoking a cigarette and looking up at her beautiful eyes. Suddenly he threw his cigarette away, took hold of her hand, and said to her. 'Virginia, a wife should have no secrets from her husband.'

'Dear Cecil! I have no secrets from you.'

'Yes, you have,' he answered, smiling, 'you have never told me what happened to you when you were locked up with the ghost.'

'I have never told any one, Cecil,' said Virginia gravely.

'I know that, but you might tell me.'

'Please don't ask me, Cecil, I cannot tell you. Poor Sir Simon! I owe him a great deal. Yes, don't laugh, Cecil, I really do. He made me see what Life is, and what Death signifies, and why Love is stronger than both.'

The Duke rose and kissed his wife lovingly.

'You can have your secret as long as I have your heart,' he murmured.

'You have always had that, Cecil.'

'And you will tell our children some day, won't you?'

Virginia blushed.

Barnsfather's Syndrome

RICHARD GORDON

PARIS WAS A DISAPPOINTMENT. Young Mr Edgar Barnsfather FRCS had expected to find himself in the Champs-Elysées, jammed between the Arc de Triomphe and the Eiffel Tower, with the Folies Bergère opposite. The medical conference was in an angular, concrete hotel like a hospital, a five-minute bus-ride from the airport terminal. He had never been to France before. He arrived in late afternoon, and queued for his conference documents in the hotel foyer behind a fat, ruddy, gingery, rustic-looking practitioner in tweeds.

'Awful bore, these conferences,' said the fat doctor genially.

'I wouldn't know,' Edgar replied meekly. 'I've never attended one.'

'I'm only here for the beer. Exactly like everyone else. Dreadful rackets, all scientific meetings. A most damning reflection on the way we have to live. The doctors go along for a jolly, which they can set against their income-tax. Some sinister drug company subsidizes it all for the publicity. As for the hotel, at this time of the year they'd entertain a convention of cannibals to let their empty bedrooms.'

Edgar could not help feeling shocked. 'I think myself privileged to be delivering a paper.'

'Really? What about?'

'Barnsfather's syndrome. Pseudoperforation in young adults.'

'Ah! You're a surgeon?'

Edgar nodded. 'I'm a registrar at the Percival Pott.'

'An excellent London hospital.' The tweedy doctor smiled over half-moon glasses. 'And what *is* Barnsfather's syndrome?'

'I've a paper about it in the latest *BMJ*.' Edgar's voice was twisted painfully between pride and modesty. 'The first I've published, actually. I collected a series of young persons admitted with the signs and symptoms of acute perforated peptic ulcer. Abdominal pain, rigidity, vomiting, that sort of thing. But nothing physically wrong.

All psychological. Stress, you know. Very interesting. Some were even operated upon. But perhaps this is not in your line?' he apologized.

'Not really.'

'And what do you do in the profession?'

'Oh, I just go on being President of the Royal College of Therapeutics.'

A pretty French girl in a thin white blouse stood behind a long table with piles of plastic-covered folders, each emblazoned in gold with the name of the drug company and the products it hoped the assembly would go home to prescribe. When Edgar introduced himself, she smiled delightedly and pinned to his lapel a card saying E BARNSFARTER.

'Have a nice time,' she said.

He stared at the lace edging her bra. He was full of unsurgical thoughts. It was his first night in two years of marriage away from his wife. The girl had given him such a lovely smile. 'Is there anything to do in the evenings?'

'There are excursions by autobus to the Opéra and Comédie française.'

'I mean of a more . . . er, intimate nature.'

'You like the *boxe*? There is a tournament just near the hotel.' She smiled delightedly at the next doctor. 'Have a nice time.'

Edgar bought a postcard of Napoleon's tomb, addressed it to his wife in Putney, but could find nowhere to post it. He slipped it in the pocket of his John Collier suit. He would take it home to put on the mantelpiece. It would save postage. He went up to his cuboid bedroom. It was getting dark. He gazed through the double-glazing at the wintry fields, the brightly-lit motorway, the ugly anonymous buildings which fringe all airports. Apart from seeing people drive on the right, he could have stayed at home.

He sat down with *Le Canard Enchaîné*, which he had extravagantly bought at Heathrow to get in the mood. He had been irritated at hardly understanding a word, having imagined that anyone with his intelligence and O-levels could read French. In the plane, he had thrown back his head and laughed loudly over the pages, just to show that he could, until the other passengers started staring at him oddly. So he had read through all the leaders in the *British Medical Journal*, his pale, domed forehead stamped with critical furrows.

He went carefully through the printed conference programme, received from the girl downstairs. He would be speaking the following afternoon to the psychosomatic section, between a surgeon from Chicago on the digestive processes of confused rats and a professor from Milan on phantom tapeworms in nuns.

He drew the *BMJ* from his briefcase, its handle secured at one end with a surgical suture. The learned pages fell open at the paper on Barnsfather's syndrome. He read it again all the way through, as though returning to the oft-folded sheets of a love-letter.

He sighed, staring through the window at the cars flicking along the motorway. This would be the first conference in a lifetime full of them. He might be a mere surgical registrar, but one day he would ease himself into a professorial chair. Everyone in the hospital told him that he was far more use in a lab than an operating theatre. He looked at his watch. It was dinnertime. He could savour the famed French cuisine.

Edgar crossed the foyer towards a notice saying:

INTERNATIONAL GASTROENTEROLOGISTS AND
CHOLECYSTOLOGISTS OFFICIAL DINNER

'Monsieur?' icily demanded a man in striped trousers at the door.

'Dinner,' Edgar explained. *'Dîner. Comprenez?'*

'Monsieur has an invitation? This is the dinner for the officials of the Congress. I assure monsieur that he will find an excellent dinner in the hotel restaurant.'

The restaurant was a long room hung with brown plastic curtains, so dim nobody could see the food or read the menu. He ordered *cervelle au beurre noir*, because he was fond of kidneys. He chose half a bottle of Beaujolais, because it was the only name he recognized. When the dish appeared, he realized that he had made an error in anatomy. The wine tasted peculiar, but he was too timid to complain. He ventured afterwards into the bar, but it was jammed with doctors drinking free brandy and noisier than students. He went to his room, undressed and read *Recent Advances in Surgery* until he fell asleep.

He woke. The curtains were drawn, the room pitch dark. He felt terrible.

He groaned, clasping his stomach. It was the brains, the wine. Some vile, explosive chemical reaction had occurred between the two. Brains always solidified in alcohol. That was how pathologists kept them, in pots.

He gasped. Colic tore at him with tiger's claws. He lay back on his pillow, breathing quickly. He was ill. He was also a doctor. He must decide what was wrong with him.

Intestinal obstruction? Appendicitis? Meckel's diverticulitis? Acute pancreatitis? Alarming diagnoses leapt through his mind, like questions fired at students over the bedside. The referred pain of coronary thrombosis, perhaps? Or of acute meningitis? Bellyache could be anything.

The tiger leapt again. He sensed sweat on his brow. He groped in the darkness. His watch said it was barely midnight. He fumbled for the telephone.

'*Allo?*' said a woman's voice.

'*Je suis malade.*'

'*Vous êtes Monsieur qui?*'

'*Malade.* Ill. Kaput. OK?'

'Monsieur wants room service?'

'No, I want a doctor.'

'*Oui*, monsieur. Which doctor?'

'Any doctor.'

'But monsieur! The hotel tonight is full of doctors.'

Edgar bit this thumb-nail. It was like having a riot at the police ball and dialling 999 for the squad cars. 'Has the hotel a doctor? One who comes when the guests are taken *malade!*'

'*Mais bien sûr*, monsieur. But he is in Paris.'

'Get him,' commanded Edgar, as another pang exploded in his stomach. An hour passed. The pains were worse. He was dying.

He picked up the telephone again.

'*Allo?*' said a man.

'*Je suis presque mort.*'

'*Ah! Monsieur désire quelque chose à boire?*'

Edgar put down the telephone. He rose, reaching for the red-spotted dressing-gown his wife had given him for Christmas. He staggered to the lift, descending with his forehead resting on the cool metal side. The foyer was empty. Edgar knew his materialisation was alarming, but desperate diseases needed desperate remedies.

'Why, there's the surgeon,' exclaimed the ruddy-faced President of the Royal College of Therapeutics. 'Sleepwalking, eh? Or astray on your way to some nice lady's bedroom? You surgical registrars, all guts and gonads. Or is there a fire?'

The official dinner was breaking up. From the door earlier barred to him drifted twenty or so doctors in dinner-jackets, all chattering noisily and slapping each other on the back.

'I'm ill,' said Edgar shortly.

'*Ill?*' The President was amazed. 'But you can't be ill here. We're all off duty. Enjoying ourselves at some crooked drug company's expense. Excellent dinner, Harry, don't you think?' he enquired of a tall man swaying beside him. 'I'm so fond of *cailles à la gourmande*. But of course, I should never dream of paying for them.'

'The wine was fine, Sir Marmaduke,' said the tall doctor, an American.

'I'm *so* glad you liked it. I chose it myself,' disclosed the President smugly. 'I must confess a favouritism towards claret rather than burgundy, and the Château Figeac '72 *is* very good. On the other hand, the champagne they gave us – I say,' he added irritably, as Edgar groaned loudly. 'Can't you do all that sort of thing in your room?'

'I'm in agony.' Edgar doubled up. 'I've got an acute abdomen.'

'Really? Well, I suppose you should know. I'm only a physician. I never feel at home below the umbilicus.'

'Sir, Sir Marmaduke –' Edgar staggered towards him imploringly. 'Can't you help me? I think I'm dying.'

'My dear fellow, of course, if *that's* the case,' said Sir Marmaduke more amiably, blowing into Edgar's strained face billows of brandy. 'One has one's Hippocratic tradition, and all that, eh? Human life must be preserved, however unworthy. Better have a dekko at your belly. Just jump up there.' He indicated the table previously supervised by the girl with the see-through blouse. He pulled up Edgar's mauve pyjama top and pulled down his pyjama trousers. The other doctors crowded round. It was an unexpected after-dinner entertainment.

'Where does it hurt?' asked Sir Marmaduke, staggering steeply forward and pressing hard.

'Ouch!' screamed Edgar.

'Jolly interesting. You've got a retroperitoneal abscess.'

'Can anyone have a feel?' murmured Harry.

'My dear fellow, help yourself.'

'You're wrong, Sir Marmaduke,' Harry disagreed. 'It's a case of haemoperitoneum.'

'Don't really think so, my dear old boy.' Sir Marmaduke had his eyes closed. 'Patient would be more collapsed.'

'Ah! But they collapse and die suddenly. Like that.' Harry tried to snap his fingers, but missed.

'Excuse, please.' A Japanese doctor wriggled to the front, grinning. 'Please?' he asked, hand poised over Edgar's goose-pimples.

'Dear Saki-san, do plunge in. I'm sure we can all benefit from your oriental wisdom.'

'Please,' decided the Japanese. 'Clear case, hernia foramen of Winslow.'

'Now *that's* a jolly good diagnosis,' agreed Sir Marmaduke warmly. 'Any improvement on a herniated foramen of Winslow, gentlemen?' he invited, looking round.

'*Ja so*, we haf the jaundice?' asked another doctor, pulling down Edgar's eyelid.

'*Mon cher confrère*,' suggested another. 'This case reminds me of one I saw some years ago in Algeria. Ruptured amoebic cyst of the liver. Has your patient lived abroad?'

Edgar shook his head violently.

'Well, that is not necessary to get amoeba,' the French doctor consoled himself. 'My case was fatal, by the way. They nearly always are.'

'How about Legionnaires' pneumonia?' remarked another brightly. 'It's very popular just now.'

'Lassa fever can present like this,' came a voice from the back. 'Though of course I've never seen a case, nor even done a post-mortem on one. They whisk the bodies away so quickly in metal coffins.'

'Well, I must be toddling off to bed,' said Sir Marmaduke. 'Delightful evening. Delightful chaps. Don't forget the golf tomorrow, Harry. Anything to avoid the bloody papers.'

'What about me?' cried Edgar, sitting up.

Sir Marmaduke seemed to have forgotten him. 'I should get a glass of hot water from room service. Do you the world of good. Old remedies are best. If you're not better in the morning, toddle along to my suite and we'll have another prod.'

The doctors disappeared, yawning. Edgar crawled to the lift. He fell into his bedroom. He dialled Putney.

There was a long wait. 'Who's that?' began his wife suspiciously.

'Edgar.'

She gasped. 'Did you miss your plane? God knows, you insisted on getting there early enough.'

'I'm in Paris –'

'What do you mean, phoning?' she demanded crossly. 'It's dreadfully expensive. And at this hour, too. You scared me to death. Or perhaps you imagined I was out for the night,' she added cuttingly, 'and were just checking up on me?'

'I'm ill.'

'There're plenty of doctors to look after you.'

'They're all drunk.'

'What's the matter?' she asked with more concern.

'I've some sort of abdominal catastrophe. I'm coming home. There's a plane at five a.m. I'll try and get on it.'

'But what about your paper?'

'It'll be printed in the Congress proceedings. I should have liked to read it, but . . . what's the point, if I'm dead by tonight?'

'Oh, Edgar!' she cried. 'I'd no idea you were as bad as that.'

'I am. I must see a sober English doctor as soon as possible.'

'Oh, Edgar!' she said again, bursting into tears.

Groaning, gurgling, gagging, Edgar collected his luggage, ordered a taxi, staggered into the airport, changed his ticket, relaxed in his seat on the half-empty plane. He slept, exhausted.

He woke with the stewardess gently shaking him. 'Where am I?' he cried in panic.

'We've just landed at Heathrow. Don't worry, sir,' she said caringly. 'The captain had a radio message about you. You're in good hands.'

She tenderly helped him to the aircraft door. He found himself sitting on a fork-lift truck. Two uniformed men were waiting below with a stretcher. They slid him into an ambulance, which instantly raced across the tarmac with light flashing and horn blaring. A young man with glasses was leaning over him.

'I'm a doctor,' said Edgar.

'Are you? Well, so am I. Your wife alerted the airport. An acute abdomen, isn't it? I'd better take a look at it.'

He felt Edgar's tummy in silence. 'H'm.'

'What's the diagnosis?' Edgar asked anxiously.

'Without doubt, I'd say a clear case of Barnsfather's syndrome. There was a lot of guffle about it in this week's *BMJ*.'

The Machine Stops

E.M. FORSTER

PART ONE: THE AIR-SHIP

IMAGINE, IF YOU CAN, A SMALL ROOM, hexagonal in shape, like the cell of a bee. It is lighted neither by window nor by lamp, yet it is filled with a soft radiance. There are no apertures for ventilation, yet the air is fresh. There are no musical instruments, and yet, at the moment that my meditation opens, this room is throbbing with melodious sounds. An armchair is in the centre, by its side a reading-desk – that is all the furniture. And in the armchair there sits a swaddled lump of flesh – a woman, about five feet high, with a face as white as a fungus. It is to her that the little room belongs.

An electric bell rang.

The woman touched a switch and the music was silent.

'I suppose I must see who it is,' she thought, and set her chair in motion. The chair, like the music, was worked by machinery, and it rolled her to the other side of the room, where the bell still rang importunately.

'Who is it?' she called. Her voice was irritable, for she had been interrupted often since the music began. She knew several thousand people; in certain directions human intercourse had advanced enormously.

But when she listened into the receiver, her white face wrinkled into smiles, and she said:

'Very well. Let us talk, I will isolate myself. I do not expect anything important will happen for the next five minutes – for I can give you fully five minutes, Kuno. Then I must deliver my lecture on "Music during the Australian Period".'

She touched the isolation knob, so that no one else could speak to her. Then she touched the lighting apparatus, and the little room was plunged into darkness.

'Be quick!' she called, her irritation returning. 'Be quick, Kuno; here I am in the dark wasting my time.'

But it was fully fifteen seconds before the round plate that she held in her hands began to glow. A faint blue light shot across it, darkening to purple, and presently she could see the image of her son, who lived on the other side of the earth, and he could see her.

'Kuno, how slow you are.'

He smiled gravely.

'I really believe you enjoy dawdling.'

'I have called you before, mother, but you were always busy or isolated. I have something particular to say.'

'What is it, dearest boy? Be quick. Why could you not send it by pneumatic post?'

'Because I prefer saying such a thing. I want —'

'Well?'

'I want you to come and see me.'

Vashti watched his face in the blue plate.

'But I can see you!' she exclaimed. 'What more do you want?'

'I want to see you not through the Machine,' said Kuno. 'I want to speak to you not through the wearisome Machine.'

'Oh, hush!' said his mother, vaguely shocked. 'You mustn't say anything against the Machine.'

'Why not?'

'One mustn't.'

'You talk as if a god had made the Machine,' cried the other. 'I believe that you pray to it when you are unhappy. Men made it, do not forget that. Great men, but men. The Machine is much, but it is not everything. I see something like you in this plate, but I do not see you. I hear something like you through this telephone, but I do not hear you. That is why I want you to come. Come and stop with me. Pay me a visit, so that we can meet face to face, and talk about the hopes that are in my mind.'

She replied that she could scarcely spare the time for a visit.

'The airship barely takes two days to fly between me and you.'

'I dislike airships.'

'Why?'

'I dislike seeing the horrible brown earth, and the sea, and the stars when it is dark. I get no ideas in an airship.'

'I do not get them anywhere else.'

'What kind of ideas can the air give you?'

He paused for an instant.

'Do you not know four big stars that form an oblong, and three stars close together in the middle of the oblong, and hanging from these stars, three other stars?'

'No, I do not. I dislike the stars. But did they give you an idea? How interesting; tell me.'

'I had an idea that they were like a man.'

'I do not understand.'

'The four big stars are the man's shoulders and his knees. The three stars in the middle are like the belts that men wore once, and the three stars hanging are like a sword.'

'A sword?'

'Men carried swords about with them, to kill animals and other men.'

'It does not strike me as a very good idea, but it is certainly original. When did it come to you first?'

'In the airship —' He broke off, and she fancied that he looked sad. She could not be sure, for the Machine did not transmit *nuances* of expression. It only gave a general idea of people – an idea that was good enough for all practical purposes, Vashti thought. The imponderable bloom, declared by a discredited philosophy to be the actual essence of intercourse, was rightly ignored by the Machine, just as the imponderable bloom of the grape was ignored by the manufacturers of artificial fruit. Something 'good enough' had long since been accepted by our race.

'The truth is,' he continued, 'that I want to see these stars again. They are curious stars. I want to see them not from the airship, but from the surface of the earth, as our ancestors did, thousands of years ago. I want to visit the surface of the earth.'

She was shocked again.

'Mother, you must come, if only to explain to me what is the harm of visiting the surface of the earth.'

'No harm,' she replied, controlling herself. 'But no advantage. The surface of the earth is only dust and mud, no life remains on it, and you would need a respirator, or the cold of the outer air would kill you. One dies immediately in the outer air.'

'I know; of course I shall take all precautions.'

'And besides —'

'Well?'

She considered, and chose her words with care. Her son had a queer temper, and she wished to dissuade him from the expedition.

'It is contrary to the spirit of the age,' she asserted.

'Do you mean by that, contrary to the Machine?'

'In a sense, but — '

His image in the blue plate faded.

'Kuno!'

He had isolated himself.

For a moment Vashti felt lonely.

Then she generated the light, and the sight of her room, flooded with radiance and studded with electric buttons, revived her. There were buttons and switches everywhere – buttons to call for food, for music, for clothing. There was the hot-bath button, by pressure of which a basin of (imitation) marble rose out of the floor, filled to the brim with a warm deodorized liquid. There was the cold-bath button. There was the button that produced literature. And there were of course the buttons by which she communicated with her friends. The room, though it contained nothing, was in touch with all that she cared for in the world.

Vashti's next move was to turn off the isolation-switch, and all the accumulations of the last three minutes burst upon her. The room was filled with the noise of bells, and speaking-tubes. What was the new food like? Could she recommend it? Had she had any ideas lately? Might one tell her one's own ideas? Would she make an engagement to visit the public nurseries at an early date? – say this day month.

To most of these questions she replied with irritation – a growing quality in that accelerated age. She said that the new food was horrible. That she could not visit the public nurseries through press of engagements. That she had no ideas of her own but had just been told one – that four stars and three in the middle were like a man: she doubted there was much in it. Then she switched off her correspondents, for it was time to deliver her lecture on Australian music.

The clumsy system of public gatherings had been long since abandoned; neither Vashti nor her audience stirred from their rooms. Seated in her armchair she spoke, while they in their armchairs heard her, fairly well, and saw her, fairly well. She opened with a humorous account of music in the pre-Mongolian epoch, and went on to describe the great outburst of song that followed the Chinese conquest. Remote and primaeval as were the methods of I-San-So and the Brisbane school, she yet felt (she said) that study of them might repay the musician of today: they had freshness; they had, above all, ideas.

Her lecture, which lasted ten minutes, was well received, and at its conclusion, she and many of her audience listened to a lecture on the sea; there were ideas to be got from the sea; the speaker had donned a respirator and visited it lately. Then she fed, talked to many friends, had a bath, talked again, and summoned her bed.

The bed was not to her liking. It was too large, and she had a feeling for a small bed. Complaint was useless, for beds were of the same dimension all over the world, and to have had an alternative size would have involved vast alterations in the Machine. Vashti isolated herself – it was necessary, for neither day nor night existed under the ground – and reviewed all that had happened since she had summoned the bed last. Ideas? Scarcely any. Events – was Kuno's invitation an event?

By her side, on the little reading-desk, was a survival from the ages of litter – one book. This was the Book of the Machine. In it were instructions against every possible contingency. If she was hot or cold or dyspeptic or at a loss for a word, she went to the book, and it told her which button to press. The Central Committee published it. In accordance with a growing habit, it was richly bound.

Sitting up in the bed, she took it reverently in her hands. She glanced round the glowing room as if some one might be watching her. Then, half ashamed, half joyful, she murmured 'O Machine! O Machine!' and raised the volume to her lips. Thrice she kissed it, thrice inclined her head, thrice she felt the delirium of acquiescence. Her ritual performed, she turned to page 1367, which gave the times of the departure of the airships from the island in the southern hemisphere, under whose soil she lived, to the island in the northern hemisphere, whereunder lived her son.

She thought, 'I have not the time.'

She made the room dark and slept; she awoke and made the room light; she ate and exchanged ideas with her friends, and listened to music and attended lectures; she made the room dark and slept. Above her, beneath her, and around her, the Machine hummed eternally; she did not notice the noise, for she had been born with it in her ears. The earth, carrying her, hummed as it sped through silence, turning her now to the invisible sun, now to the invisible stars. She awoke and made the room light.

'Kuno!'

'I will not talk to you,' he answered, 'until you come.'

'Have you been on the surface of the earth since we spoke last?'

His image faded.

Again she consulted the book. She became very nervous and lay back in her chair palpitating. Think of her as without teeth or hair. Presently she directed the chair to the wall, and pressed an unfamiliar button. The wall swung apart slowly. Through the opening she saw a tunnel that curved slightly, so that its goal was not visible. Should she go to see her son, here was the beginning of the journey.

Of course she knew all about the communication-system. There was nothing mysterious in it. She would summon a car and it would fly with her down the tunnel until it reached the lift that communicated with the airship station: the system had been in use for many, many years, long before the universal establishment of the Machine. And of course she had studied the civilization that had immediately preceded her own – the civilization that had mistaken the functions of the system, and had used it for bringing people to things, instead of for bringing things to people. Those funny old days, when men went for change of air instead of changing the air in their rooms! And yet – she was frightened of the tunnel: she had not seen it since her last child was born. It curved – but not quite as she remembered; it was brilliant – but not quite as brilliant as a lecturer had suggested. Vashti was seized with the terrors of direct experience. She shrank back into the room, and the wall closed up again.

'Kuno,' she said, 'I cannot come to see you. I am not well.'

Immediately an enormous apparatus fell on to her out of the ceiling, a thermometer was automatically inserted between her lips, a stethoscope was automatically laid upon her heart. She lay powerless. Cool pads soothed her forehead. Kuno had telegraphed to her doctor.

So the human passions still blundered up and down in the Machine. Vashti drank the medicine that the doctor projected into her mouth, and the machinery retired into the ceiling. The voice of Kuno was heard asking how she felt.

'Better.' Then with irritation: 'But why do you not come to me instead?'

'Because I cannot leave this place.'

'Why?'

'Because, any moment, something tremendous may happen.'

'Have you been on the surface of the earth yet?'

'Not yet.'

'Then what is it?'

'I will not tell you through the Machine.'

She resumed her life.

But she thought of Kuno as a baby, his birth, his removal to the public nurseries, her one visit to him there, his visits to her – visits which stopped when the Machine had assigned him a room on the other side of the earth. 'Parents, duties of,' said the book of the Machine, 'cease at the moment of birth. P. 422327483.' True, but there was something special about Kuno – indeed there had been something special about all her children – and, after all, she must brave the journey if he desired it. And 'something tremendous might happen.' What did that mean? The nonsense of a youthful man, no doubt, but she must go. Again she pressed the unfamiliar button, again the wall swung back, and she saw the tunnel that curved out of sight. Clasping the Book, she rose, tottered on to the platform, and summoned the car. Her room closed behind her: the journey to the northern hemisphere had begun.

Of course it was perfectly easy. The car approached and in it she found armchairs exactly like her own. When she signalled, it stopped, and she tottered into the lift. One other passenger was in the lift, the first fellow creature she had seen face to face for months. Few travelled in these days, for, thanks to the advance of science, the earth was exactly alike all over. Rapid intercourse, from which the previous civilization had hoped so much, had ended by defeating itself. What was the good of going to Pekin when it was just like Shrewsbury? Why return to Shrewsbury when it would be just like Pekin? Men seldom moved their bodies; all unrest was concentrated in the soul.

The airship service was a relic from the former age. It was kept up, because it was easier to keep it up than to stop it or to diminish it, but it now far exceeded the wants of the population. Vessel after vessel would rise from the vomitories of Rye or of Christchurch (I use the antique names), would sail into the crowded sky, and would draw up at the wharves of the south – empty. So nicely adjusted was the system, so independent of meteorology, that the sky, whether calm or cloudy, resembled a vast kaleidoscope whereon the same patterns periodically recurred. The ship on which Vashti sailed started now at sunset, now at dawn. But always, as it passed above Rheims, it would neighbour the ship that served between Helsingfors and the Brazils, and, every third time it surmounted the Alps, the fleet of Palermo would cross its track behind. Night and day, wind and storm, tide and earthquake, impeded man no longer. He had harnessed Leviathan. All the old literature, with its praise of Nature, and its fear of Nature, rang false as the prattle of a child.

Yet as Vashti saw the vast flank of the ship, stained with exposure to the outer air, her horror of direct experience returned. It was not quite like the airship in the cinematophote. For one thing it smelt – not strongly or unpleasantly, but it did smell, and with her eyes shut she should have known that a new thing was close to her. Then she had to walk to it from the lift, had to submit to glances from the other passengers. The man in front dropped his Book – no great matter, but it disquieted them all. In the rooms, if the Book was dropped, the floor raised it mechanically, but the gangway to the airship was not so prepared, and the sacred volume lay motionless. They stopped – the thing was unforeseen – and the man, instead of picking up his property, felt the muscles of his arm to see how they had failed him. Then some one actually said with direct utterance: 'We shall be late' – and they trooped on board, Vashti treading on the pages as she did so.

Inside, her anxiety increased. The arrangements were old-fashioned and rough. There was even a female attendant, to whom she would have to announce her wants during the voyage. Of course a revolving platform ran the length of the boat, but she was expected to walk from it to her cabin. Some cabins were better than others, and she did not get the best. She thought the attendant had been unfair, and spasms of rage shook her. The glass valves had closed, she could not go back. She saw, at the end of the vestibule, the lift in which she had ascended going quietly up and down, empty. Beneath those corridors of shining tiles were rooms, tier below tier, reaching far into the earth, and in each room there sat a human being, eating, or sleeping, or producing ideas. And buried deep in the hive was her own room. Vashti was afraid.

'O Machine! O Machine!' she murmured, and caressed her Book, and was comforted.

Then the sides of the vestibule seemed to melt together, as do the passages that we see in dreams, the lift vanished, the Book that had been dropped slid to the left and vanished, polished tiles rushed by like a stream of water, there was a slight jar, and the airship, issuing from its tunnel, soared above the waters of a tropical ocean.

It was night. For a moment she saw the coast of Sumatra edged by the phosphorescence of waves, and crowned by lighthouses, still sending forth their disregarded beams. These also vanished, and only the stars distracted her. They were not motionless, but swayed to and fro above her head, thronging out of one skylight into another, as if the universe and not the airship was careening. And, as often happens on clear nights, they seemed now to be in perspective, now on a plane; now piled tier beyond tier into the infinite heavens, now concealing infinity, a roof limiting for ever the visions of men. In either case they seemed intolerable. 'Are we to travel in the dark?' called the passengers angrily, and the attendant, who had been careless, generated the light, and pulled down the blinds of pliable metal. When the airships had been built, the desire to look direct at things still lingered in the world. Hence the extraordinary number of skylights and windows, and the proportionate discomfort to those who were civilized and refined. Even in Vashti's cabin one star peeped through a flaw in the blind, and after a few hours' uneasy slumber, she was disturbed by an unfamiliar glow, which was the dawn.

Quick as the ship had sped westwards, the earth had rolled eastwards quicker still, and had dragged back Vashti and her companions towards the sun. Science could prolong the night, but only for a little, and those high hopes of neutralizing the earth's diurnal revolution had passed, together with hopes that were possibly higher. To 'keep pace with the sun,' or even to outstrip it, had been the aim of the civilization preceding this. Racing aeroplanes had been built for the purpose, capable of enormous speed, and steered by the greatest intellects of the epoch. Round the globe they went, round and round, westward, westward, round and round, amidst humanity's applause. In vain. The globe went eastward quicker still, horrible accidents occurred, and the Committee of the Machine, at the time rising into prominence, declared the pursuit illegal, unmechanical, and punishable by Homelessness.

Of Homelessness more will be said later.

Doubtless the Committee was right. Yet the attempt to 'defeat the sun' aroused the last common interest that our race experienced about the heavenly bodies, or indeed about anything. It was the last time that men were compacted by thinking of a power outside the world. The sun had conquered, yet it was the end of his spiritual dominion. Dawn, midday, twilight, the zodiacal path, touched neither men's lives nor their hearts, and science retreated into the ground, to concentrate herself upon problems that she was certain of solving.

So when Vashti found her cabin invaded by a rosy finger of light, she was annoyed, and tried to adjust the blind. But the blind flew up altogether, and she saw through the skylight small pink clouds, swaying against a background of blue, and as the sun crept higher, its radiance entered direct, brimming down the wall, like a golden sea. It rose and fell with the airship's motion, just as waves rise and fall, but it advanced steadily, as a tide advances. Unless she was careful, it would strike her face. A spasm of horror shook her and she rang for the attendant. The attendant too was horrified, but she could do nothing; it was not her place to mend the blind. She could only suggest that the lady should change her cabin, which she accordingly prepared to do.

People were almost exactly alike all over the world, but the attendant of the airship, perhaps owing to her exceptional duties, had grown a little out of the common. She had often to address passengers with direct speech, and this had given her a certain roughness and originality of manner. When Vashti swerved away from the sunbeams with a cry, she behaved barbarically – she put out her hand to steady her.

'How dare you!' exclaimed the passenger. 'You forget yourself!'

The woman was confused, and apologized for not having let her fall. People never touched one another. The custom had become obsolete, owing to the Machine.

'Where are we now?' asked Vashti haughtily.

'We are over Asia,' said the attendant, anxious to be polite.

'Asia?'

'You must excuse my common way of speaking. I have got into the habit of calling places over which I pass by their unmechanical names.'

'Oh, I remember Asia. The Mongols came from it.'

'Beneath us, in the open air, stood a city that was once called Simla.'

'Have you ever heard of the Mongols and of the Brisbane school?'

'No.'

'Brisbane also stood in the open air.'

'Those mountains to the right – let me show you them.' She pushed back a metal blind. The main chain of the Himalayas was revealed. 'They were once called the Roof of the World, those mountains.'

'What a foolish name!'

'You must remember that, before the dawn of civilization, they seemed to be an impenetrable wall that touched the stars. It was supposed that no one but the gods could exist above their summits. How we have advanced, thanks to the Machine!'

'How we have advanced, thanks to the Machine!' said Vashti.

'How we have advanced, thanks to the Machine!' echoed the passenger who had dropped his Book the night before, and who was standing in the passage.

'And that white stuff in the cracks? – what is it?'

'I have forgotten its name.'

'Cover the window, please. These mountains give me no ideas.'

The northern aspect of the Himalayas was in deep shadow: on the Indian slope the sun had just prevailed. The forests had been destroyed during the literature epoch for the purpose of making newspaper-pulp, but the snows were awakening to their morning glory, and clouds still hung on the breasts of Kinchinjunga. In the plain were seen the ruins of cities, with diminished rivers creeping by their walls, and by the sides of these were sometimes the signs of vomitories, marking the cities of today. Over the whole prospect airships rushed, crossing and intercrossing with incredible *aplomb*, and rising nonchalantly when they desired to escape the perturbations of the lower atmosphere and to traverse the Roof of the World.

'We have indeed advanced, thanks to the Machine,' repeated the attendant, and hid the Himalayas behind a metal blind.

The day dragged wearily forward. The passengers sat each in his cabin, avoiding one another with an almost physical repulsion and longing to be once more under the surface of the earth. There were eight or ten of them, mostly young males, sent out from the public nurseries to inhabit the rooms of those who had died in various parts of the earth. The man who had dropped his Book was on the homeward journey. He had been sent to Sumatra for the purpose of propagating the race. Vashti alone was travelling by her private will.

At midday she took a second glance at the earth. The airship was crossing another range of mountains, but she could see little, owing to clouds. Masses of black rock hovered below her, and merged indistinctly into grey. Their shapes were fantastic; one of them resembled a prostrate man.

'No ideas here,' murmured Vashti, and hid the Caucasus behind a metal blind.

In the evening she looked again. They were crossing a golden sea, in which lay many small islands and one peninsula.

She repeated, 'No ideas here,' and hid Greece behind a metal blind.

PART TWO: THE MENDING APPARATUS

By a vestibule, by a lift, by a tubular railway, by a platform, by a sliding door – by reversing all the steps of her departure did Vashti arrive at her son's room, which exactly resembled her own. She might well declare that the visit was superfluous. The buttons, the knobs, the reading-desk with the Book, the temperature, the atmosphere, the illumination – all were exactly the same. And if Kuno himself, flesh of her flesh, stood close beside her at last, what profit was there in that? She was too well-bred to shake him by the hand.

Averting her eyes, she spoke as follows:

'Here I am. I have had the most terrible journey and greatly retarded the development of my soul. It is not worth it, Kuno, it is not worth it. My time is too precious. The sunlight almost touched me, and I have met with the rudest people. I can only stop a few minutes. Say what you want to say, and then I must return.'

'I have been threatened with Homelessness,' said Kuno.

She looked at him now.

'I have been threatened with Homelessness, and I could not tell you such a thing through the Machine.'

Homelessness means death. The victim is exposed to the air, which kills him.

'I have been outside since I spoke to you last. The tremendous thing has happened, and they have discovered me.'

'But why shouldn't you go outside?' she exclaimed. 'It is perfectly legal, perfectly mechanical, to visit the surface of the earth. I have lately been to a lecture on the sea; there is no objection to that; one simply summons a respirator and gets an Egression-permit. It is not the kind of thing that spiritually-minded people do, and I begged you not to do it, but there is no legal objection to it.'

'I did not get an Egression-permit.'

'Then how did you get out?'

'I found out a way of my own.'

The phrase conveyed no meaning to her, and he had to repeat it.

'A way of your own?' she whispered. 'But that would be wrong.'

'Why?'

The question shocked her beyond measure.

'You are beginning to worship the Machine,' he said coldly. 'You think it irreligious of me to have found out a way of my own. It was just what the Committee thought, when they threatened me with Homelessness.'

At this she grew angry. 'I worship nothing!' she cried. 'I am most advanced. I don't think you irreligious, for there is no such thing as religion left. All the fear and the superstition that existed once have been destroyed by the Machine. I only meant that to find out a way of your own was — Besides, there is no new way out.'

'So it is always supposed.'

'Except through the vomitories, for which one must have an Egression-permit, it is impossible to get out. The Book says so.'

'Well, the Book's wrong, for I have been out on my feet.'

For Kuno was possessed of a certain physical strength.

By these days it was a demerit to be muscular. Each infant was examined at birth, and all who promised undue strength were destroyed. Humanitarians may protest, but it would have been no true kindness to let an athlete live; he would never have been happy in that state of life to which the Machine had called him; he would have yearned for trees to climb, rivers to bathe in, meadows and hills against which he might measure his body. Man must be adapted to his surroundings, must he not? In the dawn of the world our weakly must be exposed on Mount Taygetus, in its twilight our strong will suffer euthanasia, that the Machine may progress, that the Machine may progress, that the Machine may progress eternally.

'You know that we have lost the sense of space. We say "space is annihilated," but we have annihilated not space, but the sense thereof. We have lost a part of ourselves. I determined to recover it, and I began by walking up and down the platform of the railway outside my room. Up and down, until I was tired, and so did recapture the meaning of "Near" and "Far". "Near" is a place to which I can get quickly *on my feet*, not a place to which the train or the airship will take me quickly. "Far" is a place to which I cannot get quickly on my feet; the vomitory is "far," though I could be there in thirty-eight seconds by summoning the train. Man is the measure. That was my first lesson. Man's feet are the measure for distance, his hands are the measure for ownership, his body is the measure for all that is lovable and desirable and strong. Then I went further: it was then that I called to you for the first time, and you would not come.

'This city, as you know, is built deep beneath the surface of the earth, with only the vomitories protruding. Having paced the platform outside my own room, I took the lift to the next platform and paced that also, and so with each in turn, until I came to the topmost, above which begins the earth. All the platforms were exactly alike, and all that I gained by visiting them was to develop my sense of space and my muscles. I think I should have been content with this – it is not a little thing, – but as I walked and brooded, it occurred to me that our cities had been built in the days when men still breathed the outer air, and that there had been ventilation shafts for the workmen. I could think of nothing but these ventilation shafts. Had they been destroyed by all the food-tubes and medicine-tubes and music-tubes that the Machine has evolved lately? Or did traces of them remain? One thing was certain. If I came upon them anywhere, it would be in the railway-tunnels of the topmost story. Everywhere else, all space was accounted for.

'I am telling my story quickly, but don't think that I was not a coward or that your answers never depressed me. It is not the proper thing, it is not mechanical, it is not decent to walk along a railway-tunnel. I did not fear that I might tread upon a live rail and be killed. I feared something far more intangible – doing what was not contemplated by the Machine. Then I said to myself, "Man is the measure," and I went, and after many visits I found an opening.

'The tunnels, of course, were lighted. Everything is light, artificial light; darkness is the exception. So when I saw a black gap in the tiles, I knew that it was an exception, and rejoiced. I put in my arm – I could put in no more at first – and waved it round and round in ecstasy. I loosened another tile, and put in my head, and shouted into the darkness: "I am coming, I shall do it yet," and my voice reverberated down endless passages. I seemed to hear the spirits of those dead workmen who had returned each evening to the starlight and to their wives, and all the generations who had lived in the open air called back to me, "You will do it yet, you are coming."'

He paused, and, absurd as he was, his last words moved her. For Kuno had lately asked to be a father, and his request had been refused by the Committee. His was not a type that the Machine desired to hand on.

'Then a train passed. It brushed by me, but I thrust my head and arms into the hole. I had done enough for one day, so I crawled back to the platform, went down in the lift, and summoned my bed. Ah what dreams! And again I called you, and again you refused.'

She shook her head and said:

'Don't. Don't talk of these terrible things. You make me miserable. You are throwing civilization away.'

'But I had got back the sense of space and a man cannot rest then. I determined to get in at the hole and climb the shaft. And so I exercised my arms. Day after day I went through ridiculous movements, until my flesh ached, and I could hang by my hands and hold the pillow of my bed outstretched for many minutes. Then I summoned a respirator, and started.

'It was easy at first. The mortar had somehow rotted, and I soon pushed some more tiles in, and clambered after them into the darkness, and the spirits of the dead comforted me. I don't know what I mean by that. I just say what I felt. I felt, for the first time, that a protest had been lodged against corruption, and that even as the dead were comforting me, so I was comforting the unborn. I felt that humanity existed, and that it existed without clothes. How can I possibly explain this? It was naked, humanity seemed naked, and all these tubes and buttons and machineries neither came into the world with us, nor will they follow us out, nor do they matter supremely while we are here. Had I been strong, I would have torn off every garment I had, and gone out into the outer air unswaddled. But this is not for me, nor perhaps for my generation. I climbed with my respirator and my hygienic clothes and my dietetic tabloids! Better thus than not at all.

'There was a ladder, made of some primaeval metal. The light from the railway fell upon its lowest rungs, and I saw that it led straight upwards out of the rubble at the bottom of the shaft. Perhaps our ancestors ran up and down it a dozen times daily, in their building. As I climbed, the rough edges cut through my gloves so that my hands bled. The light helped me for a little, and then came darkness and, worse still, silence which pierced my ears like a sword. The Machine hums! Did you know that? Its hum penetrates our blood, and may even guide our thoughts. Who knows? I was getting beyond its power. Then I thought: "This silence means that I am doing wrong." But I heard voices in the silence, and again they strengthened me.' He laughed. 'I had need of them. The next moment I cracked my head against something.'

She sighed.

'I had reached one of those pneumatic stoppers that defend us from the outer air. You may have noticed them on the airship. Pitch dark, my feet on the rungs of an invisible ladder, my hands cut; I cannot explain how I lived through this part, but the voices still comforted me, and I felt for fastenings. The stopper, I suppose, was about eight feet across. I passed my hand over it as far as I could reach. It was perfectly smooth. I felt it almost to the centre. Not quite to the centre, for my arm was too short. Then the voice said: "Jump. It is worth it. There may be a handle in the centre, and you may catch hold of it and so come to us your own way. And if there is no handle, so that you may fall and are dashed to pieces – it is still worth it: you will still come to us your own way." So I jumped. There was a handle, and –'

He paused. Tears gathered in his mother's eyes. She knew that he was fated. If he did not die today he would die tomorrow. There was not room for such a person in the world. And with her pity disgust mingled. She was ashamed at having borne such a son, she who had always been so respectable and so full of ideas. Was he really the little boy to whom she had taught the use of his stops and buttons, and to whom she had given his first lessons in the Book? The very hair that disfigured his lip showed that he was reverting to some savage type. On atavism the Machine can have no mercy.

'There was a handle, and I did catch it. I hung tranced over the darkness and heard the hum of these workings as the last whisper in a dying dream. All the things I had cared about and all the people I had spoken to through tubes appeared infinitely little. Meanwhile the handle revolved. My weight had set something in motion and I span slowly, and then –

'I cannot describe it. I was lying with my face to the sunshine. Blood poured from my nose and ears and I heard a tremendous roaring. The stopper, with me clinging to it, had simply been blown out of the earth, and the air that we make down here was escaping through the vent into the air above. It burst up like a fountain. I crawled back to it – for the upper air hurts – and, as it were, I took great sips from the edge. My respirator had flown goodness knows where, my clothes were torn. I just lay with my lips close to the hole, and I sipped until the bleeding stopped. You can imagine nothing so curious. This hollow in the grass – I will speak of it in a minute, – the sun shining into it, not brilliantly but through marbled clouds, – the peace, the nonchalance, the sense of space, and, brushing my cheek, the roaring fountain of our artificial air! Soon I spied my respirator, bobbing up and down in the current high above my head, and higher still were many airships. But no one ever looks out of airships, and in any case they could not have picked me up. There I was, stranded. The sun shone a little way down the shaft, and revealed the topmost rung of the ladder, but it was hopeless trying to reach it. I should either have been tossed up again by the escape, or else have fallen in, and died. I could only lie on the grass, sipping and sipping, and from time to time glancing around me.

'I knew that I was in Wessex, for I had taken care to go to a lecture on the subject before starting. Wessex lies above the room in which we are talking now. It was once an important state. Its kings held all the southern coast from the Andredswald to Cornwall, while the Wansdyke protected them on the north, running over the high ground. The lecturer was only concerned with the rise of Wessex, so I do not know how long it remained an international power, nor would the knowledge have assisted me. To tell the truth I could do nothing but laugh, during this part. There was I, with a pneumatic stopper by my side and a respirator bobbing over my head, imprisoned, all three of us, in a grass-grown hollow that was edged with fern.'

Then he grew grave again.

'Lucky for me that it was a hollow. For the air began to fall back into it and to fill it as water fills a bowl. I could crawl about. Presently I stood. I breathed a mixture, in which the air that hurts predominated whenever I tried to climb the sides. This was not so bad. I had not lost my tabloids and remained ridiculously cheerful, and as for the Machine, I forgot about it altogether. My one aim now was to get to the top, where the ferns were, and to view whatever objects lay beyond.

'I rushed the slope. The new air was still too bitter for me and I came rolling back, after a momentary vision of something grey. The sun grew very feeble, and I remembered that he was in Scorpio – I had been to a lecture on that too. If the sun is in Scorpio, and you are in Wessex, it means that you must be as quick as you can, or it will get too dark. (This is the first bit of useful information I have ever got from a lecture, and I expect it will be the last.) It made me try frantically to breathe the new air, and to advance as far as I dared out of my pond. The hollow filled so slowly. At times I thought that the fountain played with less vigour. My respirator seemed to dance nearer the earth; the roar was decreasing.'

He broke off.

'I don't think this is interesting you. The rest will interest you even less. There are no ideas in it, and I wish that I had not troubled you to come. We are too different, mother.'

She told him to continue.

'It was evening before I climbed the bank. The sun had very nearly slipped out of the sky by this time, and I could not get a good view. You, who have just crossed the Roof of the World, will not want to hear an account of the little hills that I saw – low colourless hills. But to me they were living and the turf that covered them was a skin, under which their muscles rippled, and I felt that those hills had called with incalculable force to men in the past, and that men had loved them. Now they sleep – perhaps for ever. They commune with humanity in dreams. Happy the man, happy the woman, who awakes the hills of Wessex. For though they sleep, they will never die.'

His voice rose passionately.

'Cannot you see, cannot all you lecturers see, that it is we that are dying, and that down here the only thing that really lives is the Machine? We created the Machine, to do our will, but we cannot make it do our will now. It has robbed us of the sense of space and of the sense of touch, it has blurred every human relation and narrowed down love to a carnal act, it has paralysed our bodies and our wills, and now it compels us to worship it. The Machine develops – but not on our lines. The Machine proceeds – but not to our goal. We only exist as the blood corpuscles that course through its arteries, and if it could work without us, it would let us die. Oh, I have no remedy – or, at least, only one – to tell men again and again that I have seen the hills of Wessex as Ælfrid saw them when he overthrew the Danes.

'So the sun set. I forgot to mention that a belt of mist lay between my hill and other hills, and that it was the colour of pearl.'

He broke off for the second time.

'Go on,' said his mother wearily.

He shook his head.

'Go on. Nothing that you say can distress me now. I am hardened.'

'I had meant to tell you the rest, but I cannot: I know that I cannot: goodbye.'

Vashti stood irresolute. All her nerves were tingling with his blasphemies. But she was also inquisitive.

'This is unfair,' she complained. 'You have called me across the world to hear your story, and hear it I will. Tell me – as briefly as possible, for this is a disastrous waste of time – tell me how you returned to civilization.'

'Oh – that!' he said, starting. 'You would like to hear about civilization. Certainly. Had I got to where my respirator fell down?'

'No – but I understand everything now. You put on your respirator, and managed to walk along the surface of the earth to a vomitory, and there your conduct was reported to the Central Committee.'

'By no means.'

He passed his hand over his forehead, as if dispelling some strong impression. Then, resuming his narrative, he warmed to it again.

'My respirator fell about sunset. I had mentioned that the fountain seemed feebler, had I not?'

'Yes.'

'About sunset, it let the respirator fall. As I said, I had entirely forgotten about the Machine, and I paid no great attention at the time, being occupied with other things. I had my pool of air, into which I could dip when the outer keenness became intolerable, and which would possibly remain for days, provided that no wind sprang up to disperse it. Not until it was too late did I realize what the stoppage of the escape implied. You see – the gap in the tunnel had been mended; the Mending Apparatus; the Mending Apparatus, was after me.

'One other warning I had, but I neglected it. The sky at night was clearer than it had been in the day, and the moon, which was about half the sky behind the sun, shone into the dell at moments quite brightly. I was in my usual place – on the boundary between the two atmospheres – when I thought I saw something dark move across the bottom of the dell, and vanish into the shaft. In my folly, I ran down. I bent over and listened, and I thought I heard a faint scraping noise in the depths.

'At this – but it was too late – I took alarm. I determined to put on my respirator and to walk right out of the dell. But my respirator had gone. I knew exactly where it had fallen – between the stopper and the aperture – and I could even feel the mark that it had made in the turf. It had gone, and I realized that something evil was at work, and I had better escape to the other air, and, if I must die, die running towards the cloud that had been the colour of a pearl. I never started. Out of the shaft – it is too horrible. A worm, a long white worm, had crawled out of the shaft and was gliding over the moonlit grass.

'I screamed. I did everything that I should not have done, I stamped upon the creature instead of flying from it, and it at once curled round the ankle. Then we fought. The worm let me run all over the dell, but edged up my leg as I ran. "Help!" I cried. (That part is too awful. It belongs to the part that you will never know.) "Help!" I cried. (Why cannot we suffer in silence?) "Help!" I cried. Then my feet were wound together, I fell, I was dragged away from the dear ferns and the living hills, and past the great metal stopper (I can tell you this part), and I thought it might save me again if I caught hold of the handle. It also was enwrapped, it also. Oh, the whole dell was full of the things. They were searching it in all directions, they were denuding it, and the white snouts of others peeped out of the hole, ready if needed. Everything that could be moved they brought – brushwood, bundles of fern, everything, and down we all went intertwined into hell. The last things that I saw, ere the stopper closed after us, were certain stars, and I felt that a man of my sort lived in the sky. For I did fight, I fought till the very end, and it was only my head hitting against the ladder that quieted me. I woke up in this room. The worms had vanished. I was surrounded by artificial air, artificial light, artificial peace, and my friends were calling to me down speaking-tubes to know whether I had come across any new ideas lately.'

Here his story ended. Discussion of it was impossible, and Vashti turned to go.

'It will end in Homelessness,' she said quietly.

'I wish it would,' retorted Kuno.

'The Machine has been most merciful.'

'I prefer the mercy of God.'

'By that superstitious phrase, do you mean that you could live in the outer air?'

'Yes.'

'Have you ever seen, round the vomitories, the bones of those who were extruded after the Great Rebellion?'

'Yes.'

'They were left where they perished for our edification. A few crawled away, but they perished, too – who can doubt it? And so with the Homeless of our own day. The surface of the earth supports life no longer.'

'Indeed.'

'Ferns and a little grass may survive, but all higher forms have perished. Has any airship detected them?'

'No.'

'Has any lecturer dealt with them?'

'No.'

'Then why this obstinacy?'

'Because I have seen them,' he exploded.

'Seen *what*?'

'Because I have seen her in the twilight – because she came to my help when I called – because she, too, was entangled by the worms, and, luckier than I, was killed by one of them piercing her throat.'

He was mad. Vashti departed, nor, in the troubles that followed, did she ever see his face again.

PART THREE: THE HOMELESS

During the years that followed Kuno's escapade, two important developments took place in the Machine. On the surface they were revolutionary, but in either case men's minds had been prepared beforehand, and they did but express tendencies that were latent already.

The first of these was the abolition of respirators.

Advanced thinkers, like Vashti, had always held it foolish to visit the surface of the earth. Airships might be necessary, but what was the good of going out for mere curiosity and crawling along for a mile or two in a terrestrial motor? The habit was vulgar and perhaps faintly improper: it was unproductive of ideas, and had no connection with the habits that really mattered. So respirators were abolished, and with them, of course, the terrestrial motors, and except for a few lecturers, who complained that they were debarred access to their subject-matter, the development was accepted quietly. Those who still wanted to know what the earth was like had after all only to listen to some gramophone, or to look into some cinematophote. And even the lecturers acquiesced when they found that a lecture on the sea was none the less stimulating when compiled out of other lectures that had already been delivered on the same subject. 'Beware of first-hand ideas!' exclaimed one of the most advanced of them. 'First-hand ideas do not really exist. They are but the physical impressions produced by love and fear, and on this gross foundation who could erect a philosophy? Let your ideas be second-hand, and if possible tenth-hand, for then they will be far removed from that disturbing element – direct observation. Do not learn anything about this subject of mine – the French Revolution. Learn instead what I think that Enicharmon thought Urizen thought Gutch thought Ho-Yung thought Chi-Bo-Sing thought Lafcadio Hearn thought Carlyle thought Mirabeau said about the French Revolution. Through the medium of these ten great minds, the blood that was shed at Paris and the windows that were broken at Versailles will be clarified to an idea which you may employ most profitably in your daily lives. But be sure that the intermediates are many and varied, for in history one authority exists to counteract another. Urizen must counteract the scepticism of Ho-Yung and Enicharmon, I must myself counteract the impetuosity of Gutch. You who listen to me are in a better position to judge about the French Revolution than I am. Your descendants will be even in a better position than you, for they will learn what you think I think, and yet another intermediate will be added to the chain. And in time' – his voice rose – 'there will come a generation that has got beyond facts, beyond impressions, a generation absolutely colourless, a generation

> *seraphically free*
> *From taint of personality,*

which will see the French Revolution not as it happened, nor as they would like it to have happened, but as it would have happened, had it taken place in the days of the Machine.'

Tremendous applause greeted this lecture, which did but voice a feeling already latent in the minds of men – a feeling that terrestrial facts must be ignored, and that the abolition of respirators was a positive gain. It was even suggested that airships should be abolished too. This was not done, because airships had somehow worked themselves into the machine's system. But year by year they were used less, and mentioned less by thoughtful men.

The second great development was the re-establishment of religion.

This, too, had been voiced in the celebrated lecture. No one could mistake the reverent tone in which the peroration had concluded, and it awakened a responsive echo in the heart of each. Those who had long worshipped silently, now began to talk. They described the strange feeling of peace that came over them when they handled the Book of the Machine, the pleasure that it was to repeat certain numerals out of it, however little meaning those numerals conveyed to the outward ear, the ecstasy of touching a button, however unimportant, or of ringing an electric bell, however superfluously.

'The Machine,' they exclaimed, 'feeds us and clothes us and houses us; through it we speak to one another, through it we see one another, in it we have our being. The Machine is the friend of ideas and the enemy of superstition; the Machine is omnipotent, eternal; blessed is the Machine.' And before long this allocution was printed on the first page of the Book, and in subsequent editions the ritual swelled into a complicated system of praise and prayer. The word 'religion' was sedulously avoided, and in theory the Machine was still the creation and the implement of man. But in practice all, save a few retrogrades, worshipped it as divine. Nor was it worshipped in unity. One believer would be chiefly impressed by the blue optic plates, through which he saw other believers; another by the mending apparatus, which sinful Kuno had compared to worms; another by the lifts, another by the Book. And each would pray to this or to that, and ask it to intercede for him with the Machine as a whole. Persecution – that also was present. It did not break out, for reasons that will be set forward shortly. But it was latent, and all who did not accept the minimum known as 'undenominational Mechanism' lived in danger of Homelessness, which means death, as we know.

To attribute these two great developments to the Central Committee, is to take a very narrow view of civilization. The Central Committee announced the developments, it is true, but they were no more the cause of them than were the kings of the imperialistic period the cause of war. Rather did they yield to some invincible pressure, which came no one knew whither, and which, when gratified, was succeeded by some new pressure equally invincible. To such a state of affairs it is convenient to give the name of progress. No one confessed the Machine was out of hand. Year by year it was served with increased efficiency and decreased intelligence. The better a man knew his own duties upon it, the less he understood the duties of his neighbour, and in all the world there was not one who understood the monster as a whole. Those master brains had perished. They had left full directions, it is true, and their successors had each of them mastered a portion of those directions. But Humanity, in its desire for comfort, had over-reached itself. It had exploited the riches of nature too far. Quietly and complacently, it was sinking into decadence, and progress had come to mean the progress of the Machine.

As for Vashti, her life went peacefully forward until the final disaster. She made her room dark and slept; she awoke and made the room light. She lectured and attended lectures. She exchanged ideas with her innumerable friends and believed she was growing more spiritual. At times a friend was granted Euthanasia, and left his or her room for the homelessness that is beyond all human conception. Vashti did not much mind. After an unsuccessful lecture, she would sometimes ask for Euthanasia herself. But the death-rate was not permitted to exceed the birth-rate, and the Machine had hitherto refused it to her.

The troubles began quietly, long before she was conscious of them.

One day she was astonished at receiving a message from her son. They never communicated, having nothing in common, and she had only heard indirectly that he was still alive, and had been transferred from the northern hemisphere, where he had behaved so mischievously, to the southern – indeed, to a room not far from her own.

'Does he want me to visit him?' she thought. 'Never again, never. And I have not the time.'

No, it was madness of another kind.

He refused to visualize his face upon the blue plate, and speaking out of the darkness with solemnity said:

'The Machine stops.'

'What do you say?'

'The Machine is stopping, I know it, I know the signs.'

She burst into a peal of laughter. He heard her and was angry, and they spoke no more.

'Can you imagine anything more absurd?' she cried to a friend. 'A man who was my son believes that the Machine is stopping. It would be impious if it was not mad.'

'The Machine is stopping?' her friend replied. 'What does that mean? The phrase conveys nothing to me.'

'Nor to me.'

'He does not refer, I suppose, to the trouble there has been lately with the music?'

'Oh no, of course not. Let us talk about music.'

'Have you complained to the authorities?'

'Yes, and they say it wants mending, and referred me to the Committee of the Mending Apparatus. I complained of those curious gasping sighs that disfigure the symphonies of the Brisbane school. They sound like some one in pain. The Committee of the Mending Apparatus say that it shall be remedied shortly.'

Obscurely worried, she resumed her life. For one thing, the defect in the music irritated her. For another thing, she could not forget Kuno's speech. If he had known that the music was out of repair – he could not know it, for he detested music – if he had known that it was wrong, 'the Machine stops' was exactly the venomous sort of remark he would have made. Of course he had made it at a venture, but the coincidence annoyed her, and she spoke with some petulance to the Committee of the Mending Apparatus.

They replied, as before, that the defect would be set right shortly.

'Shortly! At once!' she retorted. 'Why should I be worried by imperfect music? Things are always put right at once. If you do not mend it at once, I shall complain to the Central Committee.'

'No personal complaints are received by the Central Committee,' the Committee of the Mending Apparatus replied.

'Through whom am I to make my complaint, then?'

'Through us.'

'I complain then.'

'Your complaint shall be forwarded in its turn.'

'Have others complained?'

This question was unmechanical, and the Committee of the Mending Apparatus refused to answer it.

'It is too bad!' she exclaimed to another of her friends. 'There never was such an unfortunate woman as myself. I can never be sure of my music now. It gets worse and worse each time I summon it.'

'I too have my troubles,' the friend replied. 'Sometimes my ideas are interrupted by a slight jarring noise.'

'What is it?'

'I do not know whether it is inside my head, or inside the wall.'

'Complain, in either case.'

'I have complained, and my complaint will be forwarded in its turn to the Central Committee.'

Time passed, and they resented the defects no longer. The defects had not been remedied, but the human tissues in that latter day had become so subservient, that they readily adapted themselves to every caprice of the Machine. The sigh at the crisis of the Brisbane symphony no longer irritated Vashti; she accepted it as part of the melody. The jarring noise, whether in the head or in the wall, was no longer resented by her friend. And so with the mouldy artificial fruit, so with the bath water that began to stink, so with the defective rhymes that the poetry machine had taken to emitting. All were bitterly complained of at first, and then acquiesced in and forgotten. Things went from bad to worse unchallenged.

It was otherwise with the failure of the sleeping apparatus. That was a more serious stoppage. There came a day when over the whole world – in Sumatra, in Wessex, in the innumerable cities of Courland and Brazil – the beds, when summoned by their tired owners, failed to appear. It may seem a ludicrous matter, but from it we may date the collapse of humanity. The Committee responsible for the failure was assailed by complainants, whom it referred, as usual, to the Committee of the Mending Apparatus, who in its turn assured them that their complaints would be forwarded to the Central Committee. But the discontent grew, for mankind was not yet sufficiently adaptable to do without sleeping.

'Some one is meddling with the Machine –' they began.

'Some one is trying to make himself king, to reintroduce the personal element.'

'Punish that man with Homelessness.'

'To the rescue! Avenge the Machine! Avenge the Machine!'

'War! Kill the man!'

But the Committee of the Mending Apparatus now came forward, and allayed the panic with well-chosen words. It confessed that the Mending Apparatus was itself in need of repair.

The effect of this frank confession was admirable.

'Of course,' said a famous lecturer – he of the French Revolution, who gilded each new decay with splendour – 'of course we shall not press our complaints now. The Mending Apparatus has treated us so well in the past that we all sympathize with it, and will wait patiently for its recovery. In its own good time it will resume its duties. Meanwhile let us do without our beds, our tabloids, our other little wants. Such, I feel sure, would be the wish of the Machine.'

Thousands of miles away his audience applauded. The Machine

still linked them. Under the seas, beneath the roots of the mountains, ran the wires through which they saw and heard, the enormous eyes and ears that were their heritage, and the hum of many workings clothed their thoughts in one garment of subserviency. Only the old and the sick remained ungrateful, for it was rumoured that Euthanasia, too, was out of order, and that pain had reappeared among men.

It became difficult to read. A blight entered the atmosphere and dulled its luminosity. At times Vashti could scarcely see across her room. The air, too, was foul. Loud were the complaints, impotent the remedies, heroic the tone of the lecturer as he cried: 'Courage! courage! What matter so long as the Machine goes on? To it the darkness and the light are one.' And though things improved again after a time, the old brilliancy was never recaptured, and humanity never recovered from its entrance into twilight. There was an hysterical talk of 'measures,' of 'provisional dictatorship,' and the inhabitants of Sumatra were asked to familiarize themselves with the workings of the central power station, the said power station being situated in France. But for the most part panic reigned, and men spent their strength praying to their Books, tangible proofs of the Machine's omnipotence. There were gradations of terror – at times came rumours of hope – the Mending Apparatus was almost mended – the enemies of the Machine had been got under – new 'nerve-centres' were evolving which would do the work even more magnificently than before. But there came a day when, without the slightest warning, without any previous hint of feebleness, the entire communication-system broke down, all over the world, and the world, as they understood it, ended.

Vashti was lecturing at the time and her earlier remarks had been punctuated with applause. As she proceeded the audience became silent, and at the conclusion there was no sound. Somewhat displeased, she called to a friend who was a specialist in sympathy. No sound: doubtless the friend was sleeping. And so with the next friend whom she tried to summon, and so with the next, until she remembered Kuno's cryptic remark, 'The Machine stops.'

The phrase still conveyed nothing. If Eternity was stopping it would of course be set going shortly.

For example, there was still a little light and air – the atmosphere had improved a few hours previously. There was still the Book, and while there was the Book there was security.

Then she broke down, for with the cessation of activity came an unexpected terror – silence.

She had never known silence, and the coming of it nearly killed her – it did kill many thousands of people outright. Ever since her birth she had been surrounded by the steady hum. It was to the ear what artificial air was to the lungs, and agonizing pains shot across her head. And scarcely knowing what she did, she stumbled forward and pressed the unfamiliar button, the one that opened the door of her cell.

Now the door of the cell worked on a simple hinge of its own. It was not connected with the central power station, dying far away in France. It opened, rousing immoderate hopes in Vashti, for she thought that the Machine had been mended. It opened, and she saw the dim tunnel that curved far away towards freedom. One look, and then she shrank back. For the tunnel was full of people – she was almost the last in that city to have taken alarm.

People at any time repelled her, and these were nightmares from her worst dreams. People were crawling about, people were screaming, whimpering, gasping for breath, touching each other, vanishing in the dark, and ever and anon being pushed off the platform on to the live rail. Some were fighting round the electric bells, trying to summon trains which could not be summoned. Others were yelling for Euthanasia or for respirators, or blaspheming the Machine. Others stood at the doors of their cells fearing, like herself, either to stop in them or to leave them. And behind all the uproar was silence – the silence which is the voice of the earth and of the generations who have gone.

No – it was worse than solitude. She closed the door again and sat down to wait for the end. The disintegration went on, accompanied by horrible cracks and rumbling. The valves that restrained the Medical Apparatus must have been weakened, for it ruptured and hung hideously from the ceiling. The floor heaved and fell and flung her from her chair. A tube oozed towards her serpent fashion. And at last the final horror approached – light began to ebb, and she knew that civilization's long day was closing.

She whirled round, praying to be saved from this, at any rate, kissing the Book, pressing button after button. The uproar outside was increasing, and even penetrated the wall. Slowly the brilliancy of her cell was dimmed, the reflections faded from her metal switches. Now she could not see the reading-stand, now not the Book, though she held it in her hand. Light followed the flight of sound, air was following light, and the original void returned to the cavern from which it had been so long excluded. Vashti continued to whirl, like the devotees of an earlier religion, screaming, praying, striking at the buttons with bleeding hands.

It was thus that she opened her prison and escaped – escaped in the spirit: at least so it seems to me, ere my meditation closes. That she escapes in the body – I cannot perceive that. She struck, by chance, the switch that released the door, and the rush of foul air on her skin, the loud throbbing whispers in her ears, told her that she was facing the tunnel again, and that tremendous platform on which she had seen men fighting. They were not fighting now. Only the whispers remained, and the little whimpering groans. They were dying by hundreds out in the dark.

She burst into tears.

Tears answered her.

They wept for humanity, those two, not for themselves. They could not bear that this should be the end. Ere silence was completed their hearts were opened, and they knew what had been important on the earth. Man, the flower of all flesh, the noblest of all creatures visible, man who had once made god in his image, and had mirrored his strength on the constellations, beautiful naked man was dying, strangled in the garments that he had woven. Century after century had he toiled, and here was his reward. Truly the garment had seemed heavenly at first, shot with the colours of culture, sewn with the threads of self-denial. And heavenly it had been so long as it was a garment and no more, so long as man could shed it at will and live by the essence that is his soul, and the essence, equally divine, that is his body. The sin against the body – it was for that they wept in chief; the centuries of wrong against the muscles and the nerves, and those five portals by which we can alone apprehend – glozing it over with talk of evolution, until the body was white pap, the home of ideas as colourless, last sloshy stirrings of a spirit that had grasped the stars.

'Where are you?' she sobbed.

His voice in the darkness said, 'Here.'

'Is there any hope, Kuno?'

'None for us.'

'Where are you?'

She crawled towards him over the bodies of the dead. His blood spurted over her hands.

'Quicker,' he gasped, 'I am dying – but we touch, we talk, not through the Machine.'

He kissed her.

'We have come back to our own. We die, but we have recaptured life, as it was in Wessex, when Ælfrid overthrew the Danes. We know what they know outside, they who dwelt in the cloud that is the colour of a pearl.'

'But, Kuno, is it true? Are there still men on the surface of the earth? Is this – this tunnel, this poisoned darkness – really not the end?'

He replied:

'I have seen them, spoken to them, loved them. They are hiding in the mist and the ferns until our civilization stops. Today they are the Homeless – tomorrow —'

'Oh, tomorrow – some fool will start the Machine again, tomorrow.'

'Never,' said Kuno, 'never. Humanity has learnt its lesson.'

As he spoke, the whole city was broken like a honeycomb. An airship had sailed in through the vomitory into a ruined wharf. It crashed downwards, exploding as it went, rending gallery after gallery with its wings of steel. For a moment they saw the nations of the dead, and, before they joined them, scraps of the untainted sky.

Lappin and Lapinova

VIRGINIA WOOLF

THEY WERE MARRIED. THE WEDDING march pealed out. The pigeons
fluttered. Small boys in Eton jackets threw rice; a fox terrier sauntered
across the path; and Ernest Thorburn led his bride to the car through
that small inquisitive crowd of complete strangers which always
collects in London to enjoy other people's happiness or unhappiness.
Certainly he looked handsome and she looked shy. More rice was
thrown, and the car moved off.

That was on Tuesday. Now it was Saturday. Rosalind had still to
get used to the fact that she was Mrs Ernest Thorburn. Perhaps she
never would get used to the fact that she was Mrs Ernest Anybody,
she thought, as she sat in the bow window of the hotel looking over
the lake to the mountains, and waited for her husband to come down
to breakfast. Ernest was a difficult name to get used to. It was not the
name she would have chosen. She would have preferred Timothy,
Antony, or Peter. He did not look like Ernest either. The name
suggested the Albert Memorial, mahogany sideboards, steel engravings of the Prince Consort with his family – her mother-in-law's
dining-room in Porchester Terrace in short.

But here he was. Thank goodness he did not look like Ernest – no.
But what did he look like? She glanced at him sideways. Well, when
he was eating toast he looked like a rabbit. Not that anyone else
would have seen a likeness to a creature so diminutive and timid in
this spruce, muscular young man with the straight nose, the blue
eyes, and the very firm mouth. But that made it all the more amusing.
His nose twitched very slightly when he ate. So did her pet rabbit's.
She kept watching his nose twitch; and then she had to explain,
when he caught her looking at him, why she laughed.

'It's because you're like a rabbit, Ernest,' she said. 'Like a wild
rabbit,' she added, looking at him. 'A hunting rabbit; a King Rabbit;
a rabbit that makes laws for all the other rabbits.'

Ernest had no objection to being that kind of rabbit, and since it amused her to see him twitch his nose – he had never known that his nose twitched – he twitched it on purpose. And she laughed and laughed; and he laughed too, so that the maiden ladies and the fishing man and the Swiss waiter in his greasy black jacket all guessed right; they were very happy. But how long does such happiness last? they asked themselves; and each answered according to his own circumstances.

At lunch time, seated on a clump of heather beside the lake, 'Lettuce, rabbit?' said Rosalind, holding out the lettuce that had been provided to eat with the hard-boiled eggs. 'Come and take it out of my hand,' she added, and he stretched out and nibbled the lettuce and twitched his nose.

'Good rabbit, nice rabbit,' she said, patting him, as she used to pat her tame rabbit at home. But that was absurd. He was not a tame rabbit, whatever he was. She turned it into French. 'Lapin,' she called him. But whatever he was, he was not a French rabbit. He was simply and solely English – born at Porchester Terrace, educated at Rugby; now a clerk in His Majesty's Civil Service. So she tried 'Bunny' next; but that was worse. 'Bunny' was someone plump and soft and comic; he was thin and hard and serious. Still, his nose twitched. 'Lappin,' she exclaimed suddenly; and gave a little cry as if she had found the very word she looked for.

'Lappin, Lappin, King Lappin,' she repeated. It seemed to suit him exactly; he was not Ernest, he was King Lappin. Why? She did not know.

When there was nothing new to talk about on their long solitary walks – and it rained, as everyone had warned them that it would rain; or when they were sitting over the fire in the evening, for it was cold, and the maiden ladies had gone and the fishing man, and the waiter only came if you rang the bell for him, she let her fancy play with the story of the Lappin tribe. Under her hands – she was sewing; he was reading – they became very real, very vivid, very amusing. Ernest put down the paper and helped her. There were the black rabbits and the red; there were the enemy rabbits and the friendly. There was the wood in which they lived and the outlying prairies and the swamp. Above all there was King Lappin, who, far from having only the one trick – that he twitched his nose – became as the days passed an animal of the greatest character; Rosalind was always finding new qualities in him. But above all he was a great hunter.

'And what,' said Rosalind, on the last day of the honeymoon, 'did the King do today?'

In fact they had been climbing all day; and she had worn a blister on her heel; but she did not mean that.

'Today,' said Ernest, twitching his nose as he bit the end off his cigar, 'he chased a hare.' He paused; struck a match, and twitched again.

'A woman hare,' he added.

'A white hare!' Rosalind exclaimed, as if she had been expecting this. 'Rather a small hare; silver grey; with big bright eyes?'

'Yes,' said Ernest, looking at her as she had looked at him, 'a smallish animal; with eyes popping out of her head, and two little front paws dangling.' It was exactly how she sat, with her sewing dangling in her hands; and her eyes, that were so big and bright, were certainly a little prominent.

'Ah, Lapinova,' Rosalind murmured.

'Is that what she's called?' said Ernest – 'the real Rosalind?' He looked at her. He felt very much in love with her.

'Yes; that's what she's called,' said Rosalind. 'Lapinova.' And before they went to bed that night it was all settled. He was King Lappin; she was Queen Lapinova. They were the opposite of each other; he was bold and determined; she wary and undependable. He ruled over the busy world of rabbits; her world was a desolate, mysterious place, which she ranged mostly by moonlight. All the same, their territories touched; they were King and Queen.

Thus when they came back from their honeymoon they possessed a private world, inhabited, save for the one white hare, entirely by rabbits. No one guessed that there was such a place, and that of course made it all the more amusing. It made them feel, more even than most young married couples, in league together against the rest of the world. Often they looked slyly at each other when people talked about rabbits and woods and traps and shooting. Or they winked furtively across the table when Aunt Mary said that she could never bear to see a hare in a dish – it looked so like a baby: or when John, Ernest's sporting brother, told them what price rabbits were fetching that autumn in Wiltshire, skins and all. Sometimes when they wanted a gamekeeper, or a poacher or a Lord of the Manor, they amused themselves by distributing the parts among their friends.

Ernest's mother, Mrs Reginald Thorburn, for example, fitted the part of the squire to perfection. But it was all secret – that was the point of it; nobody save themselves knew that such a world existed.

Without that world, how, Rosalind wondered, that winter could she have lived at all? For instance, there was the golden-wedding party, when all the Thorburns assembled at Porchester Terrace to celebrate the fiftieth anniversary of that union which had been so blessed – had it not produced Ernest Thorburn? and so fruitful – had it not produced nine other sons and daughters into the bargain, many themselves married and also fruitful? She dreaded that party. But it was inevitable. As she walked upstairs she felt bitterly that she was an only child and an orphan at that; a mere drop among all those Thorburns assembled in the great drawing-room with the shiny satin wallpaper and the lustrous family portraits. The living Thorburns much resembled the painted; save that instead of painted lips they had real lips; out of which came jokes; jokes about schoolrooms, and how they had pulled the chair from under the governess; jokes about frogs and how they had put them between the virgin sheets of maiden ladies. As for herself, she had never even made an apple-pie bed. Holding her present in her hand she advanced toward her mother-in-law sumptuous in yellow satin; and toward her father-in-law decorated with a rich yellow carnation. All round them on tables and chairs there were golden tributes, some nestling in cotton wool; others branching resplendent – candlesticks; cigar boxes; chains; each stamped with the goldsmith's proof that it was solid gold, hall-marked, authentic. But her present was only a little pinchbeck box pierced with holes; an old sand caster, an eighteenth-century relic, once used to sprinkle sand over wet ink. Rather a senseless present she felt – in an age of blotting paper; and as she proffered it, she saw in front of her the stubby black handwriting in which her mother-in-law when they were engaged had expressed the hope that 'My son will make you happy.' No, she was not happy. Not at all happy. She looked at Ernest, straight as a ramrod with a nose like all the noses in the family portraits; a nose that never twitched at all.

Then they went down to dinner. She was half hidden by the great chrysanthemums that curled their red and gold petals into large tight balls. Everything was gold. A gold-edged card with gold initials intertwined recited the list of all the dishes that would be set one after another before them. She dipped her spoon in a plate of clear golden fluid. The raw white fog outside had been turned by the lamps into a golden mesh that blurred the edges of the plates and gave the pineapples a rough golden skin. Only she herself in her white wedding dress peering ahead of her with her prominent eyes seemed insoluble as an icicle.

As the dinner wore on, however, the room grew steamy with heat. Beads of perspiration stood out on the men's foreheads. She felt that her icicle was being turned to water. She was being melted; dispersed; dissolved into nothingness; and would soon faint. Then through the surge in her head and the din in her ears she heard a woman's voice exclaim, 'But they breed so!'

The Thorburns – yes; they breed so, she echoed; looking at all the round red faces that seemed doubled in the giddiness that overcame her; and magnified in the gold mist that enhaloed them. 'They breed so.' Then John brawled:

'Little devils! . . . Shoot 'em! Jump on 'em with big boots! That's the only way to deal with 'em . . . rabbits!'

At that word, that magic word, she revived. Peeping between the chrysanthemums she saw Ernest's nose twitch. It rippled, it ran with successive twitches. And at that a mysterious catastrophe befell the Thorburns. The golden table became a moor with the gorse in full bloom; the din of voices turned to one peal of lark's laughter ringing down from the sky. It was a blue sky – clouds passed slowly. And they had all been changed – the Thorburns. She looked at her father-in-law, a furtive little man with dyed moustaches. His foible was collecting things – seals, enamel boxes, trifles from eighteenth-century dressing tables which he hid in the drawers of his study from his wife. Now she saw him as he was – a poacher, stealing off with his coat bulging with pheasants and partridges to drop them stealthily into a three-legged pot in his smoky little cottage. That was her real father-in-law – a poacher. And Celia, the unmarried daughter, who always nosed out other people's secrets, the little things they wished to hide – she was a white ferret with pink eyes, and a nose clotted with earth from her horrid underground nosings and pokings. Slung round men's shoulders, in a net, and thrust down a hole – it was a pitiable life – Celia's; it was none of her fault. So she saw Celia. And then she looked at her mother-in-law – whom they dubbed The Squire. Flushed, coarse, a bully – she was all that, as she stood returning thanks, but now that Rosalind – that is Lapinova – saw her, she saw behind her the decayed family mansion, the plaster peeling off the walls, and heard her, with a sob in her voice, giving thanks to her children (who hated her) for a world that had ceased to exist. There was a sudden silence. They all stood with their glasses raised; they all drank; then it was over.

'Oh, King Lappin!' she cried as they went home together in the fog, 'if your nose hadn't twitched just at that moment, I should have been trapped!'

'But you're safe,' said King Lappin, pressing her paw.

'Quite safe,' she answered.

And they drove back through the Park, King and Queen of the marsh, of the mist, and of the gorse-scented moor.

Thus time passed; one year; two years of time. And on a winter's night, which happened by a coincidence to be the anniversary of the golden-wedding party – but Mrs Reginald Thorburn was dead; the house was to let; and there was only a caretaker in residence – Ernest came home from the office. They had a nice little home; half a house above a saddler's shop in South Kensington, not far from the tube station. It was cold, with fog in the air, and Rosalind was sitting over the fire, sewing.

'What d'you think happened to me today?' she began as soon as he had settled himself down with his legs stretched to the blaze. 'I was crossing the stream when – '

'What stream?' Ernest interrupted her.

'The stream at the bottom, where our wood meets the black wood,' she explained.

Ernest looked completely blank for a moment.

'What the deuce are you talking about?' he asked.

'My dear Ernest!' she cried in dismay. 'King Lappin,' she added, dangling her little front paws in the firelight. But his nose did not twitch. Her hands – they turned to hands – clutched the stuff she was holding; her eyes popped half out of her head. It took him five minutes at least to change from Ernest Thorburn to King Lappin; and while she waited she felt a load on the back of her neck, as if somebody were about to wring it. At last he changed to King Lappin; his nose twitched; and they spent the evening roaming the woods much as usual.

But she slept badly. In the middle of the night she woke, feeling as if something strange had happened to her. She was stiff and cold. At last she turned on the light and looked at Ernest lying beside her. He was sound asleep. He snored. But even though he snored, his nose remained perfectly still. It looked as if it had never twitched at all. Was it possible that he was really Ernest; and that she was really married to Ernest? A vision of her mother-in-law's dining-room came before her; and there they sat, she and Ernest, grown old, under the engravings, in front of the sideboard. . . . It was their golden-wedding day. She could not bear it.

'Lappin, King Lappin!' she whispered, and for a moment his nose seemed to twitch of its own accord. But he still slept. 'Wake up, Lappin, wake up!' she cried.

Ernest woke; and seeing her sitting bolt upright beside him he asked: 'What's the matter?'

'I thought my rabbit was dead!' she whimpered. Ernest was angry.

'Don't talk such rubbish, Rosalind,' he said. 'Lie down and go to sleep.'

He turned over. In another moment he was sound asleep and snoring.

But she could not sleep. She lay curled up on her side of the bed, like a hare in its form. She had turned out the light, but the street lamp lit the ceiling faintly, and the trees outside made a lacy network over it as if there were a shadowy grove on the ceiling in which she wandered, turning, twisting, in and out, round and round, hunting, being hunted, hearing the bay of hounds and horns; flying, escaping . . . until the maid drew the blinds and brought their early tea.

Next day she could settle to nothing. She seemed to have lost something. She felt as if her body had shrunk; it had grown small, and black and hard. Her joints seemed stiff too, and when she looked in the glass, which she did several times as she wandered about the flat, her eyes seemed to burst out of her head, like currants in a bun. The rooms also seemed to have shrunk. Large pieces of furniture jutted out at odd angles and she found herself knocking against them. At last she put on her hat and went out. She walked along the Cromwell Road; and every room she passed and peered into seemed to be a dining-room where people sat eating under steel engravings, with thick yellow lace curtains, and mahogany sideboards. At last she reached the Natural History Museum; she used to like it when she was a child. But the first thing she saw when she went in was a stuffed hare standing on sham snow with pink glass eyes. Somehow it made her shiver all over. Perhaps it would be better when dusk fell. She went home and sat over the fire, without a light, and tried to imagine that she was out alone on a moor; and there was a stream rushing; and beyond the stream a dark wood. But she could get no further than the stream. At last she squatted down on the bank on the wet grass, and sat crouched in her chair, with her hands dangling empty, and her eyes glazed, like glass eyes, in the firelight. Then there was the crack of a gun. . . . She started as if she had been shot. It was only Ernest, turning his key in the door. She waited, trembling. He came in and switched on the light. There he stood, tall, handsome, rubbing his hands that were red with cold.

'Sitting in the dark?' he said.

'Oh, Ernest, Ernest!' she cried, starting up in her chair.

'Well, what's up now?' he asked briskly, warming his hands at the fire.

'It's Lapinova . . .' she faltered, glancing wildly at him out of her great startled eyes. 'She's gone, Ernest. I've lost her!'

Ernest frowned. He pressed his lips tight together. 'Oh, that's what's up, is it?' he said, smiling rather grimly at his wife. For ten seconds he stood there, silent; and she waited, feeling hands tightening at the back of her neck.

'Yes,' he said at length. 'Poor Lapinova . . .' he straightened his tie at the looking-glass over the mantelpiece.

'Caught in a trap,' he said, 'killed,' and sat down and read the newspaper.

So that was the end of that marriage.

The Three Strangers

THOMAS HARDY

AMONG THE FEW FEATURES OF agricultural England which retain an appearance but little modified by the lapse of centuries, may be reckoned the long, grassy and furzy downs, coombs, or ewe-leases, as they are called according to their kind, that fill a large area of certain counties in the south and south-west. If any mark of human occupation is met with hereon, it usually takes the form of the solitary cottage of some shepherd.

Fifty years ago such a lonely cottage stood on such a down, and may possibly be standing there now. In spite of its loneliness, however, the spot, by actual measurement, was not three miles from a county-town. Yet that affected it little. Three miles of irregular upland, during the long inimical seasons, with their sleets, snows, rains, and mists, afford withdrawing space enough to isolate a Timon or a Nebuchadnezzar; much less, in fair weather, to please that less repellent tribe, the poets, philosophers, artists, and others who 'conceive and meditate of pleasant things.'

Some old earthen camp or barrow, some clump of trees, at least some starved fragment of ancient hedge is usually taken advantage of in the erection of these forlorn dwellings. But, in the present case, such a kind of shelter had been disregarded. Higher Crowstairs, as the house was called, stood quite detached and undefended. The only reason for its precise situation seemed to be the crossing of two footpaths at right angles hard by, which may have crossed there and thus for a good five hundred years. Hence the house was exposed to the elements on all sides. But, though the wind up here blew unmistakably when it did blow, and the rain hit hard whenever it fell, the various weathers of the winter season were not quite so formidable on the down as they were imagined to be by dwellers on low ground. The raw rimes were not so pernicious as in the hollows, and the frosts were scarcely so severe. When the shepherd and his family who tenanted the house were pitied for their sufferings from the exposure, they said that upon the whole they were less inconvenienced by 'wuzzes and flames' (hoarses and phlegms) than when they had lived by the stream of a snug neighbouring valley.

The night of March 28, 182–, was precisely one of the nights that were wont to call forth these expressions of commiseration. The level rainstorm smote walls, slopes, and hedges like the clothyard shafts of Senlac and Crecy. Such sheep and outdoor animals as had no shelter stood with their buttocks to the winds; while the tails of little birds trying to roost on some scraggy thorn were blown inside-out like umbrellas. The gable-end of the cottage was stained with wet, and the eavesdroppings flapped against the wall. Yet never was commiseration for the shepherd more misplaced. For that cheerful rustic was entertaining a large party in glorification of the christening of his second girl.

The guests had arrived before the rain began to fall, and they were all now assembled in the chief or living room of the dwelling. A glance into the apartment at eight o'clock on this eventful evening would have resulted in the opinion that it was as cosy and comfortable a nook as could be wished for in boisterous weather. The calling of its inhabitant was proclaimed by a number of highly-polished sheep-crooks without stems that were hung ornamentally over the fireplace, the curl of each shining crook varying from the antiquated type engraved in the patriarchal pictures of old family Bibles to the most approved fashion of the last local sheep-fair. The room was lighted by half-a-dozen candles, having wicks only a trifle smaller than the grease which enveloped them, in candlesticks that were never used but at high-days, holy-days, and family feasts. The lights were scattered about the room, two of them standing on the chimneypiece. This position of candles was in itself significant. Candles on the chimneypiece always meant a party.

On the hearth, in front of a back-brand to give substance, blazed a fire of thorns, that crackled 'like the laughter of the fool.'

Nineteen persons were gathered here. Of these, five women, wearing gowns of various bright hues, sat in chairs along the wall; girls shy and not shy filled the window-bench; four men, including Charley Jake the hedge-carpenter, Elijah New the parish-clerk, and John Pitcher, a neighbouring dairyman, the shepherd's father-in-law, lolled in the settle; a young man and maid, who were blushing over tentative *pourparlers* on a life-companionship, sat beneath the corner-cupboard; and an elderly engaged man of fifty or upward moved restlessly about from spots where his betrothed was not to the spot where she was. Enjoyment was pretty general, and so much the more prevailed in being unhampered by conventional restrictions. Absolute confidence in each other's good opinion begat perfect ease, while the finishing stroke of manner, amounting to a truly princely serenity, was lent to the majority by the absence of any expression or trait denoting that they wished to get on in the world, enlarge their minds, or do any eclipsing thing whatever – which nowadays so generally nips the bloom and *bonhomie* of all except the two extremes of the social scale.

Shepherd Fennel had married well, his wife being a dairyman's daughter from a vale at a distance, who brought fifty guineas in her pocket – and kept them there, till they should be required for ministering to the needs of a coming family. This frugal woman had been somewhat exercised as to the character that should be given to the gathering. A sit-still party had its advantages; but an undisturbed position of ease in chairs and settles was apt to lead on the men to such an unconscionable deal of toping that they would sometimes fairly drink the house dry. A dancing-party was the alternative; but this, while avoiding the foregoing objection on the score of good drink, had a counterbalancing disadvantage in the matter of good victuals, the ravenous appetites engendered by the exercise causing immense havoc in the buttery. Shepherdess Fennel fell back upon the intermediate plan of mingling short dances with short periods of talk and singing, so as to hinder any ungovernable rage in either. But this scheme was entirely confined to her own gentle mind: the shepherd himself was in the mood to exhibit the most reckless phases of hospitality.

The fiddler was a boy of those parts, about twelve years of age, who had a wonderful dexterity in jigs and reels, though his fingers were so small and short as to necessitate a constant shifting for the high notes, from which he scrambled back to the first position with sounds not of unmixed purity of tone. At seven the shrill tweedle-dee of this youngster had begun, accompanied by a booming ground-bass from Elijah New, the parish-clerk, who had thoughtfully brought with him his favourite musical instrument, the serpent. Dancing was instantaneous, Mrs Fennel privately enjoining the players on no account to let the dance exceed the length of a quarter of an hour.

But Elijah and the boy in the excitement of their position quite forgot the injunction. Moreover, Oliver Giles, a man of seventeen, one of the dancers, who was enamoured of his partner, a fair girl of thirty-three rolling years, had recklessly handed a new crown-piece to the musicians, as a bribe to keep going as long as they had muscle and wind. Mrs Fennel seeing the steam begin to generate on the countenances of her guests, crossed over and touched the fiddler's elbow and put her hand on the serpent's mouth. But they took no notice, and fearing she might lose her character of genial hostess if she were to interfere too markedly, she retired and sat down helpless. And so the dance whizzed on with cumulative fury, the performers moving in their planet-like courses, direct and retrograde, from apogee to perigee, till the hand of the well-kicked clock at the bottom of the room had travelled over the circumference of an hour.

. While these cheerful events were in course of enactment within Fennel's pastoral dwelling an incident having considerable bearing on the party had occurred in the gloomy night without. Mrs Fennel's concern about the growing fierceness of the dance corresponded in point of time with the ascent of a human figure to the solitary hill of Higher Crowstairs from the direction of the distant town. This personage strode on through the rain without a pause, following the little-worn path which, further on in its course, skirted the shepherd's cottage.

It was nearly the time of full moon, and on this account, though the sky was lined with a uniform sheet of dripping cloud, ordinary objects out of doors were readily visible. The sad wan light revealed the lonely pedestrian to be a man of supple frame; his gait suggested that he had somewhat passed the period of perfect and instinctive agility, though not so far as to be otherwise than rapid of motion when occasion required. At a rough guess, he might have been about forty years of age. He appeared tall, but a recruiting sergeant, or other person accustomed to the judging of men's heights by the eye, would have discerned that this was chiefly owing to his gauntness, and that he was not more than five-feet-eight or nine.

Notwithstanding the regularity of his tread there was caution in it, as in that of one who mentally feels his way; and despite the fact that it was not a black coat nor a dark garment of any sort that he wore, there was something about him which suggested that he naturally belonged to the black-coated tribes of men. His clothes were of fustian, and his boots hobnailed, yet in his progress he showed not the mud-accustomed bearing of hobnailed and fustianed peasantry.

By the time that he had arrived abreast of the shepherd's premises the rain came down, or rather came along, with yet more determined violence. The outskirts of the little settlement partially broke the force of wind and rain, and this induced him to stand still. The most salient of the shepherd's domestic erections was an empty sty at the forward corner of his hedgeless garden, for in these latitudes the principle of masking the homelier features of your establishment by a conventional frontage was unknown. The traveller's eye was attracted to this small building by the pallid shine of the wet slates that covered it. He turned aside, and, finding it empty, stood under the pent-roof for shelter.

While he stood the boom of the serpent within the adjacent house, and the lesser strains of the fiddler, reached the spot as an accompaniment to the surging hiss of the flying rain on the sod, its louder beating on the cabbage-leaves of the garden, on the straw hackles of eight or ten beehives just discernible by the path, and its dripping from the eaves into a row of buckets and pans that had been placed under the walls of the cottage. For at Higher Crowstairs, as at all such elevated domiciles, the grand difficulty of housekeeping was an insufficiency of water; and a casual rainfall was utilized by turning out, as catchers, every utensil that the house contained. Some queer stories might be told of the contrivances for economy in suds and dishwaters that are absolutely necessitated in upland habitations during the droughts of summer. But at this season there were no such exigencies; a mere acceptance of what the skies bestowed was sufficient for an abundant store.

At last the notes of the serpent ceased and the house was silent. This cessation of activity aroused the solitary pedestrian from the reverie into which he had lapsed, and, emerging from the shed, with an apparently new intention, he walked up the path to the house-door. Arrived here, his first act was to kneel down on a large stone beside the row of vessels, and to drink a copious draught from one of them. Having quenched his thirst he rose and lifted his hand to knock, but paused with his eye upon the panel. Since the dark surface of the wood revealed absolutely nothing, it was evident that he must be mentally looking through the door, as if he wished to measure thereby all the possibilities that a house of this sort might include, and how they might bear upon the question of his entry.

In his indecision he turned and surveyed the scene around. Not a soul was anywhere visible. The garden-path stretched downward from his feet, gleaming like the track of a snail; the roof of the little well (mostly dry), the well-cover, the top rail of the garden gate, were varnished with the same dull liquid glaze; while, far away in the vale, a faint whiteness of more than usual extent showed that the rivers were high in the meads. Beyond all this winked a few bleared lamplights through the beating drops – lights that denoted the situation of the county-town from which he had appeared to come. The absence of all notes of life in that direction seemed to clinch his intentions, and he knocked at the door.

Within, a desultory chat had taken the place of movement and musical sound. The hedge-carpenter was suggesting a song to the company, which nobody just then was inclined to undertake, so that the knock afforded a not unwelcome diversion.

'Walk in!' said the shepherd promptly.

The latch clicked upward, and out of the night our pedestrian appeared upon the door-mat. The shepherd arose, snuffed two of the nearest candles, and turned to look at him.

Their light disclosed that the stranger was dark in complexion and not unprepossessing as to feature. His hat, which for a moment he did not remove, hung low over his eyes, without concealing that they were large, open, and determined, moving with a flash rather than a glance round the room. He seemed pleased with his survey, and, baring his shaggy head, said, in a rich deep voice, 'The rain is so heavy, friends, that I ask leave to come in and rest awhile.'

'To be sure, stranger,' said the shepherd. 'And faith, you've been lucky in choosing your time, for we are having a bit of a fling for a glad cause – though, to be sure, a man could hardly wish that glad cause to happen more than once a year.'

'Nor less,' spoke up a woman. 'For 'tis best to get your family over and done with, as soon as you can, so as to be all the earlier out of the fag o't.'

'And what may be this glad cause?' asked the stranger.

'A birth and christening,' said the shepherd.

The stranger hoped his host might not be made unhappy either by too many or too few of such episodes, and being invited by a gesture to a pull at the mug, he readily acquiesced. His manner, which, before entering, had been so dubious, was now altogether that of a careless and candid man.

'Late to be traipsing athwart this coomb – hey?' said the engaged man of fifty.

'Late it is, master, as you say. – I'll take a seat in the chimney-corner, if you have nothing to urge against it, ma'am; for I am a little moist on the side that was next the rain.'

Mrs Shepherd Fennel assented, and made room for the self-invited comer, who, having got completely inside the chimney-corner, stretched out his legs and his arms with the expansiveness of a person quite at home.

'Yes, I am rather cracked in the vamp,' he said freely, seeing that the eyes of the shepherd's wife fell upon his boots, 'and I am not well fitted either. I have had some rough times lately, and have been forced to pick up what I can get in the way of wearing, but I must find a suit better fit for working-days when I reach home.'

'One of hereabouts?' she inquired.

'Not quite that – further up the country.'

'I thought so. And so be I; and by your tongue you come from my neighbourhood.'

'But you would hardly have heard of me,' he said quickly. 'My time would be long before yours, ma'am, you see.'

This testimony to the youthfulness of his hostess had the effect of stopping her cross-examination.

'There is only one thing more wanted to make me happy,' continued the newcomer. 'And that is a little baccy which I am sorry to say I am out of.'

'I'll fill your pipe,' said the shepherd.

'I must ask you to lend me a pipe likewise.'

'A smoker, and no pipe about 'ee?'

'I have dropped it somewhere on the road.'

The shepherd filled and handed him a new clay pipe, saying, as he did so, 'Hand me your baccy-box – I'll fill that too, now I am about it.'

The man went through the movement of searching his pockets.

'Lost that too?' said his entertainer, with some surprise.

'I am afraid so,' said the man with some confusion. 'Give it to me in a screw of paper.' Lighting his pipe at the candle with a suction that drew the whole flame into the bowl, he resettled himself in the corner and bent his looks upon the faint steam from his damp legs, as if he wished to say no more.

Meanwhile the general body of guests had been taking little notice of this visitor by reason of an absorbing discussion in which they were engaged with the band about a tune for the next dance. The matter being settled, they were about to stand up when an interruption came in the shape of another knock at the door.

At sound of the same the man in the chimney-corner took up the poker and began stirring the brands as if doing it thoroughly were the one aim of his existence; and a second time the shepherd said, 'Walk in!' In a moment another man stood upon the straw-woven doormat. He too was a stranger.

This individual was one of a type radically different from the first. There was more of the commonplace in his manner, and a certain jovial cosmopolitanism sat upon his features. He was several years older than the first arrival, his hair being slightly frosted, his eyebrows bristly, and his whiskers cut back from his cheeks. His face was rather full and flabby, and yet it was not altogether a face without power. A few grog-blossoms marked the neighbourhood of his nose. He flung back his long drab greatcoat, revealing that beneath it he wore a suit of cinder-gray shade throughout, large heavy seals, of some metal or other that would take a polish, dangling from his fob as his only personal ornament. Shaking the water-drops from his low-crowned glazed hat, he said, 'I must ask for a few minutes' shelter, comrades, or I shall be wetted to my skin before I get to Casterbridge.'

'Make yourself at home, master,' said the shepherd, perhaps a trifle less heartily than on the first occasion. Not that Fennel had the least tinge of niggardliness in his composition; but the room was far from large, spare chairs were not numerous, and damp companions were not altogether desirable at close quarters for the women and girls in their bright-coloured gowns.

However, the second comer, after taking off his greatcoat, and hanging his hat on a nail in one of the ceiling-beams as if he had been specially invited to put it there, advanced and sat down at the table. This had been pushed so closely into the chimney-corner, to give all available room to the dancers, that its inner edge grazed the elbow of the man who had ensconced himself by the fire; and thus the two strangers were brought into close companionship. They nodded to each other by way of breaking the ice of unacquaintance, and the first stranger handed his neighbour the family mug – a huge vessel of brown ware, having its upper edge worn away like a threshold by the rub of whole generations of thirsty lips that had gone the way of all flesh, and bearing the following inscription burnt upon its rotund side in yellow letters —

THERE IS NO FUN
UNTiLL i CUM.

The other man, nothing loth, raised the mug to his lips, and drank on, and on, and on – till a curious blueness overspread the countenance of the shepherd's wife, who had regarded with no little surprise the first stranger's free offer to the second of what did not belong to him to dispense.

'I knew it!' said the toper to the shepherd with much satisfaction. 'When I walked up your garden before coming in, and saw the hives all of a row, I said to myself, "Where there's bees there's honey, and where there's honey there's mead." But mead of such a truly comfortable sort as this I really didn't expect to meet in my older days.' He took yet another pull at the mug, till it assumed an ominous elevation.

'Glad you enjoy it!' said the shepherd warmly.

'It is goodish mead,' assented Mrs Fennel, with an absence of enthusiasm which seemed to say that it was possible to buy praise for one's cellar at too heavy a price. 'It is trouble enough to make – and really I hardly think we shall make any more. For honey sells well, and we ourselves can make shift with a drop o' small mead and metheglin for common use from the comb-washings.'

'O, but you'll never have the heart!' reproachfully cried the stranger in cinder-gray, after taking up the mug a third time and setting it down empty. 'I love mead, when 'tis old like this, as I love to go to church o' Sundays, or to relieve the needy any day of the week.'

'Ha, ha, ha!' said the man in the chimney-corner, who, in spite of the taciturnity induced by the pipe of tobacco, could not or would not refrain from this slight testimony to his comrade's humour.

Now the old mead of those days, brewed of the purest first-year or maiden honey, four pounds to the gallon – with its due complement of white of eggs, cinnamon, ginger, cloves, mace, rosemary, yeast, and processes of working, bottling, and cellaring – tasted remarkably strong; but it did not taste so strong as it actually was. Hence, presently, the stranger in cinder-gray at the table, moved by its creeping influence, unbuttoned his waistcoat, threw himself back in his chair, spread his legs, and made his presence felt in various ways.

'Well, well, as I say,' he resumed, 'I am going to Casterbridge, and to Casterbridge I must go. I should have been almost there by this time; but the rain drove me into your dwelling, and I'm not sorry for it.'

'You don't live in Casterbridge?' said the shepherd.

'Not as yet; though I shortly mean to move there.'

'Going to set up in trade, perhaps?'

'No, no,' said the shepherd's wife. 'It is easy to see that the gentleman is rich, and don't want to work at anything.'

The cinder-gray stranger paused, as if to consider whether he would accept that definition of himself. He presently rejected it by answering, 'Rich is not quite the word for me, dame. I do work, and I must work. And even if I only get to Casterbridge by midnight I must begin work there at eight tomorrow morning. Yes, het or wet, blow or snow, famine or sword, my day's work tomorrow must be done.'

'Poor man! Then, in spite o' seeming, you be worse off than we?' replied the shepherd's wife.

''Tis the nature of my trade, men and maidens. 'Tis the nature of my trade more than my poverty. . . . But really and truly I must up and off, or I shan't get a lodging in the town.' However, the speaker did not move, and directly added, 'There's time for one more draught of friendship before I go; and I'd perform it at once if the mug were not dry.'

'Here's a mug o' small,' said Mrs Fennel. 'Small, we call it, though to be sure 'tis only the first wash o' the combs.'

'No,' said the stranger disdainfully. 'I won't spoil your first kindness by partaking o' your second.'

'Certainly not,' broke in Fennel. 'We don't increase and multiply every day, and I'll fill the mug again.' He went away to the dark place under the stairs where the barrel stood. The shepherdess followed him.

'Why should you do this?' she said reproachfully, as soon as they were alone. 'He's emptied it once, though it held enough for ten people; and now he's not contented wi' the small, but must needs call for more o' the strong! And a stranger unbeknown to any of us. For my part, I don't like the look o' the man at all.'

'But he's in the house, my honey; and 'tis a wet night, and a christening. Daze it, what's a cup of mead more or less? There'll be plenty more next bee-burning.'

'Very well – this time, then,' she answered, looking wistfully at the barrel. 'But what is the man's calling, and where is he one of, that he should come in and join us like this?'

'I don't know. I'll ask him again.'

The catastrophe of having the mug drained dry at one pull by the stranger in cinder-gray was effectually guarded against this time by Mrs Fennel. She poured out his allowance in a small cup, keeping the large one at a discreet distance from him. When he had tossed off his portion the shepherd renewed his inquiry about the stranger's occupation.

The latter did not immediately reply, and the man in the chimney-corner, with sudden demonstrativeness, said, 'Anybody may know my trade – I'm a wheelwright.'

'A very good trade for these parts,' said the shepherd.

'And anybody may know mine – if they've the sense to find it out,' said the stranger in cinder-gray.

'You may generally tell what a man is by his claws,' observed the hedge-carpenter, looking at his own hands, 'My fingers be as full of thorns as an old pin-cushion is of pins.'

The hands of the man in the chimney-corner instinctively sought the shade, and he gazed into the fire as he resumed his pipe. The man at the table took up the hedge-carpenter's remark, and added smartly, 'True; but the oddity of my trade is that, instead of setting a mark upon me, it sets a mark upon my customers.'

No observation being offered by anybody in elucidation of this enigma the shepherd's wife once more called for a song. The same obstacles presented themselves as at the former time – one had no voice, another had forgotten the first verse. The stranger at the table, whose soul had now risen to a good working temperature, relieved the difficulty by exclaiming that, to start the company, he would sing himself. Thrusting one thumb into the armhole of his waistcoat, he waved the other hand in the air, and, with an extemporizing gaze at the shining sheep-crooks above the mantelpiece, began: –

> 'O my trade it is the rarest one,
> > Simple shepherds all –
> My trade is a sight to see;
> For my customers I tie, and take them up on high,
> And waft 'em to a far countree!'

The room was silent when he had finished the verse – with one exception, that of the man in the chimney-corner, who, at the singer's word, 'Chorus!' joined him in a deep bass voice of musical relish –

'And waft 'em to a far countree!'

Oliver Giles, John Pitcher the dairyman, the parish-clerk, the engaged man of fifty, the row of young women against the wall, seemed lost in thought not of the gayest kind. The shepherd looked meditatively on the ground, the shepherdess gazed keenly at the singer, and with some suspicion; she was doubting whether this stranger were merely singing an old song from recollection, or was composing one there and then for the occasion. All were as perplexed at the obscure revelation as the guests at Belshazzar's Feast, except the man in the chimney-corner, who quietly said, 'Second verse, stranger,' and smoked on.

The singer thoroughly moistened himself from his lips inwards, and went on with the next stanza as requested: –

'My tools are but common ones,
   Simple shepherds all –
 My tools are no sight to see:
A little hempen string, and a post whereon to swing,
 Are implements enough for me!'

Shepherd Fennel glanced round. There was no longer any doubt that the stranger was answering his question rhythmically. The guests one and all started back with suppressed exclamations. The young woman engaged to the man of fifty fainted half-way, and would have proceeded, but finding him wanting in alacrity for catching her she sat down trembling.

'O, he's the —!' whispered the people in the background, mentioning the name of an ominous public officer. 'He's come to do it! 'Tis to be at Casterbridge jail tomorrow – the man for sheep-stealing – the poor clock-maker we heard of, who used to live away at Shottsford and had no work to do – Timothy Summers, whose family were a-starving, and so he went out of Shottsford by the high-road, and took a sheep in open daylight, defying the farmer and the farmer's wife and the farmer's lad, and every man jack among 'em. He' (and they nodded towards the stranger of the deadly trade) 'is come from up the country to do it because there's not enough to do in his own county-town, and he's got the place here now our own county man's dead; he's going to live in the same cottage under the prison wall.'

The stranger in cinder-gray took no notice of this whispered string of observations, but again wetted his lips. Seeing that his friend in the chimney-corner was the only one who reciprocated his joviality in any way, he held out his cup towards that appreciative comrade, who also held out his own. They clinked together, the eyes of the rest of the room hanging upon the singer's actions. He parted his lips for the third verse; but at that moment another knock was audible upon the door. This time the knock was faint and hesitating.

The company seemed scared; the shepherd looked with consternation towards the entrance, and it was with some effort that he resisted his alarmed wife's deprecatory glance, and uttered for the third time the welcoming words, 'Walk in!'

The door was gently opened, and another man stood upon the mat. He, like those who had preceded him, was a stranger. This time it was a short, small personage, of fair complexion, and dressed in a decent suit of dark clothes.

'Can you tell me the way to —?' he began: when, gazing round the room to observe the nature of the company amongst whom he had fallen, his eyes lighted on the stranger in cinder-gray. It was just at the instant when the latter, who had thrown his mind into his song with such a will that he scarcely heeded the interruption, silenced all whispers and inquiries by bursting into his third verse: –

> 'Tomorrow is my working day,
> > Simple shepherds all –
> Tomorrow is a working day for me:
> For the farmer's sheep is slain, and the lad who did it ta'en,
> > And on his soul may God ha' merc-y!'

The stranger in the chimney-corner, waving cups with the singer so heartily that his mead splashed over on the hearth, repeated in his bass voice as before: –

> 'And on his soul may God ha' merc-y!'

All this time the third stranger had been standing in the doorway. Finding now that he did not come forward or go on speaking, the guests particularly regarded him. They noticed to their surprise that he stood before them the picture of abject terror – his knees trembling, his hand shaking so violently that the door-latch by which he supported himself rattled audibly: his white lips were parted, and his eyes fixed on the merry officer of justice in the middle of the room. A moment more and he had turned, closed the door, and fled.

'What a man can it be?' said the shepherd.

The rest, between the awfulness of their late discovery and the odd conduct of this third visitor, looked as if they knew not what to think, and said nothing. Instinctively they withdrew further and further from the grim gentleman in their midst, whom some of them seemed to take for the Prince of Darkness himself, till they formed a remote circle an empty space of floor being left between them and him –

'. . . circulus, cujus centrum diabolus.'

The room was so silent – though there were more than twenty people in it – that nothing could be heard but the patter of the rain against the window-shutters, accompanied by the occasional hiss of a stray drop that fell down the chimney into the fire, and the steady puffing of the man in the corner, who had now resumed his pipe of long clay.

The stillness was unexpectedly broken. The distant sound of a gun reverberated through the air – apparently from the direction of the county-town.

'Be jiggered!' cried the stranger who had sung the song, jumping up.

'What does that mean?' asked several.

'A prisoner escaped from the jail – that's what it means.'

All listened. The sound was repeated, and none of them spoke but the man in the chimney-corner, who said quietly, 'I've often been told that in this county they fire a gun at such times; but I never heard it till now.'

'I wonder if it is *my* man?' murmured the personage in cinder-gray.

'Surely it is!' said the shepherd involuntarily. 'And surely we've zeed him! That little man who looked in at the door by now, and quivered like a leaf when he zeed ye and heard your song!'

'His teeth chattered, and the breath went out of his body,' said the dairyman.

'And his heart seemed to sink within him like a stone,' said Oliver Giles.

'And he bolted as if he'd been shot at,' said the hedge-carpenter.

'True – his teeth chattered, and his heart seemed to sink; and he bolted as if he'd been shot at,' slowly summed up the man in the chimney-corner.

'I didn't notice it,' remarked the hangman.

'We were all a-wondering what made him run off in such a fright,' faltered one of the women against the wall, 'and now 'tis explained!'

The firing of the alarm-gun went on at intervals, low and sullenly, and their suspicions became a certainty. The sinister gentleman in cinder-gray roused himself. 'Is there a constable here?' he asked, in thick tones. 'If so, let him step forward.'

The engaged man of fifty stepped quavering out from the wall, his betrothed beginning to sob on the back of the chair.

'You are a sworn constable?'

'I be, sir.'

'Then pursue the criminal at once, with assistance, and bring him back here. He can't have gone far.'

'I will, sir, I will – when I've got my staff. I'll go home and get it, and come sharp here, and start in a body.'

'Staff! – never mind your staff; the man'll be gone!'

'But I can't do nothing without my staff – can I, William, and John, and Charles Jake? No; for there's the king's royal crown a painted on en in yaller and gold, and the lion and the unicorn, so as when I raise en up and hit my prisoner, 'tis made a lawful blow thereby. I wouldn't 'tempt to take up a man without my staff – no, not I. If I hadn't the law to gie me courage, why, instead o' my taking up him he might take up me!'

'Now, I'm a king's man myself, and can give you authority enough for this,' said the formidable officer in gray. 'Now then, all of ye, be ready. Have ye any lanterns?'

'Yes – have ye any lanterns? – I demand it!' said the constable.

'And the rest of you able-bodied —'

'Able-bodied men – yes – the rest of ye!' said the constable.

'Have you some good stout staves and pitchforks —'

'Staves and pitchforks – in the name o' the law! And take 'em in yer hands and go in quest, and do as we in authority tell ye!'

Thus aroused, the men prepared to give chase. The evidence was, indeed, though circumstantial, so convincing, that but little argument was needed to show the shepherd's guests that after what they had seen it would look very much like connivance if they did not instantly pursue the unhappy third stranger, who could not as yet have gone more than a few hundred yards over such uneven country.

A shepherd is always well provided with lanterns; and, lighting these hastily, and with hurdle-staves in their hands, they poured out of the door, taking a direction along the crest of the hill, away from the town, the rain having fortunately a little abated.

Disturbed by the noise, or possibly by unpleasant dreams of her baptism, the child who had been christened began to cry heart-brokenly in the room overhead. These notes of grief came down through the chinks of the floor to the ears of the women below, who jumped up one by one, and seemed glad of the excuse to ascend and comfort the baby, for the incidents of the last half-hour greatly oppressed them. Thus in the space of two or three minutes the room on the ground-floor was deserted quite.

But it was not for long. Hardly had the sound of footsteps died away when a man returned round the corner of the house from the direction the pursuers had taken. Peeping in at the door, and seeing nobody there, he entered leisurely. It was the stranger of the chimney-corner, who had gone out with the rest. The motive of his return was shown by his helping himself to a cut piece of skimmer-cake that lay on a ledge beside where he had sat, and which he had apparently forgotten to take with him. He also poured out half a cup more mead from the quantity that remained, ravenously eating and drinking these as he stood. He had not finished when another figure came in just as quietly – his friend in cinder-gray.

'O – you here?' said the latter, smiling. 'I thought you had gone to help in the capture.' And this speaker also revealed the object of his return by looking solicitously round for the fascinating mug of old mead.

'And I thought you had gone,' said the other, continuing his skimmer-cake with some effort.

'Well, on second thoughts, I felt there were enough without me,' said the first confidentially, 'and such a night as it is, too. Besides, 'tis the business o' the Government to take care of its criminals – not mine.'

'True; so it is. And I felt as you did, that there were enough without me.'

'I don't want to break my limbs running over the humps and hollows of this wild country.'

'Nor I neither, between you and me.'

'These shepherd-people are used to it – simple-minded souls, you know, stirred up to anything in a moment. They'll have him ready for me before the morning, and no trouble to me at all.'

'They'll have him, and we shall have saved ourselves all labour in the matter.'

'True, true. Well, my way is to Casterbridge; and 'tis as much as my legs will do to take me that far. Going the same way?'

'No, I am sorry to say! I have to get home over there' (he nodded indefinitely to the right), 'and I feel as you do, that it is quite enough for my legs to do before bedtime.'

The other had by this time finished the mead in the mug, after which, shaking hands heartily at the door, and wishing each other well, they went their several ways.

In the meantime the company of pursuers had reached the end of the hog's-back elevation which dominated this part of the down. They had decided on no particular plan of action; and, finding that the man of the baleful trade was no longer in their company, they seemed quite unable to form any such plan now. They descended in all directions down the hill, and straightway several of the party fell into the snare set by Nature for all misguided midnight ramblers over this part of the cretaceous formation. The 'lanchets,' or flint slopes, which belted the escarpment at intervals of a dozen yards, took the less cautious ones unawares, and losing their footing on the rubbly steep they slid sharply downwards, the lanterns rolling from their hands to the bottom, and there lying on their sides till the horn was scorched through.

When they had again gathered themselves together the shepherd, as the man who knew the country best, took the lead, and guided them round these treacherous inclines. The lanterns, which seemed rather to dazzle their eyes and warn the fugitive than to assist them in the exploration, were extinguished, due silence was observed; and in this more rational order they plunged into the vale. It was a grassy, briery, moist defile, affording some shelter to any person who had sought it; but the party perambulated it in vain, and ascended on the other side. Here they wandered apart, and after an interval closed together again to report progress. At the second time of closing in they found themselves near a lonely ash, the single tree on this part of the coomb, probably sown there by a passing bird some fifty years before. And here, standing a little to one side of the trunk, as motionless as the trunk itself, appeared the man they were in quest of, his outline being well defined against the sky beyond. The band noiselessly drew up and faced him.

'Your money or your life!' said the constable sternly to the still figure.

'No, no,' whispered John Pitcher. ''Tisn't our side ought to say that. That's the doctrine of vagabonds like him, and we be on the side of the law.'

'Well, well,' replied the constable impatiently; 'I must say something, mustn't I? and if you had all the weight o' this undertaking upon your mind, perhaps you'd say the wrong thing too! – Prisoner at the bar, surrender, in the name of the Father – the Crown, I mane!'

The man under the tree seemed now to notice them for the first time, and, giving them no opportunity whatever for exhibiting their courage, he strolled slowly towards them. He was, indeed, the little man, the third stranger; but his trepidation had in a great measure gone.

'Well, travellers,' he said, 'did I hear ye speak to me?'

'You did; you've got to come and be our prisoner at once!' said the constable. 'We arrest 'ee on the charge of not biding in Casterbridge jail in a decent proper manner to be hung tomorrow morning. Neighbours, do your duty, and seize the culpet!'

On hearing the charge the man seemed enlightened, and, saying not another word, resigned himself with preternatural civility to the search-party, who, with their staves in their hands, surrounded him on all sides, and marched him back towards the shepherd's cottage.

It was eleven o'clock by the time they arrived. The light shining from the open door, a sound of men's voices within, proclaimed to them as they approached the house that some new events had arisen in their absence. On entering they discovered the shepherd's living room to be invaded by two officers from Casterbridge jail, and a well-known magistrate who lived at the nearest country-seat, intelligence of the escape having become generally circulated.

'Gentlemen,' said the constable, 'I have brought back your man – not without risk and danger; but every one must do his duty! He is inside this circle of able-bodied persons, who have lent me useful aid, considering their ignorance of Crown work. Men, bring forward your prisoner!' And the third stranger was led to the light.

'Who is this?' said one of the officials.

'The man,' said the constable.

'Certainly not,' said the turnkey; and the first corroborated his statement.

'But how can it be otherwise?' asked the constable. 'Or why was he so terrified at sight o' the singing instrument of the law who sat there?' Here he related the strange behaviour of the third stranger on entering the house during the hangman's song.

'Can't understand it,' said the officer coolly. 'All I know is that it is not the condemned man. He's quite a different character from this one; a gauntish fellow, with dark hair and eyes, rather good-looking, and with a musical bass voice that if you heard it once you'd never mistake as long as you lived.'

'Why, souls – 'twas the man in the chimney-corner!'

'Hey – what?' said the magistrate, coming forward after inquiring particulars from the shepherd in the background. 'Haven't you got the man after all?'

'Well, sir,' said the constable, 'he's the man we were in search of, that's true; and yet he's not the man we were in search of. For the man we were in search of was not the man we wanted, sir, if you understand my everyday way; for 'twas the man in the chimney-corner!'

'A pretty kettle of fish altogether!' said the magistrate. 'You had better start for the other man at once.'

The prisoner now spoke for the first time. The mention of the man in the chimney-corner seemed to have moved him as nothing else could do. 'Sir,' he said, stepping forward to the magistrate, 'take no more trouble about me. The time is come when I may as well speak. I have done nothing; my crime is that the condemned man is my brother. Early this afternoon I left home at Shottsford to tramp it all the way to Casterbridge jail to bid him farewell. I was benighted, and called here to rest and ask the way. When I opened the door I saw before me the very man, my brother, that I thought to see in the condemned cell at Casterbridge. He was in this chimney-corner; and jammed close to him, so that he could not have got out if he had tried, was the executioner who'd come to take his life, singing a song about it and not knowing that it was his victim who was close by, joining in to save appearances. My brother threw a glance of agony at me, and I knew he meant, "Don't reveal what you see; my life depends on it." I was so terror-struck that I could hardly stand, and, not knowing what I did, I turned and hurried away.'

The narrator's manner and tone had the stamp of truth, and his story made a great impression on all around. 'And do you know where your brother is at the present time?' asked the magistrate.

'I do not. I have never seen him since I closed this door.'

'I can testify to that, for we've been between ye ever since,' said the constable.

'Where does he think to fly to? – what is his occupation?'

'He's a watch-and-clock-maker, sir.'

''A said 'a was a wheelwright – a wicked rogue,' said the constable.

'The wheels of clocks and watches he meant, no doubt,' said Shepherd Fennel. 'I thought his hands were palish for's trade.'

'Well, it appears to me that nothing can be gained by retaining this poor man in custody,' said the magistrate; 'your business lies with the other, unquestionably.'

And so the little man was released off-hand; but he looked nothing the less sad on that account, it being beyond the power of magistrate or constable to raze out the written troubles in his brain, for they concerned another whom he regarded with more solicitude than himself. When this was done, and the man had gone his way, the night was found to be so far advanced that it was deemed useless to renew the search before the next morning.

Next day, accordingly, the quest for the clever sheep-stealer became general and keen, to all appearance at least. But the intended punishment was cruelly disproportioned to the transgression, and the sympathy of a great many country-folk in that district was strongly on the side of the fugitive. Moreover, his marvellous coolness and daring in hob-and-nobbing with the hangman, under the unprecedented circumstances of the shepherd's party, won their admiration. So that it may be questioned if all those who ostensibly made themselves so busy in exploring woods and fields and lanes were quite so thorough when it came to the private examination of their own lofts and outhouses. Stories were afloat of a mysterious figure being occasionally seen in some old overgrown trackway or other, remote from turnpike roads; but when a search was instituted in any of these suspected quarters nobody was found. Thus the days and weeks passed without tidings.

In brief, the bass-voiced man of the chimney-corner was never recaptured. Some said that he went across the sea, others that he did not, but buried himself in the depths of a populous city. At any rate, the gentleman in cinder-gray never did his morning's work at Casterbridge, nor met anywhere at all, for business purposes, the genial comrade with whom he had passed an hour of relaxation in the lonely house on the slope of the coomb.

The grass has long been green on the graves of Shepherd Fennel and his frugal wife; the guests who made up the christening party have mainly followed their entertainers to the tomb; the baby in whose honour they all had met is a matron in the sere and yellow leaf. But the arrival of the three strangers at the shepherd's that night, and the details connected therewith, is a story as well known as ever in the country about Higher Crowstairs.

March 1883.

All Creatures Great and Small

JAMES HERRIOT

THEY DIDN'T SAY ANYTHING ABOUT this in the books, I thought, as the snow blew in through the gaping doorway and settled on my naked back.

I lay face down on the cobbled floor in a pool of nameless muck, my arm deep inside the straining cow, my feet scrabbling for a toe hold between the stones. I was stripped to the waist and the snow mingled with the dirt and the dried blood on my body. I could see nothing outside the circle of flickering light thrown by the smoky oil lamp which the farmer held over me.

No, there wasn't a word in the books about searching for your ropes and instruments in the shadows; about trying to keep clean in a half bucket of tepid water; about the cobbles digging into your chest. Nor about the slow numbing of the arms, the creeping paralysis of the muscles as the fingers tried to work against the cow's powerful expulsive efforts.

There was no mention anywhere of the gradual exhaustion, the feeling of futility and the little far-off voice of panic.

My mind went back to that picture in the obstetrics book. A cow standing in the middle of a gleaming floor while a sleek veterinary surgeon in a spotless parturition overall inserted his arm to a polite distance. He was relaxed and smiling, the farmer and his helpers were smiling, even the cow was smiling. There was no dirt or blood or sweat anywhere.

That man in the picture had just finished an excellent lunch and had moved next door to do a bit of calving just for the sheer pleasure of it, as a kind of dessert. He hadn't crawled shivering from his bed at two o'clock in the morning and bumped over twelve miles of frozen snow, staring sleepily ahead till the lonely farm showed in the headlights. He hadn't climbed half a mile of white fellside to the doorless barn where his patient lay.

I tried to wriggle my way an extra inch inside the cow. The calf's head was back and I was painfully pushing a thin, looped rope towards its lower jaw with my finger tips. All the time my arm was being squeezed between the calf and the bony pelvis. With every straining effort from the cow the pressure became almost unbearable, then she would relax and I would push the rope another inch. I wondered how long I would be able to keep this up. If I didn't snare that jaw soon I would never get the calf away. I groaned, set my teeth and reached forward again.

Another little flurry of snow blew in and I could almost hear the flakes sizzling on my sweating back. There was sweat on my forehead too, and it trickled into my eyes as I pushed.

There is always a time at a bad calving when you begin to wonder if you will ever win the battle. I had reached this stage.

Little speeches began to flit through my brain. 'Perhaps it would be better to slaughter this cow. Her pelvis is so small and narrow that I can't see a calf coming through', or 'She's a good fat animal and really of the beef type, so don't you think it would pay you better to get the butcher?' or perhaps 'This is a very bad presentation. In a roomy cow it would be simple enough to bring the head round but in this case it is just about impossible.'

Of course, I could have delivered the calf by embryotomy – by passing a wire over the neck and sawing off the head. So many of these occasions ended with the floor strewn with heads, legs, heaps of intestines. There were thick textbooks devoted to the countless ways you could cut up a calf.

But none of it was any good here, because this calf was alive. At my furthest stretch I had got my finger as far as the commissure of the mouth and had been startled by a twitch of the little creature's tongue. It was unexpected because calves in this position are usually dead, asphyxiated by the acute flexion of the neck and the pressure of the dam's powerful contractions. But this one had a spark of life in it and if it came out it would have to be in one piece.

I went over to my bucket of water, cold now and bloody, and silently soaped my arms. Then I lay down again, feeling the cobbles harder than ever against my chest. I worked my toes between the stones, shook the sweat from my eyes and for the hundredth time thrust an arm that felt like spaghetti into the cow; alongside the little dry legs of the calf, like sandpaper tearing against my flesh, then to the bend in the neck and so to the ear and then, agonizingly, along the side of the face towards the lower jaw which had become my major goal in life.

It was incredible that I had been doing this for nearly two hours; fighting as my strength ebbed to push a little noose round that jaw. I had tried everything else – repelling a leg, gentle traction with a blunt hook in the eye socket, but I was back to the noose.

It had been a miserable session all through. The farmer, Mr Dinsdale, was a long, sad, silent man of few words who always seemed to be expecting the worst to happen. He had a long, sad, silent son with him and the two of them had watched my efforts with deepening gloom.

But worst of all had been Uncle. When I had first entered the hillside barn I had been surprised to see a little bright-eyed old man in a pork pie hat settling down comfortably on a bale of straw. He was filling his pipe and clearly looking forward to the entertainment.

'Now then, young man,' he cried in the nasal twang of the West Riding. 'I'm Mr Dinsdale's brother. I farm over in Listondale.'

I put down my equipment and nodded. 'How do you do? My name is Herriot.'

The old man looked me over, piercingly. 'My vet is Mr Broomfield. Expect you'll have heard of him – everybody knows him, I reckon. Wonderful man, Mr Broomfield, especially at calving. Do you know, I've never seen 'im beat yet.'

I managed a wan smile. Any other time I would have been delighted to hear how good my colleague was, but somehow not now, not now. In fact, the words set a mournful little bell tolling inside me.

'No, I'm afraid I don't know Mr Broomfield,' I said, taking off my jacket and, more reluctantly, peeling my shirt over my head. 'But I haven't been around these parts very long.'

Uncle was aghast. 'You don't know him! Well you're the only one as doesn't. They think the world of him in Listondale, I can tell you.' He lapsed into a shocked silence and applied a match to his pipe. Then he shot a glance at my goose-pimpled torso. 'Strips like a boxer does Mr Broomfield. Never seen such muscles on a man.'

A wave of weakness coursed sluggishly over me. I felt suddenly leaden-footed and inadequate. As I began to lay out my ropes and instruments on a clean towel the old man spoke again.

'And how long have you been qualified, may I ask?'

'Oh, about seven months.'

'Seven months!' Uncle smiled indulgently, tamped down his tobacco and blew out a cloud of rank, blue smoke. 'Well, there's nowt like a bit of experience, I always says. Mr Broomfield's been doing my work now for over ten years and he really knows what he's about. No, you can 'ave your book learning. Give me experience every time.'

I tipped some antiseptic into the bucket and lathered my arms carefully. I knelt behind the cow.

'Mr Broomfield always puts some special lubricating oils on his arms first,' Uncle said, pulling contentedly on his pipe. 'He says you get infection of the womb if you just use soap and water.'

I made my first exploration. It was the burdened moment all vets go through when they first put their hand into a cow. Within seconds I would know whether I would be putting on my jacket in fifteen minutes or whether I had hours of hard labour ahead of me.

I was going to be unlucky this time; it was a nasty presentation. Head back and no room at all; more like being inside an undeveloped heifer than a second calver. And she was bone dry – the 'waters' must have come away from her hours ago. She had been running out on the high fields and had started to calve a week before her time; that was why they had had to bring her into this half-ruined barn. Anyway, it would be a long time before I saw my bed again.

'Well now, what have you found, young man?' Uncle's penetrating voice cut through the silence. 'Head back, eh? You won't have much trouble, then. I've seen Mr Broomfield do 'em like that – he turns calf right round and brings it out back legs first.'

I had heard this sort of nonsense before. A short time in practice had taught me that all farmers were experts with other farmers' livestock. When their own animals were in trouble they tended to rush to the phone for the vet, but with their neighbours' they were confident, knowledgeable and full of helpful advice. And another phenomenon I had observed was that their advice was usually regarded as more valuable than the vet's. Like now, for instance, Uncle was obviously an accepted sage and the Dinsdales listened with deference to everything he said.

'Another way with a job like this,' continued Uncle, 'is to get a few strong chaps with ropes and pull the thing out, head back and all.'

I gasped as I felt my way around. 'I'm afraid it's impossible to turn a calf completely round in this small space. And to pull it out without bringing the head round would certainly break the mother's pelvis.'

The Dinsdales narrowed their eyes. Clearly they thought I was hedging in the face of Uncle's superior knowledge.

And now, two hours later, defeat was just round the corner. I was just about whacked. I had rolled and grovelled on the filthy cobbles while the Dinsdales watched me in morose silence and Uncle kept up a non-stop stream of comment. Uncle, his ruddy face glowing with delight, his little eyes sparkling, hadn't had such a happy night for years. His long trek up the hillside had been repaid a hundredfold. His vitality was undiminished; he had enjoyed every minute.

As I lay there, eyes closed, face stiff with dirt, mouth hanging open, Uncle took his pipe in his hand and leaned forward on his straw bale. 'You're about beat, young man,' he said with deep satisfaction. 'Well, I've never seen Mr Broomfield beat but he's had a lot of experience. And what's more, he's strong, really strong. That's one man you couldn't tire.'

Rage flooded through me like a draught of strong spirit. They right thing to do, of course, would be to get up, tip the bucket of bloody water over Uncle's head, run down the hill and drive away; away from Yorkshire, from Uncle, from the Dinsdales, from this cow.

Instead, I clenched my teeth, braced my legs and pushed with everything I had; and with a sensation of disbelief I felt my noose slide over the sharp little incisor teeth and into the calf's mouth. Gingerly, muttering a prayer, I pulled on the thin rope with my left hand and felt the slipknot tighten. I had hold of that lower jaw.

At last I could start doing something. 'Now hold this rope, Mr Dinsdale, and just keep a gentle tension on it. I'm going to repel the calf and if you pull steadily at the same time, the head ought to come round.'

'What if the rope comes off?' asked Uncle hopefully.

I didn't answer. I put my hand in against the calf's shoulder and began to push against the cow's contractions. I felt the small body moving away from me. 'Now a steady pull, Mr Dinsdale, without jerking.' And to myself, 'Oh God, don't let it slip off.'

The head was coming round. I could feel the neck straightening against my arm, then the ear touched my elbow. I let go the shoulder and grabbed the little muzzle. Keeping the teeth away from the vaginal wall with my hand, I guided the head till it was resting where it should be, on the fore limbs.

Quickly I extended the noose till it reached behind the ears. 'Now pull on the head as she strains.'

'Nay, you should pull on the legs now,' cried Uncle.

'Pull on the bloody head rope, I tell you!' I bellowed at the top of my voice and felt immediately better as Uncle retired, offended, to his bale.

With traction the head was brought out and the rest of the body followed easily. The little animal lay motionless on the cobbles, eyes glassy and unseeing, tongue blue and grossly swollen.

'It'll be dead. Bound to be,' grunted Uncle, returning to the attack.

I cleared the mucus from the mouth, blew hard down the throat and began artificial respiration. After a few pressures on the ribs, the calf gave a gasp and the eyelids flickered. Then it started to inhale and one leg jerked.

Uncle took off his hat and scratched his head in disbelief. 'By gaw, it's alive. I'd have thowt it'd sure to be dead after you'd messed about all that time.' A lot of the fire had gone out of him and his pipe hung down empty from his lips.

'I know what this little fellow wants,' I said. I grasped the calf by its fore legs and pulled it up to its mother's head. The cow was stretched out on her side, her head extended wearily along the rough floor. Her ribs heaved, her eyes were almost closed, she looked past caring about anything. Then she felt the calf's body against her face and there was a transformation; her eyes opened wide and her muzzle began a snuffling exploration of the new object. Her interest grew with every sniff and she struggled on to her chest, nosing and probing all over the calf, rumbling deep in her chest. Then she began to lick him methodically. Nature provides the perfect stimulant massage for a time like this and the little creature arched his back as the coarse papillae on the tongue dragged along his skin. Within a minute he was shaking his head and trying to sit up.

I grinned. This was the bit I liked. The little miracle. I felt it was something that would never grow stale no matter how often I saw it. I cleaned as much of the dried blood and filth from my body as I could, but most of it had caked on my skin and not even my finger nails would move it. It would have to wait for the hot bath at home. Pulling my shirt over my head, I felt as though I had been beaten for a long time with a thick stick. Every muscle ached. My mouth was dried out, my lips almost sticking together.

A long, sad figure hovered near. 'How about a drink?' asked Mr Dinsdale.

I could feel my grimy face cracking into an incredulous smile. A vision of hot tea well laced with whisky swam before me. 'That's very kind of you, Mr Dinsdale, I'd love a drink. It's been a hard two hours.'

'Nay,' said Mr Dinsdale looking at me steadily, 'I meant for the cow.'

I began to babble. 'Oh yes, of course, certainly, by all means give her a drink. She must be very thirsty. It'll do her good. Certainly, certainly, give her a drink.'

I gathered up my tackle and stumbled out of the barn. On the moor it was still dark and a bitter wind whipped over the snow, stinging my eyes. As I plodded down the slope, Uncle's voice, strident and undefeated, reached me for the last time.

'Mr Broomfield doesn't believe in giving a drink after calving. Says it chills the stomach.'

The Red Signal

AGATHA CHRISTIE

'NO, BUT HOW TOO THRILLING,' SAID pretty Mrs Eversleigh, opening her lovely, but slightly vacant, blue eyes very wide. 'They always say women have a sixth sense; do you think it's true, Sir Alington?'

The famous alienist smiled sardonically. He had an unbounded contempt for the foolish pretty type, such as his fellow guest. Alington West was the supreme authority on mental disease, and he was fully alive to his own position and importance. A slightly pompous man in full figure.

'A great deal of nonsense is talked, I know that, Mrs Eversleigh. What does the term mean – a sixth sense?'

'You scientific men are always so severe. And it really is extraordinary the way one seems to positively know things sometimes – just know them, feel them, I mean – quite uncanny – it really is. Claire knows what I mean, don't you, Claire?'

She appealed to her hostess with a slight pout, and a tilted shoulder.

Claire Trent did not reply at once. It was a small dinner party – she and her husband, Violet Eversleigh, Sir Alington West, and his nephew Dermot West, who was an old friend of Jack Trent's. Jack Trent himself, a somewhat heavy, florid man with a good-humoured smile and a pleasant lazy laugh, took up the thread.

'Bunkum, Violet! Your best friend is killed in a railway accident. Straight away you remember that you dreamed of a black cat last Tuesday – marvellous, you felt all along that something was going to happen!'

'Oh, no, Jack, you're mixing up premonitions with intuition now. Come, now, Sir Alington, you must admit that premonitions are real?'

'To a certain extent, perhaps,' admitted the physician cautiously. 'But coincidence accounts for a good deal, and then there is the invariable tendency to make the most of a story afterward.'

'I don't think there is any such thing as premonition,' said Claire

Trent rather abruptly. 'Or intuition or a sixth sense or any of the things we talk about so glibly. We go through life like a train rushing through the darkness to an unknown destination.'

'That's hardly a good simile, Mrs Trent,' said Dermot West, lifting his head for the first time and taking part in the discussion. There was a curious glitter in the clear gray eyes that shone out rather oddly from the deeply tanned face. 'You've forgotten the signals, you see.'

'The signals?'

'Yes, green if it's all right, and red – for danger!'

'Red – for danger – how thrilling!' breathed Violet Eversleigh.

Dermot turned from her rather impatiently. 'That's just a way of describing it, of course.'

Trent stared at him curiously. 'You speak as though it were an actual experience, Dermot, old boy.'

'So it is – has been, I mean.'

'Give us the yarn.'

'I can give you one instance. Out in Mesopotamia, just after the Armistice, I came into my tent one evening with the feeling strong upon me. Danger! Look out! Hadn't the ghost of a notion what it was all about. I made a round of the camp, fussed unnecessarily, took all precautions against an attack by hostile Arabs. Then I went back to my tent. As soon as I got inside, the feeling popped up again stronger than ever. Danger! In the end I took a blanket outside, rolled myself up in it, and slept there.'

'Well?'

'The next morning, when I went inside the tent, first thing I saw was a great knife arrangement – about half a yard long – struck down through my bunk, just where I would have lain. I soon found out about it – one of the Arab servants. His son had been shot as a spy. What have you got to say to that, Uncle Alington, as an example of what I call the red signal?'

The specialist smiled noncommittally. 'A very interesting story, my dear Dermot.'

'But not one that you accept unreservedly?'

'Yes, yes, I have no doubt but that you had the premonition of danger, just as you state. But it is the origin of the premonition I dispute. According to you, it came from without, impressed by some outside source upon your mentality. But nowadays we find that nearly everything comes from within – from our subconscious self.'

'I suggest that by some glance or look this Arab had betrayed himself. Your conscious self did not notice or remember, but with your subconscious self it was otherwise. The subconscious never forgets. We believe, too, that it can reason and deduce quite independently of the higher or conscious will. Your subconscious self, then, believed that an attempt might be made to assassinate you, and succeeded in forcing its fear upon your conscious realization.'

'That sounds very convincing, I admit,' said Dermot, smiling.

'But not nearly so exciting,' pouted Mrs Eversleigh.

'It is also possible that you may have been subconsciously aware of the hate felt by the man toward you. What in old days used to be called telepathy certainly exists, though the conditions governing it are very little understood.'

'Have there been any other instances?' asked Claire of Dermot.

'Oh! yes, but nothing very pictorial – and I suppose they could all be explained under the heading of coincidence. I refused an invitation to a country house once, for no other reason than the "red signal." The place was burned out during the week. By the way, Uncle Alington, where does the subconscious come in there?'

'I'm afraid it doesn't,' said Sir Alington, smiling.

'But you've got an equally good explanation. Come, now. No need to be tactful with near relatives.'

'Well, then, nephew, I venture to suggest that you refused the invitation for the ordinary reason that you didn't much want to go, and that after the fire, you suggested to yourself that you had had a warning of danger, which explanation you now believe implicitly.'

'It's hopeless,' laughed Dermot. 'It's heads you win, tails I lose.'

'Never mind, Mr West,' cried Violet Eversleigh. 'I believe in your Red Signal. Is the time in Mesopotamia the last time you had it?'

'Yes – until –'

'I beg your pardon?'

'Nothing.'

Dermot sat silent. The words which had nearly left his lips were: 'Yes, until tonight.' They had come quite unbidden to his lips, voicing a thought which had as yet not been consciously realized, but he was aware at once that they were true. The Red Signal was looming up out of the darkness. Danger! Danger close at hand!

But why? What conceivable danger could there be here? Here in the house of his friends? At least – well, yes, there was that kind of danger. He looked at Claire Trent – her whiteness, her slenderness, the exquisite droop of her golden head. But that danger had been there for some time – it was never likely to get acute. For Jack Trent was his best friend, and more than his best friend, the man who had saved his life in Flanders and been recommended for the VC for doing so. A good fellow, Jack, one of the best. Damned bad luck that he should have fallen in love with Jack's wife. He'd get over it some day, he supposed. A thing couldn't go on hurting like this forever. One could starve it out – that was it, starve it out. It was not as though she would ever guess – and if she did guess, there was no danger of her caring. A statue, a beautiful statue, a thing of gold and ivory and pale-pink coral – a toy for a king, not a real woman.

Claire – the very thought of her name, uttered silently, hurt him. He must get over it. He'd cared for women before. *But not like this!* said something. *Not like this.* Well, there it was. No danger there – heartache, yes, but not danger. Not the danger of the Red Signal. That was for something else.

He looked round the table and it struck him for the first time that it was rather an unusual little gathering. His uncle, for instance, seldom dined out in this small, informal way. It was not as though the Trents were old friends; until this evening Dermot had not been aware that he knew them at all.

To be sure, there was an excuse. A rather notorious medium was coming after dinner to give a séance. Sir Alington professed to be mildly interested in spiritualism. Yes, that was an excuse, certainly.

The word forced itself on his notice. An excuse. Was the séance just an excuse to make the specialist's presence at dinner natural? If so, what was the real object of his being here? A host of details came rushing into Dermot's mind, trifles unnoticed at the time, or, as his uncle would have said, unnoticed by the conscious mind.

The great physician had looked oddly, very oddly, at Claire more than once. He seemed to be watching her. She was uneasy under his scrutiny. She made little twitching motions with her hands. She was nervous, horribly nervous, and was it, could it be, frightened? Why was she frightened?

With a jerk he came back to the conversation round the table. Mrs Eversleigh had got the great man talking upon his own subject.

'My dear lady,' he was saying, 'what *is* madness? I can assure you that the more we study the subject, the more difficult we find it to pronounce. We all practice a certain amount of self-deception, and when we carry it so far as to believe we are the Czar of Russia, we are shut up or restrained. But there is a long road before we reach that point. At what particular spot on it shall we erect a post and say, "On this side sanity, on the other madness"? It can't be done, you know. And I will tell you this – if the man suffering from a delusion happened to hold his tongue about it, in all probability we should never be able to distinguish him from a normal individual. The extraordinary sanity of the insane is an interesting subject.'

Sir Alington sipped his wine with appreciation and beamed upon the company.

'I've always heard they are very cunning,' remarked Mrs Eversleigh. 'Loonies, I mean.'

'Remarkably so. And suppression of one's particular delusion has a disastrous effect very often. All suppressions are dangerous, as psychoanalysis has taught us. The man who has a harmless eccentricity, and can indulge it as such, seldom goes over the border line. But the man –' he paused – 'or woman who is to all appearance perfectly normal, may be in reality a poignant source of danger to the community.'

His gaze travelled gently down the table to Claire and the back again.

A horrible fear shook Dermot. Was that what he meant? Was that what he was driving at? Impossible, but –

'And all from suppressing oneself,' sighed Mrs Eversleigh. 'I quite see that one should be very careful always to – to express one's personality. The dangers of the other are frightful.'

'My dear Mrs Eversleigh,' expostulated the physician, 'you have quite misunderstood me. The cause of the mischief is in the physical matter of the brain – sometimes arising from some outward agency such as a blow, sometimes, alas, congenital.'

'Heredity is so sad,' sighed the lady vaguely. 'Consumption and all that.'

'Tuberculosis is not hereditary,' said Sir Alington dryly.

'Isn't it? I always thought it was. But madness is! How dreadful. What else?'

'Gout,' said Sir Alington, smiling. 'And colour blindness – the latter is rather interesting. It is transmitted direct to males, but is latent in females. So while there are many colour-blind men, for a woman to be colour blind, it must have been latent in her mother as well as present in her father – rather an unusual state of things to occur. That is what is called sex-limited heredity.'

'How interesting. But madness is not like that, is it?'

'Madness can be handed down to men or women equally,' said the physician gravely.

Claire rose suddenly, pushing back her chair so abruptly that it overturned and fell to the ground. She was very pale, and the nervous motions of her fingers were very apparent.

'You – you will not be long, will you?' she begged. 'Mrs Thompson will be here in a few minutes now.'

'One glass of port and I will be with you,' declared Sir Alington. 'To see this wonderful Mrs Thompson's performance is what I have come for, is it not? Ha, ha! Not that I needed any inducement.' He bowed.

Claire gave a faint smile of acknowledgement and passed out of the room with Mrs Eversleigh.

'Afraid I've been talking shop,' remarked the physician as he resumed his seat. 'Forgive me, my dear fellow.'

'Not at all,' said Trent perfunctorily.

He looked strained and worried. For the first time Dermot felt an outsider in the company of his friend. Between these two was a secret that even an old friend might not share. And yet the whole thing was fantastic and incredible. What had he to go upon? Nothing but a couple of glances and a woman's nervousness.

They lingered over their wine but a very short time, and arrived up in the drawing-room just as Mrs Thompson was announced.

The medium was a plump middle-aged woman, atrociously dressed in magenta velvet, with a loud, rather common voice.

'Hope I'm not late, Mrs Trent,' she said cheerily. 'You did say nine o'clock, didn't you?'

'You are quite punctual, Mrs Thompson,' said Claire in her sweet, slightly husky voice. 'This is our little circle.'

No further introductions were made, as was evidently the custom. The medium swept them all with a shrewd, penetrating eye.

'I hope we shall get some good results,' she remarked briskly. 'I can't tell you how I hate it when I go out and I can't give satisfaction, so to speak. It just makes me mad. But I think Shiromako – my Japanese control, you know – will be able to get through all right tonight. I'm feeling ever so fit, and I refused the Welsh rarebit, fond of cheese though I am.'

Dermot listened, half-amused, half-disgusted. How prosaic the whole thing was! And yet, was he not judging foolishly? Everything, after all, was natural – the powers claimed by mediums were natural powers, as yet imperfectly understood. A great surgeon might be wary of indigestion on the eve of a delicate operation. Why not Mrs Thompson?

Chairs were arranged in a circle, lights so that they could conveniently be raised and lowered. Dermot noticed that there was no question of tests, or of Sir Alington satisfying himself as to the conditions of the séance. No, this business of Mrs Thompson was only a blind. Sir Alington was here for quite another purpose. Claire's mother, Dermot remembered, had died abroad. There had been some mystery about her – Hereditary –

With a jerk he forced his mind back to the surroundings of the moment.

Everyone took their places, and the lights were turned out, all but a small red-shaded one on a far table.

For a while nothing was heard but the low, even breathing of the medium. Gradually it grew more and more stertorous. Then, with a suddenness that made Dermot jump, a loud rap came from the far end of the room. It was repeated from the other side. Then a perfect crescendo of raps was heard. They died away, and a sudden high peal of mocking laughter rang through the room.

Then silence, broken by a voice utterly unlike that of Mrs Thompson, a high-pitched, quaintly inflected voice.

'I am here, gentlemen,' it said. 'Yes, I am here. You wish to ask me things?'

'Who are you? Shiromako?'

'Yes. I Shiromako. I pass over long ago. I work. I very happy.'

Further details of Shiromako's life followed. It was all very flat and uninteresting, and Dermot had heard it often before. Everyone was happy, very happy. Messages were given from vaguely described relatives, the description being so loosely worded as to fit almost any contingency. An elderly lady, the mother of someone present, held the floor for some time, imparting copybook maxims with an air of refreshing novelty hardly borne out by her subject matter.

'Someone else want to get through now,' announced Shiromako. 'Got a very important message for one of the gentlemen.'

There was a pause, and then a new voice spoke, prefacing its remarks with an evil, demoniacal chuckle.

'Ha, ha! Ha, ha, ha! Better not go home. Take my advice.'

'Who are you speaking to?' asked Trent.

'One of you three. I shouldn't go home if I were him. Danger!
Blood! Not very much blood – quite enough. No, don't go home.'
The voice grew fainter. *'Don't go home!'*

It died away completely. Dermot felt his blood tingling. He was
convinced that the warning was meant for him. Somehow or other,
there was danger abroad tonight.

There was a sigh from the medium, and then a groan. She was
coming round. The lights were turned on, and presently she sat
upright, her eyes blinking a little.

'Go off well, my dear? I hope so.'

'Very good indeed, thank you, Mrs Thompson.'

'Shiromako, I suppose?'

'Yes, and others.'

Mrs Thompson yawned.

'I'm dead beat. Absolutely down and out. Does fairly take it out
of you. Well, I'm glad it was a success. I was a bit afraid something
disagreeable might happen. There's a queer feel about this room
tonight.'

She glanced over each ample shoulder in turn, and then shrugged
them uncomfortably.

'I don't like it,' she said. 'Any sudden deaths among any of you
people lately?'

'What do you mean – among us?'

'Near relatives – dear friends? No? Well, if I wanted to be melo-
dramatic, I'd say that there was death in the air tonight. There, it's only
my nonsense. Goodbye, Mrs Trent. I'm glad you've been satisfied.'

Mrs Thompson in her magenta velvet gown went out.

'I hope you've been interested, Sir Alingon,' murmured Claire.

'A most interesting evening, my dear lady. Many thanks for the
opportunity. Let me wish you good night. You are all going on to a
dance, are you not?'

'Won't you come with us?'

'No, no. I make it a rule to be in bed by half past eleven. Good
night. Good night, Mrs Eversleigh. Ah, Dermot, I rather want to
have a word with you. Can you come with me now? You can rejoin
the others at the Grafton Galleries.'

'Certainly, Uncle. I'll meet you there, then, Trent.'

Very few words were exchanged between uncle and nephew during
the short drive to Harley Street. Sir Alington made a semi-apology

for dragging Dermot away, and assured him that he would only detain him a few minutes.

'Shall I keep the car for you, my boy?' he asked, as they alighted.

'Oh, don't bother, Uncle. I'll pick up a taxi.'

'Very good. I don't like to keep Charlson up later than I can help. Goodnight, Charlson. Now where the devil did I put my key?'

The car glided away as Sir Alington stood on the steps searching his pockets.

'Must have left it in my other coat,' he said at length. 'Ring the bell, will you? Johnson is still up, I dare say.'

The imperturbable Johnson did indeed open the door within sixty seconds.

'Mislaid my key, Johnson,' explained Sir Alington. 'Bring a couple of whiskies and sodas into the library.'

'Very good, Sir Alington.'

The physician strode on into the library and turned on the lights. He motioned to Dermot to close the door.

'I won't keep you long, Dermot, but there's just something I want to say to you. Is it my fancy, or have you a certain – *tendresse*, shall we say, for Mrs Jack Trent?'

The blood rushed to Dermot's face.

'Jack Trent is my best friend.'

'Pardon me, but that is hardly answering my question. I dare say that you consider my views on divorce and such matters highly puritanical, but I must remind you that you are my only near relative and my heir.'

'There is no question of a divorce,' said Dermot angrily.

'There certainly is not, for a reason which I understand perhaps better than you do. That particular reason I cannot give you now, but I do wish to warn you. She is not for you.'

The young man faced his uncle's gaze steadily. 'I do understand – and permit me to say, perhaps better than you think. I know the reason for your presence at dinner tonight.'

'Eh?' The physician was clearly startled. 'How did you know that?'

'Call it a guess, sir. I am right, am I not, when I say that you were there in your – professional capacity.'

Sir Alington strode up and down.

'You are quite right, Dermot. I could not, of course, have told you so myself, though I am afraid it will soon be common property.'

Dermot's heart contracted. 'You mean that you have – made up your mind?'

'Yes, there is insanity in the family – on the mother's side. A sad case – a very sad case.'

'I can't believe it, sir.'

'I dare say not. To the layman there are few if any signs apparent.'

'And to the expert?'

'The evidence is conclusive. In such a case the patient must be placed under restraint as soon as possible.'

'My God!' breathed Dermot. 'But you can't shut anyone up for nothing at all.'

'My dear Dermot! Cases are only placed under restraint when their being at large would result in danger to the community.'

'Danger?'

'Very grave danger. In all probability a peculiar form of homicidal mania. It was so in the mother's case.'

Dermot turned away with a groan, burying his face in his hands. Claire – white and golden Claire!

'In the circumstances,' continued the physician comfortably, 'I felt it incumbent on me to warn you.'

'Claire,' murmured Dermot. 'My poor Claire.'

'Yes, indeed, we must all pity her.'

Suddenly Dermot raised his head.

'I say I don't believe it. Doctors make mistakes. Everyone knows that. And they're always keen on their own specialty.'

'My dear Dermot,' cried Sir Alington angrily.

'I tell you I don't believe it – and anyway, even if it is so, I don't care. I love Claire. If she will come with me, I shall take her away – far away – out of the reach of meddling physicians. I shall guard her, care for her, shelter her with my love.'

'You will do nothing of the sort. Are you mad?'

Dermot laughed scornfully. '*You* would say so.'

'Understand me, Dermot.' Sir Alington's face was red with suppressed passion. 'If you do this thing – this shameful thing – I shall withdraw the allowance I am now making you, and I shall make a new will leaving all I possess to various hospitals.'

'Do as you please with your damned money.' said Dermot in a low voice. 'I shall have the woman I love.'

'A woman who –'

'Say a word against her and, by God, I'll kill you!' cried Dermot.

A slight chink of glasses made them both swing round. Unheard by them in the heat of their argument, Johnson had entered with a tray of glasses. His face was the imperturbable one of the good servant, but Dermot wondered just exactly how much he had overheard.

'That'll do, Johnson,' said Sir Alington curtly. 'You can go to bed.'

'Thank you, sir. Good night, sir.'

Johnson withdrew.

The two men looked at each other. The momentary interruption had calmed the storm.

'Uncle,' said Dermot. 'I shouldn't have spoken to you as I did. I can quite see that from your point of view you are perfectly right. But I have loved Claire Trent for a long time. The fact that Jack Trent is my best friend has hitherto stood in the way of my ever speaking of love to Claire herself. But in these circumstances that fact no longer counts. The idea that any monetary conditions can deter me is absurd. I think we've both said all there is to be said. Good night.'

'Dermot –'

'It is really no good arguing further. Good night, Uncle Alington.'

He went out quickly, shutting the door behind him. The hall was in darkness. He passed through it, opened the front door and emerged into the street, banging the door behind him.

A taxi had just deposited a fare at a house farther along the street and Dermot hailed it, and drove to the Grafton Galleries.

In the door of the ballroom he stood for a minute, bewildered, his head spinning. The raucous jazz music, the smiling women – it was as though he had stepped into another world.

Had he dreamed it all? Impossible that that grim conversation with his uncle should have really taken place. There was Claire floating past, like a lily in her white-and-silver gown that fitted sheathlike to her slenderness. She smiled at him, her face calm and serene. Surely it was all a dream.

The dance had stopped. Presently she was near him, smiling up into his face. As in a dream he asked her to dance. She was in his arms now, the raucous melodies had begun again.

He felt her flag a little.

'Tired? Do you want to stop?'

'If you don't mind. Can we go somewhere where we can talk? There is something I want to say to you.'

Not a dream. He came back to earth with a bump. Could he ever have thought her face calm and serene? It was haunted with anxiety, with dread. How much did she know?

He found a quiet corner, and they sat down side by side.

'Well,' he said, assuming a lightness he did not feel, 'you said you had something you wanted to say to me?'

'Yes.' Her eyes were cast down. She was playing nervously with the tassel of her gown. 'It's difficult –'

'Tell me, Claire.'

'It's just this. I want you to – to go away for a time.'

He was astonished. Whatever he had expected, it was not this.

'You want me to go away? Why?'

'It's best to be honest, isn't it? I know that you are a – a gentleman and my friend. I want you to go away because I – I have let myself get fond of you.'

'Claire.'

Her words left him dumb – tongue-tied.

'Please do not think that I am conceited enough to fancy that you – would ever be likely to fall in love with me. It is only that – I am not very happy – and – oh! I would rather you went away.'

'Claire, don't you know that I have cared – cared damnably – every since I met you?'

She lifted startled eyes to his face.

'You cared? You have cared a long time?'

'Since the beginning.'

'Oh!' she cried. 'Why didn't you tell me? Then! When I could have come to you! Why tell me now when it's too late. No, I'm mad – I don't know what I'm saying. I could never have come to you.'

'Claire, what did you mean when you said "now that it's too late"? Is it – is it because of my uncle? What he knows?'

She nodded, the tears running down her face.

'Listen, Claire, you're not to believe all that. You're not to think about it. Instead, you will come away with me. I will look after you – keep you safe always.'

His arms went round her. He drew her to him, felt her tremble at his touch. Then suddenly she wrenched herself free.

'Oh, no, please. Can't you see? I couldn't now. It would be ugly – ugly – ugly. All along I've wanted to be good – and now – it would be ugly as well.'

He hesitated, baffled by her words. She looked at him appealingly.

'Please,' she said. 'I want to be good.'

WIthout a word, Dermot got up and left her. For the moment he was touched and racked by her words beyond argument. He went for his hat and coat, running into Trent as he did so.

'Hallo, Dermot, you're off early.'

'Yes, I'm not in the mood for dancing tonight.'

'It's a rotten night,' said Trent gloomily. 'But you haven't got my worries.'

Dermot had a sudden panic that Trent might be going to confide in him. Not that – anything but that!

'Well, so long,' he said hurriedly. 'I'm off home.'

'Home, eh? What about the warning of the spirits?'

'I'll risk that. Good night, Jack.'

Dermot's flat was not far away. He walked there, feeling the need of the cool night air to calm his fevered brain. He let himself in with his key and switched on the light in the bedroom.

And all at once, for the second time that night, the feeling of the Red Signal surged over him. So overpowering was it that for the moment it swept even Claire from his mind.

Danger! He was in danger. At this very moment, in this very room!

He tried in vain to ridicule himself free of the fear. Perhaps his efforts were secretly halfhearted. So far, the Red Signal had given him timely warning which had enabled him to avoid disaster. Smiling a little at his own superstition, he made a careful tour of the flat. It was possible that some malefactor had got in and was lying concealed there. But his search revealed nothing. His man, Milson, was away, and the flat was absolutely empty.

He returned to his bedroom and undressed slowly, frowning to himself. The sense of danger was acute as ever. He went to a drawer to get out a handkerchief, and suddenly stood stock still. There was an unfamiliar lump in the middle of the drawer.

His quick nervous fingers tore aside the handkerchiefs and took out the object concealed beneath them.

It was a revolver.

With the utmost astonishment Dermot examined it keenly. It was of a somewhat unfamiliar pattern, and one shot had been fired from it lately. Beyond that he could make nothing of it. Someone had placed it in that drawer that very evening. It had not been there when he dressed for dinner – he was sure of that.

He was about to replace it in the drawer, when he was startled by a bell ringing. It rang again and again, sounding unusually loud in the quietness of the empty flat.

Who could be coming to the front door at this hour? And only one answer came to the question – an answer instinctive and persistent.

Danger – danger – danger.

Led by some instinct for which he did not account, Dermot switched off his light, slipped on an overcoat that lay across a chair, and opened the hall door.

Two men stood outside. Beyond them Dermot caught sight of a blue uniform. A policeman!

'Mr West?' asked one of the two men.

It seemed to Dermot that ages elapsed before he answered. In reality it was only a few seconds before he replied in a very fair imitation of his servant's expressionless voice, 'Mr West hasn't come in yet.'

'Hasn't come in yet, eh? Very well, then, I think we'd better come in and wait for him.'

'No, you don't.'

'See here, my man. I'm Inspector Verall of Scotland Yard, and I've got a warrant for the arrest of your master. You can see it if you like.'

Dermot perused the proffered paper, or pretended to do so, asking in a dazed voice, 'What for? What's he done?'

'Murder. Sir Alington West of Harley Street.'

His brain in a whirl, Dermot fell back before his redoubtable visitors. He went into the sitting-room and switched on the light. The inspector followed him.

'Have a search round,' he directed the other man. Then he turned to Dermot. 'You stay here, my man. No slipping off to warn your master. What's your name, by the way?'

'Milson, sir.'

'What time do you expect your master in, Milson?'

'I don't know, sir, he was going to a dance, I believe. At the Grafton Galleries.'

'He left there just under an hour ago. Sure he's not been back here?'

'I don't think so, sir. I fancy I should have heard him come in.'

At this moment the second man came in from the adjoining room. In his hand he carried the revolver. He took it across to the inspector in some excitement. An expression of satisfaction flitted across the latter's face.

'That settles it,' he remarked. 'Must have slipped in and out without your hearing him. He's hooked it by now. I'd better be off. Cawley, you stay here, in case he should come back again, and you can keep an eye on this fellow. He may know more about his master than he pretends.'

The inspector bustled off. Dermot endeavored to get the details of the affair from Cawley, who was quite ready to be talkative.

'Pretty clear case,' he vouchsafed. 'The murder was discovered almost immediately. Johnson, the manservant, had only just gone up to bed when he fancied he heard a shot, and came down again. Found Sir Alington dead, shot through the heart. He rang us up at once and we came along and heard his story.'

'Which made it a pretty clear case?' ventured Dermot.

'Absolutely. This young West came in with his uncle and they were quarreling when Johnson brought in the drinks. The old boy was threatening to make a new will, and your master was talking about shooting him. Not five minutes later the shot was heard. Oh, yes, clear enough.'

Clear enough indeed. Dermot's heart sank as he realized the overwhelming evidence against him. And no way out save flight. He set his wits to work. Presently he suggested making a cup of tea. Cawley assented readily enough. He had already searched the flat and knew there was no back entrance.

Dermot was permitted to depart to the kitchen. Once there he put the kettle on, and chinked cups and saucers industriously. Then he stole swiftly to the window and lifted the sash. The flat was on the second floor, and outside the window was the small wire lift used by tradesmen which ran up and down on its steel cable.

Like a flash Dermot was outside the window and swinging himself down the wire rope. It cut into his hands, making them bleed, but he went on desperately.

A few minutes later he was emerging cautiously from the back of the block. Turning the corner, he cannoned into a figure standing by the sidewalk. To his utter amazement he recognized Jack Trent. Trent was fully alive to the perils of the situation.

'My God! Dermot! Quick, don't hang about here.'

Taking him by the arm, he led him down a by street, then down another. A lonely taxi was sighted and hailed and they jumped in, Trent giving the man his own address.

'Safest place for the moment. There we can decide what to do next to put those fools off the track. I came round here, hoping to be able to warn you before the police got here.'

'I didn't even know that you had heard of it. Jack, you don't believe –'

'Of course not, old fellow, not for one minute. I know you far too well. All the same, it's a nasty business for you. They came round asking questions – what time you got to the Grafton Galleries, when you left, and so on. Dermot, who could have done the old boy in?'

'I can't imagine. Whoever did it put the revolver in my drawer, I suppose. Must have been watching us pretty closely.'

'That séance business was damned funny. 'Don't go home.' Meant for poor old West. He did go home, and got shot.'

'It applies to me, too.' said Dermot. 'I went home and found a planted revolver and a police inspector.'

'Well, I hope it doesn't get me, too,' said Trent. 'Here we are.'

He paid the taxi, opened the door with his latchkey, and guided Dermot up the dark stairs to his den, a small room on the first floor.

He threw open the door and Dermot walked in, while Trent switched on the light, and came to join him.

'Pretty safe here for the time being,' he remarked. 'Now we can get our heads together and decide what is best to be done.'

'I've made a fool of myself,' said Dermot suddenly. 'I ought to have faced it out. I see more clearly now. The whole thing's a plot. What the devil are you laughing at?'

For Trent was leaning back in his chair, shaking with unrestrained mirth. There was something horrible in the sound – something horrible, too, about the man altogether. There was a curious light in his eyes.

'A damned clever plot,' he gasped out. 'Dermot, you're done for.'

He drew the telephone toward him.

'What are you going to do?' asked Dermot.

'Ring up Scotland Yard. Tell 'em their bird's here – safe under lock and key. Yes, I locked the door when I came in and the key's in my pocket. No good looking at the other door behind me. That leads into Claire's room, and she always locks it on her side. She's afraid of me, you know. Been afraid of me for a long time. She always knows when I'm thinking about that knife – a long, sharp knife. No, you don't –'

Dermot had been about to make a rush at him, but the other had suddenly produced a revolver.

'That's the second of them,' chuckled Trent. 'I put the first in your drawer – after shooting old West with it – What are you looking at over my head? That door? It's no use, even if Claire were to open it – and she might to you – I'd shoot you before you got there. Not in the heart – not to kill, just wing you, so that you couldn't get away. I'm a jolly good shot, you know. I saved your life once. More fool I. No, no, I want you hanged – yes, hanged. It isn't you I want the knife for. It's Claire – pretty Claire, so white and soft. Old West knew. That's what he was here for tonight, to see if I were mad or not. He wanted to shut me up – so that I shouldn't get at Claire with a knife. I was very cunning. I took his latchkey and yours, too. I slipped away from the dance as soon as I got there. I saw you come out of his house, and I went in. I shot him and came away at once. Then I went to your place and left the revolver. I was at the Grafton Galleries again almost as soon as you were, and I put the latchkey back in your coat pocket when I was saying good night to you. I don't mind telling you all this. There's no one else to hear, and when you're being hanged I'd like you to know I did it. There's not a loophole of escape. It makes me laugh – God, how it makes me laugh! What are you thinking of? What the devil are you looking at?'

'I'm thinking of some words you quoted just now. You'd have done better, Trent, not to come home.'

'What do you mean?'

'Look behind you.'

Trent spun round. In the doorway of the communicating room stood Claire – and Inspector Verall.

Trent was quick. The revolver spoke just once – and found its mark. He fell forward across the table. The inspector sprang to his side, as Dermot stared at Claire in a dream. Thoughts flashed through his brain disjointedly. His uncle – their quarrel – the colossal misunderstanding – the divorce laws of England which would never free Claire from an insane husband – 'we must all pity her' – the plot between her and Sir Alington which the cunning of Trent had seen through – her cry to him, 'Ugly – ugly – ugly!' Yes, but now –

The inspector straightened up.

'Dead,' he said vexedly.

'Yes,' Dermot heard himself saying, 'he was always a good shot.'

The Gold Bug

EDGAR ALLAN POE

MANY YEARS AGO, I CONTRACTED AN intimacy with a Mr William Legrand. He was of an ancient Huguenot family, and had once been wealthy; but a series of misfortunes had reduced him to want. To avoid the mortification consequent upon his disasters, he left New Orleans, the city of his forefathers, and took up his residence at Sullivan's Island, near Charleston, South Carolina.

This island is a very singular one. It consists of little else than the sea sand, and is about three miles long. Its breadth at no point exceeds a quarter of a mile. It is separated from the mainland by a scarcely perceptible creek, oozing its way through a wilderness of reeds and slime, a favourite resort of the marsh-hen. The vegetation, as might be supposed, is scant, or at least dwarfish. No trees of any magnitude are to be seen. Near the western extremity, where Fort Moultrie stands, and where are some miserable frame buildings, tenanted, during summer, by the fugitives from Charleston dust and fever, may be found, indeed, the bristly palmetto; but the whole island, with the exception of this western point, and a line of hard, white beach on the sea-coast, is covered with a dense undergrowth of the sweet myrtle so much prized by the horticulturist of England. The shrub here often attains the height of fifteen or twenty feet, and forms an almost impenetrable coppice, burthening the air with its fragrance.

In the inmost recess of this coppice, not far from the eastern or more remote end of the island, Legrand had built himself a small hut, which he occupied when I first, by mere accident, made his acquaintance. This soon ripened into friendship – for there was much in the recluse to excite interest and esteem. I found him well educated, with unusual powers of mind, but infected with misanthropy, and subject to perverse moods of alternate enthusiasm and melancholy. He had with him many books, but rarely employed them. His chief

amusements were gunning and fishing, or sauntering along the beach
and through the myrtles, in quest of shells or entomological specimens
– his collection of the latter might have been envied by a Swammer-
damm. In these excursions he was usually accompanied by an old
Negro, called Jupiter, who had been manumitted before the reverses
of the family, but who could be induced, neither by threats nor by
promises, to abandon what he considered his right of attendance upon
the footsteps of his young 'Massa Will'. It is not improbable that the
relatives of Legrand, conceiving him to be somewhat unsettled in
intellect, had contrived to instil this obstinacy into Jupiter, with a
view to the supervision and guardianship of the wanderer.

The winters in the latitude of Sullivan's Island are seldom very
severe, and in the fall of the year it is a rare event indeed when a
fire is considered necessary. About the middle of October, 18 –, there
occurred, however, a day of remarkable chilliness. Just before sunset
I scrambled my way through the evergreens to the hut of my friend,
whom I had not visited for several weeks – my residence being, at
that time, in Charleston, a distance of nine miles from the island,
while the facilities of passage and repassage were very far behind
those of the present day. Upon reaching the hut I rapped, as was my
custom, and getting no reply sought for the key where I knew it was
secreted, unlocked the door, and went in. A fine fire was blazing
upon the hearth. It was a novelty, and by no means an ungrateful
one. I threw off an overcoat, took an armchair by the crackling logs,
and awaited patiently the arrival of my hosts.

Soon after dark they arrived, and gave me a most cordial welcome.
Jupiter, grinning from ear to ear, bustled about to prepare some
marsh-hen for supper. Legrand was in one of his fits – how else shall
I term them? – of enthusiasm. He had found an unknown bivalve,
forming a new genus, and, more than this, he had hunted down and
secured, with Jupiter's assistance, a *scarabæus* which he believed
to be totally new, but in respect to which he wished to have my
opinion on the morrow.

'And why not tonight?' I asked, rubbing my hands over the blaze,
and wishing the whole tribe of *scarabæi* at the devil.

'Ah, if I had only known you were here!' said Legrand, 'but it's so
long since I saw you; and how could I foresee that you would pay
me a visit this very night of all others? As I was coming home I met
Lieutenant G —, from the fort, and, very foolishly, I lent him the
bug; so it will be impossible for you to see it until the morning. Stay

here tonight, and I will send Jup down for it at sunrise. It is the loveliest thing in creation!'

'What? – sunrise?'

'Nonsense! no! – the bug. It is of a brilliant gold colour – about the size of a large hickory-nut – with two jet black spots near one extremity of the back, and another, somewhat longer, at the other. The *antennæ* are –'

'Dey aint *no* tin in him, Massa Will, I keep a tellin' on you,' here interrupted Jupiter; 'de bug is a goole-bug, solid, ebery bit of him, inside and all, sep him wing – neber feel half so hebby a bug in my life.'

'Well, suppose it is, Jup,' replied Legrand, somewhat more earnestly, it seemed to me, than the case demanded; 'is that any reason for your letting the birds burn? The colour' – here he turned to me – 'is really almost enough to warrant Jupiter's idea. You never saw a more brilliant metallic lustre than the scales emit – but of this you cannot judge till tomorrow. In the meantime I can give you some idea of the shape.' Saying this, he seated himself at a small table, on which were a pen and ink, but no paper. He looked for some in a drawer, but found none.

'Never mind,' he said at length, 'this will answer;' and he drew from his waistcoat pocket a scrap of what I took to be very dirty foolscap, and made upon it a rough drawing with the pen. While he did this, I retained my seat by the fire, for I was still chilly. When the design was complete, he handed it to me without rising. As I received it, a loud growl was heard, succeeded by scratching at the door. Jupiter opened it, and a large Newfoundland, belonging to Legrand, rushed in, leaped upon my shoulders and loaded me with caresses; for I had shown him much attention during previous visits. When his gambols were over, I looked at the paper, and, to speak the truth, found myself not a little puzzled at what my friend had depicted.

'Well!' I said, after contemplating it for some minutes, 'this *is* a strange *scarabæus*, I must confess; new to me; never saw anything like it before – unless it was a skull, or a death's-head, which it more nearly resembles than anything else that has come under *my* observation.'

'A death's-head!' echoed Legrand. 'Oh – yes – well, it has something of that appearance upon paper, no doubt. The two upper black spots

look like eyes, eh? and the longer one at the bottom like a mouth –
and then the shape of the whole is oval.'

'Perhaps so,' said I; 'but, Legrand, I fear you are no artist. I must
wait until I see the beetle itself, if I am to form any idea of its
personal appearance.'

'Well, I don't know,' said he a little nettled, 'I draw tolerably –
should do it at least – have had good masters, and flatter myself that
I am not quite a blockhead.'

'But, my dear fellow, you are joking then,' said I, 'this is a very
passable *skull* – indeed, I may say that it is a very *excellent* skull,
according to the vulgar notions about such specimens of physiology
– and your *scarabæus* must be the queerest *scarabæus* in the
world if it resembles it. Why, we may get up a very thrilling bit of
superstition upon this hint. I presume you will call the bug *scarabæus caput hominis*, or something of that kind – there are many
similar titles in the Natural Histories. But where are the *antennæ* you
spoke of?"

'The *antennæ*!' said Legrand, who seemed to be getting unaccountably warm upon the subject; 'I am sure you must see the
antennæ. I made them as distinct as they are in the original insect,
and I presume that is sufficient.'

'Well, well,' I said, 'perhaps you have – still I don't see them'; and
I handed him the paper without additional remark, not wishing to
ruffle his temper; but I was much surprised at the turn affairs had
taken; his ill humour puzzled me – and, as for the drawing of the
beetle, there were positively no *antennæ* visible, and the whole
did bear a very close resemblance to the ordinary cuts of a death's-
head.

He received the paper very peevishly, and was about to crumple
it, apparently to throw it in the fire, when a casual glance at the
design seemed suddenly to rivet his attention. In an instant his face
grew violently red – in another as excessively pale. For some minutes
he continued to scrutinize the drawing minutely where he sat. At
length he arose, took a candle from the table, and proceeded to seat
himself upon a sea-chest in the furthest corner of the room. Here
again he made an anxious examination of the paper, turning it in
all directions. He said nothing, however, and his conduct greatly
astonished me; yet I thought it prudent not to exacerbate the growing
moodiness of his temper by any comment. Presently he took from
his coat pocket a wallet, placed the paper carefully in it, and deposited

both in a writing desk, which he locked. He now grew more composed in his demeanour; but his original air of enthusiasm had quite disappeared. Yet he seemed not so much sulky as abstracted. As the evening wore away he became more and more absorbed in reverie, from which no sallies of mine could arouse him. It had been my intention to pass the night at the hut, as I had frequently done before, but, seeing my host in this mood, I deemed it proper to take leave. He did not press me to remain, but, as I departed, he shook my hand with even more than his usual cordiality.

It was about a month after this (and during the interval I had seen nothing of Legrand) when I received a visit at Charleston, from his man, Jupiter. I had never seen the good old Negro look so dispirited, and I feared that some serious disaster had befallen my friend.

'Well, Jup,' said I, 'what is the matter now? – how is your master?'

'Why, to speek de troof, massa, him not so berry well as mought be.'

'Not well! I am truly sorry to hear it. What does he complain of?'

'Dar! dat's it! – he neber 'plain of notin' – but him berry sick for all dat.'

'*Very* sick, Jupiter! – why didn't you say so at once? Is he confined to bed?'

'No, dat he aint! – he aint 'fin'd nowhar – dat's just whar de shoe pinch – my mind is got to be berry hebby 'bout poor Massa Will.'

'Jupiter, I should like to understand what it is you are talking about. You say your master is sick. Hasn't he told you what ails him?'

'Why, massa, 'taint worf while for to git mad about de matter – Massa Will say noffin at all aint de matter wid him – but den what make him go about dis here way, wid he head down and he soldiers up, and as white as a gose? And den he keep a syphon all de time —'

'Keeps a what, Jupiter?'

'Keeps a syphon wid de figgurs on de slate – de queerest figgurs I ebber did see. Ise getting' to be skeered, I tell you. Hab for to keep mighty tight eye 'pon him 'noovers. Todder day he gib me slip 'fore de sun up and was gone the whole ob de blessed day. I had a big stick ready cut for to gib him deuced good beating when he did come – but Ise sich a fool dat I hadn't de heart arter all – he looked so berry poorly.'

'Eh? – what? – ah yes! – upon the whole I think you had better not be too severe with the poor fellow – don't flog him, Jupiter – he

can't very well stand it – but can you form no idea of what has
occasioned this illness, or rather this change of conduct? Has anything
unpleasant happened since I saw you?'

'No, massa, dey aint bin noffin onpleasant *since* den – 't was '*fore*
den I'm feared – 't was de berry day you was dare.'

'How? what do you mean?'

'Why, massa, I mean de bug – dare now.'

'The what?'

'De bug – I'm verry sartain dat Massa Will bin bit somewhere
'bout de head by dat goole-bug.'

'And what cause have you, Jupiter, for such a supposition?'

'Claws enuff, massa, and mouff too. I nebber did see sich a deuced
bug – he kick and he bite ebery ting what cum near him. Massa
Will cotch him fuss, but had for to let him go 'gin mighty quick, I
tell you – den was de time he must ha' got de bite. I didn't like de
look ob de bug mouff, myself, nohow, so I wouldn't take told ob him
wid my finger, but I cotch him wid a piece ob paper dat I found. I
rap him up in de paper and stuff a piece of it in he mouff – dat was
de way.'

'And you think, then, that your master was really bitten by the
beetle, and that the bite made him sick?'

'I don't think noffin' about it – I nose it. What make him dream
'bout de goole so much, if 'taint 'cause he bit by the goole-bug? Ise
heerd 'bout dem goole-bugs 'fore dis.'

'But how do you know he dreams about gold?'

'How I know? why, 'cause he talk about it in he sleep – dat's how
I nose.'

'Well, Jup, perhaps you are right; but to what fortunate circumstances am I to attribute the honour of a visit from you today?'

'What de matter, massa?'

'Did you bring any message from Mr Legrand?'

'No, massa, I bring dis here pissel'; and here Jupiter handed me a
note which ran thus:

'MY DEAR –
    'Why have I not seen you for so long a time? I hope you have not
been so foolish as to take offence at any little *brusquerie* of mine; but
no, that is improbable.
    'Since I saw you I have had great cause for anxiety. I have something
to tell you, yet scarcely know how to tell it, or whether I should tell
it at all.

'I have not been quite well for some days past, and poor old Jup annoys me, almost beyond endurance, by his well meant attentions. Would you believe it? – he had prepared a huge stick the other day, with which to chastise me for giving him the slip, and spending the day, *solus*, among the hills on the mainland. I verily believe that my ill looks alone saved me a flogging.

'I have made no addition to my cabinet since we met.

'If you can, in any way, make it convenient, come over with Jupiter. *Do* come. I wish to see you *tonight*, upon business of importance. I assure you that it is of the *highest* importance.

> Ever yours,
> 'WILLIAM LEGRAND.'

There was something in the tone of this note which gave me great uneasiness. Its whole style differed materially from that of Legrand. What could he be dreaming of? What new crotchet possessed his excitable brain? What 'business of the highest importance' could *he* possibly have to transact? Jupiter's account of him boded no good. I dreaded lest the continued pressure of misfortune had, at length, fairly unsettled the reason of my friend. Without a moment's hesitation, therefore, I prepared to accompany the Negro.

Upon reaching the wharf, I noticed a scythe and three spades, all apparently new, lying in the bottom of the boat in which we were to embark.

'What is the meaning of all this, Jup?' I inquired.

'Him syfe, massa, and spade.'

'Very true; but what are they doing here?'

'Him de syfe and de spade what Massa Will sis 'pon my buying for him in de town, and de debbil's own lot of money I had to gib for 'em.'

'But what, in the name of all that is mysterious, is your "Massa Will" going to do with scythes and spades?'

'Dat's more dan *I* know, and debbil take me if I don't b'lieve 'tis more dan he know, too. But it's all cum ob de bug.'

Finding that no satisfaction was to be obtained of Jupiter, whose whole intellect seemed to be absorbed by 'de bug', I now stepped into the boat, and made sail. With a fair and strong breeze we soon ran into the little cove to the northward of Fort Moultrie, and a walk of some two miles brought us to the hut. It was about three in the afternoon when we arrived. Legrand had been awaiting us in eager expectation. He grasped my hand with a nervous *empressement* which alarmed me and strengthened the suspicions already entertained. His countenance was pale even to ghastliness, and his deep-set eyes glared with unnatural lustre. After some inquiries respecting his health, I asked him, not knowing what better to say, if he had yet obtained the *scarabæus* from Lieutenant G —.

'Oh, yes,' he replied, colouring violently, 'I got it from him the next morning. Nothing should tempt me to part with that *scarabæus*. Do you know that Jupiter is quite right about it?'

'In what way?' I asked, with a sad foreboding at heart.

'In supposing it to be a bug of *real gold*.' He said this with an air of profound seriousness, and I felt inexpressibly shocked.

'This bug is to make my fortune,' he continued, with a triumphant smile; 'to reinstate me in my family possessions. Is it any wonder, then, that I prize it? Since Fortune has thought fit to bestow it upon me, I have only to use it properly, and I shall arrive at the gold of which it is the index. Jupiter, bring me that *scarabæus*!'

'What! de bug, massa? I'd rudder not go fer trubble dat bug; you mus' git him for your own self.' Hereupon Legrand arose, with a grave and stately air, and brought me the beetle from a glass case in which it was enclosed. It was a beautiful *scarabæus*, and, at that time, unknown to naturalists – of course a great prize in a scientific point of view. There were two round black spots near one extremity of the back, and a long one near the other. The scales were exceedingly hard and glossy, with all the appearance of burnished gold. The weight of the insect was very remarkable, and, taking all things into consideration, I could hardly blame Jupiter for his opinion respecting it; but what to make of Legrand's concordance with that opinion, I could not, for the life of me, tell.

'I sent for you,' said he, in a grandiloquent tone, when I had completed my examination of the beetle, 'I sent for you that I might have your counsel and assistance in furthering the views of Fate and of the bug –'

'My dear Legrand,' I cried, interrupting him, 'you are certainly unwell, and had better use some little precautions. You shall go to bed, and I will remain with you a few days, until you get over this. You are feverish and –'

'Feel my pulse,' said he.

I felt it, and to say the truth, found not the slightest indication of fever.

'But you may be ill and yet have no fever. Allow me this once to prescribe for you. In the first place go to bed. In the next —'

'You are mistaken,' he interposed. 'I am as well as I can expect to be under the excitement which I suffer. If you really wish me well, you will relieve this excitement.'

'And how is this to be done?'

'Very easily. Jupiter and myself are going upon an expedition into the hills, upon the mainland, and, in this expedition, we shall need the aid of some person in whom we can confide. You are the only one we can trust. Whether we succeed or fail, the excitement which you now perceive in me will be equally allayed.'

'I am anxious to oblige you in any way,' I replied; 'but do you mean to say that this infernal beetle has any connection with your expedition into the hills?'

'It has.'

'Then, Legrand, I can become a party to no such absurd proceeding.'

'I am sorry – very sorry – for we shall have to try it by ourselves.'

'Try it by ourselves! The man is surely mad! – but stay! – how long do you propose to be absent?'

'Probably all night. We shall start immediately, and be back, at all events, by sunrise.'

'And you will promise me, upon your honour, that when this freak of yours is over, and the bug business (good God!) settled to your satisfaction, you will then return home and follow my advice implicitly, as that of your physician.'

'Yes; I promise; and now let us be off, for we have no time to lose.'

With a heavy heart I accompanied my friend. We started about four o'clock – Legrand, Jupiter, the dog, and myself. Jupiter had with him the scythe and spades – the whole of which he insisted upon carrying – more through fear, it seemed to me, of trusting either of the implements within reach of his master, than from any excess of industry or complaisance. His demeanour was dogged in the extreme, and 'dat deuced bug' were the sole words which escaped his lips during the journey. For my own part, I had charge of a couple of dark lanterns, while Legrand contented himself with the *scarabæus*, which he carried attached to the end of a bit of whipcord, twirling it to and fro, with the air of a conjuror, as he went. When I observed this last, plain evidence of my friend's aberration of mind, I could scarcely refrain from tears. I thought it best, however, to humour his fancy, at least for the present, or until I could adopt some more energetic measures with a chance of success. In the meantime, I endeavoured, but all in vain, to sound him in regard to the object of the expedition. Having succeeded in inducing me to accompany him, he seemed unwilling to hold conversation upon any topic of minor importance, and to all my questions vouchsafed no other reply than 'we shall see!'

We crossed the creek at the head of the island by means of a skiff, and, ascending the high grounds on the shore of the mainland, proceeded in a north-westerly direction, through a tract of country excessively wild and desolate, where no trace of a human footstep was to be seen. Legrand led the way with decision; pausing only for an instant, here and there, to consult what appeared to be certain landmarks of his own contrivance upon a former occasion.

In this manner we journeyed for about two hours, and the sun was just setting when we entered a region infinitely more dreary than any yet seen. It was a species of tableland, near the summit of an almost inaccessible hill, densely wooded from base to pinnacle, and interspersed with huge crags that appeared to lie loosely upon the soil, and in many cases were prevented from precipitating themselves into the valleys below, merely by the support of the trees against which they reclined. Deep ravines, in various directions, gave an air of still sterner solemnity to the scene.

The natural platform to which we had clambered was thickly overgrown with brambles, through which we soon discovered that it would have been impossible to force our way but for the scythe; and Jupiter, by direction of his master, proceeded to clear for us a path to the foot of an enormously tall tulip tree, which stood, with some eight or ten oaks, upon the level, and far surpassed them all, and all other trees which I had then ever seen, in the beauty of its foliage and form, in the wide spread of its branches, and in the general majesty of its appearance. When we reached this tree, Legrand turned to Jupiter, and asked him if he thought he could climb it. The old man seemed a little staggered by the question, and for some moments made no reply. At length he approached the huge trunk, walked slowly around it, and examined it with minute attention. When he had completed his scrutiny, he merely said –

'Yes, massa, Jup climb any tree be ebber see in he life.'

'Then up with you as soon as possible, for it will soon be too dark to see what we are about.'

'How far mus go up, massa?' inquired Jupiter.

'Get up the main trunk first, and then I will tell you which way to go – and here – stop! take this beetle with you.'

'De bug, Massa Will! – de goole-bug!' cried the Negro, drawing back in dismay – 'what for mus tote de bug way up de tree? – d–n if I do!'

'If you are afraid, Jup, a great big Negro like you, to take hold of a harmless little dead beetle, why you can carry it up by this string – but, if you do not take it up with you in some way, I shall be under the necessity of breaking your head with this shovel.'

'What de matter now, massa?' said Jup, evidently shamed into compliance; 'always want for to raise fuss wid old nigger. Was only funnin anyhow. *Me* feered de bug! what I keer for de bug?' Here he took cautiously hold of the extreme end of the string, and, maintaining the insect as far from his person as circumstances would permit, prepared to ascend the tree.

In youth, the tulip-tree or *Liriodendron Tulipiferum*, the most magnificent of American foresters, has a trunk peculiarly smooth, and often rises to a great height without lateral branches; but, in its riper age, the bark becomes gnarled and uneven, while many short limbs make their appearance on the stem. Thus the difficulty of ascension, in the present case, lay more in semblance than in reality. Embracing the huge cylinder, as closely as possible, with his arms and knees, seizing with his hands some projections, and resting his naked toes upon others, Jupiter, after one or two narrow escapes from falling, at length wriggled himself into the first great fork, and seemed to consider the whole business as virtually accomplished. The *risk* of the achievement was, in fact, now over, although the climber was some sixty or seventy feet from the ground.

'Which way mus go now, Massa Will?' he asked.

'Keep up the largest branch – the one on this side,' said Legrand. The Negro obeyed him promptly, and apparently with but little trouble; ascending higher and higher, until no glimpse of his squat figure could be obtained through the dense foliage which enveloped it. Presently his voice was heard in a sort of halloo.

'How much fudder is got for go?'

'How high up are you?' asked Legrand.

'Ebber so fur,' replied the Negro; 'can see de sky fru de top ob de tree.'

'Never mind the sky, but attend to what I say. Look down the trunk and count the limbs below you on this side. How many limbs have you passed?'

'One, two, tree, four, fibe – I done pass fibe big limb, massa, pon dis side.'

'Then go one limb higher.'

In a few minutes the voice was heard again, announcing that the seventh limb was attained.

'Now, Jup,' cried Legrand, evidently much excited, 'I want you to work your way out upon that limb as far as you can. If you see anything strange let me know.'

By this time what little doubt I might have entertained of my poor friend's insanity was put finally at rest. I had no alternative but to conclude him stricken with lunacy, and I became seriously anxious about getting him home. While I was pondering upon what was best to be done, Jupiter's voice was again heard.

'Mos feerd for to venture pon dis limb berry far – 'tis dead limb putty much all de way.'

'Did you say it was a *dead* limb, Jupiter?' cried Legrand in a quavering voice.

'Yes, massa, him dead as de doornail – done up for sartain – done departed dis here life.'

'What in the name of heaven shall I do?' asked Legrand, seemingly in the greatest distress.

'Do!' said I, glad of an opportunity to interpose a word, 'why, come home and go to bed. Come now! – that's a fine fellow. It's getting late, and, besides, you remember your promise.'

'Jupiter,' cried he, without heeding me in the least, 'do you hear me?'

'Yes, Massa Will, hear you ebber so plain.'

'Try the wood well, then, with your knife, and see if you think it *very* rotten.'

'Him rotten, massa, sure nuff,' replied the Negro in a few moments, 'but not so berry rotten as mought be. Mought venture out leetle way pon de limb by myself, dat's true.'

'By yourself! – what do you mean?'

'Why, I mean de bug. 'Tis *berry* hebby bug. S'pose I drop him down fuss, and den de limb won't break wid just de weight ob one nigger.'

'You infernal scoundrel!' cried Legrand, apparently much relieved, 'what do you mean by telling me such nonsense as that? As sure as you drop that beetle I'll break your neck. Look here, Jupiter, do you hear me?'

'Yes, massa, needn't hollo at poor nigger dat style.'

'Well! now listen! – if you will venture out on the limb as far as you think safe, and not let go the beetle, I'll make you a present of a silver dollar as soon as you get down.'

'I'm gwine, Massa Will – deed I is,' replied the Negro very promptly – 'mos out to the eend now.'

'*Out to the end!*' here fairly screamed Legrand; 'do you say you are out to the end of that limb?'

'Soon be to de eend massa – o-o-o-o-oh! Lor-gol-a-marcy! what *is* dis here pon de tree?'

'Well!' cried Legrand, highly delighted, 'what is it?'

'Why taint noffin but a skull – somebody bin lef him head up de tree, and de crows done gobble ebery bit of de meat off.'

'A skull, you say! – very well, – how is it fastened to the limb? – what holds it on?'

'Sure nuff massa; mus look. Why dis berry curous sarcumstance, pon my word – dare's a great big nail in de skull, what fastens ob it on to de tree.'

'Well now, Jupiter, do exactly as I tell you – do you hear?'

'Yes, massa.'

'Pay attention, then – find the left eye of the skull.'

'Hum! hoo! dat's good! why dey ain't no eye lef at all.'

'Curse your stupidity! Do you know your right hand from your left?'

'Yes, I knows dat – knows all bout dat – 'tis my lef hand what I chops de wood wid.'

'To be sure! you are left-handed; and your left eye is on the same side as your left hand. Now, I suppose, you can find the left eye of the skull, or the place where the left eye has been. Have you found it?'

Here was a long pause. At length the Negro asked:

'Is de lef eye of de skull pon de same side as de lef hand side of de skull too? – cause de skull ain't got not a bit ob a hand at all – nebber mind! I got de lef eye now – here de lef eye! what mus do wid it?'

'Let the beetle drop through it, as far as the string will reach – but be careful and not let go your hold of the string.'

'All dat done, Massa Will; mighty easy ting for to put de bug fru de hole – look out for him dare below!'

During this colloquy no portion of Jupiter's person could be seen; but the beetle, which he had suffered to descend, was now visible at the end of the string, and glistened, like a globe of burnished gold, in the last rays of the setting sun, some of which still faintly illumined the eminence upon which we stood. The *scarabæus* hung quite clear of any branches, and, if allowed to fall, would have fallen at our feet. Legrand immediately took the scythe, and cleared with it a circular space, three or four yards in diameter, just beneath the insect, and, having accomplished this, ordered Jupiter to let go the string and come done from the tree.

Driving a peg, with great nicety, into the ground, at the precise spot where the beetle fell, my friend now produced from his pocket a tape-measure. Fastening one end of this at that point of the trunk of the tree which was nearest the peg, he unrolled it till it reached the peg and thence further unrolled it, in the direction already established by the two points of the tree and the peg, for the distance of fifty feet – Jupiter clearing away the brambles with the scythe. At the spot thus attained a second peg was driven, and about this, as a centre, a rude circle, about four feet in diameter, described. Taking now a spade himself, and giving one to Jupiter and one to me, Legrand begged us to set about digging as quickly as possible.

To speak the truth, I had no especial relish for such amusement at any time, and, at that particular moment, would most willingly have declined it; for the night was coming on, and I felt much fatigued with the exercise already taken; but I saw no mode of escape, and was fearful of disturbing my poor friend's equanimity by a refusal. Could I have depended, indeed, upon Jupiter's aid, I would have had no hesitation in attempting to get the lunatic home by force; but I was too well assured of the old Negro's disposition, to hope that he would assist me, under any circumstances, in a personal contest with his master. I made no doubt that the latter had been infected with some of the innumerable Southern superstitions about money buried, and that his phantasy had received confirmation by the finding of the *scarabæus*, or, perhaps, by Jupiter's obstinacy in maintaining it to be 'a bug of real gold'. A mind disposed to lunacy would readily be led away by such suggestions – especially if chiming in with favourite preconceived ideas – and then I called to mind the poor fellow's speech about the beetle's being 'the index of his fortune'. Upon the whole, I was sadly vexed and puzzled, but, at length, I concluded to make a virtue of necessity – to dig with a good will, and thus the sooner to convince the visionary, by ocular demonstration, of the fallacy of the opinions he entertained.

The lanterns having been lit, we all fell to work with a zeal worthy a more rational cause; and, as the glare fell upon our persons and implements, I could not help thinking how picturesque a group we composed, and how strange and suspicious our labours must have appeared to any interloper who, by chance, might have stumbled upon our whereabouts.

We dug very steadily for two hours. Little was said; and our chief embarrassment lay in the yelpings of the dog, who took exceeding interest in our proceedings. He, at length, became so obstreperous that we grew fearful of his giving the alarm to some stragglers in the vicinity, – or, rather, this was the apprehension of Legrand; – for myself, I should have rejoiced at any interruption which might have enabled me to get the wanderer home. The noise was, at length, very effectually silenced by Jupiter, who, getting out of the hole with a dogged air of deliberation, tied the brute's mouth up with one of his suspenders, and then returned, with a grave chuckle, to his task.

When the time mentioned had expired, we had reached a depth of five feet, and yet no signs of any treasure became manifest. A general pause ensued, and I began to hope that the farce was at an end. Legrand, however, although evidently much disconcerted, wiped his brow thoughtfully and recommenced. We had excavated the entire circle of four feet diameter, and now we slightly enlarged the limit, and went to the farther depth of two feet. Still nothing appeared. The gold-seeker, whom I sincerely pitied, at length clambered from the pit, with the bitterest disappointment imprinted upon every feature, and proceeded, slowly and reluctantly, to put on his coat, which he had thrown off at the beginning of his labour. In the meantime I made no remark. Jupiter, at a signal from his master, began to gather up his tools. This done, and the dog having been unmuzzled, we turned in profound silence toward home.

We had taken, perhaps, a dozen steps in this direction, when, with a loud oath, Legrand strode up to Jupiter, and seized him by the collar. The astonished Negro opened his eyes and mouth to the fullest extent, let fall the spades, and fell upon his knees.

'You scoundrel!' said Legrand, hissing out the syllables from between his clenched teeth – 'you infernal black villain! – speak, I tell you! – answer me this instant, without prevarication! – which – which is your left eye?'

'Oh, my golly, Massa Will! aint dis here my lef eye for sartain?' roared the terrified Jupiter, placing his hand upon his **right** organ of vision, and holding it there with a desperate pertinacity, as if in immediate dread of his master's attempt at a gouge.

'I thought so! – I knew it! hurrah!' vociferated Legrand, letting the Negro go and executing a series of curvets and caracols, much to the astonishment of his valet, who, arising from his knees, looked, mutely, from his master to myself, and then from myself to his master.

'Come! we must go back,' said the latter, 'the game's not up yet'; and he again led the way to the tulip-tree.

'Jupiter,' said he, when we reached its foot, 'come here! Was the skull nailed to the limb with the face outward, or with the face to the limb?'

'De face was out, massa, so dat de crows could get at de eyes good, widout any trouble.'

'Well, then, was it this eye or that through which you dropped the beetle?' – here Legrand touched each of Jupiter's eyes.

''Twas dis eye, massa – de lef eye – jis as you tell me,' – and here it was his right eye that the Negro indicated.

'That will do – we must try again.'

Here my friend, about whose madness I now saw, or fancied that I saw, certain indications of method, removed the peg which marked the spot where the beetle fell, to a spot about three inches to the westward of its former position. Taking, now, the tape-measure from the nearest point of the trunk to the peg, as before, and continuing the extension in a straight line to the distance of fifty feet, a spot was indicated, removed, by several yards, from the point at which we had been digging.

Around the new position a circle, somewhat larger than in the former instance, was now described, and we again set to work with the spade. I was dreadfully weary, but, scarcely understanding what had occasioned the change in my thoughts, I felt no longer any great aversion from the labour imposed. I had become most unaccountably interested – nay, even excited. Perhaps there was something, amid all the extravagant demeanour of Legrand – some air of forethought, or of deliberation, which impressed me. I dug eagerly, and now and then caught myself actually looking, with something that very much resembled expectation, for the fancied treasure, the vision of which had demented my unfortunate companion. At a period when such vagaries of thought most fully possessed me, and when we had been at work perhaps an hour and a half, we were again interrupted by the violent howlings of the dog. His uneasiness, in the first instance, had been, evidently, but the result of playfulness or caprice, but he now assumed a bitter and serious tone. Upon Jupiter's again attempting to muzzle him, he made furious resistance, and, leaping into the hole, tore up the mould frantically with his claws. In a few seconds he had uncovered a mass of human bones, forming two complete skeletons, intermingled with several buttons of metal, and what appeared to be the dust of decayed woollen. One or two strokes of a spade upturned the blade of a large Spanish knife, and, as we dug farther, three or four loose pieces of gold and silver coin came to light.

At sight of these the joy of Jupiter could scarcely be restrained, but the countenance of his master wore an air of extreme disappointment. He urged us, however, to continue our exertions, and the words were hardly uttered when I stumbled and fell forward, having caught the toe of my boot in a large ring of iron that lay half buried in the loose earth.

We now worked in earnest, and never did I pass ten minutes of more intense excitement. During this interval we had fairly unearthed an oblong chest of wood, which, from its perfect preservation and wonderful hardness, had plainly been subjected to some mineralizing process – perhaps that of the bichloride of mercury. This box was three feet and a half long, three feet broad, and two and a half feet deep. It was firmly secured by bands of wrought iron, riveted, and forming a kind of open trelliswork over the whole. On each side of the chest, near the top, were three rings of iron – six in all – by means of which a firm hold could be obtained by six persons. Our utmost united endeavours served only to disturb the coffer very slightly in its bed. We at once saw the impossibility of removing so great a weight. Luckily, the sole fastenings of the lid consisted of two sliding bolts. These we drew back – trembling and panting with anxiety. In an instant, a treasure of incalculable value lay gleaming before us. As the rays of the lanterns fell within the pit, there flashed upward a glow and a glare, from a confused heap of gold and of jewels, that absolutely dazzled our eyes.

I shall not pretend to describe the feelings with which I gazed. Amazement was, of course, predominant. Legrand appeared exhausted with excitement, and spoke very few words. Jupiter's countenance wore, for some minutes, as deadly a pallor as it is possible, in the nature of things, for any Negro's visage to assume. He seemed stupefied – thunderstricken. Presently he fell upon his knees in the pit, and burying his naked arms up to the elbows in gold, let them there remain, as if enjoying the luxury of a bath. At length with a deep sigh, he exclaimed, as if in a soliloquy:

'And dis all cum ob de goole-bug! de putty goole-bug! de poor little goole-bug, what I boosed in dat sabage kind ob style! Aint you shamed ob yourself, nigger! – answer me dat!'

It became necessary, at last, that I should arouse both master and valet to the expediency of removing the treasure. It was growing late, and it behoved us to make exertion, that we might get everything housed before daylight. It was difficult to say what should be done, and much time was spent in deliberation – so confused were the ideas of all. We, finally, lightened the box by removing two-thirds of its contents, when we were enabled, with some trouble, to raise it from the hole. The articles taken out were deposited among the brambles, and the dog left to guard them, with strict orders from Jupiter, neither, upon any pretence, to stir from the spot, nor to open his mouth until our return. We then hurriedly made for home with the chest; reaching the hut in safety, but after excessive toil, at one o'clock in the morning. Worn out as we were, it was not in human nature to do more immediately. We rested until two, and had supper; starting for the hills immediately afterwards, armed with three stout sacks, which, by good luck, were upon the premises. A little before four we arrived at the pit, divided the remainder of the booty, as equally as might be, among us, and, leaving the holes unfilled, again set out for the hut, at which, for the second time, we deposited our golden burthens, just as the first faint streaks of the dawn gleamed from over the tree-tops in the East.

We were now thoroughly broken down; but the intense excitement of the time denied us repose. After an unquiet slumber of some three or four hours' duration, we arose, as if by preconcert, to make examination of our treasure.

The chest had been full to the brim, and we spent the whole day, and the greater part of the next night, in a scrutiny of its contents. There had been nothing like order or arrangement. Everything had been heaped in promiscuously. Having assorted all with care, we found ourselves possessed of even vaster wealth than we had at first supposed. In coin there was rather more than four hundred and fifty thousand dollars – estimating the value of the pieces, as accurately as we could, by the tables of the period. There was not a particle of silver. All was gold of antique date and of great variety – French, Spanish, and German money, with a few English guineas, and some counters, of which we had never seen specimens before. There were several very large and heavy coins, so worn that we could make nothing of their inscriptions. There was no American money. The value of the jewels we found more difficult in estimating. There were diamonds – some of them exceedingly large and fine – a hundred and ten in all, and not one of them small; eighteen rubies of remarkable brilliancy; – three hundred and ten emeralds, all very beautiful; and twenty-one sapphires, with an opal. These stones had all been broken from their settings and thrown loose in the chest. The settings themselves, which we picked out from among the other gold, appeared to have been beaten up with hammers, as if to prevent identification. Besides all this, there was a vast quantity of solid gold ornaments: nearly two hundred massive finger and earrings; rich chains – thirty of these, if I remember; eighty-three very large and heavy crucifixes; five gold censers of great value; a prodigious golden punch-bowl, ornamented with richly chased vine leaves and Bacchan-alian figures; with two sword handles exquisitely embossed, and many other smaller articles which I cannot recollect. The weight of these valuables exceeded three hundred and fifty pounds avoirdupois; and in this estimate I have not included one hundred and ninety-seven superb gold watches; three of the number being worth each five hundred dollars, if one. Many of them were very old, and as timekeepers valueless; the works having suffered more or less from corrosion – but all were richly jewelled and in cases of great worth. We estimated the entire contents of the chest, that night, at a million and a half of dollars; and upon the subsequent disposal of the trinkets and jewels (a few being retained for our own use), it was found that we had greatly undervalued the treasure.

When, at length, we had concluded our examination, and the intense excitement of the time had, in some measure, subsided, Legrand, who saw that I was dying with impatience for a solution of this most extraordinary riddle, entered into a full detail of all circumstances connected with it.

'You remember,' said he, 'the night when I handed you the rough sketch I had made of the *scarabæus*. You recollect also, that I became quite vexed at you for insisting that my drawing resembled a death's head. When you first made this assertion, I thought you were jesting; but afterwards I called to mind the peculiar spots on the back of the insect, and admitted to myself that your remark had some little foundation in fact. Still, the sneer at my graphic powers irritated me – for I am considered a good artist – and, therefore, when you handed me the scrap of parchment, I was about to crumple it up and throw it angrily into the fire.'

'The scrap of paper, you mean,' said I.

'No; it had much of the appearance of paper, and at first I supposed it to be such, but when I came to draw upon it, I discovered it at once to be a piece of very thin parchment. It was quite dirty, you remember. Well, as I was in the very act of crumpling it up, my glance fell upon the sketch at which you had been looking, and you may imagine my astonishment when I perceived, in fact, the figure of a death's-head just where, it seemed to me, I had made the drawing of the beetle. For a moment I was too much amazed to think with accuracy. I knew that my design was very different in detail from this – although there was a certain similarity in general outline. Presently I took a candle, and seating myself at the other end of the room, proceeded to scrutinize the parchment more closely. Upon turning it over, I saw my own sketch upon the reverse, just as I had made it. My first idea, now, was mere surprise at the really remarkable similarity of outline – at the singular coincidence involved in the fact that, unknown to me, there should have been a skull upon the other side of the parchment, immediately beneath my figure of the *scarabæus* and that this skull, not only in outline, but in size, should so closely resemble my drawing. I say the singularity of this coincidence absolutely stupefied me for a time. This is the usual effect of such coincidences. The mind struggles to establish a connection – a sequence of cause and effect – and, being unable to do so, suffers a species of temporary paralysis. But, when I recovered from this stupor, there dawned upon me gradually a conviction which startled me even far more than the coincidence. I began distinctly, positively, to remember that there had been *no* drawing upon the parchment when I made my sketch of the *scarabæus*. I became perfectly certain of this; for I recollected turning up first one side and then the other, in search of the cleanest spot. Had the skull been then there, of course I could not have failed to notice it. Here was indeed a mystery which I felt it impossible to explain; but, even at that early moment, there seemed to glimmer, faintly, within the most remote and secret chambers of my intellect, a glow-worm-like conception of that truth which last night's adventure brought to so magnificent a demonstration. I arose at once, and putting the parchment securely away, dismissed all further reflection until I should be alone.

'When you had gone, and when Jupiter was fast asleep, I betook myself to a more methodical investigation of the affair. In the first place I considered the manner in which the parchment had come into my possession. The spot where we discovered the *scarabœus* was on the coast of the mainland, about a mile eastward of the island, and but a short distance above high water mark. Upon my taking hold of it, it gave me a sharp bite, which caused me to let it drop. Jupiter, with his accustomed caution, before seizing the insect, which had flown toward him, looked about him for a leaf, or something of that nature by which to take hold of it. It was at this moment that his eyes, and mine also, fell upon the scrap of parchment, which I then supposed to be paper. It was lying half buried in the sand, a corner sticking up. Near the spot where we found it, I observed the remnants of the hull of what appeared to have been a ship's longboat. The wreck seemed to have been there for a very great while; for the resemblance to boat timbers could scarcely be traced.

'Well, Jupiter picked up the parchment, wrapped the beetle in it, and gave it to me. Soon afterwards we turned to go home, and on the way met Lieutenant G —. I showed him the insect, and be begged me to let him take it to the fort. Upon my consenting, he thrust it forthwith into his waistcoat pocket, without the parchment in which it had been wrapped, and which I had continued to hold in my hand during his inspection. Perhaps he dreaded my changing my mind, and thought it best to make sure of the prize at once – you know how enthusiastic he is on all subjects connected with Natural History. At the same time, without being conscious of it, I must have deposited the parchment in my own pocket.

'You remember that when I went to the table, for the purpose of making a sketch of the beetle, I found no paper where it was usually kept. I looked in the drawer, and found none there. I searched my pockets, hoping to find an old letter, when my hand fell upon the parchment. I thus detail the precise mode in which it came into my possession; for the circumstances impressed me with peculiar force.

'No doubt you will think me fanciful – but I had already established a kind of *connection*. I had put together two links of a great chain. There was a boat lying upon a sea-coast, and not far from the boat was a parchment – *not a paper* – with a skull depicted upon it. You will, of course, ask "where is the connection?" I reply that the skull, or death's-head, is the well-known emblem of the pirate. The flag of the death's-head is hoisted in all engagements.

'I have said that the scrap was parchment, and not paper. Parchment is durable – almost imperishable. Matters of little moment are rarely consigned to parchment; since, for the mere ordinary purpose of drawing or writing, it is not nearly so well adapted as paper. This reflection suggested some meaning – some relevancy – in the death's-head. I did not fail to observe, also, the *form* of the parchment. Although one of its corners had been, by some accident, destroyed, it could be seen that the original form was oblong. It was just such a slip, indeed, as might have been chosen for a memorandum – for a record of something to be long remembered and carefully preserved.'

'But,' I interposed, 'you say that the skull was *not* upon the parchment when you made the drawing of the beetle. How then do you trace any connection between the boat and the skull – since this latter, according to your own admission, must have been designed (God only knows how or by whom) at some period subsequent to your sketching the *scarabæus?*'

'Ah, hereupon turns the whole mystery; although the secret, at this point, I had comparatively little difficulty in solving. My steps were sure, and could afford but a single result. I reasoned, for example, thus. When I drew the *scarabæus*, there was no skull apparent upon the parchment. When I had completed the drawing I gave it to you, and observed you narrowly until you returned it. *You*, therefore, did not design the skull, and no one else was present to do it. Then it was not done by human agency. And nevertheless it was done.

'At this stage of my reflections I endeavoured to remember, and *did* remember, with entire distinctness, every incident which occurred about the period in question. The weather was chilly (oh, rare and happy accident!), and a fire was blazing upon the hearth. I was heated with exercise and sat near the table. You, however, had drawn a chair close to the chimney. Just as I had placed the parchment in your hand, and as you were in the act of inspecting it, Wolf, the Newfoundland, entered, and leaped upon your shoulders. With your left hand you caressed him and kept him off, while your right, holding the parchment, was permitted to fall listlessly between your knees, and in close promixity to the fire. At one moment I thought the blaze had caught it, and was about to caution you, but, before I could speak, you had withdrawn it, and were engaged in its examination. When I considered all these particulars, I doubted not for a moment that *heat* had been the agent in bringing to light, upon the parchment, the skull which I saw designed upon it. You are well aware that chemical preparations exist, and have existed time out of mind, by means of which it is possible to write upon either paper or vellum, so that the characters shall become visible only when subjected to the action of fire. Zaffre, digested in *aqua regia*, and diluted with four times its weight of water, is sometimes employed; a green tint results. The regulus of cobalt, dissolved in spirit of nitre, gives a red. These colours disappear at longer or shorter intervals after the material written upon cools, but again become apparent upon the reapplication of heat.

'I now scrutinized the death's-head with care. Its outer edges – the edges of the drawing nearest the edge of the vellum – were far more *distinct* than the others. It was clear that the action of the caloric had been imperfect or unequal. I immediately kindled a fire, and subjected every portion of the parchment to a glowing heat. At first, the only effect was the strengthening of the faint lines in the skull; but, upon persevering in the experiment, there became visible, at the corner of the slip, diagonally opposite to the spot in which the death's-head was delineated, the figure of what I at first supposed to be a goat. A closer scrutiny, however, satisfied me that it was intended for a kid.'

'Ha! ha!' said I, 'to be sure I have no right to laugh at you – a million and a half of money is too serious a matter for mirth – but you are not about to establish a third link in your chain – you will not find any especial connection between your pirates and a goat – pirates, you know, have nothing to do with goats; they appertain to the farming interest.'

'But I have just said that the figure was *not* that of a goat.'

'Well, a kid then – pretty much the same thing.'

'Pretty much, but not altogether,' said Legrand. 'You may have heard of one *Captain* Kidd. I at once looked upon the figure of the animal as a kind of punning or hieroglyphical signature. I say signature; because its position upon the vellum suggested this idea. The death's-head at the corner diagonally opposite, had, in the same manner, the air of a stamp, or seal. But I was sorely put out by the absence of all else – of the body to my imagined instrument – of the text for my context.'

'I presume you expected to find a letter between the stamp and the signature.'

'Something of that kind. The fact is, I felt irresistibly impressed with a presentiment of some vast good fortune impending. I can scarcely say why. Perhaps, after all, it was rather a desire than an actual belief; – but do you know that Jupiter's silly words, about the bug being of solid gold, had a remarkable effect upon my fancy? And then the series of accidents and coincidences – these were so *very* extraordinary. Do you observe how mere an accident it was that these events should have occurred upon the *sole* day of the year in which it has been, or may be sufficiently cool for fire, and that without the fire, or without the intervention of the dog at the precise moment in which he appeared, I should never have become aware of the death's-head, and so never the possessor of the treasure.'

'But proceed – I am all impatience.'

'Well; you have heard, of course, the many stories current – the thousand vague rumours afloat about money buried, somewhere upon the Atlantic coast, by Kidd and his associates. These rumours must have had some foundation in fact. And that the rumours have existed so long and so continuous, could have resulted, it appeared to me, only from the circumstance of the buried treasure still *remaining* entombed. Had Kidd concealed his plunder for a time, and afterward reclaimed it, the rumours would scarcely have reached us in their present unvarying form. You will observe that the stories told are all about money-seekers, not about money-finders. Had the pirate recovered his money, there the affair would have dropped. It seemed to me that some accident – say the loss of a memorandum indicating its locality – had deprived him of the means of recovering it, and that this accident had become known to his followers, who otherwise might never have heard that treasure had been concealed at all, and who, busying themselves in vain, because unguided, attempts to regain it, had first given birth, and then universal currency, to the reports which are now so common. Have you ever heard of any important treasure being unearthed along the coast?'

'Never.'

'But that Kidd's accumulations were immense, is well known. I took it for granted, therefore, that the earth still held them; and you will scarcely be surprised when I tell you that I felt a hope, nearly amounting to certainty, that the parchment so strangely found involved a lost record of the place of deposit.'

'But how did you proceed?'

'I held the vellum again to the fire, after increasing the heat, but nothing appeared. I now thought it possible that the coating of dirt might have something to do with the failure: so I carefully rinsed the parchment by pouring warm water over it, and having done this, I placed it in a tin pan, with the skull downward, and put the pan upon a furnace of lighted charcoal. In a few minutes, the pan having become thoroughly heated, I removed the slip, and, to my inexpressible joy, found it spotted, in several places, with what appeared to be figures arranged in lines. Again I placed it in the pan, and suffered it to remain another minute. Upon taking it off, the whole was just as you see it now.'

Here Legrand, having reheated the parchment, submitted it to my inspection. The following characters were rudely traced, in a red tint, between the death's-head and the goat:

'53‡‡†305))6*; 4826)4‡.)4‡; 806*; 48†8¶60))85; 1‡(;:‡*8†83(88)5*†;
46(;88*96*?;8)*‡(;485); 5*†2:*‡(;4956*2(5*–4)8¶8*; 4069285);)6†8)
4‡‡.1(‡9; 48081; 8:8‡1; 48†85;4)485†528806*81(9;48;(88;4(‡?34;48)
4‡;161;:188;‡?;'

'But,' said I, returning him the slip, 'I am as much in the dark as ever. Were all the jewels of Golconda awaiting me upon my solution of this enigma, I am quite sure that I should be unable to earn them.'

'And yet,' said Legrand, 'the solution is by no means so difficult as you might be led to imagine from the first hasty inspection of the characters. These characters, as any one might readily guess, form a cipher – that is to say, they convey a meaning; but then from what is known of Kidd, I could not suppose him capable of constructing any of the more abstruse cryptographs. I made up my mind, at once, that this was of a simple species – such, however, as would appear, to the crude intellect of the sailor, absolutely insoluble without the key.'

'And you really solved it?'

'Readily; I have solved others of an abstruseness ten thousand times greater. Circumstances, and a certain bias of mind, have led me to take interest in such riddles, and it may well be doubted whether human ingenuity can construct an enigma of the kind which human ingenuity may not, by proper application, resolve. In fact, having once established connected and legible characters, I scarcely gave a thought to the mere difficulty of developing their import.

'In the present case – indeed in all cases of secret writing – the first question regards the *language* of the cipher; for the principles of solution, so far, especially, as the more simple ciphers are concerned, depend upon, and are varied by, the genius of the particular idiom. In general, there is no alternative but experiment (directed by probabilities) of every tongue known to him who attempts the solution, until the true one be attained. But, with the cipher now before us all difficulty was removed by the signature. The pun upon the word 'Kidd' is appreciable in no other language than the English. But for this consideration I should have begun my attempts with the Spanish and French, as the tongues in which a secret of this kind would most naturally have been written by a pirate of the Spanish main. As it was, I assumed the cryptograph to be English.

'You observe there are no divisions between the words. Had there been divisions the task would have been comparatively easy. In such cases I should have commenced with a collation and analysis of the shorter words, and, had a word of a single letter occurred, as is most likely (*a* or *I*, for example), I should have considered the solution as assured. But, there being no division, my first step was to ascertain the predominant letters, as well as the least frequent. Counting all, I constructed a table thus:

Of the character 8 there are 33.

;	,,	26.
4	,,	19.
‡)	,,	16.
*	,,	13.
5	,,	12.
6	,,	11.
?(	,,	10.
†1	,,	8.
0	,,	6.
92	,,	5.
:3	,,	4.
?	,,	3.
¶	,,	2.
-.	,,	1.

'Now, in English, the letter which most frequently occurs is *e*.

Afterwards, the succession runs thus: *a o i d h n r s t u y c f g l m w b k p q x z*. *E* predominates so remarkably, that an individual sentence of any length is rarely seen, in which it is not the prevailing character.

'Here, then, we have, in the very beginning, the groundwork for something more than a mere guess. The general use which may be made of the table is obvious – but, in this particular cipher, we shall only very partially require its aid. As our predominant character is 8, we will commence by assuming it as the *e* of the natural alphabet. To verify the supposition, let us observe if the 8 be seen often in couples – for *e* is doubled with great frequency in English – in such words, for example, as 'meet', 'fleet' 'speed', 'seen', 'been', 'agree', etc. In the present instance we see it doubled no less than five times, although the cryptograph is brief.

'Let us assume 8, then, as *e*. Now, of all *words* in the language, 'the' is most usual; let us see, therefore, whether there are not repetitions of any three characters, in the same order of collocation, the last of them being 8. If we discover repetitions of such letters, so arranged, they will most probably represent the word 'the'. Upon inspection, we find no less than seven such arrangements, the characters being ;48. We may, therefore assume that ; represents *t*, 4 represents *h*, and 8 represents *e* – the last being now well confirmed. Thus a great step has been taken.

'But, having established a single word, we are enabled to establish a vastly important point; that is to say, several commencements and terminations of other words. Let us refer, for example, to the last instance but one, in which the combination ;48 occurs – not far from the end of the cipher. We know that the ; immediately ensuing is the commencement of a word, and, of the six characters succeeding this 'the', we are cognizant of no less than five. Let us set these characters down, thus, by the letters we know them to represent, leaving a space for the unknown –

t eeth.

'Here we are enabled, at once, to discard the '*th*', as forming no portion of the word commencing with the first *t*; since, by experiment of the entire alphabet for a letter adapted to the vacancy, we perceive that no word can be formed of which this *th* can be a part. We are thus narrowed into

t ee,

and, going through the alphabet, if necessary, as before, we arrive at the word 'tree', as the sole possible reading. We thus gain another letter, r, represented by (, with the words 'the tree' in juxtaposition.

'Looking beyond these words, for a short distance, we again see the combination ;48, and employ it by way of *termination* to what immediately precedes. We have thus this arrangement:

the tree ;4(‡34 the,

or, substituting the natural letters, where known, it reads thus:

The tree thr‡?3h the.

'Now, if, in place of the unknown characters, we leave blank spaces, or substitute dots, we read thus:

the tree thr . . .h the,

when the word '*through*' makes itself evident at once. But this discovery gives us three new letters, o, u, and g, represented by ‡, ?, and 3.

'Looking now, narrowly, through the cipher for combinations of known characters, we find, not very far from the beginning, this arrangement,

83(88, or egree,

which, plainly, is the conclusion of the word 'degree', and gives us another letter, d, represented by †.

'Four letters beyond the word 'degree', we perceive the combination

;46(;88*.

'Translating the known characters, and representing the unknown by dots, as before, we read thus:

th.rtee.,

an arrangement immediately suggestive of the word 'thirteen', and again furnishing us with two new characters, i and n, represented by 6 and *.

'Referring, now, to the beginning of the cryptograph, we find the combination,

53‡‡†.

'Translating as before, we obtain

.good,

which assures us that the first letter is A, and that the first two words are 'A good'.

'It is now time that we arrange our key, as far as discovered, in a tabular form, to avoid confusion. It will stand thus:

5	represents	a
†	„	d
8	„	e
3	„	g
4	„	h
6	„	i
*	„	n
‡	„	o
(	„	r
;	„	t
?	„	u

'We have, therefore, no less than eleven of the most important letters represented, and it will be unnecessary to proceed with the details of the solution. I have said enough to convince you that ciphers of this nature are readily soluble, and to give you some insight into the *rationale* of their development. But be assured the specimen before us appertains to the very simplest species of cryptograph. It now only remains to give you the full translation of the characters upon the parchment, as unriddled. Here it is:

'*A good glass in the bishop's hostel in the devil's seat forty-one degrees and thirteen minutes northeast and by north main branch seventh limb east side shoot from the left eye of the death's-head a bee-line from the tree through the shot fifty feet out.*'

'But,' said I, 'the enigma seems still in as bad a condition as ever. How is it possible to extort a meaning from all this jargon about "devil's seats", "death's-heads", and "bishop's hostels"?'

'I confess,' replied Legrand, 'that the matter still wears a serious aspect, when regarded with a casual glance. My first endeavour was to divide the sentence into the natural division intended by the cryptographist.'

'You mean, to punctuate it?'

'Something of that kind.'

'But how was it possible to effect this?'

'I reflected that it had been a *point* with the writer to run his words together without division, so as to increase the difficulty of solution. Now, a not over-acute man, in pursuing such an object, would be nearly certain to overdo the matter. When, in the course of his composition, he arrived at a break in his subject which would naturally require a pause, or a point, he would be exceedingly apt to run his characters, at this place, more than usually close together. If you will observe the MS., in the present instance, you will easily detect five such cases of unusual crowding. Acting upon this hint, I made the division thus:

'A good glass in the bishop's hostel in the devil's seat – forty-one degrees and thirteen minutes – northeast and by north – main branch seventh limb east side – shoot from the left eye of the death's-head – a bee-line from the tree through the shot fifty feet out.'

'Even this division,' said I, 'leaves me still in the dark.'

'It left me also in the dark,' replied Legrand, 'for a few days; during which I made diligent inquiry, in the neighbourhood of Sullivan's Island, for any building which went by the name of the "Bishop's Hotel"; for, of course, I dropped the obsolete word "hostel". Gaining no information on the subject, I was on the point of extending my sphere of search, and proceeding in a more systematic manner, when, one morning, it entered into my head, quite suddenly, that this "Bishop's Hostel" might have some reference to an old family, of the name of Bessop, which, time out of mind, had held possession of an ancient manor house, about four miles to the northward of the island. I accordingly went over to the plantation, and reinstituted my inquiries among the older Negroes of the place. At length, one of the most aged of the women said that she had heard of such a place as *Bessop's Castle*, and thought that she could guide me to it, but that it was not a castle, nor a tavern, but a high rock.

'I offered to pay her well for her trouble, and, after some demur, she consented to accompany me to the spot. We found it without much difficulty, when, dismissing her, I proceeded to examine the place. The "castle" consisted of an irregular assemblage of cliffs and rocks – one of the latter being quite remarkable for its height as well as for its insulated and artificial appearance. I clambered to its apex, and then felt much at a loss as to what should be next done.

'While I was busied in reflection, my eyes fell upon a narrow ledge in the eastern face of the rock, perhaps a yard below the summit upon which I stood. This ledge projected about eighteen inches, and was not more than a foot wide, while a niche in the cliff just above it gave it a rude resemblance to one of the hollow-backed chairs used by our ancestors. I made no doubt that here was the "devil's seat" alluded to in the MS., and now I seemed to grasp the full secret of the riddle.

'The "good glass", I knew, could have reference to nothing but a telescope; for the word "glass" is rarely employed in any other sense by seamen. Now here, I at once saw, was a telescope to be used, and a definite point of view, *admitting no variation*, from which to use it. Nor did I hesitate to believe that the phrases, "forty-one degrees and thirteen minutes", and, "northeast and by north" were intended as directions for the levelling of the glass. Greatly excited by these discoveries, I hurried home, procured a telescope, and returned to the rock.

'I let myself down to the ledge, and found that it was impossible to retain a seat upon it except in one particular position. This fact confirmed my preconceived idea. I proceeded to use the glass. Of course, the "forty-one degrees and thirteen minutes" could allude to nothing but elevation above the visible horizon, since the horizontal direction was clearly indicated by the words "northeast and by north". This latter direction I at once established by means of a pocket-compass; then, pointing the glass as nearly at an angle of forty-one degrees of elevation as I could do it by guess, I moved it cautiously up or down, until my attention was arrested by a circular rift or opening in the foliage of a large tree that overtopped its fellows in the distance. In the centre of this rift I perceived a white spot, but could not, at first, distinguish what it was. Adjusting the focus of the telescope, I again looked, and now made it out to be a human skull.

'Upon this discovery I was so sanguine as to consider the enigma solved; for the phrase "main branch, seventh limb, east side," could refer only to the position of the skull upon the tree, while "shoot from the left eye of the death's-head" admitted, also, of but one interpretation, in regard to a search for buried treasure. I perceived that the design was to drop a bullet from the left eye of the skull, and that a bee-line, or, in other words, a straight line, drawn from the nearest point of the trunk through "the shot" (or the spot where the bullet fell), and thence extended to a distance of fifty feet, would indicate a definite point – and beneath this point I thought it at least *possible* that a deposit of value lay concealed.'

'All this,' I said, 'is exceedingly clear, and, although ingenious, still simple and explicit. When you left the Bishop's Hotel, what then?'

'Why, having carefully taken the bearings of the tree, I turned homeward. The instant that I left "the devil's seat", however, the circular rift vanished; nor could I get a glimpse of it afterward, turn as I would. What seems to me the chief ingenuity in this whole business, is the fact (for repeated experiment has convinced me it *is* a fact) that the circular opening in question is visible from no other attainable point of view than that afforded by the narrow ledge upon the face of the rock.

'In this expedition to the "Bishop's Hotel" I had been attended by Jupiter, who had, no doubt, observed, for some weeks past, the abstraction of my demeanour, and took especial care not to leave me alone. But, on the next day, getting up very early, I contrived to give him the slip, and went into the hills in search of the tree. After much toil I found it. When I came home at night my valet proposed to give me a flogging. With the rest of the adventure I believe you are as well acquainted as myself.'

'I suppose,' said I, 'you missed the spot, in the first attempt at digging, through Jupiter's stupidity in letting the bug fall through the right instead of through the left eye of the skull.'

'Precisely. This mistake made a difference of about two inches and a half in the "shot" – that is to say, in the position of the peg nearest the tree; and had the treasure been *beneath* the "shot" the error would have been of little moment; but the "shot", together with the nearest point of the tree, were merely two points for the establishment of a line of direction; of course the error, however trivial in the beginning, increased as we proceeded with the line, and by the time we had gone fifty feet threw us quite off the scent. But for my deep-seated impressions that treasure was here somewhere actually buried, we might have had all our labour in vain.'

'But your grandiloquence, and your conduct in swinging the beetle – how excessively odd! I was sure you were mad. And why did you insist upon letting fall the bug, instead of a bullet, from the skull?'

'Why, to be frank, I felt somewhat annoyed by your evident suspicious touching my sanity, and so resolved to punish you quietly, in my own way, by a little bit of sober mystification. For this reason I swung the beetle, and for this reason I let it fall from the tree. An observation of yours about its great weight suggested the latter idea.'

'Yes, I perceive; and now there is only one point which puzzles me. What are we to make of the skeletons found in the hole?'

'That is a question I am no more able to answer than yourself. There seems, however, only one plausible way of accounting for them – and yet it is dreadful to believe in such atrocity as my suggestion would imply. It is clear that Kidd – if Kidd indeed secreted this treasure, which I doubt not – it is clear that he must have had assistance in the labour. But this labour concluded, he may have thought it expedient to remove all participants in his secret. Perhaps a couple of blows with a mattock were sufficient, while his coadjutors were busy in the pit; perhaps it required a dozen – who shall tell?'

The Station

H.E. BATES

FOR THIRTY SECONDS AFTER THE lorry had halted between the shack and the petrol pumps the summer night was absolutely silent. There was no wind; the leaves and the grass stalks were held in motionless suspense in the sultry air. And after the headlights had gone out the summer darkness was complete too. The pumps were dead white globes, like idols of porcelain; there was no light at all in the station. Then, as the driver and his mate alighted, slamming the cabin doors and grinding their feet on the gravel, the light in the station came suddenly on: a fierce electric flicker from the naked globe in the shack, the light golden in one wedge-shape shaft across the gravel pull-in. And seeing it the men stopped. They stood for a moment with the identical suspense of the grass and the trees.

The driver spoke first. He was a big fellow, quite young, with breezy blue eyes and stiff untrained hair and a comic mouth. His lips were elastic: thin bands of pink india-rubber that were for ever twisting themselves into grimaces of irony and burlesque, his eyes having that expression of comic and pained astonishment seen on the painted faces of Aunt Sallies in shooting galleries.

His lips twisted to the shape of a buttonhole, so that he whispered out of one corner, 'See her? She heard us come. What'd I tell you?'

The mate nodded. He too was young, but beside the driver he was boyish, his cheeks pink and smooth and shiny as white cherries, his hair yellow and light and constantly ruffled up like the fur of a fox-cub. And unlike the driver's his lips and eyes were quite still; so that he had a look of intense immobility.

He could see the woman in the shack. Short white casement curtains of transparent lace on brass rods cut across the window, but above and through them he could see the woman clearly. She was big-shouldered and dark, with short black hair, and her face was corn-coloured under the light. She seemed about thirty; and that astonished him.

'I thought you said she was young,' he said.

'So she is.' The driver's eyes flashed white. 'Wait'll you git close. How old d'ye think she is?'

'Thirty. More.'

'Thirty? She's been here four years. And was a kid when she was married, not nineteen. How's that up you?'

'She *looks* thirty.'

'So would you if you'd kept this bloody shack open every night for four year. Come on, let's git in.'

They began to walk across the gravel, but the driver stopped.

'And don't forget what I said. She's bin somebody. She's had education. Mind your ups and downs.'

And when they opened the door of the shack and shuffled in, the driver first, the mate closing the door carefully behind him, the woman stood behind the rough-carpentered counter with her arms folded softly across her chest, in an attitude of unsurprised expectancy. The counter was covered with blue squared oilcloth, tacked down. By the blue alarm clock on the lowest of the shelves behind it, the time was four minutes past midnight. At the other end of the shelf a flat shallow kettle was boiling on an oilstove. The room was like an oven. The woman's eyes seemed curiously drowsy, as though clouded over with the steam and the warm oil fumes. And for half a minute nothing happened. She did not move. The men stood awkward. Then the driver spoke. His india-rubber mouth puckered comically to one side, and his eye flicked in a wink that was merely friendly and habitual.

'Well, here we are again.'

She nodded; the drowsiness of her eyes cleared a little. All the same there was something reserved about her, almost sulky.

'What would you like?' she said.

'Give me two on a raft and coffee,' the driver said.

'Two on a raft and coffee,' the woman said. She spoke beautifully, without effort, and rather softly. 'What's your friend going to have?'

The mate hesitated. His eyes were fixed on the woman, half consciously, in admiration. And the driver had to nudge him, smiling his india-rubber smile of comic irony, before he became aware of all that was going on.

'Peck up,' the driver said.

'That'll do me,' the mate said.

'Two on a raft twice and coffee,' the woman said. 'Is that it?'

Though the mate did not know it for a moment, she was addressing him. He stood in slight bewilderment, as though he were listening to a language he did not understand. Then as he became aware of her looking at him and waiting for an answer the bewilderment became embarrassment and his fair cherry-smooth cheeks flushed very red, the skin under the short golden hairs and his neck flaming. He stood dumb. He did not know what to do with himself.

'I'm afraid I don't know your friend's name or his tastes yet,' the woman said. 'Shall I make it two poached twice and coffee?'

'Just like me. Forgot to introduce you,' the driver said. His mouth was a wrinkle of india-rubber mocking. 'Albie, this is Mrs Harvey. This is Albert Armstrong. Now mate on Number 4, otherwise Albie.'

The woman smiled, and in complete subjection and fascination the boy smiled too.

'Are you sure that's all right?' she said. 'Poached and coffee? It sounds hot to me.'

'Does me all right,' the driver said.

'I could make you a fresh salad,' she said. And again she was speaking to the mate, with a kind of soft and indirect invitation. 'There would be eggs in that.'

'I'll have that,' the mate said.

'What?' the driver said. His eyes were wide open, his mouth wide also in half-serious disgust, as though the mate had committed a sort of sacrilege. 'You don' know what's good.'

'So you'll have the salad?' the woman said.

'Yes, please.'

'I can give you the proper oil on it, and vinegar. You can have fruit afterwards if you'd like it.'

'Fruit?' the driver said. 'What fruit?'

She took the kettle from the oilstove and poured a little hot water into the coffee-pot and then a little into each of the egg poachers. 'Plums,' she said.

'Now you're talking,' the driver said. 'Plums. Some sense. Now you *are* talking.'

'Go and get yourself a few if you like them so much.'

'Show me. Show me a plum tree within half a mile and I'm off.'

'Go straight down the garden and it's the tree on the left. Pick as many as you like.'

The driver opened the door, grinning. 'Coming, Albie?'

'You're not afraid of the dark, are you?' the woman said.

This time she was speaking to the driver. And suddenly as he stood there at the door, grimacing with comic irony at her, his whole head and face and neck and shoulders became bathed in crimson light, as though he had become the victim of a colossal blush. Startled, he lifted up his face and looked up at the shack from the outside. The bright electric sign with the naked letters saying simply *The Station* was like a fire of scarlet and white. At intervals it winked and darkened, on and out, scarlet to darkness, *The Station* to nothing. The driver stood with uplifted face, all scarlet, in surprised admiration.

'Blimey, that's a winner. When'd you get that?'

'It's new this week.'

'It's a treat. It makes no end of a difference. How's it you didn't have it on when we came in?'

'I keep forgetting it. I'm so used to sitting here in the dark I can't get used to it. It's a bit uncanny.'

The driver went down the shack steps, into the night. The woman, busy with the eggs, and the boy, leaning against the counter, could see him standing back, still faintly crimson, in admiration of the eternal winking light. And for a minute, as he stood there, the station was completely silent, the August darkness like velvet, the sultry night air oppressing all sound except the soft melancholy murmur of the simmering kettle. Then the woman called:

'You'd better get your plums. The eggs won't be two minutes.'

The driver answered something, only barely audible, and after the sound of his feet crunching the gravel the silence closed in again.

It was like a stoke-room in the shack. The smells of coffee and eggs and oil were fused into a single breath of sickening heat. Like the driver, the boy stood in his shirtsleeves. He stood still, very selfconscious, watching the woman breaking the eggs and stirring the coffee and finally mixing in a glass bowl the salad for himself. He did not know what to do or say. Her thin white dress was like the silky husk of a seed-pod, just bursting open. Her ripe breasts swelled under it like two sun-swollen seeds. And he could not take his eyes away from them. He was electrified. His blood quivered with the current of excitement. And all the time, even though she was busy with the eggs on the stove, and the mixing of the salad, and very often not looking at him, she was aware of it. Looking up sometimes from the stove or the salad she would look past him, with an air of arrested dreaminess, her dark eyes lovely and sulky. The deliberation of it maddened him. He remembered things the driver had said as they came along the road. The words flashed in his mind as though lit up by the electricity of his veins. 'She's a peach, Albie. But I'll tell you what. One bloody wink out o' place and you're skedaddled. She won't have it. She's nice to the chaps because it's business, that's all. See what I mean, Albie? She'll look at you fit to melt your bleedin' heart out, but it don't mean damn all. She wants to make that station a success, that's all. That's why she runs the night shack. Her husband runs the day show and she's second house, kind of. It's her own idea. See?'

And suddenly his thoughts broke off. The lights in his brain, as it were, went out. His mind was blank. She was looking at him. He stood transfixed, his veins no longer electric but relapsed, his blood weak.

'Like it on the lorry?' she said.

'Yes.' He hardly spoke.

She had finished making the salad and she pushed the bowl across the counter towards him before speaking again.

'You're not very old for the job, are you?'

'I'm eighteen.'

'Get on with old Spike?'

'Yes.'

'Isn't it lonely at first? They all say it's lonely when they first begin.'

'I don't mind it.'

'What's your girl say to it?'

It was as though the electric sign had been suddenly turned on him as it had been turned on the driver. He stood helpless, his face scarlet.

'I ain't got a girl.'

'What? Not a nice boy like you?' She was smiling, half in mockery. 'I know you must have.'

'No.'

'Does she love you much?' She looked at him in mock seriousness, her eyes lowered.

'I ain't got one.'

'Honest?' She pushed the bottles of oil and vinegar across the counter towards him. 'I'll ask Spike when he comes in.'

'No, don't say anything to Spike,' he begged. 'Don't say nothing. He's always kidding me about her, anyway.'

'You said you hadn't got a girl.'

'Well —'

She took two plates from the rack behind the counter and then knives and forks from the drawer under the counter and then laid them out.

'Does she hate it when you're on nights?' she said.

'Yes.'

'What's she like – dark or fair?'

'Dark.'

'Like me?'

He could not answer. He only gazed straight at her in mute embarrassment and nodded. Every word she uttered fired him with passionate unrest. The current in his blood was renewed again. He felt himself tightened up. And she could see it all.

'You'd better call Spike,' she said. 'The eggs are ready.'

He moved towards the door. Then he turned and stopped. 'Don't say nothing,' he said.

'All right.'

He stood at the door, his face scarlet under the winking sign, and called out for Spike, singing the word, 'Spi-ike!' And he could hear the sound echoing over the empty land in the darkness. There was a smell of corn in the air, stronger and sweeter even than the smell of the heat and cooking in the shack. It came in sweet waves from across the invisible fields in the warm night air.

'I know how you feel,' she said.

He turned sharply. 'How?'

'Come and eat this salad and cool down a bit.'

He came from the door to the counter in obedience, pulling out a stool and sitting on it.

'Oil and vinegar?' she said. 'The coffee will be ready by the time Spike comes.'

'How do I feel?' he insisted.

'You know.'

'Yes, but how do you know?'

'I've felt like it myself.'

She stood with her arms folded and resting on the counter edge, and leaning slightly forward, so that he could see her breasts beneath the open dress. She looked at him with a kind of pity, with tenderness, but half amused. He saw the breasts rise and fall with the same slow and almost sulky passion as she looked at him. He stared from her breasts to her face, and she stared back, her eyes never moving. And they stood like that, not moving or speaking, but only as it were burning each other up, until suddenly Spike came in.

The woman stood up at once. Spike's cupped hands were full of plums.

'They're green,' the woman said.

'By God, if I didn't think they was tart.'

'Didn't you find the right tree? On the left?'

'I couldn't see a blamed thing.'

'Eat your eggs. I'll get a torch and we'll go down and get some ripe ones before you go.'

'Eggs look good an' all,' Spike said.

The men ate in silence, the woman busy with bread and coffee. The boy put vinegar on his salad, but not oil, and once, noticing it, she unstoppered the oil bottle and pushed it across to him. It was her only sign towards him. The old manner of pity and intimacy had vanished. She was the proprietress; they were the drivers come in to eat. She stood almost aloof, busy with odd things at the far end of the counter. And the boy sat in fresh bewilderment, at a loss, and in wonder about her.

They each drank two cups of coffee and when the cups were finally empty she said:

'If you're ready we can go down and get the plums. But I don't want to hurry you.'

'I'm fit,' Spike said. 'And, my God, the eggs were a treat. You missed a treat Albie, not having eggs.'

'The salad was all right.'

'I'll get the torch,' the woman said. 'You go out that door and I'll meet you round the back.'

She went out of the shack by a door behind the counter, and the boy followed Spike through the front door, under the electric sign. Outside, behind the shack, the sweet smell of ripened corn and night air seemed stronger than ever. At the side of the shack and a little behind it, the bungalow stood out darker than the darkness. And after a minute the torch appeared from the bungalow and began to travel towards the men. The boy could see it shining white along the cinder path and on the woman's feet as she came along.

'You walk down the path,' she said. 'I'll show the light.'

Spike began to walk down the path, the boy following him, and then the woman. The shadows strode like giants over the garden and were lost beyond the yellow snake fence in the dark land. The garden was short, and in a moment they all three stood under the plum tree, the woman shining the torch up into the branches, the tree turned to an immense net of green and silver.

'I'll shine, Spike,' she said. 'You pick them. If they're soft and they lift off they're ripe.'

'This is better,' Spike said. His mouth was already full of plums. 'I struck one match to every blamed plum when I came down.'

The woman stood a little away from the tree, shining the torch steadily, making a great ring of white light across which little moths began to flutter like casual leaves. The boy stood still, not attempting to move, as though he were uninvited.

'What about you?' she said.

And again he could feel the old softness of sympathy and pity and insinuation in her voice, and again his blood leapt up.

'I'm about full up,' he said.

'Take some for the journey.'

He stood still, electrified.

'Take some to eat on the way. Look here, come round the other side. They're riper.'

She moved round the tree, shining the torch always away from her. He followed her in silence, and then in silence they stood against the plum branches, in the darkness behind the light. He saw her stretch up her arm into the silver leaves, and then lower it again.

'Where's your hand?' she was whispering. 'Here. It's a beauty.' The soft ripe plum was between their hands. Suddenly she pressed it hard against his hands, and the ripe skin broke and the juice trickled over his fingers. 'Eat it, put it in your mouth,' she said. He put the plum into his mouth obediently, and the sweet juice trickled down over his lips and chin as it had already trickled over his hands.

'Was that nice?' she said softly.

'Lovely.'

'Sweet as your girl?'

It seemed suddenly as if his blood turned to water. She was touching him. She took his hand and laid it softly against her hip. It was firm and strong and soft. It had about it a kind of comforting maturity. He could feel all the sulky strength and passion of her whole body in it. Then all at once she covered his hand with her own, stroking it up and down with her fingers, until he stood helpless, intoxicated by the smell of corn and plums and the night warmth and her very light, constant stroking of his hand.

'Shine the light,' Spike called. 'I can't see for looking.'

'I'm shining,' she said. 'Albie wants to see too.'

'Getting many, Albie?'

'He's filling his pockets.'

She began to gather plums off the tree with her free hand as she spoke, keeping her other hand still on his, pressing it against her by an almost mechanical process of caressing. He reached up and tore off the plums too, not troubling if they were ripe, filling one pocket while she filled the other, the secrecy and passion of her movements half demoralizing him, and going on without interruption until Spike called:

'Albie! Plums or no plums, we shall have to get on th' old bus again.'

'All right.'

The boy could hardly speak. And suddenly as the woman took her hand away at last he felt as if the life in him had been cut off, the tension withdrawn, leaving his veins like dead wires.

He stumbled up the path behind Spike and the woman and the light. Spike was gabbling:

'The sweetest plums I ever tasted. When we come back I'll take a couple of pounds and the missus'll pie 'em.'

'When will you be back?'

'The night after tomorrow.'

'They'll be plenty,' she said.

She said nothing to the boy, and he was dumb.

'Let's pay you,' Spike said.

'A shilling for you, and ninepence for the salad,' she said.

'Salad's cheaper,' Spike said. 'I'll remember that. What about the plums?'

'The plums are thrown in.'

They paid her. Then she stood on the shack steps while they crunched across the pull-in and climbed up into the cab, the bright red sign flashing above her.

'That sign's a treat,' Spike called. 'You could see it miles off.'

'I'm glad you like it,' she called. 'Good night.'

Spike started up, and almost before the boy could realize it the lorry was swinging out into the road, and the station was beginning to recede. He sat for some moments without moving. Then the lorry began to make speed and the smell of corn and plums and the summer land began to be driven out by the smells of the cab, the petrol and oil and the heat of the engine running. But suddenly he turned and looked back.

'The light's out,' he said.

Spike put his head out of the cab and glanced back. The sign was still flashing but the shack itself was in darkness.

'She's sitting in the dark,' he said. 'She always does. She says it saves her eyes and the light and she likes it better.'

'Why?'

'Better ask her.' Spike put a plum in his mouth. 'I don't know.'

'What's her husband doing, letting her run the place at night, and sit there in the dark?'

'It's her own idea. It's a paying game an' all, you bet your life it is.'

The boy took a plum from his pocket and bit it slowly, licking the sweet juice from his lips as it ran down. He was still trembling.

And glancing back again he could see nothing of the station but the red sign flashing everlastingly out and on, scarlet to darkness, *The Station* to nothing at all.

My Enemy's Enemy

KINGSLEY AMIS

'YES, I KNOW ALL ABOUT THAT, TOM,' the Adjutant said through a mouthful of stew. 'But technical qualifications aren't everything. There's other sides to a Signal officer's job, you know; especially while we're still pretty well static. The communications are running themselves and we don't want to start getting complacent. My personal view is, and has been from the word go, that your friend Dally's a standing bloody reproach to this unit, never mind how much he knows about the six-channel and the other boxes of tricks. That's a lineman-mechanic's job, anyway, not an officer's. And I can tell you for a fact I mean to do something about it, do you see?' He laid down his knife, though not his fork and took three or four swallows of wine.

'Well, your boy Cleaver doesn't impress me all that much, Bill,' Thurston, who hated the Adjutant, said to him. 'The only time we've tried him on duty he flapped.'

'Just inexperience, Tom,' the Adjutant said. 'He'd soon snap out of that if we gave him command of the section. Sergeant Beech would carry him until he found his feet.'

'Mm, I'd like to see that, I must say. The line duty officer getting his sergeant out of bed to hold his hand while he changes a valve.'

'Now look here, old boy.' The Adjutant levered a piece of meat out from between two teeth and ate it. 'You know as well as I do that young Cleaver's got the best technical qualifications of anyone in the whole unit. It's not his fault he's been stuck on office work ever since he came to us. There's a fellow that'd smarten up that bunch of goons and long-haired bloody mathematical wizards they call a line maintenance section. As it is, the NCOs don't chase the blokes and Dally isn't interested in chasing the NCOs. Isn't interested in anything but his bloody circuit diagrams and test-frames and what-have-you.'

To cover his irritation, Thurston summoned the Mess corporal, who stood by the wall in a posture that compromised between that of an attendant waiter and the regulation stand-at-ease position. The Adjutant had schooled him in Mess procedure, though not in Mess etiquette. 'Gin and lime, please, Gordon. . . . Just as well in a way he is interested in line apparatus, isn't it, Bill? We'd have looked pretty silly without him during the move out of Normandy and across France. He worked as hard as any two of the rest of us. And as well.'

'He got his bouquet from the Colonel, didn't he? I don't grudge him that, I admit he did good work then. Not as good as some of his chaps, probably, but still, he served his turn. Yes, that's exactly it, Tom, he's served his —'

'According to Major Rylands he was the lynchpin of the whole issue,' Thurston said, lighting a cigarette with fingers that were starting to tremble. 'And I'm prepared to take his word for it. The war isn't over yet, you know. Christ knows what may happen in the spring. If Dally isn't around to hold the line-maintenance end up for Rylands, the whole unit might end up in a mess with the Staff jumping on its back. Cleaver might be all right, I agree. We just can't afford to take the risk.'

This was an unusually long speech for anyone below the rank of major to make in the Adjutant's presence. Temporarily gagged by a mouthful of stew, that officer was eating as fast as he could and shaking his forefinger to indicate that he would as soon as possible propose some decisive amendment to what he had just been told. With his other hand he scratched the crown of his glossy black head, looking momentarily like a tic-tac man working through his lunchbreak. He said indistinctly: 'You're on to the crux of the whole thing, old boy. Rylands is the root of all the trouble. Bad example at the top, do you see?' Swallowing, he went on: 'If the second-in-command goes round looking like a latrines detail and calling the blokes by their Christian names, what can you expect? You can't get away from it, familiarity breeds contempt. Trouble with him is he thinks he's still working in the Post Office.'

A hot foam of anger seemed to fizz up in Thurston's chest. 'Major Rylands is the only field officer in this entire unit who knows his job. It is due to him and Dally, plus Sergeant Beech and the lineman-mechs., that our line communications have worked so smoothly during this campaign. To them and to no one else. If they can go on doing that, they can walk about with bare arses for all I care.'

The Adjutant frowned at Thurston. After running his tongue

round his upper teeth, he said: 'You seem to forget, Tom, that I'm responsible for the discipline of officers in this unit.' He paused to let the other reflect on the personal implications of this, then nodded to where Corporal Gordon was approaching with Thurston's drink.

As he signed the chit, Thurston was thinking that Gordon had probably been listening to the conversation from the passage. If so, he would probably discuss it with Hill, the Colonel's batman, who would probably report it to his master. It was often said, especially by Lieutenant Dalessio, the 'Dally' now under discussion, that the Colonel's chief contact with his unit was through the rumours and allegations Hill and, to a less extent, the Adjutant took to him. A tweak of disquiet made Thurston drink deeply and resolve to say no more for a bit.

The Adjutant was brushing crumbs off his battledress, which was of the greenish hue current in the Canadian Army. This little affectation, like the gamboge gloves and the bamboo walking-stick, perhaps suited a man who had helped to advertise men's clothes in civilian life. He went on to say in his rapid quacking monotone: 'I'd advise you, Tom, not to stick your neck out too far in supporting a man who's going to be out of this unit on his ear before very long.'

'Rylands, you mean?'

'No no no. Unfortunately not. But Dally's going.'

'That's gen, is it?'

'Not yet, but it will be.'

'I don't follow you.'

The Adjutant looked up in Gordon's direction, then leaned forward across the table to Thurston. 'It only needs one more thing,' he said quietly, 'to turn the scale. The CO's been watching Dally for some time, on my suggestion. I know the old man pretty well, as you know, after being in his company for three years at North Midland Command. He's waiting to make up his mind, do you see? If Dally puts up a black in the near future – a real black – that'll be enough for the CO. Cleaver'll get his chance at last.'

'Suppose Dally doesn't put up a black?'

'He will.'

'He hasn't yet, you know. The terminal equipment's all on the top line, and Dally knows it inside out.'

'I'm not talking about that kind of a black. I'm talking about the administrative and disciplinary side. Those vehicles of his are in a shocking condition. I thought of working a snap 406 inspection on one of them, but that wouldn't look too good. Too much like discrimination. But there'll be something. Just give me time.'

Thurston thought of saying that those vehicles, though covered with months-old mud and otherwise offensive to the inspecting eye, were in good running order, thanks to the efficiency of the section's transport corporal. Instead, he let his mind wander back to one of the many stories of the Colonel's spell as a company commander in England. Three weeks running he had presented his weekly prize of £1 for the smartest vehicle to the driver of an obsolete wireless truck immobilized for lack of spare parts. The company sergeant-major had won a bet about it.

'We'll have some fun then, Tom, old boy,' the Adjutant was saying in as festive a tone as his voice allowed. He was unaware that Thurston disliked him. His own feelings towards Thurston were a mixture of respect and patronage: respect for Thurston's Oxford degree and accent, job at a minor public school, and competence as a non-technical officer; patronage for his practice of reading literary magazines and for his vaguely scholarly manner and appearance. The affinity between Thurston's unmilitary look and the more frankly ragamuffin demeanour of Dalessio could hardly explain, the Adjutant wonderingly felt, the otherwise unaccountable tendency of the one to defend the other. It was true that they'd known each other at the officer's training unit at Catterick, but what could that have to do with it? The Adjutant was unaccustomed to having his opinions contested and he now voiced the slight bafflement that had been growing on him for the last few minutes. 'It rather beats me,' he said, 'why you're taking this line about friend Dally. You're not at all thick with him. In fact he seems to needle you whenever he speaks to you. My impression is, old boy, for what it's worth, you've got no bloody use for him at all. And yet you stick up for him. Why?'

Thurston amazed him by saying coldly: 'I don't see why the fact that a man's an Italian should be held against him when he does his job as well as anyone in the sodding Army.'

'Just a minute, Tom,' the Adjutant said, taking a cigarette from his silver case, given him by his mistress in Brussels. 'That's being a bit unfair, you know. You ever heard me say a word about Dalessio being an Eyeteye? Never. You were the one who brought it up. It makes no difference to me if a fellow's father's been interned, provided —'

'Uncle.'

'All right, uncle, then. As I say, that's no affair of mine. Presumably he's okay from that point of view or he'd never have got here. And that's all there is to it as far as I'm concerned. I'm not holding it against him, not for a moment. I don't quite know where you picked up that impression, old boy.'

Thurston shook his head, blushing slightly. 'Sorry, Bill,' he said. 'I must have got it mixed. It used to get on my wick at Catterick, the way some of the blokes took it out of him about his pal Musso and so on. I suppose it must be through that somehow, in a way, I keep feeling people have got it in for him on that score. Sorry.' He was not sorry. He knew quite certainly that his charge was well-founded, and that the other's silence about Dalessio's descent was a matter of circumspection only. If anyone in the Mess admired Mussolini, Thurston suspected, it was the Adjutant, although he kept quiet about that as well. It was tempting to dig at his prejudices on these and other questions, but Thurston did his best never to succumb to that temptation. The Adjutant's displeasure was always strongly urged and sometimes, rumour said, followed up by retaliatory persecution. Enough, dangerously much, had already been said in Dalessio's defence.

The Adjutant's manner had grown genial again and, with a muttered apology, he now offered Thurston a cigarette. 'What about another of those?' he asked, pointing his head at Thurston's glass.

'Thank you, I will, but I must be off in a minute. We're opening that teleprinter to the Poles at twenty-hundred and I want to see it's working.'

Two more officers now entered the Mess dining-room. They were Captain Bentham, a forty-year-old Regular soldier who had been a company sergeant-major in India at the outbreak of war, and Captain Rowney, who besides being in charge of the unit's administration was also the Mess's catering officer. Rowney nodded to Thurston and grinned at the Adjutant, whose Canadian battledress he had been responsible for securing. He himself was wearing a sheepskin jacket, made on the Belgian black market. 'Hello, William,' he said. 'Won the war yet?' Although he was a great chum of the Adjutant's, some of his remarks to him, Thurston had noticed, carried a curious vein of satire. Bentham sat stolidly down a couple of places along the table, running his hands over his thin grey hair.

'Tom and I have been doing a little plotting,' the Adjutant said.

'We've decided a certain officer's career with this unit needs terminating.'

Bentham glanced up casually and caught Thurston's eye. This, coming on top of the Adjutant's misrepresentation of the recent discussion, made Thurston feel slightly uncomfortable. That was ludicrous, because he had long ago written Bentham off as of no particular account, as the most uninteresting type of Regular Army ex-ranker, good only at cable-laying, supervising cable-laying and looking after the men who did the actual cable-laying. Despite this, Thurston found himself saying: 'It wasn't quite like that,' but at that moment Rowney asked the Adjutant a question, and the protest, mild as it was, went unheard.

'Your friend Dally, of course,' the Adjutant answered Rowney.

'Why, what's he been up to?' Bentham asked in his slow Yorkshire voice. 'Having his hair cut?'

There was a general laugh, then a token silence while Gordon laid plates of stew in front of the new arrivals. His inquiry whether the Adjutant wanted any rice pudding was met with a facetious and impracticable instruction for the disposal of that foodstuff by an often-quoted route. 'Can't you do better than that, Jack?' the Adjutant asked Rowney. 'Third night we've had Chinese wedding-cake this week.'

'Sorry, William. My Belgian friend's had a little misunderstanding with the civvy police. I'm still looking round for another pal with the right views on how the officers of a liberating army should be fed. Just possess your soul in patience.'

'What's this about Dally?' Bentham persisted. 'If there's a move to give him a wash and a change of clothes, count me in.'

Thurston got up before the topic could be reopened. 'By the way, Jack,' he said to Rowney, 'young Malone asked me to remind you that he still hasn't had those cigarettes for the blokes he's lent to Special Wireless.'

Rowney sighed, 'Tell him it's not my pigeon, will you, Thomas? I've been into it all with him. They're under Special Wireless for everything now.'

'Not NAAFI rations. He told me you'd agreed to supply them.'

'Up until last week. They're off my hands now.'

'Oh no, they're not,' Thurston said nastily. 'According to Malone, they still haven't had last week's.'

'Well, tell him —'

'Look, Jack, you tell him. It's nothing to do with me, is it?'

Rowney stared at him. 'All right, Thomas,' he said, abruptly diving his fork into his stew. 'I'll tell him.'

Dodging the hanging lampshade, which at its lowest point was no more than five feet from the floor, Thurston hurried out, his greatcoat over his arm.

'What's eating our intellectual friend?' Rowney asked.

The Adjutant rubbed his blue chin. 'Don't know quite. He was behaving rather oddly before you blokes came in. He's getting too sort of wrapped up in himself. Needs shaking up.' He was just deciding, having previously decided against it, to inflict some small but salutary injustice on Thurston through the medium of unit orders. He might compel the various sections to start handing in their stores records for check, beginning with Thurston's section and stopping after it. Nice, but perhaps a bit too drastic. What about pinching his jeep for some tiresome extra duty? That might be just the thing.

'If you ask me,' Bentham was saying, 'he's too bloody stuck-up by half. Wants a lesson of some kind, he does.'

'You're going too far there, Ben,' the Adjutant said decisively. He disliked having Bentham in the Officers' Mess, declaring its tone to be thereby lowered, and often said he thought the old boy would be much happier back in the Sergeants' Mess with people of his own type. 'Tom Thurston's about the only chap round here you can carry on a reasonable intelligent discussion with.'

Bentham, unabashed, broke off a piece of bread and ran it round his plate in a way that Thurston and the Adjutant were, unknown to each other, united in finding unpleasant. 'What's all this about a plot about Dally?' he asked.

'You got that, Reg?' Dalessio asked. 'If you get any more interference on this circuit, put it back on plain speech straight away. Then they can see how they like that. I don't believe for a bloody moment the line's been relaid for a single bastard yard. Still, it's being ceased in a week or two, and it never was of the slightest importance, so there's no real worry. Now, what about the gallant Poles?' He spoke with a strong Glamorganshire accent diversified by an occasional Italian vowel.

'They're still on here,' Reg, the lineman-mechanic, said, gesturing towards the test teleprinter. 'Want to see 'em?'

'Yes, please. It's nearly time to switch 'em through to the teleprinter room. We'll get that done before I go.'

Reg bent to the keyboard of the machine and typed:

HOW U GETTING ON THERE READING ME OK KKKK

There was a humming pause while Reg scratched his armpit and said: 'Gone for a piss, I expect. . . . Ah, here he is.' In typical but inextinguishably eerie fashion the teleprinter took on a life of its own, performed a carriage-return, moved the glossy white paper up a couple of lines, and typed:

4 CHRISTS SAKE QUIT BOTHERING ME NOT 2000 HRS YET KKK

Dalessio, grinning to himself, shoved Reg out of the way and typed:

CHIEF SIGNAL OFFICER BRITISH LIBERATION ARMY ERE WATCH YR LANGUAGE MY MAN KKKK

Without hestitation the distant operator typed:

U GO AND SCREW YRSELF JACK SORRY I MEAN SIR

At this Dalessio went into roars of laughter, digging his knuckle into one deep eye-socket and throwing back his large dark head. It was exactly the kind of joke he liked best. He rotated a little in the narrow aisle between the banks of apparatus and test-panels, still laughing, while Reg watched him with a slight smile. At last Dalessio recovered and shouldered his way down to the phone at the other end of the vehicle.

'Give me the teleprinter room, please. What? Who? All right, I'll speak to him. . . . Terminal Equipment, Dalessio here. Yes. Oh, really? It hasn't?' His voice changed completely, became that of a slightly unbalanced uncle commiserating with a disappointed child: 'Now isn't that just too bad? Well, I do think that's hard lines. Just when you were all excited about it, too, eh?' Over his shoulder he squealed to Reg, in soprano parody of Thurston's educated tones: 'Captain Thurston is tewwibly gwieved that he hasn't got his pwinter to the Poles yet. He's afwaid we've got some howwid scheme on over heah to depwive him of it. . . . All right, Thurston, I'll come over. Yes, now.'

Reg smiled again and put a cigarette in his mouth, striking the match, from long habit, on the metal 'No Smoking' notice tacked up over the ventilator.

'Give me one of those, Reg, I want to cool my nerves before I go into the beauty parlour across the way. Thanks. Now listen: switch

the Poles through to the teleprinter room at one minute to eight
exactly, so that there's working communication at eight but not
before. Do Thurston good to bite his nails for a few minutes. Put it
through on number . . .' – his glance and forefinger went momentarily
to a test-frame across the aisle – 'number six. That's just been rewired.
Ring up Teleprinters and tell 'em, will you? See you before I go off.'

It was dark and cold outside and Dalessio shivered on his way over
to the signal office. He tripped up on the cable which ran shin-high
between a line of blue-and-white posts outside the entrance, and
applied an unclean expression to the Adjutant, who had had this
amenity provided in an attempt to dignify the working area. Inside
the crowded, brilliantly lighted office, he was half-asphyxiated by
the smoke from the stove and half-deafened by the thumping of date-
stamps, the ringing of telephones, the enraged bark of one sergeant
and the loud, tremulous singing of the other. A red-headed man was
rushing about bawling 'Emergency Ops for Z Corps' in the accents
of County Cork. Nobody took any notice of him: they had all dealt
with far too many Emergency Ops messages in the last eight months.

Thurston was in his office, a small room partitioned off from the
main one. The unit was occupying what had once been a Belgian
military school and later an SS training establishment. This building
had obviously formed part of the original barrack area, and Thurston
often wondered what whim of the Adjutant's had located the offices
and stores down here and the men's living-quarters in former offices
and stores. The cubicle where Thurston spent so much of his time
had no doubt been the abode of the cadet, and then *Unter-offizier*, in
charge of barrack-room. He was fond of imagining the heavily built
Walloons and high-cheeked Prussians who had slept in here, and had
insisted on preserving as a historical document the chalked *Wir
kommen zurück* on the plank wall. Like his predecessors, he fancied,
he felt cut off from all the life going on just outside the partition,
somehow isolated. 'Alone, withouten any company,' he used to quote
to himself. He would laugh then, sometimes, and go on to think of
the unique lavatory at the far end of the building, where the defecator
was required to plant his feet on two metal plates, grasp two handles,
and curve his body into the shape of a bow over a kind of trough.

He was not laughing now. His phone conversation with Dalessio
had convinced him, even more thoroughly than phone conversations
with Dalessio commonly did, that the other despised him for his lack
of technical knowledge and took advantage of it to irritate and

humiliate him. He tried to reread a letter from one of the two married women in England with whom, besides his wife, he was corresponding, but the thought of seeing Dalessio still troubled him.

Actually seeing Dalessio troubled him even more. Not for the first time it occurred to him that Dalessio's long, matted hair, grease-spotted, cylindrical trouser legs and ill-fitting battle-dress blouse were designed as an offensive burlesque of his own neat but irremediably civilian appearance. He was smoking, too, and Thurston himself was punctilious in observing inside his office the rule that prohibited smoking on duty until ten at night, but it was no use telling him to put it out. Dalessio, he felt, never obeyed orders unless it suited him. 'Hallo, Thurston,' he said amiably. 'Not still having a baby about the Poles, I hope?'

'I don't think I ever was, was I? I just wanted to make sure what the position was.'

'Oh, you wanted to make sure of that, did you? All right, then. It's quite simple. Physically, the circuit remains unchanged, of course. But, as you know, we have ways of providing extra circuits by means of electrical apparatus, notably by utilizing the electron-radiating properties of the thermionic valve, or vacuum-tube. If a signal is applied to the grid . . .'

Thurston's phone rang and he picked it up gratefully. 'Signal master?' said the voice of Brigadier the Lord Fawcett, the largest and sharpest thorn in the side of the entire Signals unit. 'I want a special despatch-rider to go to Brussels for me. Will you send him round to my office for briefing in ten minutes?'

Thurston considered. Apart from its being over a hundred miles to Brussels, he suspected that the story told by previous special DRs who had been given this job was probably quite true: the purpose of the trip was to take in the Brigadier's soiled laundry and bring back the clean stuff, plus any wines, spirits and cigars that the Brigadier's Brussels agent, an RASC colonel at the headquarters of the reserve Army Corps, might have got together for him. But he could hardly ask the Lord Fawcett to confirm this. Why was it that his army career seemed littered with such problems? 'The regular DR run goes out at oh-five-hundred, sir,' he said in a conciliatory tone. 'Would that do instead, perhaps?'

'No, it certainly would not do instead. You have a man available, I take it?'

'Oh yes, sir.' This was true. It was also true that the departure of this man with the dirty washing would necessitate another, who might have been driving all day, being got out of the section billet and condemned, at best to a night on the signal-office floor, more likely to a run half across Belgium in the small hours with a genuine message of some kind. 'Yes, we have a man.'

'Well, I'm afraid in that case I don't see your difficulty. Get him round to me right away, will you?'

'Very good, sir.' There was never anything one could do.

'Who was that?' Dalessio asked when Thurston had rung off.

'Brigadier Fawcett,' Thurston said unguardedly. But Dally probably didn't know about the laundry rumour. He had little to do with the despatch-rider sections.

'Oh, the washerwoman's friend. I heard a bit about that from Beech. Not on the old game again, is he? Sounded as if he wanted a special DR to me.'

'Yes, he did.' Thurston raised his voice. 'Prosser!'

'Sir!' came from outside the partition.

'Ask Sergeant Baker to come and see me, will you?'

'Sir.'

Dalessio's large pale face became serious. He pulled at his moustache. Eventually he said: 'You're letting him have one, are you?' If asked his opinion of Thurston, he would have described him as a plausible bastard. His acquiescence in such matters as this, Dalessio would have added, was bloody typical.

'I can't do anything else.'

'I would. There's nothing to it. Get God's Adjutant on the blower and complain. He's an ignorant bloody oaf, we know, but I bet he'd take this up.'

Thurston had tried this, only to be informed at length that the job of Signals was to give service to the Staff. Before he could tell Dalessio about it, Baker, the DR sergeant, arrived to be acquainted with the Lord Fawcett's desires. Thurston thought he detected a glance of protest and commiseration pass between the other two men. When Baker had gone, he turned on Dalessio almost savagely and said: 'Now look, Dally, leaving aside the properties of the thermionic bleeding valve, would you kindly put me in the picture about this teleprinter to the Poles? Is it working or isn't it? Quite a bit of stuff has piled up for them and I've been holding it in the hope the line'll be through on time.'

'No harm in hoping,' Dalessio said. 'I hope it'll be working all right, too.' He dropped his fag end on the swept floor and trod on it.

'Is it working or is it not?' Thurston asked very loudly. His eyes wandered up and down the other's fat body, remembering how it had looked in a pair of shorts doing physical training at the officers' training unit. It had proved incapable of the simplest tasks laid upon it, crumpling feebly in the forward-roll exercise, hanging like a crucified sack from the wall-bars, climbing by slow and ugly degrees over the vaulting-horse. Perhaps its owner had simply not felt like exerting it. That would have been bloody typical.

Before Dalessio could answer, a knock came at the plywood door Thurston had had made for his cubicle. In response to the latter's bellow, the red-headed man came in. 'Sergeant Fleming sent to tell you, sir,' he said, 'we're just after getting them Polish fellows on the printer. You'll be wanting me to start sending off the messages we have for them, will you, sir?'

Both Thurston and Dalessio looked up at the travelling-clock that stood on a high shelf in the corner. It said eight o'clock.

'That's just about all, gentlemen,' the Colonel said. 'Except for one last point. Now that our difficulties from the point of view of communication have been removed, and the whole show's going quite smoothly, there are other aspects of our work which need attention. This unit has certain traditions I want kept up. One of them, of course, is an absolutely hundred-per-cent degree of efficiency in all matters affecting the disposal of Signals traffic, from the time the In-Clerk signs for a message from the Staff to the time we get . . .'

He means the Out-Clerk, Thurston thought to himself. The little room where the officers, warrant-officers and senior NCOs of the unit held their conferences was unheated, and the Colonel was wearing his knee-length sheepskin coat, another piece of merchandise supplied through the good offices of Jack Rowney in Exchange, perhaps, for a few gallons of petrol or a couple of hundred cigarettes; Malone's men's cigarettes, probably. The coat, added to the CO's platinum-blond hair and moustache, increased his resemblance to a polar bear. Thurston was in a good mood, having just received the letter which finally buttoned up arrangements for his forthcoming leave: four days with Denise in Oxford, and then a nice little run up to Town for five days with Margot. Just the job. He began composing a nature note on the polar bear: 'This animal, although of poor intelligence, possesses considerable cunning of a low order. It displays the utmost ferocity when menaced in any way. It shows fantastic patience in pursuit of its prey, and a vindictiveness which . . .'

The Colonel was talking now about another tradition of his unit, its almost unparalleled soldier-like quality, its demonstration of the verity that a Signals formation *of any kind* was not a collection of down-at-heel scientists and long-haired mathematical wizards. Thurston reflected it was not for nothing that the Adjutant so frequently described himself as the Colonel's staff officer. Yes, there he was, Arctic-fox or, if they had them, Arctic jackal, smiling in proprietary fashion at his chief's oratory. What a bunch they all were. Most of the higher ranking ones had been lower-ranking officers in the Territorial Army during the 'thirties, the Colonel, for instance, a captain, the Adjutant a second lieutenant. The war had given them responsibility and quick promotion, and their continued enjoyment of such privileges rested not on their own abilities, but on those of people who had arrived in the unit by a different route: Post Office engineers whipped in with a commission, older Regular soldiers promoted from the ranks, officers who had been the conscripts of 1940 and 1941. Yes, what a bunch. Thurston remembered the parting words of a former sergeant of his who had been posted home a few months previously: 'Now I'm going I suppose I can say what I shouldn't. You never had a dog's bloody chance in this lot unless you'd been at North Midland Command with the Adj. and the CO. And we all know it's the same in that Mess of yours. If you'd been in the TA like them you were a blue-eyed boy, otherwise you'd had it from the start. It's all right, sir, everybody knows it. No need to deny it.'

The exception to the rule, presumably, was Cleaver, now making what was no doubt a shorthand transcript of the Colonel's harangue. Thurston hated him as the Adjutant's blue-eyed boy and also for his silky hair, his Hitler Youth appearance and his thunderous laugh. His glance moved to Bentham, also busily writing. Bentham, too, fitted into the picture, as much as the Adjutant would let him, which was odd when compared with the attitude of other Regulars in the Mess. But Bentham had less individuality than they.

'So what I propose,' the Colonel said, 'is this. Beginning next week the Adjutant and I will be making a series of snap inspections of section barrack rooms. Now I don't expect anything in the nature of spit-and-polish, of course. Just ordinary soldierly cleanliness .and tidiness is all I want.'

In other words, just ordinary spit-and-polish, Thurston thought, making a note for his sergeant on his pad just below the polar-bear *vignette*. He glanced up and saw Dalessio licking the flap of an envelope; it was his invariable practice to write letters during the Colonel's addresses, when once the serious business of line-communications had been got through. Had he heard what had just been said? It was unlikely.

The conference broke up soon afterwards and in the Mess ante-room, where a few officers had gathered for a drink before the evening meal, Thurston was confronted by an exuberant Adjutant who at once bought him a drink. 'Well, Tom,' he said, 'I reckon that fixes things up nice and neat.'

'I don't follow you, Bill.'

'Step number one in cooking your friend Dally's goose. Step number two will be on Monday, oh-nine-thirty hours, when I take the Colonel round the line-maintenance billet. You know what we'll find there, don't you?'

Thurston stared blankly at the Adjutant, whose eyes were sparkling, like those of a child who has been promised a treat. 'I still don't get you, Bill.'

'Use your loaf, Tommy. Dally's blokes' boudoir, can't you imagine what it'll be like? There'll be dirt enough in there to raise a crop of potatoes, fag-ends and night buckets all over the shop and the rest of it. The Colonel will eat Dally for his lunch when he sees it.'

'Dally's got three days to get it cleaned up, though.'

'He would have if he paid attention to what his Commanding Officer says. But I know bloody well he was writing a letter when that warning was given. Serves the bastard right, do you see? He'll be off to the mysterious East before you can turn round.'

'How much does the Colonel know about this?'

'What I've told him.'

'You don't really think it'll work, do you?'

'I know the old man. You don't, if you'll excuse my saying so.'

'It's a lousy trick and you know it, Bill,' Thurston said violently. 'I think it's completely bloody.'

'Not at all. An officer who's bolshie enough to disobey a CO's order deserves all he gets,' the Adjutant said, looking sententious. 'Coming in?'

Still fuming, Thurston allowed himself to be led into the dining-room. The massive green-tiled stove was working well and the room was warm and cheerful. The house had belonged to the commandant of the Belgian military school. Its solid furniture and tenebrous landscape pictures had survived German occupation, though there was a large burn in the carpet that had been imputed, perhaps rightly, to the festivities of the *Schutz Staffel*. Jack Rowney, by importing photographs of popular entertainers, half-naked young women and the Commander-in-Chief, had done his best to document the Colonel's thesis that the Officers' Mess was also their home. The Adjutant, in excellent spirits, his hand on Thurston's shoulder, sent Corporal Gordon running for a bottle of Burgundy. Then, before they sat down, he looked very closely at Thurston.

'Oh, and by the way, old boy,' he said, a note of menace intensifying the quack in his voice, 'you wouldn't think of tipping your friend Dally the wink about this little treat we've got lined up for him, would you? If you do, I'll have your guts for garters.' Laughing heartily, he dug Thurston in the ribs and added: 'Your leave's due at the end of the month, isn't it? Better watch out you don't make yourself indispensable here. We might not be able to let you go, do you see?'

Early on Monday morning Thurston was walking up from the signal office towards the area where the men's barrack rooms were. He was going to find his batman and arrange to be driven some twenty miles to the department of the Advocate-General's branch which handled divorce. The divorce in question was not his own, which would have to wait until after the war, but that of his section cook, whose wife had developed an immoderate fondness for RAF and USAAF personnel.

Thurston was thinking less about the cook's wife than about the fateful inspection, scheduled to take place any minute now. He realized he had timed things badly, but his trip had only just become possible and he hoped to be out of the area before the Colonel and the Adjutant finished their task. He was keen to do this because the sight of a triumphant Adjutant would be more than he could stand, especially since his conscience was very uneasy about the whole affair. There were all sorts of reasons why he should have tipped Dalessio off about the inspection. The worst of it was, as he had realized in bed last night, when it was too late to do anything about it, that his irritation with Dalessio over the matter of the Polish teleprinter had been a prime cause of his keeping quiet about it. He remembered actually thinking more than once that a thorough shaking-up would do Dalessio no harm, and that perhaps the son of an Italian café proprietor in Cascade, Glamorganshire, had certain disqualifications for the role of British regimental officer. He twisted up his face when he thought of this and started wondering just why it was that the Adjutant was persecuting Dalessio. Perhaps the latter's original offence had been his habit of doing bird-warbles while the Adjutant and Rowney listened to broadcast performances of *The Warsaw Concerto*, the intermezzo from *Cavalleria Rusticana* and other sub-classics dear to their hearts. Cheeping, trilling and twittering, occasionally gargling like a seagull, Dalessio had been told to shut up or get out and had done neither.

Thurston's way took him past the door of the notorious line-maintenance billet. There seemed to be nobody about. Then he was startled by the sudden manifestation of two soldiers carrying brooms and a bucket. One of them had once been in his section and had been transferred early that year to one of the cable sections, he had forgotten which one. 'Good morning, Maclean,' he said.

The man addressed came sketchily to attention. 'Morning, sir.'

'Getting on all right in No. 1 Company?'

'Yes, thank you, sir, I like it fine.'

'Good. What are you fellows up to so early in the morning?'

They looked at each other and the other man said: 'Cleaning up, sir. Fatigue party, sir.'

'I see; right, carry on.'

Thurston soon found his batman, who agreed with some reluctance to the proposed trip and said he would see if he could get the jeep down to the signal office in ten minutes. The jeep was a bone of contention between Thurston and his batman, and the batman always won, in the sense that never in his life had he permitted Thurston to drive the jeep in his absence. He was within his rights, but Thurston often wished, as now, that he could be allowed a treat occasionally. He wished it more strongly when a jeep with no exhaust and with seven men in it came bouncing down the track from the No. 1 Company billet area. They were laughing and two of them were pretending to fight. The driver was a lance-corporal.

Suddenly the laughing and fighting stopped and the men assumed an unnatural sobriety. The reason for this was provided by the immediate emergence into view of the Colonel and the Adjutant, moving across Thurston's front.

They saw him at once; he hastily saluted and the Adjutant, as usual, returned the salute. His gaze met Thurston's under lowered brows and his lips were gathered in the fiercest scowl they were capable of.

Thurston waited till they were out of sight and hurried to the door of the line-maintenance billet. The place was deserted. Except in illustrations to Army manuals and the like, he had never seen such perfection of order and cleanliness. It was obviously the result of hours of devoted labour.

He leant against the door post and began to laugh.

'I gather the plot against our pal Dally misfired somewhat,' Bentham said in the Mess dining-room later that day.

Thurston looked up rather wearily. His jeep had broken down on the way back from the divorce expert and his return had been delayed for some hours. He had made part of the journey on the back of a motorbike. Further, he had just read a unit order requiring him to make the jeep available at the Orderly Room the next morning. It wasn't his turn yet. The Adjutant had struck again.

'You know, I'm quite pleased,' Bentham went on, lighting a cigarette and moving towards the stove where Thurston stood.

'Oh, so am I.'

'You are? Now that's rather interesting. Surprising, even. I should have thought you'd be downcast.'

Something in his tone made Thurston glance at him sharply and put down the unit order. Bentham was standing with his feet apart in an intent attitude. 'Why should you think that, Ben?'

'I'll tell you. Glad of the opportunity. First of all I'll tell you why it misfired, if you don't already know. Because I tipped Dally off. Lent him some of my blokes and all, to get the place spick and span.'

Thurston nodded, thinking of the two men he had seen outside the billet that morning. 'I see.'

'You do, do you? Good. Now I'll tell you why I did it. First of all, the Army's not the place for this kind of plotting and scheming. The job's too important. Secondly, I did it because I don't like seeing an able man taken down by a bunch of ignorant jumped-up so-called bloody gentlemen from the Territorial Army. Not that I hold any brief for Dalessio outside his technical abilities. As you know, I'm a

Regular soldier and I disapprove most strongly of anything damn slovenly. It's part of my nature now and I don't mind either. But one glance at the Adj.'s face when he was telling me the form for this morning and I knew where my duty lay. I hope I always do. I do my best to play it his way as a rule for the sake of peace and quiet. But this business was different. Wasn't it?'

Thurston had lowered his gaze. 'Yes, Ben.'

'It came as a bit of shock to me, you know, to find that Dalessio needed tipping off.'

'How do you mean?'

'I mean that I'd have expected someone else to have told him already. I only heard about this last night. I was the only one here later on and I suppose the Adj. felt he had to tell someone. I should have thought by that time someone else would have let the cat out of the bag to Dally. You, for instance. You were in on this from the start, weren't you?'

Thurston said nothing.

'I've no doubt you have your reasons, your excuses for not letting on. In spite of the fact that I've always understood you were the great one for pouring scorn on the Adj. and Rowney and Cleaver and the rest of that crowd. Yes, you could talk about them till you were black in the face, but when it came to doing something, talking where it would do some good, you kept your mouth shut. And, if I remember rightly, you were the one who used to stick up for Dally when the others were laying into him behind his back. You know what I think? I don't think you care tuppence. You don't care beyond talking, any road. I think you're really quite sold on the Adj.'s crowd, never mind what you say about them. Chew that over. And chew this over and all. I think you're a bastard, just like the rest of 'em. Tell that to your friend the Adjutant, Captain bloody Thurston.'

Thurston stood there for some time after Bentham had gone, tearing up the unit order and throwing the pieces into the stove.

ACKNOWLEDGEMENTS

The publishers would like to thank the following authors, publishers and others for their permission to reproduce the copyright material included in this volume: *No Kaddish for Weinstein* by Woody Allen. Reprinted by permission of the author, Elm Tree Books and Random House Inc. © 1975 by Woody Allen. *Alopecia* by Fay Weldon. Reprinted by permission of the author, the author's agents and Macmillan, London and Basingstoke. © Fay Weldon 1984. *February 1999: Ylla* by Ray Bradbury. Reprinted by permission of Don Congdon Associates. Copyright © 1950 by Ray Bradbury, renewed 1978. *According to Celsus* by Mary Renault. Reprinted by permission of Authur Barker/Weidenfeld & Nicholson Ltd and Curtis Brown Ltd on behalf of the Estate of Mary Renault. © 1976 by Mary Renault. *Flight* from *The Long Valley* by John Steinbeck. Reprinted by permission of Curtis Brown Ltd of London on behalf of the estate of John Steinbeck and Viking Penguin Inc. Copyright 1938, renewed © 1966 by John Steinbeck. *Murder. 1986* by P.D. James. Reprinted by permission of the author and Elaine Greene Ltd. © 1970 by P.D. James. *The Landlady* from *The Best of Roald Dahl*, published by Michael Joseph Ltd, Penguin Books Ltd and Alfred A. Knopf, Inc. Reprinted by permission of the author, Michael Joseph Ltd, Penguin Books Ltd and Alfred A. Knopf Inc. © 1959 by Roald Dahl. *Something Special* by Iris Murdoch. Reprinted by permission of the author, W. H. Allen & Co. Ltd and Viking Penguin Inc. © 1957 by Iris Murdoch. *Parthenope* by Rebecca West. Reprinted by permission of A. D. Peters & Co. Ltd. © 1977 by Rebecca West. *Mortmain* by Graham Greene. Reprinted from *Collected Stories* by permission of the author, William Heinemann Ltd, The Bodley Head Ltd and Viking Penguin Inc. *The Baby Party* by F. Scott Fitzgerald. Reprinted from *The Rich Boy* by permission of The Bodley Head Ltd and Charles Scribner's Sons. *The Reunion* by Margaret Drabble. Reprinted by permission of A. D. Peters & Co. Ltd.© 1968 by Margaret Drabble. *The Dead* by James Joyce. Reprinted from *Dubliners* by permission of the Executors of the James Joyce Estate, Jonathan Cape Ltd and Viking Penguin Inc. Copyright 1916 by B.W. Huebsch, Definitive text © 1967 by the Estate of James Joyce. *The Blood of the Lamb* by Bernice Rubens. Reprinted by permission of A. D. Peters & Co. Ltd and Robin Dalton Associates Ltd. © 1976 by Bernice Rubens. *Suffer the Little Children* by Stephen King. Reprinted by permission of Kirby McCauley Ltd. *The New Girlfriend* by Ruth Rendell. Reprinted by permission of A. D. Peters & Co. Ltd. *Odour of Chrysanthemums* by D. H. Lawrence. Reprinted by permission of Laurence Pollinger Ltd, William Heinemann Ltd, Viking Penguin Inc and the Estate of Mrs Frieda Lawrence Ravagli. *Mysterious Kôr* by Elizabeth Bowen. Reprinted by permission of Jonathan Cape Ltd and Alfred A. Knopf Inc., on behalf of the Estate of Elizabeth Bowen. *Strictly from Hunger* by S. J. Perelman. Reprinted by permission of A. D. Peters & Co. Ltd, the Estate of S. J. Perelman and Curtis Brown Ltd. *Kiss me*

GREAT SHORT STORIES